Devil's Knight S

Books 5 - 8

Wall Street Journal and *USA Today* Bestselling Author
Winter Travers

Also By Winter Travers

Devil's Knights Series:
Loving Lo
Finding Cyn
Gravel's Road
Battling Troy
Gambler's Longshot
Keeping Meg
Fighting Demon
Unraveling Fayth
Forever Lo (December 10th 2019)

Skid Row Kings Series:
DownShift
PowerShift
BangShift

Fallen Lords MC Series
Nickel
Pipe
Maniac
Wrecker
Boink
Clash
Freak
Slayer
Brinks (January 2019)

Kings of Vengeance MC
Drop a Gear and Disappear
Lean Into It

Powerhouse MA Series
Dropkick My Heart
Love on the Mat
Black Belt in Love
Black Belt Knockout

Nitro Crew Series
Burndown
Holeshot
Redlight
Shutdown

Sweet Love Novellas
Sweet Burn
Five Alarm Donuts

Stand Alone Novellas
Kissing the Bad Boy
Daddin' Ain't Easy
Silas: A Scrooged Christmas
Wanting More
Mama Didn't Raise No Fool

Boxset Table of Contents

Gambler's Longshot
Devil's Knights Series
Book 5
Winter Travers

Chapter 1
Gambler

"I swear, woman, you need to get your ass back in that house, now!"

"And I swear, man, I don't know how many times I need to tell you, but you are not the God damn boss of me!"

That was it. I'd had enough. I had never met a woman more infuriating than Gwen. No matter what I told her, she threw it back at me, telling me to shove it up my ass.

"The damn cat will come back. There's no fucking point in traipsing all around the woods looking for it. It's two fucking o'clock in the morning." I continued following Gwen, pushing branches and brush out of the way.

"It's not just a cat, he's Mr. Tuna," she shot back at me. Like that made perfect sense. Don't even get me started on the ridiculous name she had given the cat. Half the time she called it Mr. T. Ridiculous.

"For Christ sake, Gwen, stop!" I yelled, grabbing her arm and ducked as a branch she had been holding back swung back, hitting me in the face.

She whirled around and stumbled into my arms and grabbed onto my shoulders. "I can't stop until I find Mr. Tuna. There is nothing you can say that will make me stop looking for him." She looked up at me, her eyes huge and doe-eyed. "That cat is all I have," she whispered, a lone tear sliding down her cheek. Gwen looked entirely different than when she is all dolled up at the salon. She still had a rock-a-billy look to her but softened. I was shocked when she had opened the door to me tonight. The tight white shorts that barely covered her ass and tight white tank top gave me a half chubby instantly.

Of course, as soon as she had opened her mouth and started bitching at me, my chubby friend deflated. Now with her soft, warm body pressed against me it had my chubby friend taking notice. Gwen was half a foot shorter than me, and I was always looking down into her doe eyes. Her eyes were something wet dreams were made of. She could convey so much with just her eyes.

Right now they were leaking tears and begging me to help her.

Son of a bitch, not tears. I could handle anything but tears. "He'll come back, doll."

"You don't know that. He could be lost and wandering around hurt. We need to find him," she pleaded.

"All right, we'll look for the damn cat, but can we please go back to the house for five minutes and put warmer clothes on?"

"Fine, but only for a minute, that's it." She pulled out of my arms and headed back towards the house.

Her firm ass taunted me the whole way, wagging in my face. She still had the tight shorts and tank on and managed to slip a pair of sandals on her feet as she dashed out the door after her damn cat. My boots were haphazardly pulled on my feet, the laces whipping around. Thankfully I hadn't gotten ready for bed yet and still had jeans and a tee on.

Just as we stepped onto the porch of her house, a motorcycle pulled into her driveway and killed the engine.

"Stay here," I grunted. I knew the only reason for Hammer to be here was not a good one.

"You lose your phone or something?" Ham called.

I patted my pocket where I usually kept my phone and felt nothing. "Shit, I left it in the house. I didn't have time to grab it." Just as I was getting ready for bed, Gwen had screamed bloody murder, and I hightailed it down the hall to see what the hell was going on. My only thought was to get to her and see if she needed help.

"Shits going down. You and Gwen need to get to the clubhouse now."

"What the hell do you mean?"

"Someone tried to fucking blow up Meg's house tonight."

"Holy shit," I groaned, running my fingers through my hair. There was only one person who would try to blow up Meg's house. The Assassins.

"Someone tried to hurt Meg?" Gwen called, panic in her voice.

"They tried, but they're all ok. King wants everyone at the clubhouse. Lockdown."

I nodded my head, knowing exactly what Ham meant. He cranked his bike back and headed back to town.

"We need to pack up and get to the clubhouse. Pack for at least a week, if not more," I ordered, marching up the steps, standing one step below Gwen.

"What? Why the hell for? I don't have anyone chasing after me. I can stay here. Plus, I'm not leaving until I find Mr. Tuna." She propped her hands on her hips, pure attitude.

"This isn't a fucking option, Gwen. Pack and we leave. The cat will be fine. It's an animal; it can survive outside."

"No way, no how. The only way I leave is if Mr. Tuna is with me." She glared at me.

"For fucks sake, we find the cat and then we leave, deal?"

She held her hand out to me, and we shook on it. "Deal."

"Get a can of cat food or tuna and let's find the little shit," I ordered. She ran into the house, the screen door slamming shut behind her.

I turned around, looking over her front yard and groaned. Of course, Gwen had to live out in the country. There wasn't a neighbor in sight, and she was surrounded by cornfields on one side and woods on the other. This was going to take all night.

I listened, trying to hear the little shit. Gwen came banging out of the front door, and I held my hand up, telling her to stop. She covered her mouth with her hand and whispered, "Do you hear him?"

"Quiet," I grunted. I heard the wind rushing around me, but I could also hear a soft meow. I kept listening, trying to figure out which way to go. I slowly walked around the back of the house, the meowing getting louder and louder.

Gwen was pressed to my back, one hand holding a can of tuna and the other gripping my arm. "I hear him," she whispered.

I looked around, trying to figure out where the hell he was. Thankfully the little shit was bright white and was easy to see in the dark. He was sitting at the back door, meowing to be let in.

"Mr. Tuna!" Gwen shouted, running around me and up the short steps to the back door. "I thought we'd never find you," she cooed, picking the cat up and cradled it to her chest. They both acted like they hadn't seen each other in days when it had only been twenty minutes.

"You think we could continue this happy little reunion in the house while you pack a bag?"

"Don't mind him, Mr. Tuna. He's just a crab ass. He did help find you, though," Gwen cooed, rubbing her forehead against the cat's fur.

"We don't have time for this, Gwen. We found the cat, now pack."

"Dick," Gwen hissed as she whizzed by me, her precious cat tucked in her arms.

I followed behind, wondering what the hell I had done to deserve the sick and twisted punishment of Gwen Lawson. Lord help me.

'*'*'*'*'*'*'*'*'*'*'*

Chapter 2

Gwen

"What an ass," I vented to Mr. T, who laid on my bed, sprawled out on the pillow licking his paws.

I tossed my black crinoline skirt at the suitcase I had on the bed and walked back into my closet. Trying to pack when you had no idea how long you were going to be gone was hard. I needed to pack enough clothes for work and for whatever else we might do. Hopefully, Gambler would let me come back to my house to get more clothes if I needed them.

I grabbed three more skirts and four pairs of jeans and started folding everything to fit. I was going to need to bring two suitcases.

Mr. T pounced on my poofy skirt and rolled around, batting at it. I reached over, pulling him out of the tulle and cradled him to my chest. He meowed his protest of leaving the tulle cave and batted at my hand. "Don't you be an ass, too, Mr. T," I scolded, scratching him behind his ears. He purred, leaning into my hand, the tulle cave forgotten.

If only I could scratch Gambler behind his ear and do whatever I wanted. Right now, no matter what I said, he fought me tooth and nail about it. The same could be said of him, though. Ninety percent of the time I wanted to pop him in the nose and tell him to shove it where the sun doesn't shine.

I had never met a man that infuriated me so much. It had to do with the fact that the first time I had met him, he sauntered into my salon like he owned the place and told me what was going to happen and gave no room for argument. Ass.

"Doll, you about done? You've been packing for twenty minutes!" Gambler shouted through the door.

"I'll take another twenty minutes if I damn well feel like," I shouted back, flipping off the door. He couldn't see me, but it was satisfying none the less. Mr. T jumped from my arms and laid back down on my pillow.

I shut the first suitcase, tossed it on the floor and pulled another one out from under my bed. Now came the hard decision, shoes. I didn't want to leave any of my babies behind. I, Gwen Lawson, had a major shoe fetish. Heels were my utter weakness, but a cute pair of tennis shoes had been known to make me swoon a time or two.

"You got ten minutes, and we are leaving with or without all the shit you're packing," Gambler yelled. I heard him retreat down the hall, probably grabbing a beer from the fridge.

"Oh, hey!" I yelled, opening the door and peeked my head out. "Can you go down to the basement and grab Mr. T's carrier? He gets a little anxious on car rides if he's not in his carrier."

Gambler stopped walking and shook his head. He kept his back turned to me and mumbled under his breath. All I made out of it was a six pack of beer and General Tso's Chicken as he ran his fingers through his hair and headed in the direction of the basement.

I ducked back into my room, wondering if I should ever leave Mr. T. with Gambler. I'd be afraid I'd come home to a homemade Chinese dinner and no more Mr. T.

"You are not eating my cat!" I yelled, opening the door and dashed down the hall to the basement door that was wide open. "Did you hear me?"

The light down in the basement was dim, and all I could see was Gambler's shadow wandering around looking for Mr. T's pet carrier. Just as I was about to tell him where to look for it, he walked over to the stairs, the carrier in hand.

"You done packing?" he gruffed, walking up the stairs.

"No, I still need to pick out shoes." I backed up as he neared the top of the stairs and bumped against the door.

"Easy, doll." Gambler grabbed my arm and steadied me. My eyes connected with his and I couldn't look away. This wasn't the first time this had happened to me. There was something about his deep, dark brown eyes that held me captive. I had never seen a brown so hypnotizing before.

"I should go pack my shoes," I mumbled but didn't move.

"Put some pants on too, doll. I don't want you going to the clubhouse looking like that."

"What?" I asked. Looking like what? I was in my freakin' pajamas which were just shorts and a tank top. Nothing scandalous.

"Trust me when I say this, doll. You walk into that clubhouse looking like that, I'm going to have to protect you from more than the Assassins. Every man in there who doesn't have an ol' lady will be all over you like white on rice."

"I'm in my pajamas, and I don't even have any makeup on. You're crazy."

Gambler moved closer, his face inches away from mine. "You think because you ain't got makeup on that none of those guys will look at you?"

I nodded my head yes, unable to speak. Gambler's eyes were even more captivating up close. I was speechless. Speechlessness and I did not go together. There was always something to be said. Except now.

"When those guys lay their eyes on your plump, lush ass and perfect tits hanging out of that tank top, they aren't even going to make it to your face before they pin you against a wall and have their way with you."

"But…what…how would you know?" I whispered.

"Because I've been fighting the urge since I walked through that door tonight. You're lucky I'm a God damn gentleman. Otherwise, I'd have you bent over that kitchen table right now." He dropped the pet carrier at our feet and cupped my chin in his hand. "I need to know what you taste like," he growled.

"But you hate me," I breathed out, his lips hovering over mine.

"You got a smart mouth, doll, and I'd like to bend you over my knee for it, but I sure as hell don't hate you."

"Oh," I repeat. I was speechless.

His hand caressed my cheek, his other hand loosening his grip, not forcing me to stay, but I didn't want to move.

He brushed his lips against mine and, as much as I'd like to deny it, I moaned as his hand delved into my hair, his lips assaulting me. He wrapped his arm around my waist and pulled me to him, our bodies flush. I wrapped my arms around his neck and held on.

I heard him growl low in his throat as he deepened the kiss, his tongue taking over my mouth, taking everything and making me want more. I was so into the kiss, I swear I could hear AC/DC playing "Highway to Hell." Wait, "Highway to Hell" was not the song I would imagine when kissing Gambler.

I backed away, pulling my lips away from Gambler and shook my head. I didn't hear it anymore and thought I must be going crazy.

"Get back here, doll," he growled, grabbing me by the neck, his lips claiming mine again. Just as I was about to get lost in Gambler again, "Highway to Hell" started playing again. "Stop," I said, pulling away. "Your phone is going off."

"Ignore it." He grabbed me by the waist, but I leaned back and pushed on his chest.

"No, that's, at least, the second time it's gone off. It might be important."

Gambler stopped pulling me to him and his eyes cleared of the lust that had turned them almost black. He shook his head and let me go. I stumbled back into the kitchen, somehow missing the feel of Gambler's arms wrapped around me. "Uh, sorry, doll. I shouldn't have done that," he mumbled, running his fingers through his jet black hair.

"Oh, ok," I whispered. I reached up, my fingertips brushing against my lips. I agree it probably wasn't the best time for Gambler to kiss me, but I definitely wouldn't fight him if he did it again.

His phone started blaring again from the table, and we both stared at it.

"Go finish packing, we leave in ten minutes," he ordered, the first one snapping out of the daze our kiss had put us in.

I slowly walked back to my room, Gambler rumbling into his phone. I was almost to my room when he yelled, "Make sure you change. You're not leaving this house looking like that."

I halted in my tracks, and I felt my blood boil. I stomped my foot and stormed into my room, slamming the door behind me. Childish yes, but dammit did Gambler piss me off.

One minute ago I was putty in his hands, and now I was ready to rip his dick off and feed it to Mr. T.

He wanted me to change? I'll give him change.

''*'*'*'*'*'*'*'*'*

Chapter 3
Gambler

One hour.

It took her one fucking hour until she walked out of her bedroom and when she did my jaw hit the floor.

She walked out of her room looking like a nineteen fifties pin-up model. She had a low-cut black dress on that her tits were about to fall out of and swayed around her perfectly toned legs. Her hair was curled and pinned up to her head, and her makeup was perfectly applied. Don't even get me started on her shoes. I never knew a pair of shoes could scream 'fuck me' like her's did. She looked like she was ready to go out, not go to the clubhouse and go to sleep.

"I'm ready," she murmured, smoothing her skirt down.

"The question is what exactly are you ready for?"

She puffed her chest out, and my eyes stayed glued to her chest, hopeful to get a glimpse at her tits if they popped out. "You're a dick."

"I've been called worse. Now tell me where the hell you think you are going looking like that?"

"To the clubhouse."

I shook my head and couldn't believe this woman. I knew she had done this just to spite me because I told her to change, but my reason for her changing was a damn good one. "This isn't a game, Gwen. I didn't tell you to change just to piss you off."

She rolled her eyes at me and walked back into her room. She walked back out with a coat thrown over her shoulders and two suitcases trailing behind her. "What the fuck did you pack? We're going to the clubhouse, not the damn jungle. You've probably got enough packed for a month."

"Doubtful. The small one is just shoes."

One of her suitcases was just shoes? Who the hell has that many shoes, let alone insists packing them. "How many pairs of shoes did you bring?"

"5 pairs of heels, 3 pairs of boots, 3 pairs of tennis shoes, and 6 pairs of flats. Oh, and three pairs of house shoes."

Gwen had just packed twenty pairs of shoes. Motherfucking twenty. "What the hell are house shoes?"

She rolled her eyes at me again, and I was ready to lay her over my knee and let her know what I thought of her attitude. "Slippers, Gambler."

"Then say fucking slippers." I grabbed the suitcases out of her hands and made my way down the hall. "You're gonna have to drive your car. I'll follow behind you. Just take it easy and everything should be fine."

"This is utterly ridiculous, Gambler. I don't even know why I'm being included in this lockdown business. No one is after me," she sassed, walking back into her room.

"Gwen, for fucks sake, can we get the hell out of here? I'm God damn tired!" I hollered, opening the door.

"Don't get your panties in a bunch, I just had to grab Mr. T. and my purse." She tossed her bag at my chest, knocking the wind out of me with how heavy the fucking thing was.

"You got fucking rocks in here?" I picked her purse up off the floor and weighed it in my hand. The damn thing had to at least weigh ten pounds.

"No, dick. I have makeup and other important things in there."

"Like what?"

"None of your damn business is what." She crammed Mr. T. into the carrier and picked it up, the damn cat meowing in protest. "I got Mr. T., you grab the rest."

"Leave the cat and I'll grab him after I put this stuff in your car."

"I can carry something," she insisted.

"I never said you couldn't. Drop the cat and get your ass in the car." I was losing all patience.

"Do you think I'm some helpless girl who can't carry anything?" She popped her hip out and rested her hand on it. Pure fucking attitude.

"No, Gwen, I'm pretty sure you are anything but helpless, I was just trying to be God damn nice."

"I didn't ask you to be nice to me!" Why the fuck was she yelling at me? I was trying to be a gentleman, and this is what it got me?

I wasn't going to take her fucking attitude anymore. "Get your ass in that car right now. You have five seconds before I throw you over my shoulder, and we leave with what's only on your back. No clothes, shoes, or fucking cat. You got me?"

Gwen took a step back, her face paling. I didn't mean to yell at her but fuck me. No matter what I did, she fought me. "Four seconds," I warned, taking a step towards her.

She squeaked as I took another step and set the cat down. She side stepped around me and dashed out the door.

I ran my fingers through my hair, wondering how the hell I was going to make it through sharing a room with this woman.

I heard her car door slam and knew she was waiting for me. I turned off all the lights and grabbed the cat carrier. I swung the door shut behind me, flipping the lock up before it shut.

I tucked the carrier under my arm and pulled the two suitcases behind me. "Pop the trunk," I hollered when I got to the front of her car. She drove a little Beetle that matched her to a T. It was pitch black, with blacked out wheels and tint. It wasn't a Beetle you saw every day. Just like everything else in Gwen's life, there was a definite edge to it.

She swung out of the car, walked around to the front and opened the trunk for me. "So you'll let me open the trunk for you, I see." She propped her hands on her hips and watched me toss the suitcases into the car.

"You want the cat in the front or back seat?" I asked, slamming the lid shut.

"I'm surprised you didn't try to shove him into the trunk."

"Front or back, doll?"

"Front," she huffed out as she slid back into the driver's seat and slammed the door shut.

I opened the passenger side door and set the cat down who had been meowing protests the whole time. Thank God I didn't have to be in the same car as the little shit. I probably would have thrown it out the window halfway to town.

"All right, take it slow and drive straight to the clubhouse. I'll be right behind you the whole time." Gwen stared straight ahead and didn't look at me. "You hear me?"

"Loud and clear, Gambler."

I slammed her door shut and shook my head. She started up her car and peeled out of the driveway, kicking up dust and gravel. Her taillights disappeared down the road as I jogged over to my bike and swung a leg over it. I cranked it up, thankful I had packed up my bag and put it in my saddlebags before.

I gunned it out of her driveway and drove like a bat out of hell trying to catch up with her. I caught up with her, the glow of her red taillights ten car lengths ahead of me. I honestly had no idea what the hell I was going to do with her. I knew I wanted to know what her heavenly body felt like underneath mine, but I didn't know if I would live through all the sass and attitude she threw at me all the time. I wasn't lying when I said I wanted to put her over my knee and spank the sass right out of her.

She rolled through the stop sign at the end of the road and squealed her tires, heading into town. Never mind me telling her to take it slow and make sure I'm behind her. I pulled through the stop sign, too, making sure no one was coming and rocketed after Gwen.

Gwen had just made up my mind what I was going to do with her. I had never met a woman before who could resist me. Be it a friend or lover, I could always win them over. After the kiss we had shared, I knew there was more to Gwen than what she showed. She came off as kick ass and tough, but I knew underneath all the rockabilly attitude, there was a woman I wanted to get to know.

And whether Gwen liked it or not, I was going to see what she was trying too hard to keep away from me.

''*'*'*'*'*'*'*'*'*'*

Chapter 4
Gwen

I was tired. Like, *drain*ed.

When we had finally made it to the clubhouse, only King, Troy, and Rigid were awake. Gambler had dropped my bags by the door and had told me he would be right back. That was forty-five minutes ago, and my eyelids were heavy and my eyes scratchy. I was edging past tried, falling into exhaustion.

I was sprawled out on the couch with the T.V. muted, a late night infomercial playing. My whole plan of getting all dressed up and strutting into the clubhouse had been foiled by the fact the only guys who had seen my entrance were all in a relationship and had eyes only for their women.

"Let's go, doll. I'm dead on my feet."

I looked over the back of the couch and saw Gambler standing at the edge of the living room. "It's about time."

"Save the sass for the morning, doll. I don't have it in me to deal with it right now. I've been going since five o'clock yesterday morning."

"Ew, what an ungodly time to wake up," I groaned, standing up and pulling my two suitcases behind me.

Gambler grabbed one out of my hand and headed down the hall. "I had a bunch of shit to deal with over at the body shop."

We came to the end of the hall and took a left, passing three doors before he pulled his keys out of his pocket and opened the fourth door.

"It ain't much but it's mine," Gambler mumbled, pushing the door open.

I walked in, as he reached in and flicked the light switch on. He wasn't kidding when he said it wasn't much. There was a bed directly in front of me with a huge T.V. hanging on the wall to the left of the door. There was a dresser and a desk to the right and a closed door next to the bed. "Simplistic."

"Is that the nice way of saying boring?" Gambler laughed, pulling my suitcases in and setting Mr. T's cage on the bed. I pushed the door shut and walked over to Mr. T, who was meowing like crazy. He had dozed in his cage while I waited for Gambler, but he was wide awake now.

"It's not boring, just simple." I pulled Mr. T out of his cage and set him on the bed. He cautiously walked around the bed, his eyes round and big, wondering where the hell we were.

"Call it whatever you want, doll. I'm gonna hit the head, I'm ready for bed."

I looked around wondering where the hell Gambler was going to sleep. "Um, where exactly are you sleeping?" I asked as he opened the bathroom door.

He turned around and looked at me, a grin spreading across his lips. "Right there, doll." He pointed to the bed, and my stomach dropped. Shit.

"OK, so where am I going to sleep?"

"Well," he grabbed the hem of his shirt and pulled it over his head and tossed it on the floor. "Right now your only options are the bed or the floor."

"This place is huge, there has to be another bed that I can sleep in."

"They're all full, doll. That is unless you want to share a bed with Hammer. I'm sure he won't mind you sneaking into his bed with him."

"I don't want to sleep with anyone, especially not Hammer. Can't you sleep on the floor, I thought you were a gentleman." I crossed my arms over my chest, unwilling to sleep with anyone. "Or, you can go and sleep with Hammer."

"Dream on, doll. My ass is going to be in that bed in less than two minutes. So you need to decide where the hell your head is going to lay tonight." He turned around, walked into the bathroom and swung the door shut behind him.

Shit. Fuck. Shit. I didn't want to sleep with Gambler tonight. Gah, why were the gods against me tonight? First, I couldn't control myself when Gambler kissed me, and now I was being forced to sleep with him. Not at all how I had planned my night going. I heard the toilet flush and the water turn on. I only had probably thirty seconds before Gambler walked in shirtless and possibly with no pants on.

I grabbed the empty pet carrier and set it next to the desk. I pulled my suitcase onto the bed and rummaged through it, trying to find my pajamas. I was going to have to sleep with Gambler. There was really no way around it. As much as I wanted to make him sleep on the floor, I knew I couldn't do that to him.

With my pajamas and makeup bag in hand, I stood at the bathroom door waiting for him to come out. I bent over, tucking my clothes under my arm and slid my heels off. Just as I got the second one off, Gambler walked out of the bathroom, my head level with his crotch. Just lovely.

"That's one way to greet someone when they walk out of the bathroom," he chuckled.

I stood up, almost smashing my head into his leg, and stood face to face with him. Well, it wasn't exactly face to face. It was more face to chest. Without my heels on I was much shorter than Gambler. "I was taking my shoes off."

"Sure," Gambler said, walking around me, "keep telling yourself that, doll."

I stormed into the bathroom and slammed the door shut behind me. Fuck he was an infuriating man. I dropped my makeup bag on the side of the sink and looked in the mirror. My hair was still perfectly pinned and my makeup perfect, but I felt like I had been run over by a Mac truck. I grabbed a makeup wipe out of my bag and started erasing my hour worth of hard work.

After all my makeup was off, I unpinned my hair, dropping the discarded bobby pins into my makeup, a couple missing their target when I threw them, but I didn't pick up. Hopefully Gambler steps on them and wonders where the hell they came from.

I brushed out my hair, feeling the sleek smoothness under my fingers and grabbed my clothes off the back of the toilet.

I didn't really have conventional pajamas. Most of the time it was an old vintage tee and booty shorts. When Gambler had unexpectedly come over tonight, I was already dressed for bed, and he got a glimpse of my shortest booty shorts. Hell, he saw me in them the whole time. His eyes flared when his gaze ran up and down my body. I knew what I was working with and how to flaunt it. I had a nice rack, thick thighs, and a nice ass. I had to say I think Gambler agreed. I had just recently dyed my hair a deep midnight blue that every time the sun or light hit it just right the dark blue shined.

I stepped out of my dress and hung it over the shower rod, deciding I would hang it up in the morning. As I slipped on my tee and shorts, my long day really hit me, and I felt like I was ready to fall over. After tossing my hair up in a messy knot on the top of my head, I turned off the light and opened the door to pitch dark.

"About time," I heard grumbled from the darkness.

"I was in there for ten minutes." If Gambler was grumbling about ten minutes, he was going to shit a brick when he saw how long it took me to get ready in the morning. "Why did you turn off the lights? I can't even see my hand in front of my face."

"Jesus," he mumbled. I heard him reach around, and then his phone lit up the room. "Get your ass in bed, doll."

"Where's Mr. T.?" I asked, looking around the floor for him.

"His fluffy ass is under the covers, purring like there's no tomorrow."

"You let him under the covers?" I was utterly shocked. From what I had seen of Gambler and Mr. T together, they weren't fans of each other

"He didn't really give me much choice. As soon as I pulled the covers back, he sprang up on the bed and burrowed to the bottom of the bed."

I walked to the bed and pulled the covers back, Mr. T staring back at me. "Hey pretty man," I cooed.

"Jesus Christ, you did not just call the cat pretty man."

My eyes snapped to Gambler, "He's my cat, I'll call him whatever I want."

"You know what, I think we just need to stop talking to each other altogether. Although I'm sure you'd get pissed at me for breathing too loud then."

He was probably right. "You do breathe too loud."

Gambler rolled his eyes and shut the light off on his phone. "Sleep, now," he ordered.

I slipped under the warm comforter, laying on my side and Mr. T crawled to my bent knees and cuddled into me. I was facing Gambler but couldn't see him. "Why is it so dark in here?"

"Because it's night time, doll. That's what happens."

"I know that, dick. I meant why don't you have a night light on?"

"Do I look like a fucking five-year-old who needs a night light, doll?"

"No, it's just that I typically need some kind of light on to sleep." I always left a light on in my living room, plus I had a night light in the hallway and my bedroom. I may come off as a badass, but I still had stupid, irrational fears. Darkness was one of them.

"I know, whenever I slept at your house after you feel asleep I had to turn off all the God damn lights just to get some rest."

"Hey! You can't turn off my lights."

"Gwen."

"What?"

"Can we finish this argument in the morning? When I said I was exhausted, I meant it." I could hear how tired he was, and I felt bad that I was keeping him awake.

"Yeah, I'm sorry," I whispered.

"Nothing to be sorry for, doll. I just need some sleep. I'm sure you do, too."

I opened my mouth to argue with him that I wasn't tired, but I stopped and realized I was tired too. What the hell was wrong with me? He was right, every time he said something to me I had to disagree with him, even if I was wrong. "Night, Gambler," I whispered.

"Night, doll." He rolled over, his back to me and his breathing evens out within minutes, and I knew he was asleep.

Mr. T was purring contently cuddled up to me, and I closed my eyes. Maybe I was ridiculous with Gambler. He never really did anything to me to warrant the attitude I threw at him all the time. He just drove me crazy. He was always telling me what to do. I think what really drove me crazy was he only told me what to do because he was trying to be nice.

I never had anyone who told me what to do who had my best interest at heart. I sighed, wondering what the hell was wrong with me. I finally had a guy who tried to be nice and treat me right and what did I do? Call him a dick all the time.

"Do I have to turn on the goddamn bathroom light so you will stop huffing and puffing over there?" Gambler growled.

"I thought you were sleeping?" I whispered. I didn't mean to wake him up.

"I'm not." Jeez, he sounded annoyed. "You want the light on or not?"

Um, I totally wanted the light on, but I didn't want Gambler to go out of his way to make me happy. I decided not to say anything and prayed he would go back to sleep, and I would try to get a handle on my sighing.

Gambler whipped the cover back, scaring both Mr. T. and me, got out of bed and stalked over to the bathroom. The light flicked on, illuminating half the room. I turned over, catching a glimpse of his back that was heavily tattooed, as he pulled the door almost shut, leaving it open a crack. It was perfect. It didn't light up the whole room, but it helped to make the room not so dark.

He stomped back over to his side of the bed and slid back under the covers, tossing them over us. "Sleep," he growled.

Mr. T cuddled back up to me and was purring within seconds. I tucked my hands under my cheek and closed my eyes. I was out in minutes.

''*'*'*'*'*'*'*'*'*'*'*

Gambler

I heard light snoring and thanked God she was finally asleep. Gwen was always going a mile a minute, even while lying in bed trying to go to sleep. I could hear all the thoughts swirling around in her head before I turned on the bathroom light.

I was amazed she didn't put up more of a fight when I told her that she would have to sleep with me. I'm sure if she actually would have put up a fuss I could have found somewhere else to sleep, but I wasn't going to let her know that.

Turning over, I saw her beautiful face that was always throwing sass at me, finally relaxed and looked peaceful. Two weeks ago she had dyed her hair dark blue and somehow pulled it off. I had never met someone like her before that was always changing something about the way they look. Whether it was her hair, nails, makeup or clothes, you never knew what Gwen was going to look like every morning.

The only time I saw her not all gussied up was right before she went to bed or right when she woke up. She didn't stay relaxed and casual for long. Her clothes were some kind of armor for her. What she was protecting herself from I had no clue.

She talked about her aunt often, telling me she was the whole reason she had moved to Rockton. I didn't know much except her aunt had raised Gwen and her sister, and she felt it was her job to take care of her now. The aunt had a stroke two months ago and was just recently getting back to normal. I had yet to meet her, but I knew it was only a matter of time that I would be able to.

Gwen went to see her, at least, three times a week, and I would be going with her this week since King wanted someone with each of the girls at all times.

She rolled over in her sleep, cuddling into me, resting her head on my shoulder. She sighed contently and continued to snore. I wrapped my arm around her, pulling her to me and kissed her on the top of her head.

I know I had told her after our kiss that it was a mistake, but I was wrong. Kissing her was probably one of the best choices I had made in a while.

She tossed her arm over my stomach, and I wondered what the tough chick who fought me at every turn would think about the sleepy, sweet Gwen, who was curled to me, sleeping peacefully.

I closed my eyes, willing sleep to come and pushing all thoughts of Gwen's soft, sexy body pressed against me out of my mind.

It took a long fucking time to fall asleep.

''*'*'*'*'*'*'*'*'*'*

Chapter 5

Gwen

"Holy shit, did you have to drug her to sleep in the same bed as you?"

"No, I just knocked her over the head and had my way with her."

"Ah, nice."

What the hell was I listening to? I cracked one eye open and looked right into Mr. T's eyes. He let out an 'I'm hungry' meow and batted his paw at me.

"I got some shit to take care of. You think you can hang out with Gwen for an hour or so?" Gambler asked, his footsteps sounding like they were headed out the door.

"Yeah, Troy and I were going to grab some lunch. I'm sure Gwen will want to come with us." My brain unfogged a bit and realized Gambler was talking to Marley.

"Thanks. Just stay with Troy and don't let her out of your sight." The door slammed shut, and there was quiet.

"I know you're awake, bitch."

Shit, I didn't think I moved at all. How the hell did she know I was awake? I had every intention of faking sleep so Marley would go away, and then I could actually go back to sleep. "It's all a figment of your imagination," I chanted, waving my arm back and forth.

"Hmm, so you sleeping with Gambler last night is also part of this figment of my imagination, too?" Marley grabbed the covers and pulled them off and tossed them on the floor.

"Yes, you're sleep walking. Go back to sleep, Marley, you're drunk."

Marley tossed her head back giggling and jumped on the bed. "How did I go from sleep walking to drunk?"

"Drunk sleepwalking. That explains it all. Now leave me, I need my beauty sleep." I grabbed Mr. T and cuddled him to me, burying my face in his fur.

"It's almost noon. You need to get your ass up and go to lunch with Troy and me. Plus, I need to fill you in on everything that happened with Troy last night."

"From the sounds of it, I would say things went well with Troy last night if that silly smile on your face is any indication."

"Oh, things went way more than well." Marley laid down next to me, grabbing Gambler's pillow and crammed it under her head. "Hmm, Gambler smells good," she said, burying her face in the soft pillow.

"I wouldn't know," I mumbled, lying. I totally knew how good Gambler smelled. I had woken up a couple of hours ago, surprised that I was wrapped around Gambler, my head resting on his bare chest.

"I bet you don't know," Marley laughed, tossing the pillow at me. "Up. Now." Marley rolled off the bed and stood up, straightening her clothes.

"You are such a bitch."

"No, I'm not. You're just pissed I walked in on you sleeping with Gambler."

"Whatever. You think we can swing by the shop after lunch?" I asked, running my fingers through my hair.

"Oh, I know that look!" Marley exclaimed, pointing her finger at me.

"What? What look?" What the hell was she talking about?

"The same look you got the last time you changed your hair. What are we going to do this time?" Marley clapped her hands, a smile lighting up her face.

"Um, maybe highlights?"

"Blonde?"

"Eh, been there."

"Blood red?" I could tell Marley was getting more and more excited with each guess.

"Nope."

"Purple? I don't know how well that will show up with the midnight blue you have right now." Marley bit her lip, studying my hair.

"I've done purple so many times. No purple."

"I give. Tell me," she ordered, propping her hands on her hips.

I grabbed a strand of hair and twirled it around my finger. I knew as soon as I say it, Marley was going to flip. I had been needing a change but didn't know what I wanted to do. It had just popped into my head, and I knew it was exactly what I needed. "Orange."

Marley's jaw dropped, and I knew I had shocked her. "Wow. Like all over?"

"Kind of like peek-a-boo. Here and there, mostly underneath." I ran my fingers through my hair, feathering it out.

"Holy shit, I'm excited! Get up, let's go! I'd say let's skip lunch, but I know Troy is starving. You get dressed, I'm gonna go check on Meg." Marley dashed from the room, not waiting for a response.

I stretched out, Mr. T meowing in protest. I stood up, pulling my hair up into a messy knot on the top of my head and looked around the room.

It was just as plain as I thought it was last night, you couldn't even tell whose room it was. Right now it looked like I lived here, not Gambler. All of my crap was spread out on the bathroom sink, and my top suitcase was open, clothes hanging out of it.

Gambler really was a mystery to me. All I knew about him was the little he had told me and what I had picked up from being around him.

I grabbed my suitcase and threw it on the bed and unzipped it, clothes busting out of it. I really did have a shoe and clothing addiction. I couldn't help it. It was unbelievable what a fabulous pair of shoes paired with the perfect skirt could do to boost your mood.

I grabbed my cropped jeans, white button down shirt and a red bandana to tie my hair back with.

As I slipped on the jeans and shirt, I felt like I was channeling Rosie the Riveter from those magazine ads from the fifties. I grabbed a black pair of flats and slid my feet into them.

After fifteen minutes of quick swiping on eyeshadow and lip gloss, I tied my hair back with the bandana and grimaced. I had puffy bags under my eyes, and I just looked tired. I may have gotten seven hours of sleep, but you sure couldn't tell by looking at me.

I flipped the bathroom light off and grabbed my purse as I walked past Mr. T, who was sprawled out on top of the bed and gave him a quick pat on the head.

I quick set up his kitty litter, cursing myself for not doing it earlier. I'm surprised Mr. T wasn't crossing his legs, giving me the evil eye.

"Hey, you ready?" Marley asked, sticking her head in the room.

"Yeah, I just had to get Mr. T. all set up." I grabbed my purse, hitching it up on my shoulder and slipped out the door, making sure it was shut behind me.

"Troy's waiting in the truck. I told him after lunch we were headed to the salon."

"I'm sure he was excited about that," I laughed, following Marley down the long hall and into the common room.

"Ha, you're right. I told him I would make it up to him later." Marley glanced back at me, winking.

No one was in the large common room, only the TV playing quietly, as we walked past. I had never seen this part of the clubhouse without someone in it. "Where is everyone?"

"The guys are in church, and Meg and Cyn are in Lo's room watching TV. I think Ethel is in the kitchen."

"Did you want to see if Cyn and Meg wanted to come?'

"I did. They said next time. They were in the middle of Dirty Dancing and said they weren't moving until the end."

We walked out the front door, straight into Troy's truck that he had idling smack dab in front of the front door.

"Door to door service, ladies," Troy smirked as Marley climbed in, placing a kiss on Troy's cheek.

"Well, aren't you just a gentleman." I hoisted myself up into the jacked up truck and slammed the door shut. "Think your truck is high enough?" I asked, buckling my seat belt.

"Women like big hair, men like big trucks." Troy winked at me over Marley's head and laughed.

"I think big hair went out in the eighties," Marley snickered.

"Yeah, well, big trucks sure as hell didn't." Troy pulled out of the parking lot and headed to the diner across town.

By the time we had pulled into the parking lot of the restaurant, my stomach was growling with hunger, and I was ready to eat an elephant.

First, on my to-do list was to order the biggest stack of pancakes ever, devour them, and then head to the salon to give into the change I needed so badly. I was feeling restless and had no idea why.

Hopefully, it only had to do with my hair and not about a tall, handsome man who was taking up too much of my time.

''*'*'*'*'*'*'*'*'*

32

Chapter 6

Gambler

I hated the way it smelled here. It felt like death was hanging overhead, the stench of lives lost surrounding me.

The grave was overgrown when I had shown up, and I immediately trimmed away the grass and brushed off the loose leaves and debris that always seemed to gather around the headstone.

I hated coming here, but it also was something I had to do. It had been almost a month since I had come here and it was eating me alive that I had waited so long.

My fingertips grazed over the name engraved on the cold stone, tracing the name of one of the first women I had ever loved.

Evelyn Margret Holmes

1984-2009

She was only twenty-five when she had left too soon. I still remember that day like it was yesterday.

"Sorry, I haven't been by in a while, Evie. Things have been crazy at the clubhouse." I paused, expecting an answer, knowing I wouldn't get one. "I talked to mom the other day. She said she came out to see you last week. From the looks of the grass, it must have been a quick stop to see you."

I glanced around, seeing the undertaker's blue truck enter the far gate and slowly pass by. He raised his hand in hello but didn't stop. "I'll have to talk to Bernie and let him know he needs to take better care when he mows. Although the snow will be flying soon."

I ran my fingers through my hair, trying to find more to say. "I told you King met someone, right? Well, now Rigid fell in love with Meg's best friend, Cyn. Gravel finally hooked up with Ethel and Gravel's daughter moved back into town. She works at a salon and started dating Meg's other best friend. Somehow her boss got mixed up in all the shit swirling around the club, and now I'm supposed to keep an eye on her. Her name is Gwen. You'd really like her. She's got a style all her own just like you did."

Maybe that was why I was so drawn to Gwen but pushed her away at the same time. She reminded me so much of Evie when she was alive. Evie was always the life of the party, making friends with everyone. She always wore the craziest clothes, but always made them look good. I never thought I would meet someone like Evie again, and then I met Gwen.

The wind picked up, sending a chill with it that made me pull my coat tight around me. It was definitely fall now. The leaves were changing colors and the days were getting shorter. "I hope you're happy wherever you are, Evie. I miss you every day." My words floated away, silence the only response.

I grabbed the shears I always brought with me and headed back to my bike, sticking them into my saddlebag. I didn't know the next time I would find time to come out and talk to Evie, but I knew it would be soon. I never could stay away from her for too long.

As I swung my leg over the bike, my phone dinged, a message coming through.

I swiped the screen and brought up the text Troy had just sent me. *At the salon. You might want to get here when you can.*

Why the hell would I need to get to the salon? I had asked Troy to keep an eye on Gwen for me while I went to church and then headed out here. I had already been gone three hours and wouldn't be back for another hour.

Be back in an hour. I'll meet you at the salon. I pocketed my phone, not waiting for a response and cranked up my bike. I glanced one last time at Evie's grave, wishing things could be different but knew things had happened the way they did for a reason.

Evie was meant to be in my life for only a short time, but it was some of the best moments of my life.

I roared out of the cemetery, leaving Evie behind, headed for the woman who was so much like Evie, but not. When I had lost Evie, I had almost died. I had never known a loss like that before, and her death had left a gaping hole in my heart. I hoped I never felt that again. I knew the only way to never feel that again was to never love again. I had been doing a pretty damn good job of it these past seven years, but I had a feeling Gwen was going to have something different to say about my heart being closed off. She might be the one person who could make me love again. Hopefully, I would make it out alive this time again. With only knowing Gwen a short time, I knew she could be the one thing to bring me to my knees and make me beg for mercy.

''*'*'*'*'*'*'*'*'

34

Chapter 7
Gwen

"Holy shit, you look hot. I wanna do that. Can I do that?" Marley rambled to Troy.

"Do whatever you want, sunshine. Although you and Gwen might look like twins if you do orange like her."

"I'm down with that. Gwen is a sexy Rosie the Riveter."

I busted out laughing, assuming my attempt to look like Rosie had been accomplished this morning. "I'm gonna run to the bathroom quickly and then we can head out."

"Okay. I'm gonna grab the color book and figure out what color I want to go with," Marley mumbled, walking over to the front desk and started digging through the pile of binders I had stacked on the bottom shelf.

I slipped into the bathroom, lightly shutting the door behind me and looked in the mirror.

I had done it. I had put peek-a-boo orange in my hair, and it looked sick. After Marley had dyed it, she had blown it out and curled it, making the orange strands stand out.

She had put it half up and then folded my bandana, knotting it, on the top of my head, to hold my hair back. The orange popped out against the black of my hair, and I freakin' loved it. It was exactly what I needed.

I fluffed my hair, glancing one last time in the mirror and headed back out to Marley and Troy. "Do you think we could swing by the store and pick up some-" I stopped mid-sentence when I saw Gambler standing where Marley and Troy were. When the hell did he get here?

"We can go wherever you want, doll. You're on the back of my bike now." Gambler was leaning against the front desk, his arms crossed over his chest as his eyes roamed up my body.

Thank goodness I had taken the time to get ready today and not just slap on some yoga pants and call it good. "Marley and Troy can take me where I need to go. They were the ones who brought me here."

"I know who brought you here, doll. I've known where you've been all day."

"How the hell have you known that? I haven't seen you all day." I crossed my arms over my chest, annoyance rolling off of me.

"Text." Son of a bitch. Troy had probably been sending Gambler messages all day about what we were doing.

"Hmph, whatever. So you get to know where I am at all times, but you can disappear for hours without anyone knowing where you are?"

"The people who needed to know knew where I was."

"Apparently, I was not one of the ones who needed to know where you were." I have no idea why that bothered me so much, but it did.

"No, doll. I had some things to take care of. That's all you need to know."

"Hardly seems fair."

"Not much in life is fair. You done playing with your hair?"

Playing with my hair? What an ass. What I did with hair was way more than playing. I doubt Gambler could even do a simple braid. I turned hair into works of art. "Is that what you think I do, play with hair?"

Gambler held his hands up, knowing he was treading on delicate ground. "I didn't mean anything by it."

"Yeah, well, my playing with my hair pays the bills and keeps the lights on."

Gambler walked towards me, the tip of his boots touching the tips of my flats. He reached up, grabbing a strand of orange hair and twirled it around his finger. "Orange?"

Gah, why did he have to get so close? I could smell his cologne float around me, distracting me from the fact I was mad at him five seconds ago. "Yes, orange."

"You know you picked my favorite color, doll?"

I did? Oh shit. I had seen the tank on his bike a week ago and noticed how it was a burnt orange that I loved, but I didn't know it was his favorite color. "It's just a color I picked out." Lie, lie, lie, Gwen. I felt my face heat, hoping Gambler wouldn't see through my lie.

"Hmm, I guess I'll give you that one for right now." He leaned down as I looked up and our eyes locked. "My favorite color or not, doll, you look like a smokin' hot fifties pin-up model."

"Rockabilly," I whispered.

"What, doll?"

"The way I dress, it's called Rockabilly." Not a lot of people knew what that was, especially people in Rockton. When I had moved here to live by my aunt, I had shocked the town. I loved the era of the fifties and the way I dressed reflected that. I wasn't a true rockabilly because I just couldn't get into the music from the forties and fifties. I liked it, but I tended to lean more toward more modern music.

"Well, whatever the fuck it's called, I like it. Especially on you."

"Thank you," I whimpered as his arms snaked around me. This was not good. Not good at all. Being wrapped up in Gambler's arms made me forget my own name, let alone the fact this man drove me crazy with every word that came out of his mouth.

He stroked my back, and I relaxed into his arms and held onto his biceps. "You hungry, doll?"

Hungry? Was I hungry? I had no freakin' clue. All I knew was I wanted to feel Gambler's lips on mine again. "Um, I don't know."

"You don't know if you're hungry?" Gambler smirked.

Sweet Jesus, I needed to pull it together. I had been in the arms of men before and able to keep it together. What the hell was it about Gambler that made me lose it? "Yes, I'm hungry," I said, clearing my throat and tried to step back from Gambler.

His arms tightened around me, and he pulled me closer. "Not so fast, doll." He leaned down, his lips a breath away.

"What are we doing, Gambler?"

"Right now?"

I nodded my head yes, unable to form another sentence.

His eyes searched my face, and I saw something change. "Nothing, we're doing nothing." Gambler pulled away and turned his back to me. He hung his head down and ran his fingers through his hair.

I stumbled backward, not expecting the change in him. I brushed my fingertips against my lips, wishing he would have let go and kissed me.

This was for the best. Getting tangled up with Gambler was a dead end street that was only going to end up in heartache.

"I'll just grab my purse and then we can go get something to eat," I mumbled, walking into the small back room, not waiting for Gambler to answer.

I grabbed my purse and leaned against the small counter, tilting my head back. What the hell was I doing? Was I really wishing for Gambler to kiss me?

The last time I had given in to what my body had wanted, it had started out fantastic, but then crashed and burned. I couldn't go through what I had gone through before. I had told myself after Matt that I would never fall for another man who would just break my heart.

I couldn't let Gambler in. I was still broken from the last time.

''*'*'*'*'*'*'*'*'*

Chapter 8
Gambler

Son of a bitch.

God dammit that woman got under my skin in a second and made me forget everything I had been telling myself.

As soon as I had seen her, all I wanted to do was pin her to the wall and take everything she had to offer. Her soft, warm body in my arms almost tipped me over the edge.

She mumbled something about grabbing her purse, but I couldn't even turn around to look at her. I needed to get control. I didn't want to need Gwen the way I did. I didn't want the attraction that made me search her out in a crowded room. I just wanted my life to go back to the way it was before Gwen had barged in and started throwing her sass all over and making my body beg for her.

I'd take her to get something to eat and then head back to the clubhouse where there was always someone around, and it would keep me from putting my hands on her.

"I'm ready," she chirped from behind me, apparently not as affected as I was.

I rubbed my hands down my face and tried to pull my head out of my ass and get it together. "Where do you feel like eating?" I asked, turning around to look at her. She really did look like a fifties pin-up goddess.

"Why don't we get pizza and take it back to the clubhouse. I'm sure everyone else is hungry."

"Sounds like a plan, doll, but we're going to have to get it delivered. I don't think we can carry ten pizzas on my bike," I laughed.

"Oh, that's right. Well, then we might as well head back to the clubhouse, and then we can see what everyone wants." She walked towards the front door, making sure everything was turned off and stood by the door waiting for me. "You coming?" she asked, cocking her head to the side, smiling at me.

I shook my head, trying to get the image of her swinging hips as she walked out of my head and grabbed my keys out of my pocket as I walked by her. I slipped out the door, waiting for her to shut and lock it and then walked over to my bike.

"Ever been on a motorcycle?" I grabbed the helmet I had in the saddlebag and handed it to her.

"This is going to give me helmet hair," she complained, handing it back to me.

"I don't give a shit about the fact it's going to wreck your hair. All I care about is that it's going to protect your head in case we crash." I grabbed it from her and set it on her head, snapping the strap shut.

"You don't have to be such a dick," she sassed at me as she adjusted the helmet, trying to fix her hair.

"I'm keeping you safe. If that means I'm a dick, I'm okay with that." I swung my leg over the motorcycle and waited for her to climb on.

"Um," she said, tapping me on the shoulder, "I haven't been on a motorcycle in a long time."

"Swing your leg over and hold on," I smirked, looking over my shoulder at her.

"I'm sure there's more to it than that. If we crash, it's your fault, not mine. I told you it's been awhile." She swung her leg over, kicking me in the side and finally sat down behind me.

"Next time try it without kicking me," I laughed, cranking up the bike.

"You know what, I can totally call Marley to come and pick me up." Gwen sat back from me. I looked over my shoulder and saw her with her arms crossed over her chest glaring at me.

"You're my responsibility, doll. Not Troy's. Where I go, you go. End of story." I yelled over the roar of the engine. I reached back, grabbing her arms and wrapped them around my waist. "Hold on!" I grabbed the handlebars and pulled onto the street. Gwen's arms tightened around me, and I knew she wasn't going to let go until the bike stopped, no matter how pissed off at me she was.

"You're still a dick," she yelled in my ear. I gunned the throttle making Gwen yelp in surprise and wrap her arms around me even tighter.

Good, maybe if she thought I was a dick she would swing those hips at someone else, and I could go back to the way things were before I walked into her salon and she tipped my world on its side.

'''*'*'*'*'*'*

Gwen

Hold on. Jesus Christ. I was holding on alright. I had the strangest feeling that I was seconds away from death and having the best time of my life. I glanced down, the pavement speeding past underneath us, the white line a blur.

I had never been on a motorcycle before, but not for a lack of trying. I begged my aunt for two years to get a motorcycle when I was sixteen, but she had solidly refused. She told me when I was eighteen I could get a motorcycle with my own money. Well, eighteen hit and as much as I wanted a bike, the money was never there to get one. Plus, living in Illinois meant I would still have to buy a car for the winter months, so it just made sense to only have a car since I couldn't afford both. Holding on for my life was either curing the need for a motorcycle or feeding the urge. The jury was still out.

Gambler drove like the bike was an extension of his body. He maneuvered the curves with ease, rolling to stops and then rocketing off. We were only five minutes away from the clubhouse, but Gambler took the long way, basically driving to the other side of town and then to the clubhouse.

"Um, I think there might be a quicker way to get to the clubhouse than the one you just took," I said, clambering off the bike and unsnapping the helmet. I took it off, shoving it into Gambler's hands.

"Eh, felt like going for a ride, doll." He shrugged, hanging the helmet from the handlebars.

"No, you wanted to see how many times you could make me shriek."

Gambler leaned in, his lips inches away from mine. "I admit nothing, doll. Just felt like going for a ride."

"You're a dick," I spat back.

"So you keep saying, but I doubt you have anything to back that up."

"Dick."

"Doll."

"I hate you." Ugh, this man was turning me into a pissed off five-year-old.

"No, you don't. You just hate the fact that I was right, and I was only trying to keep you safe. You're on the back of my bike, you wear a helmet. King, Rigid, and Gravel have the same rule for when their ol' ladies are on the back of their bikes."

"I'm not you're ol' lady. Ever."

"I never said you were."

"Ahh, I fucking hate you!" I stomped off, pissed that Gambler could evoke such a strong response out of me. I could barely remember the reason I was so pissed at him. I ripped open the door to the clubhouse and walked over to the couch where Cyn and Meg were sitting.

"Love the hair!" Meg gushed, pulling me out of my pissed off mood.

"Thanks, I needed a change." I fluffed my hair, running my fingers through it.

"Told you it was killer," Marley said, walking out of the kitchen.

"Thanks for leaving me with dickhead, Marley." I crossed my arms over my chest.

"Hey," Marley held her hands up, "I tried to stay, but Troy told me we had to go. Plus, it's Gambler. Not like I left you with the some stranger."

"No, not a stranger, but definitely a dick."

"Look, I'm sorry. I figured things were cool with you two since I found you in his bed this morning." Marley plopped down in the recliner and popped open the footrest.

"What? What the hell did I miss?" Cyn asked, looking between Marley and me.

"Shit, I totally forgot to tell you guys. I caught Gwen and Gambler in bed this morning."

"Damn girl, you work fast. Not as fast as Marley though," Meg laughed.

"Bitch," Marley yelled, throwing a pillow at Meg.

"First and last one-night stand, night, sunshine?" Troy bragged, walking out of the kitchen, his mouth full.

"Damn straight," Marley laughed. Troy fell into the recliner next to Marley, tossing his arm around her.

"Look, I need help. Meg, do you think that you could talk to King and try to see if there is someone else who can watch me until this, this … whatever the hell is going on is over." I waved my arms around, not knowing what the hell to call what all this going on was. I knew the bare facts; that the Assassins were after the Knights for some bullshit reason, and now everyone was in danger until they figured out what the hell to do.

"I can ask, but I don't think it's going to help. Lo likes to keep club business away from me. Although the club business tried to blow up my house last night, so maybe he might listen to me."

"Please, Meg. You can make that man do anything you want. Flash him some boob and he'll be putty in your hands. I'm begging you. If I have to spend any more time with Gambler, I will not be held responsible for my actions."

"All right. I'll see what I can do tonight. You'll have to deal with him till I talk to Lo."

I glanced over my shoulder at Gambler, who had just walked in the front door. God dammit, why the hell did the man have to look so good? His jeans were molded to his legs, and his t-shirt was just tight enough to remind me what he looked like shirtless, it made me want to walk over and rip it off. This man was fucking with my head, and it was driving me crazy.

One more day. I could totally handle being around him for one more day without throwing myself at him.

He crooked his finger for me to come over and I rolled my eyes. What the hell did the man want now?

"What?" I asked, walking over to him.

He reached into his back pocket and grabbed his wallet. "Find out what everyone wants and order pizza." I glanced down as he opened his wallet and my eyes bugged out at the wad of cash he thumbed through. He handed me five twenties and shoved his wallet back in his pocket.

"I need one hundred dollars for pizza?" I asked, shocked, grabbing the money.

"You need more, come find me before the guy gets here and let me know."

"Um, I don't think I'll need any more money." I folded the money up and put it in my pocket. "Can't I just order a bunch of different pizzas and let them go at it?"

"Whatever you want, doll. Just make sure you get one with everything on it and make sure I get a piece." Gambler winked at me and headed down the hall to the bedrooms.

"Did I hear pizza?" Marley asked, walking up to me.

"Um, yeah," I mumbled watching Gambler's retreating back.

"Yes!" Marley pumped her fist in the air. "You want me to order? I'm tight with the owner." Marley pulled her phone out of her pocket and started pushing buttons.

"How the hell are you tight with the pizza guy?"

"I order like three times a week." Marley held her finger up, silencing me. "Mike! It's Marley! How are you?" Marley walked away talking to whoever the hell Mike was like they were best friends.

I looked around seeing people milling around, most of them I knew, but there were a couple that I had never seen before. I glanced at the clock on the wall seeing it was almost five and wondered where the day went. There was a guy behind the bar handing out drinks, and I decided a drink was just exactly what I needed.

Gambler had told me to make myself at home, and if I were at home, I would definitely be getting the bottle of vodka out of the cabinet tonight.

"What'll it be, darlin'?" the guy behind the bar asked.

"Gin and tonic. Make it a double." He moved behind the bar grabbing the bottles he needed and started making my drink. "So, what's your name?"

"Demon. I'm the V.P."

I was taken back by the fact that the vice president of the club was making me a drink. I really didn't know a lot about MC's, but I kind of figured the vice president making you a drink was not the norm. "You often sling drinks for the club?"

"Ha. No, not really. It's Turtle's night to be behind the bar, but he's over in the shop finishing up an El Camino, and I told him I would cover for him until he finishes up." He set my drink down in front of me, and I took a sip. Pure heaven.

"Well, if it's any consolation, the next time I see you behind the bar I'm going to have you make me five drinks because that is the best gin and tonic I have ever had."

"Gotcha. If all else fails, I can be a bartender." Demon winked at me, his eyes sparkling with humor.

Demon walked away, taking drink orders from other club members, each of them ribbing him about being behind the bar.

I turned around, leaning against the bar, propping my elbows up. Marley and Troy were toe to toe, wrapped in each other's arms. They both had their heads thrown back laughing. I was happy for Marley. She deserved to find her happy ending. Lord knew she had gone through enough to finally find Troy.

My phone buzzed, letting me know I had a text message and pulled it out of my pocket. I turned back to the bar, setting my drink down and opened the message.

I put my two-week notice in today.

Yes! It was about time Paige got up here. Paige was my older sister who still lived in Rhyton. I had been pestering her for the past year that she needed to move to Rockton.

Hell yes! When will you be here? You're moving in with me, right?

LOL. We'll see. I'm not sure I can live with your neat freakiness. We barely made it through childhood without killing each other.

I hated to admit it, but Paige was right. It really was a miracle we had lived to see adulthood. While I was a neat freak and wanted everything in its place, Paige was the complete opposite and seemed to thrive in messy chaos.

OK. If anything, I'll help you find a place to live.

"What put that smile on your face, doll?"

I whirled around, scared by Gambler sneaking up on me. "Jesus, you scared the bejeebus out of me."

Gambler smirked at me and signaled to Demon. Demon grabbed a bottle of whiskey and poured it into a glass full of ice and set it in front of Gambler.

"Sorry, doll. Didn't mean to scare you." He took a sip of his drink and set it down next to mine. "What's got you smiling at your phone like a loon?"

"Oh, um, just my sister. I think she might actually be moving up here in a couple of weeks."

"No shit?" I nodded my head yes and grabbed my drink. "She gonna live with you?"

"Um, I'm trying to convince her to move in with me, but she says we'd clash. She does have a point. Growing up, it's amazing we didn't kill each other." I took a sip of my drink and swirled the liquid in the glass around.

"What made her decide to finally move here?"

"I've been trying to convince her to move here since I did. Ever since our aunt got sick, I've been slowly wearing her down. She put her two-week notice in at work today, so now it's official." I knew I was smiling like a crazy person, but I was so damn excited that Paige was moving here.

"I'm happy for you, doll." He took a sip of his drink and looked me up and down. "You order that pizza?"

"Um," I glanced over his shoulder and saw Marley walking back into the main room. "Marley said she was going to order it. Something about being tight with the owner. Although I really doubt it's going to cost as much as you gave me." I dug into my pocket and handed the money back to him.

He shook his head and drained his glass empty. "Wanna bet?"

"What? No. Just take the money back. You can pay the guy." He set his glass on the bar, signaling to Demon he needed a refill and grabbed the money out of my hand. "Let's make a bet, doll. They don't call me Gambler for nothing." He grabbed a stool, pulling it out for me and motioned for me to sit down.

I hoisted myself up on the stool and set my drink on the bar. "All right, what kind of bet? What happens when I win?"

"Ha. You mean *if* you win. I bet you that the pizza will be more than what I gave you."

"I'll take that bet because I know you are wrong. Now, I repeat, what do I get when I win?"

"You pick, doll. Just like I'll pick what I want when I win."

"Huh," I folded my arms over my chest and rolled my eyes at him. "Well, I wouldn't waste too much time thinking about what you want because you are so going to lose."

"We'll see, doll." He held his hand out for me to shake, a smirk playing on his lips.

I grabbed his hand, shaking it firmly and couldn't wait to see his face when he lost. There was no way this was a bet he was going to win. "You do this often? Make poor bets?"

"You'll see. I never make a bet I know I can't win." He released my hand and grabbed the drink Demon had refilled.

"Oh shit. I know that look. You just made a bet with him, didn't you?" Demon asked, leaning against the bar.

"Hell yeah, I did. Plus, it's a bet he's going to lose. I better think of what I want." I propped my head up on my arm I had rested on the bar.

"You're gonna learn real quick, darlin', that Gambler is not a person you want to make a bet against unless you know for a fact you'll win. He's brutal with what he wants when he wins," Demon warned, shaking his head.

"I'm sure I'll be okay. He handed me over one hundred dollars for pizza and told me I'll probably need more."

Demon just shook his head and walked away. I started doubting my decision when Demon didn't stay to reassure me that I was right. Oh shit.

"Oh my God. Marley told me about your hair, but it looks even more incredible than I pictured." I spun around on my stool and saw Meg and Cyn standing there.

"Oh, you like? It's a bit different, but I like it." I fluffed up my hair, forgetting I had even colored it today.

"It's amazing. Do you think you could put bright purple in mine? Remy told me I was too old to do crazy colors anymore, but I don't care. I'll be the eighty-year-old in the nursing home rocking pink hair and pushing my life alert button to see if any hot firemen show up."

Cyn leaned against the bar and crossed her arms over her chest. "That seems like a pretty accurate guess at what you'll be like."

"I know. I can't wait." Meg rubbed her hands together and laughed like a crazy villain from a cartoon.

"What do you two ladies want to drink?" Demon asked, filling a beer glass for one of the guys.

"Two Old Fashions, extra cherries," Meg called out.

"Sour or sweet?" Demon reached under the bar and grabbed two empty glasses.

"Um, just make it one. And Meg always drinks sweet. I'll have a Sprite or something." Cyn grabbed a barstool behind her and plopped down on it. "I'm so friggin tired, I'm afraid after a drink I'll pass out."

"You're going to make me drink alone, aren't you?" Meg complained.

"Just for tonight. Plus, Gwen is drinking, and I'm sure Marley will be, too. You can relive the bathroom incident the last time you drank with her. Just tell Demon to start brewing a pot of coffee." Cyn laughed, grabbing the Sprite Demon set in front of her.

"Um, do I want to know?" I asked.

"You're going to learn real quick, doll, that when Meg and Cyn are around, craziness is almost guaranteed to ensue. It's best just to stand back and watch." I looked over my shoulder at Gambler, and he threw a wink at me. I turned back to Cyn and Meg and felt him move behind me, putting his arm on the back of my chair.

"Good, sounds like fun." I know Gambler was trying to warn me, but Cyn and Meg look like a hell of a good time that I wanted in on. "Oh, I never got to ask. Are you ok? How bad is your house?"

Meg waved her hand at me and took a drink. "Eh, it's kind of messed up. They tossed it onto the front porch so of course, the porch is toast, but thankfully it didn't really hurt the house and we were all safe. I'm more pissed at the fact my favorite chair is now smithereens. It was the perfect chair to sit in, sipping cocktails and watch Lo work on his bike."

"She's going on and on about the damn chair again, isn't she?" King walked up behind Meg and wrapped his arms around her, kissing her on the side of the head.

"Eh, he knows me so well." She shrugged her shoulders and drained half of her glass in one drink.

"Well, thank God you were all okay, and I'm sure you can find another chair. It's the perfect reason to go shopping," I laughed. I tried to take a sip of my drink but was surprised that all that was left was ice cubes. Gambler grabbed it out of my hand and set it on the bar, shaking his head at me.

"Going down like water, doll."

"It was a long day," I said, shrugging my shoulders at him.

"Pizza will be here in probably ten minutes. Mike said he'll put a rush on it. I told him we had twenty hungry bikers." Marley walked up to our group, a wine cooler dangling from her fingertips.

"How much was it?" I asked.

"One-."

"Eh!" Gambler threw his hand up, silencing Marley. "We'll wait till the guy gets here."

Marley looked at Gambler like he was crazy but didn't finish her sentence. "Okay."

"Is that really all you are going to drink tonight? I almost got blew up. We need to celebrate. Shots!" Meg yelled, raising her hand in the air. She stood on the ring of her bar stool and leaned over the bar, grabbing the first bottle she touched.

"Hey, hey, hey. My bar, my rules." Demon grabbed the bottle out of her hand, setting it back down.

"Okay, whatever," she said, sitting back down. "We need shots. Buttery Nipples, four of them," Meg ordered.

"I swear to Christ, she doesn't hear a word I say," Cyn mumbled, standing up. "Make it three, Demon. I'm headed back to Rigid's room. I'll be out for some pizza later." Cyn shuffled down the hall, not waiting for a response.

"She okay?" King asked, watching Cyn disappear down the hall.

"She's been a crab ass lately. I think she's coming down with something. She was fine this morning when we were watching movies." Meg's eyes also watched Cyn walk away.

"Maybe someone should check on her," Marley said.

"I'm sure Rigid won't be far behind. He had some shit to finish in the shop. Once he gets his ass in here, we'll let him know about Cyn." King pulled his phone out of his pocket, glancing at it and shoved it into his pocket.

"You waiting for an important call?" Meg asked, grabbing the three shots Demon poured and handed them to Marley and me.

"Just checking to make sure I didn't miss any calls, babe."

"Okay! Let's toast!" Meg raised her glass. "To the fact that my ass is not a toasty human marshmallow right now." Meg clinked her glass against ours and tossed her shot back. Marley and I followed suit, the shot going down smoothly.

Marley started coughing the instant she drank it, and Gambler patted her on the back.

"Yo, pizza is here!" a guy by the door yelled.

"Oh hell yes, time for me to win a bet." I set my drink down and beelined to the door, dodging people and trying to not to spill their drinks. "How much is it?" I asked, pushing the guy who had opened the door out of the way.

The delivery boy's eyes were bugged out, and he looked at me in shock, "Ugh, that'll be one ninety-nine and fifty-four cents," he mumbled, thrusting the receipt at me.

"What the fuck." I scanned the receipt, counting 15 pizzas were ordered. "Holy shit."

"Why do you look so shocked, doll?" Gambler asked, coming up behind me, resting his hand on my hip.

"Because you were fucking right! Who the hell orders fifteen pizzas?"

"I do. Have you seen how many people are here? I doubt this will even be enough. I plan on devouring half of one by myself." Marley walked up, rubbing her hands together.

"Uh, you think I could get some help carrying these in?" The delivery boy looked around, his eyes huge saucers of awe as he looked at all the bikers.

"Roam, Ham, Turtle. Help bring the pizzas in," King yelled. The three guys filed out the door with Marley following behind, hot on the heels of the delivery guy.

"I do believe this means I won," Gambler said, pulling out the money he had handed me before. He opened his wallet and pulled out an extra twenty.

"It really wasn't a fair bet because I'm sure you've ordered pizza for this many people before. The most I've ever ordered for is four people. The bet is off," I huffed, crossing my arms over my chest. I knew Gambler wasn't going to let it go, but I had to try. I was terrified of what he was going to want for winning.

"Another thing you don't know about me, doll," he leaned in his face an inch away from mine. "I collect on every bet. Every time."

"This wasn't fair."

"Demon tried to warn you, doll. He knows I'm ruthless. I guess you just figured that out, too. I'll let you know what I want when I think of it." He winked at me and walked out the door.

Son of a bitch. I had no idea what Gambler was going to want from me. The possibilities were endless of the things he could want.

"Lost that bet, didn't you darlin'?" Demon asked, walking up to me.

"Hell yes. You could have warned me a little better. I didn't get a danger Will Robinson vibe from you at all. I thought you were just joking. Now I have to wait and see what Gambler is going to want since he won." I crossed my arms over my chest, pouting.

"I wouldn't worry too much about it. Gambler's a good guy most of the time." Demon winked at me, a smirk plastered on his face.

"It's the 'most of the time' I'm worried about." Gambler and guys walked passed us, there arms full of pizza boxes and set them down on the pool table. Marley walked in the door, one pizza box in her hands, the lid open.

"Couldn't wait?" I asked.

"I can never wait for pizza. Roam wanted me to grab a couple. I told him I was only out there for my dinner." She took a bite of a slice, cheese stringing from her face. "So fucking good," she mumbled her mouth full.

I reached into her box to grab a slice, but she slammed the lid shut on my hand. "No touchy." She waved her finger at me and walked away. Jesus, remember not to get between Marley and her pizza.

"Doll, come eat before these fuckers eat it all," Gambler called, a slice raised to his mouth.

Oh, Jesus. Why the hell did he have to look so sexy? Why did he have to make me want things I promised myself I would never want again? Gambler had trouble and heartbreaker written all over him. I needed to remember that.

Gambler was a one-way street to heartbreak. Time to find a detour around him.

But first, I needed a drink.

''*'*'*'*'*'*'*'*'*'*

Chapter 9
Gambler

"I've only had four drinks," Gwen said holding five fingers up in my face.

"That's five, doll."

"No, it's five." All I could do is shake my head and laugh.

After the pizza had come, Gwen had polished off half a pizza all by herself and slammed two gin and tonics in a matter of minutes. Throw in Meg yelling shots every ten minutes, Gwen was hammered.

"Let's get you to bed, doll. I really don't think you want to sleep on a pool table tonight." I had been trying to wrangle Gwen down the hall to my room, but she had veered over to the pool table and was now sprawled out on top of it. People had slept on the pool table before, but never in the middle of Roam and Demon's game.

"I think I can get it around her arm if she doesn't move," Roam said, closing one eye, squinting, and lined up his shot.

"Son of a bitch," I grabbed Gwen off the table seconds before Roam's pool stick connected with the ball. I tossed her over my shoulder and headed down the hall.

"Wait, wait, I didn't say byeeee to Meg. Or Marley." She pounded on my back, trying to make me stop.

I detoured over to Meg and Marley, who were sitting on top of the bar and swung Gwen around to see them.

"Gambler says I have to go to bed. He's a pooper. A party. I mean, aw fuck. I don't know," she rattled on, not able to put two sentences together.

"King is trying to get me into bed, too." Meg reached out, petting Gwen's head. "He's bossy but sooo hot. Like a taco, hot."

Marley burst out laughing, tossing her head back, falling off the bar. Thankfully Turtle was walking by, and he broke her fall. "Oh no, I broke the turtle," Marley laughed, shakily getting up off the floor.

"I think it's everyone's time for bed," Troy said, walking around the bar, helping Turtle off the floor.

"What the hell just happened?" he asked, watching Marley lean heavily against the bar.

"I think we should have cut them off two drinks ago." Troy patted Turtle on the back and walked over to Marley to help steady her.

"Okay, doll, time for bed." I nodded at Troy and King, knowing they were going to have as much fun as I was about to have hauling Gwen to bed.

"Bye, Ladies! You all kick ass!" Gwen called as we walked down the hall. We turned the corner to my room, and she fell silent.

"You okay, doll?"

She patted my leg but didn't say anything.

I grabbed my keys out of my pocket and opened the door, pushing it open with my foot. I flipped the light switch on and saw Mr. T sitting in the middle of the bed, waiting for us.

I slid Gwen down till her feet touched the floor, but I didn't let go of her. "Why were you so nice tonight," she mumbled into my neck.

"Did you want me to be an ass, doll?"

"Hmm, most guys would have."

"I'm not most guys. You had fun, nothing to get mad at." She leaned back, her hair all over the place, covering her face. I brushed it aside, her eyes closed, and she hummed under her breath.

"You're smooookin' hot. Tall, hot, and nice. Stop it." She reached up and punched me in the shoulder.

"You said hot twice," I laughed.

"That's because it needs to be said twice. Better make it three. You're hot." She ran her fingers through her hair, cascading it all around her face again and tried blowing the piece that had fallen on her face out of the way.

"You're hot, too, doll." I brushed her hair out of her face again, and she smiled up at me. "Let's get you ready for bed. You wanna use the bathroom first?" It would have been the perfect time to kiss Gwen again, but I knew she was totally tanked, and I didn't want to take advantage of her.

"Pee then cuddles." She pushed out of my arms and stumbled to the bathroom, thankfully making it without falling.

Cuddles? Gwen must *really* be drunk. Most of the times it felt like she was seconds away from scratching my eyes out.

"Gambler?" My head whipped to the door, and I listened closely. "Gambler?" I heard her quietly mumble.

"You need me, doll?"

"I shouldn't want you, but I do."

What the hell? Drunk Gwen was confusing as fuck. "So you want me to come in, or you're good?"

"Come in, I need help," she whined. I heard a thump against the wall, and I bolted to the door, throwing it open.

Gwen was slumped over on the floor, her cheek pressed against the cold tile of the floor. I knelt down next to her and gently shook her shoulder. Her eyes fluttered open, and she moaned. "Tell me what you need, doll."

"To go back five hours and not drink so much," she complained, shutting her eyes again.

"I can't help you with that, but I can help you get undressed and into bed. I'll get you some water and Tylenol too."

"Hmm, let's just stay here. I'm hot."

"Not happening. You'll end up with a sore neck and smelling like pine sol in the morning. Come on, babe." I gently helped her sit up and rested her against the wall. "You okay there for a second?" I asked, standing up and looked down at her.

"Oh yeah. Totally good," she said, holding her fingers up in a peace sign. I laughed because honestly, this was one of the funniest things I had seen in a while. I opened the medicine cabinet, glancing over my shoulder, making sure Gwen hadn't slumped over again and grabbed the bottle of Tylenol down and filled a glass with water. "Be right back," I mumbled as I stepped out the door and set the pills and water next to the bed.

"Gambler," she called, panic in her voice

"I'm coming, doll."

"Oh, I thought you left," she mumbled, closing her eyes again.

"I told ya I was going to the other room, doll. Did you fall asleep for fifteen seconds?" I laughed, bending down, gathering her in my arms and lifted her up.

"Whoa, who knew you were hot and strong," she whispered, resting her head on my shoulder.

"You weigh nothing, doll. I'm pretty sure I could pick two of you up."

"Hardly, my butt is big, and I got pudge."

"Pudge?" I asked, not knowing what the hell she was talking about. I set her down on the bed, and she fell back, sprawling out on the bed.

She lifted her shirt up and pointed at her stomach. "This is pudge." She put her hand on her stomach and giggled it. "Jiggly pudge," she laughed.

"You're crazy. Give me a foot." She held her leg up, and I quickly slid off her shoe and repeated the same with the other foot. "We need to get you out of these clothes. You OK with me undressing you?"

"Whatever, it's not like it's something you haven't seen before," she said, waving her hand around.

I just shook my head, not wanting to get into a fight with Gwen when she was drunk. "Sit up for one second, doll." She held her hands up for me to grab but didn't make any moves. I grabbed her arms that were limp like wet spaghetti and pulled her up. "Hold on to my neck," I ordered, lacing her fingers behind my neck.

She held on as I pulled the hem of her t-shirt up and lifted her arms from my neck as I pulled the shirt up. I tossed her shirt behind my back and pushed her back to lay down. I tried my hardest not to focus on her pale orange bra that pushed her breasts up, putting them on display. I popped the button of her jeans and slid the zipper down. Fuck me. Matching panties. I gritted my teeth and tried to focus on the task at hand. Get Gwen undressed and in bed.

"Who would have thought I'd be letting you into my pants this soon," she giggled, smothering her mouth with her hand. Her eyes danced with laughter, and I had never seen a more beautiful woman in my life. Wasn't it some shit that she was too far gone to even know what she was saying and doing right now.

She propped herself up on her elbows and watched as I slid her pants down her legs and over her feet. I threw them in the same direction as her shirt and pulled back the covers of the bed. "Slide in," I ordered, holding my hand out to her.

She grabbed my hand and shimmied up to the top of the bed, and I pulled the covers over her. "You need to take some Tylenol, doll. It'll help with the headache you're probably going to have in the morning."

She sat up and took the three pills I shook out of the bottle and shakily grabbed the glass of water. She popped the pills into her mouth and drained the glass of water. After she had handed it back to me, she wiped her mouth with the back of her hand and fell back into the mound of pillows.

I set the glass of water back down and headed back into the bathroom.

"Do you like me, Gambler?" Gwen called.

Shit, I thought for sure she was going to pass out again. I bent over and unlaced my boots and tried to figure out what to say. "Um, of course, I do." I did, I just didn't need her to know *how* much I liked her. I had been fighting my attraction to her all night. Every time she would laugh, she would run her fingers through her hair, cascading it all down her back making my fingers itch wanting to feel how soft her hair was.

"I wish you had some food in here, I'm starving." I was coming to find out that when Gwen was drunk, she was very random. I pulled my shirt over my head and kicked off my boots next to the shower.

"I can run and get you something from the kitchen if you're hungry," I called, running the water in the sink and splashed my face.

"There he goes being nice again," she mumbled. "Do you think there's ice cream?"

"I'm sure there is. Ever since Meg and Cyn have been hanging around, there's always food. I'm sure one of them bought ice cream." Gwen didn't answer, but I left my pants on figuring I was going to head to the kitchen. I grabbed my toothbrush, squirting toothpaste on it and gave my teeth a quick brush. I looked in the mirror and wondered what the hell I was doing. Didn't I say to myself this morning that I couldn't be with Gwen, and now I had her in my bed and was going to get her ice cream because she was craving it?

This woman was getting under my skin, and I had no idea how to stop it. All night I had stayed close to her, not wanting to leave her side. Her laugh was contagious, and she had the brothers eating out of her hand with her crazy stories from the salon and her smile that lit up the room.

I flipped the light off, not having a clue about what I was going to do about Gwen. The damn woman made me happy, and I couldn't tell you the last time that had happened. "You want me to get ice cream?" I asked, but Gwen didn't answer.

Her eyes were closed, and she was lightly snoring. Her mouth was hanging open, and she had never looked more adorable. Her hair was fanned out on the pillow, and the blanket was pulled down to her waist.

She was right when she had said that her being undressed was something I hadn't seen before, but with Gwen it was different. She wasn't some woman in my bed for a couple hours of fun and then be on her way, probably never to be seen again. Gwen made me feel things I never thought I could feel about someone.

When Evie had died, a part of me died with her. She was my only sister and was amazing. There were still days I would forget she was gone, and I'd get the urge to call her. She wasn't supposed to be taken away that soon. She was only twenty-five. She had her whole life in front of her when a semi had plowed into her on that icy morning. She was a bakery manager and she always worked early mornings. She was always out on the road it seemed before the plows could get out there.

She was driving on the highway, probably listening to that shitty pop music she always made me listen to when her life was over in a second. When I had gotten the call, I lost it. King had to drive me to the accident and hold me back when I saw her.

Her beautiful, bright, smiling face was pale and bloodied with pieces of glass scattered around her. Gwen's smile and laughter reminded me so much of Evie. Maybe that was why I needed to be around her. She brought back a part of me that I had thought died.

Gwen rolled over, turning her back to me and hugged my pillow to her. Mr. T hopped up on the bed and burrowed under the covers with his human.

Enough standing over Gwen, watching her like a stalker. I took my jeans off, throwing them over the back of the chair and turned the light off. Just as I was about to slide under the covers, I remember that Gwen needs the light on. I padded over to the bathroom, flipped the light on and shut the door, leaving a sliver of light shining into the room.

As I slid under the covers, she curled into me, her head resting on my shoulder and she hummed quietly under her breath. She settled, resting her hand on my chest, and I breathed a sigh of relief when she didn't wake up.

I shut my eyes, willing myself to fall asleep. It didn't work. All I could think about was Gwen's warm, soft body pressed against mine and how much I wanted to make her mine and never let anything happen to her.

I was falling for her, and there was nothing I could do to stop it.

''*'*'*'*'*'*'*'*'*'*

Chapter 10

Gwen

I cracked on eye open, and it felt like the whole world was spinning around me. What the hell had I done last night? I thought back, trying to remember, and all I could remember was Meg yelling shots all the time.

Oh Lord, shots had done this to me. I closed my eye, hoping that would make the world stop tilting back and forth. I moved my arm and felt my pillow move underneath me. I froze, realizing I wasn't in bed by myself.

"How bad do you feel?" Gambler rumbled.

"Like death," I croaked.

"I guess you'll have that after drinking a bottle of Southern Comfort between the three of you. I'm sure Meg and Marley are feeling the same this morning."

"I blame Meg," I groaned.

Gambler laughed and rolled towards me, his arm staying under my head. God dammit, this man even looked good right away in the morning. His hair was ruffled and sticking up, but his gorgeous eyes were shining brightly at me, a grin spread across his lips. "You want me to run and get you coffee?"

I blinked, surprised. Did he just offer to get me coffee? The almighty beverage of the gods. "Hell yes, three."

Gambler chuckled, his arm wrapping around my neck and he pulled me close. "How about you start with one and we'll see how your stomach handles that." He threw the covers back and rolled out of bed.

I glanced down and saw I was only in my bra and panties. How the hell did that happen? "Holy shit." I grabbed the covers and pulled them up to my chin. "Where the hell are my clothes?"

"Somewhere on the floor. I was more concerned with getting you into bed, not where your clothes fell."

"We didn't," I pointed between Gambler and myself, terrified I had made a terrible decision last night.

Gambler grabbed a black t-shirt out of the dresser and pulled it over his head. "No, doll. All you did was talk, a lot. Scouts honor."

"I really doubt that you were a cub scout," I scoffed.

"I plead the fifth," he turned around and winked at me. "I'll be back with your coffee. You should probably take some more Tylenol, doll, it'll help with that freight train that is running through your head right now." Gambler walked out the door, closing it tight behind him.

Okay, so we didn't have sex. I think. But what the hell did happen last night? I remember having a hell of a time with Marley and Meg and the never ending bottle of Southern Comfort, but that's it.

At one point Meg and Marley had tried to do chicken fights on King and Troy's shoulders, but both had ended up on the floor laughing their asses off when they couldn't even get on the guy's shoulders. Gambler had stayed close to my side the whole night, attentive and quiet. I figured he was staying close so I didn't embarrass myself or him. I'm sure Marley, Meg, and I were quite a sight last night.

Now, I needed to remember how the hell my clothes came off. Mr. T hopped up on the bed, stretching as he walked, his tail wagging rhythmically. "Hello, pretty man," I cooed as he bumped my hand I held out to him, rubbing against it. "Did you see how my clothes came off, pretty man?" T just purred as I rubbed his neck, ignoring my question.

"I didn't know how you like it. I drink mine black, so I just made yours that way, too." Gambler walked through the door, holding both cups in front of him.

"Black's good."

He walked over to the side of the bed and held my cup out to me. "Thank God you don't drink it with all that sissy shit like Meg and Cyn do. I swear there are fifty different kinds of creamer in the fridge." Gambler curled his lip in disgust and took a sip of coffee. He stared down at me, his eyes scanning me. "You still trying to figure out how your clothes came off?" He smirked.

"I'm hoping I was the one who took them off, but from what I remember, it would have been amazing if I had."

"You gonna drink that coffee, or wait till it turns cold?"

I had stuck one arm out from the blanket to grab the coffee but was afraid the blanket would fall if I made one wrong move. I know Gambler had seen me last night, but now it was different. I was sober and would remember everything. "Um, of course." I hesitantly raised my arm, and leaned forward, my chin pressed down on the blanket, praying it wouldn't fall.

"That's an interesting way to drink coffee," he laughed, walking toward the bathroom. He shut the door behind him, and I breathed a sigh of relief. I set my coffee on the bedside table and tossed the covers back and jumped from the bed. I grabbed my suitcase from under the bed and tossed it open, frantically trying to get dressed before Gambler came out of the bathroom.

I grabbed my favorite faded Def Leppard shirt and a pair of black leggings. I pulled them on quickly, thankful the shirt was baggy and covered my ass. I grabbed a hair tie, finger combing my hair and pulled it back. "I see you found some clothes."

I whirled around at Gambler's words, my arms over my head, tightening my ponytail. "Um, yeah. I plan to remember how these come off, too."

"Then I would stay away from Meg and her bottle of Southern Comfort."

"Truer words have never been spoken," I moaned as I lowered my arms.

"You got any plans today?"

"None that I know of. I normally do laundry and read on my days off."

"Well, Meg and Cyn got this crazy fucking idea that they need to go to the pumpkin patch today and wanted me to ask you if you wanted to come with."

"Are you going to come?" I wanted him to come, but I didn't.

"I think we were all going to ride out there on our bikes. Make the day of it before Meg and Cyn need to go to work."

"Isn't it too cold?"

"Just make sure you put on a coat and you'll be fine, doll. Riding in the fall is one of the best times to go." Gambler walked over to the end of the bed where he had kicked his boots off and picked them up and grabbed a pair of socks out of his dresser. "You'll be behind me so the wind shouldn't be too bad."

"Okay, I guess that sounds like fun. Are Marley and Troy coming along?" I grabbed a pair of socks out of my bag and pulled my other suitcase out from under the bed that had all my shoes in it. Thankfully I had packed a black pair of boots and had second thoughts on my decision to wear leggings. "I'm gonna change my pants," I mumbled, walking back over to my other suitcase and pulled out a pair of jeans.

"Whatever you say, doll. I'm gonna grab another cup of coffee before we take off. You want anything to eat?" He stood up, his boots already laced.

I needed to hurry the hell up. "Um, just some toast or something."

Gambler nodded his head at me and walked out the door. I pulled off my leggings, tossing them towards my open suitcase and pulled my jeans on. I traded my t-shirt for a long sleeve Henley I had packed. I took my hair down from the messy ponytail I had thrown it up and walked into the bathroom.

"Holy fuck," I moaned when I looked in the mirror. I couldn't believe that I was actually going to leave the room looking like this. I grabbed my makeup bag off the tank of the toilet and rummaged through it looking for all the necessary tools to make me look presentable.

I wiped off the makeup that was still smudged all over my face and started fresh. I forgo foundation and moved on to the heavy bags under my eyes. I smeared on concealer praying the make-up gods were on my side and topped it off with powder.

By the time I was done, I had been in the bathroom for twenty minutes and looked like I was ready to join the human world again. I grabbed my jean jacket out of my bag, shaking it out, and threw it on.

I scratched Mr. T behind his ears, checked to make sure his food bowl was full and jetted out the door, down the hall to the main room.

"It's about time you got your ass out here," Meg called as she walked out of the kitchen.

"I woke up looking like ass. It's a miracle how I look now."

"I doubt you could ever look like ass. Come on. Gambler said you needed to eat, but we all decided to stop at the diner on the way out of town and eat there." Meg threaded her arm through mine, and we walked over to the group that was gathered around the bar.

"Bout time you came out, doll." Gambler walked over to me, his eyes scanning me up and down. "Although, it was worth every second," he mumbled. I blushed under his gaze and clasped my hands in front of me.

"Um, thanks," I mumbled, unsure of what else to say.

"All right, let's hit it. Meg and Cyn need to be back by three to get to work," King called and headed to the door, Meg tucked under his arm. I didn't have a chance to ask her if she was hung over, but it didn't appear that she was. How the hell did she manage that?

"Are Marley and Troy coming with us?" I asked, glancing around trying to get a glimpse of them.

"Marley isn't used to how people from Wisconsin drink. She's nursing one hell of a hangover right now. She and Troy are staying behind," Cyn laughed as she walked past, hand in hand with Rigid.

"Oh, that sucks. Although it is true. I don't know how ya'll drink so much and still function as a human being the next day." Gambler grabbed my hand and led me out the door following Cyn and Rigid.

60

"That's how we keep warm on cold nights. Well, that and something else," Rigid laughed, handing a helmet to Cyn. She strapped it on, and I looked over at Meg, who was doing the same thing. Gambler gave me the helmet he always made me wear, and I looked at King and Rigid.

"How come ya'll don't wear helmets?" I asked as I strapped it on.

"I've never worn one. Stupid, I know. I think King and Rigid are the same. The reason you ladies need to wear one is because we need to keep y'all safe." Gambler threw his leg over the bike and climbed on.

"You know how stupid that sounds when you say that, right?" I slid on behind him and wrapped my arms around his middle and held on.

"You'll get used to it," Cyn called. "I've been arguing with Rigid for months to wear one, but he refuses. I'll wear him down one day."

All the men fire up their bikes, Gambler's bike coming to life under me, and we all headed to the edge of town where the diner was.

I was again amazed at how well Gambler handled the bike, driving it with ease and practice. When we pulled up to the restaurant, my stomach growled in protest just as Gambler killed the bike. His body shook under mine, his laughter ringing out.

"You hungry, doll?" Gambler asked.

"Damn near starved," I grumbled, sliding off the bike. "Hey, didn't I ask you to get me ice cream last night?" I asked as I watched Gambler stand up.

"Yeah, and I was almost out the door, but you passed out before I could even step foot out the door."

"Oh, well. That would explain why I'm so hungry." I pouted, sticking my lip out.

"Come on, doll, I'll feed ya," Gambler held his hand out to me, and I hesitated. It felt like he was asking for a whole lot more than just walking me to the door of the diner. I looked up from his hand, his eyes studying me. This was a test, and I didn't want to fail. "Come on, Gwen," he whispered.

I reached out, his fingers threading through mine and tugged me towards the diner. His warm hand gripped mine, and I felt something I hadn't felt in a long time. I trusted him. He held the door open for me. I walked past him, but he stopped me midway.

"You look beautiful today, doll," he whispered, pressing a kiss to the side of my head.

I looked up at him, unable to read his eyes and smiled. "Somethings are worth waiting for, I guess, right?"

"I think you're more than worth waiting for, doll. Just don't make me wait too long." He leaned down, his lips inches away. "I promise to make it worth it." He pressed his lips to mine, the sweetest kiss I had ever felt. That kiss held the promise that there was more to come, and I was damn near ready to find out just what kind of promise that was.

''*'*'*'*'*'*'*'*'*

Chapter 11
Gambler

"Three eggs, scrambled, toast, three sausage links, not the patties, two pancakes, and half a grapefruit." Gwen shut her menu and looked up at the waitress. Her pen was going a mile a minute trying to write down everything Gwen wanted.

"Um, is that it?" she asked, her pen poised to write down more.

"Can you add strawberries and whipped cream to the pancakes?"

"Sure thing, hun." The waitress turned her attention to take Cyn's order, but my eyes stayed glued to Gwen.

"You hungry, doll?"

"Beyond starved. I'm still pissed you didn't get me ice cream last night. You should have woke my ass up."

I grabbed a straw, stripping off the wrapper and stuck it in my glass of water. "I thought sleeping was more important than ice cream."

"Nothing is more important than ice cream. Ever."

"I'll remember that the next time you are drunk off your ass and demand ice cream."

"You better."

I tossed my arm over the back of the booth, pulling her to me. "What happens if I don't? Although you do have a losing bet you need to honor yet."

She turned her head towards me, a snarl on her lips. "I didn't lose. The bet was off because you lied."

"No way, doll. We shook on it. A bet is a bet." I lowered my voice, not wanting anyone to hear.

"We'll see about that," she whispered back.

"Are we going to bet on the fact of whether or not you fulfill your end of the last bet?" Stubborn as a mule. I was going to cash in her debt. Guaranteed.

"Yes."

"You do know how ridiculous this is," she just shook her head at me, not giving up. "Well, I'm assuming the terms of this bet are, you win, you don't have to fulfill the old bet. If I win, you have to do two things for me."

"Deal, because you are not going to win." She grabbed my hand, shaking it and pulled away from me. "You're going down, Gambler."

I leaned towards her, nose to nose. "Oh, I plan on it, doll, and I'm going to enjoy it just as much as you are." Her jaw dropped at my words, and she reared back.

I sat back, smug, knowing that I was going to get Gwen right where I wanted her whether she liked it or not.

''*'*'*'*'*'*'*'*'*'*'*'*'

Gwen

"Oh shit, things are getting interesting over there," Meg called, smirking at me as she emptied two packets of sugar into her coffee.

"Y'all want coffee?" The waitress asked the pot lifted, waiting.

I looked around seeing everyone else had their cups filled and were staring at Gambler and me, "Black," we said at the same time. Cyn and Meg broke down into a fit of giggles while King and Rigid just shook their heads.

After the waitress had filled our cups, I had to make an escape and get my wits about me. "I'm gonna run to the restroom before the food comes." I bumped Gambler, urging him to get his ass out of my way.

"Running away, doll?" he whispered as he slid out of the booth.

"You wish," I hissed back. I hightailed it to the bathroom, shutting the door behind me. I leaned against the door, resting my head back and screamed when there was a knock on the door. "Someone's in here," I hollered when they knocked again.

"We know, now let us the hell in." Wait, was that Meg? We, who the hell was we?

I turned the handle on the door, and before I could pull it open, it was being pushed into, and I took a step back before I got plowed over.

"Scoot in, woman. This bathroom is tiny," Meg ordered as she shut the door behind her as Cyn and her crowded in.

"Because it's only meant for one person," I said, standing in the corner between the sink and the wall.

"Would you squish over, I'm gonna have to straddle the toilet," Cyn complained.

"Just sit on the damn toilet. That'll give us more room." Meg ordered, lowering the seat and Cyn sat down.

"I can't believe this is happening," I said, running my fingers through my hair. All I wanted to do was go to the bathroom to get away from Gambler for a second, and now I was crowded into a four by four bathroom with Mutt and Jeff.

"Believe it. It's easier that way," Cyn advised, crossing her legs.

"So what's the deal with you and Gambler?" Meg said, crossing her arms over her chest, except she knocked Cyn in the head as she did it.

"Would you watch what the hell you are doing?" Cyn rubbed the side of her head, scowling at Meg.

"You've got a hard head, you'll be fine," Meg said, waving Cyn off. "Now, back to you and Gambler." Her eyes bore into me, almost like she was trying to read my mind.

"Oh Jesus, Meg. Stop trying to read her mind," Cyn said, punching Meg in the leg.

"Hey, you never know if you can read minds unless you try." Meg flipped off Cyn and stuck her tongue out at her.

I was in the twilight zone. I had to be in another dimension, because in my normal life, I never would be trapped in a tiny bathroom with Cyn and Meg. "Um, nothing is going on with Gambler and me," I mumbled, hoping Cyn and Meg would leave.

"I'm not buying it. I saw the way that man was looking at you earlier." Meg tried moving closer but stepped on Cyn's foot.

"For all that is holy, would you stop moving?! There's nowhere to fucking go, Meg!" Cyn cursed, grabbing her foot and rubbed it.

"Sorry, but you know you have snow skis for feet. It was inevitable I would step on them."

"You did not just go there. You have the same size feet as I do!"

"Details," Meg mumbled.

"I swear to God it's a good thing I love you, or I would definitely rethink you being Godmother to my baby." Cyn glared at Meg and put both of her feet on the ground.

"I've got time before that. At least a year."

"More like eight months," Cyn muttered.

"Plenty of time," Meg looked back at me, ready to pounce on the whole Gambler issue. Except, she didn't, because it finally sunk in what Cyn had just said. Holy shit, Cyn was pregnant. That explained her mood swings and weird eating habits lately. Not to mention the wanting to sleep all the time. She had a baby Rigid in the oven.

Meg's jaw dropped open, and she made a weird baaing sound. Not exactly the reaction I expected from her.

"Are you gonna say anything or just act like a sheep until I pop this baby out?"

"You… You have a…" Meg rocked her arms, pretending to hold a baby and pointed at Cyn.

"Jesus Christ, she's resorted to charades now," Cyn said, rolling her eyes.

Meg slapped her hand over her mouth and screamed. "At least, she's making a different noise now," I laughed as Cyn slapped her leg again.

"Knock it off, you didn't act like this the first time I was pregnant." I didn't know all the details, but I knew Cyn had been pregnant by her asshole of an ex before she met Rigid.

"That's because this time, you're having a baby with someone you love. I was over the moon excited the last time, too, but now I get to be excited for Rigid, too. Oh, my God, you are going to have the cutest babies!" Meg clapped her hands together and bounced on the balls of her feet. "This is the most fantastic thing ever."

"It does feel different now. Rigid is so careful with me he's driving me insane. He told me today is my last ride on his bike until the baby comes. I swear he's going to wrap me in bubble wrap." Cyn put her hand on her stomach, rubbing it.

"Congratulations," I said, leaning down, wrapping her up in a hug. Cyn's pregnancy was way more exciting than whatever the hell was going on with Gambler and me.

Meg wrapped her arms around Cyn and I and squeezed the hell out us. "I'm gonna be an auntie. I can spoil the shit out of him and then give him back when he's naughty. Win, win."

"Oh Lord, it's already starting," Cyn wheezed out.

"Babe," King called out as he pounded on the door.

"Shit," Meg stepped back and wiped the tears from her eyes. "You made me cry, bitch," she laughed.

"I'm always on the verge of tears lately. Welcome to the club." Cyn stood up, bumping into Meg and I and reached for a paper towel. She wiped her eyes and tossed it in the garbage. "We never did hear about you and Gambler."

I backed up, my back against the wall, and shrunk down under their stares. "Don't look at me like that. I have no freakin' clue."

"Well, do you like him?" Meg asked, crossing her arms over her chest.

"The man drives me insane."

"Do you think he's hot?"

Ugh, that was an understatement. I thought he was the most gorgeous man I had ever seen. "He's okay."

"I think you think he's more than okay. What the hell is the problem?"

"Babe, the food is here. If you want to be back in time for work tonight, we need to eat and get a move on," King said through the door.

Meg stomped her foot and whirled around, and yanked open the door. "We're in the middle of something, Lo."

"Cyn's pregnant. Come freak out at the table," King said, grabbing her hand.

Meg sputtered, struggling to get a sentence out. "You… how… tell… You knew and didn't tell me!"

"I found out five minutes ago when I wondered what the hell you three were doing, and Rigid said Cyn probably told y'all she's pregnant. Let's go." King tugged her arm, and she stumbled behind him, looking over her shoulder at us.

"We're talking later, Gwen," she vowed, determination lacing her voice.

Cyn stood up, stretching her back as she walked out of the bathroom. "She's right, by the way. You're not getting out of this that easy." Cyn winked at me and made her way back over to the table, sliding in next to Rigid. He wrapped his arm around her and pulled her close, whispering in her ear.

I smiled, seeing the love between the two and knowing they were going to be incredible parents.

I glanced at Gambler, his back turned to me and breathed a heavy sigh. Uh. What the hell was I doing with Gambler? I liked him. I truly did.

Gambler turned around, his eyes searching for me. I flicked off the bathroom light and made my way back to the table. His eyes watched me the whole way, studying the way I walked, his eyes flaring as I put a little more sway in my walk.

I had enough. I wanted Gambler. I knew, right then and there, that this man might hurt me, but he was going to be worth the pain.

''*'*'*'*'*'*'*'*

Chapter 12

Gambler

We were cruising down the road, the wind cutting through me, and Gwen was pressed to my back, holding on. We had just left the restaurant and pulled on the highway, King leading us to the pumpkin place. I never thought I would say that I was going to a pumpkin patch, but here I was. Marley and Troy were meeting us there and planned on hauling all the pumpkins back in Troy's truck.

Before we had gotten on the bike, I had handed Gwen her helmet, but she didn't grab it. "What are we doing, Gambler?"

"We gotta get on the road, doll. Put the helmet on."

"That's not what I meant. I mean, what are we," she pointed between the two if us, "what the hell is going on?"

I stared down at her, helmet in between us. Jesus, I didn't expect that question. I was still trying to figure out what the hell we were, and now Gwen wanted to know. "Um, well, I'm not sure."

"You're not sure?"

"Well, what are you thinking?"

She glanced to the left and cleared her throat. "I'm not sure either," she mumbled.

I threw my head back, laughing at the fact that she also had no idea what the hell was going on between us. Although when it came down to it, we both knew what was going on, we were just fighting it tooth and nail. "God dammit, I fucking like you, Gwen. I don't know what the hell to do with that, but I fucking like you."

Gwen turned her head back to me, her eyes laughing at me. "You fucking like me?"

"Yeah."

"Well," she pushed her blowing hair out of her face and smiled. "I fucking like you, too, Gambler. Half the time I don't know if I wanna kick you in the shin, or kiss you till you shut up."

"We can try the second option first," I smirked, pulling her into my arms. The helmet was sandwiched between us, but I had Gwen in my arms, somewhat.

"I know you're going to hurt me, Gambler. Hopefully, we can make some good memories for when the pain sets in I have something to remember you," she whispered.

"I got no plans of hurting you, Gwen, but I can promise I'll give you as many good memories as possible." I leaned down, my lips brushing against hers. She reached for the helmet and tossed it on the ground.

"Let's make one right now," she whispered, reaching up, threading her fingers through my hair. Her lips touched mine, and I knew I was a goner. If being with Gwen was going to feel like this, I didn't know what the hell I was thinking running from her before.

"Woo!" I heard yelled from behind us. I deepened the kiss, not wanting to let Gwen go. She moaned low, her body pressed against mine. My dick begged to be buried in her sweet pussy after only kissing her. Once I got her naked, Lord knows what would happen.

"Told ya something was going on," Cyn said, cutting into our little world.

Gwen pulled away, her lips wet and tempting. I pressed one last kiss to them, reminding myself that there was always later. She let go of my hair, trailing her fingers down my shirt, sending shivers down my spine at her words. "I'm gonna need more later," she purred, her eyes filled with desire.

"As soon as we're done with this pumpkin shit, there'll be more, doll. So much more." She backed away from me, her eyes studying me as she grabbed the helmet off the ground and strapped it on.

"Promises, promises, Gambler. Let's hope you can keep all of them."

I heard King crank his bike up, and I knew it was time to go. I swung my leg over my bike, not even having to wait five seconds before I felt Gwen's warm body pressed against mine.

"How long until we get there?" Gwen called over the roar of the motorcycle.

"About half an hour," I said, turning my head so she could hear me.

I felt her hands sneak into the pockets of my jacket, pressing against my stomach.

"My hands are cold," she mumbled into my ear and burrowed into my back. It was rather cold to be out riding today, and I knew this would probably be one of the last times Gwen and I rode this year before the snow started falling.

We were five miles away from our exit when I noticed a black van behind us, weaving in and out of traffic. King and Rigid were a few car lengths ahead of us, riding side by side.

Just as I glanced in my mirror to see where the van was, I saw an arm reach out the passenger side window, a gun pointed at Gwen and me.

I swerved to the left, then to the right, knowing if I kept moving they wouldn't be able to get a shot off at us.

"Gambler?" I heard Gwen call, panic in her voice. I didn't want to worry her, but I didn't know what the hell we were dealing with. I speed up, taking the shoulder around the car in front of us, the van also going faster and squeezing itself through two cars, keeping up alongside me. I slowed down, not wanting the van to catch up to King and Rigid. The van slowed down with us, the car that was separating us slamming on its brakes when the guy in the van pulled the gun out again, pointing it at us. I speed up, zig-zagging, trying to lose the van. Gwen's arms tightened around me, holding on as I went faster and faster, trying to shake the van.

I could tell the two guys in the van were getting impatient when they swerved at us, attempting to run us off the road.

I heard two gun shots and looked over, the guy now taking aim at my tires, trying to make me wreck.

We were a mile from our exit, and I knew I had to do something. Just as I was about to slam on the brakes, I heard another shot fired from the gun, and I felt a sharp, burning sting in my leg. I glanced down, blood staining my jeans. Shit.

"Gambler!" Gwen screeched as I revved the throttle, knowing I need to get off the road. All I remember was hearing one more shot and then the world went dark as I felt a stabbing pain in my neck and prayed to God that I didn't kill Gwen.

''*'*'*'*'*'*'*'*'*'

Chapter 13

Gwen

I don't know how, but I swear to God I could feel Gambler getting shot.

When Gambler had first started swerving, I had no idea what he was doing. I thought maybe he was trying to scare me a bit, not knowing that I had been on a motorcycle many times before.

I finally realized what was going on when the black van sped up, and a gun came out of the window, attached to a very pissed off Mexican man.

When Gambler's body had gone limp, I knew I had to do something or we were going to crash, bad. I reach for the handlebars, squashing Gambler. I knocked his hands off the handlebars, the fact that he had let go so easily scared the shit out of me, but I knew I couldn't focus on that right now. My hands gripped the bars just as the bike started to shake and sway. I tried coasting to a stop, avoiding traffic and causing an even worse accident than we were about to have.

I bumped over to the shoulder, rocks kicking up under the tires. I hit the brakes, and I knew as soon as I did it, I had made a mistake. The wheels skidded, and I tried to correct it, but I couldn't.

We skidded, leaning over to the left, and I saw the road come up and rip my leg apart, feeling like burning coals as the gravel and dirt embedded in my leg. I let go of the handlebars and held onto Gambler. The bike skidded ahead of us as Gambler and I rolled into the ditch. My head banged on the road, thankfully protected by the helmet Gambler insisted I always wear.

When we finally came to a stop, my arms were still wrapped around his body I heard him moan, and I thanked God that he was still alive. We had both just laid the bike down, but he had also been shot, maybe twice.

I heard the screeching of tires, and I immediately panicked, thinking that whoever had shot at us had come to finish the job.

"Call nine one one, now!" I heard bellowed. I craned my neck, trying to see who was talking, but we were too far down in the ditch to see the road. Two sets of black boots came stomping down the embankment skidding to a stop next to Gambler and me.

I held Gambler tight to me and closed my eyes, afraid to see who had found us. "Gwen, it's us darlin', nothing is going to happen to y'all. Meg is calling an ambulance right now." I opened my eyes and looked up into King's face.

"Thank God," I cried.

"Where are you hurt? Did you get shot?" Rigid asked, kneeling on the other side of me.

"Um, I'm hurt, but Gambler was shot. Once for sure in the neck, and I think in the leg too. You have to help him!"

"We will, darlin'. You're gonna have to let him go, though." Rigid said, prying my arms away from Gambler. I didn't realize how tight I had been holding on to him until I tried loosening my arms and my muscles relaxed, crying out in relief.

"Can you move?" King asked me.

I took stock of my body, trying to figure out if anything was broken. I was bleeding, bruised, and sore, but I didn't think anything was broken. "I think I'm okay," I said hoarsely.

"I just want you to lie here until the ambulance comes." Rigid gently lifted Gambler off of me and laid him next to me. Gambler's eyes fluttered open, and I cried out, thankful he was conscious.

Rigid looked at his neck, trying to see how bad he had been hit. "I think it just grazed him. I'm not sure, but it doesn't look like there is an entry wound."

"What about his leg?" I asked, trying to sit up, but my arms shook, and I collapsed onto the ground.

"Gwen, you need to just lay down," King ordered. He undid the helmet on my head, gently taking it off. He took off his coat, folded it up and slid it under my head. "Stay still."

"The ambulance will be here in five minutes," Meg called.

"I want you and Cyn to stay up there and wait for it to come. It might miss us if we're all down here," King called.

"Is everyone okay?"

"Gwen is banged up, and Gambler got shot. He's losing a lot of blood; we need to get him out of here as fast as we can."

Gambler groaned, and I tried to get up again, but King held me down. "I'm not going to tell you again, Gwen. Stay still. There could be something wrong with you that we can't see. Stay. Still."

"She's stubborn as shit," Gambler wheezed.

"Gambler," I cried. I had never been so relieved to hear his voice before.

"Gwen," he gasped.

"Stop trying to talk, brother. The ambulance should be here any minute." Rigid pressed down on his shoulder when he attempted to sit up. "Stop trying to move. I don't know what's all wrong with y'all."

"My ribs." Gambler moved his hand, grasping his left side. That was the side we had fallen on. I tried to hold onto Gambler as much as I could, but I knew he had taken the brunt of the fall.

"Probably broke a few. Just lay still. If you move wrong, you might puncture a lung."

King stood up and walked over to the edge of the ditch. "I hear sirens, babe. You see it yet?"

"I see cars pulling over up there." I heard Meg say.

"There it is!" Cyn called.

The next ten minutes were a whirlwind of poking, prodding, and twenty questions. As they were loading Gambler up onto a gurney, another ambulance arrived to take me to the hospital. Gambler was still conscious and answering questions the whole time. He tried insisting that I go in the first ambulance, but the paramedics ignored him and loaded him up while he protested.

"All right, we're going to slide this board under you, and then we'll get you loaded up." I glanced to the left, watching the woman paramedic who had been talking to me the whole time, explaining everything as it happened.

"We're going to the same hospital as Gambler, right?"

"Gambler? You mean the other guy who was just here? Of course. We'll try to get ya'll in close rooms, too, as long as he doesn't need to be on a different floor." The paramedic finished writing on her clipboard and shoved it into her bag. "Just stay still and relax. As far we can tell there isn't any internal bleeding."

I was hoisted up and carried over to the ambulance and raised in. "We'll meet you at the hospital," Meg called as the back doors slammed shut.

I closed my eyes, trying not to worry about Gambler. They had figured that he had broken a couple of ribs from the fall and, of course, other bumps, bruises, and cuts. He was just grazed by the bullet in his neck and his leg didn't appear to have hit any major arteries. We were both okay for the most part.

I felt the ambulance pull off the shoulder and head to the hospital. Somehow a day of relaxing fun had turned into ambulance rides and gun shots.

''*'*'*'*'*'*'*'*

73

Chapter 14
Gambler

"I need to know how Gwen is. I don't care about me. Just tell me if she's okay," I pleaded with the nurse who was taking my blood pressure.

"I can't say anything about other patients unless you are family. I told you once you're up to it and if she agrees, I'll take you over to see her." The nurse scribbled something down on her clipboard and clipped it to the end of the bed and walked out of the room.

I had been here for over an hour, and I hadn't been able to find out any information on Gwen. King had come, and I told him to not come back until he had information on Gwen. I was afraid he was running into the same problem I was, none of us were her family.

I glanced around the room and spotted the phone next to the bed. I knew what I was about to do was a longshot, but I didn't have much choice.

I picked up the receiver and called the front desk of the hospital.

"Rockton General, how may I direct your call?"

"I need to speak to a Gwen Lawson. She was in a car accident today. I'm her brother."

"Hold please." The line clicked over to cheesy jazz music, and I waited for two minutes before she came back on the line.

"We have her in room two fourteen. Would you like me to ring you over to her room?"

Hell yeah! "Yes, please." The shit music came back on, but this time, I didn't mind it because I knew the next person I talked to was going to be Gwen.

"Hello?" Jesus, freakin' Meg.

"Put Gwen on the phone."

"Gambler? What the hell are you doing calling? Aren't you in a room just down the hall?"

"Yeah, but they won't tell me anything about Gwen. I called pretending to be her brother, and they patched me over to her room. Put her on the phone."

"Jeez, desperate much?" she scoffed. "Gambler wants you," I heard Meg say as she handed the phone to Gwen.

"Gambler?" Gwen asked, surprised.

"It's me, doll. The damn nurse won't tell me how you are doing so I got creative and rang the front desk and said I was your brother."

Gwen laughed, "You must have been desperate."

"I just need to know if you're okay, doll."

"I'm okay. Just bumps and bruises. My leg is pretty shredded, but it's all superficial. I think I'll be out of here in a little bit. What about you?"

I adjusted the blanket that was draped over me and slowly raised my other arm over my head, careful not to hurt my neck. There was an enormous bandage on the left side of my neck where the bullet had ripped open my skin. The doctor had said if it had hit me a half an inch to left I wouldn't be here anymore. "I'm hanging in there. I think I'm going to need to spend the night tonight, but I should be out of here in the morning."

"Oh crap, the nurse just came in. I'll call you back. What room are you in?"

I looked around, trying to see a room number. "I don't know, doll. I'll call you back in twenty minutes, that ok?" I don't know why I needed to call her back. I had found out that she was okay, that was all I needed to know.

"Okay. Bye," she whispered. The dial tone of the phone sounded in my ear, and I replaced the receiver on the table.

Now, what the hell was I supposed to do? I glanced at the clock, seeing it was only half past three. I flipped the TV on, flipping through the channels till I found a marathon of *Fast and Loud*. Hammer, Slider, and Gravel had stopped by earlier but had left to go scope out the cafeteria for any good food. I told them they were on a hopeless mission, but they still went.

I glanced at the clock again, seeing it had only been five minutes since I talked to Gwen. I laid my head back on the pillow and watched the TV waiting for fifteen minutes to go by. Not even ten minutes later I was passed out, the medicine they had given me finally kicking in. I never got to call Gwen back.

''*'*'*'*'*'*'*'*'*

Chapter 15

Gwen

"Are you sure you want us to leave you here?"

I glanced over my shoulder at Marley and Troy, who were standing behind me in the hallway.

"Yeah, I'll be fine. Hell, the hospital is probably the safest place for me." I had just been released and was standing in the door to Gambler's room. He had never called me back, and I was worried that something had happened to him. Thankfully all that had happened to him was that he fell asleep.

"Do you want me to bring you some more clothes?" I glanced down at the yoga pants and shirt Marley had in Troy's truck and shook my head.

"I'll be fine. Gambler said he should be released tomorrow so this will be fine until then." Thankfully the pants were stretchy enough I could squeeze my ass into them, and the shirt was baggy.

"Okay, well, I guess we'll see you tomorrow. Call me if you need anything, okay?" Marley said, her voice laced with concern.

"Will do. I think we all just need to relax." I glanced back into Gambler's room, seeing he was still sleeping.

"Troy has to head to work, but remember, if you need me, just call." Marley wrapped her arms around me, squeezing the hell out of me. "I'm so glad you're okay," she whispered.

I hugged her back, thankful that today wasn't as bad as it could have been. "Me too," I said, stepping back. Troy threw his arm over her shoulder, and they walked down the hall arm in arm.

I stepped into the room, mindful of being quiet as I shut the door and looked around. His room was set up just like mine was, and I walked over to the chair that was next to the bed. I sat down gingerly and stretched my legs out in front of me. My leg protested pain shooting up it, and I grimaced. Fuck that hurt. My leg didn't hurt that bad until they had washed it out and scrubbed it clean of all the dirt and gravel. Now it was tender and painful.

There was a knock on the door and the same nurse who had taken care of me walked in the room. She looked at me in surprise and smiled. "I should have known you would come down here." She walked over to the sink and washed her hands.

"I wanted to make sure he was okay," I said meekly, afraid she was going to tell me I had to leave.

She grabbed paper towels and dried her hands as she studied me. "You're fine, hun. No need to look like I'm the bouncer about to kick you out," she laughed. She grabbed his chart from the bottom of the bed, and I breathed a sigh of relief. "That chair you're sitting in folds down into a bed. Probably not the comfiest, but it'll be better than the floor," she said as she studied the chart. She grabbed her pen out of her pocket and scribbled something down.

"It'll be okay if I spend the night?"

"Of course, hun. Just no parties," she winked at me and walked over to the machines that were hooked up to Gambler.

"He's going to be okay, right?"

"As far as I can tell he should be good. It'll take a bit to recover, but nothing I don't think he can't handle." She scribbled something on the clipboard and looked up at me. "How long have you two been together? He was asking to see you the whole time, too."

"Oh, well, I'm not really sure we're even together." I looked down at my hands clasped in my lap and bit my lip. Jeez, this was such a messed up situation.

"Oh, well, maybe y'all figure things out now." She smiled at me sympathetically, setting the clipboard at the end of the bed and walked out of the room, quietly shutting the door.

Figure things out? Lord knew if that would happen. When Gambler had passed out on the bike, I had panicked thinking the worse, and as much as I tried to tell myself that didn't mean anything, I couldn't deny it anymore. Gambler meant something to me. The way I felt about him was something new and scary.

I grabbed the remote from the side of the bed and turned up the volume. He was watching some car show I had never seen before, but you really couldn't go wrong with hot guys and cars.

After two episodes, my stomach started growling, and I was seriously considering wandering around in search of food.

Just as I grabbed my wallet off the floor, Gambler stirred next to me, his head turning towards the door. I watched his hand as he flexed his fingers, and I wondered if he was awake.

"Shit," he cursed his voice gravely from sleep.

Well, that answered my question. He turned his head to the table beside me and looked at the time. "Fuck."

"Is something wrong?" I asked.

His eyes shot to me, "What the hell?"

"Um, did you need something?" I had no idea what he meant by 'what the hell.' Maybe he didn't expect me to be here, or he didn't want me here.

"I forgot to call you." He cleared his throat, and his eyes traveled all over my body, taking in my less than stellar appearance and baggy clothes.

"Oh, that's okay. I might have missed it if you had called. I got discharged right after I got off the phone with you." I clasped my hands in my lap, searching for what else to say.

"You're okay to go home?"

"So they say. My leg is pretty beaten up, but I'm good. I'm sure tomorrow I'll be pretty stiff."

"I think stiff might be an understatement, doll," he winked at me, his gorgeous smile spreading across his lips.

"You might be right although you might have it a bit worse than me." I motioned to the bandage on his neck and felt the tears coming. I had no idea why I was about to cry. I think it was finally hitting me that today could have turned out a lot worse than it did.

I glanced away, my eyes trying to focus on the TV, but they were blurred by the tears that I couldn't hold back. I tried swiping them away as they rained down my cheeks, but there were too many to catch.

My world felt like it was about to end, and I had no idea how to stop it. Gambler was okay, I kept reminding myself.

"Gwen," Gambler quietly called to me. All I could do was shake my head and sob. "Gwen, come here."

"I… can't," I hiccuped.

"I need to hold you right now, Gwen. Don't make me get out of this bed. I think I'd be pretty shaky right now."

Deep breaths. Everything and everyone was fine. I counted backward from ten trying to calm the panic that was trying to overtake me.

"Son of a bitch," Gambler grumbled under his breath.

I saw him toss the blanket off him and try to swing his legs out of the bed. "What the hell are you doing?" I demanded, shooting up from my chair.

"You need me, and I can't fucking get to you right now." He tried to sit up and grimaced in pain, holding his stomach.

"Gambler, stop it!" I gently pushed on his shoulder and grabbed the corner of the blanket he had tossed off. I pulled it up over his legs, noticing the large bandage on his leg, but blocked from my mind how he had gotten it. "You don't need to worry about me right now," I scolded, tucking him back in.

"Get in here with me," he ordered, tossing back the blanket again.

"No, you're crazy. You need to rest, not have me smushed in that bed with you."

"I'm not taking no for an answer, doll. I want you in this bed with me. I may not be able to do what I really wanted to do to you the next time I had you in bed, but I can still damn sure hold you."

"Gambler, I can't. I'm-"

"Gwen, get in the fucking bed." I looked him in the eye, and I knew he wasn't messing around.

"Gambler, if I hurt you by climbing in that bed, I don't think I'll be able to live with myself."

"You won't hurt me," he grabbed my hand, tugging me closer to the bed. "I need to make sure you're fine, and the only way it's going to sink in that we're both alive and not dead is if I hold you in my arms. I need you right now, Gwen."

The tears sprung back, swelling and building. "I need you, too," I choked out.

I slipped off my shoes, tucking them under the bed, and pulled the covers back more. Gambler slowly slid over to the other side of the bed gingerly. I slid in, clinging to the edge of the bed, afraid to touch him.

"Gwen, you better get your ass next to me in two seconds, or you can guarantee when I'm feeling better I'll bend you over my knee and spank that pretty ass."

"You can try," I scoffed, scooting over next to him.

His shirt was off, and I cuddled up under his arm he was holding out and rested my head against his shoulder, mindful of his neck. "How bad does it hurt?" I asked, looking up at him.

His head was tilted down, his eyes studying me. "I'm pretty doped up right now, doll. I don't feel much."

I pinched his side, and he jumped under my touch. "What the hell did you do that for?"

"Just wanted to see if you would feel it," I laughed, leaning up, brushing a kiss on his cheek.

"You're crazy. They sure you don't have a concussion?" He rubbed his side and smiled at me.

"Positive," I mumbled. "So, are you going to tell me what the hell that was today, or am I going to have to pump Meg for information?" I rested my head back on his shoulder and traced over his tattoos on his chest with my fingertips.

"We don't know much, yet. I know it was the Assassins, but we don't know why they went after you and I. Their main beef has always been with Rigid, but they could have confused me with him today, or, they could just be going after anyone with the Devil's Knights patch."

"So this isn't over yet?" I asked, worried that something worse could happen next time.

"I don't think so, doll. I know King was going to put a couple of calls in and see what he can find out."

"So now we sit like ducks waiting to be attacked again."

"This isn't going to happen again. This is the last time the Assassins are going to get the jump on us."

I snuggled deeper into Gambler's arms, feeling safer than I should. Even though I knew there was no way for him to guarantee to keep us safe, I knew he would die trying. "I trust you, Gambler," I whispered.

He leaned over, burying his nose in my hair and breathed a sigh of relief. "You have no idea how much that means to me, doll."

I did know how much it meant because I never trusted anyone. Gambler was the first in a very long time who I had given my trust to. I just prayed that I wasn't wrong.

''*'*'*'*'*'*'*'*'*'*

Chapter 16
Gambler

"Woman, for the last freakin' time, I'm all right!"

"No, you're not! It's only been two weeks since you were shot! There is no way you are driving your bike today." Gwen crossed her arms over her chest, pushing up her tits that were already hanging out of her shirt.

We had just woken up, and she was driving me crazy with her rumpled, sexy hair and sleepy look on her face. Although, right now she was more pissed off than sleepy. It had been over two weeks since we had crashed, and I was about to go fucking crazy.

Don't get me wrong, I loved Gwen fawning over me, but sometimes a man needed a rest. She had insisted I not ride my bike whenever we need to go anywhere, and I had been okay with that for a while, but now I was done with it.

I pulled a shirt out of my dresser and pulled it over my head. "Gwen, I'm going. I need to go."

She was sitting in the middle of the bed, arms crossed looking like a pissed off vixen. Every minute I spent with her, the more I didn't want to let her go. We didn't fight and argue at every turn anymore, but it wasn't like much else had changed.

It was almost like we were in limbo, each waiting for the other one to make a move.

"It's too cold to go for a ride, anyway. It's fifty degrees out. You'll freeze your balls off."

"Not like I'm using them," I mumbled under my breath as I grabbed my cut off the chair and pulled it on. I tossed open the door to the closet and grabbed my leather jacket out.

Okay, so another reason I was ready to get the fuck out of here was Gwen. I had never had such a case of blue balls in my life. She drove me crazy with her short shorts and tank tops she wore to bed. Then rubbing all over me while she slept and woke up like she just hadn't basically molested me while she slept. Don't even get me started on what she wore when she was awake.

"Well, then I'm coming with you," Gwen crawled to the end of the bed, her sweet tits swaying under her barely their tank top, and I couldn't take it anymore.

"Stop!" She froze, balancing on all fours, her shocked face staring at me. "Get your ass back in bed, and I'll be back later. I'm taking Roam and Slider with me. I'll be fine." I stormed out of the room, the door banging against the door as I walked down the hall.

I couldn't take it anymore. She had to know what she was doing to me. I was a man with only so much self-control before I would snap. I needed to make her mine, but I'd be damned if that was what she wanted. She treated me like a fucking friend, not like someone she wanted to fuck the shit out of.

"Let's go," I growled, walking past Slider and Roam, who were drinking coffee at the bar. They both set their cups down and followed me out the door, no questions asked. All the guys could tell I was ready to fucking explode each time they talked to me.

I tossed my leg over my bike, knowing all eyes were on me, but I didn't fucking care. Ninety percent of these fuckers were getting pussy every night while I laid in my bed every night with the most gorgeous woman I had ever known and woke up with blue balls every morning.

"Where we headed?" Slider asked, walking over to his bike.

"Not a fucking clue. I just need to clear my head." I cranked up my bike, not waiting for a response. I just needed to drive and not think. I looked over my shoulder making sure Roam was ready to go. Slider and Roam both cranked up their bikes, and it was finally time to get the fuck out of here.

I headed out of town, not knowing where the hell I was headed but thankful to be headed where ever the hell it was. I needed to ride till I forgot the past two weeks and maybe ride Gwen out of my system.

Who the fuck knew how long that would take. That woman had made me her's, and she hadn't even touched me yet. What the fuck?

''*'*'*'*'*'*'*'*'*

Gwen

I sat in the middle of the rumpled bed wondering what the hell just happened. I was only trying to help. Gambler was hurt, and I was just trying to go out of my way to make him comfortable.

I could tell the past couple of days he was growing restless, but I guess I didn't know how much.

"Hey, where the hell did Gambler head off to?" Meg asked, walking into the room.

"Um, not sure," I mumbled, wiping the tears that had been flowing down my cheeks.

"Hey, what the hell is wrong?" she asked, sitting on the end of the bed.

"Oh, nothing. I guess I must have gotten on Gambler's nerves."

Meg jumped and grabbed the box of Kleenex out of the bathroom and handed them to me. "I'm sure he just needed a break, babe. Don't stress about it."

"It's kind of hard not to when he just yelled at me. It's just that things have been almost strained between us these past few weeks. I have no idea what to say or do around him. The only time things seem to be chill between us is when we are in bed."

"Oh, well, at least, you've got the whole sex thing going for you." Meg winked at me and plopped down on the bed, laying down across the foot of the bed.

"Please, we cuddle, that's it," I scoffed. I blew my nose and wiped my eyes and tossed the box of Kleenex on the nightstand. I turned back to Meg, and her jaw was hanging wide open.

"You mean to tell me all you guys do is sleep? What the hell happened between the parking lot of the restaurant and now? You both looked like you were ready to rip each other's clothes off that day."

"I have no idea what happened. It's like I just freeze around him. I want him so fucking bad, but I have no idea how to tell him. I spend so much time with him you would think that I would just be able to say it, but I can't. I'm one of those chicks I can't stand who want something but don't know how to go after it." I grabbed a pillow from the head of the bed and set it on my lap.

"I think you should just rip his clothes off the next time you see him, and he'll take the rest from there."

"I'm pretty sure that's what it's all going to come down to." My phone rang, and I grabbed it off the nightstand and saw it was Paige calling. "I gotta take this, it's my sister," I mumbled as I swiped left and put the phone to my ear. Meg waved her hand at me and grabbed her phone out of her pocket and started texting someone.

"Hello?"

"Are you sure you're ready for me to move to Rockton?"

"I am more than ready. When do you leave?"

"Let's see, today is Friday, and I have about two or three more days of packing, so I hope to be there by Wednesday at the latest."

"It's about freakin' time. I let Aunt Rose know last week you were coming. She's over the moon to have us both back in the same town again."

"I can't wait to see her. So, how's it going with your motorcycle man?"

Ugh, not this again. I never should have told Paige about Gambler. I didn't really see any way around it, though. "There's not much to tell."

"Ha! I don't believe that for a second. I'm sure you've got him eating out of your hand already. I can't wait to meet the man who finally made you settle down."

I wouldn't really say I was settled down. I mean, I was living in the clubhouse of a motorcycle club. Not exactly settled. "It's nothing, Paige."

"Hmm, well, I guess I'll just have to be the judge of that when I get there."

"Ugh, there's nothing to judge."

"Suuure. Well, I need to get back to packing. I just wanted to make sure you still wanted me up there before I start packing all my Mary Moo Moo's."

Oh, jeez. "Pack the Mary Moo Moo's. There's no turning back after you do. Call me Monday."

I hung the phone up and tossed it on the bed.

"What the fuck is a Mary Moo Moo?" Meg asked, her eyes as big as saucers.

I burst out laughing realizing I probably sounded crazy talking to Paige. "They're these figurines of cows that my sister collects."

"Who the hell collects figurines of cows?"

"Um, Paige and my aunt apparently," I laughed.

"Oh, well. That's different. I'll have to check out her cows when she gets into town."

"I'll let her know to expect you," I laughed.

"You up to blowing this pop stand today?" Meg asked, sitting up.

"I guess." I had no idea when Gambler was going to be back, so I suppose it was probably good to be distracted and not mope around all day.

"I just texted Cyn and Marley and asked if they wanted to go to the mall. They're down. Lo and Rigid are going to come along, too."

"Okay, just let me get dressed and grab a cup of coffee." I scooted out of the bed and walked over to my suitcase that was in the corner. I really needed to get my clothes out of this suitcase, but I was too scared to ask Gambler if I could use some closet space.

"I'm gonna go make some more coffee." Meg rolled off the bed and straightened her shirt. "I wouldn't worry about Gambler, Gwen. I'm pretty sure you just scare the shit out of him, and he has no idea what to do."

"Well, I hope you're right." I flipped open the suitcase and started rummaging through it, trying to find something that wasn't too wrinkled. "I'll meet you in the kitchen in a couple of minutes." Meg walked out, leaving the door open and headed down the hall.

I sat back on my butt and wondered what the hell I was going to do. I obviously needed to do something different than what I had been doing.

Gambler knew I liked him, so I had no idea why the hell it was so hard for us to be together.

I had been hurt in the past by so many douchebags that I was definitely hesitant to let go, but I knew that Gambler was going to be worth any heartbreak.

I grabbed my black leggings and red button down shirt that had tiny black polka dots all over it and tossed it on the bed. I pulled out my other suitcase out from under the bed looking for the perfect shoes. I was in a shitty mood, so I needed to dress to the nines to make myself feel better. My four-inch patent leather heels called to me as I grabbed them and knew these were going to be just the thing to get me out of this funk.

I grabbed my clothes and shoes and headed into the bathroom, stripped down, and hopped into the shower. I quickly washed, shampooed, and conditioned and was out in record time. I knew everyone was waiting for me, so I blew out my hair and tied it back with a red bandana. Did a quick swipe of mascara, eyeliner, and eyeshadow and topped everything off with my favorite lip gloss.

As I slipped my feet into my heels, they gave me a confidence I hadn't had in a while.

I stood up, looking at myself in the mirror and smiled. It was time to take the plunge with Gambler.

''*'*'*'*'*'*'*'*

Chapter 17
Gambler

I should have known that I would end up here. I hadn't been by to visit Evie in a while. Slider and Roam had held back at the bottom of the hill, knowing I needed time alone. We had driven for over an hour before I realized I was headed straight here.

Her stone was covered with fallen leaves and dead grass. I pulled off my leather glove and used it to brush the stone off. The flowers I had laid there last time were gone and replaced by bright pink daisies my mom always left. She must have been here in the past couple of days. She was always better at getting out here to see Evie than I was.

"I'm sorry I haven't been out here in a while, Evie. I was in an accident a couple of weeks ago, and Gwen had me on a short leash." I looked up at the sky, regret washing over me like it did each time I came here. I should get out to see her every week, but life always seemed to get in the way.

"I don't know what to do with her, Evie. I wish you were here to help me figure things out. You always were the one who told me if a girl was worth it or not. You had that special sense to you." I had always had Evie meet my girlfriends and knew she would give it to me straight about them. Ninety-nine percent of them she told me to let them go. She was right, too. There was only one girl she ever told me was worth it, but it turned out that girl didn't think I was worth it. Go figure.

"She scares the fucking shit out of me, Evie. I've never been with someone who makes me want to give them everything. I'm pretty sure I'd die just to see her beautiful smile one more time." I knelt down, my knee sinking into the wet ground, soaking through my jeans. "When we crashed, all I could think was if anything happened to Gwen, I wouldn't be able to go on." My heart squeezed in my chest just thinking about Gwen dying. The last time I had ever felt that kind of pain was when Evie had died. "I need to let her go, but I fucking can't. I feel like I'll drown in her and never want to come up for air. She's going to destroy me either way." I bowed my head down, a fucking tear streaking down my cheek.

The wind picked up, swirling the fallen leaves around me and the chill cut through my leather jacket, reminding me that it really wasn't the best weather to be riding, but I needed to clear my head. "Maybe I should have mom meet her. I haven't been by to see her in over a month." I tried to get out to see mom at least once a month, but just like with visiting Evie, life got in the way. I pulled my phone out of my pocket and dialed my mom.

She picked up on the second ring, her voice eager to hear from me. "Anthony?"

"Yeah, it's me, Ma. I'm up here with Evie." I pulled the collar of my coat tighter around me, realizing Gwen might have been right about going for a ride today.

"Oh, I was just up there to see her two days ago. I talked to Hank about keeping her grave cleaner. He said he would personally make sure it wouldn't be such a mess the next time I came up."

"It was pretty good when I came today. Just some leaves." Keeping Evie's grave clear and clean was my mother's number one vice. I think she felt that it was the one way she could still feel connected to Evie and protect her.

"Good, good. How are you? I haven't heard from you in a while. The occasional text or call would not go under-appreciated."

"I know, Ma. I was actually calling to see if you would want to have dinner next week with Gwen and me."

"Gwen? Who is Gwen?" Her voice peaked with curiosity, and I knew she was dying to know what was going on. I had never mentioned anyone to her since Evie had passed.

"Um, well, I think she's a girl I'm seeing." I ran my fingers through my hair and winced at how stupid I sounded. I was thirty-seven years old, and I didn't even know if I was seeing someone.

"Oh my," she whispered. "This is huge for you, Anthony."

"I know, Ma. I don't know what the hell I'm doing. I came to see Evie hoping she would give me answers, but talking to a stone only makes me look crazy."

"Oh, Anthony, you don't look crazy. You go there for the same reason I do. You feel close to her for a little bit, but it also helps you to get things out. It helps to clear my head when I go out there. When Evie was alive, when I talked to her I felt the same way. She was always the best listener."

I thought about what my mom had just said, and she was right. Although I didn't get an answer from Evie, I got all my thoughts out. All the things that were bothering me were now laid out before me, and I could see things more clearly. "She did always listen, Ma, but as soon as you were done, she let you know what she thought," I laughed.

"She sure did." My mom went quiet, thinking about Evie. "I'd love to meet your Gwen, Anthony. I'm sure I'll love her. If she's good enough to capture your attention, she has to be pretty special."

"She's definitely something else." I shook my head, realizing Gwen drove me crazy, but I fucking loved it. "We'll be out Thursday night, that ok?"

"It's perfect. I'll make sure to get home early from work and make something special."

"Don't go to too much trouble, Ma. I know you're tired when you get off of work." Ma was a school counselor and treated each and every one of those kids like they were her own.

"Don't worry about it. Just be here by six. That will give me plenty of time."

"Alright, Ma, I'll see you then." I hung the phone up and shoved it into my pocket. I stood up, brushing the grass off my jeans and ran my fingers through my hair.

"I really wish you were here, Evie. I think you'd really like Gwen. I'll be back in a couple of weeks." I walked away from her grave and down the hill where Slider and Roam were waiting for me.

"You 'aight, brother?" Roam asked.

"Nothing a bottle of Jack and a couple hands of poker can't fix," I laughed.

"Who was she to you?" Slider asked, nodding up the hill.

I glanced over my shoulder at where I just came from and sighed. I've never really told any of the newer brothers about Evie. King, Demon, Gravel, and Roam knew about her, but that was it. "She's my sister. Died 6 years ago."

"Sorry, man."

"Yeah, me too." I walked over to my bike and swung my leg over and glanced at Roam and Slider. "You guys good for driving for a bit longer?"

"I got nothing but time, brother. You lead, we'll follow. We know you got shit bugging ya right now," Roam replied, saying exactly the right thing.

This was what I loved about this club. Even when it was freezing fucking cold, my brothers were there for me, riding around so I could sort my head out. "We'll just take the long way home. I pissed Gwen off when I left, and I should probably get back sooner rather than later."

"King texted me and said they were all headed to the mall. He said Demon was keeping an eye on Gwen."

"Demon?" Roam nodded his head, a shit eating grin spreading across his face. "I'm sure he'll take good care of her while you're gone."

Motherfucker. What the hell was that supposed to mean? Demon didn't like Gwen. Hell, even if he did, he better keep his fucking hands off of Gwen. "What time did he text you?"

"He must have texted me about fifteen minutes after we took off. I'm sure everything is fine, brother. He can't do much with her at the mall."

"He better not do anything with her!" I roared, pissed the fuck off. I hadn't even had the chance to make her mine and already I was going to have to mark my fucking territory. "Demon knows I'm with Gwen."

"Then you shouldn't have anything to worry about as long as Gwen knows that, too." Slider slipped his sunglasses on his face and smirked at me.

"You're both fuckers, you know that, right?" I cranked up my bike and headed out the gate. It was going to take at least an hour to get back to Gwen.

"Yo! I need to stop for gas!" Roam yelled at me.

I waved my hand at him, letting him know I had heard. Fuck me, better make that over an hour to get home now.

Demon better know that Gwen was mine. If he didn't, I'd sure as shit let him know. No one was touching Gwen but me.

''*'*'*'*'*'*'*

Chapter 18
Gwen

"That'll be two hundred thirty-seven dollars and fifteen cents," the cashier said. I forked over the money and grabbed the four bags she handed me. "Have a nice day."

"You too," I mumbled, shocked by the fact on how much I had just spent at Victoria's Secret. I figured out what her secret was. The shit was fucking expensive.

"Lo is going to flip when he sees what I bought. He isn't going to know what hit him," Meg purred, peaking into her bag.

"Ugh, I hate you both. I couldn't buy anything because I'm about to blow up into a whale," Cyn groaned, standing up from the bench that was outside the store.

"You could have come in with us," Meg chided, looping her arm through Megs. "Preggo can still be sexy." She leaned down and rubbed Cyn's belly

Cyn swatted her hand away and rolled her eyes. "All I feel right now is bloated. Bloated is not sexy."

"I bet Rigid still thinks you're sexy," Marley said, walking out of the store, her arms laden down with bags.

"I could put a bag over my head, and Rigid would still tell me I'm the sexiest woman. It gets annoying."

We all looked at Cyn like she was insane. What the hell was she talking about? I would love to have a man who would think I am sexy no matter what. "What the hell are you talking about?"

"Yeah, girl. I think we need to check your temperature or something."

"Ugh, I didn't mean it like that. It's just… oh shit, I don't even know what I'm saying. I've become such a bitch since I've become pregnant. It will be a miracle if Rigid is still with me by the time I pop this baby out."

"Oh, Cyn. It's just hormones, honey. I went through it when I had Remy. One minute I was a raging bitch, and then the next I was sweet as pie. You just need to realize when you're a complete bitch and reel it in. Rigid is not going to leave you. That man is so in love with you, he'd die before he left you." Meg wrapped her arm around Cyn's shoulders and pulled her into a hug.

"I'm sorry, guys. I've really ruined our shopping trip," Cyn cried.

"Oh shit, here comes the waterworks," Marley mumbled next to me. Right on cue, Cyn burst into tears, blubbering all over Meg's shoulder.

"Remind me never to get pregnant. I don't think Troy could handle the hormones or the tears."

"As long as you remind me of the same thing," I smirked. Marley held her hand out to me, and we shook on it.

"Oh Jesus, Gambler is wearing off on you if you two just made a bet," Demon said, walking up to us. He stood next to Marley and me, watching Meg and Cyn.

"No bet. Just agreeing to remind each other of the wonders of being pregnant," Marley said, motioning to Cyn.

"What the hell is wrong?" Rigid thundered, pushing past us. He pulled Cyn out of Meg's arms and wrapped himself around her.

"I'm so… so… sorry," Cyn hiccuped. "I'm such a bitch to you," she wailed.

Rigid rubbed her back, whispering to her. I turned away, not able to watch because I was so jealous that Cyn had such a wonderful man. Don't get me wrong, I was happy she had that, but it just made me realize that I didn't have that.

"Oh jeez, Rigid told me about this," King said, walking up with a Sears bag in one hand and an enormous pretzel in the other. He stood next to me, giving me the play by play of what was going on.

"Ugh, she just wiped her nose on his sleeve," he said, cringing. "Oh jeez, Meg's searching for something in her purse. Lord knows what she's going to pull out of there. Could be a fucking stuffed penguin for all I know. Last night I asked her for a pen, and it took her ten minutes to find one. Although, in the search for the pen, she found three check stubs, five packs of gum, ten fruit snacks, an old romance novel, and twenty-three green Skittles."

"Twenty-three green Skittles?" Who the hell has only green Skittles in their purse?

"Yup," King took a huge bite of the pretzel and laughed. "Not a fucking clue why they were all green either. She was just as surprised as I was. She said it was probably Troy the last time they went to the movies. They're always doing stupid shit to each other."

Well, I guess that made sense, sort of. "Did she ever find a pen?"

"Yeah, a green one," King burst out laughing.

"He told you about the Skittles, didn't he?" Meg asked walking over to King.

"Babe, it was fucking hilarious. Even you were shocked when you found the Skittles."

Meg grabbed the pretzel from him and tore a piece off and shoved it in her mouth, mumbling about Troy.

"Yo, I just got a text from Roam. He said they should be back to the clubhouse in forty-five minutes," Demon said, his phone in hand.

My ears perked up at the mention of Roam, knowing that Gambler was with him.

"Alright, you ready to head back, babe?" King asked, wrapping his arm around Meg.

"I wanted to hit up Torrid yet. I promise it'll only take ten minutes. Scouts honor." Meg held her hand up with the pretzel in it, salt falling to the floor.

"I know how you are shopping. Ten minutes turns into an hour and three more stores."

"We already hit up all the other stores I wanted to go to. Torrid and then we can go home, and I'll show you what I just bought." Meg leaned into King, trailing a finger down his shirt. She licked her lips and winked.

King was a goner as soon as she licked her lips. He wrapped both arms around her and kissed the hell out of her. She dropped the pretzel as she delved her fingers into his hair and held on.

"Jesus Christ. Get a fucking room," Demon grumbled, shoving his phone back in his pocket. King reached out, putting his hand on Demon's face and pushed him away.

"What the fuck?" he growled.

"Mind your own fucking business, brother," King mumbled, pulling away from Meg.

"Five minutes, tops," Meg breathed out, holding five fingers up.

"Five minutes for what?" Rigid asked, walking over with Cyn under his arm. Her eyes were red and puffy, but she had, at least, stopped crying.

"Meg promised King we would only spend five minutes in Torrid," Marley explained, pulling her phone out of her purse.

"Yeah, well, she promised that, not me," Cyn sassed, her hands propped on her hips.

"I'm with Cyn," I said, lacing my arm through hers.

"I'm good with whatever," Marley said, shoving her phone back in her pocket. "Troy isn't going to be back to the clubhouse for at least an hour."

"You've been overruled, King. Five minutes is barely enough time to make it past the sales tables." Cyn smirked.

King's eyes traveled over all of us, scowling. "Meg."

Meg shrugged her shoulders and held her hands up. "Hey, who am I to argue?" Meg glanced at Cyn and winked.

"Just one time I'd like a day where I don't have to deal with your crazy ass."

"Maybe one day, but today is not that day," Meg laughed, grabbing Cyn's other arm and pulled us in the direction of Torrid. "Give me half an hour and I'll give you an answer to the question you asked me before," Meg called over her shoulder.

"Oh my fucking God! You still haven't answered him?" Cyn said, her jaw dropped open.

"We were busy with kidnappings and houses blowing up. Me marrying Lo wasn't high on my priority list," Meg muttered.

Holy shit! Meg and King were going to get married! How fucking awesome! "Do you have a date set yet?"

"Pfft, first I need to say yes."

Cyn yanked on Meg's arm, stopping her in her tracks. "Your ass better say yes."

"I have no idea what my ass is going to say. But I'm pretty sure my mouth is going to say yes."

Cyn squealed and raised her arms up in the air, tossing up devil horns. "Fuck yes! I so get to be your maid of honor!"

"You're gonna have to be co-maid of honor with Mel."

Cyn pouted but nodded her head yes. "I'm good with that. Your sister is pretty cool."

"I'm glad you approve. Now let's get a move on." Meg grabbed Cyn's arm again, and we continued to the store.

"Wait for me, bitches!" Marley yelled from behind us. I looked over my shoulder to see Marley sprinting to catch up with us, her long blonde hair flowing behind her. She threaded her arm through mine, and we were walking four wide down the mall. I'm pretty sure no one could get past us if they wanted.

"What the hell was all the squealing about?" Marley asked.

"Meg's going to marry King."

"It's about time he puts a ring on it," Cyn mumbled.

"We haven't even been together for a year."

"Yeah, well, it doesn't matter how long you two have been together. You're a match made in heaven with that man." Cyn opened her purse and pulled out a pack of gum, offering us each a piece.

I grabbed one and popped it into my mouth as I looked behind us, King, Rigid, and Demon trailing about twenty feet away. Three gorgeous men and none of them were mine. Not that I wanted any of them, but it would have been nice to have Gambler here.

I turned back around and sighed. Ugh, it was partly my fault why Gambler wasn't here. I should have pulled my head out of my ass and told the man what I wanted. Now I had pissed him off with all my nagging.

Oy. It was time to do some fixing. I already had a plan working in my head that included my new purchases at Victoria's Secret. Maybe I could find something to top off my plan to make Gambler mine.

All my cards were on the table. It was time to go all in on Gambler.

''*'*'*'*'*'*'*'*'*

Chapter 19

Gambler

Two fucking hours later and we were finally pulling up to the clubhouse. I swear to Christ Slider and Roam were trying to keep me away from the clubhouse. We had ended up stopping at two gas stations because when we stopped for Roam the first time, Slider didn't need gas but then forty-five minutes later we needed to stop for him and then he decided he was hungry so we ate at the fucking diner that was connected.

Longest two fucking hours of my life.

I glanced around the parking lot, seeing Gwen's little Beetle and all the other girls's cars were there, too.

I had no idea what the fuck I was going to do, but I had to do something. I couldn't go on with Gwen driving me crazy and not finding any release.

I turned back to the clubhouse to see Turtle walking out the door, lighting a cigarette. "It's about time ya'll got back. Meg's in the kitchen cooking dinner, trying to teach Marley how to not burn water and Cyn and Gwen are challenging all the guys to a pool tournament. I do have to say, that Gwen sure does have some fine assets." Turtle winked and took a long drag.

What the fuck did he just say? Here I was worrying about Demon and come to find out I have to worry about the whole fucking club possibly going after Gwen. I swung my leg over my bike and stalked to the door.

"Yo! Calm down, Gambler!" I heard Roam call, but I didn't fucking listen. The only way I was going to get these fuckers to lay off Gwen was to fucking take what was mine.

I swung open the door and saw red when my eyes connected with Gwen's ass that was pointed at the fucking door as she bent over the pool table lining up her shot. She was wearing skin tight pants and sky-high heels that made my blood boil and made me want to rip all her clothes off and fuck her in just the heels.

All eyes were on her as she wiggled her ass and took her shot. I could only imagine what she looked like from the front laid out on the pool table. She drove me crazy in her see through tank tops and short shorts at night. All of those nights didn't compare to this moment right now. Fully clothed and covered, she drove me absolutely insane.

She jumped up from the table, arms in the air after she made the shot and spun around. An enormous grin on her face until her eyes connected with mine. The color drained from her face, and I could tell she was surprised to see me.

She took a step towards me, and I shook my head no. I stalked toward her, my eyes only on her. Everyone else in the club faded away.

"I didn't know if-" she started to ramble but stopped when I stooped down, put my shoulder in her stomach and lifted her up. I didn't miss a step as I tossed her over my shoulder and headed toward the hallway.

"Dinner will be done in half an hour y'all," Meg said, walking out of the kitchen and right into me.

"Save us a plate. We're gonna be a while," I mumbled, walking around her.

"Oh shit, it's about to go down," Meg said in awe. "Don't come out until y'all know what the hell you two are!" she hollered at my retreating back.

"Gambler?"

I didn't say anything. I had no idea what to say to Gwen right now that wouldn't make me sound like some caveman. All I wanted to do was pound on my chest and scream mine.

"Are you mad at me?"

I grabbed my keys out of my pocket and unlocked my door. I flipped the light switch on and tossed Gwen on the bed.

"What the hell do you think you're doing?" she demanded as she bounced on the bed, her hair falling in her face.

"I don't have a fucking clue what I'm doing anymore, Gwen! You're driving me fucking crazy!" I ran my fingers through my hair and paced in front of the bed.

"Me?! What about you? This morning you blow up at me and roar off on your bike and now come back and carry me off like some caveman, and I'm just supposed to be okay with this? You're confusing the shit out of me!" she wailed, rolling off the bed and getting in my face.

"I don't know what the hell you want!"

"Like I know what you want?"

"I come back from visiting my dead sister's grave and find you spread out on the fucking pool table putting on a God damn show!" I roared.

"How the hell was I supposed to know that was where you went? And, I wasn't spread out on the pool table! I was playing pool!" Her eyes flared with annoyance, and she poked her finger into my chest.

"You better think twice before you do that again, doll," I warned, grabbing her hand.

"Oh yeah, what the hell are you going to do about it? Drive off and leave me all alone again?"

"I didn't leave you alone. I needed to clear my fucking head."

"Well, fucking tell me that! You left here, and I thought I did something wrong." She crossed her arms over her chest and glared at me.

"You fucking did! I can't get you out of my fucking head! You brush up against me, fawn over me, and don't even get me started how you wrap yourself around me when you sleep. I fucking need you and I can't God damn have you!"

"Who the hell says you can't have me?"

"Me! I know you're going to fucking destroy me. Something will happen, and you'll be gone, and then I'll be right back where I was when I lost Evie. I can't fucking love someone and lose them again."

Gwen gasped, and her eyes widened. "Who was Evie?" she whispered.

"My sister. I loved her, and she died. She was the last person I loved besides my mom. I can't give that to someone again, Gwen, and you deserve more than what I can fucking give you."

"Don't you think I should be the fucking judge of what I deserve?"

"You don't know what you're asking for, Gwen. I see the way you watch King, Rigid, and Troy with the girls. I know you want that, and I don't think I can give that to you."

"Don't tell me what I fucking want! I want you, and I don't care if you think I deserve someone else!"

"You don't know what you are asking for," I growled. I was at the end of my patience with her. I could only warn her and fight with her so much.

"Give me what I want!"

"Don't push me, Gwen."

She stepped closer, her head tilted back a bit. Even with heels on I was still taller than her. "Take it, Gambler. Take me."

I couldn't do it anymore. I couldn't deny myself the one thing I needed and wanted. I grabbed her around the waist and spun her around, slamming her against the door. "This makes you mine, Gwen. There's no going back." This was her last chance to change her mind.

"I've never wanted anything more in my life," she whispered.

I slammed my mouth down on her's and groaned as she instantly opened, yielding to me. My hands immediately went to her ass, lifting her up. She wrapped her legs around my waist, her heels digging into my back. "I wanna fuck you with just the heels on," I growled.

She wrapped her legs around me tighter and tossed her head back as I trailed kisses down her neck, tasting what I had been craving.

I reached up, grabbing one side of her shirt and ripped it open. She gasped in surprise but didn't stop me as I pulled her bra down and devoured her perfect tit. "Gambler," she moaned, arching her body into me.

She tugged at her shirt, twisting out of it and tossed it on the floor. I reached behind her, trying to free her perfect tits and moaned as her bra hit the floor. "You're not allowed to ever put clothes on again."

A laugh bubbled out of her, and she cradled my face in her hands. "That sounds good now, but I'm pretty sure the first one of your friends to see me naked will end up dead."

"You're probably right. I'll just have to keep you in my room and never let you out."

"Now that has promise," she said, nibbling on my bottom lip.

"Don't tempt me, doll. Slide down, we both have too many clothes on right now for this to go the way I want."

"So demanding," she purred unwrapping her legs from me. Her feet touched the floor, but she kept her arms wrapped around my neck. "Everything off but the heels?"

"Heels stay, the rest better be off in ten seconds." I pulled my coat and cut off, turning around and tossed them on the bed. I turned back around, tugging my shirt over my head to see Gwen hopping from foot to foot pulling her pants off. I glimpsed a tiny purple triangle of cloth covering her sweet pussy, and I swear I could have cum in my jeans right there.

I watched as she struggled to pull her pants over the heels. Her pants were skin tight, and there was no way she was going to get them off. "Stop," I said, kneeling down in from of her. I grabbed her right foot, slipping her heel off and then her pant leg. I did the same with the left and then put both heels back on.

"What about my panties?" she asked as I stood up.

"They stay on for now." I unbuttoned my jeans, watching as she bit her bottom lip. I leaned down, quickly unlacing my boots and kicked them off. Her tongue snaked out, licking her lips as I tugged my jeans down, my underwear coming down with them. "This first time is going to go fast, doll. I've wanted you for over a month. I'm pretty sure my dick is going to explode when it feels your tight pussy." I pulled my pants down the rest of the way, my dick rock hard and bobbing.

Gwen took a step towards me, her hand reaching out. "No." She stopped in her tracks, confusion crossing her face. "Turn around, brace your hands on the door," I ordered.

She hesitantly turned around, her eyes not leaving mine until she was entirely turned around. "I want to touch you, Gambler. Please," she begged as she put her hands on the door.

"I told you I'm on the edge, doll. One touch from you and this is going to be over before we even start." I stepped forward and trailed a finger down the center of her back. "So smooth," I murmured.

Her body shivered under my touch, a moan escaping from her lips. Her head fell forward and her back arched. "You're torturing me," she whispered.

"Now you know how I've felt every night you wrapped your sweet, soft body around me." I wrapped my arms around her and pulled her to me. "Spread your legs, doll." She shuffled her feet a couple of inches apart and waited. Her breathing was shallow and short, and I knew she needed this just as much as I did.

I reached around and cupped her pussy, her lips drenched with her desire. "So wet for me," I murmured as I parted her slick lips. She trembled in my arms, and I placed my other hand on her stomach. My dick was cradled in the crack of her ass, and it took all my self-control not to bend her over and plow into her. "I'm going to make you come all over my hand," I whispered, "and then you're going to come even harder around my dick."

A tremor rocked through her body, and she tossed her head back, exposing her neck to me. I slipped a finger inside her as I trailed kisses down her neck.

"Gambler," she moaned as I pumped my finger in and out. I added another finger, and her tight pussy pulsed around them, making my dick rock hard and beg to be buried inside her. I flicked her clit with my thumb, her pussy drenched with her desire.

"Are you gonna cum for me, doll?" I growled in her ear.

"Yes," she hissed as I worked her clit, bringing her closer and closer to the edge. She threw her arms over her head and wrapped them around my head and held on. "I'm so close."

She arched her back, pressing her sweet ass into my rock hard dick. She rocked her body with the thrusting of my fingers, moans, and mewls of pleasure gasping from her lips.

"Cum for me, Gwen. Now," I demanded as I bit down on her earlobe. I pinched her clit, and she exploded around my fingers, her screams of ecstasy surrounding me. Her body bucking with every wave of pleasure that washed over her.

"Gambler," she moaned as her body came down, small tremors still taking over her body. She leaned back into me, the full weight of her pressed against me. "Holy fuck," she cursed, resting her head on my shoulder.

"That was the sexiest thing I've ever seen," I growled, kissing her neck.

"Hmm it sure felt good," she purred.

"Are you okay to stand?" I asked, trailing my hands up her body and cupped her perfect tits.

"As long as you hold me up," she laughed.

"Hmm, I had plans of bending you over right here."

"Jesus Christ," she gasped as another tremor rocked through her body. "Just the thought of you bending me over could make me cum."

"How about my dick makes you cum next, doll. Next time we can see if you can cum from just my voice." I stepped back, holding onto her arms making sure she was steady enough to stand. "You good, doll?"

She nodded her head and looked over her shoulder at me. "Never better."

I put my hand on the small of her back and slowly pushed her down till she was bent over, her ass in the air. "I've dreamed of seeing you like this. Bent over, ready and waiting for me," I murmured, running my hand over the fullness of her ass.

"Take me, Gambler," she begged.

I stroked my cock as I caressed her ass, spreading her cheeks, seeing her dripping wet pussy waiting for me. I stepped forward, my dick nudging the tight rose of her ass. She gasped, a slow moan escaping her lips as I trailed my dick down the crack of her ass and lined my dick up with her sweet pussy.

I slammed into her, unable to take things slow any longer. "Hold onto your ankles, baby." I watched as her hands slid down her legs, and she wrapped her fingers around her delicate ankles. I rocked slowly in and out of her, eager to fuck the shit out of her, but not wanting it to be over that quickly.

"Harder," she moaned.

"I go harder, and I'll be done in ten seconds," I gritted out.

"Not to freak you out, but you don't have a condom on." Holy fuck! I pulled out but was stopped when Gwen reached, holding my legs so I couldn't pull out all the way. "I'm on the pill, and there is no way we are going to use a condom after I felt how perfect you fit inside me."

"Jesus fucking Christ, Gwen. How the hell am I supposed to stop after you said that?"

"You're not. That's exactly why I said it. If you stop, I'll kill you," she threatened. She dug her nails into my leg, tightening her grip.

I slowly sunk back into her as she tossed her head back. "Fuck," I moaned as she squeezed the walls of her pussy around my dick.

"Fuck me hard, Gambler. Make it better than anything I've ever felt."

She didn't have to tell me twice. "Can you reach down and put your hands on the floor?" She reached down without a word, but we both moaned as she leaned forward, and I slipped even further into her. "Hold on, doll. I'm gonna fuck the shit out of you."

I pulled out and slammed back into her, her body rocking forward. She braced her hands farther apart and waited for more. I slowly slid out, leaving only the tip inside her. She rocked her body backward and slammed down on my dick. "Fuck me, Gambler. I don't want gentle. I want everything you can give me."

I growled at her words, wondering how the hell I had gotten so lucky to find this perfect woman. I grabbed her waist, my fingertips digging into her hips and slammed into her, the tight walls of her pussy contracting around me. I thrust in and out, each one better than the last.

"Yes," she moaned, as I pounded into her, reaching for my release. I reached around, parted the lips of her pussy and flicked her clit. "Gambler," she screamed. She stumbled forward as her orgasm crashed into her, but I caught her by her hips as I slammed into her one last time as I came in her tight, sweet pussy that was milking every last drop of cum from me. "Holy fuck," I groaned, throwing my head back. I leaned forward, covering her body with mine, and lifted her up, helping her stand up.

Her head limply laid on my shoulder, her breathing labored and short. "I have no idea what that position was called, but we need to do that again. Soon."

"First, I need to sit down before I fall down, doll." I leaned over, lifting her into my arms and turned around and laid her on the bed. She kicked her shoes off, scooted up to the pillows and pulled the covers back. She slipped under them and held the sheet back, waiting for me.

"You do know it's only four o'clock, right?"

She shrugged her shoulders and patted the mattress. "Who said anything about sleeping?"

''*'*'*'*'*'*'*'*'*

Chapter 20
Gwen

I was beyond exhausted, but I wanted more. I don't think I would ever get tired of this man. Gambler looked down at me, smirking, and my heart melted a little bit. That fucking smirk drove me crazy. I grabbed his arm and tugged him down on the mattress.

He crawled on top of me, caging me in with his arms and trapping me with his body. "You're just a little vixen, aren't you, doll?"

"Only for you," I purred, reaching up, stroking his cheek. He had a weeks worth of stubble, and it drove me mad. Each day he became more and more gorgeous. "I like this," I murmured.

He leaned his cheek into my hand, "Maybe I'll keep it for a while since you seem to be a fan of it."

"I wonder what it would feel like everywhere."

Gambler leaned down, rubbing his cheek against the side of my breast. "You mean here?" he mumbled.

The scratchy roughness drove me crazy as he worked his way down my stomach, raining kisses as he went. "Hmm, maybe just a little lower," I cooed.

"Here?" He nipped at my side.

"Closer."

He kneeled in between my legs, spreading them wide. "Right here?" he whispered, a breath away from my core. I dug my fingers into the bed and nodded my head. "I need to hear you, doll. Tell me where you want it."

"Make me cum," I pleaded, arching my back.

"Hmm, I've already done that twice." He parted the lips of my pussy, his breath teasing me. "How should I make you come?"

Oh my God. Just his voice was setting me on the brink of coming. One touch from him and I knew I was going to go off like a rocket. "Your tongue. I need your tongue," I pleaded. He flicked my clit with the tip of his tongue, and a tremor rocked my body.

"Like that?" I looked down my body to see Gambler smirking at me, his eyes burning with desire.

"More. I need more," I panted.

"Whatever you want, doll. It's all yours." His head disappeared, and he sucked my clit into his mouth, his tongue swirling, and kneading.

I dug my heels into the bed, lifting my body up, reaching for more. Gambler put his hand on my stomach, pushing me down back on the bed. His hand glided up, grabbing my breast, pinching the nipple in between his fingers. I was in fucking heaven and hell all at the same time. I had never felt the way Gambler made me feel before, but it was pure torture, and I wanted more.

Gambler looked up, his eyes connecting with mine. I bit my lip as I caught a glimpse of his tongue flicking my clit. "Fuck me," he groaned, raising his head. "I bet your fucking mouth was made for my dick." He grabbed my hand, pulling me up and rolled us over so I was sprawled out on top of him.

"Hmm, I liked what you were doing," I pouted, kissing his neck.

He grabbed my ass, "Flip around, doll, I want you sucking my cock while I eat that sweet pussy." He smacked my ass and pressed a kiss to my forehead.

I moaned as I slid down his body and swung my leg over his body and came face to face with his rock hard dick. He didn't need to tell me twice to do anything. Everything he wanted was the same thing I needed. I slid his cock into my mouth, moaning as he spread the lips of my pussy and flicked my clit with his finger. "So wet," he mumbled. His tongue swirled around my clit, and I dug my nails into his thighs, holding on as he brought me to the edge with one touch. I bobbed my head up and down, my tongue feeling every ridge and vein of his cock.

Gambler grabbed my ass, pulling me down and buried his face in my pussy, licking and devouring every inch. "I'm gonna cum," I moaned, raising my head and stroked him with my hand.

"Mouth," Gambler muffled, slapping my ass.

I slid him back into my mouth as my hand stroked his shaft. I swirled my tongue around the tip and sucked hard as I moved my hand faster. I heard Gambler moan and knew he was just as close as I was. "Faster," he panted. "I want to cum down your throat while you scream my name."

There he goes again making me want to come from just his voice. I slide all the way down until he hit the back of my throat and swallowed. Gambler roared, his balls tightening and his dick pulsed under my tongue. He nipped at my clit and tipped me over the edge, my orgasm slamming into me as his cum coated my throat.

His fingers dug into my ass as he thrust into my mouth wringing every last drop of cum from him. My arms shook as I tried to hold myself, my orgasm rocking my body harder than the last time.

"God dammit, you are unbelievable."

I swirled my tongue one last time around the head of his dick, making sure not to miss a drop of his sweet cum and laid my head on his thigh. "No, I think you're the amazing one for making me cum three times in less than an hour."

He stroked my back, trailing his fingers in lazy circles. "Happy to be of service," he laughed, his body shaking under me.

I rolled off and face planted in the mattress, completely rung out. "You do know I'll be needing daily service from now on."

Gambler laughed even harder and sat up. He reached for me, grabbing my arms and pulled me into his lap. He brushed the hair out of my face and stroked my cheek. "Only if you promise to service me."

"I'm sure that can be arranged," I leaned up, my lips brushing against him. "I think you might have broken me for the rest of the night, though."

"I doubt that. I say we rest, get some dinner, and then maybe I can do some more service. You do know I'm a mechanic, so I like to be very thorough in my work. Check under the hood," he trailed his tongue between my breasts, "check the spark plus," his tongue snaked out, swirling around my nipple, "and you can't forget about checking the undercarriage." His hand cupped my pussy, and another tremor of anticipation ran through me. How the hell did this man manage to make me cum three times and still leave me wanting more?

"I guess I better rest and prepare for my full inspection." I rested my head on his chest, the steady beating of his heart calming and lulling me to sleep.

I finally gave in to what I wanted, and the world didn't end. Maybe I would get my happy ending after all.

''*'*'*'*'*'*'*'*'*

Chapter 21
Gambler

"Salsa?" Gwen asked, sitting back down in my lap as she poured a shit ton of salsa on her nachos.

After we had recovered by taking an hour nap, we managed to find our clothes we had tossed all over the room and ventured out to the kitchen. Meg was just about to put a plate up for us as we walked in.

We both piled our plates high and headed over to the table where Roam, Hammer, Slider, and King were playing poker. "Go get another chair," King said to Hammer as we set our plates down.

"No, we're good," Gwen said, waving her hand at Ham to sit down.

"Doll, where the hell are you going to sit?"

"On you."

Which lead us to now. She perched on my knee and shoveled a forkful into her mouth.

"How they hell do you eat so much?" Ham asked, his eyes following Gwen's every move.

Roam slapped him upside the head and scoffed, "Don't you have any common sense?" he asked.

"What the hell was that for?" he asked, rubbing his head. "I just wanted to know how she had such a smokin' body when she eats like a God damn truck driver. That's her third plate."

Gwen laughed next to me and took a swig of the margarita Meg had handed to her when we walked out of the kitchen. Meg had been up twice to fill her glass up. Apparently, it was a bottomless margarita. "Gambler worked up my appetite." She winked at me as she piled more food on her fork.

"Alright, I'm done. Next time I make tacos someone else is doing the dishes. I make too big of a mess to clean up myself," Meg laughed, carrying the big pitcher of margaritas in one hand and her glass in the other. She set it in front of Gwen and plopped down in King's lap.

"I would have helped you," Gwen said, shoveling the last of her food in her mouth. I really must have worked her appetite up. I was on my second plate, and I was full.

"Eh, that was more directed at Lo than you," Meg laughed, taking a drink.

"I told you what needed to happen before I'd do the dishes again." King set his cards down and wrapped his arms around Meg. "All I need to hear is one little word out of that pretty little mouth."

Meg rolled her eyes but didn't say anything. "Dude, you promised you would answer him if he let you go in Torrid today. Never mind the fact that we almost spent an hour in there. Answer the man!" Cyn yelled from the couch. Rigid was sitting in the corner of the couch, and Cyn was laying down, her head in his lap as he rubbed her stomach.

"You're not helping!" Meg yelled. "I thought you were supposed to be my ride or die bitch. Now you're just throwing me to the wolves."

"King is far from a wolf," Cyn countered.

"They do realize you're sitting right here?" I asked King.

He just shrugged his shoulders and picked up his cards. "I'm used to it. Cyn will probably get an answer out of her before I will." Meg grabbed his cards out of his hands and tossed them on the table. "Babe," he called as he watched his cards scatter and fall on the floor.

"Ask me again," she demanded.

"What?" King said.

"Ask me again. Do it."

"Meg, I don't want to do this if you're just going to say yes to make everyone else happy. I'm good with how we are. Forget I even asked." King lifted Meg off his lap and headed for the bar. I could tell he was either pissed off or disappointed. Either way, he wasn't in a good mood anymore.

Meg looked around, shocked. "You take it back?"

King picked up a bottle of Jim Beam and filled his glass. "I don't want to make you do something you don't want. I don't take it back, but I'm not going to hassle you about it anymore. When you're ready, let me know."

"But I am ready."

King shook his head and set his glass down. "If you were ready, babe, you would have already said yes."

I looked around the poker table, and Roam, Ham, and Slider each looked like they wanted to slide under the table and disappear. Gwen was sitting next to me her jaw hanging open, looking at Meg and King. I had no idea what the hell was going on, but it was either going to end good or bad. Right now I would have betted on bad.

"I wanna say yes," Meg insisted, stomping her foot.

"No, ya don't. A man shouldn't have to ask a woman five times to marry him before he gets an answer. I love you, Meg, and I'm not going anywhere, but I can only take so much rejection before I get the point. Marriage is a no."

"But that's not what I want," she wailed, throwing her arms up in the air.

"Well, then fucking tell me what you want. I hear more from your friends of what you want than you!"

"God dammit, Lo! I fucking love you, and you better believe your ass is going to marry me! I don't care what anyone else says or thinks. Stop listening to them, and listen to me!" Everyone went silent. Cyn and Rigid sat up from the couch and peered over the back of it.

Marley and Troy came walking down the hallway but stopped in their tracks when they saw Meg and King squared off on each other.

"God dammit, Meg. This is what you want? In front of everybody?"

"I don't care who's in this room right now besides you. If you're here, it's what I want. I don't want anyone else." Tears were streaming down her face as she waited.

King ran his fingers through his hair, his eyes never leaving Meg. "I fucking love you. With everything I am and will be, I love you. I want to wake up every morning next to you in our big ass bed and every night I want you next to me in that big ass bed so we can do it all over again the next day. I love your son, I love your dog, but most of all I love you. Without you I'm nothing and with you I'm everything. Marry me?"

Meg nodded her head, her hand covering her mouth. Holy shit, King had some moves. He even had me wanting to say yes.

Gwen reached for her napkin and blotted her eyes. I pulled her hair out of my way and kissed her neck. "You okay, doll?"

She nodded her head and buried her face in my neck. "Meg deserves this," she mumbled.

I wrapped my arms tight around her and held her close.

"Is that a yes?" King asked.

Meg nodded her head again and sobbed. I glanced over at Troy and Marley, who both had huge grins plastered on their faces and Cyn was quietly crying as Rigid rubbed her back.

"It's about fucking time," King mumbled. He closed the distance between them and lifted her in her arms and swung her around.

"Well, I guess that's one way to get engaged," Roam said, taking a sip from his beer.

Gwen spit out the sip of margarita she took and busted out laughing. "What the hell, doll?" I asked, wiping off my hands she had just spat over.

"Roam is right. That really was a Meg way to get engaged. Holler and yell at each other and then get engaged," Cyn laughed.

"Oh shut up," Meg said, flipping the bird at all of us. "You all knew I was going to say yes," she scoffed.

King reached into his back pocket and pulled his wallet. "Good man, he knows as soon as she says yes to just hand his wallet over to her. Exhibit A of why the hell I will *never* get married." Slider wiped his mouth with the back of his palm and raised his glass up to Meg and King.

"I'm not giving her my fucking wallet," King grumbled as he searched through his wallet. "I knew that when she said yes, it was going to be in some crazy way. That's why I kept the ring in my pocket." King pulled it out and got down on one knee. "Megan Marie Grain, ever since you've come into my life, nothing has been the same. You're the reason I laugh and smile every day. Will you marry me?"

And, just like in true Meg fashion, she nodded her head yes and tackled him to the ground. "Yes, yes, yes a thousand times!" she yelled.

"Well, I didn't know we were going to get a show with our tacos," Gwen said, turning her head to look at me.

"Neither did I, doll," I brushed my lips against her's, craving her taste.

She threaded her fingers through my hair and pulled me close. "Last one to the bedroom is a rotten egg." She jumped up from my lap and sprinted down the hall without looking back.

"What the fuck?" Slider said, watching Gwen run away.

I shook my head and grabbed our empty plates and carried them to the kitchen. "Hey, where are you going?" Cyn called. "We need to celebrate!"

I shook my head and wiped my pants on my jeans. "I think Gwen has her own kind of celebration in mind," I called, raising my hand over my head and headed down the hall.

I rubbed my hands together hopeful that by the time I made it to our room, Gwen would have her clothes off and spread out on the bed for me.

Today had ended completely different from how it started. It had started out with Gwen, and I ready to claw each other's eyes out, and now all I wanted to do was rip her clothes off and bury myself in her for hours.

I turned the handle on the door and pushed it open. And to top the night off, Gwen was laid out on the bed wearing nothing but a smile and her high heels.

Let the celebration begin.

''*'*'*'*'*'*'*'*'*

Chapter 22
Gwen

"How many boxes can one woman have?" I groaned, lifting up another box from the trunk of Paige's car.

"I don't know, doll. She's your sister." Gambler grabbed the box from my arms and set it on top of the last one in the trunk and lifted them both.

"I could have taken that," I whined, slamming the lid shut.

"I know. Doesn't mean you have to." Gambler winked at me and head into the two bedroom place Paige had found the day she arrived in town. It was two blocks away from my salon and over the pet store. Plus, our aunt lived only five minutes away, so it was perfect.

I glanced into the backseat of her car, double-checking to make sure we didn't miss anything and headed into the house. "I think that's it, Paige," I said, shutting the door behind me. It was two weeks away from Thanksgiving, and there was a definite chill in the air. I pulled my cardigan tight around me and rubbed my hands together.

"You want these in the kitchen?" Gambler asked.

"Um, I'm not really sure what they are," Paige mumbled standing up from unpacking a box that was full of cow figurines. Yes, the whole collection of Mary Moo Moo's had made the move with Paige.

Gambler shook the box, and it sounded like silverware rattling around. "I think I'll just set it in the kitchen," he mumbled.

Paige had gotten into town yesterday, and it had been a whirlwind, to say the least.

Before Paige arrived, Gambler and I spent most of our time in his room surfacing only to go to work and eat. I never thought that Gambler would be so demanding and dominate. I was falling quick and fast for the man I was terrified to love.

He anticipated all my needs and gave me everything I could ever want or need. I was in a blissful haze that I never wanted to leave.

A pounding on the door made me jump, "That must be Meg and Marley," I mumbled, opening the door.

Meg stood on the other side with King next to her. "Don't ask. Apparently shit has gone down, and I'm not allowed to leave the clubhouse on my own." Meg rolled her eyes and walked into the small living room.

King followed Meg in, looking annoyed and ready to wring her neck. "I'm sorry me keeping you safe is inconvenient for you, babe."

"Ugh, I don't mean it, Lo. I'm a bitch today, apparently. I'm sick of having to look over my shoulder all the time and worrying if someone is going to get hurt again." Meg ran her fingers through her hair and sighed. I couldn't agree with her more. Every time Gambler would go to work I was terrified something would happen.

"As soon as Leo and his sister get here, things will change. He said they should be here this weekend and that he had some interesting information for us. We just need to make it two more days." King took his coat off and tossed it on the back of the couch. "Where's Gambler?"

I pointed to the kitchen, and King headed that way. Meg sat down next to me and held her hand out to Paige. "I'm Meg. That big hunk in the kitchen is King, he belongs to me."

Paige shook her hand and laughed. "Good to know."

"He's also her fiancé," I chimed in, sitting on the couch.

Meg waved her hand at me, shushing me. "Ignore her."

"Oh, he's not your fiancé?" Paige asked, confused.

"He is, but I don't feel it necessary to tell everyone I meet like Gwen here does. I figure with me saying he belongs to me was good enough." Meg stuck her tongue out at me and flipped me off.

I was coming to realize if Meg flipped you off, it was her way of saying she liked you. Strange, but so Meg. "Is Marley coming?"

"Naw, her and Troy were cuddled up at the clubhouse watching TV. She said she'll get over to meet Paige the next couple of days."

Paige stood up and carried a box over to her bookshelf Gambler had put together earlier. "It's the cows!" Meg hollered as she watched Paige line them up on the shelf.

Paige laughed and shook her head. "I'm assuming Gwen informed you about my cows?"

"She sure did, and I had no idea what the hell she was talking about. I did ask Ethel, and she knew what they were. I'm apparently out of the loop."

"Where has Ethel been?" I asked, grabbing the other box of cows and took them over to Paige.

"Somehow Gravel and her are able to stay at her house. King said he doesn't think they'll go after them. King takes me over there every couple days to keep me from going crazy being cooped up at the clubhouse. He either loves me, or he knows I'll cut him if he doesn't let me out," Meg laughed.

"The answer is a little bit of both, babe." King and Gambler walked back into the living room, both looking at what Paige was doing. They both apparently had never seen a Mary Moo Moo before. I had grown up with them, so I didn't think they were strange at all.

"I gotta make a couple of phone calls, babe. You good in here with your girls?" King asked, pulling his phone out of his pocket.

"Go, shoo. We'll holler if we need anything. Like pizza or wine," Meg said, waving her hand at him. King leaned down, pressing a kiss to the side of her head and walked out the door.

"I'll be right outside, doll." Gambler wrapped his arms around me and kissed me like he hadn't seen me in years.

I grabbed his biceps and held on. It was the only thing I could do when Gambler kissed me. The man knew what he was doing with his mouth.

He pulled back, a smirk playing on his lips. "Miss me," he winked and walked out the door.

"Holy hell," Meg said, her jaw dropped. "I think Gambler just made me swoon." She fanned herself with her hand and pulled her shirt away trying to get air under it.

"For the record, even though you are my sister, that was pretty freakin' hot." Paige set her empty box on the floor and took the one I was holding out of my hands.

"When I finally let myself be with Gambler, I never imagined he would be the way he is." I grabbed another box and opened it seeing more cows. I now knew that when I wondered how the hell Paige could have so much stuff, I realized half the boxes were filled with cows.

"Oh, do tell how Gambler is." Meg grabbed a pillow off the couch and stuffed it under her head and laid down.

"I thought you came here to help unpack?" I asked.

"I'd much rather hear how Gambler is than put shit away. No offense, Paige."

Paige laughed and shook her head. "I'm not worried. I don't need everything put away right away. I can't tell you the last time I just hung out and chilled with friends. We can talk, and I can organize my cows."

"I think we might have to get you a new hobby."

"It's useless, Meg. Paige and my aunt have been obsessed with these damn cows since they came out." I grabbed another box off the floor and wasn't surprised to see it stuffed full with more cows.

"You mean to tell me you're not down with the cows?" Meg laughed. "Although you two really don't look anything alike. Paige is all sexy, sweet, innocence while you're sexy pinup. The only way I can tell you two are related is your eyes."

"Muddy brown," Paige and I said at the same time. We both hated our eye color.

"Dude," Meg said, sitting up. "Your eyes are like dark pools of chocolate. Or that could be my hunger talking." Meg scratched her head and laughed. "But anyway, your eyes rock."

Paige and I both laughed. "You are right that we are nothing alike. Except when we were growing up, Gwen *always* tried to dress like me. That is until she met Matt Crown and everything changed."

"Shut up," I yelled, grabbing a pillow off the couch and threw it at her.

"Hey, watch the cows," she whined, throwing her body in front of the bookcase.

"No one wants to hear about Matt." I crossed my arms over my chest and glared at Paige. I hadn't thought about Matt in ages, and I didn't want to start now.

"Matthew Crown was the first ever to turn Gwen's head, and she was stuck on him for years. I'm talking six years, here."

"Wow, six years. When did you two meet?"

"Oh my God, I can't believe we are talking about this. I totally regret talking you into moving up here. Pack all this shit up and go."

"Oh, hush, woman," Paige threw her empty box on the floor and took the full from one my hands. "She was fifteen when she met him. He moved in next door to us and Gwen was totally smitten."

"Who the hell says smitten?" I mumbled, collapsing on the floor next to Meg.

"I do. Now shut up. If you don't want to tell the story, then I will."

"It's all lies," I said, looking at Meg.

Meg just shook her head and wrapped her arms around my shoulders. "Hush, it's story time." She put her finger over my mouth and winked.

"Sooo, back to what I was saying. Matt was the complete and total bad boy. He was two years older than Gwen and, in my opinion, was a complete and total ass. Drop dead gorgeous, but still an ass."

"Ugh, they totally lose points when they're asses," Meg agreed.

"Now our Gwen was nothing to scoff about. Even when I was eighteen, and she was fifteen, her boobs were bigger than mine. Matt took one look at both of us and also became totally smitten with Gwen."

"There's that fucking word again," I muttered.

Paige rolled her eyes but kept going. "I'm not all sure what happened because I did move away from home, but things were going pretty good for these two until one night Matt went to a party by himself and had a little bit too much to drink. At this point, they were five years into their love/infatuation and Gwen thought rainbows and ponies shot out of Matt's ass. I knew better."

"You did not. Nobody expected it to happen."

"I saw it coming. I couldn't pinpoint exactly what was about to happen, but I knew."

"Holy freakin' shit! Would one of you please tell me what the hell happened!" Meg gripped my arm, anxiously waiting.

It was a definite doozy what happened. Paige could say it till she was blue in the face that she knew, but I doubt she did. Even Matt's own mom didn't know. "Matt was gay."

"What!?!? You dated a gay guy for six years! Wait, you said after five years you found out. You stayed with him even when you knew he was gay?"

"She sure did. Matt was too much of a chicken to come out of the closet. He begged and pleaded with Gwen to stay with him."

"Wait, hold the fucking gay train up a minute here. Did you have sex with him before all this came out?" Meg turned to me, her eyes bulging out of her head.

"Um, yeah."

"So how the hell did he have sex with you? Was he like bi or something? How the hell did he get hard?" Meg lifted her pinkie finger and wiggled it.

"I found out he had a good imagination," I winced, closing my eyes. Ugh, telling people about my sham of a relationship was not the shining moment of my life I wanted to talk about.

Hi, my name is Gwen, and I was so blind that I couldn't see that the man I was sleeping with every night was secretly picturing The Rock every time we had sex. Nope, not what I want people to know.

"Can we please stop talking about this? I was a fool and an idiot and trust me, I learned from it."

Paige sat down next to me and put her arm around my shoulder. "Nobody thinks you're a fool, hun. We all think Matt was an ass for lying to you for so long."

"Hell yeah, how the hell were you supposed to know he preferred salami to tuna?"

Paige and I burst out laughing, tears streaming down our faces.

"I thought you girls were unpacking?" I looked up and saw Gambler and King walk through the door.

"We were, but then we had to take a trip down memory lane about Gw-." I elbowed Paige to shut her up.

"We were just talking, and Meg made a joke," I said, as Paige glared at me while she rubbed her side. I did not need Gambler knowing about my six-year mistake.

Imagine thinking you've found the man of your dreams, at fifteen no less, and then you decide to surprise him by showing up at a party and find him making out with a guy. Talk about a shock. Then I was an even bigger fool for staying with him for another year. We were both shocked when I walked in that room on him. Matt swore that was the first time he had kissed another guy. He insisted that he had too much to drink, and one thing led to another. I could only imagine what would have happened if I hadn't walked in when I did.

He still called me a couple times of year to check up on me. I know he felt guilty for doing what he did to me, and that was his way to make himself feel better. I always answered the phone when he called, but I never called him.

"What was the joke?" Gambler asked, sitting down on the couch.

Paige, Meg and I looked back and forth, scrambling for a joke.

"Uh, well, you know…" Paige trailed off, her hands held out in front of her.

"And then it, um, you know…" I wasn't much better at thinking on the spot.

"Pig fell in the mud!" Meg yelled. We all looked at her like she was crazy and her face turned bright red. "It was a dirty joke," she said, shrugging her shoulders.

Paige snorted and burst out laughing while King and Gambler rolled their eyes. "I feel like this is the whole drunk Marley and the coffee pot in the bathroom again. When am I going to learn that I can't leave you alone for that long?" King walked over to her and held his hand out. She grabbed on, and he pulled her up and wrapped his arms around her. "What am I going to do with you?" he whispered. Meg wrapped her arms around his neck and whispered something in his ear. I could only imagine what came out of Meg's mouth.

"Watch this," Gambler said, nudging me with his foot and pointed to King and Meg. "Five, four, three, two, one," he mouthed.

"Well, it's time to get the fuck out of here," King boomed, grabbing Meg's hand and pulling her to the door.

"But I didn't help unpack anything," Meg laughed.

"You can come back tomorrow if I'm done with you by then."

"Oh, well, bye girls!" Meg waved as King pushed her out the door, waved to Gambler and slammed the door shut behind him.

"How the hell did you know that was going to happen?" I asked, standing up.

"Cause I heard what she was whispering to him."

"What did she say?" I mean, I could take a guess at what she said, but I wanted to know what Gambler heard. It probably had something to do with salami and tuna if I knew Meg.

"I'll show you when we get back to our room." Gambler reached forward, snagging my hand and pulled me into his lap.

I slapped his hand away as he traveled up my leg and laughed. "No, none of that right now. I need to help Paige. Our only other help just left, so now it's all on us."

"Um, I'm gonna order pizza," Paige mumbled, walking into the kitchen.

"Now you just embarrassed my sister," I scolded, hitting him in the chest.

Gambler grabbed my hand and pressed a kiss to my palm. "It's not my fault I can't keep my hands off you." He buried his face in my hair and rubbed my back.

I leaned into him, missing his touch. It was crazy how much I missed him when he had been within shouting distance of me. "I think I'm going crazy, Gambler."

"Hmm, how so, doll?"

"I hate when you're not touching me."

"Then I guess I'll have to do a better job of always being by you."

"You do know that is completely unrealistic, right?" I giggled, as he rolled us onto the couch, his body covering me.

"I already told you I'm going to lock you in my room and keep you naked. I don't think me touching you all the time is out of line." He leaned down, his lips brushing mine.

"You do realize we are on my sister's couch, and she is fifteen feet away?"

"Does that mean you don't like this?" He nipped my earlobe and chills ran through me. "Or this?" He trailed kisses down my neck, and I arched my back, pressing into him, begging for more. "Then I guess I better stop." He pulled away from me, but I grabbed his shoulders and pulled him back.

"Just one more kiss," I whispered.

"There's always time for one more kiss," he whispered.

"Okay, I've stayed out for as long as I can," Paige said, walking back into the room, her hand covering her eyes. "Please put all clothes on and get off my sister."

Gambler grunted and pulled away from me. He sat on the end of the couch and ran his fingers through his hair. "Sorry, Paige," he mumbled.

I sat up, a bit dazed, "Um, did you order the pizza?" I pulled my shirt down that I hadn't even realized Gambler had pulled up and swung my feet off the couch and sat up.

"Yeah, it should be here in half an hour. I figure if we keep working, we'll be done in no time, and you shouldn't have to come back tomorrow."

By the time the pizza arrived, Paige had all her cows unpacked, Gambler was working on putting all the boxes in the rooms they belonged, and I was aimlessly unpacking the kitchen, still needing the man who had almost taken me on my sister's couch.

Gambler was wearing me down, making me rethink everything I thought I knew about him. Gambler was turning into the man I always wanted. I just hoped it stayed that way.

''*'*'*'*'*'*'*'*'*'*'*'*'*

118

Chapter 23
Gambler

"Leo just pulled up. Get your ass out here," King barked into the phone.

"I'll be right there." I hung the phone up and tossed it on the bedside table. I looked down at Gwen, who was sprawled out on top of me, quietly snoring.

She had spent all day at her sister's yesterday, leaving Marley to take care of the shop. Turtle had stayed with Gwen while I helped King and Demon get everything ready for Leo's sister Fayth and nephew coming today.

The past couple days had been busy, and it seemed the only time we spent together was when we were sleeping. It was only seven thirty, and I already needed to leave her.

I slipped out from under her, careful not to wake her up, and laid her head on my pillow. She moaned in her sleep but grabbed the pillow and wrapped her arms around it. I didn't know what I did to get her in my bed, but I was going to do everything I could to keep her there.

After I had my clothes and boots on, I slipped back over to the bed and pressed a kiss to the side of her head and brushed her hair from her face. She looked like an angel when she slept, peaceful and carefree. I kissed her one last time, half hoping she would wake up, but didn't.

"It's about fucking time you haul your ass out of that room," Hammer called when I walked into the main room.

"Fuck off. You wouldn't want to leave your room either if you had what I do." I grabbed an empty cup and filled it with steaming coffee.

"Ha! You were the only one who had a chance with her. Lucky fucker," Hammer mumbled walking over to the bar. He grabbed a plate and piled it high with waffles, eggs, and bacon.

"Who the hell cooked?" My stomach growled as I saw Slider, Demon, and Gravel shoveling food into their mouths.

"Meg. She woke up, made breakfast and now she's back in bed," King explained walking into the kitchen with his empty plate.

"And I can tell you right now she is not a morning person. As soon as she walked out of her room this morning she threatened to stab me if I talked to her. Freaking crazy," Slider said as he picked up his coffee cup and walked over to the coffee pot.

"You might not want to talk smack about the chick who feeds you ninety percent of the time," Gravel laughed.

"Eh, not making fun, just giving out a warning." Slider shrugged his shoulders and took a sip of his coffee.

I walked over to the food and mounded my plate full, sat down at the table and tucked in to eat. "I thought Leo was here?" I asked, my mouth full, looking around.

"He should be here in half an hour. I remember how I was when Meg and I hooked up. I figured you would need the extra time to say goodbye."

"She was still sleeping. She's been working hard and then helping her sister getting settled in, I think she's been running on empty."

"You didn't tell her you were leaving?" King asked.

I shook my head no and forked in a load of eggs into my mouth. "She knew what I had going on today. She said she was just going to run to the salon with Marley to take care of a couple of appointments, and then she was just going to head back here and relax. I'm good."

King just shook his head and grinned. "If that's what you think, brother."

I don't know what the big deal was. I had let Marley know where I would be today, she seemed fine with it. I glanced at the clock seeing it was a quarter to eight. It probably wouldn't hurt to wake Gwen quick to say I was headed out.

"Yo! Leo is here," Turtle said, sticking his head into the door. Shit, there went telling Gwen I was leaving.

"Let's go. First stop is a couple of offices we found for him. Leo setting up an office in town could be a good thing." King set his cup down and headed out the door.

We all followed, Hammer piling up all our dishes and carrying them to the sink.

I glanced down the hall, thinking I could quick sneak down to our room, but if she woke up, I knew it wasn't going to be a quick kiss and then be gone. She was going to want me to stay, and I wouldn't want to leave.

I felt my pocket, making sure I had my phone and planned on calling her in a little bit when I knew she would be awake. That would have to do.

''*'*'*'*'*'*'*'*'*

Gwen

I woke up, and I knew he wasn't in bed. I cracked one eye open and rolled over to look at the bathroom and saw the door open, Gambler not in there. I glanced at the clock and saw it was nine o'clock. Shit! I needed to be at the salon in fifteen minutes. I whipped the covers back and jumped out of bed.

After a quick brush of my hair and teeth, I swiped on some eyeshadow, and I was rummaging through my bag trying to find something to wear.

"Hey, you ready to go?" Marley stuck her head into my room, a smile plastered on her face. Someone apparently didn't oversleep like I did.

"Yeah, I just need to throw some clothes on," I mumbled. I grabbed a vintage Betty Boop long sleeve tee and a pair of jeans and dashed back into the bathroom.

"The guys left pretty early this morning," Marley called through the door.

Well, at least, Marley knew what time the men left. I didn't even remember Gambler leaving the bed. Who knows if he even said goodbye. Yesterday at Paige's had worn me out. Although we finally had all her stuff put away, so it was definitely worth it. She was here to stay, and I couldn't be happier. "What time did they leave?" I pulled my shirt over my head and fluffed my hair. I needed a shower but didn't have time. I grabbed a stray bandana from the bottom of my bag and tied it up in my hair. "This is as good as it's going to get today," I said to the mirror and headed back to my suitcase to find shoes.

"Um, I think it was over an hour ago."

I opened my shoe suitcase and saw it was empty. What the hell? I glanced at the floor and saw ninety percent of my shoes were scattered around. Oh shit. When the hell did I get so messy? Normally I was so neat and orderly it drove people crazy. If I didn't know any better, it looked like Paige was staying here.

I spied my black Mary Jane's sticking out from under the bed, grabbed them and slid them on my feet. After I had got done at the salon, I was going to have to clean up. "Okay, I'm ready. I just need a cup of coffee for the road, and then we can hit it. Are we taking Troy's truck?" I asked as we walked down the hall.

"Yeah, he hates my car. Plus, I love his truck. It's a win, win," she laughed.

I grabbed a travel cup, filled it to the brim and snapped the lid on.

We headed out to the truck that Troy had idled at the door and climbed in. I rubbed my arms as I waited for Marley to get in and figured I should have grabbed a coat. We were having an unseasonably warm winter for Wisconsin, but it was still a bit chilly in the morning. I glanced at the clock on the dash and knew I didn't have time to run back in. Oh well, it looked like I would just have to turn the heat up a bit.

"How long is this going to take?" Troy asked as we headed out of the driveway.

"Probably two hours. I think we have six girls we need to do, although they all want pretty basic updos." I flipped the visor down and checked my face. I should have taken more time with my makeup. I always liked to go to work dressed up because my appearance represented what I was capable of, but I just didn't have the time this morning. "You don't like spending time with Marley when she's at work?"

"It's not that I don't like spending time with Marley, it's just that I never thought I would spend so much fucking time inside a salon. I come home smelling like hair dye and shampoo."

Marley reached over and patted his cheek. "Oh, my poor Troy. Does all this girl time bother you? Should I bring a football, baseball and some Penthouses the next time?"

"Yeah, just what I want to do, hold my balls, read porn and watch you cut hair. My life is complete." Troy rolled his eyes and grabbed Marley's hand. "It's a damn good thing I love you." He pressed a kiss to the back of her palm and held her hand in his lap. Marley leaned over and pressed a kiss to his cheek.

"I love you, too," she mumbled.

I looked out the window and rested my head against the glass. Son of a bitch, I missed Gambler. It had only been a couple of hours since he left to go take care of club business, and I felt like a clingy bitch because I was upset he didn't tell me he was leaving. Shit.

We pulled up in front of the shop as I scolded myself for being so dependent. I vowed to myself when Matt and I broke up that I would never rely on a man so much again. Now here I was moping around, pining after a guy again.

"Oh crap, they're early."

I glanced at the front of the shop and saw a group of woman crowded around the door, looking through the glass, none of them looking happy. I pushed my sunglasses up my nose and realized this was not going to be a good morning.

I was a sad sack pining over Gambler, and now I had a feeling I was about to deal with Bridezilla. This day could be over any time now.

''*'*'*'*'*'*'*'*'*'*'*

Chapter 24
Gambler

"Man, this is the fourth fucking office building we've looked at. You think he's ever going to pick one?" Hammer sat next to me in one of the shop's trucks, eating a banana. Don't ask me where the hell he got a banana from.

"Well, seeing as this is the last available building in Rockton, this one is going to be it or nothing."

"We've been at this shit for four hours, and we still have to help move his sister in. We're not gonna be done till fucking dinner time, and I'm fucking starving." Hammer chomped down on his banana, chewing with his mouth open. I swear he had ten brain cells, and five of them were slowly dimming.

"First off, chew with your fucking mouth shut." I reached over and smacked him on the back of the head. "Secondly, this shit better not take that long. I forgot to plug my phone in last night, and the motherfucker died before we even made it to the first office."

"You can use mine if you want." Hammer patted his left pocket, and his eyes grew big. He patted his right pocket. "Shit, I must have left it back at the clubhouse."

I shook my head and ran my fingers through my hair. Son of a bitch. I didn't know if Gwen was going to be pissed or understand why I hadn't called her all day. "No worries, brother. I just wanted to check in with Gwen."

"You two finally together, huh?" Hammer wiggled his eyebrows at me as he took an enormous bite.

"Yeah, for the most part."

"What the hell does that mean? She warms your bed every night."

"Yeah, she does, but…" I ran my fingers through my hair again and sighed.

"But what? What else is there?"

"A whole lot more, brother, but I don't know if Gwen wants to give me more."

Hammer's jaw dropped open, and he gaped at me. "Holy shit, not you too. You're gonna be like King and Rigid, aren't you?"

"King and Rigid got a good thing, brother. Nothing wrong with wanting what they have, especially if it's with someone like Gwen." I pictured Gwen lying in bed this morning when I left, and I knew that was what I wanted to wake up to every morning.

"If you say so. I think I'm going to stick with my bike and freedom." Hammer folded up the banana peel and tossed it out the window. "Having one woman holds ya down, and that's not something I want."

"To each their own, brother." I turned my head, looked out the window and saw King, Demon, and Leo finally walk out of the office building. Besides Hammer and I keeping an eye on things, Leo also had his own men riding along today. Leo said he hadn't heard anything from the Assassins since Troy had been kidnapped, but he was very cautious that they were now going to go after Leo.

Going after Leo and the Banachi's would be a huge mistake, but as we had seen in the past, The Assassins were not a smart bunch. Things had been quiet since they had tried to kill Gwen and I. We still didn't know if they were going after anyone in the Knights now, or if they again mistook the wrong people for Rigid and Cyn.

King walked over to our truck, and I rolled the window down. "He's going with this one. It's not exactly what he wanted, but he said he can make the improvements needed."

"Nice. So, now what? Is the sister in town yet?" I asked, grabbing my pack of smokes and pulled one out.

"Yeah, he said she was about three hours behind in the U-Haul. She's been at the house for almost an hour now. We head over there, help get her all set up and then we can head back to the clubhouse."

"Sweet. You good with riding with Gravel?"

"Yeah, we're good. He's a grumpy fucking bear right now, but I can handle it."

"What the hell is up his ass? He hasn't seemed too happy these past couple of weeks." Gravel had walked into the clubhouse this morning acting like someone had pissed in his cheerios.

"Not sure, brother. I'll try to talk to him and see if he'll tell me anything. I know we're all getting sick of looking over our shoulders so maybe that's just got him wound tight right now."

"Could be." I glanced over King's shoulder and saw Leo sitting in his car, waiting. "We better head out." I nodded at Leo and King turned around.

King patted the top of the truck and walked over to Gravel. "What do you think has got Gravel so ticked?" Hammer asked as I started the truck.

"Don't know, brother. Could be a bunch of shit, or it could be Gravel just being Gravel."

"Yeah, you're probably right." Hammer reached down into the side of the door and pulled out another banana.

"Dude, where the hell are you getting these bananas from?" I asked, shocked as he pulled out two more.

"I knew it was going to be a long day, so I grabbed the bunch of bananas that was sitting on the counter before we left. Pretty smart, huh?" He peeled another banana and ate half of it in one bite.

Yeah, Hammer wasn't going to think he was very smart when he got back to the clubhouse and Meg rips him a new asshole for eating all the bananas she was going to use to make banana cream bars. "Yeah, you sure are a smart one," I laughed, shifting into drive and followed behind Leo and his goons.

We headed in the direction of Fayth's house while Hammer rambled on about all the benefits of eating bananas. "Dude, these suckers are loaded with potassium. One of these and…"

I tuned out Hammer, knowing he was just rambling and not looking for a response. I glanced at the clock on the dash and groaned. The more time that went by, the more I doubted Gwen would be okay with me not calling her. I was sure she had probably called me, but there was no way for me to know until I got my phone charged.

Let's hope when I got back to the clubhouse Gwen wasn't ready to rip me a new asshole like Meg was going to do to Hammer.

''*'*'*'*'*'*'*

Gwen

"Who the hell eats a whole bunch of bananas? Like, I'm talking a big bunch of bananas. At least 9!" Meg flailed her arms around as she yelled and searched the kitchen for the mysterious missing bananas.

"I feel like this is a case for Scooby Doo and the gang," Cyn laughed, plopping down on a stool by the bar.

"This is not a time to make jokes," Meg called from the kitchen.

I was standing in the doorway to the kitchen, exhausted from a long day of dealing with Bridezilla, but I was thoroughly entertained at the moment. "I haven't seen Scooby Doo in ages. Is it still on TV?" I asked.

"Oh yeah. It's definitely still on. I make Rigid watch it with me sometimes. He always bitched because I make him watch the new episodes, and he says they have nothing on the old ones." Cyn grabbed her glass of water and took a drink.

Marley stood on the other side of the bar from Cyn, her head propped in her hand as she leaned against the bar. "I always had a thing for Shaggy."

Cyn spat her water out and slammed her glass down. Meg leaned out the doorway to the kitchen, and we all stared at Marley. "What the hell did you say?" Cyn asked, wiping water off her chin.

Marley wiped her hand off that was covered with water with a bar towel and handed it to Cyn. "Um, I had a thing for Shaggy?"

"You do realize Shaggy is a cartoon, right?" Meg asked.

"Of course," she propped her hands on her hips and stared us down. "Come on. You mean to tell me there's not a cartoon character that y'all don't think is hot?"

Cyn, Meg and I looked at each other and shrugged our shoulders. "Well, I guess if you put it that way." Meg tapped her finger on her chin and hummed. "I suppose I'd have to go with Batman. He's all tall, dark, and handsome."

"Eh, I'm going with the Hulk," Cyn said as she propped her feet up on the stool in front of her.

"Dude, you just looked at me like I was insane for saying Shaggy, but you just named a huge, nine foot, lime green giant who gets pissed off then transforms into said monster." Marley shook her head and grabbed the towel, tossing it into the sink.

Cyn held her hands up and shrugged. "I can't help what I like."

"That would explain why she's into Rigid. I swear we should have painted him green for Halloween and made him pass out candy as the Hulk," I said, walking into the kitchen.

"I am so making him do that after I pop this baby out," Cyn giggled, rubbing her belly.

I grabbed a bag of chips, and the huge bowl of guacamole Meg had made earlier and headed to the bar. "Question," I said, ripping open the bag of chips. "Who the hell dyes his hair?"

"I do now. Before me, he said he did it himself, although I have a sneaky suspicion he either had one of the club girls do it or Demon."

"Demon? Why the hell would you say that?" Meg asked, walking behind the bar, grabbing bottles and setting them on the top.

"Because Demon mentioned a couple of weeks ago to Rigid that it looked like he was due to have his hair dyed. Now, you tell me why the hell he would say that?"

"I am so picturing Rigid sitting in the bathroom, on the toilet, a towel draped over his shoulders and Demon rubbing blue shit in his hair," Meg laughed.

Marley and Cyn burst out laughing, and I couldn't help but laugh too. "Oh my God," I groaned.

"Ugh, not the picture I wanted. I'd like to believe Rigid and Demon are more manly than that." Marley dipped her chip in the guacamole and moaned. "This is the best shit, ever."

"Yeah, well, you should try my banana cream bars. Wait, you can't because someone ate all the fucking bananas!" Meg yelled, her eyes traveling over all of us.

"Ugh, and now we're back to the bananas," Cyn laughed, shaking her head.

"I can tell you right now there is no way I could eat nine bananas, so turn your eyes elsewhere," I said, wagging my fingers at her.

"Well, I can tell you one thing, I am going to find out who ate my bananas, and when I do they will pay."

Cyn laughed and loaded her chip with a mound of guacamole. "Sure you will. More like just make them run to the store and buy you more."

"Hey, you never said who you thought was hot as a cartoon," Marley said, pointing her finger at me. Meg and Cyn both nodded their heads as they chewed.

"Oh, that's easy. Johnny Bravo all the way." Couldn't tell I'd ever thought about this before.

"Isn't that the guy with the oddly shaped body and way blonde hair?" Meg asked.

"Yeah."

"I have no idea who the hell that is," Marley said.

"You're kidding me. Someone grab their phone and educate Marley here. Shaggy has nothing on Johnny Bravo." Cyn pulled her phone out of her pocket and asked Google who Johnny Bravo is.

"Why the hell are you googling Johnny Bravo?" Troy asked, walking into the common room.

"Because Gwen had the hots for him," Meg said, walking past Troy and into the kitchen.

"He's a cartoon," Troy said, confused.

"Well, in that case, you *really* don't want to know who Marley had a thing for," Cyn said, rolling her eyes.

"Who the hell is it? I bet it's Batman, isn't it?" Troy crossed his arms over his chest and stared down Marley.

"Dude! That was mine!" Meg yelled from the kitchen.

"I should have known," Troy mumbled.

"You're never going to guess it," Cyn mumbled.

"Okay!" Marley yelled. "It's Shaggy, alright? I never thought it was weird until I told these three."

Troy threw his head back and laughed. "I always had a thing for Velma."

Cyn's jaw dropped. "You're kidding me. You two are like a match made in heaven."

Troy walked around the bar and wrapped his arms around Marley. "It's only a little weird you had the hots for Shaggy," Troy mumbled.

"Oh! Here, I've got Johnny Bravo!" Cyn held her phone up and shoved it in Marley's face.

Marley grabbed the phone and laughed. "At least, Shaggy looks human, this guy has a triangle for a body and like no facial features."

I grabbed the phone out of her hands and scoffed. "Come on, he thought all the ladies wanted him, and he had confidence for days." Although I did have to admit, I remembered him a bit differently.

"Lo just texted me. He said they'll be here in ten minutes." Meg walked out of the kitchen, her nose buried in her phone.

I pulled my phone out, wondering if I had missed a call from Gambler but there was nothing. I had called him more than five times today, but it went to voicemail each time. Each time I called him, I got a little bit more pissed off.

"Nothing yet?" Marley asked.

I shook my head no and shoved my phone back in my pocket. "It's nothing. He told me he was going to be busy today."

"Yeah, well, the prick could have at least called once." We all looked at Cyn, shocked. "Hey," she said, holding her hands up. "I just call it like I seem 'em."

"Damn, Cyn is one friend you want on your side," Marley laughed.

"Yeah, she definitely is a ride or die bitch." Meg put her arm around Cyn's shoulders and laughed.

"You putting the moves on my woman?" We all turned around to see Rigid standing in the doorway, smirking.

"Well, if you wouldn't leave her alone so much I wouldn't have to."

Rigid looked at his wrist, "I've only been gone seven hours."

"Since when did you get a watch?" Cyn asked.

Rigid laughed and held up his arm that didn't have a watch on it. "You got me."

"Lo just called and said ten minutes. What the hell are you doing here?" Meg asked.

"I left a couple of minutes before they did. I hitched a ride with Gambler and Hammer. Never again will I do that. The three of us crammed into that truck was not a good idea. Plus, I kept stepping on banana peels." Rigid walked over to Cyn and put his hands on her belly. "How's my little biker?" he mumbled.

"I knew it! Your boyfriend ate all of my bananas!" Meg turned around glaring and pointing at me.

"Hey! Gambler is his own man."

"I'm gonna beat the bananas out of him," Meg threatened.

"Who, Hammer?" I whirled around at Gambler's voice and smiled. I was still annoyed he hadn't called me all day, but dammit did he look good. He still hadn't shaved, and he was wearing his signature jeans, tee, and boots. Plus, a leather coat since the weather had turned cold. Although, if you looked at any of the guys in the club, that seemed to be standard attire. Except they all appeared to have their own spin on it.

"What the hell does Hammer have to do with you eating all my bananas?"

"The fact that I had to sit in that God damn truck all day watching him mow down on them."   "Oh, shit." Meg turned her head to me. "I take back what I said."

"What the hell did Meg say now?" King asked, walking in from the shop. He closed the door behind him and took his coat off. Leather jackets seemed to be another thing the guys all added to their uniforms in the winter time.

"Someone ate all my bananas, and I'm pretty sure it was Hammer."

"I wouldn't doubt it. The fucker is a God damn garbage disposal."

I tuned everyone out when Gambler started walking over to me. Remember you're mad at him, Gwen, I reminded myself. But the closer he got, the more my anger disappeared, and all I wanted was to be in his arms.

"Nice of you to call."

"I tried, doll." He pulled his phone out of his pocket and handed it to me. "I forgot to plug it in last night. It died an hour after I left and I was stuck with Hammer all day. Motherfucker left his here."

"You couldn't borrow someone else's?" I crossed my arms over my chest and cocked my hip out.

"Well, if you're going to play that way, doll, if you were really concerned you could have had Meg call King to talk to me?" Gambler crossed his arms, mimicking me.

My blood boiled, pissed the hell of by the fact he thinks I should have tried harder to talk to him. "So you mess up, and I have to go out of my way to talk to you? I was busy at work today and didn't have time to try to play leap frog on the damn phone."

Gambler took a step towards me, closing the distance between us. His eyes darkened, and he grabbed my arm, "You might want to be careful what you say next, doll. I've been on edge all day not able to talk to you, and now when I can, all I get is sass."

I tugged my arm, trying to get away, but he tightened his grip and pulled my body flush against him. He plastered his hand to my ass and held me close. I looked up, his face tilted down at me. "Don't be a dick, Gambler," I spat out. He was cranky he couldn't talk to me, well, so was I.

"You got one more try, doll," he warned.

"Dick!" I shouted in his face.

Gambler growled low, and I knew I might have made a mistake. "Bad move," he whispered. He pushed me away, surprising me so I stumbled over my feet, and he put his shoulder in my stomach and lifted me up. "What the hell are you doing? I don't want to go anywhere with you!" I pounded on his back, but he didn't stop.

"I warned you twice. I'm not taking your sass about this." He swatted me on the ass and headed down the hallway. "Anyone knocks on our door, all they're going to meet is my fist," Gambler growled as we walked past everyone by the bar. I really couldn't see them except for their feet, though.

"Whoa, Hulk smash," Cyn yelled.

"What the hell does that mean?" I heard Rigid ask.

"Your girl has got a thing for the Hulk." I heard Meg say as we turned the corner down the hall. I really wish I could have heard what Rigid's reaction was.

"Gambler put me down. I can God damn walk."

"You won't be able to when I get done with you." He reached into his pocket and pulled his keys out. I swatted at his hand, and he dropped them. He went still, and this was the second time in five minutes I regretted my actions. "You're really trying my patience today, Gwen."

"Sorry," I gulped.

"I think you need to be taught a lesson," He growled. He set me down on my feet and pressed me against the wall. He caged me in with his arms and body making it so there was no escape. I looked up and down the hallway, hoping one of the girls had followed us, but they hadn't.

"No one is coming to save you, doll." My eyes snapped to his, and a shiver ran through my body. I swallowed hard, a little terrified, but a whole lot turned on.

"I'm not sure if I want to be saved," I whispered.

Gambler growled low and slammed his lips down on mine. His fingers delved into my hair, pulling my bandana off, tossing it on the floor. He tilted my head back, his lips devouring me. I held on to his arms and moaned as his tongue snaked into my mouth. "Wrap your legs around me," he mumbled against my lips. He grabbed my ass, and I swung my legs around his waist as he pressed me against the wall. "Why can't I get enough of you?"

I pressed my lips to his, not wanting to answer. I knew the reason why I couldn't get enough of him, I was falling in love with him. Did Gambler feel the same way? I didn't have a clue. "Maybe we should take this to your room."

"Not yet," he mumbled, trailing kisses down my neck. He grabbed the hem of my shirt and yanked it over my head.

"Whoa, whoa," I protested. I crossed my arms over my chest and looked down the hallway. "Gambler, what if someone comes down the hall?'

"No one is coming down here. I told them to leave us the fuck alone."

I pushed on his shoulder, and he lifted his head. "No, you told him not to knock on our door. Last I checked," I looked up and down the hall, "we're not in your room."

"Gwen."

"What?'

"Shut up." His lips claimed mine again, and all thought except for Gambler left me. I wrapped my arms around his neck and held on. I arched my hips, squeezing my legs tighter around him. His hands kneaded my breasts through my bra, and I moaned as he raised my bra and his head lowered. His mouth sought out my nipple, and I ran my fingers through his hair.

"Yes," I moaned as he rocked his hips against me. "I need you, Gambler."

"I'm gonna set you down, and you have ten seconds to get your pants off, okay?"

I nodded my head yes, unable to talk. I was about to have sex in a hallway that anyone could walk down, and all I could think about was how fast I could get my pants off.

My feet touched the floor, and I ripped open the fly of my jeans, slid down the zipper and tore them down my legs. Thankfully I had slipped on a pair of flats when I got home so they just fell off when I pushed my jeans down.

Gambler had his pants pulled down to his knees, and he was stroking his dick as he watched me. "You're mine," he growled as he stroked one last time. He prowled to me, his hands grabbing my ass and he hoisted me up. "Ride me."

I didn't have to be told twice. I reached down, stroking his rock, hard dick. He leaned back, and I guided his cock in and slowly sunk down on him. I threw my head back and moaned as he reached places that drove me insane. Gambler kissed my neck as he kneaded my ass. "Ah, I don't know how you do it, Gambler."

"Do what, doll?" He sucked on my neck, driving me, even more, crazy.

"All I can see is you. You make the world disappear." I buried my fingers in his hair, lifting his head to mine. "What have you done to me?"

"I'm making you fall in love with me. I'm not letting you go. Stop questioning it, and just let go." He kissed me long and deep, giving me everything I needed in just that one kiss. Gambler had just said he wasn't going to let me go, and I wasn't freaking out, trying to figure out how to push him away. "You ready to ride me?"

"God yes," I moaned. I steadied myself by putting my hands on his shoulders and used my legs wrapped around him as leverage and pulled myself up. Gambler gritted his teeth and put his hands under my ass and helped to lift me up.

"Fuck, you're like a fucking vise like this," he groaned as I slid back down. "Fuck," he said, closing his eyes.

I lifted up again and slid back down, over and over. My climax built with each movement as I slammed down on his dick, faster and faster. "I need to cum," I breathed out, "please."

"Not yet, doll, not yet," Gambler chanted as he took over, thrusting up as I slammed down. "I want you to cum all over my dick while I cum inside you. Together," he growled. His lips claimed mine, taking everything I had to give.

"Who do you belong to?" he asked against my lips. "Tell me."

"You," I whispered.

"Louder. I need to hear it."

"You, I belong to you," I moaned on the brink of ecstasy.

"I can't let you go, I need you." I fell over the edge at his words. Words I needed to hear. My orgasm slammed into me, taking my breath away. Gambler threw his head back groaning as he fell over the edge with me. He slowing thrusted, the walls of my pussy pulsing and contracting as I milked every drop of cum from him.

He stumbled forward, my back hitting the wall. "Holy fuck," he gasped, catching his breath.

I leaned forward, wrapping my arms around him and held on. I loved Gambler, and I was going to hold on like I could lose him at any second.

''*'*'*'*'*'*'*'*

Chapter 25
Gambler

"We should really get in your room," Gwen mumbled into my chest.

"I'm not sure my legs will make it." I had my knees locked and was sure as soon as I tried to walk, I was going to fall over. Gwen had taken everything I had to give, and I was drained to the point of exhaustion.

"Set me down, you grab the key, and we can haul ass into the room."

I shook my head no and buried my face in her hair. "Five more-"

"Meg, stay the hell away from their room!" We heard called. My head snapped back and I looked at Gwen whose eyes were bugged out.

"Fuck," she whispered, hitting me in the shoulder. "Let me the hell down!" She dropped her legs from my waist, and I unlocked my knees and scrambled to find the key. Apparently, while we were going at it, I must have kicked it. My eyes darted all over, hoping to glance the white key fob and saw it ten feet down the hall. I lunged for it, my fucking pants still around my knees.

"Quick!" Gwen whispered, panicking to grab her shirt and bra.

"Someone needs to check on her! Gambler was a dick to her." Meg whined, her voice getting closer. I sprinted to the door, Gwen at my back as I fumbled with the key and finally got it in the lock and twisted the handle open. Gwen pushed me in, and we landed in a heap on the floor. Gwen kicked her leg, connecting with the door and it swung shut.

"That was close," Gwen laughed, laying down next to me.

"We still had about ten seconds." I reached over and pulled Gwen to my side. She rested her head on my shoulder and looked up at me.

"I suppose you think ten seconds is a long time."

"It doesn't even sound like King let her down here." We both listened, our breathing the only thing we heard. "He must have headed her off at the turn in the hall."

"Thank God," Gwen murmured.

"I'm sorry I didn't call you today, doll." I looked into her beautiful face, and a grin spread across her lips.

"You don't sound like the guy outside my door five minutes ago who demanded I shut up and fucked me breathless."

"You do crazy things to me, doll. Your attitude drives me insane. All I want to do is fuck it out of you when you start mouthing off." I brushed her hair out of her face and slid my thumb over her soft lips. "I meant what I said out there. I'm not letting you go, even if you want to leave. I'll just have to find ways to convince you to love me."

"I think you're crazy, but I don't think I'll need much convincing to stick around," she smirked. "Oh yeah?" I laughed. I reached over, tickling her side and she squealed, pushing my hand away.

"No, you don't fight fair!" she laughed, fighting me.

"Gwen!" Shit, I guess King didn't hold Meg off.

"Stop it," she hissed at me. "Meg is going to think you're hurting me."

"Yeah, because people always laugh when they are getting hurt," I laughed, both hands attacking her now. I rolled her over, pinning her to the floor and straddled her hips. "I'm not letting you up until you get rid of Meg."

"You're crazy," she gasped as I doubled my efforts. "I'm fine, Meg. Gambler's just yelling at me."

"What?" Meg called.

"Why you little liar." I grabbed her arms and pinned them over her head. "You better tell her the truth before I turn you over my knee and give you the spanking you deserve."

"Never," she laughed, wiggling underneath me. "Gambler says he's going to spank me, Meg!"

I held her wrists with one hand and put my other hand over her mouth. "Did you just lick me?" I asked, pulling my hand away.

"Fair warning. You put your hand on my mouth, you will get licked." She stuck her tongue out at me and bucked her hips trying to get out from under me.

"King, get over here!" Meg called.

"Oh shit, you're in trouble now, she's getting King," Gwen taunted.

"Oh yeah, watch this."

"Gambler," King said.

"Yo!"

"You good?"

"Never better. Just working the attitude out of Gwen." Gwen squeaked, outraged. "We'll be out for dinner in a couple of minutes."

"Get, now," I heard King mumble. I heard Meg stomp down the hallway, their voices fading.

"You do know my attitude, as you put it, is not going anywhere, right?"

I let go of Gwen's wrists and cupped my hands around her face. "I hope not, it's one of my favorite things about you." I leaned down and gently pressed a kiss to her lips.

"What else do you like about me?"

"You fishing for compliments, doll?"

"No, it's just nice to hear sometimes what you like about me."

"All right," I said, leaning back. "One, you have legs for days. I'm talking you could wrap 'em around me twice." Gwen laughed, her cheeks blushing. "Two, your fucking hair. I have no idea what the hell you do to it, but I seriously want to bury my face in it every time you're near."

"It's shampoo, Gambler," she laughed.

"Yeah, well, I think it's also you, too. You make everything better."

"I think you're just partial because I'm warming your bed right now."

"Wrong. You are more than warming my bed."

"Then what the hell am I doing?"

"Becoming part of my life."

"Don't you think it's a little too soon to be talking like that? We've known each other what, a month, five weeks?"

"Well, you are meeting my mom tomorrow, so I would have to say that means something." I had made plans to see her last week, but Gwen had to work late, and we couldn't make it.

"Ugh, I feel like I'm going to puke every time you mention meeting your mom. Can't we do that like next year?"

"You do realize that this is the middle of November and next year isn't that far off, right?"

"Well, even if we only wait that long I'll be fine."

"Gwen," I growled, "we're having dinner with my mom tomorrow. I want you to be there."

"You need a haircut," she said, sitting up. She reached up and brushed her fingertips against the ends of my hair.

"Stop trying to distract me." I turned my head and kissed her palm. "I don't want to wait, Gwen. You never know what is going to happen in life. If anything taught me that, it was losing Evie. She was here one day and then she was gone the next. I'm not letting that happen to me again."

"You can't guarantee I'll be here, Gambler."

"That's not what I mean. I just know that the time I do have, I want to make the most of it. I want to know that if I were to die tomorrow, I wouldn't have any regrets."

"You think I could be a regret you have? You could regret giving me so much time down the road."

"Gwen, stop trying to talk me out of wanting to spend time with you."

She rolled her eyes and crossed her arms over her chest. "I'm not doing that; I just don't see why we have to rush into things."

"And I don't see why we just can't be together already. I want you and you want me. What the hell is holding you back? I'm all in, Gwen. It's time for you to place your bet. Are you here, doing this with me, or are you going to disappear once we get all the Assassin shit sorted out?"

She pushed my chest, knocking me to the side and scrambled off the floor. She grabbed her bra and slid her arms into it. "I need some air, Gambler. We went from just having fun to have a discussion about the rest of my life. I can't decide this so easily."

"That's the thing, Gwen, this should be an easy answer. I don't doubt it for a second that I want to be with you."

"Well good for you, Gambler. I'm sorry that I'm not as decisive as you are." She grabbed her jeans and hopped from one foot to the other as she pulled them on.

"You're blowing this way out of proportion, Gwen. You're acting like I've announced we're getting married."

Gwen just shook her head and shoved her feet into her shoes. "I can't do this right now."

I jumped up from the floor and grabbed her. "Then when the hell are you going to be able to do it, Gwen? Why can't you just say you want to be with me?"

"Because I've already done that once in my life and it was a huge mistake. I don't think I can do it again."

"You know what is really crazy about this whole thing?" She shook her head no and pulled out of my arms. "I have no idea what you are talking about. How am I supposed to be different from what you had in the past if I don't know what happened? I'm pitted against something I can't fight because I have no idea what it is."

"I need to go, Gambler. I need to get out of here." She ran her fingers through her hair and looked around like a caged animal.

I had no idea what was going through her head right now. We were fine and then we weren't. "You can't leave by yourself right now, Gwen."

"Then someone can come with me."

"Just let me get my shirt on and-"

"No! Someone that isn't you. I'm just going to go to the salon."

"What the hell are you going to do at the salon right now? It's closed."

Gwen shook her head and stepped to the door. "I own the fucking salon, Gambler, I can go there whenever I want, closed or not. I'll meet you out at the bar." She twisted the door handle, tossed it open and took off down the hall.

I looked around the room trying to figure what the hell just happened. I didn't even know what to do. I was fighting something I didn't even do.

I grabbed my boots, laced them up and grabbed my keys. If Gwen didn't want to be with me right now, she was, at least, going to have one of the brothers with her. I headed down the hall, and my eyes searched for Gwen, but I didn't see her.

"Where the hell did Gwen go?" I asked King.

"She said she was going to wait in the car for you."

"Son of a bitch," I ran to the door just in time to see her taillights pull out of the driveway. "Fuck!"

"What the hell is going on?" King walked over, Meg behind him.

"I don't have a fucking clue."

"Well, where the hell is she going? She's by herself." Meg pushed past King and I and looked down the street.

"Shit, I should go after her, but she said she doesn't want to be with me right now." Son of a bitch. I knew she was mad at me right now, but why the hell did she have to leave?

"Demon," King called. Demon walked out from behind the bar and over to King. "I'm gonna need you to follow Gwen."

"Where the hell did she go?" he asked, pulling his keys out of his pocket.

"She said she wanted to go to the salon. I would head there." I pulled my phone out, wanting to send her a message but the fucking thing was dead. "God dammit!" I chucked my phone across the parking lot, and it smashed against the dumpster by the ditch. This all started because of my fucking phone. Now I couldn't even call her because the damn thing was still dead.

"I'll keep an eye on her," Demon mumbled. He walked over to one of the shop trucks and took off.

"So what the hell did you do to her?" Meg asked, her hands propped on her hips.

"I didn't do a damn thing other than telling her I want to fucking be with her."

"So she just took off? That doesn't make any sense!" Meg bitched.

"It makes sense to me," King said, walking over to Meg. "Head back in babe. I'm gonna talk to Gambler for a bit."

"I don't want to. All I want to do is kick Gambler in the nuts right now for hurting Gwen." Meg glared at me so now I not only had Gwen pissed off at me, now Meg was too.

"I didn't do anything to her, Meg. I fucking swear. All I wanted to do was take her to see my mom tomorrow, and she freaked out, saying we were rushing things."

King grabbed Meg and whispered something in her ear. She stomped her foot and pointed her finger at King. "You better be right," she said. She stomped past me, glaring the whole time.

I pulled out a cigarette and stuck it in the corner of my mouth. I patted my pocket for my lighter and realized I left it in the truck. "Catch," King said, tossing one to me.

"What the hell do you have a lighter for?" I asked as I lit the end.

"It was sitting on the end of the bar. I figured it was Hammer's so I grabbed it to fuck with him," King smirked.

"Thanks," I muttered.

"So, that really all that happened with Gwen?"

"Yeah. I told her I didn't want to dick around anymore. I want to fucking be with her, and she freaked. Told me she didn't know if she was ready for that. Something how she had been fucked over before."

"Meg did the same fucking thing."

"Oh yeah, that why you laid off of her for a bit?" We had all known that Meg and King had taken a break, but we never really knew why.

"She kept pinning all the shit her ex did on me. Even though I hadn't even done anything. Shit was whacked in her head. She needed to work through that shit before I could even think about being with her for good."

"I don't even know what the hell happened to her before me. She never mentioned anything about an ex. It's fucking bullshit."

"She'll come around, brother. You just need to give her some time."

"Fuck that. I'm not waiting weeks for her to come back to me. No offense, King, but two weeks is fourteen days too long." Wait two fucking weeks to talk to Gwen? I don't fucking think so.

"I'm not saying you need to wait that long, but don't go at her half-cocked, pissed off at the world. All that is going to do is push her away more."

"I'm not fucking pissed; I just want to know what the fuck is going on!"

"Yeah, you don't sound pissed at all," King laughed. "Look, go after her if you want, but you need to fucking listen to what she wants instead of telling her what you want." King patted me on the back and headed back into the clubhouse.

I looked up at the sky and had no idea what the fuck I was going to do. King was right in everything he said, but I couldn't wait. I had no idea what the hell it was that had Gwen running. The Gwen I had come to know would never run from something.

I needed to find out what the fuck was going on.

''*'*'*'*'*'*'*'*'*'*

Chapter 26
Gwen

I needed to order more bleach and rubber gloves. I chewed the end of the pen and glanced around the shop. I had only turned on the back lights over the supply area, and the rest of the salon was dimly lit.

Demon had pulled up in front of the shop over two hours ago. He had knocked on the door, told me he would be out front if I needed him and that was where he had stayed.

I had done inventory on everything in the shop, and now I had nothing to distract me from thinking about Gambler. I had run, plain and simple. He had scared the shit out of me with talk of his mom. He had mentioned it before, but I had ended up working late so I was hoping it would be forgotten. Obviously not.

I plopped down in a chair and slowly spun myself around. Time to sort shit out in my head.

Question 1. Was I over Matt? (I had to start at the root of my problem.)

Answer. Hell Yes.

Question 2. Was I over what Matt did to me? i.e. Lie for *years*.

Answer. Undecided. Although I was over Matt, I think I really wasn't over the fact someone could lie to me for so long, and I was the idiot that couldn't tell. I think that was what I was most worried about happening again. If Gambler lied to me, I probably wouldn't be able to tell. Apparently, when I love someone, I'm blinded to the point where I think they're perfect.

So, was I over what Matt had done to me? No.

Question 3. Gambler hadn't lied to me yet, so why was I punishing him for what Matt had done to me?

Answer. Because I was too fucking terrified it would happen again. Damn Matt. He really screwed me up.

Question 4. Did I want to be with Gambler? (This question was a doozy.)

Answer. Yes. Wait, did I really just admit to it that fast? I put my foot down and stopped spinning. I think I had just had a major breakthrough.

I wanted to be with Gambler. I really did. Now how the hell was I going to tell him that after I basically just ran away?

I looked out the window and saw another shop truck pull up. Fuck. Gambler got out and walked over to Demon. Looked like I wasn't going to have to wait very long to tell Gambler. Shit.

''*'*'*'*'*'*'*'*'*

Gambler

I lasted a whole two hours before I couldn't take it anymore.

"Dammit, you couldn't have waited another twenty minutes before you showed up?" Demon cursed as I walked up to his truck.

"Two hours was long enough. Who won the bet?" I knew those fuckers back at the clubhouse would find some way to bet on my misery.

"Fucking Speed won. Cyn, Meg, and Marley even got in on the action. The pot was fucking big, brother. It would have been nice to have that extra cushion in my wallet."

"What she been up to in there?" I asked, looking over my shoulder at the salon.

"Looked like she was counting shit for a while, and she just sat down a couple of minutes ago. And from the look on her face, I'd say she just saw you."

"Yeah, I think you might be right," I laughed. Gwen was sitting in one of the barber chairs, sprawled out on it, her foot pushing her back and forth. Her arms were crossed over her chest, and she looked pissed. "Maybe I should drive around the block a couple of times. See if she'll cool off a bit more."

She got up from the chair, walked to the front door, unlocked it and sat back down. "I'm pretty sure she wants you to go in. Now, I can't tell if she wants to apologize or kill you," Demon laughed.

"Alright, you staying here or heading back?"

"I'll hang here for a bit. Maybe grab some Chinese from down the street."

"Sounds good, I might need you for backup if Gwen decides to kick my ass."

Demon laughed and started up the truck. "I think you'll be good, brother, just listen to her. I'm gonna grab some food, and I'll be back."

Demon headed down the street, and I turned back to the salon. Gwen was staring me down, waiting. I crossed the street and stood in front of the door. "Just listen," I mumbled to myself.

I pulled the door open and locked it behind me.

"Making it so I can't get out?"

"Um, no. Making it so *I* can't get out."

"Hmm," she hummed. I sat down in the chair next to her and spun around so I was facing her.

"Get some work done?"

"I did inventory. I haven't done it since summer, so it needed to be done."

I nodded my head and slowly spun around in my chair. "I was worried about you."

"You didn't need to, I had Demon watching me."

"I know. King sent him. He was worried about you being alone."

She put her foot on my chair when I was face to face with her, stopping me from spinning. "King sent him, or you did?"

"King did, although if he hadn't, I would have."

"Why did you come then if you knew that Demon was making sure I was safe?"

"I came to collect on the two bets you lost." A grin spread across my lips as it dawned on her I could ask her to do anything I wanted. Twice.

"You don't play fair, Gambler."

"I never said I did, doll."

She crossed her arms over her chest and stared me down. Even pissed off Gwen was hot. "Spit it out, what do you want?"

"Well," I ran my fingers through my hair and grinned. "I could use a haircut, free of charge of course."

"That's what you want, a haircut?"

"For the first one, don't forget about the second bet you lost."

Gwen growled but didn't say anything. She got up from her chair and walked to the mirror that was in front of my chair. "I have to admit I didn't think you were going to say haircut."

"Well, I figured, we're in a salon, you're a hairdresser, what better place to do it?"

She grabbed a cape, shook it out and snapped it over my shoulders. "I guess I can't argue with that logic." She spun me around to face the mirror and ran her fingers through my hair. "How short do you want it?"

"Up to you, doll. I trust you." She hummed as she grabbed a comb, spray bottle and scissors from the counter and wet my hair. "Now, time for the second bet you lost."

"Really, while I'm cutting your hair?" She set the spray bottle down and started cutting.

"Yeah, I think it's a perfect time."

"You know I could accidentally chop off all your hair right now?"

"There's that attitude I love so much."

"Hmm, just spit out what you want."

"Tell me why you're scared. Tell me why you ran. Tell me who the hell I have to beat up for making you doubt falling in love with me."

Her scissors stopped mid cut and her eyes connected with mine. "Ugh, that's three questions."

"Tell me, Gwen. I want to know. I need to know."

She licked her lips and looked back at my hair. She started cutting my hair again but didn't talk. It took her almost five minutes before she said anything. "His name was Matt."

"Tell me more, doll."

"I met him when I was a teenager. He moved next door to me when I was fifteen. I fell in love with him the second I saw him." I growled low in my throat but didn't say anything.

"I was with him for six years."

"That's a mighty long time, doll."

"Yeah," she murmured. "Six years too long." She worked on my hair, cutting the sides, combing them over. "Everything was good for five years. Matt was the perfect boyfriend. He's the one who got me into riding. The first time I rode on his motorcycle I wanted one of my own."

"I didn't know you wanted to ride, doll."

"Yup. I planned on getting one when I graduated, but life just kept getting in the way. Riding on the back of yours had made me get the itch again to get on one again."

"We'll get you set up this summer. Chicks who ride are hot," I winked at her in the mirror, and she laughed.

"Maybe. I kind of like being on the back of yours." That sounded promising. I wasn't going to be back on my bike until April, and that was five months away.

"So what happened, doll?"

I watched her in the mirror as she ran my hair through her fingers, enjoying her touch. "Matt told me he was going to a party one night, but I had to work late, so he went by himself." Uh oh, this did not sound like it was going to end well. "I ended up getting off early and decided to head out to the party he was at." She set her scissors down in front of the mirror and ran the comb through my hair. "It was one of our friends that was throwing the party. The friend had told me he had seen Matt arrive about an hour before, but he hadn't seen him in a bit. I just wandered around looking for him. Then I opened a bedroom door and walked in on two guys kissing."

"So you didn't find Matt?"

Gwen laughed and shook her head. "Oh, I found him alright. He was one of the guys who was kissing."

What the fuck! "He was bi? Did you know?"

"That would be a negative. It never once crossed my mind in five years that Matt was gay. He was the perfect bad boy. Rough around the edges with just the right amount of sweet. I'm sure his boyfriend, Juan, appreciates it." A laugh bubbled out of her, a smirk on her lips.

"So, you said you were with him for six years, but you found him with a guy a year before that."

"Yeah, about that. I was an idiot and stayed with him because he was too afraid to tell anyone."

"Pretty selfish of him to ask you to stay with him."

"It's not like he made me. It wasn't exactly a hard thing to do either. He was my best friend and my boyfriend for so long that he just stopped being my boyfriend and stayed my friend. At least for that last year." She tossed the comb in front of me and propped her hands on her hips. "All done." She unsnapped the cape and whipped it off me. She tossed in the chair she was sitting in before and watched me in the mirror.

I turned my head to the left and right, checking out what she had done. My eyes connected with hers, and I nodded my head. "Pretty fucking good, doll. You should do this full-time."

She laughed swatting me on the shoulder. "I just might do that."

She worked on cleaning the scissor and comb, putting everything back where it belonged, and I watched her. "So, you think I have this big secret that is going to push you away, right?"

"I don't know. I think I have a little self-doubt in myself, too. Paige swears she knew there was something off about Matt, but she could never put her finger on it." She turned around and leaned against the small counter in front of the mirror. "I had no indication at all until I saw Matt getting it on with another guy, that he was gay. Never saw it coming."

"Doll, you can't blame yourself for the fact that he lied to you for so long."

She shrugged her shoulders and turned back around. "I gave him everything I had, and he lied to me the whole time. I can't do that again."

"So you're never going to trust anyone again?"

"It's less painful that way."

I grabbed her hand and tugged her into my lap. She straddled my lap, and I saw there were tears in her eyes. "Doll, he's not worth your tears."

"I know that," she sniffed. "I stopped crying over him a long time ago."

"Then why the tears?"

"Because I'm afraid to love you, but I'm afraid to lose you." She wiped her eyes and smiled. "I think this is what they call being stuck between a rock and a hard place."

"Gwen, do you want to be with me?"

"Yes. Completely." Yes!

"Then stop worrying about everything else. I can promise I don't have a huge secret that no one knows that is going to rip us apart. You know about Evie, and that is something I never tell anyone."

She reached up, cupping my cheek. "I'm sorry about your sister," she whispered.

And this was why I loved Gwen. Hard as nails, but the most loving woman. "Thank you, baby." I leaned into her hand, relishing her touch. Whenever she freely touched me, it was like a small battle won. "I miss her every day, but it helped me realize I needed to live my life how I wanted because you never knew when it was going to be taken away."

"You know what you want, and you take it," she smiled big, "me included."

"Yeah, doll. You are the one thing I know I want. Now, tomorrow, fifty years from now. I need you."

"I'm terrified, Gambler. Except I can't say no anymore. I say I don't want to fall in love with you when I already have."

My body went still at her words. She was crying again, but she had a huge grin on her face. She already loved me?

She already loved me.

Thank you, God.

’’*’*’*’*’*’*’*’*

Chapter 27
Gwen

I waited.

Then I waited some more. Gambler just stared at me, not saying a word. Okay, I might regret just telling him that I loved him. Except wasn't that what he wanted me to do? Let go of worrying and just go for it. Well, I loved him.

"Now would be a good time to say something."

"Pants off, now."

I reared back, pushing against his chest and looked at him like he was crazy. "What the hell do you mean pants off? That's not exactly the thing you say to someone when they tell you they love you for the first time."

"It is when I want to be inside you the first time I say it." He bucked his hips under me, prompting me to get up. I scurried off his lap and watched as he unzipped his pants. "Ten seconds, doll."

I scrambled out of my pants because I knew the tone in his voice. Gambler wasn't playing. I loved when he talked to me like that. He knew what he wanted from me, and he was going to take it. This man drove me crazy in the best way possible.

"Shirt, too. I want to see you."

"Gambler, the damn street is right there." I dropped my pants to the floor and stepped out of them.

"Worry about me, not the damn street. Shirt, now."

I grabbed the hem and pulled it over my head. "You're crazy. Absolutely insane."

"But you love me," he smirked. He leaned forward and pulled his shirt over his head. "Hop on, doll."

Sitting in my salon chair, Gambler was naked as the day he was born with a raging hard-on. I was never going to be able to look at this chair again without blushing. I stood between his legs and reached for his dick. He may want me to climb up, but first, I wanted to have my own fun. His cock was hard, throbbing and hot in my hand. I stroked him up and down as he groaned under my touch. I sunk down to my knees and licked my lips.

"Oh my fucking God," he growled as I leaned forward and slid his dick all the way to the back of my throat. "Damn, your mouth is perfect, doll."

I glanced up, my eyes connecting with his as he watched his dick disappear in and out of my mouth. My tongue stroked him as I sped up, my head bobbing up and down.

He threaded his fingers through my hair and gripped my head. He took control, setting the pace. "I'll die without you," he whispered, closing his eyes.

I swallowed as he hit the back of my throat, and he moaned low and deep. He sat forward, lifting my head up. "Ride me, now," he demanded. I stood up, and he grabbed my hips, pulling me onto his lap.

"I wanted you to cum in my mouth," I purred, grabbing his dick. I stroked him up and down, as I licked my lips, his eyes watching my every move.

"Next time, I need to be in that tight pussy."

I rose up on my knees that were on either side of his body and slowly slid down on his cock, filling me. I leaned forward, my forehead resting against Gambler's forehead. "Tell me again why I ran away from this?" I laughed.

Gambler grabbed my ass and squeezed. "Doll, right now all I can think about is how tight your pussy is around my dick. Fuck the past, this, right here," he thrust his hips up, "is all I'm worried about."

I grabbed onto his shoulders, slowly pushing myself up. "Then you forgive me?" I held myself up, just the tip of his cock in me.

"Are you withholding that pussy from me until I say yes?"

"Tell me you love me."

"No," he growled, his hands holding my hips, his fingers digging into me. "Give me that pussy."

I shook my head, no, but he thrust his hips, slamming back into me. I moaned as he bottomed out, "Not fair."

"I don't see you complaining too much, doll," he gritted out. His jaw was clenched as he lifted me off then thrust up and he brought me back down. My eyes shut, and my head rolled to the side as I fell into a haze of desire. He leaned forward, trailing kisses up my collar bone. "This needs to come off." He nipped at my bra, pulling the strap down with his teeth.

I reached behind me, unhooking the bra and tossed it on the floor. "You do realize anyone walking by can see me, right?" I purred, cupping my breasts as I looked out the window.

"No one is going to walk by. Eyes to me," he growled.

My eyes snapped to him, and a grin spread across my lips. "You're awfully demanding."

"We've gone over this before. I'm demanding when it's something I want. Right now, I want you." He leaned forward, his mouth devouring my breast. His hands stayed on my hips, helping to move me up and down on his dick.

"Don't stop," I moaned. Gambler sped up, bouncing me up and down, grunting each time I slid back down. I grabbed onto his shoulders, steadying myself. I dug my knees into the chair and held on.

"Say it," he growled.

"No," I moaned. I tossed my head back, moaning as he took me closer and closer to the edge with each thrust.

"Tell me you love me."

I shook my head no, unable to talk. I don't know how Gambler did it, but each time he took me, it was better than the last.

"I'm gonna cum, doll. Tell me," he demanded.

"I love you!" I cried as I tipped over the edge, drowning in Gambler.

"I love you. I'll love you till the day I die," he gritted out, his teeth clenched. He had thrust three more times before he cried out, filling me with his cum. "Mine," he chanted over and over.

I collapsed forward, resting my head on his shoulder. "That was fucking amazing," I breathed out.

Gambler thrust one last time, holding me tight and staying buried deep inside me. "I love you," he whispered into my ear.

I wrapped my arms around his shoulders and cried my eyes out. I cried for the girl so many years ago who had her heart broken and never really healed. I cried for the simple fact that I finally felt like I had found a place that felt like home. And I cried for the sheer fact that I had found the man who was going to be everything I thought didn't exist. "I love you, too."

"You're crying all over me, doll," Gambler laughed. I sat back, pushing against his chest. He reached up and wiped every tear that fell away. "No crying, Gwen. I love you."

"I couldn't get you to say it, and now you won't shut up," I laughed.

He shrugged his shoulders and smirked. "It sounds pretty good coming out of my mouth. You're probably going to hear it all the time now."

"Promise?" I whispered, pressing a kiss to his lips.

"At least fifty times a day, doll."

"I guess that's just something I'll have to get used to." I laid my head back on his shoulders, this time smiling and not bawling my eyes out.

"You think you could get one of these chairs for my room? That was the best sex I've ever had. Well, except for that one night you woke me up with your mouth, and then I took you against the wall three hours ago."

"These chairs are over two thousand dollars. I think we'll have to come here if you want to do that again." Headlights flashed through the window, and I scooted down Gambler's lap, ducking.

"Doll, they can't see you," he laughed, wrapping his arms around me. My stomach growled loud, and I looked Gambler right in the eye. "Am I supposed to ignore that?" He asked, smirking.

"No," I laughed. "I can't help it I'm starving. I didn't grab anything to eat when I left, and all I did was inventory the past two hours."

"See, that's what you get when you run away from me."

"Hungry?" I laughed.

"Yes, exactly. How about we each throw our clothes on, and I'll run down the street and order Chinese while you shut down the shop."

"Sounds like a solid plan." I pushed against Gambler, trying to stand up but he didn't let me go. "Let me up. Can you not hear my stomach sounding like a beluga whale?"

"Yeah, doll, I hear it," he laughed. "First, I'm gonna need something from you."

"Hmm, I bet I know what it is."

"Oh yeah, you think you're really ready to bet against me again? I did just collect from you two times."

I crossed my arms over my chest and glared at him. "Trust me, I remember."

"Well, how about no more bets anymore, at least for a bit. I just placed a huge wager on a longshot, and I thankfully won."

"Oh yeah, what did you win?" I had a feeling I was going to have to keep an eye on Gambler and all his betting in the future. Although it did seem that he won most of his bets. I wonder what he bet on that he won now.

"You. You were my longshot bet, doll. I came here tonight, and I had no idea what the hell was going to go on. All I knew was that I couldn't stay away from you any longer."

"So, I'm your winnings?"

"Yeah, doll. You were my most risky bet, but the most rewarding."

I leaned forward, my lips brushing against his. "Thank God you're a betting man." Gambler threaded his fingers through my hair, pressing his lips to mine and gave me everything in that one kiss.

Someone I could trust, love, have fun with and have the best sex ever with. If you asked me, we were both winners in that longshot bet.

''*'*'*'*'*'*'*'*'*'*

Chapter 28

Gwen

I had just put everything away from Gambler's haircut when I heard a noise in the back. Gambler had left ten minutes ago to grab the food, and I hadn't expected him back yet.

I looked out the front window of the shop, glancing up and down the street but didn't see anything. I figured it must have just been something settling back in the storeroom and brushed it off.

My phone ding in my pocket, and I pulled it out, seeing Meg had texted me. I plopped down in the salon chair Gambler and I had used and opened up the text message.

You and Gambler make up and have wild monkey sex yet? Leave it to Meg to get straight to the point.

We're all good.

But did you have wild monkey sex?

I'm not answering that. Meg cracked me up.

You guys soooo had wild monkey sex.

Is there a reason for you texting me other than talking about hot monkey sex?

Yeah. Oh, my God. I laughed at her one-word response. She was a straight up nut.

And that would be?????

You wanna be a bridesmaid?

Really? Me? Wow, I didn't expect her to ask me that. I had only known her for a couple of months, although I did feel really close to her and all the other the girls.

Yes, you. The wedding is New Year's Eve by the way. What?!?! New Year's Eve? That was just over a month away.

This New Years?

Yes, you think Lo is going to wait over a year? He said Christmas, I countered with New Year's Eve.

Holy Cow! That's awesome! Yes, I'll be your bridesmaid!

Sweet. I'll let you get back to sweaty monkey sex. TTYL

Wow, Meg and King were getting married. Hell yes! And, I got to be a bridesmaid. Plus, now I get to get all dolled– I whirled around in my chair when I heard something fall in the back. What the fuck was that?

I heard the click of a gun being cocked and froze. "Throw your phone on the floor and slowly turn around." I couldn't see anyone, but I knew they had to be in the back room. I tossed my phone on the floor and slowly turned in my chair.

"We've waited a long time for those Knights to leave one of their women alone. Although you're not the one we want." The man walked out of the shadows of the back hall, and he held a gun pointed directly at me.

I clasped my hands in my lap and prayed for Gambler to come back. "How… how did…did you… get in… here?" I stuttered. I was petrified with fear.

"You need better locks around here. Anyone could get in." He walked closer to me, and I knew right away he was part of the Assassins.

"Please don't hurt me," I whispered as he walked closer, only a few feet away from me.

"I'm not here to hurt you. I'm here to give you a message."

I nodded my head, unable to talk. If he wasn't going to hurt me, then why the hell did he have a gun pointed at me?

He sat in the chair across from me, the gun still trained on me. "Do you know who you hang around?" I shook my head, no, not knowing the right answer to the question. "They're murderers," he spat out. "That is who you decide to spend your time with."

I had no idea what he was talking about, and I honestly didn't want to know. As much as I didn't want to believe that anyone with the Devil's Knights was a murderer, I knew that if they did have to do anything like what this guy was saying, the person deserved it. I had spent time with everyone in that club, and there was no way that I was wrong about this. The Devil's Knights were not murderers. "If that's what you believe."

"They are!" He yelled at me. He waved the gun at me, his hand shaking. His eyes flared with anger, and I knew I hadn't said the right thing.

"Okay," I whispered.

"Damn right, but you want to know who we're going after to destroy?" I just stared at him, waiting for him to continue. "Rigid. Rigid is the one who went after my cousin and took him away from my family. Rigid is the one I am going to destroy." He stood up, standing right in front of me. He leaned down, his face an inch away from me. "You tell Rigid and all those Knights you think that are going to keep you safe, I'm coming for his woman and his niño."

154

I gasped at his words. Not only terrified for myself right now but for Cyn and her baby, too. I knew Rigid would die before anything would happen to Cyn. But the man who was standing in front of me seemed like one crazy fucker.

"Stand up," he ordered, waving the gun at me. I stood up, my legs shaking underneath me. "Move." He nodded to the back of the shop. He shoved the gun into my back, prompting me to walk.

"Please don't hurt Cyn," I pleaded as we walked.

"Stupid woman, you have no idea what they've done. My cousin died because of that puta." We stopped in front of the bathroom, and he pushed me inside. "Make sure you deliver my message." He slammed the door shut, but he didn't move away. I listened, trying to hear what he was doing. He stomped to the left and then I heard something being dragged on the floor, scraping it. Something slammed against the bathroom door, and I screamed. "No getting out, puta," he sneered. I heard him move to the back door and then silence.

I tried pushing the door open, but it was blocked by my file cabinet he had pushed in front of the door. Shit. I pounded on the door, hoping Gambler was back, but he wasn't. Double shit.

I leaned against the door and slid down, wrapping my arms around my knees. My mind was whirling with everything the guy had told me. I couldn't believe that King and all the guys were murderers. I held my head in my hands and ran my fingers through my hair.

I went over everything the guy had told me and my blood boiled at the thought of him hurting Cyn and her baby. I had known that Cyn's ex had hurt her, but I never really got all the details of what happened.

I leaned my head against the door and sighed. The only thing I could do right now is wait for Gambler and get the answers to all my questions then. I just hoped Cyn was going to be okay until I told Gambler the message.

Come on, Gambler. I need you.

''*'*'*'*'*'*'*'*'*

155

Chapter 29
Gambler

"Soy sauce or anything else I can help you with?"

"No, I'm fine," I turned away from the counter and walked over to the storefront window. If I had known that fucking Cherry worked here, I would have told Gwen she was going to have to be hungry till we went somewhere else to eat.

"I haven't been able to make it out to the clubhouse lately. I've heard the parties aren't happening as much anymore."

I glanced over my shoulder to see Cherry come out from behind the counter and lean against it. I couldn't believe I use to think this chick was hot. Now she just looked slutty and wore out. "We've become more selective about who comes to the club." I turned back around and watched the traffic drive by. It was more interesting than talking to Cherry.

"Hmm, I bet King's girlfriend has something to do with that."

I shrugged my shoulders, not wanting to give her the satisfaction of talking about Meg. Meg, Cyn, and Cherry all hated each other. Cyn's asshat of an ex was Cherry's brother who had met an untimely end at the hands of Rigid and the club.

"I don't know why he would settle for–"

"Is my food done?" I cut her off, not wanting to hear her bitch fest about Meg. Cherry was delusional if she thought that King was going to leave Meg for her.

Cherry glared at me and thankfully didn't continue. "I'll go check," she snarled.

I sighed, wondering what the hell we were all thinking to have Cherry in the clubhouse. Thankfully I had never tapped that, but I knew some of the other brothers weren't that lucky to say that. Demon being one of them.

Cherry yelled in the back, asking about the food and I smirked. The last we had known, Cherry was working at the plant that Meg and Cyn worked at. Obviously, things hadn't worked out there, and now she was slinging Chinese food.

I looked down the street toward the salon and watched a black van slowly drive by. A Mexican man was driving, and he watched me as he slowly cruised by, a snarl on his lips. He spat out the window at me and took off once he passed the restaurant.

I pulled my phone out of my pocket and called Gwen. It rang until her voicemail picked up. I instantly ended the call and hit send again. Still no answer. Something wasn't right. I ripped open the door and ran down the street to the shop.

The phone was pressed to my ear as I called the shop, thinking she might not hear her cell ringing. I skidded at the door of the shop and heard the phone ringing but didn't see Gwen anywhere in the shop.

"Yo!" I turned around and saw Demon pull up to the curb.

"Gwen's not answering the phone," I yelled, yanking on the door. It was still locked so I grabbed my keys and quickly opened the door. I heard Demon slam his door behind me and run across the street.

"I got your back," he said. He pulled a gun out of the waistband of his jeans and looked up and down the street. "I've been driving around and haven't seen anything, but that don't mean shit." He nodded at me to go in, and I pulled the door open.

"Gwen!" I called, looking around. Nothing seemed to be out of place, but that didn't mean nothing was wrong.

"I'm gonna walk around to the back," Demon ducked out the door and slinked around the side of the building.

"Gwen!" I called again. I walked forward, kicking something on the floor. It skidded across the ground, hitting the wall. I reached down, picked it up and realized it was Gwen's phone.

"Gambler!" I heard a door bang against something as she called for me.

I headed to the back room and saw a file cabinet pushed up against the door. "What the fuck?" I shoved the cabinet out of the way, and Gwen threw open the door of the bathroom and threw her arms around me.

"What the fuck happened?" I asked as I ran my hands all over her body.

"I was texting Meg, and then I heard something fall in the backroom. I turned around, and a guy was standing there, pointing a gun at me."

Rage boiled inside me as soon as I heard he was pointing a gun at her. "Did he say who he was?"

She shook her head no and leaned back, "No, he was a short guy and Mexican. He said I needed to tell you he is coming for Cyn and her baby. He kept calling everyone in the Knights murderers."

I gritted my teeth and knew exactly who was just here. "Fucking Big A. He's not sending his minions to take care of shit anymore. He came himself."

"He was infuriated, Gambler. He said the Knights were going to pay for killing his cousin. He asked me if I knew you were all murderers."

Her body quaked in my arms, and I held her tighter. I buried my face in her hair. "I'm so sorry I wasn't here, doll. I'm so sorry."

She sniffled, wiping her nose on my shoulder. "It's not your fault, Gambler. I'm just worried. He didn't hurt me this time, but he seemed so desperate. It was like his eyes were filled with hate and anger.

We figured the assassins were getting more desperate, especially when they went after Gwen and me before, but I don't think we knew what kind of crazy we were dealing with. "Did he hurt you anywhere?"

"No, he just kept the gun on me the whole time. He shoved me into the bathroom, but that didn't hurt. He just scared me more than anything. I don't know how he got in."

"He busted the lock on the back door." Gwen and I both turned around to see Demon walk in, the broken handle in his hand. "I should have walked around the building when I showed up before, Gwen. This is all my fault."

Demon was right, he should have checked things out, but I probably would have done the same thing if I were him. He could see her through the glass the whole time so there really wasn't a point to walk around the building. "It's not your fault, brother. I didn't think he would go after Gwen either. I'm sure he's been waiting for us to leave one of the girls alone, and Gwen just happened to be the unlucky one."

Gwen was still wrapped up in my arms, turned sideways. "Even if you would have done a walk around, I don't think you would have saw it, Demon. I had heard a noise before he came in, but I didn't think anything of it."

"Why didn't you call me when you heard the noise?"

"Because I thought it was something settling or something in the back. I had just moved everything around for inventory. I wasn't thinking that it was someone breaking in. I've known all along the Assassins were a problem, but I thought that I was on the sidelines, not important to them."

"Well, I think after this, it's safe to say that no one is safe." Demon dropped the door handle in the garbage and pulled his phone out. "I'll give King a heads up and then we can work on securing that door before we head back." Demon walked back out the door, leaving it open.

"I'm sorry I didn't call you. The noise wasn't that loud, so I just ignored it."

"You're fine, doll." She shivered in my arms and laid her head on my shoulder. "I'm pretty sure I saw him leaving. I was standing at the window of the Chinese place when a black van rolled by."

"This is all so crazy, Gambler." She tilted her head back and looked me in the eye. "He said Rigid killed his cousin, did he?" Her gorgeous eyes looked up at me, needing answers.

"Anything I say to you, Gwen, stays between us. That includes not telling Meg, Cyn or Marley. I have no idea what they know, but I don't want them finding out from you."

"I promise I won't say anything."

I ran my fingers through my hair and walked her over to the chair we were sitting in earlier. I pulled her into my lap, and she curled up, wrapping her arms around my neck. "Do you know what happened to Cyn?"

"Not the details. I know she lost her baby."

"She lost her baby because her asshat of an ex beat the hell out of her when she told him she was pregnant. They were already broken up because he was cheating on her the whole time."

"Oh my God, poor, Cyn."

"Yeah, doll. She went through some shit after that. Her ex knew he fucked up and went to his cousin Big A, the guy who was here tonight and helped him hide. Troy found him, then Rigid and the rest of the club paid him a visit."

"Did… did you help?" she stuttered, her eyes huge.

I brushed the hair out of her face and pressed a kiss to the side of her head. "I was there, doll. I had to be there for my brother."

She buried her face in my chest and wrapped her arms around my neck. "He hurt Cyn and took away her baby," she whispered.

"He did."

"He deserved what he got."

"We're not murderers, doll. But when someone hurts someone we love, we take matters into our own hands."

She trailed her hand up my chest and cupped my cheek. She lifted her head, my lips a breath away from her's. "You wronged a right. You did what needed to be done," she whispered.

"We couldn't let him get away with it."

She nodded her head yes and threaded her fingers through my hair. "I love you, Gambler."

I slammed my lips down on her's, not knowing what to say. I love you didn't seem to fit what I was feeling for Gwen. My chest felt like it was going to explode, and all I wanted to do was bury myself in Gwen. There had never been anything in my life that had ever made me feel this way. "I love you more than anything in this world," I growled against her lips.

"You know people are going to think we're crazy for falling in love so fast," she laughed.

"I could give a shit what people think. As long as you're happy I don't care."

"Yo!" Demon called, walking back into the shop. "King said he doesn't want to tell the girls right now, especially Cyn."

"We have to tell Cyn, he said he's coming for her." Gwen jumped out of her chair and put her hands on her hips.

"Doll, relax." Gwen glared at me but didn't say anything else.

"Right now, only Gwen is to know about what happened. Rigid isn't going to let Cyn out of his sight, and she'll always have two other club members with her including Rigid. King isn't going to let anything happen to her." Demon walked over to the front desk and started searching through the drawers. "You got a tool box or something, babe? We need to get that door fixed for the night."

"It's in the back, but we're not done talking about keeping this from the girls, especially Cyn."

Demon crouched down and pulled out a roll of duct tape. "Yeah, we are done talking about it, babe, because it's club business. That's what King wants, and that's what is going to happen. If you want to tell the girls, you will not only have Gambler to deal with but King also. Meg may make him look like a teddy bear, but I can guarantee you that he is not."

"I'm not part of the club, I don't have to listen to him." She stomped her foot as Demon walked by.

"No, you don't, but you're dating a member of the club. You think King wants you to not tell the girls for the hell of it. He's doing it to protect them." Demon shook his head and walked into the backroom.

"This is bullshit," she hissed at me.

"Gwen, knock it off. It's not like you have to lie to them. Just don't tell them. I really doubt King is going to keep this away from them for that long."

"I don't like this at all." She crossed her arms over her chest and glared at me. "Damn, Meg just asked me to be in her wedding, and now I have to lie to her."

"Gwen, for the damn fifth time, it's not lying. Don't. Tell. Her." Jesus. Gwen had barely known Meg and the girls, but she was rather fiercely protective of them.

"I'm giving you one week to tell them before I do."

Gwen's attitude was out ten-fold tonight. "Two weeks and then you can say something. I'm not arguing with you over this."

"What if King wanted me to keep a secret from you, would you be okay with that?"

"No, because that is different than this. I'm a part of the club, and King wouldn't keep this away from me. The only reason you know is because you were involved in it. I'm not going to say it again. Let it drop."

"Gambler, I just think–"

"Gwen! Stop, now." I ordered.

She stopped mid-sentence, and I swear to God she growled.

Oh shit.

''*'*'*'*'*'*'*

Chapter 30

Gwen

One kick to the nuts and I'd have him on his knees. One kick.

I couldn't believe that I was going to have to keep this from Meg, Cyn, and Marley. I worked every day with Marley. We talked all the time. He didn't think that something like this was going to come up. The only reason I was going to agree not to tell the girls was because Cyn didn't need the extra stress right now since she wasn't very far along in her pregnancy. "Two weeks, and then I'm letting it out," I vowed, holding up two fingers.

"Two weeks. I bet before that King will have already told them. He just needs some time to figure some shit out first. I promise."

Hmph. I wasn't happy, but I understood where King was coming from. "Fine," I pouted, crossing my arms over my chest.

"Thank you, doll." He walked over and wrapped me up in a hug. I may love this man, but that didn't mean I had to agree with everything he said. I knew with him being connected to the club that there were going to be times where he couldn't tell me things, but I didn't think that I would have to keep secrets. "I love you," he mumbled into my hair.

"I love you, too, Gambler. Hey," I said, pulling back, "what's your real name?"

"Just call me Gambler, doll. Only my mom calls me by my real name, and I hate it."

"No, you're going to have to tell me. You promised no secrets."

Gambler sighed, and I knew I got him. "It's Anthony."

"Anthony? Tony?" I smirked. He didn't look like an Anthony, but I could totally see calling him Tony.

"Gambler, doll. Just Gambler."

I leaned forward, whispering in his ear. "Can I call you Anthony when you're pounding into me, making me cum?"

"I'm pretty sure at that point, doll, with my dick buried inside you, I'll answer to Edgar or anything else you want to call me."

"Oh, I know! How about I call you Antonio in a Spanish accent. Oh, Antonio!" I shouted, throwing my head back.

"What the fuck are you two doing?" Demon asked. We both turned around to see Demon standing there, my neon pink tool box in his hand. "Who the fuck is Antonio?"

Gambler busted out laughing and pulled me close. "Nobody you know, brother."

"Let's get this shit done so we can get back to the clubhouse. King is waiting for us." Demon headed out the back and started banging on the door.

"Demon sure does like to boss you around."

"He's the VP, doll. He can." Gambler slid his arm around my shoulders and walked me over to the front desk. "Get your shit ready while Demon and I take care of the door. I've got your phone in my pocket." He pulled it out and handed it to me.

"Thanks. I just need to go to the bathroom and grab my purse." He leaned in, pressing a kiss to my lips and headed out back to help Demon.

"About fucking time you rip yourself away from her." I heard Demon grumble. I shook my head and headed to the bathroom. I glimpsed Gambler helping Demon as I walked into the bathroom and he threw a wink at me. I blushed, my face turning red and slammed the door shut behind me when I heard Demon cussing at Gambler for not paying attention when he had swung the hammer, nailing Demon on the thumb.

I had never really spent much time with Demon before, but I never knew he was such a crank ass. He definitely needed to get laid.

I looked in the mirror, fluffing my hair and laughed. What a day. A bride from hell, fighting with Gambler, making up with Gambler, held at gunpoint (the definite downfall of my day), fighting with Gambler again, and then we made up.

I had a feeling from here on out that was going to be how my days would go. Well, minus the being held at gunpoint. Gambler and I might go at it, arguing and pressing each other's buttons, but when we made up, boy did we make up.

"Doll, you ready?" Gambler hollered.

I grinned at myself in the mirror, never looking happier.

Was I ready?

You bet your ass I was ready for whatever life had in store for me as long as Gambler was with me.

He said he had never bet on such a longshot before, but the same could be said for me.

I whirled around as the door opened and Gambler stood on the other side, smirking at me. "Just looking at yourself in the mirror, doll?"

Such a smart ass. I reached up, threading my fingers through his hair and kissed him with everything I had. I loved this man, and nothing could come between us. He bet on me, won, and now I was his forever.

Win, win.

''*'*'*'*'*'*'*'*'*

Chapter 31
Meg

One hour.

One fucking hour.

Lo had left our bed over an hour ago after he got a phone call. I asked him, as he was hopping back into his jeans and boots, what the hell was going on. All he told me was he had some club shit to take care of. I had glanced at the clock, seeing it was ten o'clock and wondered what kind of club business he would have then.

I had grabbed my phone and shot a message off to Cyn, seeing if Rigid was gone, too, but she never responded. She had probably passed out as soon as her head had hit the pillow. She was only a couple of months along, but that baby seemed to be draining all of her energy.

I swung my legs out of bed, my feet hitting the cold hardwood floor, and a chill ran through me. I turned on the bedside lamp, and the light bounced off my ring, making it sparkle. I held my hand up, moving my finger in the light, watching the light dance and smiled.

December thirty-first I was going to marry the man I loved. Lo hadn't believed that I had agreed to get married that soon, but I figured how much could things change if we got married? I loved him, and he loved me, Remy, and Blue. What more could a girl want?

"You still up, babe?" Lo asked, walking through the door.

"When you're used to working and staying up till eleven o'clock every night, Lo, you tend to stay up late even if you're not working."

"What's with the sass, babe?" He asked as he shut the door, locking it behind him and pulled his shirt over his head.

God dammit Lo looked good. We had just got done having sex when the phone rang, and I already wanted him again. "The sass, as you call it, has to do with the fact that you got a phone call, didn't tell me what the hell was going on and left."

"I told you it was club business."

"I don't care if it's club business. I've watched Sons of Anarchy, Jax told Tara shit."

Lo busted out laughing and shook his head at me. "You do realize that is a TV show and not real life, right?"

I waved my hand at him, not wanting to get into the same fight we always had when I brought up Sons. "Whatever, that's not the point. The point is that you're not telling me what the hell is going on."

"Meg, I don't need to tell you what is going on. It has to do with the club, and that is where it's going to stay. I'm not talking about this anymore." He unbuttoned his pants, tossed them on the back of the desk chair and climbed into bed.

"Is anyone hurt?"

Lo sighed and grabbed my pillow, smashing it behind his head. Bastard always stole my pillow, but he let me sleep and drool on him every night. It was a good compromise. "No one is hurt."

"Does it have to do with the Banachi's?" I knew Lo had helped Leo move his sister in today so it might be a possibility that something had come up with them.

"No, nothing to do with Leo."

Damn. I was running out of things to guess. "The Assassins?"

"Meg, I'm not playing twenty questions with you. I'm damn tired, and right now, all I want to do is turn on the TV, watch a movie, and sleep."

This wasn't working. I switched off the light and slid back under the covers. "I'm sorry you're tired, hunny," I purred, running my hand up his bare chest.

Lo grabbed my hand and pulled me on top of him. "As much as I like you touching me, babe, I'm not going to tell you what the hell is going on." We were nose to nose, and I could tell that I really wasn't going to get anywhere with Lo. At least not tonight. "I promise that everything will be fine, you just need to trust me."

"Fine," I whispered, laying down on top of him. "Can I, at least, pick what movie we are going to watch?"

"Anything you want, babe," he laughed.

"Put on Mad Max." Lo reached over, grabbing the remote of the nightstand and started the DVD that was already in the machine.

"You do know this is the third time we've watched this movie in two weeks, right?" He asked as the opening previews started to play.

"I know. I just like it." I rolled off Lo, settling under his arm and rested my head on his shoulder.

I watched the movie mindlessly, not actually paying attention to what was going on. I glanced up at Lo, his eyes already at half mast, ready to sleep then glanced at my ring.

I was getting married in less than six weeks, and my fiancé was keeping secrets from me. From what I could tell, one of them was a dousey.

Now, I just needed to figure out how to get it out of him and then marry his sexy ass. It looked like the next six weeks were going to be busy.

’’*’*’*’*’*’*’*

Lo

Shit.

The End
for now...

Keeping Meg
Devil's Knights Series
Book 6

Winter Travers

Keeping Meg

Chapter 1
Meg

"Purple."

"No, I look like Barney the fucking dinosaur in purple. How about orange?"

"You only want orange, so it'll match your hair. The wedding is five weeks away. Your hair will probably be three different colors by then," Cyn said, sitting down at the table next to Marley.

"Well, we're all in this wedding, so we need to agree on a color. I vote red." I rolled my eyes and wrote down purple on the sheet of paper in front of me.

We were all gathered around one of the tables at the clubhouse, chowing down on Firecracker chicken and trying to decide what colors I wanted for the wedding. I really didn't know why we were discussing it; it was going to be purple. End of story.

"I vote blue," Cyn said, grabbing her bottle of water and twisting the cap open.

"Gee, I wonder why blue?" I said, turning around to look at Rigid, who was playing pool with Lo. Lo leaned over the table to line up his shot, his jeans stretching across his ass and his shirt taut over his shoulders. God dammit that man looked good. I turned back around and looked at Cyn. "Did you dye his hair? He looks extra blue today."

Cyn snorted as she took a drink. "I'll have to let him know you noticed. He had me do it last night. It was all good until he started freaking out about the fumes rolling off his head. He stood in the hallway until it was time to rinse."

"Oh my God, I wish I could have seen it," Marley snorted. "Does he know he can come to the salon, and I could do it for him?"

"He said salons are girly shit."

"Tell me the next time he wants to dye his hair, and I'll bring everything home with me. I'm sure he's using shit dye, too." Gwen picked up her plate and headed to the kitchen.

"Can you grab me some more?" Cyn asked, holding her plate up.

"Only because you're pregnant, otherwise you'd be on your own," Gwen mumbled, grabbing her plate.

"I know, I need to take advantage of you guys as much as I can," Cyn winked at her.

"Doll, grab me another beer while you're up," Gambler called, shaking his empty bottle at her.

Gwen flipped him off and headed into the kitchen. "I can't tell if those two love each other or not," Marley laughed.

"I think they're a match made in heaven if you take out the constant arguing and bitching," I snorted.

"It's love, dammit," Gambler called. "She's just got an attitude I need to work out of her once in a while. That's my favorite part," he snickered, elbowing Lo.

"Oh, Lord," Cyn mumbled.

"Alright, back to the color, ladies. It's purple. Barney be damned. You can be my dino bitches for all I care. Colors are Purple and black."

"Did you really just call us your dino bitches?" Cyn asked.

"You're fucking crazy," Marley laughed.

I waved my hand at them, already knowing I was a bit crazy. It was part of my charm. "Moving on. Next Saturday we'll go look for dresses. I need to look for myself, too."

"Ahh, this is so exciting. Do you know what you want your dress to look like? Mermaid, drop waist, A-line, ball gown, tea-length, mini, or trumpet?" Marley gushed, her hands clasped in front of her

We all looked at her, our jaws hanging open. "They make that many kinds of wedding dresses?" Cyn asked, shocked.

"Oh, yeah, those and more. I've always loved weddings and already have my dress picked out for when I get married."

"Um, I want a dress," I mumbled, no idea which of the ones she said to pick. Although I could probably rule mini out right now. "Preferably one that won't make me look fat."

"Does Troy know about your obsession with getting married?"

"My obsession is with the wedding, not getting married."

"There's a difference?" I asked, confused as hell.

"Yes, I just want to have a killer party and look hot as hell."

"Alright, bitches. We've lined our stomachs with yummy, spicy chicken and rice, it's time for a little tequila!" Gwen ducked behind the bar, grabbing two bottles and brought them over to the table.

"Babe, I thought this was a strategy meeting with your girls to figure shit out for the wedding?" Lo asked, walking over, a smirk playing on his lips as he watched Gwen grab four shot glasses and drop them on the table next to the bottles.

"Hey, we totally planned shit. Our wedding colors are purple and black, these are my dino bitches, and we're going shopping next Saturday."

"I'd say a productive meeting indeed," Gwen said, filling each shot glass and handing them out. "Come on, King, you guys have got over five weeks to get this shit planned. How hard can it be? Have a drink, relax." Gwen filled another shot glass and handed it to Lo.

He took it and looked at me. "This wedding shit is all on you, babe. You want flowers and a huge party, I'm good with that. As long as you're my wife on December 31st, I'll be happy."

And this was why I was in love with Logan Birch. No matter what happened, I was going to marry this man and live happily ever after.

Right?

————

Chapter 2
Lo

"Babe, you are so tanked," I laughed as I watched Meg stumble out of her pants. She held onto the wall, her pants around her ankles, her eyes shut.

"Shhh, you make the room spin when you talk," she whispered.

"No, I'm pretty sure that's the 8 shots of tequila doing that to you." I pulled my shirt over my head and tossed it over the desk chair. "You want me to get you some water and Tylenol?"

Meg nodded her head and moaned, waving her hand at me.

"I don't know why the hell you did tequila tonight, babe." I walked into the bathroom and opened the huge bottle of Tylenol Meg had bought on her recent trip to Costco. Whenever she went there, we were always stocked up on the weirdest shit. Let's not get into the fifty rolls of toilet paper she bought the last time. "Here, take these, and climb into bed."

She grabbed the pills and the bottle of water I was holding out to her. "You're a saint," she whispered, twisting the cap off.

"And you're a nut, babe."

"But you love me," she said, handing the bottle back to me. "Now, help me get out of these clothes before I fall over." She leaned heavily against the wall, slowly sinking down.

"No more tequila for you. From now on, it's Southern Comfort and Whiskey for you." I grabbed her hand, pulling her to me. She rested her hands on my shoulders and held on.

"You know me so well," she whispered. I pulled her shirt over her head and tossed it on the floor.

"Step out of your pants." She lifted one foot and then the other and finally stepped out of them.

"My pants are like a Chinese fire trick."

"Babe?"

"You know, those things where you stick your finger in each end, and then you're stuck."

"You mean finger handcuffs?"

"Yeah, that, too." She wrapped her arms around me and rested her head on my shoulder.

"Where the hell did you get fire from?"

"Chinese fire drill."

"I'm not following you at all." Meg's craziness intensified when she drank. It's a miracle for me to understand her most times she drinks.

"I don't know. Don't be ass dumb."

"Dumbass?"

"Yeah, that, too." She patted me on the chest and yawned. "I'm going to fall asleep on you," she mumbled.

"You fall asleep on me every night, babe. Except let's do it in the bed." I leaned down and swung her up into my arms and walked over to the bed.

"You're gonna hurt yourself one of these days if you keep doing that," she mumbled, burrowing under the covers.

I pulled my jeans off, tossing them on top of my shirt and flipped the light off. I slid under the covers, Meg instantly cuddling up to me and rested her head on my shoulder. "You're crazy, babe." I grabbed her pillow and shoved it under my head.

"Is there ever going to be a night where you don't steal my pillow?"

"No."

"Maybe I want my own pillow."

"If you don't have a pillow then you have to lay on me."

"Fucking sweet Lo is out tonight," she murmured. "Maybe sweet Lo will tell me the secret hard ass Lo is hiding from me."

I shook my head and leaned back into the pillows. "Not happening. If you need to know, I'll tell you. This isn't something you need to know."

Meg sighed, her body relaxing into me. "Next time I'm getting you drunk, and then I know I'll get it out of you."

"You can try," I laughed.

"I love you, Logan," she sighed.

"I love you, too, babe." She rested her hand on my heart, and I knew she was out when her breathing evened out.

I closed my eyes, trying to sleep, but all I could here was Meg's damn dog, Blue, snoring at the foot of the bed. I tossed one of the pillows from my behind my head at him, and he thankfully stopped snoring.

For five seconds.

Fuck.

————

Chapter 3
Meg

"I want eggs."

"Then you might want to get your head off the table and get in the kitchen before Marley burns all the food," Troy laughed.

"I heard that, asshole!" Marley yelled from the kitchen.

I covered my ears and groaned. Ugh, I blame Gwen for this. I was absolutely miserable. Tequila was firmly on my no-fly list from now on. "You can cook, go cook me eggs. You're supposed to be my best friend."

"Look," Troy whispered. I raised my head, wondering why the hell he was suddenly whispering. "She's got it in her head she needs to learn how to cook, but she has *no* sense of time. The box says ten minutes, and she starts doing something, forgets about it and then we're ordering pizza. I. Need. Help."

Poor Troy. He looked so desperate. His eyes darted nervously to the kitchen, fearful Marley would hear him. "You need to let her learn, Troy. I don't know what to tell you."

"Can't you help her or something. Go in there and just watch the pan. Honestly, she can get it all going, but if there are even five minutes of cook time, she's off doing something else, completely forgetting about the pan on the stove until it sets the fire alarm off."

"Oh my God, you are going to make me go in there with a raging hangover and watch Marley cook aren't you?"

"If you value our friendship at all, you will not ignore my pleas of desperation."

I dropped my head to the table again and groaned. "You owe me big for this," I muffled into the table.

"I will be a God damn bridesmaid for you if you get your ass in that kitchen and protect my eggs. I will *not* eat frozen pizza for breakfast another morning."

"I feel that has happened more mornings than I think."

"Frozen pizza four times this past week and its only Thursday."

"Wow, we're starting the week on Sunday, right?" I asked, counting in my head. Troy nodded my head, and I had to feel sorry for him. "Well, at least she got it right one morning."

Troy shook his head no and leaned back in his chair. "I woke up before her and made *her* breakfast. You know that I am not a morning person. I don't wake up before eight for anything."

"Okay, okay, I'm going. But I'll tell you right now, purple is not your color, so we'll have to figure out something else besides you being my bridesmaid. Plus, I'm sure Hammer doesn't want to walk you down the aisle."

Troy flipped me off as I stood up from the table, hunched over and shuffled to the kitchen. The smell of burning toast reached my nose, and I feared I might be too late to save Troy from frozen pizza. "Need any help?"

"He sent you, didn't he?" Marley asked, slamming the spatula down.

Shit. Abort, abort! "No, not at all. I need coffee. Gwen killed me with the tequila last night. Coffee is a must." I reached up into the cabinet, pulled a cup down, and grabbed the coffee pot. I glanced at it, wary Marley had made it. If she couldn't cook, could she make coffee? I had a fifty/fifty chance of taking a sip and spitting it out. I filled my cup half full and set it down. I wasn't sure if I was in a gambling mood. I turned back around to see Marley pulling two pieces of toast from the toaster and toss them in the garbage. "You want me to make the eggs while you do toast?" It sounded like I was trying to be helpful, right?

"Sure. I already had to scrap one batch of scrambled eggs." She grabbed the loaf of bread and stuck two more in the toaster. I glanced at the bag, seeing there was only half a loaf left. I had just bought it yesterday. I had to assume there had been a few toast fatalities before I had stumbled in.

"I just don't get it. I follow the directions exactly but everything always burns." Marley reached in the fridge and handed me the eggs.

"Milk, too," I said.

"What the hell do you need milk for?" She asked, handing it to me.

Didn't everyone put milk in their eggs? "Um, I splash a little."

Marley nodded her head and slammed the fridge shut. "I should probably watch how you do this. I just throw some eggs in a bowl, stir them up and toss them in the pan."

I made a face as I grabbed the salt and pepper down from the cabinet. "I just add a little extra to my eggs." I walked over to the pantry, grabbed an onion and then opened the fridge to grab the green pepper I had in there.

"You're putting all that in the eggs?"

"Yeah. I could give you the recipe if you want." Was that too obvious? I didn't want Troy to have to suffer through flavorless eggs. I love Marley to death, but Troy was right. Marley needed help in the kitchen.

"Sure, if you get the time. I know you're busy with all the wedding plans."

I grabbed a knife and hacked the onion in half. "It shouldn't be a problem. I'm planning a wedding, but it's not going to be huge." I peeled the skin off the onion and started chopping it. "I figure we'll get married at the church and then come back here for the party."

"I can't wait to see Troy in a tux."

Umm, how to break it to Marley that tuxes were so not happening. Lo had put his foot down two seconds after we set a date that he would be dead before he wore a tux.

"Yeah, about that. I'm not really sure what the guys are wearing. Lo said he was going to take care of that."

"Seriously?" The toast popped up, and Marley pushed the handle down again.

"No!" I yelled, pointing my knife at her.

She held her hands up, her eyes bugging out of her head. "Dude! What the hell?"

"Ugh," I mumbled, setting the knife down. I suppose that was a bit drastic. "don't put the toast down again. I'm sure it's good. Just slap some butter on it."

"Really? Troy said he liked the toast dark, so I always do it twice."

I shook my head and turned back to the cutting board. Fucking Troy was shooting himself in the foot. I bet she kept burning the toast and instead of telling her, he just told her he liked it. Dumbass. "I would try it once and see what he says. Maybe you'll be surprised."

She shrugged her shoulders and stuck two more pieces in. We worked in silence together, me whipping and cooking the eggs while she conquered making toast. One step at a time. Today toast, hopefully tomorrow eggs. "So, back to the tuxes. You really think King isn't going to wear one?"

"I can pretty much guarantee that Lo will not wear one." I put the pan on the stove, turning the heat to low and dropped some butter into it. "Plus, I don't know if I want Lo in a tux. He's sexy as hell just in his jeans and tees." I reached for my coffee and took a hesitant sip. Surprisingly not bad.

"Oh girl, I would pay money to see Troy in a suit."

I poured the eggs into the pan and gently stirred them. "Well, you might have to bribe Lo, and it's going to have to be a significant amount. I don't think that man is budging."

"Why don't you turn the heat up?" Marley peaked over my shoulder.

"Low and slow when it comes to eggs. Low and slow." The eggs slowly started to cook, and I continued to stir them, not stopping.

"This is going to take forever. I typically crank the burner up and let em roll. Scrambled eggs in five minutes."

I just shook my head and continued to stir.

"Hey, babe." I glanced in the doorway and saw Lo standing there. Hot damn he looked good. He had gotten up early to work on paperwork for the shop, and I hadn't seen him since.

"Hey, handsome," I blushed.

"You wanna head over to your house after breakfast and figure out what we all need to do to fix the porch?" Oh, my poor porch. I used to love sitting out there, and the Assassins had decided to blow it the hell up.

"Yeah, the eggs should be ready in a couple of minutes." Lo nodded his head and headed back out to sit by Troy.

"You're telling me you don't want to see that man in a tux?" Marley asked, pulling two more pieces of toast out and putting two more in. We really needed to get a bigger toaster. Two pieces at a time took forever. She smothered them with butter and piled them on top of the other pieces.

"As long as Lo is there, I don't care what he's wearing."

"Aww, you two are so sweet together," Marley gushed.

I grimaced, realizing how big of a sap I sounded. I grabbed a big plate down from the cabinet and set it next to the stove. "Don't let Lo hear you call him cute. He'll probably drop and do ten push-ups and fart just to prove he's not cute."

Marley busted out laughing, waving the buttery knife at me. "You're crazy."

I shrugged my shoulders and continued to stir the eggs. "Like I haven't been told that before." I lifted the pan off the stove and dumped them onto the plate. I had scrambled two dozen eggs, and they overflowed on the plate. I grabbed a plate off the stack Marley grabbed and scooped the rest onto it. "I'll eat these."

I grabbed the platter of eggs and toast and headed out to the table. "Eggs, boys," I said, setting the plate down.

Troy looked at them like he was ready to cry. I'm sure he was happy to see I had made the eggs and not Marley. I'm sure he had been eating hard, flavorless eggs since Marley started cooking. Lo grabbed me and pulled me into his lap.

"I missed you this morning, babe. You feeling okay?" he asked, brushing my hair back and pressed a kiss to the side of my head.

"Yeah, I didn't even feel you leave the bed this morning." I rubbed my cheek against his and smiled. "Hmm, you didn't shave today."

"No, I just threw some clothes on and headed out to the shop."

I reached up, rubbing his cheek. "Scruffy Lo is sexy. Makes me wonder what this feels like somewhere else."

"Let me eat my breakfast, and I'll show you." He winked, pressing a kiss to my lips.

"Hmm, promises, promises," I murmured, getting up from his lap.

Lo slapped my ass and pulled me back in his lap. He cupped my cheek and whispered, "That pussy is mine as soon as we're done checking out the porch. I miss being in that big ass bed with you."

Right to my core every time he talked to me like that. "Eat fast," I whispered.

He crushed his lips to mine, wrapping his arms around me. "I love you," he mumbled against my mouth.

"The feeling is definitely mutual," I purred, running my fingers through his hair.

"Do you think you two could keep your hands off each other for ten minutes while I eat?" Troy asked, pointing his fork at us, his mouth full.

"The same goes for you two when we're watching a movie on the couch, and you decide to cop a feel. Take it to the damn bedroom," Lo growled.

Troy flipped off Lo and tucked back into the plate of food in front of him that was mounded up with eggs and toast.

"Eat, I'm gonna get dressed." Lo kissed me on the side of the head, and I stood up.

"Fifteen minutes, babe," he mumbled, filling his plate.

"Yeah, yeah." I ducked into the kitchen, filled my coffee cup and headed down the hall to our room.

"Hey," Cyn mumbled, stumbling out of her room.

"You feeling okay?" Cyn looked green and ready to pass out.

"Surprisingly feeling better than I did ten minutes ago. This baby makes me toss chunks every morning. As soon as my eyes open, I'm praying to the porcelain gods."

"I'm sorry, hun. I know there's coffee in the kitchen, and I just made a huge batch of eggs."

Cyn turned an unnerving shade of green and shook her head. "Just coffee," she mumbled, holding her stomach. She had a little bump that had just popped out in the last couple of days, and she looked freakin' adorable.

"Okay, I'm headed over to my house for a bit with Lo after breakfast, but you wanna hang out after?"

"We'll see. I see a nap in my future for sure. Maybe a movie or something?"

I nodded my head, yes, and she walked down the hall to the kitchen. I felt terrible for her. This pregnancy was kicking her ass. I ducked into Lo's room, flipping the light switch on and headed into the bathroom.

"Oh, sweet Jesus. Did I look like this out there?" I groaned, staring into the mirror. I had tossed my hair up into a haphazard bun after I had rolled out of bed and stumbled to the kitchen, coffee, and eggs my only thought. I really should have looked in the mirror before.

My skin was all splotchy and red, and I looked like I had been run over by an elephant. Seriously not good. Shower, I needed to shower. After I had twisted the water on to scorching hot, I stripped my clothes off and slipped into the shower. The water poured over me, hot and steamy. I closed my eyes and tilted my head back under the water. Ahh, this was exactly what I needed. Nothing besides coffee helped to wake me up like a shower. Of course, the only way this could be better is if Lo was in here with me.

I grabbed the soap, lathering up in my hands and ran it over my body, imagining it was Lo caressing me. Ugh, I needed to get out of the shower.

———

Chapter 4
Lo

"You break and tell her what's going on with the Assassins yet?" Troy asked as he shoveled the last of the eggs into his mouth.

I leaned back in my chair, sipping my coffee. "No. But not for her lack of trying. I swear she's going to withhold sex from me soon. I can tell you right now, that shit will not fly."

Troy looked over his shoulder into the kitchen, making sure Marley wasn't behind him. "You really think it's that big of a deal that we can't tell the girls what's going on?"

"No, I don't think it's that big of a deal, but Rigid doesn't want to stress out Cyn anymore than she is right now. Hopefully, when we meet with Leo tomorrow, we'll know more and be able to tell the girls. Right now, all we know is Big A spewed some shit at Gwen. I need to find out more."

"Well," Troy pushed his plate away and patted his stomach. He just ate like he wasn't going to eat for the rest of the week. "all I can tell you is the longer you keep it from Meg, the harder she's going to try to get it out of you."

"I think I know Meg, brother."

Troy put his hands up and shrugged. "Yeah, you've been friends with her for years. You totally know her better than I do." Troy stood up and headed outside, slamming the door behind him.

Son of a bitch. I didn't want Troy pissed at me, but it really fucking irritated me when he acted like he was her personal pit bull. What he was saying made sense, but I didn't want to tell Meg anything till I knew more. "Son of a bitch." I set my coffee cup down and ran my fingers through my hair.

"You ready?" Meg asked, wrapping her arms around my neck from behind. She placed a kiss on my cheek and moaned. "I'm more than ready," she purred, running her hands up and down my chest.

"Hmm, what got you all excited, babe?"

"Well," she whispered in my ear, "I was in the shower, and I was lathering soap all over me, and all I could think about was what this scruff is going to feel like when you eat me out." I grabbed her arm, twisting her around and pulled her into my lap. Her arm knocked my cup, coffee splashing over the side. "Whoopsie," she whispered.

"What else did you do in the shower?" I didn't fucking care she just spilled hot coffee on my hand, I was much more concerned about what she had been doing when I wasn't there to watch.

"Hmm, wouldn't you like to know."

"I'll just make you show me when we get to your house."

"It's your house, too, Lo," she mumbled, trailing a finger down my chest. "You did move in with me."

I had, to a point. I still had stuff at the clubhouse, though. "You're avoiding my question."

She shrugged her shoulders but didn't say anything.

"What if I say your house is my house, will you tell me what else you did?"

Her eyes flared, and I knew I had her. "Not only will I tell you, but I will also definitely show you, too." She leaned forward, pressing a kiss to my lips and smiled.

"Let's go home, babe." I lifted her up in my arms and carried her out the door. "Keys?" She pulled them out of her pocket, and I opened the driver's side door to her truck.

"You're driving, aren't you?" she pouted, scooting over to the middle of the seat.

"Yes, I'm still worried about you driving since the whole drive-thru incident." I slid in, slamming the door behind me and started the truck.

"Hey! That was not my fault at all! That pencil dick in the drive thru was being an ass. He started it." Meg crossed her arms over her chest and stuck her bottom lip out.

I threw my arm over the back of the seat and looked out the back window as I backed out of the parking spot. "Babe, you're twenty years older than him."

She glared at me, her eyes flaring, and I knew that was not the right thing to say. "You might want to think very carefully about the next words that come out of your mouth, Logan Birch."

I shifted into drive and headed out the driveway to Meg's. "I plead the fifth," I mumbled.

"Wise choice," she humphed, crossing her arms over her chest. "How bad do you think the porch will be to fix?"

"I think the whole damn thing is going to need to be replaced." Meg groaned but didn't say anything. I knew she loved that damn porch, and it sucked the fucking Assassins blew the damn thing up. "We'll get it fixed, babe, and have you back to drinking coffee on it every morning."

"Good. I'd also like to live in my house again, not just drop by once a week to pick up clothes." I knew living at the clubhouse was wearing thin for everyone, but we didn't have a choice. We never knew when the Assassins would strike next.

"Soon." I grabbed her hand and pressed a kiss to the back of it.

Something had to give with the Assassins. We just had to figure out their weakness.

———

Chapter 5
Meg

I was out of coffee. How in the hell did that happen?

"Babe, what the fuck are you doing?"

I had left Lo on the porch and wandered into the house hoping to make a pot of coffee and wallow in my porch troubles. Lo was right, it was a total loss. Fucking Assassins.

I banged the cabinet door shut and leaned against the counter. This day was sucking ass, and it wasn't even half over. "I'm out of coffee," I mumbled.

Lo pressed his body against my back and wrapped his arms around me. "You need me to run to the store to get some?"

I leaned my head back and rested it on his shoulder. How the hell did I get so lucky to find this man? I already had two cups of coffee, and I really didn't need any more, but he was more than willing to run to the store for me. "No, I'll survive. I'll pick some up the next time I grocery shop for the house."

"There might be something else that could replace your coffee for the day."

"Oh yeah, and what would that be?"

He brushed his lips against my ear and a shiver ran through my body. "I seem to remember you wondering what my beard would feel like in other places," he growled, trailing kisses down my neck and all thoughts of coffee flew out the window.

"Hmm, you did say you've been missing our big bed." I turned around and wrapped my arms around his neck. He pressed me against the counter, grabbing the hem of my shirt and tugged it over my head.

"I've missed having you all to myself." He reached around, unhooking my bra and tossed it on the floor. His green eyes darkened with desire, and he licked his lips. "I still can't believe you're all mine, babe."

I delved my fingers into his hair and arched my back as he sucked a nipple into his mouth and flicked it with his tongue. "I'm always yours, Lo. No matter where we are."

"I know. It's just nice that I can strip you naked whenever I want when we're at your house."

"Except when Remy is home," I laughed, pushing him back. "How about we take this to the bed?" I suggested.

He leaned in, nuzzling my neck. "I like the way you think." He pressed a kiss to my lips then hoisted me over his shoulders and headed to the bedroom.

"You're going to give yourself a hernia one day if you keep lifting me. I was not made for lifting." He tossed me on the bed and crawled up and covered me with his body.

"You know what happens when you put yourself down, babe. That pretty little ass of yours meets my hand, and I spank all that bullshit out of your head." He leaned back and popped open the button of my jeans.

"Watch your head," I warned as I looked at the fan blades whoosh past his head. We both loved the big bed, the only problem was that it was so tall, that the fan was capable of taking your head off if you weren't careful.

"I got it." He worked my pants down my legs and tossed them on the floor. "There's only one head you should be worrying about right now," he winked.

"Cheesy, Lo. So cheesy," I laughed.

He leaned down, pressing kisses to the inside of my legs and a shiver ran through my body as he rubbed his scruff against me. "You know you like it."

"I must confess," I moaned as his lips grazed over my pussy, "that I am a fan of all things Lo, even your cheesiness."

He tugged on the waistband of my underwear and slowly dragged them down. "No matter how many times I see you naked, it's always better than the last."

And this is where my heart explodes into a million pieces, and I know Logan Birch is the man for me. "God dammit, I love you, Lo," I whispered.

"I never doubted it." He tossed my underwear over his shoulder and spread my legs apart. "Put your arms above your head."

I slowly raised my arms and clasped my hands over my head. "I like touching you, though, Lo."

"You will, babe. For now, it's all about you." He parted the lips of my pussy, and a low growl came from his throat. "So fucking wet." He swiped a finger through my wet pussy, flicking my clit.

I bucked my hips, wanting more. "Logan," I moaned.

"Hmm, it's been too long since I tasted you." He laid down, his head between my legs and his scruffy face rubbed the inside of my legs. "Knees up, spread wider."

I raised my legs and dug my heels into the bed. He wrapped his arms around my hips and pressed kisses on my legs. "I want to touch you," I pleaded. I loved threading my fingers through his hair and holding on.

"Hands stay up, or I put you over my lap." A shiver ran through my body at his words, and I clasped my hands even tighter.

"You're a tease," I gasped as his tongue flicked my clit. My hips bucked, and it took all my self-control not to grab his head and grind my pussy on his face.

"Stay still or I'll tie you to the bed." He grasped my hips and held me down as his tongue assaulted my clit. I threw my head back, grabbing the quilt, twisting it in my hands as moans of ecstasy fell from my lips with every flick of his tongue.

"Say my name, Meg. I want you to fucking scream it," he growled, lifting his head as his finger took over, driving me more insane as he sped up.

"Lo," I gasped as I slammed my eyes shut, pleasure rocking my body.

"You coming on my dick or my face, babe?" God damn I loved when he asked me that. Either way was going to be fucking amazing.

"Dick," I moaned, "I want your hard dick in me."

I moaned low as his tongue took over again, the warmth of his breath on my pussy driving me closer to the edge. He sucked my clit into his mouth, and I shouted out his name.

He pushed away from me, and I opened my eyes to figure out what the hell he was doing. I pushed up on my elbows and watched as he shucked off his jeans, tossing them in the ever growing pile of clothes on the bed and crawled back up my body. "You ready for me?"

All I could do was nod my head yes and wrap my arms around his bare shoulders. His hand snaked down between us, and he grabbed his rock hard dick, stroking it up and down. I licked my lips as I watched his hand and nodded my head.

"You trust me, babe?" I again nodded my head, not really listening as I watched a small drop wet the tip of his dick. He backed away from me, his hand still on his cock and stood up. "Come here," he ordered.

I shimmied to the side of the bed and stood up, facing him. He turned me around, my back to his front and pushed me back, bending me over. He ran his hands up and down my back and squeezed my ass. "Put your hands above your head, and hold the fuck on." He kicked my legs apart and stepped between them. He reached down, stroking my pussy as he lined his dick up and teased my clit with the tip. "I'm going to make you scream my name, Meg. So loud the neighbors will hear you."

I moaned into the blanket, knowing that Lo was more than capable of making me do that. He pushed in slowly, and I dug my hands into the bed and moaned low as he pushed all the way in. Lo reached around and parted the lips of my pussy and flicked my clit over and over as he thrust in and out. "Say my name," he growled.

I shook my head no and bit my lip, not wanting to give in to him yet. "So fucking stubborn," he growled, doubling his efforts, slamming into me as he pinched my clit. He was driving me crazy, and I knew I was only going to be able to hold on for so long before we both fell over the edge. "Say it."

My hips reared back into him with each thrust of his hips, and he grabbed my hair, fisting into his hand and pulled my head back. The sharp tug on my head mixed with the thrusting of his hips tipped me over the edge when he pinched my clit again, and I chanted his name over and over. "Lo! Oh God, Lo! Logan," I screamed.

He grunted over and over as he drilled into me. He let go of my hair and grabbed onto my hips. "Mine," he gasped, groaning low as his cum poured into me, filling me fuller with each thrust. "Mine," he whispered again, collapsing on top of me.

We both were panting, trying to catch our breath. "How… the hell… do you manage… to make it better than… the last?"

"You felt that, too, huh?" He pressed kisses down my back as he ran his fingers up and down my side.

"I feel it every time, Lo. I always think it can't get any better, and then you blow my mind the next time."

He pressed one final kiss to my shoulder and rolled off me and climbed up on the bed, pulling me with him. He wrapped his arms around me and pulled me to his side. "I love you, Logan," I whispered, laying my head down on his shoulder.

"I love you, too, Meg."

"You think we could stay the night here tonight?" I asked, grabbing the edge of the blanket and pulling it over us.

"Babe, you know being at the clubhouse is the safest place to be."

"I know, but remember how you said you miss having me all to yourself, I feel the same way. At least when you're here, I don't have to share you with the club."

Lo pressed a kiss to the side of my head and sighed. "Dammit, Meg. I can never say no to you. One night and then we're back at the clubhouse until this Assassin shit gets tied up."

"Yes!" I shouted, springing up and raising my hands.

Thwack! The fan blade smacked me upside the head and knocked me back down on the bed. I fell on top of Lo, holding the side of my head, "Man down, man down," I mumbled into his chest.

"Jesus Christ, Meg," Lo laughed, wrapping his arms around me. "You almost just knocked yourself out, babe."

"It's not funny," I pouted, slugging him in the shoulder. "It's this damn bed. I swear to Christ one of these times I'm going to decapitate myself."

"This damn bed is your fault."

"Ugh, just shut up and get me some ice, please."

"Let me look at it. You might have a concussion." I rolled off him, and he sat up and gently prodded the side of my head. "I think you'll just have a goose egg on the side of your head for the next couple of days," he laughed, shaking his head. "Let me see your eyes."

"I got hit on the side of the head, Lo, not in the eye."

Lo shook his head and just grabbed my chin, looking me in the eye. "If your pupils are dilated, babe, it means you have a concussion."

"Oh, I didn't know that," I said, opening my eyes wide.

"You look fine. Probably just gonna have one hell of a headache." He stood up and opened the dresser drawer and grabbed a pair of underwear out.

"I don't get you naked the whole night?"

"No, babe." He pulled them on and grabbed his jeans off the floor.

"Hey," I said, sitting up, "you weren't wearing any underwear. You must have thought I was a sure thing."

"You are a sure thing. Just like I'm a sure thing for you. All you need to do is bat those pretty eyes at me, and I'll do whatever you ask."

Hmm, he'll do whatever I ask, huh? I batted my eyes and pulled the blanket off, exposing my breasts. "Then tell me what everyone is keeping from me."

Lo threw his head back, laughing and walked out of the room. "Nice try," he called over his shoulder.

"Dammit," I cursed, falling back onto the bed. Not only had I just cracked my skull open on the damn fan, I still couldn't get Lo to tell me what the hell was going on.

Shit.

———

Chapter 6
Lo

"Dinner, Lo!" Meg called.

I tossed my crowbar down and wiped my hands on my pants. My hands were numb from working in the cool, fall weather and the sun was almost set.

"Holy shit." I spun around and caught Meg before she fell out the front door. I had managed to tear down the whole front porch, and it was now a pile of wood and debris on the side of the house. "You said you were going to do a little work out here before dinner. I guess I didn't realize that meant tearing the whole thing down." She pushed off my shoulders and grabbed the door frame, pulling herself back in the house. "How the hell are we supposed to get in the house now, Lo?"

"Backdoor. Plus, it's only going to be like this for a week or two. I figure while you're doing wedding shit, the brothers and I can work on getting the deck done."

"I'm sure Remy would help, too."

"I'll shoot him a text in a little bit and see if he's free this weekend." I know Meg wanted me to get along with her son and we did. Meg had raised him to be a good kid and it was easy to get along with him. He had the same personality as his mom; laidback.

"Dinner's done, Lo," she said again, leaning against the door frame. It was times like these that I fell more in love with Meg. I never once thought that I would have the life I do. A drop dead gorgeous woman telling me dinner was made, standing in the door of the house we were going to share together. I was one lucky mother fucker.

"What did you make, babe?" I grabbed the last three boards off the ground and tossed them into the pile.

"Chicken Parmesan, garlic rolls, and Mexican Cheesecake for dessert."

Another reason I was a lucky fucker, Meg cooked like a fucking five-star chef. "What makes your cheesecake Mexican?" I hoisted myself up into the house and Meg backed up, making room for me.

"You'll have to wait until dessert to figure that out."

"Or I could eat my dessert first."

"You can't. The cheesecake is still cooling, and if you eat dessert first, your dinner will get cold."

I grabbed her around the waist and pulled her to me. "Just one bite. That's all, I promise."

"Tell me what you're keeping from me, and I'll cut you a big ass piece."

Damn, this woman was fucking relentless. "Nope. I can wait till after dinner." I pressed a kiss to the side of her head and ducked around, missing her swinging arm.

"I hate you, Lo. I don't understand why you can't tell me. I'm sure it's nothing, and you're making it a bigger deal than what it really is." She propped her arms on her hips and tapped her foot. Even pissed off and telling me she hated me, Meg still looked hot as hell.

"It isn't a big deal, Meg, that's why I don't need to tell you."

"I'm not going to be in a relationship where you're constantly keeping things from me, Lo. I'm not some fragile flower that you need to protect and keep secrets from." She crossed her arms over her chest and sighed.

I hated that I couldn't tell Meg about Big A and what happened at the salon, but knew it was better if she didn't know until I knew what the hell was going on. With my luck, she and Cyn would go Nancy Drew on my ass and try to figure out how to get rid of the Assassins. I walked over to her and put my hands on her shoulders and looked her in the eye. "Do you trust me, Meg?"

"Lo, this isn't about trust."

"Yes, it is, Meg. Do you trust me to do what's right for you?"

"Gah, yes, OK, I trust you."

"Then trust that I will tell you what you need to know, and if I have to keep a secret from you, know that they only reason I am is because it's club business, and I'm keeping you safe. Sometimes the less you know, the better, babe."

She closed her eyes and leaned her head back. "You make sense, Lo, but it really bothers me that there are going to be times where you are going to know things, and I'll be clueless." There weren't going to be many times that I was going to have to keep secrets from Meg. Now, if this would have been five years ago when the Knights were heavy into drugs and gun running, then yes there would be lots of things Meg wouldn't know.

"Babe, open your eyes and look at me." She opened her eyes and tilted her head down. "Trust me. Trust that I am doing right by you, and when the time comes, I will tell you what happened."

"Ugh, fine. I trust you, but just know, you are going to make me go crazy."

"That's a risk I'm willing to take seeing as you're already half crazy."

She wrapped her arms around my neck and leaned in. "You know what's even crazier, Lo?" I shook my head no and brushed the hair out of her face. "The fact that you want to marry my crazy ass."

"Hmm, you may be right, babe, but I'm totally fine with being crazy if it means I get you." I pressed a kiss to her lips, and she threaded her fingers through my hair.

"I guess you could have one bite of cheesecake before dinner," she whispered against my lips.

"Maybe I could have a bite of something else, too." I nipped at her bottom lip, my hands grabbing her ass, lifting her up and she wrapped her legs around my waist.

"Dinners going to get cold, Lo," she moaned, tilting her head to the side, giving me better access as I rained kisses down her neck.

"Dinner can fucking wait," I growled, turning around and headed back to the bedroom.

She squealed as I tossed her on the bed and climbed on top of her. "I guess we can always rewarm it," she purred.

"There's always later. I'm hungry for something else right now."

Dinner was ice cold by the time we resurfaced from the bedroom. It was well worth it.

———————

Chapter 7
Meg

"Oh for Christ's sake, get your ass in the damn car."

"I am not sitting in the middle; my ass is too fat."

"You don't have an ass, Gwen. Do you think we can stop for snacks? Rigid woke me up early this morning and kept me, shall we say, busy." Cyn wiggled her eyebrows and plopped down into the passenger seat.

"If I'm not back in eight hours, send out the cavalry." Lo chuckled next to me and shook his head.

"Did you call ahead to the dress shop and warn them that y'all were coming?"

"I made an appointment. I hope they're prepared for us. I need to find a wedding dress and all the girls need to get their dresses, too. I'm fucking worried Cyn is going to walk down the aisle in a big ol' sack I paint purple." I watched as Cyn swung her legs into the car and slammed the door shut. In the past two weeks, her baby bump had started showing, and it seemed almost every day it grew.

Lo wrapped his arm around me and pulled me close. "I'm sure you'll find something, babe."

"Hmm, I hope so. I wish your mom would have been able to come."

"She said she had an appointment scheduled she couldn't miss. You know she wants to be here."

I leaned my head against his shoulder and sighed. "I miss your mom, Lo. She doesn't hang out at the clubhouse much anymore."

"I plan on swinging by there while you're on the hunt for the great white dress, see what she and Gravel have been up to. He hasn't been at the clubhouse much either."

"Maybe they just want to spend time with each other. They missed out on being together for so many years, perhaps they're making up for it now."

"Are you coming with, or am I going to have to pick your dress out by myself?" Cyn yelled.

"I better go; the natives are getting restless." I pressed a kiss to Lo's cheek and grabbed the door handle.

"Not so fast, babe." Lo grabbed me around the waist and wrapped his arms around me. "I'm gonna need a better kiss than that," he growled. He slammed his lips down on mine, pushed me up against the car, and I completely slipped into the *Lo Daze*.

I delved my fingers into his hair, holding on while he devoured my lips.

"Oh, sweet Jesus. We're never going to make it to the appointment on time if King won't take his hands off her." I heard Cyn mumble through the open window.

"I think it's sweet. It's good to know that King still has it in him."

I tossed my head back, busting out laughing at Marley's words.

"Dude, how the hell old do you think King is?" Gwen asked Marley.

"I don't know. Forty?"

"Should I let them know you're older than me?" Lo rumbled.

"Do it, and I kill you," I warned.

"Actually Marley, Meg is—"

"Doing Lo a favor by being with him since he's *so* old. I mean, whew, Lo is way older than I am," I cut Lo off. No way in hell was I going to willingly tell anyone that I was older than Lo.

Lo leaned in, his lips touching my ear. "You just earned yourself a little time over my lap, babe."

A shiver ran through my body at his words, and I knew my white lie was going to be worth it. "Promises, promises," I cooed. I grabbed the door handle, pulling it open and slid into the car, slamming the door shut. "Say hi to your mom and Gravel for me."

"Will do, babe. Have fun." Lo tapped the top of the car and stepped back, crossing his arms over his chest.

"About fucking time. I'm starving." I glanced over at Cyn, watching as she pulled a granola bar out of her purse and ripped it open.

"We just got done eating breakfast. How the hell are you starving right now?" I shifted the car into reverse and backed up.

"I blame the baby. He's a bottomless pit. I eat and then fifteen minutes later I'm starving." She ripped off a piece of granola bar and chomped down on it.

"Well, do you have enough snacks in your purse to get through until we are done dress shopping?" Gwen asked from the back seat.

"Hopefully. Although, I could really go for some Dip 'N Dots."

"Dude, it's ten thirty in the morning. Who the hell has ice cream in the morning?"

"Little Caleb does." She rubbed her belly and shoved the rest of her bar in her mouth.

"Yesterday you were calling him Jolio. Now it's Caleb?" I asked, totally confused.

"Rigid and I can't agree on a name, so every day we pick a name and call the baby that to see if it's something we both like. So far we haven't been able to find any that we both like."

"What about Cody?" Marley suggested.

"Eh, no."

"Wait, why are you only doing boy names? Do you know what you're having yet?" Gwen piped in.

"No clue what we're having, but we both want a boy. That is the only thing that we can agree on."

"Well, if it's a girl, I like Ella." I always told myself that if I were ever to get pregnant again and it was a girl, Ella would have been her name. I could now pawn that name off on Cyn because my baby factory had been shut down ten years ago.

"Oh, I love that," Marley sighed.

"Hmm, I'll have to run it by Rigid, but I like it, too. Now, think of a boy name."

Cyn, Gwen, and Marley all tossed names around on the way to the bridal store, none of them agreeing on any.

"I'm telling you, Shia is the way to go," Marley slid out of the car and slammed her door shut.

"She's only saying that because yesterday she and Troy had a Transformers marathon." Gwen grabbed her purse out of the backseat and headed into the shop.

"Is your sister meeting us here?" Cyn asked.

"Yeah, let me check my phone." I grabbed my phone out of my purse and saw that she had texted me ten minutes ago saying she was here.

"So, we get to meet your sister. Is she anything like you? Crazy and fun?" Marley asked.

"Oh, you're in for a treat. Meg's sister is the complete opposite of her. Married for years and she has five kids," Cyn informed Marley.

"But is she fun? I've met some married women that are crazier than a tornado in Oklahoma." Gwen held the door open, and we all headed in.

"Jackie is everything I am not. Plus, she's one hell of a time. She may be married and have five kids, but she still knows how to have fun. I promise, between us four and her, we are going to have a good time today."

We walked to the front desk to check in, and we were surrounded by hundreds of wedding dresses, my eyes bugging out by all the choices. Three-quarters of the store were varying shades of white wedding dresses and the other quarter of the store were the bridesmaid dresses. That was where I spotted Jackie, flipping through the racks.

"It's about time you guys got here. I've already got a stack of dresses I want to try on, and half of them are not appropriate for a mother of five." Jackie winked at me, and I knew this was going to be one hell of an afternoon.

Lo

"Yo, King!" I glanced over my shoulder as I walked into the clubhouse and saw Hammer headed towards me with the club phone in his hand. "Leo needs to talk to you."

I grabbed the phone from him and put it to my ear. "Leo."

"King. How are things in Rockton today?"

"Quiet for the time being." Quiet that was making me uneasy. The last time there was silence from the Assassins, Meg's porch got blown up.

"Good, good. I'm keeping my men in town, making sure nothing happens before I know about it. That is also the reason I'm calling right now. All my men are busy, and I need some help."

"Shoot." Leo had already helped us, so I had no problem helping him with whatever he needed.

"It's my sister, Fayth. My damn nephew is giving her a run for her money right now, and I'm not there to help. I had to head back to Chicago for a couple of days, and he's taken this opportunity of my absence to wreak havoc."

It was times like these I was thankful Meg had raised such a good kid. I didn't have to worry about Remy doing stupid shit. "So what exactly do you need us to do?"

"Fayth said she heard Marco on the phone this morning making plans to meet with some of the drug runners from down here. I don't know what the hell this kid is thinking." I could hear the annoyance in his voice, and I knew annoying Leo Banachi was not a wise thing to do.

"You want us to run them out of town?"

"No. I'm meeting with the leader of these little rats and plan on getting Marco out of this fucking mess. What I need from you is to send a couple of guys over to my sister's house and keep an eye on the fucker until I get there tomorrow."

I scrubbed my hand down my face and tried to figure out who the hell I was willing to give up for a day. "Slider and Hammer could stay over there until you get back. I'm sure they won't be happy to be babysitting a seventeen-year-old, but they'll do it."

"I'll owe you one, King. I know babysitting isn't what you guys want to be doing right now. I'll let Fayth know that they'll be over." I shoved the phone back in my pocket and ran my fingers through my hair. Babysitting a seventeen-year-old, great.

"You want me to grab Slider so you can tell us both about your phone call?" Hammer asked.

"I'm right here." I looked to my right and saw Slider walking into the common room. "What's up?"

"Leo just called. He had to go out of town for a couple of days, and he's having some problems with his nephew. I want you two to head over there and keep an eye on the little fucker until Leo gets back in town."

"How the hell long is that going to be? I had plans tonight." Slider crossed his arms over his chest, already pissed off.

"Fucking cancel them. Get your shit packed and head over there. Call Demon and let him know what's going on once you get settled. I'm heading over to Ma's to see what the hell has been up with Gravel lately."

"Fucking bullshit," Slider mumbled under his breath as he walked back to his room with Hammer following.

I shot off a text to Demon, letting him know what the hell was going on and letting him know Slider would be calling him, and I would be over at Gravel's.

I ran my fingers through my hair and sighed. I would be fucking happy when all this bullshit with the Assassins was over, and shit could go back to the way it was. I was getting too old for this shit.

———

Chapter 8
Meg

"Twirl."

"Twirling isn't going to make that dress look any better," Gwen called from the racks of dresses behind me.

"It looked so good on the hanger." Jackie stood in front of me, her hands propped on her hips.

"Ugh!" I tossed my hands up in the air and stomped my foot. "This is beyond hopeless! There isn't one single dress in this store that looks good on me."

"Calm down, we have four more dresses in the fitting room to try on, and Gwen is out searching for more. Your dress is here; we just have to find it. We need to find it today in case you need any alterations done." Jackie shooed me with her hand, and I headed back to the dressing room.

"She didn't like that one either?" Cyn asked. She was sprawled out on the mini couch they had in the dressing room, fanning herself with her hand. A half-eaten bag of Funyuns cradled in her arm and a can of soda next to her.

"Eh, I didn't like it either. I look like a God damn cupcake. The pouf of this dress clashes with the pouf of my ass and thighs."

"Not this one either?" The saleslady asked, sweeping into the room, closing the door behind her.

"No, Barb, I'm 0 and 12 at this point." Yes, that's right. I had tried on twelve dresses, and none of them were right. I wasn't even picky. They all just looked like shit on me.

"Don't give up just yet, my dear. I know we have something that will sweep your man off his feet." Oh Barb, so optimistic.

"Shouldn't King be swiping you off your feet, not the other way around?" Cyn mumbled.

"What was that, dear?"

I glared at Cyn, daring her to repeat what she said. Barb was well past sixty and sweet to a fault. "Oh nothing," Cyn chirped, throwing a chip at me.

"Well, let's get you in something you haven't tried yet, shall we? I found this in the back, and I hope it'll be just what you're looking for."

"Alright, Barb, hit me with it."

"First, we need to put this on," she reached out the door and grabbed a different bustier. "We need to get those girls up where they belong."

Cyn burst out into giggles, and my jaw dropped. I thought my girls were in a pretty good position, thank you very much. Hell, Lo never complained about them. "Uh, are you sure that's the right size?" I asked as she held it up and stepped towards me. I scurried backward, afraid of the damn thing. It was going to squeeze the hell out of me, that is if we could even get the thing on.

"Oh, trust me, dear. It laces up, we'll be able to make it as tight as we need it to be."

Cyn stood up, wiping the chip crumbs off on her jeans and unzipped the back of the dress I had on. "The cupcake dress is no more," she laughed, helping me step out and draped it over the couch.

"All right, young lady. I'm going to need you to take this side, and I'll take the other, and we'll hopefully meet in the middle." The way Barb talked half the time, I felt that I should possibly be offended, but then she would say something nice. She was giving me whiplash. "Take off your other bra, dear."

I reached the back clasped, unhooking it and tossed it over my shoulder as I held my boobs in my arms. Wedding dress shopping sure wasn't turning out to be as fun as I thought it would be.

Barb and Cyn grabbed a side of the new torture device and moved behind me. "Are your breasts in the cups, dear?" I lifted the ol' girls up, resting them in the cups, and I felt like I was going to suffocate.

"Um, they're kind of high, Barb."

"That's where they're supposed to be, dear." There she goes again, possibly insulting me, but I'm not really sure. "Now suck in, and don't breathe until I say so."

"Wait—" Barb yanked on the laces, and my breath whooshed out. "Can't breathe," I wheezed.

"Just a little bit more, dear, and we'll have you in that dress lickety split." She tugged one more time, and I was pretty sure she broke a couple of ribs. "There, I'll grab the dress." She flitted out of the dressing room, and I fought for breath.

"Holy fuck, Meg. You have like a serious hourglass figure."

I didn't care if I looked like a goddamn supermodel, I couldn't breathe. I waved my hand behind me, trying to get Cyn's attention, letting her know I was about to pass out. "I... my ribs... tell Lo... I love... him." I collapsed to my knees, clutching at my stomach. Barb had managed to shove and squish me into this bodice that was three sizes too small, but it was going to kill me.

"Fuck, fuck, fuck," Cyn chanted. "Don't die on me!" I could feel her clawing at my back, frantically trying to untie the ties. "Jesus Christ, it's like Fort Knox back here. It's like she triple knot tied the fucker."

I closed my eyes and saw spots as my lungs fought to suck air back into them. This was it, this was how I was going to die. Death by wedding dress.

"I've got it, I've got– Ah, fuck. Hold on. My fingers are too fat to get this last knot untied." I reached behind me, frantically clawing at my back, grasping for anything to tug on. I needed to get this fucking thing off.

"Stop, you keep knocking the damn laces out of my hand, bitch." Cyn knocked my hands away and more panic set in.

"Well, here it is," Barb swept into the room with a huge dress draped over her arm and stopped dead in her tracks when she saw Cyn and me on the floor. "What on earth are you two doing?"

"You're killing her, Barb."

"Oh, posh. She just needs to get used to it."

"Barb, I swear to God, if you don't help me get my best friend out of this torture device, I will shove that fucking wedding dress down your throat. Get your ass over here, now!"

Barb scurried over, kneeling behind me. "I didn't even make it as tight as it should be," she mumbled under her breath. I was going to kill Barb if she didn't get me out of this fucking contraption.

"I got it, I got it!" Cyn yelled. I felt the ties loosen, and I was able to suck a little bit of air into my lungs. "Just fucking pull, Barb, who cares if the fucking laces are even or not." I felt the laces tug all the way off, and I fell forward, my chest heaving with the deep breaths I was dragging into my lungs. The corset fell off, and I was laying on the floor, topless. I had reached an all new level of classy.

"What in the hell is going on here?" I looked up and saw Gwen, Marley and Jackie standing in the door of the dressing room, all looking horrified. I glanced behind me, seeing Cyn flat on her ass, holding her stomach while Barb was on all fours, her skirt hitched up her legs.

"Why the hell are your boobs out?" I glared at Jackie and wrapped my arms around my boobs, trying to contain them.

"Barb tried to kill me. Cyn saved my life. I think we're done for the day, ladies. I didn't try on anything I liked." I laid my head down on the floor, light-headed from the loss of air, and a bit disappointed I didn't find my dress.

"Not so fast. While you were in here dying, I was out there scouring the racks for the perfect dress." Gwen ducked out of the room while Jackie and Marley plopped down on the mini couch.

"Can I have some chips?" Jackie asked, picking up the bag that Cyn had dropped on the floor. "I didn't know we were bringing snacks. I totally would have brought my amazing spinach dip that I make."

"Hmm, I love spinach dip. You should totally make some for the wedding." Marley reached into the bag and popped a chip in her mouth. "Although that might be a lot seeing as I know all the guys from the club are coming and they can eat a ton."

"Around sixty people are coming. Lo and I don't want anything huge. Although he gave an open invitation to his old chapter, so who knows how many guys will show up from there." My breathing had finally returned to normal, and I didn't feel like I was going to pass out anymore.

"Here it is!" Gwen swept into the room, holding up the most beautiful dress I had ever seen. It was an A-line, strapless, white dress, and get this, it had gorgeous, small dark purple flowers. All. Over. It.

Everyone gasped when they saw it, and I knew that was going to be the dress I walked down the aisle to Lo in. "You didn't tell me you wanted color," Barb snapped, standing up. "I would have brought that dress in right away if I knew you were looking for purple."

But that was the thing, I didn't know I was looking for purple. I knew that I wanted the bridesmaids to be in purple, but never really thought about what I wanted my dress to look like. "Oh put a sock in it, Barb," Cyn snarled. "You and your backhanded comments can take a hike. I'll get her in the dress." I looked over my shoulder and watched Cyn stumble up off the floor. Barb stormed out of the room and slammed the door shut.

"You do realize I need to buy this dress from her. Pissing her off might not be the best idea." Cyn shrugged her shoulders and picked up the bra I had been wearing before. It was also a corset, but it was nowhere near the torture device that Barb had managed to squeeze me into. "Stand up. Let's get this show on the road."

I awkwardly stood up, keeping my hand over my chest and grabbed the bra out of Cyn's hand and wrapped it around my front while Cyn fastened it in the back. "Open the dress, Gwen." Gwen eagerly ripped off the plastic bag, taking the dress off the hanger and unzipped the back. She held it open, and I gingerly stepped into it.

"Holy shit," Jackie gasped, her hand covering her mouth, "You look fucking amazing." Cyn and Gwen shimmied it up my body and zipped up the back.

I clamped my eyes shut, afraid to look in the mirror. The dress looked amazing on the hanger, and it felt perfect on my body, but I was so scared that I would look in the mirror, and it would look like a potato sack on me.

"King is going to shit when he sees you in that."

"Shit, Cyn? Really, that was the best word you could come up with?" Gwen asked, propping her hands on her hips.

"More like pop a wood and have her right then and there." Jackie stood up and walked around me, studying the dress. "I'm happy I finally get to see you get married this time, plus I'm even more happy it's not to a jackass like Hunter again."

Hunter and I had married at the courthouse with only our parents as witnesses. Shall we say the family wasn't exactly ecstatic with the fact I was nineteen and pregnant? By the time Remy was born, everything was fine in my family, but it was a tense few months when I had told them I was pregnant. "I'm afraid to turn around and look," I whined, running my hands up and down the dress.

"Turn your ass around and look at it. I swear to God you look gorgeous." Gwen put her hands on my shoulders and looked me in the eyes. "Do it." She slowly spun me around, and I gasped as my reflection came into view.

"Christ on a cracker, I look amazing." Cyn jumped up and down, clapping like a seal while Marley and Jackie cackled on the couch. "I can't believe that's me." I really did look beautiful. The dress hugged my curves perfectly, and the strapless bodice kept the girls under wraps and helped slim my typically boxy shoulders.

"Now to figure out the shoes. Are you doing heels or flats?" Jackie asked.

I only wore heels when I was going out, and that was few and far between. I think that last time I had worn them was when Lo and the guys from the club had crashed Cyn's 'Thank God I didn't marry that asshat' party. "Flats, but not the kind you are thinking of." I bent over and grabbed my purse off of the floor by the small couch. I fished out the picture I had found in a magazine a week ago and held it to my chest. "No matter what any of you say, I am wearing these shoes, and I will not be swayed."

"Come on, come on. Show us the picture," Marley goaded, holding her hand out. I stuck it in Marley's hand and closed my eyes when she screeched.

"Holy shit she's wearing purple Chucks," she wailed. I was pretty sure the whole bridal shop knew what shoes I was wearing.

"No, you're not. Not with that dress!" Gwen cried, outraged. Here I thought she would be the one who was down with my shoe choice.

"Yup. I totally am. Besides, no one is going to see them unless I lift my dress up, and that isn't happening until after the party," I winked.

"I, for one, love it." Cyn plucked the picture out of Marley's hand and studied it. "They even say 'Bride' on the back."

"Mom is going to flip when she sees those."

"Mom is going to love them because she loves Lo. And, she doesn't have to pay for anything for the wedding so I can wear whatever I want." I stuck my tongue out at Jackie, and she threw her head back, giggling. I had forgotten how much fun I had when I was with my sister. We still lived in the same town, but we never managed to see each other enough. She had a huge family. She was always running around, doing things, and I was, well, I was Meg, living my screwed up but always fun life.

"When did King meet your parents? How come I wasn't invited?" Cyn asked.

"Probably because they wanted to meet King, not Meg's friend," Marley laughed.

"I've met Meg's parents before," Cyn pouted. "I was just wondering why I didn't know he had met Karla and Mike."

"He met them when you and Rigid were just starting to get it on. I figured you would rather be with Rigid then go hang out with my parents." I stared at myself in the mirror, not believing what I was seeing. I was finally going to be that girl who got to walk down the aisle to the man of her dreams.

"Okay!" Marley said, standing up. "Now it's time for the bridesmaids! Now, you go sit out there, and we are going to give you a bit of a fashion show." Marley opened the door, reaching for the hangers full of colorful dresses that were hanging on a hook outside the door and pulled them in.

"Yes! This was just what I was waiting for." Jackie stood up and took her jacket off, tossing it on the couch. "Shoo, bridey, we'll be out in a jiff." She pushed me out the door and slammed it shut.

"Hey!" I protested, "You could at least hand me the chips!" The door opened and a hand, I'm assuming it was Jackie's, held the bag out and I snatched it up. "Thank you, I think," I grumbled to myself.

I plopped down on the big couch that was in front of the dressing room and fanned my dress out around me. The beautiful and intricate stitching of each and every flower was amazing, and the dark rich shade of purple was perfection.

I opened the bag of chips, mindful of my dress, and popped a chip into my mouth. Here I was sitting on a couch in a bridal shop, wearing a fabulous wedding dress, waiting for my best girls to come out and show me their picks for dresses. I don't think this day could get any better.

———————

Chapter 9
Lo

I pulled up to my mom's house and didn't see her car in the driveway and sighed. I should have called before I came out here, but I figured she would be home. Hopefully, she was home. Otherwise, I had just driven out here for nothing. I pulled my leather jackets tight around me and headed up the sidewalk.

Gravel had packed up everything off the porch, getting ready for winter and mom had already put a fake tree up where her favorite chair generally sat. I tried the handle, opening the door, "Ma! You home?" All the lights were on, but there wasn't an answer.

I walked in and shut the door behind, wondering why the door was unlocked and all the lights were on. "Ma, you here?"

"Logan," I heard whimpered.

"Mom? Where the hell are you?" I called. I listened again, trying to figure out where she was but didn't hear anything.

I sprinted into the kitchen and saw my mom propped up against the cupboards, shards of glass surrounding her. "Mom," I kneeled down beside her, and she lifted her head to look at me. She looked tired and worn out, and her eyes were glassy. I grabbed her hand, needing to touch her, making sure she was still with me. Her hands were ice cold but her fingers wrapped around mine, holding on tight. "What happened?"

"I'm... just weak," she gasped.

Weak? What the hell did she mean weak? She was one of the strongest women I knew, inside and out. "We need to call an ambulance, Ma. You shouldn't be weak. Something isn't right." I pulled my phone out of my pocket, and she knocked it out of my hand. It skidded across the floor and hit the fridge. "Ma, you need to go to the hospital."

"No, I don't, Lo. I'm all right."

"You're not fine if I come over and find you laying on the kitchen floor."

"I wasn't laying down," she mouthed off. Even possibly dying and my mother was still being a pain in my ass.

"What the hell happened?" I looked over my shoulder and saw Gravel standing at the entrance of the kitchen, two plastic grocery bags dangling from his fingertips. "I thought I told you to sit your ass on that couch and not move, woman."

Mom waved her hand at Gravel and rested her head on the cabinet behind her. "I needed a drink. You left me with nothing to drink."

"I was only gone for twenty minutes; I didn't think I needed to leave you with a survival kit."

"Well, now you know," she laughed. She fucking laughed.

"What the hell is going on?" I roared. "I come over and find my mother on the floor, and all you two are going on about is the fact he didn't leave you with a drink."

"Calm down, Lo. Everything will be fine. I'm just weak after my treatments, and apparently getting a drink is too taxing on me."

They were talking like I knew what was going on when in fact I didn't have a fucking clue. Gravel walked into the kitchen, setting the bags down on the table and grabbed the broom from beside the fridge. "Get off the floor, Lo, and grab the dustpan. We need to get this cleaned up before Ethel gets hurt."

"She's already hurt," I bellowed.

"She's not hurt, Lo."

"Don't you dare call me Lo. Only two people call me that, and you are not one of them."

"Alright, son." My blood boiled. Usually, I didn't mind if he called me Lo or son, but right now I was pissed the fuck off by the fact he knew what the hell was wrong with my mom, and I didn't have a fucking clue.

"Tell me what the fuck is going on!"

"Logan Birch, knock it off and help Gravel clean up. I'll explain everything when I'm not sitting in a pile of broken glass." She scowled at me, somehow pissed off. I grabbed the dustpan and kneeled down, collecting the shards as Gravel swept them up.

"Help your mother to the couch. I'll get some drinks."

I pressed the dustpan into his chest, and he wrapped his hand around it. "Here," I growled. Gravel just shook his head and backed away.

After kneeling down, I wrapped an arm around her shoulders and hoisted her up. She leaned heavily against me, seeming as though her legs couldn't even hold her up. "Put me in my chair." I gingerly set her down, making sure not to move faster than she could and stood back, looking down at her. She looked so fragile and tired, nothing like the mother I had known the past thirty some years.

"Sit down, Logan. There is no point in you standing over me, scowling." She shooed me away with her hand, and I sat down on the couch directly across from her.

"Tell me what is going on, mom."

Gravel walked in with three glasses in his hand, offering one to me and setting one next to mom. "I made the tea. Hopefully, it's not shit," he gruffed, sitting in the chair next to mom. After Gravel had bought mom the first chair during Meg's whole breaking the expensive ass bed, he went back and bought another chair so they could both have one.

I set my glass down on the table, not giving a shit about it. "Tell. Me. What. Is. Going. On."

"I'd change your tune real quick, boy. I know that is not how you talk to your mother."

"Gravel, stop. It's fine. You were the same way when I told you." She reached over and patted him on the leg.

"That's because the God damn doctor took fucking forever to tell us. I was ready to stab the fucker with a needle." Mom chuckled under her breath, and I just stared at her.

Her color was coming back, and she didn't look so beaten down. "Mom, please."

"Alright, just remember, I am not going to die." Gravel grunted next to her and rolled his eyes. "I meant I won't die from this, Gravel." He nodded his head, smirking at her but let her continue. "Five weeks ago, I went to the doctor's office. I have my yearly mammogram, and they found a lump." My world tipped on its side at her words, but she just kept on. "After they performed a biopsy of it, they discovered it was cancerous. I have stage II breast cancer."

Holy Fuck.

————

Chapter 10
Meg

"Okay, so we're all decided on the floor length, ¾ sleeve, plum dress, yes?" Gwen asked, twirling around in front of the mirror.

"Hell yes!" We all shouted. After three grueling hours of watching these four try on dresses, I was beyond ready to go home, slip in the shower and then slip into bed with Lo. I loved hanging out with my girls, but I missed Lo.

"All right, ladies. Let's pack it up and get the hell out of here. I will die happy if I never have to step foot in a bridal salon again."

Gwen slipped back into the dressing room while the rest of the girls gathered up their purses and coats, all talking at once about the amazing bridesmaid dress. We had managed to find a dress the same shade of purple that was on my wedding dress. We were going to look amazing the day of the wedding.

"I'll meet you guys outside." I grabbed my purse and headed out, pulling my phone out of my pocket. The last time I had heard from Lo was over three hours ago, and I missed hearing his voice.

After swiping his name, I put the phone to my ear, but it went directly to voicemail. What the hell? "Hey, it's me," I rattled off, "We're just leaving the dress shop. We should be home within the hour. I'm not sure what you wanted to do for dinner, but I thought maybe we could just hang out in our room. I miss my Lo time. See you soon, I love you." I shoved the phone back in my pocket just as the girls started pouring out the front door.

"I'm gonna head out." Jackie pulled her keys out of her purse and beeped open the locks of her SUV. "Marcus called, wanting me to bring home fried chicken and whipped cream."

"Oh, sweet Jesus, stop right there. I don't want to hear anything about your kinky sex life." I put my hands over my ears and shook my head.

Jackie hugged all the girls bye and flipped me off as she got in her car. "Ah, sisterly love," Cyn said, tossing her arm over my shoulders.

"She loves to torture me. Even though we're both grown adults, she still tries to annoy the shit out of me."

"We should stop and eat. Oh, Mexican!"

"Sorry, no can do. I plan on slipping into the *Lo Daze* and not surfacing until morning." I steered Cyn over to the car, eager to get home.

"Well, I want Mexican. Maybe I could get Rigid to help me cook."

"Oh, I can help you!" Marley called.

"Abort, abort," I whispered.

"You know what, on second thought, why don't we grab the guys and make them take us out," Gwen chimed in. I had a feeling that everyone knew about Marley's lack of cooking skills.

"Perfect idea," Cyn slid into the passenger seat while Marley and Gwen wedged themselves in the back again. "You sure you don't want to come with us? You could always have your Lo time after."

"I'm sure. I tried calling him earlier, and he didn't answer. He's probably in the garage working on paperwork or something."

The girls chatted the whole way home, gushing over the dresses we had found today, but all I could focus on was the sinking feeling in my stomach that something wasn't right.

Lo

"Yo, Cyn just called. We're all going out for Mexican. You and Meg want to come with?"

I stared at the closed door, Rigid on the other side and took a swig from the bottle of 12 year Jameson that was dangling from my fingertips. After spending more than an hour at Gravel's and Mom's, I was more than ready to go home. I didn't know what to feel or think.

She kept telling me over and over that she wasn't going to die from this, but I didn't hear it. The word cancer just kept rolling through my head, beating me down, making me feel like I had already lost her.

"King, you in there, man?" Rigid tried the handle, but I had locked the door, not wanting to be disturbed.

"I'm staying in tonight," I called. I didn't want to be out, having a good time while my mom was probably at home, throwing up and losing her hair because of the chemo she was going through.

"Suit yourself, brother." I heard his retreating footsteps and took another drink. I grabbed the stereo remote, cranking up Five Finger Death Punch.

Life sucked at the moment, and the only thing that was going to make it better was Meg and this bottle of Jameson. Meg wasn't here, so it was time to drown in Jameson.

———————

Chapter 11
Meg

"Hey, are you sure you don't want to come with us?"

This was the fifth time Cyn had asked me to go with them, and I was getting a tad bit annoyed. "I'm sure. We'll hang out tomorrow, okay?"

She nodded her head, giving me a quick hug and headed out the door, following behind Marley and Troy. I tossed my purse behind the bar and grabbed a wine cooler from the mini fridge and popped it open. Rigid had told me that Lo had gotten back from his mom's over an hour ago and headed straight to his room. Lo wasn't one to hang out in his room alone when all the other brothers were around. Something was going on, and I was worried.

The common room was quiet, everyone either going out for Mexican or out in the garage to work on cars. I headed down the long hallway, slowly making my way to our room, wary of what I was going to find.

The closer I got, the louder the music thumped, pounding against the walls. I turned the handle, but it didn't budge. I dug my keys out of my pocket, opening the door and slowly pushed it open. The room was pitch black, and the music was loud.

I felt around on the wall, searching for the light and flipped it on. The room illuminated, and my eyes landed on Lo, who was sitting in the recliner in the corner, a bottle of liquor to his lips. "Lo! Turn it down!" I yelled. He stared at me, making no moves to turn down the stereo. One look at him, and I knew he was well beyond buzzed and headed to shit faced. After walking over to the stereo and turning it down, I turned around and looked at him, my hands on my hips. "Looks like you started the party without me, hunny." A loopy grin spread across his lips, and he took another swig from the bottle.

"It's far from a party. Come here," he slurred. Even piss drunk and slurring his words this man still called to me. I went to him without hesitating and climbed up on his lap, straddling him.

I rested my hands on his shoulders. "What's going on?"

"She's dying."

"What? What do you mean she's dying?"

"Mean exactly what I mean to mean." This might be a bit harder than I thought it was going to be.

"Who is dying, Lo?"

"It's cancer, babe. It's cancer, and I can't do anything," he mumbled, burying his face in my hair. "I can't fix it."

I wrapped my arms around him, still not quite understanding what he was talking about, but I could tell it was tearing him up. "Are you talking about your mom, hunny?" I felt him nod his head yes, and my heart dropped.

Ethel had cancer. I pulled back and cupped his face with my hands. "How bad is it? Is she getting treatment?"

"Yeah. I went… I went…" He licked his lips and looked away from me.

"Do you wanna talk about it, hunny? Or maybe later?"

"I don't know what to do, Meg. I try to fix everything, be the man I know that I am, but this I can't do anything about. I can't fight it for her. I can't make her better." Tears were streaming down his cheeks, each tear ripping my heart open wider.

I reached over and grabbed the bottle from his hand and took a swig. "Holy fuck, what the fuck is that?" I asked, sputtering. I don't know how the hell Lo was drinking this shit straight up. I swear to Christ I just drank gasoline.

Lo grabbed the bottle from me and put it to his lips, taking three huge swallows. "Jameson," he slurred.

He set the bottle on the floor next to the chair and popped up the footrest, catapulting me into his chest. "Sweet Jesus, warn a girl, would ya?" I laughed, wrapping my arms around him, settling into him. I rested my head on his chest and listened to his heart beating. "Your mom is strong, handsome."

He wrapped his arms tight around me and held on like he was afraid I would slip away. "I needed you before when you called, but I didn't know what to say."

"That's all you would have needed to say, handsome. You're there for me all the time, now it's time for me to be there."

"If I lose her, I don't… I just…"

I leaned back, looking him in the eye and put a finger over his lips. "Don't even go there, handsome. Your mom is still here, and if I know her, I bet she has no plans of going anywhere for a long time."

He kissed the pad of my finger, and I laid back down, my head to his chest. "I love you with everything I am, Meg."

"I love you, too, Logan, and I promise, no matter what happens, I'll be here."

Lo

212

"I love when you hold me, handsome, but my stomach is about to start rioting." Meg tilted her head back, a smile on her lips. She had been in the chair with me for over an hour, just letting me hold her.

"I suppose I should feed you." I pushed the footrest down, and the chair tilted forward as Meg wrapped her arms around my neck. "You say everyone went out to eat?"

She nodded her head yes and climbed out of my lap and stood up. "Cyn and the baby were craving Mexican."

I sat back in the chair and looked Meg up and down. She was so fucking beautiful, sometimes I wondered what the hell I did to deserve her. "Did you have a good day, babe?" Here I was acting like a fucking asshole, totally ignoring Meg.

"Yeah. It was good. I found my dress and so did the girls. There was a near death experience thanks to Barb, but we all managed to walk out of the shop alive."

"I should probably be concerned that you went dress shopping and almost had a near death experience, but I'm not."

She shrugged her shoulders, "I guess you're just finally getting used to me," she laughed.

I doubted I would ever get used to Meg's crazy ways, but I wasn't so shocked anymore. After the whole getting Marley drunk and shoving her in the bathroom with a pot of coffee, I just learned to roll with the punches. "How'd you almost die, this time, babe?" I stood up and grabbed my cut that I had tossed on the bed earlier. I stumbled a bit, realizing the half bottle of Jameson still might have a bit of a hold on me.

"I love watching you when you're drunk," Meg laughed. "Your own drunkenness surprises you. I saw that you totally thought you were fine, and then you almost fell on your ass. Priceless," she giggled.

I managed to wrestle myself into my cut without falling over and sat down on the bed. Although, I'm sure it was more of a sit/fall. "Happy to entertain you," I chuckled.

She held her hand out to me, and I grabbed it as she pulled me up. "Barb tried to hide my curvy curves, sucking me into a death contraption that one of my legs couldn't fit into. Cyn and Barb both had to pull and tug to get me in. By the time they did, I was at about thirty percent oxygen level and falling. I'm pretty sure my lips turned purple." She wrapped her arm around my waist, and we headed down the hall to the kitchen.

"I hope you didn't get a dress that is going to hide all those curves I love, babe." I slid my hand down her back and cupped her ass.

"I guess you'll just have to wait and see," she giggled, grabbing my hand, leading me into the kitchen and pushing me up against the counter. Sitting or leaning was probably my best bet at the moment. "You stay there and help me figure out what to make for dinner."

"You know I'll eat whatever you make, babe."

She opened the freezer, sticking her head in, "You're half drunk. I'm betting something greasy and beyond fattening is right up your alley right now. My stomach growled at her words. She peeked her head out and laughed. "I'm going to take that as a yes." She pulled out a package of hamburger buns, tossed them on the counter and pulled out a pound of hamburger meat. "Juicy, greasy, messy, fall apart in your hand, burgers it is."

After pulling all the fixings out, Meg pulled out a beer and handed it to me. "You trying to keep me drunk?"

"Maybe I have plans to take advantage of you later." She winked at me and turned back to the counter, pattying up the burgers. "You feel like talking about your mom anymore?"

No, not really. I wish I didn't ever have to think about her and cancer again, but I knew that was reality. "What do you want to know?"

"How long has she known?"

"A month."

"What! She's known for over a month, and she didn't think that was something she should tell anyone?"

I shrugged my shoulders and took a swig of beer, "I don't know. Gravel said she didn't even tell him until the day of her first chemo appointment. To say that he was pissed is an understatement."

"What the hell, did she plan on keeping it from everyone the whole time?"

"I think so. It was almost like she was pissed when I found out. I don't believe she wants to be a burden to anyone or some shit like that. The woman took care of me all my life, now it's my turn to help take care of her. My only problem is she doesn't fucking tell me when she needs help." Damn woman was one of the most stubborn women I knew. I had to basically force her to tell me when her next chemo appointment was. After fifteen minutes of insisting knowing when it was, she finally told me. I planned to be at every appointment that I could make.

"Did you tell anyone?"

"No, she asked me not to. She said the only one I could tell was you."

"Well, that sucks. She does realize this whole clubhouse treats her like she's their mother, right?" Meg slid the burger patties onto a grill pan she had heating on the stove and grabbed an onion. She sliced it open, her knife slamming down on the board.

"I know, babe. I'm sure eventually she'll say something, but as of right now, she's asked we don't tell anyone."

She mumbled under her breath, working on the burgers and toasting the buns in the oven. I loved watching Meg cook. It was incredible how she could take something so simple as a burger and turn it into the best thing I had ever eaten. "Homemade potato chips okay?" she asked, grabbing four potatoes from the pantry. I nodded my head, tempted to tell her again I would eat anything, but I knew she heard that all the time.

"She's going to beat it. I know she will, Lo."

"She said she wasn't going to let this get her. The doctor said if she did all her treatments and shit, she should go into remission. He thinks they caught it soon enough that they can beat it."

Meg set the knife down she was using to slice the potatoes and walked over to me, resting her hands on my shoulders. "She's going to be okay. She has to be. Your mom is the person who brought us together."

"I'd like to think I would have found you eventually, but my mother finding you for me worked, too." I reached up and brushed the hair out of her face. "I did make you pretty fucking tongue tied that day." I still think back on that day, remembering Meg tripping over her words and the way her eyes had roamed over my body.

"The second I laid an eye on you, my brain stopped working, and all I could think of was where those tattoos on your chest started and ended." She tugged on the hem of my shirt and pulled it up, her hands gliding over my stomach. "I liked what I saw," she looked down where her hands were, "still like what I see."

"You need to figure out how hungry you are, babe. You keep doing what you're doing, we won't be eating dinner for hours."

"Hmm," she hummed, her fingertips grazing over my nipples. "I'm hungry for both food," she glanced over her shoulder at the burgers cooking away, "and you," she purred, looking back at me. She pressed her lips to mine, teasing me with what I wanted, but slipped away before I could take it.

"Did you just choose food over me?" I chuckled.

"Not really, I mean sort of. Although, it's not like the option was only food or only Lo. I just decided food now, Lo all night," she purred, glancing at me over her shoulder.

Son of a bitch, I loved this woman.

———————

Chapter 12
Meg

"I don't know how you did it, babe, but that was the best fucking burger I've ever had." Lo fell face first on the bed, his arms and legs sprawled out.

"Seasoning and don't pack your meat too hard."

Lo flipped over, a grin spread across his lips. "So that's your secret, you know how to handle the meat."

"Shh, don't tell anyone," I winked, walking into the bathroom. "I'm gonna shower quick, try not to pass out before I get out. I've got plans for you."

"Hmm, I'll be right here." I closed the door and leaned against it. I reached over, flipping on the light switch, and finally breathed.

When Lo had told me about his mom, all I wanted to do was curl up in a ball and cry. Except I couldn't do that, because Lo needed me to be strong for him. From what he had told me, Ethel was going to be okay, but it was still terrifying. The word cancer was terrifying by itself. When the name of someone you loved was tacked on to it, it took on a whole new meaning.

"Babe, let me in."

I spun around, ripping open the door, fearful that Lo was about to be sick. During dinner, he had managed to drink three more beers. "Are you okay?"

He was leaning against the doorframe, his arms crossed over his chest. "I think I'm about as good as you are."

"Well, if you're going to puke, I think I'm a little better than you are."

"I can't remember the last time I puked from drinking. I can hold my own. I meant are you okay."

God dammit, I was supposed to be the strong one for Lo, and here he was, making sure I was okay. This man was amazing, and I was unworthy of him. "I'm fine. I think it's kind of sinking in that your mom is sick."

"I know how you feel." He reached out and wrapped his arms around me. "Turn on the shower. I need one, too."

I turned around and walked over to the tub and turned on the water, adjusting the temperature till it was just right. "You know, I should be the one comforting you, not the other way around." I turned around, and my jaw dropped. In the time it had taken me to get the water just right, Lo had managed to strip all his clothes off and was standing there naked as the day he was born. Well, and also sporting a huge hard on.

"I think I know of a way you could comfort me." He reached down and stroked his cock, and I swear I came right then and there. He slid his hand up and down his hard shaft, and my desire pooled in my panties.

"Um, I think you might be thinking of a different kind of comfort."

"Take your clothes off, Meg."

"Do you really think this is the best time for this. You just found out about your mom and maybe you should… just, you know, try…" My words trailed off, and all thought left my brain as Lo squeezed a drop of precum from his ever growing dick. I licked my lips as my gaze stayed glued to his hand that was stroking his cock.

"Right now, all I want to do is forget about this whole day and lose myself in you." He stepped forward, closing the door behind him. "Clothes. Off, now."

"Lo, I really think you should think about your mom and-"

"Stop! Mention my mom one more time in the next two hours, babe, and you'll have a one-way ticket to spending the night over my knee. I'm a grown fucking man who has had the shittiest day I can remember in a long time, and all I want is you. Just give me that. Please."

I took a deep breath and closed my eyes. Lo was right. Maybe we both just needed to let go for the moment and just lose ourselves in each other. Our problems will still be there tomorrow.

I grabbed the hem of my shirt and tugged it over my head, tossing it in the corner. I reached behind me, fumbling with the clasp of my bra, managing to unhook it and sailed it over Lo's head. "I only get two hours?"

Lo growled low. "I'll take all fucking night if I have to."

"Hmm," I unbuttoned my jeans and shimmied them down my legs. "You're so demanding tonight," I purred, sliding my underwear down and flipped them away with my foot.

"I know what I want," he growled, stroking his cock faster and harder.

"Well, do you want my mouth right now?" I licked my lips again as another drop oozed out. I could never forget what he tasted like on my tongue, and right now I craved him. I slowly fell to my knees, cupping my breasts together.

"Fucking perfect," he growled, taking the three steps toward me, his dick bobbing in front of my lips. I opened my mouth, kissing the tip of his cock. His breathing became labored as I reached up, grabbing the base of his cock, and slowly worked him down my throat. He threaded his fingers through my hair and held onto my head. He moaned deep when he hit the back of my throat, and I swallowed, "Son of a bitch." My body hummed at his gruff words, and I knew I was driving him crazy, helping him forget his shitty day. "Stand up," he gently tugged on my hair and helped me up off my knees.

"Hmm, why'd you stop me?" I whispered, wrapping my arms around his waist.

"Because if I had let you go thirty more seconds, I would have gone off like a rocket. Your mouth drives me insane." He wrapped his arms around me and pulled me flush against his body. "Your whole body drives me crazy. I can barely keep my hands off you. You're like a drug I can't get enough of."

I tilted my head back, his eyes were looking down at me. "You sure do know the right words to say, Lo," I whispered.

"It's the truth, babe. I can't live without you. I don't even want to try it."

I stood on my tiptoes, pressing my lips to his, knowing I had finally found what I was always looking for. "Come on, handsome." I grabbed his hand and tugged him to the tub. "I think a shower is just what we need right now."

I tossed the curtain back and stepped in, Lo following close behind. His hands roamed over my body as the water poured over us. He grabbed the soap, lathering it between his hands and spread it all over my breasts, teasing and taunting me with every touch. "I missed you today, Meg." His hands glided over my arms leaving a soapy trail as they wrapped around me, lathering up my back.

"I missed you, too," I whispered, closing my eyes, feeling his rough yet gentle hands claim my body.

He pushed me against the wall, his arms caging me in. He cupped my chin, his thumb stroking my jaw. "Thank you for being there for me today, babe."

"You're welcome, hunny." I had never met a man so sweet that he makes me want to cry and in the next second he steals my breath away, demanding my body in every way I'll give to him.

He pressed his lips to mine, slowly assaulting all my senses. One hand cradled my face, while the other slid between our bodies, one finger separating the lips of my pussy. I gasped as he flicked my clit and one finger pumped inside me, already building my desire. "So responsive," he moaned against my lips. "Only for me."

"Yes," I whispered, closing my eyes, tucking my face into his neck.

"I'm gonna make you cum, and as soon as you do, I'm gonna fuck the hell out of you until you're screaming my name, cumming again." A small tremor rocked through my body, and I knew it wouldn't be long. He flicked my clit while two fingers now pumped in and out while he assaulted my lips, taking and giving. I tossed my head back as he sped up, driving me to the brink then backing off, over and over. "You're my greedy girl, aren't you?"

I moaned at his words, knowing I should be ashamed, but I needed his touch more than my next breath. "Please," I begged.

"You're mine." He leaned in his lips on my ear. "No one gets this but me." His teeth tugged on the shell of my ear as his fingers pinched my clit and I fell over the edge, tossing my head back. He kept working me over, wringing every last tremor and moan from my lips. "Mine," he growled in my ear. I wrapped my arms around his shoulders and held on, fearful my legs wouldn't hold me up anymore.

"One down, one more to go," I smirked.

"So greedy." Lo shook his head and grabbed my ass. "Climb up, babe. Time for you to go for a ride." I managed to wrap my legs around his waist, his cock nudged between the lips of my pussy while he pinned me against the wall.

His fingers dug into my ass as he pulled away and slowly entered me. "I love when you fuck me like this," I gasped.

"I love any way you let me fuck you. Your body was made for me." I bit my lip as he pulled in and out, my desire already building again. I wrapped my arms around his neck and held on as he sped up, my breathing labored as I fought against the slow burn he was building.

"Lo," I moaned over and over. I threaded my fingers through his hair and leaned forward, resting my forehead against his forehead.

"Open your eyes. I wanna watch you cum." I bit my lip and opened my eyes, drowning in Lo's dark green eyes that were filled with desire and lust.

"Logan," I called as he slammed into me, teetering on the edge of oblivion. "I… I love… Logan… Logan," I chanted over and over. He grabbed my hair and gently tugged my head back and rained kisses down my neck, sucking and nibbling. "Logan!" I screamed as my orgasm slammed into me as he bit my neck.

"You're mine. All mine." He pounded into me, taking everything I was giving, my heart included. "I love you, only you. Forever."

I pressed a kiss to his lips, gently sucking on his bottom lip and he groaned low as his release came, filling me full. "Son of a bitch," he groaned, wrapping his arms around me, holding me close. "Every time better than the last," he whispered.

I rested my head on his shoulders and closed my eyes. This was what I always wanted. No matter the problem or obstacles we face, Lo and I were going to be there for each other. I had finally found a love that wasn't going to fade.

———

Chapter 13
Lo

"Why the hell am I always the one you send over there when this kid fucks up? Why can't you send Demon, or hell, anyone else? I'm sick of dealing with this fucking kid."

We were all gathered around the table, church winding down as I took care of the final little piece of business we needed to take care of. Leo's nephew had been causing problems again, and it was time that shit got nipped in the butt. "You're the only one I have available right now, Slider. Everyone is either working in the shop or dealing with Assassin bullshit."

"Fucking bullshit."

"Hey, just think of it this way. King made me watch out for Gwen, and now her ass is mine." Gambler sat back in his chair, a smug look on his face.

"Trust me, I don't fucking want this kid's mom. She is the complete opposite of me. It's amazing that Leo and she are related."

"He's fucking right. She's got nerd written all over her. I mean, she works at the library. How much more of a nerd could she be?" Hammer laughed.

"You're just pissed she's smarter than you, Ham, although that don't take much," Gravel grumbled, walking through the door. It was about time he showed up to church. The only reason he decided to show up today was because Meg had insisted taking Ethel to chemo and locked Gravel out of the house.

"She's not geeky, it's just... fuck, I don't know what the hell it is. I've barely spoken two words to her, and she treats me like I'm the fucking plague."

"Ah, so now we know what the problem is. Slider has finally found the one woman who can resist his charm. It's about fucking time you have to work for something in your life." Rigid stood up and grabbed his keys off the table.

"I don't want her, so I don't need to work for shit. She can hate me all she wants."

"Well, just get over there and straighten out this fucking kid. He's running around spouting shit that needs to be shut down." Leo's nephew was running around, acting like he was the drug runner in town, getting his ass into shit that he couldn't get out of. In the past three weeks, we had to get him out of four different binds that wouldn't have happened if he had just kept his mouth shut. "This is the last time I want this shit happening. I've had a talk with Leo, and he agrees that something needs to be done." Leo had been out of town more than here. Apparently, his plan of opening up shop in Rockton had been put on hold since it seemed like everything in Chicago was self-imploding. "Squash it, Slider. I don't fucking care what this chick does or doesn't do to you. Your issue is the kid, not the mom."

"Well, that's easy to say, but I'm pretty sure the kid's mom is going to have an issue with how I want to pound this kid into the ground and break his legs so he fucking stops." I had never seen Slider so irritated before. Especially over a kid and his mom.

"Then you're going to have to find a different way to handle this. Use your head, not your fists."

Slider stalked out of the room, mumbling about guns and where to hide a body. "Yo, Roam, I want you with Slider. Make sure he keeps his fucking head on straight." Roam nodded, shoving his phone in his pocket and followed Slider without protest. I wish all the brothers were like Roam. The fucker barely talked and always did what I asked him. Although he did have a tendency to disappear for weeks at a time; hence his name, Roam.

"What time were the girls supposed to be done at the salon?" Rigid asked.

"Not a fucking clue. I'm still confused why the hell they're even there right now. Meg has been going on and on about how she needs to have Gwen and Marley do a run through of everyone's hair to make sure they know what they are doing the night of the wedding. I told her she didn't need her hair done up, I'd rather her look like she does every day, and all I got was a pillow to the face and told to shut up. I wasn't about to ask her this morning what time they were going to be done."

"Yo, you fuckers done in here?" Troy was standing in the doorway, leaning against the frame.

"Yeah, what's up?" Rigid asked.

I knew why he was here, and I knew none of these fuckers were going to be happy. "We've got an appointment in half an hour. We need to fucking go. Y'all's fucking meetings take forever, talk more than fucking women," Troy said.

"What the hell do you mean, appointment? I can't remember the last time I had a fucking appointment." Rigid, Gambler, and Demon all looked confused as fuck. This was all my fault, but I would basically do anything to make Meg happy. But the thing of it was, she hadn't even asked me to do this. I just knew this was something she wanted.

"What the fuck is the appointment for?" Demon demanded.

"I can't believe you didn't fucking tell them," Troy laughed. "Oh, this is going to be good. I've at least had a week to get used to the idea. You tell them, I don't feel like getting my ass kicked today." Troy pulled out one of the empty chairs and sat down, crossing his arms over his chest.

All three guys turned to me, and I knew I had to fucking tell them. Although, maybe I could just knock them all out and drag them to the tux place. Yes, I was going to wear a fucking tux for the wedding, and I was going to make all these fuckers wear one, too. Misery loves company. "Get your asses up, we're going to the fucking tux shop."

"What the fuck! Gwen said Meg wasn't making us wear fucking tuxes. We could wear our cuts. I call fucking bullshit." Gambler stood up, slamming his chair back into the wall.

"That is what Meg said. But I know what the hell Meg wants. She wants us all in tuxes, but she knew you assholes wouldn't do it. So, I'm gonna surprise her, and I'm gonna make you fuckers do it."

"Hey! What about Slider? I'm not doing it unless he does." Fucking Rigid thought he had found an out, but he was wrong.

"Slider went yesterday and got fitted."

"Son of a bitch! You wait until Cyn and I get married, you're wearing a fucking speedo down the goddamn aisle." Rigid stormed from the room, pulling his phone out of his pocket. "Don't fucking let Meg know!" I knew he was texting Cyn about it, which was fine, as long as she didn't tell Meg.

"I can't believe how fucking whipped you are," Demon said, shaking his head as he flipped his phone over and over in his hand.

"I'm not fucking whipped; I'm just giving Meg something I know she wants but won't ask because she knows I'll fucking hate it. I'm not happy about it either, but I know the look on her face when she sees me will be worth it."

I glanced over at Gambler, who had his nose buried in his phone, his fingers typing furiously. Both Rigid and Gambler ran to their women when they had a problem. I would say they were each a bit whipped also. "If you put me in anything that is pink or purple, I will break both of your arms and steal your woman and her dog." Demon strode out of the room, shaking his head. "All of you are whipped assholes," he mumbled.

"Well, that was entertaining," Troy laughed.

"Get in the fucking truck, fuckers. Let's get this shit done and then I have something else to do." The second stop was also a surprise for Meg, but this stop I knew everyone else was going to like.

Meg

"Holy fuck, I look like Pipi Longstocking. What the hell did you do to me?"

"Relax, I already know what I'm going to do with your hair."

"Then why the hell do I look like Pipi instead of a sexy, ravishing beauty." The girls and I were gathered at the salon, going over wedding hair and plans. My ass was planted in Gwen's chair, and at the moment, I was having a mini freak out over what she was doing to my hair. "I need to look like a princess." I might also be slightly intoxicated. Slightly.

"Would you stop it," Gwen scolded, knocking my hand out of the way. "The wedding is less than two weeks away, and you've managed to go this long without being a bridezilla, don't start now." She unraveled the braids she had twisted my hair into, and my hair fanned out on my shoulders in big waves. "The day of 'I do' will be a better curling job, but this will do for today. My plan is to make you Meg on steroids."

"What the hell is that supposed to mean?" Cyn asked, sitting in the chair next to me. Marley was working on her hair, piling it up and making it cascade down the back. "Are you going to pump her up?" Cyn flexed her arms and talked like the Terminator.

"Big hair gets you closer to Jesus," Jackie called from the bathroom. Marley had just finished her hair, and she was admiring it in the mirror. "Although I think that's a southern thing."

"It is. I have a cousin down south who has the biggest hair I have ever seen. I swear it's full of all the lies and secrets she tells. Evil bitch." Jackie stuck her head out of the bathroom, and we all looked at Gwen. "What? She tried stealing my boyfriend when she came to visit."

"The gay one?" Cyn asked.

"Wait, a gay boyfriend? I feel like I've missed so much," Jackie gasped.

"No, not the gay one. Dylan was before the gay one. We were both seven and damn Alicia came up to visit and tried stealing him away. Thank God Dylan had some taste and didn't fall for her. Plus, he realized she lived over five hundred miles away. Definite deal breaker."

"Shit, Guy, is here, I don't have time to hear about the gay boyfriend." Jackie dug her phone out of her pocket and put the phone to her ear. "I'll be right out," she mumbled into the phone. "You're telling me all about the gay boyfriend at the wedding, I won't forget," she said, pointing her finger at Gwen.

"Oh great, I'm getting married, and you're looking forward to talking to Gwen about her gay boyfriend. I see where I rate."

"Oh, please. You finally got the fairytale ending, I couldn't be happier for you." A car honked its horn, and Jackie sighed, and bent over to pick up her purse. "And here I was all ready to jump his bones with my banging new hair, and all I want to do now is rip his nuts off for honking the damn horn at me. Later, girls." Jackie waved and flitted out of the salon, yelling at Guy as soon as she opened the front door.

"You don't really think she's going to rip his balls off, do you?" Marley asked. We all spun around and faced the window. Jackie was opening the passenger door, ranting and raving at Guy, who was just silently sitting there, waiting for Jackie to shut up. I had seen them like this so often, I knew what was going to happen next.

Jackie's arms were flailing and swinging around as she yelled, pointing from the shop and the truck. I could only imagine what she was saying. She finally stopped screaming and just sat there looking at Guy. He leaned over, wrapped his arms around her and kissed the living hell out of her. Jackie wrapped her arms around him, and you could see the fight drain out of her. Guy knew exactly how to handle Jackie. They had been together for so long, it was a wonder they didn't finish each other's sentences.

"Aw, I've always loved the way Guy handles Jackie. He lets her go off and then he just loves her."

"That's how King is with you, Meg," Gwen said, spinning me back around to face the mirror.

"Excuse me, I am not like Jackie. I don't go all crazy, psycho, mad on Lo."

Gwen grabbed a curling iron and a brush and started curling my hair. "No, but you do go all crazy Meg on him, and he just stands back and lets you be you. It's sweet."

"Perfect example," Marley said, "that big ass bed you and Cyn broke. King just calmly came down to the furniture shop, paid for the overpriced bed and then I'm betting proceeded to have crazy, wild monkey sex in it with you."

"Or, when you punched Hunter in the balls at that college thingy with Remy. I still would have paid to see that," Cyn mumbled.

The girls kept going on about all the crazy stuff I had done, (there was a lot), but all I did was sit there and realize Lo did put up with me. Plus, he didn't even seem to be annoyed by it. I remember when I was married to Hunter, whenever I tried to be funny or, well, just be me, he always rolled his eyes or told me to grow up. Lord knows I didn't act my age but was there really anything wrong with that. Life is too short to be all stuck up and acting like a ninety-year-old.

"Are we still dying your hair today?" Gwen asked.

"If we have time." I glanced at the clock and saw it was only one o'clock. "I think Lo said he had something to do today and wouldn't be back until tonight, so I say yes to dying my hair, that is unless you have plans with Gambler."

"Nope, he texted me about an hour ago and said the same thing. Not to expect him until tonight." She gathered all my hair and piled it on top of my head. "You want to stay with the same color or try something different?"

"Can we do different, but not too different? I am getting married in thirteen days. I probably shouldn't have bright purple hair, plus it might clash with my dress."

"I know exactly what I can do. I got some new colors in the other day, and I've been dying to try them." Gwen disappeared into the backroom, mumbling under her breath.

"I know what she has planned, and it's going to look amazing. Although it might take some time." Marley grabbed a couple of bobby pins and pushed them into Cyn's hair, securing her work of art into place. She had managed to pile all of Cyn's jet black hair on top of her head with loose pieces framing her face and stuck pretty purple flowers all over her hair. She looked amazing.

"Holy shit, I look hot," Cyn laughed. "I better send a picture to Rigid. I'm sure I'll mess it up before I see him tonight." Cyn grabbed her phone out of her purse and started having her own mini photoshoot before handing the phone to Marley and had her take pictures also.

"Okay, here we go." Gwen came walking out of the back room, pushing a cart filled with all sorts of bottles and bowls.

"Uh, is that all for me?" The last time I had my hair professionally dyed, the chick had only used two bowls and a couple of bottles, Gwen had at least six bowls and ten bottles.

"Yup, all for you. This is going to look amazing on you."

"What exactly are you going for?" Gwen parked the cart in between Cyn and I and pulled on a pair of rubber gloves.

"Have you ever seen a picture of the galaxy?"

Weird question, but who was I to question weird, I had a tendency to be weird all the time. "Um, yeah."

"You know how it's black, but then it's kind of like rainbow-ish?"

"I'd say you're going for more of an oil look. You know, when there is a puddle on the ground that had oil mixed in it, it's all swirly and rainbow-ish? I'd say that." Marley started getting everything set up, and my nerves hit me. I couldn't remember the last time I had gotten nervous about dying my hair. I think it was the fact that whatever they did with my hair, that was what I was going to look like when I got married. Galaxy, oil, rainbow-ish hair as I walked down the aisle and took pictures in. Oy.

"Um, do you think this is a good idea? I mean, maybe we should just stick to my–" Gwen spun me away from the mirror and put a finger to my lips. "I lick, you've been warned."

She quickly pulled her finger away and gave me a dirty look. "Trust us. Marley and I had no plans to let you walk down the aisle looking like rainbow bright. Now, let the fun begin." Gwen grabbed a cape and snapped it over me. "Cyn, grab her another wine cooler. I think she's losing her buzz."

Cyn gingerly stood up, handing me her phone. "Pick which one I should send to Rigid."

"You took almost fifty pictures." I scrolled through them, most of them the same except for small details. She grabbed a wine cooler from the fridge and handed it to me.

"I know. I couldn't help it; my hair looks good." I handed her back her phone and twisted open the bottle. "Drink one for me. I swear now that I can't drink, I crave wine coolers like they were water."

I chugged down half the bottle and wiped my mouth with the back of my hand. "Don't worry, in five months we'll do a girl's night after you push that baby out, and we'll have a good time."

"Okay, are you ready?" Marley and Gwen both had rubber gloves on, and both had a bowl with different colors in them. They each picked up a hair dye brush painter thing and looked at me, excitement on their faces.

"I'm ready, but if you fuck this up, I get to dye both of your hair." They looked at each other and shrugged their shoulders. But I had a little something up my sleeve. "With… box dye." The color drained from both of their faces, and they knew I was serious. Gwen and Marley always lectured me about using boxed hair dye, but it was just so damn convenient.

They both got to work, each painting different colors on my hair. It felt like it was random placement, but I knew they had a plan.

I finished off my drink and closed my eyes, listening to the girls chit chat. My mind kept going back to what Lo was doing that was going to keep him out till after dinner. He still hadn't told me the secret he was keeping from me, and it felt like he was just adding another secret to the pile.

Well, he had another thing coming. As soon as he got home, I was going to find out what both of the secrets were. If he didn't, I was really going to go crazy.

———

Chapter 14
Lo

"All right, you know the drill. No submerging in water, no direct sun, yadda yadda yadda," Buck, the tattoo artist, said as he finished wrapping up my side. I had finally gotten the bird Buck had drawn up months ago.

Rigid was on the other side of me getting his neck tattooed with a colorful peacock feather and Cyn's name underneath it. "You about done?" I asked, pulling my shirt on over my head. I grunted as I lifted my arms, the skin on my side pulling tight. I hadn't realized how big the fucking bird was until Buck had started working on it.

"Probably fifteen more minutes," the girl said who was working on him.

Troy and Gambler were both sitting in the waiting area, bullshitting with the other tattoo artist. Troy hadn't gotten a tattoo, but Gambler started an outline of a pin-up girl on his right shoulder. By the time he would be done with it, it was going to look exactly like Gwen.

"I'm gonna call Meg and let her know we'll be home in half an hour," I called, walking out the front door. I pulled my phone out of my pocket and swiped her name.

"Handsome, I miss you," she slurred into the phone. Apparently, when Meg got her hair done, she also got drunk.

"Hey, babe. You sound like you're having fun," I laughed.

"Tons, Loads. But you're not here. Do you know you're not here?"

"Yeah, I know I'm not there, although wish I was."

"Then get your ass home to me."

"I'm working on it. We're just wrapping up here and then we should be home."

"Okay. Oh, did you happen to notice I'm drunk? I blame Cyn. She's making me drink her share of the wine coolers because she… is having… a baby. Did you know that?"

I fucking loved when Meg got drunk. Her craziness escalated to a twenty and she cracked me the fuck up. Not to mention it made her horny as hell. "I did know she was pregnant, babe."

"Oh, well, she's pregnant." I threw my head back laughing. Meg was in rare form tonight. It should make it interesting for the plans I had for her later. "I gotta go. I need ice cream and Marley is demanding pizza."

"Okay. I'll see you in a bit. I love you."

"Hmm, I love you too, Logan," she sighed. I hung the phone up and shoved it back in my pocket. Son of a bitch, Meg was one of a kind. And she was all mine.

Meg

"How many of those have you had?"

"Eight. No, wait, nine. Possibly fifteen." I honestly had no clue. I think I had five at the salon, but then I also had a couple of beers, so my count was off.

"How do you go from eight to fifteen?" Marley laughed. She was standing behind the bar, trying to tie a cherry stem in a knot with just her tongue. I think she just wanted to eat a shit ton of cherries.

"Easily. eight, nine, eleven, ten, thirteen…" Wait, where did twelve go? Shit, I was beyond wasted. How in the hell had this happened? "Fifteen." Yup. Wasted.

"What do you think King is going to do when he sees how wasted we got his fiancée?" I laid my head down on the bar and pushed my empty bottle away. I think I was done for the night. Maybe.

"He thinks it's funny when she gets drunk, and he probably thinks like Rigid, he'll get laid. It's a win-win for him." Cyn grabbed my empty bottle and chucked it in the garbage. "How long until the pizza gets here? I'm starving." She walked around the bar and sat down on the stool next to me.

"Didn't you just eat all the leftover chicken from dinner last night?" I mumbled.

"It was only two pieces, it was nothing. Although I think the barbecue sauce that was on it is giving me heartburn." She rubbed her belly and grimaced.

"As soon as Gambler gets here, we are headed over to Paige's to hang out. I think she was getting Chinese, so we'll pass on the pizza," Gwen said, sitting down on the other side of me.

"Perfect, more pizza for me," Marley grinned, a stem hanging out of her mouth. "I seriously don't know how people do this."

"You do know the reason why guys are like that is because they think it shows how well the woman is with her tongue, right?" Gwen laughed, picking up a cherry and popped it in her mouth.

"Well, I may not be able to tie this little fucker into a knot, but Troy can attest that I'm good with my tongue." Marley twisted the cap back on the cherries and stuck them back in the fridge. "I might also have a gut ache from the ten plus cherries I just ate."

"Pizza is here," Gwen called when there was a loud knock on the door. Marley darted out from behind the bar and grabbed her purse on the way to the door. That woman had a serious obsession with pizza.

"Oh," she gasped as she opened the door. We all turned on our stools and saw Troy standing at the door holding the pizzas.

"I should have known you would have ordered pizza. Especially after King told me how tanked Meg was." Marley stepped back as Troy, and all the guys walked through the door.

Gambler grabbed a box off the top of the pile as he walked past Troy and opened the box, grabbing a slice. "Hey! We're going to Paige's for dinner," Gwen scolded.

He walked over, holding the piece up to her mouth and she took a huge bite. "One slice isn't going to fill me up, doll." She slapped him on the chest, and he pulled her into his arms. "You ready?" He set the box on the bar and shoved the rest of the slice into his mouth.

"Yup." Gwen grabbed her purse off the bar, hitching it over her shoulder and grabbed Gambler's hand. "Later," she called as Gambler pulled her out the door.

I spun the box around to me, opening it and grabbed a huge, cheesy slice out. "Oh, sweet Jesus," I moaned after I took a huge bite and watched Lo saunter over to me.

"Scale of one to ten, how drunk are you, babe?" He asked as he grabbed a slice from the box.

"Seven, possibly eight," I mumbled with my mouth full. I had been trying to keep it around a five, but one wine cooler led to another and here I was, shoveling my face full of pizza and trying not to fall off of my bar stool.

"Bring it down to a six in the next hour. I've got something I need to show you in my room."

I leaned forward, resting my hand on his shoulder to keep me from falling over. "I've seen everything you've got, handsome, and I am more than ready to go to our room now. Drunkenness be damned."

"Eat up and start drinking water," Lo laughed, signaling to Turtle, who was now behind the bar serving up drinks.

"Aye aye, captain," I mumbled, taking another huge bite.

Lo grabbed the stool next to me and sat down as he grabbed the water and glass of whiskey Turtle set on the bar. He turned to hand me my water and grimaced as he twisted. "What's wrong?"

Lo reached out, grabbing my hair and ran it through his fingers. "New hair?"

"Yeah. Gwen and Marley did it."

"I like it."

"Well, that's good. Now, answer my question. What's wrong?"

"I'll show you when we get to our room, babe." He tossed the shot of whiskey back and lined it up on the bar for another one. "Eat."

Well, now I didn't feel like eating because I wanted to know what the hell was wrong with Lo. "Not until you tell me why–"

"Eat," he ordered. I grabbed another slice of pizza, shoving half of it in my mouth and chew while I glared at him. "Even pissed off you're hot as hell."

I grabbed my glass of water, washing down the pizza and slammed it down on the counter. "You're killing my buzz."

"You'll get over it." Lo grabbed another slice from the box, folded it in half and ate it in two bites. "As soon as we get to the room I'll show you, promise."

"Hmm, you also promised to tell me the other secret you're keeping from me, but that hasn't happened yet."

"Because you don't need to know what that one is. The less you know, the safer you'll be." He grabbed the refilled shot Turtle set down and tossed it back.

I grabbed the box with half a pizza still in it and my glass of water. "I'll eat in our room. Let's go." I marched down the hallway, looking behind me to make sure Lo was following. He stopped to talk to Hammer and Demon, who were starting a game of pool. He had a beer in one hand and his eyes on me as he talked. "Five minutes, Logan," I warned, turning around and kept walking to Lo's room. I knew it drove him crazy when I called him Logan, so hopefully he hurried his ass up.

I balanced the pizza box on top of my glass of water, which, by the way, was not easy with me being in the eight range, and opened the bedroom door, stumbling in. After I tossed the pizza box on the bed and set my glass on the bedside table, I stripped off my pants and shirt, throwing them in the direction of the hamper and grabbed one of Lo's shirts out of the dresser. I pulled it over my head and flopped down on the bed. I grabbed Lo's pillow, shoving it under my head and curled up on my side and watched the door, waiting for Lo.

He had a lot of explaining to do. I could tell that he was hurt when he grimaced, and I noticed Lo held his side when he stood up. Something happened when he was out with the guys today, and I wanted to know what. I just hoped that it had nothing to do with the Assassins. In my head, I had been secretly wishing that they would just up and disappear. Then I wouldn't have to worry about them anymore.

I heard footsteps coming down the hall, hoping it was Lo and not someone else. I had left the door open and was laid out in only a shirt and panties. "Babe," Lo growled, leaning against the door frame. "Please tell me you've got shorts on under that shirt." I swallowed hard and decided silence was my best bet. He walked into the room, shutting the door behind him and pulled his shirt up over his head, and I gasped when I saw the huge bandage that was covering his side.

"What the hell happened?" I asked, sitting up on my knees. Lo turned away from me, peeling off the tape and tossed the bandage in the garbage. "Lo, I swear, if you're going to show me a knife wound or something, I might puke."

Lo laughed, shaking his head and turned to me.

"Holy fuck," I gasped, covering my mouth with my hand. "That's… that's…"

"That's the tattoo I've wanted to get for a couple of months. You were my caged bird who was afraid to fly when I met you."

Tears welled up in my eyes, and all I could do was stare at it. The bird was so intricately drawn but yet so simple. The wings were spread high, flying with free abandon and my name was scrawled underneath. "That's my name."

Lo nodded his head and looked down at the tattoo. "Yeah. He had your name on the wing before, but it felt like I was trying to hide your name. I don't hide you in my life, babe, I'm not going to hide your name."

"You're crazy," I cried. "You put my name on your body and everyone can see it. Well, when your shirt is off they can." I scooted further to the end of the bed, trying to get a better look at the tattoo. He stepped forward, and I put my hands on him, framing the new tattoo. "This was the important thing you had to do with the guys today?" I asked, looking up at him.

"Yeah. Rigid has been bitching he needed to get some ink done, so I went with. Gambler also got some ink, too."

"I love it." His hand reached up, cupping my face and he leaned down and placed a kiss on my lips.

"I'm glad. Now take that shirt off and get under the covers."

"So bossy," I whispered, reaching for the hem of my shirt.

"And you like it." He stepped back, popping open the button on his jeans and slid the zipper down. He definitely had a point, I thought, as I pulled my shirt over my head and tossed it on the floor. "How much did you miss me today, babe?" He pulled his jeans down his legs, stepping out of them and stood at the edge of the bed.

I licked my lips as my gaze traveled over his rock hard body and the impressive bulge that was dying to get out of his boxers. "Um, a little bit." I was trying to be coy, but I knew that wasn't going to last long before I would be begging for him to take me.

"Just a little?"

"Maybe some."

"Is some more than a little?" Lo asked, grabbing his cock, stroking it through his boxers.

My mouth went dry as I watched his hand. "Yes." I reached forward, wanting to help Lo but he batted my hand away and stepped back.

"Not before you tell me how much you missed me, babe."

"Not fair. I'm drunk."

"That doesn't mean anything besides the fact you're horny as hell. Tell me how much you missed me."

He was right about the horny part. Damn, this man knew me well. "I missed you, now come here so I can stop missing you."

"Hmm, much better." He pulled down his boxers, letting them fall to his feet. His hand stroked his cock, but he didn't step closer to me. "Take off your bra and panties."

"Are you going to come closer if I do?"

"Only one way to find out. Do it." I pulled down my panties then sat down on my ass, pulling them off. I reached behind me, unclasping my bra and tugged it down my arms. "You got what you want, now give me what I want."

"And what is it that you want, babe?" His hand kept stroking his cock, up and down, a drop of cum seeping from the tip.

"You. I want you." Lo stepped forward, and I scooted to the end of the bed, my feet touching the floor. I spread my legs, and he stepped between them, his hand stroking his cock by my mouth.

"Open," he growled. I glanced up at him, and his head was turned down, his eyes filled with desire as he watched me, waiting. I put my hands on his hips and slowly opened my mouth. I leaned forward, my tongue licking the drop of cum off the tip and he moaned as I opened my mouth and slid him into my lips. He moved his hands, threading them through my hair as I worked him down my throat, then slowly started bobbing up and down, my tongue caressing his hard shaft.

"Fucking hell," he gasped as he hit the back of my throat and I swallowed, sucking his dick in even more. His hands gripped my head and slowly lifted me up. I let Lo take control as my mouth stayed around his cock as he thrust his dick in and out of my lips. "You're mine. All mine," he moaned. He pulled completely out, his cock bobbing in between us. I reached up, wiping my mouth with the back of my hand. "Lay back on the bed." I scooted back to the middle of the bed and laid down, waiting for Lo.

He climbed up the bed and crawled up to me, pressing kisses up my body the whole way. "Are you ready for me?" He asked his lips right above my pussy.

"I'm always ready for you," I purred as he parted the lips of my pussy, his tongue zeroing in on my clit.

"I'll never get enough of your taste, babe. You drive me crazy." His mouth was on me, licking and tasting all at once. I bucked my hips, grinding my pussy into his face, unable to control myself. Lo knew just what to do to drive me crazy. I spread my legs, digging my heels into the bed, and I clutched the blanket in my fists trying to control my moans and screams.

"Lo," I gasped as he nipped my clit with his teeth, a tremor rocking through my body "More."

He sat back on his heels, wiping his mouth with the back of his hand, and I whimpered at the loss of his touch. "You'll get more when you're on top of me, riding my dick."

"Um." Shit, I hated being on top. It felt good, every position with Lo felt good, but I was just so on display when I was on top.

"Damn it, Meg. I can see that shit swirling around in your head again." He grabbed my hands and pulled me up. "Tell me."

I chewed on my lip and turned my head, not looking at him. "You see *everything* when I'm on top."

"I see everything all the time, Meg. When I take you in the shower, when I bend you over the bed, especially when I lay you out on the bed and have my way with you. I like everything."

I wrapped my arms around his neck and pressed my forehead against his forehead. "Except gravity takes over when I'm on top. I'm thirty-six years old, soon to be thirty-seven. Things are not where they use to be."

"Fucking bull shit," he growled, wrapping his arms around me and flipped us over, my body on top of him. "Fucking ride me."

"No. I don't want to." I tried sliding off, but he grabbed my arms and jackknifed off the bed, wrapping his arms around me.

"Get the bull shit out of your head and stop thinking. No one is in this room but me, so just stop. I love every curve and inch of your body. I especially love it when you're on top, riding the hell out of my dick."

"I just think–" He slammed his lips down on my mouth, cutting off any thought that I had. His tongue swept into my mouth, his fingers delved into my hair holding me still. He kissed the hell out of me, making all of my doubts and, as Lo liked to call it, bullshit melt away.

"Ride me," he growled against my lips.

I opened my eyes and looked at the man I loved and sighed. I took a deep breath and pushed on his shoulders, "Sit back and enjoy the ride." This was what Lo wanted, and I was going to give it to him.

He pressed a kiss to my lips then reclined back on his arms and watched me, waiting. "Show me what you've got."

"You better be thankful I love you," I mumbled.

"I thank God every day you're mine, babe. Every day." And that right there was why I loved this man.

I straddled his waist and slowly lowered myself down, his rock hard dick slowly entering me. I put my hands on Lo's chest and closed my eyes when I was fully seated on him. "Best feeling in the world," he growled, grabbing my hips, his fingers digging into me as he flexed his fingers.

I dropped my chin to my chest and closed my eyes. Nothing compared to being connected to Lo. He was the piece that I was missing all these years. I lifted my hips up, slowly raising off and moaned at the loss of him. "I love you," I gasped as I slid back down. I sat up, arching my back and leaned back, my hands grasping his thighs to hold myself up. I rocked my hips up and down, each movement driving me closer to the edge of madness.

"Take it, babe. Take it all," he growled low.

"Yes," I chanted over and over. Every time I lifted up, Lo thrust up as I came back down. "I need you," I moaned.

"Take it, I'm yours."

I threw my body forward, landing on his chest, face to face. My eyes connected with his and I whispered, "I love you."

He grabbed my ass and thrust up, hammering into me. "I love you, too," he moaned. He kissed me hard, his tongue invading my mouth. I ground my hips down with every thrust of his hips, searching for my release.

"More," I gasped. Lo thrust one more time, his hand reaching between us and flicked my clit. My orgasm slammed into me, throwing me over the edge. His hands grabbed my ass and thrust hard, finding his own release. My pussy milked his cock as my desire rolled through me. He grunted low, grinding his cock into me, and I felt his cum shoot into me.

I collapsed on top of him, satisfied and completely wrung out. "God." Lo's body shook underneath me, but I didn't have the energy to move. "Why are you laughing? You just completely wrecked me, and you're laughing."

"You can just call me Lo, babe. No need to call me God."

"Ha, ha, you're so funny," I muttered into his neck.

His laughing stopped, and his hand caressed my ass. "I fucking love you, Meg. I'm fucking balls deep inside you, and you still manage to make me laugh."

Hmm, what could I say, I was a comedian. "You're welcome," I sighed.

"You gonna sleep, babe?"

"Yeah."

"You wanna get cleaned up first?"

"No," I mumbled, half asleep, relaxing into his body.

"I think I might need to, though."

I opened my eyes and looked up at Lo. "What?" Whenever he asked me if I wanted to clean up or not, he let me do what I wanted.

"I think my foot is in the pizza you brought in."

"Oh fuck," I laughed, looking over my shoulder. Sure as shit, his foot and half of his leg were covered in pizza. "How the hell did you have sex like that?"

"I didn't fucking notice it until we were done. Now, all I smell is pizza, and my leg is sticking to the blanket.

I planted my face in his chest and busted out laughing. Only this would happen to me. Phenomenal sex ends with the best orgasm of my life and Lo's leg in a pizza. "Still the best sex of my life," I howled, laughing.

Lo grabbed my ass, grinding his dick into me and laughed. "Damn right, babe."

———————

Chapter 15
Lo

"What the fuck is that smell?" I was walking down the hallway to the common room with my arm around Meg's shoulders. I looked over at her, and she had her hand plugging her nose, and she was breathing through her mouth.

"Oh fuck. I bet Marley is trying to make breakfast," she wheezed.

"That's breakfast?" I asked, slowing my pace, not sure if I wanted to go any further. "It smells like a fucking tire fire was roaring in the kitchen with the slight smell of burnt bacon."

"You just paint a picture with your words, Lo. I can imagine a pile of tires burning in the kitchen with Marley roasting bacon over the flames," Meg giggled, grabbing my hand and pulling me the rest of the way to the kitchen.

The smell worsened with each step and sinking back into bed with Meg looked better and better.

"Turn back now," Demon mumbled, walking past us. "I don't know how a woman that gorgeous has no ability to cook. It was just water." Demon ran his fingers through his hair, shaking his head.

"It's like we're walking up on an accident scene," Meg mumbled.

"It was just a pot of water with a little vinegar in it. I was trying to make poached eggs for everyone," Marley wailed from the kitchen.

Meg glanced at me, and her eyes were bugged out of her head. "Poached eggs?" she whispered. "She hasn't mastered toast, but she's trying poached eggs? What the hell is Marley smoking?"

Troy stalked out of the kitchen, and I smothered my laugh with the back of my hand. "Shush." Meg turned into my body, burying her laughter in my chest.

"You didn't call the fire department, did you?" Troy asked. He was wearing only boxers, and his hair was all over the place, and it looked like he had just woken up.

"Nah, man. Everything okay?" I peeked into the kitchen and saw Marley at the sink, vigorously scrubbing a pot.

Troy ran his fingers through his hair and stepped closer. "Water. Mother fucking water."

Meg's body was shaking against me, laughter racking her body. "Did she manage to make any coffee before she tried to burn the clubhouse down."

Meg slapped my chest and finally unburied her head, and looked up at me, a goofy grin on her face. "She can make coffee. Well, at least this one time she did."

"Laugh it up," Troy growled, "but you won't be laughing when I starve to death because Marley can't even cook a simple egg."

"Well, in her defense, poached eggs aren't exactly simple. I think a plain fried egg would have been her best bet to try to make. Where the hell did she even get the idea to make poached eggs?" Meg turned around, and I wrapped my arms around her, her back to my front.

"Fucking Bobby Flay. She was watching the Food Network last night and got the bright idea to make eggs benedict for breakfast this morning."

"Eggs Benedict? Holy hell. I barely ever make that. That's like super hard. Hollandaise sauce is nothing to sneeze at."

"Well, she didn't even get to the sauce part. She put water on to boil for the poached eggs and then she decided to bring me coffee."

"You lost me. How the hell did she burn the water then?" I asked.

"When she brought me the coffee, I didn't know that she had started the water. We started talking and then she brushed up against me and then one thing leads to another and the next thing I know, the fucking fire alarm is blaring, and I'm trying to get to the stove through a cloud of smoke."

"I think I know what Marley's problem is, Troy." Meg folded her arms over her chest and leaned back into me.

"Tell me. I need to fix this. I. Am. Going. To. Starve."

"You're the problem. You keep distracting her. When she burns the pizza, where are you?"

"Well, if we're at home, usually in the kitchen with her."

"Doing what?"

"Um, well, you know."

Meg pointed her finger at him and shook her head. "Keep your damn hands off the woman for more than five seconds and I bet your problem will be solved."

"You need to leave your girl alone when she cooks, man, otherwise she's going to burn my God damn club down."

"I give up. I'm not meant to cook. I was made for pizza and cereal with the occasional pop tart thrown in which I always manage to burn." Marley walked out of the kitchen her shoulders slumped, looking utterly defeated.

"That's not true, Marley. We figured out what the problem is. Mr. Can't Keep His Hands To Himself. You need to stay away from Troy when you cook. He distracts the hell out of you." Meg walked over to Marley and draped her arm over her shoulders. "Troy is the problem."

"Wait. What… how… that…" Troy sputtered. "I'm not the one burning everything!"

"If you could keep your hands off of her for more than five minutes, there wouldn't be a problem."

"Yeah. She's right!" Marley said, pointing at Troy. "Every time I burn something it's because you grab me and have your way with me."

"I never hear you complain while I'm doing it," he growled.

"Well, that's because I can't think when you touch me," she scolded him. I shook my head, not believing that Meg was able to spin this onto Troy.

"*Lo Daze*," Meg mumbled.

"What the hell does King have to do with this?" Troy asked, just as confused as I was.

"Lo does the same thing to me. The second he touches me, I lose all train of thought and can only focus on him. You've got the *Lo Daze* except for not Lo," Meg said, turning to Marley and put her hands on her shoulders "Troy Daze. Doesn't have the same ring to it as *Lo Daze* does, though," Meg mumbled.

"This is ridiculous. I'm not keeping my damn hands off of you, Marley. If that means every damn meal I eat is going to be burnt, then so fucking be it. You're at least damn good at ordering pizza." Troy pushed Meg out of the way and wrapped Marley up in his arms.

Meg walked over to me and crossed her arms over her chest. "You're looking mighty smug, babe."

She looked up at me, a smile on her lips. "I just saved us from burnt breakfast, Lo. You should be damn happy, too."

I put my arm around her shoulders and pulled her to my side. "Good job. Although that means you gotta make breakfast now."

"I know. I'm used to being the one who always cooks." She brushed a kiss against my cheek and headed into the kitchen.

"We'll be out for breakfast later," Troy mumbled, as he and Marley headed down the hall, both of them unable to keep their hands off of each other.

"Oh, wow, what is that smell?"

"That was breakfast until your mom stepped in and fixed shit. What are you doing here?" I asked as Remy walked into the clubhouse.

"Mom told me about Ethel the other day. I tried calling her this morning to see if we could go over there, but she didn't answer. I figured I would just stop by and talk to her. Is that okay?" Remy asked, looking unsure about coming here.

I didn't want Remy to think he wasn't welcome here. He was going to start working in the garage next semester for work study in school, so I, of course, didn't mind him being here. I was just surprised to see him now. "You're good. You can come here anytime you want, you know that."

"Cool," he said, looking around, taking everything in. I suppose the common room of the clubhouse would look different to someone who had never spent time with an MC. It was basically a bar but more laid back.

"You drive here or did your dad drop you off?" Remy had been staying with his dad more since the whole locking down the clubhouse because of the Assassin bullshit.

"Dad dropped me off. He was going to go hit some golf balls with friends. I told him I would be back later." Of course, the asshole was hitting golf balls, what a fucking asshat.

"We can hit up Ma's after breakfast. You hungry?"

"Mom cooking?"

"Hell yeah," I smirked.

"Then I'm starving."

"Is that Remy I hear?" Meg asked, walking out of the kitchen wiping her hands on a kitchen towel.

"Hey, Mom. Dad dropped me off, I hope that's okay. I tried calling you this morning, but you didn't answer."

"I'm sorry, sweetie. I just woke up." She pressed a kiss to Remy's cheek and gave him a hug.

I really wanted to tell her she was a damn liar because we did not just wake up. Meg had first woken up three hours ago and proceeded to wake me up with an earth shattering blowjob that led into me eating her out and making her cum twice before I made her ride me again and then we came together. Then we fell asleep for another hour. But I guess I wouldn't say that. "You make coffee, babe?"

"Yeah, I'll grab you a cup. Sit with Lo, Rem. Breakfast will be ready in ten minutes. Marley was trying to make eggs benedict," Remy wrinkled his nose, grossed out, "but I think scrambled eggs and Canadian bacon is what I'll whip up."

"Sweet. Better than nasty poached eggs. Damn things are weird."

"Remy wants to swing by Ma's, Meg. I figured after breakfast we can hit up there and then maybe after we can go to the movies or something." I knew Meg had been missing spending time with Remy. It was just another reason why I needed to take care of the Assassin situation. Meg needed to spend time with her kid, but with not knowing what the next move from the Assassins was going to be, she had been trying to keep Remy out of everything.

"Could we?" she asked, surprised.

"Yeah, babe. Ain't got no clue what movies are playing, but you pick one, and we'll go."

"Yes!" she shouted and jumped into my arms. "That sounds perfect, Lo."

"Sweet. I'll check to see what movies are playing," Remy mumbled, pulling his phone out of his pocket as he walked over to one of the couches and plopped down.

"You're going to make this one of the best days I've had in a while," she laughed running her fingers through my hair.

"You deserve it. I feel bad you haven't had the time you need with Remy since you met me." Her life actually had been tossed upside down since she met me.

"It's not your fault, handsome. Plus, I know you're doing everything you can to make everything better."

I wrapped my arms around her and pressed her close. "I love you, babe. You need this."

"Hmm, I love you, too." She pressed a kiss to my lips, and I stepped back when she tried to deepen it.

"Kid," I said, nodding over her shoulder. "Make breakfast and then you can have the day with Remy."

"Alright, Lo. Best day ever, because I get to spend it with my two favorite guys." She turned to walk into the kitchen, and I grabbed her arm, throwing her off balance, leaving her with no choice but to wrap her arms around me.

"Every day with you is better than the last," I growled before I claimed her lips, not caring Remy was fifteen feet away.

I kissed her until she was breathless and she stumbled back, her eyes hooded and filled with desire. "You don't play fair," she whispered.

"I play for keeps, Meg. Nothing fair about that."

———————

Chapter 16
Lo

"Finish up setting up this string of lights, and then I'll grab the next strand."

Remy grabbed the lights out of my hand and headed to the front of the house to finish putting up the lights on the front porch of Ma's house.

We had been here for two hours, and it looked like it was going to be another hour before we got all of the lights set up. A half an hour after being here, Ma had started dropping hints that it was so close to Christmas, and her lights weren't up yet. Meg had volunteered Remy and me to get them set up while she stayed in the warm house chatting with Ma. I was coming to find out that Meg was one hell of a manipulator. It was a damn good thing I loved her.

We had plans to hit up the six o'clock show at the movie theater two towns over, so we weren't crunched for time, but setting up Christmas lights was not how I saw my Saturday playing out.

"You making my boy do all the work, handsome?" Meg walked out the back door and leaned over the railing of the back porch.

"Isn't that why people have kids? Put 'em to work?"

Meg laughed and brushed the hair out of her face. It was just under a week before Christmas, and it felt like winter had finally hit Wisconsin. "You should have a coat on. It's well below twenty degrees today."

She wrapped her arms around her middle and smiled down at me. "I already got one, Daddy Lo. I don't need another. Unless you're into the whole me calling you daddy thing. I read this book once, so hot. When he had her bent–"

"Babe, no. Not my thing," I cut her off.

Her smile spread across her lips, and I knew she was just fucking around with me. "You sure? Anything with you always seems to be hot. We could always try it later, Daddy," she whispered.

Her words went straight to my dick and wouldn't you know it, I was turned on as fuck, and there was no way for me to do anything about it. I shook my head and laughed, "How the hell did we go from me telling you to put a coat on, to you calling me daddy and giving me a hard-on?"

"Because I just have that effect on you. If I said hot dog just right, I bet I could make you hard." She crossed her arms over her chest and walked down the four steps and came to stand in front of me. "Hot dog," she whispered, wiggling her eyebrows.

"Naw, babe."

She leaned in closer, her lips by my ear. "Hot dog," she breathed out, her breath warm against my ear.

I wrapped my arms around her and pulled her close. "Maybe just a little. Try corn dog next time."

She busted out laughing, tossing her head back. "I think the only corn dog around here is you."

"You know you're going to pay for this later, right?"

"I hope so, Daddy," she whispered, pressing a kiss to my neck. She slipped out of my arms and looked over her shoulder as she walked to the front of the house. "You coming?"

"Not yet," I mumbled under my breath. I grabbed the last strand of lights and caught up to Meg. "Ma doing okay?" I asked, putting my arm around her shoulders.

"I think so. She's still the feisty woman that she was the first day I met her. Gravel called, so I decided to see what you boys were up to when she was talking to him."

"She say what time–" I stopped in my tracks and grabbed Meg, pulling her into my side. Remy was standing on the sidewalk in front of the house talking to someone. That someone was Big A.

"Lo, what the hell?" Meg asked, crossing her arms over her chest.

"Shush," I growled. I had no idea what the hell Big A was doing talking to Remy, but I knew I didn't want to surprise him. "Go back in the house and lock the front door."

Meg's eyes followed where I was looking. "Who the hell is talking to Remy?"

"House, now," I ordered.

"No," she said going toe to toe with me.

I kept my eyes trained on Remy and Big A, ready to make a move if Big A tried anything. "Meg." She finally sensed that something was wrong and backed down. "House. Lock it up."

"Lo, what about Remy?" She grabbed my arm and looked at Remy and Big A. Big A held his arm out, shaking hands with Remy and headed across the street and got into a dark blue sedan that was idling. Remy waved to Big A and headed up to the house.

I felt Meg move to walk to Remy, but I held her close, waiting for Big A to leave. "Listen this one fucking time, Meg. Don't move." I loved her hard-headedness, but sometimes I wanted to fucking duct tape her to a chair to make her listen to me.

Her body went solid, but she at least didn't struggle to get out of my arms. Big A pulled away from the curb and his eyes connected with mine as he tipped his head and drove off. Son of a bitch. He knew that I was here the whole time. He must have been watching Remy and me, and I didn't even fucking know it.

Remy came around the side of the house and stopped in his tracks when he saw Meg and I standing together. "Uh, everything okay?"

"I don't know," Meg mumbled. "Who were you talking to, Remy?"

"Um, he said his name was A. He was wondering about the neighborhood. He's thinking of moving in and wondered how safe it was around here."

"Son of a bitch," I cursed, running my hands through my hair. "He say anything else?"

"No. That was it."

"Lo, God dammit, tell me who the hell that was," Meg demanded, pulling out of my arms. She crossed her arms over her chest, waiting.

"It was Big A."

Meg's eyes got huge, and she gasped. "The Assassins?"

"Yeah, babe."

"What the hell was he doing talking to my son?" she demanded.

"Fuck if I know. He was probably trying to get info out of Remy."

"Um, you think I should know what the hell you're talking about?" Remy asked.

"Don't say hell," Meg scolded.

"Mom, tell me what is going on? I had no idea who that guy was, but you and King seem to know him." Remy crossed his arms over his chest, waiting for Meg or me to talk.

"I can't tell you everything that is going on, but you just need to know if you ever see that guy headed your way again, you need to get the hell out of dodge. He has a beef with the club, and he will do anything to settle the score."

"Settle what score?"

"It has to do with Cyn, hunny. Lo and the club helped Cyn, and that man doesn't like that they helped her," Meg added.

"So, someone is trying to hurt you guys, and now they might be trying to hurt me?" Fuck, I hated that it had come to this. I didn't want the bull shit from the club to touch Meg or Remy, but now it was knocking on their fucking door.

"No one is going to hurt you. I'm going to put a man on you. He'll keep watch and make sure nothing happens." I pulled my phone out of my pocket and pulled up Leo's number.

"Who are you going to have watch him? The club is spread thin already," Meg said, biting her fingernails. She was beyond worried, and I was going to do everything in my power to take that worry away from her.

"Leo. I know he has more men. He's dealing with some bull shit back in the city, but the Assassins are fucking with family now, and I'm not going to stand by and let it happen." I swiped Leo's name and put the phone to my ear. "Finish up the lights, Rem, and then we'll head to the movies."

Remy headed up the sidewalk, running his fingers through his hair, looking like he had the weight of the world on his shoulders. I had done that to him, and I was pissed off at myself.

"King, I didn't expect to hear from you today." Leo's voice came on the line, but my eyes were trained on Meg. She was pacing back and forth, mumbling under her breath.

"Shit just touched my ol' lady's family, and I do not like it. I need someone on her son at all times, but I'm spread thin."

"Say no more. I'll send two of my best men to watch her son. It's only right since you have been watching over Fayth for me."

"I appreciate it, Leo. I have no fucking clue as to which way this guy is going to go next."

"We'll get him. My men will be there by eight tonight. Can you keep an eye on him till then?"

I ran my hands through my hair and sighed, "Yeah. I got plans with them, although I don't know if we'll do them anymore."

"Don't let this fucker ruin your life, King. The second he thinks he's got you, that'll be it. Take your woman and her son out and act like everything is fine because it is. Big A isn't going to get what he wants." Leo's tone had changed, the threat evident that he wasn't going to put up with this anymore.

"Text me your men's numbers. I'll let them know where to go once they get into town."

"Will do, my friend. Enjoy your family." The line went dead, and I shoved the phone into my pocket. Enjoy my family. How the hell was I supposed to do that when I had no idea what the hell Big A was up to?

"Lo, what the hell is going on? The last you knew Big A was gone, you couldn't find him." Meg continued to pace back and forth, and I grabbed her, pulling her into my arms.

"We knew he was around, but we didn't know what he was up to. We still don't."

"Don't you think that maybe you should have told me that?"

"You know I can't tell you club business."

"When your club business walks up the steps of your mother's house and talks to my son, I think I have a right to know!" She spun out of my arms and dashed up the steps of the porch, the screen door slamming shut behind her.

"Fuck."

"She'll calm down, she always does." I whirled around at Remy's words, forgetting that he was still outside. "I'd be worried if she wasn't mad at you."

"Shouldn't that be the other way around?" I asked, walking over to Remy and picked up the end of the Christmas lights.

"No. At least not with my mom. That's how I knew she was going to divorce my dad. She stopped caring. Stopped fighting. That's also when she stopped being herself, too." Remy pulled the rest of the string out of my hands and hung it on the hooks that ran along the railing of the porch.

"How old were you when your parents divorced?"

"Twelve. Although they should have divorced long before that. Dad was an ass to Mom, and she just took it. Every year she got more and more sad."

This seemed like a lot of shit to deal with at twelve. Meg had told me her marriage had been shit but never really went into detail about it. "I'm sure your mom was just trying to do the best thing for you."

"I know. I don't blame either of them for what happened. They weren't supposed to be together. They are complete opposites and not in a good way either." He stepped back from the railing and wiped his hands on his jeans. "Is this it?"

"For today. I need to talk to your mom, and I don't want you being outside alone."

"I'm seventeen, King."

"It has nothing to do with how old you are. There's shit that's going on with the club that seems to be spilling over onto you and your mom. There's going to be two guys always with you until I take care of everything."

"Does it have to do with what happened to Cyn before?"

"That's where it started, but now it's blown up into something else completely. Just trust me to take care of you and your mom."

"My mom loves you, King. Don't mess it up." Remy walked into the house, and I turned around and leaned against the porch railing.

Life seemed to be going so well, but now everything appears to be going sideways, and I had no idea how to fix it.

Son of a bitch.

Chapter 17
Meg

"Meg, sit down and have a drink." Ethel pulled the tea out of the fridge and set it in front of me.

"I hate to break it to you, Ethel, but I think I need something a bit stronger than tea right now."

"I wasn't done yet, girl." She walked over to the cabinet above the sink and pulled down a bottle of vodka. "Everything goes with vodka, right?"

"As of right now it does," I smiled. She grabbed a tray of ice out of the freezer and two glasses from the cabinet. "Should I make one for Lo, or is he the reason you need a drink?"

"He's the reason, although it's not his fault. One of the Assassins was just out on your sidewalk talking to Remy."

"Oh no," Ethel gasped. She set the glasses and ice on the table and sat down next to me. "What the heck did Lo do?"

"Nothing. He didn't want to approach him. We walked around the house and saw Remy talking to Big A. My stomach dropped when Lo told me who he was." I grabbed two ice cubes and dropped them into my cup. "You know what gets me, Ethel? He knew."

"What do you mean he knew?"

"He was aware that the Assassins were in town, but he didn't tell me. This is what he has been hiding from me for weeks. I just knew something was going on, but he refused to tell me. He kept telling me it was club business, and he couldn't say." I dropped the other two ice cubes into Ethel's glass and grabbed the tea. Ethel put two healthy splashes of vodka into each of our glasses, and I topped them off with tea.

"Did Lo tell you when you two started dating that he couldn't tell you club business?"

"Well, yeah, but I didn't think it was a big deal back then."

"Did he say why he didn't tell you?"

I grabbed my glass and took a swig, grimacing as I set the glass down. Vodka was not my first choice in alcohol. "He's trying to keep me safe."

"And is he?"

"That's not the point, Ethel. Why is he keeping secrets from me?"

"Hunny," she reached out and rested her hand on mine. "They're not secrets. You have to realize that although Lo isn't part of a one percent club, there are still dangerous things that he does and deals with. And to him, not telling you about those dangerous things is his way of keeping you safe."

"How am I safe when the man who wants the whole club gone walked up your sidewalk and talked to my son?"

"What would you have done differently if you had known that the Assassins were in town? Would you have protected Remy any better than Lo did?"

"Well, no. But that's not the point either."

"Then tell me what the point is. Because I hear what you are saying, sweetie, but I don't think you understand the type of life that you are getting."

"I don't want secrets in my marriage. I tell Lo everything, I think he should be able to give the same to me."

Ethel grabbed her glass and sat back in her chair. "I agree. But," Oh Lord, I knew there was going to be a but in there. It had seemed that Ethel was siding with Lo. "does Lo know everything about your job?"

"Well, no, but it's not the same, Ethel."

She took a long drink from her glass and stood up. "Then you have to decide if you can live with things not being the exact same and the occasional secret kept from you. My son loves you, Meg, but you can't change the man he is. That club is a huge part of him, and if you can't handle the fact that club business stays club business, then I don't know how long you two will last. You're made for each other. You just need to let go and trust him completely." She walked out of the room, and I put my head in my hands.

I didn't know what to do. Yes, Lo had told me that club business stayed just that, but that was before when club business didn't have anything to do with me. Did I need to know the daily goings on of the garage and the strip club they were building? No. Did I need to know that there was some crazy man out there that might try to kill me and everyone I love? Yes.

"I didn't think our argument called for opening a bottle." I knew Lo was standing behind me, but I didn't turn around. I didn't know what to say anymore. He walked over to the table, grabbed the bottle and twisted the cap back on. "Remy said I should be worried if you stop talking to me. He said that's when you know you're done with someone, you stop fighting."

Oh, I had a lot of fight left in me, I just didn't know if I would be able to survive to the end. "He's a smart kid. He's all that I have, Lo." I lifted my head and looked him in the eye.

"You have me, Meg."

"The man who keeps secrets from me."

"One. One secret I kept from you. I can tell you right now, that most ol' ladies would know only half of what you know. Hell, most wouldn't even know a quarter of the shit that I tell you. So to me, one secret is nothing."

"It's something to me, Lo. One turns into two and before you know it, you have to think twice before you tell me anything because you can't keep track of the lies and secrets anymore."

"I have never once fucking lied to you," he thundered.

"How would I know?"

"Because I'm God damn telling you I haven't." I crossed my arms over my chest and looked away. "Look at me."

I shook my head, no, and I felt the tears threatening to fall. He stalked over to me and lifted my face to look up at him. "I want you safe, and if I need to keep one thing from you to keep you safe, then I will."

"I don't know how you thought not telling me that Big A was in town kept me safe. I was walking around blind, thinking that things were finally getting back to normal."

"And that is what I want for you. I don't want the shit from the club to touch you and make you worry, thinking that things aren't normal. I don't want fear and worry in your life. You have to trust me to give that to you."

"I don't like the secrets," I whispered.

Lo sighed, dropped my chin and grabbed the chair that Ethel had been sitting in. He flipped it around and sat down, straddling it. "You remember that night I got a phone call and had to deal with club shit late into the night?"

"Yeah. That's when you stopped telling me things."

Lo shook his head and looked up at the ceiling. "One thing, Meg. One damn thing that you are making into a huge deal."

"Because it's a big deal to me." I crossed my arms over my chest and glared at him.

"That night, Big A had broken into Gwen's shop and held her at gunpoint, giving her a message to give to me. He didn't hurt her, just told her that he was coming for us and to be prepared. He locked her in the bathroom of the salon and took off before Gambler came back."

My eyes got huge, and I couldn't believe what he had just told me. "Why the hell couldn't you tell me that? Gwen is my friend. She probably needs someone to talk to."

"She has Gambler to talk to about it. She is fine. You do not go to her after I'm done talking to you, questioning why she didn't tell you."

"Why didn't she tell me?"

"Because I told her not to."

I growled at his words, pissed off that he was telling my friends to keep secrets from me, too. "Is your telling me this supposed to make me less pissed at you? Because let me tell you, it's not working."

"No. Me telling you this is supposed to show you that, although you are pissed off at the Assassins and want to help Gwen, there is nothing that you can do. I have everything under control, and I don't need you trying to interfere, so then I not only have the club to worry about, but I also have you to worry about."

"If you would tell me in the first place, we wouldn't have an issue."

"And I repeat. Club business stays club business."

"And I repeat, Lo, I don't want secrets."

"It's like talking in fucking circles with you. This is not going to change. I have told you more about the club than I have ever said to anyone. If what I give you isn't enough, then I don't know if this is going to work. Will I keep a secret from you again? Yes. Do I like doing it? Hell no, but I will do whatever it takes to keep you and your son safe. I will die before I let anything that has to do with the Assassins touch you. You need to trust me, Meg. Just fucking trust me." He stood up, looking down at me. "I don't want to lose you, Meg, but I don't know what else to give you to make you happy. I'm sorry I kept that from you, but I would do it again in a heartbeat." He walked out of the kitchen, and I listened to his footsteps as he stomped across the living room and out the front door.

"Can I come with you, King?" I heard Remy ask. I couldn't hear Lo's reply, but I heard Remy grab his jacket and head out the front door.

I dropped my chin to my chest and closed my eyes. I didn't know what to think or do. Everything Lo said made sense, but it felt like if I accepted him not telling me everything all the time, I'd never be able to believe everything he said.

"You let him go, you'll regret it for the rest of your life, my girl." Ethel walked back in the kitchen, her glass empty and set it on the table. "Where the hell did the vodka go?" she asked, looking around.

"Lo put it away. Besides, I don't think I should be drinking right now."

She reached up into the cabinet and pulled the bottle down and splashed some into her glass. "Well, I'll drink yours."

"Everything okay?" Here I was freaking out some stupid thing while Ethel was dealing with cancer. I was really fucked up lately.

"Some days are better than others, hun, but Gravel makes every day good." She filled her glass to the top with tea and set the pitcher back in the fridge.

"You two really love each other, don't you?"

"With every breath I take."

"Does he tell you everything about the club?"

"No. And I don't ask him to either. I'm gonna lay it out for you, Meg, and then it's up to you." She sat down in the chair Lo had just left and set her glass on the counter. "No relationship is ever going to be perfect, no matter how bad you want it to be. You have to figure out if Lo keeping things with work from you is worth walking away from him. Would you rather have a man who lies and cheats or a man who does everything in his power to keep you safe? I know what I would choose. I just hope you make the right decision, hun. No man is perfect, but Lo is the closest you're going to get."

She walked out of the kitchen after sharing her words of wisdom, and I felt like an idiot. I stood up, dumping my glass in the sink, and leaned against the counter. I needed to get over this.

Lo didn't tell me what was going on because he was cheating on me or anything like that. He did it so I wouldn't worry. He did it to keep me safe, and I was an idiot for not understanding that.

I strode into the living room, walking out the front door and stepped out on the front porch. Lo was standing in the front yard talking on his phone, and Remy was sitting in the rocker that Ethel always sat in.

"I like you with him, mom."

"I like me with him, too, Remy."

"Then don't make the wrong choice. Don't be mad at him for something he didn't do." Dammit, even my seventeen-year-old son saw what I didn't.

"I'm not mad anymore, Remy. I just... I just don't know."

Remy stood up and walked over and put his arm around my shoulders. "It's okay, Mom. I just want you to be happy."

I rested my head on his shoulder and wondered when my son had grown up and how I had missed it. "Thank you, baby boy."

"You think we can still go to the movies with everything that's going on? King's been barking into his phone since we came out here."

"I already bought the tickets. I hope we can still go." I watched Lo pace up and down the sidewalk, and I could see the aggravation and worry roll off of him. I know Lo didn't ask for any of this, and I had no reason to blame him for Big A coming to the house.

He finally hung the phone up and shoved into his pocket. "Hey, handsome," I called.

Lo turned to look at me, uncertainty on his face. "Yeah, Meg."

"You think you can still take Remy and me to the movies? I think a night with my two favorite men is what we all need."

A smile slowly spread across Lo's lips, and I knew I had made the right decision. Lo not sharing everything about the club with me wasn't worth throwing away what we had. I loved this man, and nothing was going to make me run away from him.

"I think we can manage a night out, babe."

"Thank God," Remy whispered. "I love Ethel, mom, but it's freakin' boring here. I was afraid we were going to have to stay here all night."

I laughed as Lo made his way up the sidewalk and Remy walked back over to the rocker he had been sitting in. I jogged down the steps, right into Lo's arms and wrapped my arms around him, not wanting to let go.

"I love you, babe. With everything I am, I love you."

"I love you, too, Lo. I'm sorry I'm such a fool."

"Not a fool. I would feel the same way if I were you, that's why I hate not telling you everything, but I do it because I know I have to."

I laid my head on his shoulder and sighed. "How about from now on you just don't tell me if you're keeping something from me. Ignorance is bliss after all."

"Deal. But for the record, I didn't tell you I was keeping something from you, you just assumed I was."

"Details, Lo," I grumbled. Lo's body shook as he laughed and all I could do was smile.

Our first real fight and we managed to work our way through it. Well, I had a little help from Ethel and Remy, but I eventually saw the light.

"Alright. Grab your boy and let's get the hell out of here. If I know you, you already have everything you want to buy at the movies all picked out."

I pulled out of his arms, "You know me too well, handsome," I laughed.

He knew me, and that couldn't have made me happier.

————

Chapter 18
Lo

"Uh, you do realize we are getting married in eight days, and you just let me eat the whole concession stand at the movies? I'll never fit my ass in my dress." I glanced over at Meg, her hand holding her stomach.

"Wear your jeans down the aisle. I don't care as long as your ass is there." I shifted the car into reverse and backed out of Hunter's driveway. It was past ten o'clock, and we had just dropped Remy off. Leo's two men, Creed and Princeton were parked in front of the house, keeping an eye on things. They had said that Leo had given them strict instructions to not let Remy out of their sight.

"Hmm, as sweet as that is, Lo, I think I better wear the dress I spent hundreds of dollars on. I can always close the back up with clothespins," she giggled. We drove by Creed and Princeton, each of them nodding their heads at us. "What kind of names are those anyway?" She asked, looking over her shoulder at their car.

"I'm assuming last names."

"Oh, the mafia doesn't do names like y'all do?"

I chuckled under my breath and shook my head. "I have no clue, but I'm just assuming those are last names."

"I guess I'll have to take your word for it." She smothered a yawn with her hand and laid her head on the seat. "Are they going to be at the wedding?"

"Yeah, babe, unless we manage to get to Big A before then. I already invited Leo. He said that he'll be there."

"What about Fayth? I haven't met her yet."

"What about her?"

"Is she going to be at the wedding?"

I glanced over at her, "Do you want her to be? I don't really know her. Slider is the one who has been keeping an eye on her."

"I bet he just loves that," she laughed. "I wouldn't mind her coming."

"I'll let Slider know to ask her."

We drove in silence, each of us lost in our own thoughts. The thing that kept running through my mind was what the hell Big A was doing. I had to assume that he was going to go after our families now, but why would he do it in plain sight. It was like he wanted me to see him.

I had called Demon after fighting with Meg, letting him know what was going on and to get out on the streets and see what he could find out. I had Edge scrambling to find any and every piece of information on the Assassins, except he had been running into a dead end since day one.

"You'll get him, handsome. I know you will." Meg reached over, grabbing my hand and threaded her fingers through mine. Here I was lost in my own thoughts, and she still knew how to make me feel better.

"I hope so, babe. I'm getting sick of all of this bull shit. I just want everything back to the way it was before the Assassins came into our lives."

She squeezed my hand and scooted over to the middle of the seat and rested her head on my shoulder. "I trust you, Lo. You'll make everything right."

I put my arm around her shoulder and pulled her into my side. I hoped she was right because I was going to die trying to make everything right.

————

Chapter 19
Meg

"Oh, my sweet Jesus. Rigid is going to have to roll me to our room. Who let me eat that last piece of pie?" Cyn was sprawled out on the couch, clutching her growing stomach and groaning.

"I tried to tell you that was enough, but you threatened to cut my pinkie off if I didn't step away from the pie," I called from behind the bar.

We had just gotten done cleaning up all the dishes from Christmas dinner, and everyone was scattered around the common room of the clubhouse either playing pool, watching TV, or starting a game of poker. After a long, drawn out fight with Ethel about where we should have Christmas, she finally relented and agreed that the clubhouse was the best place. She had taken over the kitchen the whole day before, having cooked and baked her ass off.

Everyone was here beside Gwen and Gambler, who had left a couple of hours ago to spend the rest of the day with Paige and her Grandmother. Remy had also been here earlier, but he had to leave to go spend time with his dad.

"Babe, grab me a beer, would you?" Lo called, grabbing a cue stick.

"Me, too," Troy added.

I grabbed two beers out of the fridge, popped the tops and headed over to Lo. "So I'm the beer wench today?"

"Not just today, every day," Troy laughed, grabbing his beer.

I growled at Troy, glaring and Lo grabbed his beer and threw his arm over my shoulders. "Not my wench for very long," he whispered in my ear. "Soon to be my wife."

"Can we please play pool without you manhandling my best friend the whole time?" Troy complained as Lo nuzzled my neck.

"Five more days before you can call me your wife, handsome."

"Counting down the days, babe?" Lo asked, wrapping his arms around me, ignoring Troy.

"Who me?" I asked coyly.

"Hmm, you feel like playing tonight, don't you?" He nipped at my ear, and I wrapped my arms around his neck, tilting my head to the left.

"Pool or something else?"

"Hmm," he growled. "You know what I want, babe."

"Finish your game before Troy has a coronary. I'll let you unwrap your last present before bed tonight." I pulled out of his arms, throwing a wink over my shoulder and sauntered over to the couch where Cyn was laid out.

"Twenty minutes and you're mine, Meg," he called.

"I'll be right here," I replied, sitting down next to Cyn.

"You're teasing that poor man again, aren't you?"

"Eh, he can handle it. He needs to see what kind of crazy he's marrying." I grabbed the pillow that was in between us and set it on my lap.

"I think King is very much aware of the crazy that encompasses you."

"So, what's left to do in the five days before the wedding?" Ethel sat down on the couch across from us with Gravel following right behind her.

"Well, I'm going to start baking the cake in two days. Tomorrow I have to go shopping for all the taco stuff, get the meat marinating, fry up a shit ton of cinnamon nachos, and buy probably five gallons of ice cream."

"Hmm, ice cream. You should probably buy six gallons, I'm likely to eat one gallon all by myself." Cyn laid down completely, stretching her legs out and propped her feet on the pillow that was on my lap. "Make it seven."

"I can help with the cooking if you want, sweetie. I don't go to the doctor till after the wedding. I'm done with this round of chemo. Now we wait to see if it worked."

"It worked," Gravel rumbled. "And if it didn't, we'll try until the fucking cancer goes away."

Ethel waved her hand at his, shushing him. "I need something to do to occupy me. Hell, I'll blow up balloons as long as I don't have to sit in my house and worry."

"I can totally use help, Ethel. Lo was mad that I had decided to make everything myself so this will make things easier if you help."

"Great. I'll come shopping with you tomorrow. We'll take my car because it's supposed to snow."

"I have a car, too, Ethel," I laughed. "I just hate driving it."

"I'll pick you up at eight tomorrow. Lo mentioned that you took off work for the wedding."

"Yeah, I was going to try to keep working, but it's just easier to use vacation time. I have over a month's worth of time saved up, so I also took a couple days off after the wedding, too."

"Ten minutes, Meg," Lo called. I glanced over my shoulder at him, watching him shoot a ball into the pocket. He leaned against the table and crossed his arms over his chest.

The damn man looked good no matter what he was doing. "Whatever you say, handsome."

"What's Lo yelling about?" Ethel asked.

"Oh, he wants to open his last Christmas present, but I told him he had to wait until after dinner." I turned back around, a small smile on my lips.

"He's eager to open it," Cyn laughed.

"We have wedding plans we need to discuss. Tell him he can open his present out here while we plan." Ethel shook her head.

Cyn busted out laughing, "I don't think this is the type of present King wants to open in front of everybody."

"Oh, Lord, Lo," Ethel called, "keep it in your pants. I'm talking to your girl."

"Eight minutes, Ma, then she's mine."

My face turned bright red, and I couldn't believe this man could still make me blush. Although I'm sure, anyone would blush if the person they were sleeping with announced to their mother they were going to get it on. "I'll be ready at eight, Ethel. I'll make sure to bring all the lists I've been making." Blue ambled in from the body shop and collapsed at my feet, resting his head on my shoes. "Hey, big man," I mumbled, reaching down and scratching him behind his ears.

"Sounds good, hun. Did you want to come with us, Cyn?" Ethel asked.

"If you were going at say, noon, I'd totally come, Ethel. Eight o'clock does not exist to me at this point in my pregnancy. Sleep is king."

Rigid walked through the front door, his eyes immediately searching Cyn out. "You ready for bed, beautiful?" Rigid asked, walking over and kneeled in front of her. He brushed the hair out of her face and my heart melted a bit at the gentle way Rigid had with Cyn.

"I could lay down."

"You already are," I laughed.

Cyn rolled her eyes and threw the pillow she had behind her head at me. "Wyatt has been kicking the hell out of me today. Bed sounds good." Now she was calling the baby Wyatt? I would definitely have to try to talk her out of that one.

"I already told you, beautiful, we are not naming our kid Wyatt." Rigid grabbed both of her hands and help her off the couch.

"Well, we for sure aren't calling him Axel," she huffed.

Axel? What the hell were these two thinking? Have they heard of normal names? Although I wasn't really one to talk, I named my son Remington. "You two have plenty of time to figure out what to name the baby. I wouldn't stress over it," Ethel said standing up.

"We going, woman?" Gravel asked.

"Yeah. If I need to be at Meg's by eight, we should head home and get to bed."

I glanced at my watch seeing it was only a little after seven. Ethel and Gravel going to bed before eight o'clock? Seemed to me that maybe Ethel also had another present Gravel needed to unwrap. "Whatever you say, woman," Gravel mumbled walking out the front door.

"Oh, that man is just rainbows and sunshine," she sighed hitching her purse up on her shoulder. "I'll see you in the morning, hun. Bye you two," Ethel called. "Bye, ya'll!" She waved to Lo and Troy and followed Gravel out the door.

Cyn and Rigid headed down the hall to their room, both listing off names that they wanted for the baby. It was going to be a miracle if those two actually came up with a name they both agreed on in the next five months before the baby came.

"I'm ready for my present," Lo growled in my ear as he wrapped his arms around me from behind and nuzzled my neck.

"Did you finish your game?"

"Troy wandered off to find Marley. It didn't take much to find her. She's in the kitchen, trying to make some casserole for breakfast tomorrow."

My stomach instantly rolled at the idea of Marley making a casserole, and I thanked God that Ethel was picking me up at eight so I would have an excuse not to eat it. "Hmm, looks like you'll have to suffer through that on your own. Your mom is going shopping with me tomorrow for all the food for the wedding."

"I'll just sleep till noon and pray that Marley is out of the damn kitchen."

"She just needs to practice, Lo," I laughed, reaching up and running my fingers over his rough cheek. "You didn't shave today."

"She does need to practice, just not on me. That's why she has a man. He can choke her food down; I don't need to." He pressed a kiss to my hand and spun me around, his arms going around my waist. "You like when I don't shave, babe."

"Hmm, I have become partial to your beard."

He leaned down, his lips hovering above my mouth. "I want my present. Now."

"Come and get it." I pressed a kiss to his lips, pushed out of his arms and sprinted down the hall to our room.

I glanced over my shoulder right before I turned the corner and saw Lo slowing stalking down the hallway. A thrill ran through me at the blatant desire that was all over his face. I made it to our room and threw the door open. I slipped in, shutting the door behind me and sprawled out on the bed and waited for Lo.

His present wasn't going to unwrap itself.

––––––––

Chapter 20
Lo

I stalked down the hallway, my eyes on Meg right before she turned the corner and disappeared. Meg had been teasing me all day, and she was driving me crazy with every small touch and lingering glance.

These five days couldn't go fast enough before I make her mine forever and lock her in our room for three days. We couldn't have a honeymoon right now, but that didn't mean I couldn't fuck her six ways to Sunday after she said I do.

As soon as I turned the corner, I saw our door close, and I slowed my stride knowing she was either undressing or sprawling out on our bed. I hoped it was both of them.

I opened the door slowly, and the light from the hallway lit up the room, and my eyes fell on Meg, who was laid out on the bed, laying on her side. "It's about time you got here, handsome."

"I was hoping you would be undressed by the time I made it here." I closed the door behind me, leaning against the door and crossed my arms over my chest.

"Hmm, I told you that your present still needs to be unwrapped." She slid off the bed, slipping her shoes off as she walked over to me. She stood in front of me, her hands on my chest and stood on her tiptoes and pressed a kiss to my lips. "Your last present is under my clothes," she whispered against my mouth.

My hands went to her hips, pulling her to me. "I fucking love you," I growled, slamming my lips down on hers. She moaned, wrapping her arms around my neck and my hands slid around to her soft, plush ass. I lifted her up, and she wrapped her legs around my waist and deepened the kiss. I could get lost in Meg's kisses. She gave so much in each one that all I wanted to do was drown in her.

I turned around, pinning her to the door and my hands went to the hem of her shirt. I slowly pulled it up, my hands exploring her body as my tongue invaded her mouth. She lifted her arms over her head, and I pulled her shirt off, tossing it on the floor. Her tits were encased in a bra I had never seen before. It was dark purple with black lace around the edges that pushed her tits up, offering them to me. "Holy fuck."

"I thought you might like it. Wait till you see the panties."

My hands immediately went to the button of her jeans, tugging them open. She dropped her legs to the floor, her arms on my shoulders and I pulled the zipper down. I pulled her jeans down, kneeling down in front of her. I was face to face with her sweet pussy that was wrapped up in a tiny dark purple thong that matched her bra. I leaned forward, pressing a kiss to her stomach just above her panties. "Fucking perfect and mine." My hands snaked around, grabbing her bare ass, and I buried my face in her pussy, inhaling her scent.

"Lo," she gasped as I tugged on the tiny triangle of fabric that was covering her pussy. I pulled it down with my teeth, exposing her bare, sweet cunt.

She put her hands on my head, steadying herself, but also letting me know she didn't want me to move. She spread her legs, and I tugged her panties all the way off, leaving them in a puddle on the floor. I looked up at her, and her eyes were hooded with desire and her hair was hanging around her like a curtain. "I need you," she whispered, biting her lip.

Those were the only three words I needed to hear for the rest of my life. With her, I had everything I would ever need. "Keep those legs spread, babe," I ordered. I didn't give her time to respond. I buried my tongue inside her, flicking her clit and feeling her body tremble under my hands. Her fingers delved into my hair, gripping and pulling with each touch and taste of her.

I pumped my finger in and out of her, bringing her closer and closer to the edge. I wanted her to cum on my dick, but I had to taste and tease her. My touch was torture to her, but so was the taste of her on my tongue.

"Lo," she gasped as I sucked her clit into my mouth, nipping it with my teeth as I released it. Her knees buckled, and I knew she wasn't going to be standing for much longer. Her hands gripped my head, and she hung her head down, watching as I devoured her. "More, please," she begged. I pumped my finger into her one last time and pulled away. "No," she gasped, stepping towards me. "Don't stop."

"I want you coming on my dick."

"I will. Later. Right now I want to come all over your tongue," she insisted.

I stood up and pulled her into my arms. "As good as that sounds, babe, I want that sweet pussy wrapped around my dick while I fuck the hell out of you, and you scream my name so the whole clubhouse hears it."

"Oh, I think I can manage that," she whispered. I walked us backward, my arms around her, and I fell back when my calves hit the bed. I pulled her with me, needing her warm, soft body on top of me.

"You still have your clothes and boots on, Lo," she said, pushing against my chest and stood up. She pulled on the laces of my boots, pulling each one off and throwing them on the floor. I popped open the button of my jeans and tugged the zipper down just as she yanked on the hem of my jeans and pulled them down my legs. I leaned forward and pulled my shirt over my head and tossed it on the floor with our growing pile of clothes.

"Much better. Just one last piece," she mumbled, climbing up between my legs. She pulled my underwear down, and I lifted up on my elbows.

"I think you forgot one piece, babe. Bra. Off. Now," I bit off. She reached behind her back making her tits thrust forward. I watched the show she was putting on as she unhooked it and slowly worked the straps down her arms. I stroked my cock as she grabbed her lush tits, squeezing and pulling on her nipples. "We still need to get those pierced, babe. Maybe that can be your wedding gift."

"My wedding gift is pierced nipples? I think that's more of a gift for you," she laughed.

"Probably. Although I'm sure you'll like it just as I will. I won't be able to keep my mouth off of you."

"I like when you don't keep your mouth off of me." One of her hands snaked down her stomach, touching everywhere my hands itched to touch. She cupped her pussy, tossing her head back as she parted the lips of her pussy and stroked her clit. My hand sped up, watching her bring herself to ecstasy with her own touch. Just the thought of her pleasuring herself drove me mad with desire. Watching her bring herself to the edge of desire was enough to make me cum all over my hand and stomach.

"Stop," I growled, jackknifing up, grabbing her around her waist and pulled her on top of me. "So fucking hot," I groaned, burying my face in her tits. "You're supposed to be cumming around my dick, babe, not your fucking hand."

"Then get to fucking work," she laughed.

I flipped her over, covering her with my body and pinning her to the bed. Her hair was fanned out around her, and her breathing was heavy as she looked up at me, waiting for my next move. "Spread your legs," I ordered. She spread her legs, digging her heels into the mattress and put her hands over her head.

I kneeled between her legs, stroking my dick and grabbed her tit, pinching the nipple. My cock teased the lips of her pussy, and she bucked her hips, begging for me to fuck her. "How bad do you want me, babe?"

"So bad," she moaned, arching her back into my hand. I kneaded her breast and growled, watching her body trembled with need for me. She bucked her hips again, and I couldn't hold back anymore. I plunged into her, needing her. Her warm pussy tight and soaked as I thrust in and out. I groaned low as she reached down, grabbing my balls. She stroked and touched them, driving me insane.

She sat up, leaning back on her elbow and watched as my cock disappeared inside her. "I could watch that all day," she purred.

She tossed her head back as I slammed into her and I knocked her hand away, unable to handle her touch anymore without exploding too soon. "Who do you belong to?" I thundered.

"Lo… Logan. I belong to you," she trembled. I felt my orgasm building, knowing with each thrust I was closer to tipping over the edge and filling her up.

I fell on top of her, caging her in with my arms and buried my face in her neck as I searched for my release in her sweet body. She wrapped her legs around my waist, forcing my dick to hit even deeper with each thrust. Her moans and breathing became short and labored. And I knew she was close. "Cum for me," I demanded, covering her mouth with my lips. My tongue delved into her mouth, stroking and licking as my hands explored her body, touching and caressing every inch of her.

"I love you," she gasped as she exploded, her pussy squeezing me like a vice. She tossed her head back, shouting my name as I plunged into her on the edge of my release.

I pounded into her, fisting the sheets in my hands. She tilted her hips up, and I groaned low as my release slammed into me, my body trembling. She wrapped her arms around my shoulders, as I slowly pumped into her, wringing out every last ounce of pleasure from her body.

"Merry Christmas," she whispered sweetly in my ear.

"Merry Christmas, babe. This was the best Christmas that I've had in years," I mumbled into her hair.

"Hmm, you make my heart hurt when you talk like that, Lo."

"Just the truth." I rolled off the side, laying down and she snuggled into my arms, closing her eyes.

"I'm glad I get to be that for you, Lo," she mumbled.

I brushed the hair out of her face and pressed a kiss to her forehead. "You're everything to me, Meg. Without you, I know I'm nothing."

Her eyes lazily opened, a small smile spreading across her lips. "I think you're supposed to save this for the wedding day during our vows."

"I'm going to tell you every day, babe. At least ten times."

"I love you, handsome," she whispered, caressing my cheek. "I know you love me by the way you treat me. By the way, you let me be crazy but are always there to reel me in. I know you love me because I feel it in the way you look at me."

"I will fucking love you until my last breath," I promised, resting my head against her forehead. "Till the stars fall from the sky, you're mine."

———————

Chapter 21
Meg

"You want to explain to me why there are twelve crock pots in my room?" Roam asked, stalking down the hallway to me.

I was standing on a ladder that was precariously leaning to the left, trying to hang the last of the decorations for the wedding that was tomorrow. Fucking tomorrow. I tried not to freak out, but every time someone mentioned that we were down to mere hours away from me becoming Mrs. Birch, I had to fight off a panic attack. "Because I didn't know that you were going to be in town. I asked Lo where to put them, and he said your room. If you let people know where you are, you wouldn't come home to crockpots all over your room."

"Lesson learned," he laughed. "I couldn't miss the prez's wedding, though. I cut my plans short and headed back."

"Well, I'm glad you're here, Roam. But it looks like you're sleeping with twelve crock pots until tomorrow morning."

"Bunk in Slider's room. He's been staying at Fayth's so his bed is empty," Lo said, walking out of the kitchen, a beer and wine cooler in his hand.

"Who the hell is Fayth?"

"Leo's sister and Slider's pain in the ass," Hammer called. He was standing on top of the pool table hanging the last of the lanterns from the ceiling.

I had managed to put everyone to work, Lo included, who at the moment seemed was taking a break. My goal was to make the common room look more like a reception hall and less like a den of debauchery. I was basically trying to shine a turd.

"Here, babe," Lo said, holding the wine cooler up to me. If Lo had handed me a drink an hour ago, I would have yelled at him and told him to get back to work. Now, after all, the day of cleaning, cooking, and decorating the cake, a wine cooler looked pretty damn good. I grabbed it, putting it to my lips and moaned as the sweet goodness slid down my throat.

"Hmm, nectar of the Gods."

Lo shook his head, laughing at me and held the ladder. I set my drink down and finished pinning up the last of the paper lanterns.

"Alright, I managed to organize all the cars in back and made room for all the guests to park tomorrow. Please tell me I'm done and throw me one of those damn beers," Demon grumbled, walking through the front door with Edge, Rigid, and Gambler on his heels.

"I think that was the last thing I needed to be done." I mentally ran through my long list of stuff that needed to be done in my head and realized that everything was done. Everything for the tacos had been chopped, prepped, and put into containers to hold until tomorrow. The meat was ready to be put in crock pots first thing in the morning. The four tier cake that I had painstakingly slaved over was now in the office of the body shop with a warning to everyone that if they touched, licked or knocked the damn thing over, they were dead. D. E. A. D.

I glanced at the clock seeing that it was half past six. "Everyone get ready for the rehearsal dinner," I called climbing down from the ladder.

"Rehearsal dinner?" Roam asked, looking around. He was lucky I liked him. Otherwise, I would have knocked him across the head for all the questions he was asking.

"Yeah," Lo said, "Take a fucking shower and be ready to go at seven. We're headed to The Den for dinner and drinks."

Roam ambled off down the hallway, shaking his head but didn't say anything else.

"I think Cyn is already in the shower. I'm gonna see if I can sneak in before she gets out." Rigid sprinted down the hallway, dodging around Roam.

I grabbed my drink off the top of the ladder and sat down at the bar. "You gonna take a shower before we go?" Lo asked, walking around to the other side of the bar.

"Yeah. I'm pretty sure I smell like taco meat and buttercream. Both yummy things, but not together."

"I'm going to have to agree with you on that one, babe," Lo laughed, leaning across the bar, pressing a kiss to my lips.

"Thank you for all the help today," I mumbled against his lips.

"Anything for you," he smirked. "Plus I'm racking up points for later when I piss you off."

"Oh, is that how it is?" I laughed, draining the rest of my drink. I was going to need at least two more of these before we left. I was beyond exhausted, and we still had dinner and drinks to get through before I could collapse into bed tonight. A bed, might I add, that Lo was not going to be in.

Lo was going to stay at the clubhouse with all the guys, and the girls and I were all going to be camping out at Ethel's. When we were shopping, Ethel insisted that Lo and I not see each other before the wedding. No matter what I said to sway her, she said no. In the end, Lo and I both agreed that after the rehearsal dinner we wouldn't see each other until I walked down the aisle.

"Although I should try to get on my ma's good side in case she catches me sneaking into your room tonight."

"Well," I said pushing my empty bottle towards him. "If you try to sneak into my bed, I think you might have quite the surprise with Cyn sleeping with me."

"Then you'll just have to sneak out to come see me. I don't like this whole not seeing you until tomorrow."

"You can handle nineteen hours without her, Logan," Ethel scolded, walking out of the kitchen as she untied the apron around her waist.

I covered my mouth with my hand, laughing that Lo had just been busted by his mom. "I'll keep an eye on him, Ethel," Demon smirked, walking behind the bar and grabbing a beer. "He'll be too busy with all the plans I have for him tonight."

"I don't care what you do as long as I don't catch you trying to sneak up my sidewalk to see Meg."

"Ma, it's a stupid tradition."

"Humor your mother, Logan," she glared. "I'm going to grab Gravel from the shop then head home to shower. We'll meet you at The Den at seven." She breezed out the door, waving as she went.

"I'm going to see you tonight," Lo swore.

"No, you won't," Ethel snapped, sticking her head through the door she had just walked through. She slammed the door shut behind her and Demon, and Gambler and I busted out laughing.

"I think it's for the best that we listen to your mom, handsome," I laughed shaking my head.

"Humph, we'll see," he huffed. "Go shower, babe. I'll finish cleaning up here and then be into change."

"Thanks, hunny." I stood up on the bottom rung of my stool and leaned over the bar and kissed Lo.

"Bang on Gwen's door on the way by and tell her to hurry her ass up," Gambler called as I turned the corner down the hall.

I knocked on Gwen's door and two seconds after, Gwen threw the door open dressed in only a towel, and I had to assume she was expecting Gambler because she leaned against the door frame all sexy and her shoulders sagged when she saw that it was me.

"Um, Gambler said to hurry your ass up," I laughed.

"Oh, sure," she mumbled, tugging the towel up a bit higher. Gwen and Cyn had both helped me all day getting everything just right for tomorrow and were both as exhausted as I was. "I was thinking you were Gambler coming to collect on a bet he had won before."

"When are you going to learn that Gambler always wins?" I snickered. It seemed like every other day Gwen was complaining about this or that bet Gambler had won.

"This one was different. I didn't see any way possible that he could win, but the damn fucker still won."

"What was the bet?"

"He said he was going to have one of the bodyguards that are protecting Remy take Paige to the wedding as their date. I figured I knew my sister and she would say no."

"So which one did she agree to go with?"

"Princeton. The tall one with the neck tattoo. I tried telling her she had no idea what she was getting into, but she insisted that she would be fine. To say I was shocked that she had agreed is a damn understatement."

"I don't want to know what he asked for since you answered your door in your robe I can assume what it was. Just don't be late for dinner," I laughed stepping away from the door.

"Well, I'm hoping he doesn't try to collect until tomorrow. I was going to tell him the only way he wins is if Paige actually shows up with Princeton. I've got my fingers crossed hoping she chickens out the second she sees the tattoos on his neck." She closed the door, mumbling about bets and tattoos, and I headed the rest of the way to our room and headed straight to the bathroom and turned on the water.

Steam billowed out of the shower, and I turned it a bit hotter to help work out the kinks in my neck from hanging from a ladder for the past hour.

The previous four days had been a whirlwind of shopping, planning, shopping, cooking, shopping, cleaning, shopping, and baking. Did I mention shopping? I swear if I had to run to the grocery one more time, I was going to go absolutely crazy. Ethel had been a godsend helping with all of the cooking. I don't know what I thought when I had agreed to make tacos for seventy-five people. Throw in the damn cinnamon nachos, and I was completely maxed out and ready to sleep for the next three days.

I stripped off my clothes and stepped into the shower, the scalding water running over me and loosening all of my tight muscles.

"You gonna be done in half an hour, or should I tell everyone seven thirty?"

I stuck my head out of the shower curtain and saw Lo leaning against the doorframe of the bathroom. "Seven should be all right as long as you don't plan on showering with me."

"As much as I'd love to, babe, I know we wouldn't be out of here until nine o'clock then." He knew me so well.

"Seven it is then," I laughed ducking back into the shower. I grabbed the shampoo, pouring a puddle into my hand and lathered it into my hair. "You called ahead and made reservations, right?" I called.

"Yeah. I called a week ago. We have two big ass tables in the back for us."

"Good. You know how crazy the bars are on Friday for fish fries." Fish fry and Friday night went hand in hand in Wisconsin. There was always at least a half an hour wait no matter where you went on a Friday night.

"We'll be good, babe. All the hard shit is done. Now all I need to do is marry your sweet ass and lock you in our room for the next four days." I heard him turn the faucet on, and I peeked my head out, full of shampoo, to see what he was doing.

"You're not shaving, are you?" I asked.

"I was thinking about it. I figured you would want me clean shaven for tomorrow." He turned to look at me as he rubbed his cheek.

It had been two days since he had last shaved and he had just the right amount of stubble that drove me crazy. I swear Lo would look hotter than sin with a beard. "I like you with scruff." I closed one eye and squinted at him with the other as shampoo dripped down into my eye.

"Babe, two more days and I'll have a damn beard."

"Is that a problem?" I was hoping he wouldn't say it was. "It's almost January in Wisconsin. A beard is like a built-in face mask. If I could grow one, I would." I grabbed some foam from the top of my head and strategically placed it on my chin. I'm sure I looked more like a deranged Abraham Lincoln than anything else.

"Babe," Lo said, wiping the bubbles off of my chin, "leave the beard to me." He rinsed his hand off under the running water, turned it off and sauntered out of the bathroom.

"Does this mean the beard stays," I called.

"For now," he hollered back.

"Yes," I whispered pumping my fist into the air. A big chunk of hair fell into my face, blinding both of my eyes with the foamy shampoo. "Ow, ow, ow," I mumbled blindly closing the curtain and stuck my head under the hot water.

After I had managed to not blind myself and get all the shampoo out of my hair, I scrubbed myself clean while I conditioned my hair and managed to be out of the bathroom wrapped in a towel in record time.

Lo was in the closet slapping hangers back and forth, trying to find a shirt to wear. "Can't find the right Devil's Knights shirt to wear tonight?" I laughed pulling open the dresser drawer and pulled out a pair of panties and bra.

Lo looked over his shoulder at me and watched as I dropped the towel and shimmied the panties up my legs and hooked the bra around my back. "I hate when you do that," he mumbled turning back to the closet.

"Do what?" I asked pulling the straps up my arms.

"Put fucking clothes on," he murmured.

"Well, Lo," I laughed. "I don't really think you'd last very long having everyone stare at me naked."

"You're probably right," he agreed pulling a black button down shirt out of the closet and tossed it on the bed. "We leave in ten minutes. You gonna be ready?"

"Oh how you doubt me, Lo. I'll be ready by the time you are." I walked over to the closet, grabbing my dark plum sweater and my favorite pair of jeans. "I'm the girl that can be in bed sleeping one minute and five minutes later in my truck, dressed and headed to the store."

"Yeah. I saw you do that the other day. You looked hot in pajama pants, my shirt and fur boots up to your knees," Lo smirked, pulling on his jeans.

"I didn't say how I was dressed," I remembered that day. I had woken up to find that we were out of coffee, and I threw on the closest clothes I could find and hightailed it to the store. "You should have seen the stares I got," I giggled, pulling a cami over my head.

Lo pulled his shirt off and tossed it on the floor. He bent over to grab the shirt he had laid on the bed, and my eyes were drawn to the bird on his side. "I still can't believe you put my name on you."

"Believe it." He pulled his shirt on, leaving it open and stalked over to me. He wrapped his arms around me, pressing me close. "As long as your name is on me, you're mine."

"Oh, is that how that works?" I laughed.

"With me, it is."

"Cyn and I were talking the other day, and she wants to go get a tattoo after the baby comes. I had a couple of ideas of ones I want to get, too." I parted the front of his open shirt and put my hands on his chest, my fingers tracing over the flames. "I was thinking how you were King, and I saw this really cool crown design when Cyn was looking."

"A crown, babe?" He asked, looking down at me.

His eyes were studying me, and I couldn't tell if he thought it was a good idea or not. When I had shown Cyn, she thought it was hot and said Lo would probably cream himself when I told him. His reaction was definitely lacking from what she thought he would do. "Um, yeah. It's just an idea."

"It's your body." What the hell does that mean? Of course, it's my body, but he was going to be the one who would have to look at it.

"But do you think it's a good idea?"

"You getting something permanently on your body that represents me is fucking hot. I'll take you right now to get the damn thing." His arms tightened around me, and he pressed a kiss to my lips.

"I told Cyn I would go with her," I whispered, regretting I had promised her.

"You can go with her when she gets her's done, but after the wedding, I'm taking you to get that crown, babe."

"You're rather demanding."

"I know you want it now, not five months from now."

"Well, yeah," I replied, wrapping my arms around his neck. He definitely wasn't wrong. Ever since I had seen the tattoo, it was all I could think about.

"Where were you thinking about getting it?"

"Right here," I whispered, placing my hand over my heart.

His hand covered mine, and he laced his fingers through my fingers. "I'm taking you the day after the wedding to get it done."

"What am I supposed to tell, Cyn?"

"You can get another one when Cyn goes, I don't care. All I know is that you are getting that crown over your heart with me sitting right next to you."

"Have you always been this demanding?"

"Only with you." He pressed a kiss to my forehead and stepped back, buttoning his shirt. "You got five minutes, babe."

I glanced at the alarm clock on the side table and huffed. "You distracted me," I said, pointing my finger at him. I grabbed my jeans and shimmied them up my legs then pulled the sweater over my head and headed back into the bathroom. After yanking my brush through my hair and swiping on some lip gloss and eyeshadow, I had thirty seconds to throw my clothes on and find some shoes to wear other than my slippers.

"Tick tock, babe." Lo was sitting on the end of the bed scrolling through his phone waiting for me by the time I came out of the bathroom. I went straight to the closet digging around for my faux Uggs.

"I'm on time, or at least I would be if you hadn't kept bothering me while I was trying to get ready." I found the boots in the back of the closet and plopped down on my ass. "You're not allowed to be around me anymore when I get dressed," I muttered, pulling each boot on. "Alright, let's go." I stood up, my hands on my hips. "You owe me at least three drinks, if not four."

Lo shoved his phone into his pocket and grabbed my hand, dragging me down the hallway. "Lo, you're gonna pull my arm out of the socket," I whined as I tried to keep up with his pace.

"I made a bet with Gambler, and we're about to lose it," he mumbled.

We came around the corner, and I saw Gambler standing by the bar, looking down the hallway a smug look on his face. "Oh Lord, Lo. What the hell did you go and bet against Gambler for?"

"He said Gwen would be ready before you. I told him he was full of shit."

Gwen was sitting next to Gambler the same smug look on her face. How in the hell did Gwen get ready before me? She was the one that we were always waiting on. "I can't believe you bet against him. You know he only bets if he knows he'll win."

"I thought I had a shot," he whispered.

"I'm ready for my *free* steak dinner," Gambler said rubbing his stomach. "Are you, doll?"

"Hmm, I think I want lobster."

Wait, what? That was what Lo had bet? That loser had to buy dinner? I was totally fine with losing this bet because I had already planned on buying dinner for everyone. "Seeing as we're going to The Den, your choices are limited to burgers, chicken, and fish."

"That's bullshit. How the hell am I supposed to order the most expensive thing on the menu then?" Gambler scoffed.

"And I already planned on paying for your meal. You wasted that bet, Gambler," I laughed, grabbing my coat off the back of the stool I was sitting in before.

"Son of a bitch." Gambler threw back the last of his drink and slammed his empty bottle on the bar.

"We all ready to go?" Lo asked looking around. There were over twenty of us heading over there, plus Jackie and her husband meeting us there.

Lo led the way out the front door, and I stopped in my tracks when I saw the big, fat snowflakes falling from the sky. "It's snowing!" I shouted, holding my arms out. It had been such a mild winter that any flake of snow that floated down from the sky made me as happy as a nun doing squats in a cucumber patch.

"Fuck yeah," Cyn chimed in.

Everyone filed out of the clubhouse each surprised to see it snowing.

I looked around, watching everyone act like kids in the snow, Cyn and Gwen each sticking their tongues out catching the flakes while Hammer and Edge tried to collect snow off the ground and make snowballs. Lo was standing by my truck, leaning against the door, and I smiled.

This night couldn't get any better.

———————

Chapter 22
Lo

"I bet you a six pack that I can get that bartender to go home with me tonight," Hammer mumbled to Gambler.

Oh fuck, here we go. The beer was flowing good, and everyone was having a good time, Hammer included. "Bullshit. That chick won't give you the time of day other than to take your money."

"That's it," Hammer boomed, standing up and pushing his chair back. "You're gonna fucking lose, Gambler."

Hammer stumbled to the bar, knocking into Marley and Troy on the way but managed to make it without falling over. He leaned against the bar and waited for the bartender to come over. Now, it isn't that Hammer isn't a good looking guy at all, the problem came in when he opened his mouth. And, there was one other problem he hadn't identified before making the bet with Gambler.

"I'm assuming you saw the big ol' rock on her left hand?" I drawled, peeling the label off of my beer bottle.

"Spotted it the second I saw Hammer eyeing her up. I've been waiting for him to make his move."

"I think we're going to get going," Gwen said, sliding up next to Gambler. He wrapped his arm around her waist and pulled her into his lap.

"One sec, doll. First, we need to watch Hammer get his balls handed to him."

We couldn't hear what he was saying, but from the grimace on the bartender's face, we could tell that Hammer was not making the impression he thought he would.

"What the hell is he doing? Does he not see the huge rock on her finger? She could land planes with that thing," Gwen asked.

It was like a car crash. We knew we shouldn't watch, but we couldn't rip our eyes away.

"Here it comes," Gambler whispered.

The bartender reached under the bar, grabbing the water gun and sprayed Hammer right in the face. "Looks like I've got a six pack to go in the fridge," Gambler laughed, slapping the table.

"What on earth is Hammer doing?" Meg asked. She sat on the stool next to me, resting her feet on the bottom rung of my stool.

"Jackass is as bad as Turtle." I shook my head and drained the last of my beer. Hammer wiped his face off and walked over to the pool table, trying to act like he hadn't just been sprayed with water by the hot bartender.

"We're gonna go, hun. Cyn is fading fast, and I'm getting a headache." Meg's face was flushed, and she looked like she was ready to fall asleep.

"You ok, babe?" I asked, reaching out and brushing her hair behind her ear.

"Yeah. Nothing a couple of Tylenol and a soft bed won't fix." She leaned into my hand and closed her eyes. Even in a crowded bar surrounded by all our friends, all I saw was Meg.

I leaned forward, pressing a kiss to her forehead. "I'll walk you to the car."

I stood up, tossing a fifty down on the table and grabbed Meg's hand, pulling her through the sea of people and out the front door.

The door shut behind us, and I pushed her up against the wall of the building. "I seem to remember being in this same position eight months ago," she purred wrapping her arms around my neck.

"Yeah, except the difference now is I don't have to talk you into kissing me. I've finally gotten you right where I've wanted you the whole time." I caged her in with my arms on either side of her head. "Best decision I ever made was following you up to that bar."

"I have to agree with you on that. Who would have thought we would be here now the night before our wedding, standing outside a bar in the snow together?"

"I knew you were mine that first day I saw you at the store, Meg. It just took you a little bit of convincing to see things the way I do."

"Hmm, you just intimidated the hell out of me," she laughed. "Who would have thought the most handsome man I'd ever laid my eyes on would end up loving me? You were too good to be true, Lo. You still are." She stood on her tiptoes, pressing a kiss to my lips. My hands went to her head, threading my fingers through her hair and deepened the kiss. Taking what she was always willing to give.

"I can't believe you are going to be my wife tomorrow."

"Technically it's today," she whispered against my lips.

"Alright, lovebirds, time to break it the fuck up. We've still got a bachelor party to throw back at the clubhouse," Demon ordered, walking out of the bar.

It was after fucking midnight. I had no idea what the hell Demon thought we were going to do once we got back to the clubhouse. All I wanted to do was fall into bed and not wake up until it was time to marry Meg.

Meg wrapped her arms around my waist, and I felt her shivering. "Where's your coat, babe?"

"Right here," Jackie said, stumbling out of the bar holding onto Guy's arm. This was only the fourth time that I had spent time with Jackie, but I could definitely tell the family resemblance between her and Meg. They were both nuts, but you could tell they loved big. She draped the coat over Meg's shoulders and leaned into Guy, her husband. "Guy and I are going to head home. Jax has his girlfriend over, and Nel is over at her boyfriends, and we have to pick her up on the way home. I swear, they go off to college, and I'm still taking care of them. We'll be at the clubhouse around noon tomorrow." Jackie hugged, kissed and waved goodbye to everyone then headed out.

"You and your sister look nothing alike, babe, but the minute she opens her mouth, I know she's related to you."

"She sure is something else," Meg laughed.

"I'm cold, and I need a taco," Cyn whined.

"I'm taking her to the car. Hurry the hell up so she doesn't get cold," Rigid said as he picked her up and carried her to Gwen's car.

"Looks like you have a bachelor party to get to, and I need to get tacos and go to bed."

I pressed a kiss to her lips, my hands sliding around her waist and squeezed her ass. "Be careful. Edge is going to follow you guys until you get to Ethel's, okay?" Things were quiet on the Assassins front, and it was worrying the hell out of me. Gravel was going to be at Ethel's to watch the girls tonight, and I knew he wouldn't let anything happen to Meg or the girls, but I still worried. The second I stopped worrying would be the time that Big A made his move "Behave," I whispered, squeezing her ass.

"I think I should be the one saying that to you. Lord knows what Gambler has planned for the rest of the night for you."

"The only plans I have are going to bed and sleeping. You have nothing to worry about."

"Okay," she whispered. "I love you. Make sure you're waiting for me at the end of the altar."

"No other place I'd rather be, babe." She closed her eyes, my words sinking in and she pulled out of my arms and walked over to Gwen's car. She waved over the roof of the car at me then slipped into the backseat.

"Alright, fuckers. Say goodbye to your women, you pussywhipped assholes, and let's get back to the clubhouse," Demon said, rubbing his hands together. I had no idea what the hell Demon had up his sleeve, but I didn't think I wanted to know.

Gwen and Marley ripped themselves out of Gambler's and Troy's arms and headed to her car.

"You ready to be married this time tomorrow?" Troy asked.

I glanced around at Troy, Gambler, Demon, Rigid, and Hammer. "I've never been more sure of anything in my life."

"Well, fuck yeah," Troy laughed.

"I'm gonna grab the rest of the guys and then we can head back," Demon grumbled walking back into the bar.

"What the hell crawled up his ass? He not like Meg or something?" Gambler asked pulling a cigarette out of his pack.

"Naw, I think he's kind of like Slider right now. He knows the club is changing, and he doesn't know if he likes it. Slider bitches at least once a day about the fact that there aren't many parties at the clubhouse anymore. Fuckers will get used to it," Rigid replied.

I could understand where Demon and Slider were coming from, but it wasn't going to change the fact that we were all getting ol' ladies. The day would come when they will find someone like I did Meg. Although, Lord knew when that day was going to come for Demon. I knew he got burned bad in the past and didn't trust a woman as far as he could throw her. Now Slider, well, he just needed to get his head out of his ass and stop treating every woman like she was only good for one thing.

"Let's get the hell out of here," Demon shouted when he walked back out of the door.

Fuck me, I was ready for this night to be over.

———

Chapter 23
Meg

"Ugh, I think that last bean burrito was a bad idea," Cyn moaned as she slipped into bed.

We had gotten back to Ethel's over an hour ago, and we were just going to bed. Cyn had decided to order half of the menu at Taco Bell and had an impromptu picnic in the living room. There was no way that she was going to be able to eat all of the food she had ordered so of course Gwen, Marley and I had to help her eat everything.

"I would probably say eating a bean burrito at two o'clock in the morning is never a good idea," I laughed, turning off the light. Marley and Gwen were sleeping out in the living room on the sofa sleeper while Cyn and I were camping out in the guest room.

Not even two minutes after sliding into bed, Cyn was snoring, and I knew it was going to be awhile until I fell asleep.

I grabbed my phone and pulled up Lo's number and sent him a text. If I was going to be awake, I was going to make him talk to me.

I miss you. Annnnd Cyn is snoring like a chainsaw. I have no idea how Rigid sleeps with her every night. It was the damn truth. Seriously.

It only took a minute before he answered. *Miss you, too. Rigid probably falls asleep before her, so he doesn't have to listen to it.*

Smart man. I texted back.

Headed to bed?

Yeah. What are you up to? If he mentioned anything about strippers, I was going to rip Demon's balls off. I found it rather fishy how badly Demon was pushing us out the door.

Poker. Demon's big surprise was a couple of members from my old chapter coming up for the wedding.

Friends? Guy friends? I was possessive. I knew it.

Yes, babe. I'm sure he was shaking his head as he typed that.

I miss you. I was turning sappy. My sappiness also had to do with all the old fashions I drank tonight.

Miss you, too. I've just been dealt in. Get some sleep, and I'll see you tomorrow afternoon. I'll be the guy with eyes only for you.

And that was why I loved this man so much. *I love you. Don't stay up too late. I'll be the one in the white dress. ;)*

Can't wait.

I set my phone on the table next to the bed and closed my eyes. Cyn's snoring was grating on my nerves, and I elbowed her in the side, and she rolled over and thankfully the snoring stopped.

My phone dinged and lit up. I grabbed, scrambling to see what Lo had texted. *Dream of me.*

My heart melted at his words and I set the phone back down.

I fell asleep, my thoughts of Lo and the beautiful life we were going to build together.

I dreamt about tacos.

Dammit.

———

Chapter 24
Meg

"Coffee. Need coffee," I moaned as I walked into Gwen's shop. I had barely slept last night, thanks to Cyn's God awful snoring. It was a work of God that Rigid was able to get any sleep with Cyn in his bed.

"The coffee maker broke last week, and I haven't gotten a new one yet," Gwen called from the back.

I pushed my sunglasses on the top of my head and closed my eyes. "Please tell me she did not just say that."

"I'll run to the cafe down the street. What do you want?" Marley asked, grabbing her purse from under the front desk.

"Three large black coffees."

"Don't order for me. I can't have caffeine." Cyn plopped down on one of the chairs in the waiting area and rubbed her belly. "Rigid freaked out even when I was drinking decaf. The man is going to drive me insane before I even have the baby."

"I wasn't ordering for you," I mumbled. My lack of sleep needed to be remedied and the only way that was going to happen was with three cups of coffee.

"Okay, three coffees for Meg coming right up." Marley breezed out the door, and I growled at her chirpiness. It was inhuman to be so happy this early in the morning. "There's something wrong with that one."

Cyn pulled a pack of gum out of her purse and offered me a piece. "It's eleven o'clock, Meg. Most people are up by now."

"Hmm, it's still the morning."

"Alright. Who's first?" Gwen asked pushing a cart out of the backroom that was loaded full of anything you could possibly need to do hair.

"I volunteer as tribute," Cyn laughed as she struggled to stand up.

The girl was only three months, but she acted like she was nine months. Granted she was much bigger than someone normally is at three months. "Were you watching Hunger Games again?" I asked, leaning my head back and sliding my sunglasses back on.

"Yeah. Rigid loves the damn movies. I told him to read the books, they're better. But he laughed. I have to admit the thought of seeing Rigid read a book that is other than a car manual made me giggle." She sat down in the salon chair and Gwen spun her around and put a cape around her shoulders.

"Loved the movies, never read the books," Gwen replied. "I never can find the time to read. By the time I fall into bed at night, I'm either exhausted, or Gambler finds other things to keep me occupied." She smirked at me in the mirror and grabbed a comb and a huge container of bobby pins off of the cart she had wheeled out earlier and got to work on Cyn's hair.

"I think we have that problem now with our men in our lives. I used to sit on my back porch and read all day. I can't even remember the last book I picked up." The thought that I couldn't remember made me sad. I really did love to read, but I never had the time to. My life had changed so drastically from what it had been just a year ago. Would I ever be able to sit down and read a book ever again, or would I always be too busy?

"What's up with the frown?" Gwen asked as she spun Cyn around, her back now to the mirror.

"I can't remember the last book I've read."

"Yeah, you said that. Is that a big deal?" Gwen asked as she studied me in the mirror.

"No. Well, kind of. My life has changed so much to let Lo in."

"I'm sure Lo's life has changed, too."

"Really? How?"

"Well, um… you know."

"Great examples," Cyn scoffed. "Look, Meg. You and I know both know that the way these guys are now compared to how they used to be is way different." Gwen clipped half of Cyn's hair on top of her head, and it flopped down into her face. Cyn huffed, blowing the hair away. "Lo and Rigid, hell, even Gambler lived a life where the only people they had to answer to were each other. Now, they have us in their lives, complicating things, but making their lives a hell of a lot better."

"Amen," Gwen sang. "These men were lost before us, and they'd be lost again without us."

"I want to read." I felt like I had lost so much of myself. When I had agreed to be with Lo, I had found myself, but now I felt like everything I thought I was, was now gone.

"Then read, Meg. You really think Lo is the reason you stopped reading? Because you're wrong. I've seen the way that man looks at you. He'd give you anything you'd want or need without batting an eyelash. I know that look on your face. You're overthinking this. Stop it." Cyn glared at me, and I looked out the window, knowing she was right, but I couldn't help it.

"I'm gonna go look for Marley," I mumbled. I grabbed my purse and headed out the door, not listening to either Gwen or Cyn who called after me.

I pulled my coat tight around me and headed down the sidewalk. It wasn't until I was standing by my truck that I realized what I was about to do.

After I unlocked the door and slid into the driver's seat, I slammed the door shut and put the key in the ignition. Snowflakes started to fall as I looked out the windshield and felt the tears threatening to fall.

I didn't know if I could do this. I was losing myself in Lo. Just like I did with Hunter and look how that turned out. We ended up hating each other and divorced.

Cyn and Gwen poured out of the salon, and I started the truck and hit the door lock. I shifted the truck into drive as they hollered at me and I let my foot off the brake as they crossed the street. I sped past them as I watched Cyn pull her phone out of her pocket, and I knew who she was calling.

I needed to get out of here. I needed to think. I needed to figure out what I wanted.

I needed to figure out if I had just made the worst decision of my life.

Lo

"You wanna tell me why the hell I had to look all over for you, and I find you sitting on your bike in the garage?"

I glanced over my shoulder to see Demon standing in the doorway. "Too many fucking people. Can't think straight."

"What the hell do you have to think about?" Demon sauntered over to his bike that was parked next to mine and threw his leg over it. We had all been found from time to time in the garage, just sitting on our bikes in the winter. It was hard to be free for eight months of the year on our bikes then four months of being trapped in a cage.

"Do you ever think you'll settle down?"

"I had a chance to settle down years ago, and I blew it. We both fucking blew it. I couldn't see what was right in front of my nose, and she was too young."

"You're the same age as me, brother. I think there's still time for ya. Hell, look at Gravel."

"Yeah, well, Gravel and your Mom are different. Besides, we're not talking about me right now. I wanna know what the hell you have to think about on your wedding day. All your thinking should be done."

I grasped the handlebars and shook my head. "Not that kind of thinking. I know Meg is the one. I haven't doubted that since the day I met her. I'm just thinking about everything I guess. Where the club was, where we're headed. So many changes happened in such a short amount of time that I never really had a chance to just sit back and think about everything."

"Things change, brother, but as long as they change for the better, just roll with it."

"True that," I mumbled.

"Yo," Rigid called. "Cyn said she needs to talk to you. She called my phone ranting about Meg and reading. She told me to put you on the phone or she was going to name our kid Bartholomew."

Demon and I both laughed but knew that Cyn would do it in a heartbeat. Rigid walked over and handed me the phone.

"Shouldn't you be sitting in some salon getting your hair done and wrangling my bride?" I said into the phone.

"Well, that was the plan, but things seem to have taken a different turn."

"What the hell does that mean?" I could tell by the tone in her voice that something wasn't right.

"She's gone. She left the salon, got in her truck and left. I don't know what to do, King."

"What the hell do you mean she's gone?" I barked into the phone. This was not the conversation I planned on having the day of my wedding.

"We were talking about books and she suddenly got weird, saying how she use to read all the time and ever since she had been with you, she couldn't remember the last book she had read. I don't know what she's thinking right now, King. All I know is she's gone, and I have no idea where to even look for her."

"I'm getting married in four hours, Cyn, and you just told me you have no idea where the hell my bride is."

"I'm sorry, King. We tried to stop her, but she was already in her truck by the time we realized she was running."

"Fuck," I growled. I tossed the phone to Rigid and stalked to the door.

"What the fuck is going on?" Demon called.

"Fucking Meg."

"Where the hell are you going?"

"To get my Goddamn bride."

———————

Chapter 25
Meg

I didn't know where I was going when I had gotten in my truck and drove away, but I wasn't surprised when I pulled up to my house and killed the engine. I could count on one hand the days I had spent here the past month, and that just made me sad.

It wasn't Lo's fault with everything going on with the Assassins, but that didn't change the fact that I couldn't even remember the last time I had spent the night at my house.

I opened the door, numbly stepping out of the truck. "Meg! I'm surprised to see you. I thought you were getting married today."

I looked at the house next to mine and saw Larry, my neighbor, standing by his mailbox. "Just have to find something," I called. I walked around to the back of the house since the front porch was no more, and I didn't think I could hoist my ass up the three-foot drop off up to the front door.

Everything looked the same except it was all covered with a thin layer of snow that was now falling heavier. It all looked the same, but it didn't feel like it. It felt like my whole world had been tipped upside down, and I just realized that I didn't know what the hell was going on and who I was.

I stomped up the steps of the back porch, unlocked the door and dropped my coat on the floor. I waited to hear the sound of Blue coming to greet me but remembered he was at the clubhouse. Hell, my dog didn't even seem like he was mine anymore. He was always out in the garage with Lo or sleeping on the couch in the common room.

The kitchen chair skidded across the floor as I pulled it out and sat down. The clock on the stove said one o'clock. It was two hours until I was supposed to get married. I looked down at my clothes and laughed, wondering if Lo would marry me in my chuck's and jeans. That was one thing that hadn't changed. I still dressed the same.

I heard a car pull up in my driveway, not surprised that someone was already here. When I had left the salon, my phone had rung non-stop until I had turned it off. When I got to my house, I had left it in my truck, not wanting to turn it on.

I thought twice about getting up and locking the back door, but I knew if it were Lo, it wouldn't matter. He had the keys to the house. I didn't know what I was going to do or say. I didn't know what I was feeling other than I felt like I had lost myself again. When Lo and I had met, I knew who I was and what I wanted. Now I felt like I was doing the same thing I had done with Hunter. Losing myself in a man again.

The door to the car slammed shut, and I counted the seconds till I heard the back door open. I closed my eyes, not wanting to go through this. Wishing I could just disappear and not have to figure out everything that was swirling around in my head.

I heard the chair across from me scrape across the floor and then someone sat down. That someone was Lo, but I was praying it was Cyn or Troy. They talked me out of my last stupid crisis. I just hoped that I was that lucky this time.

"I love you." His words crashed into me, tearing me apart. He went straight to the words that would bring me down.

"I know," I whispered. A tear streaked down my face and fell on my jeans.

"Do you love me?"

I nodded my head yes because I couldn't deny it. That wasn't why we were here, though. I didn't doubt my love for Lo, I was afraid I was going to get lost again.

"Then you wanna tell me why I get a phone call from Cyn, who was hysterical that you ran off, and she had no idea where you were?" I shook my head no because the reason I ran wouldn't make sense to him. It hadn't made sense to Cyn or Gwen, so why would it make sense to him? "God dammit, Meg."

I opened my eyes and my eyes landed on him as he ran his fingers through his hair. He looked as handsome as ever. Jet black hair, green eyes that always reminded me of fresh cut grass and the most handsome face I had ever seen. He was my Lo. "I don't read anymore."

"I know in your head what you said makes perfect fucking sense, but out here in the real world, you're going to have to back it up and tell me what the hell that means."

I dashed away the tears that were falling with the back of my hand. "I use to come home from work every night, fall into bed and read until either my eyes got tired, or my Kindle would whack me in the face because I fell asleep." It sounded ridiculous, but it was true. Usually, I'd fall asleep, and my Kindle would fall out of my hands, waking me up and letting me know it was time to get to bed.

"Babe, I'm still not following what the hell that has to do with you and me getting married."

"I don't do that anymore. Hell, I couldn't even remember the last book I had read when Cyn and Gwen asked."

"Babe, then fucking read."

He said it like it was so easy. "But I can't. Not when I come home. You're either waiting up for me or wake up as soon as my keys hit the door. We fall into bed, you fuck me until I can't think straight and I fall asleep."

"I don't see one fucking problem with the last thing you said."

"The problem is I love to read, and I can't do it. It was my escape from life and reality. I could be a librarian who falls for the local rodeo star, the girl who's terrified of living but somehow falls into local MC and ends up someone's ol' lady–"

"Now that shit happened to you, why the fuck do you need to read about it when it's going on around you?" Lo cut me off and stood up. "Meg, you wanna read when you get home from work?" I nodded my head yes. "Then fucking read!" He boomed throwing his hands up in the air.

"It's more than reading, Lo. I don't know who I am anymore. I figured out who I was before we got together, but now I've lost her again. Don't you see? I'm not Meg, I'm King's ol' lady."

"Damn fucking straight that's a part of who you are, but you're still the same woman I met six months ago, and I wouldn't change one damn thing about you."

"But it feels different."

"Because it fucking is! You think that having a man and a shit ton more friends isn't going to change things around you? But that don't mean you fucking change! Hell, Meg. You're stuck in your damn head with all that bullshit swirling around again, aren't you?"

"It's not shit!" I wailed.

"It fucking is," he growled, getting in my face. "I love you with everything I am. I know that my life has changed and, hell, even I have fucking changed since I met you, but I wouldn't want it any other fucking way. You're mine," he bit off.

"But I'm losing myself in you. I can't do that to myself again. It'll destroy us."

"Meg, I'm so fucking wrapped up in you that I have no idea where I end and where you begin. I lost myself to you the second I saw you bent over in that damn store, waving your ass at me. That same store that every time when I drive by, I thank God he brought you into my life. I have been looking for you all my life, and I am not about to let you go because you think you've lost yourself because you don't read anymore. You can fucking read and be God damn married to me! It happens every fucking day in marriages across America!"

"You don't get it," I whined, plopping down into my chair.

Lo looked up at the ceiling and shook his head. "I get it, Meg. I get it more than you think. What happened to you when you were married to Hunter happened because you two didn't love each other anymore. Not because you lost yourself. You both stayed for as long as you did because you had a kid together." I closed my eyes and dropped my head. I hated that he knew that. I stayed in a loveless marriage because I was afraid to leave and thought that it was best for my son. "Meg," he called. I didn't want to open my eyes. He grabbed my hands, and I felt him kneel down in front of me. "Open those beautiful eyes, babe," he coaxed.

"I don't know what to say, Lo." I opened my eyes and Lo reached up, wiping the tears from my face.

"Do you love me?"

Such an easy question. "Yes."

"Then why are you running from me?"

"Because I'm scared," I whispered. "I'm afraid I'll drive you away. That after a while you'll get sick of me and then I'll be alone again, not knowing who I am. I need to keep a part of me, so I know what to do when you leave."

He sighed and shook his head. "I'm not going anywhere, Meg. Never. If I didn't want to be with you every second, I wouldn't have asked you to marry me. I would have just kept things like they were and never taken things to the next level. You wanna know why I never want to leave?" I shrugged my shoulders, not knowing why he didn't want to leave. "Because you make me whole. You make me the person I've wanted to be all of my life. I have a purpose when I wake up in the morning. You gave my life the meaning I've been searching for forever. You're. Mine."

My heart soared when I heard those words, knowing what he was saying was the truth, but I was still afraid. "I love you so much."

"Then marry me. Today."

I shook my head no and looked away. Fairy Tales weren't real, and the story that Lo was weaving was fairytale to the core.

He cupped my chin and turned my head to look at him. "Meg, I can't promise that our life is going to be perfect, and we'll never argue or fight. But I can guarantee that I'll always love you and that my place will always be next to you."

"You'll catch me when I fall? You'll be there when I make a fool of myself? You'll never leave, even when there might be something better out there for you? You'll stay?" I loved this man with everything I had, and I was terrified that he didn't love me back the same way. It was easy to say that you loved someone. It was showing it that became hard, but that was where all of the proof was.

"I'll never let you fall, Meg, except into my arms. I love when you make a fool of yourself because that's when I know I have the real Meg. The one who isn't afraid of what others think. The Meg, who would lay her life down for her son and friends. The Meg that makes me whole."

I leaned into his touch, letting his words sink in. "That includes you, too."

"What?"

"I'd lay my life down for you, too," I confided.

He leaned forward, his head resting against my forehead, his eyes locked with mine. "Will you marry me?"

Tears clouded my eyes again, but this time, because Lo still wanted to marry me. "I can't promise the shit swirling in my head will ever stop."

"As long as if you feel like you have to run, you run to me, I'll be there to quiet that shit."

"You're not supposed to see me on our wedding day. It's bad luck."

"As long as I have you, I don't care about bad luck. Marry me?"

"Your mom is going to be mad that you saw me."

"I don't care. I had to make sure my bride makes it down the aisle. Marry me?"

"How long until we can move back into my house?"

"You're ignoring my question."

"No, I'm just prolonging my answer. When can we move back home?"

"As long as you keep calling it our home, we can be in by the end of January. Marry me?"

I pushed on his shoulders, and he sat back on his heels. I slid out of my chair and knelt in front of him. "Yes," I whispered, wrapping my arms around his neck. "Yes, I'll marry you."

"It's about damn time," he whispered against my lips. His lips melted against mine, his tongue sweeping in, tasting and promising forever. Lo raised up, kicking his legs out from under him and he sat down on his ass and pulled me into his lap. "How long is it going to take you to get ready?"

"Ready for what?" I mumbled against his neck.

"To get in your dress and all that shit?"

"Hmm, probably an hour."

"Good, because you're mine for the next forty-five minutes."

"I like the sound of that," I purred, pushing him back to lay down. His hands grabbed my ass, pulling me down with him. "We've never done it on the kitchen floor before."

"I think you're right, babe. We're going to have to fix that." My fingers delved into his hair as my lips crashed down on his and his hands roamed over my body, pulling my shirt up.

"Jesus."

Lo and I froze, his hands on my bare back and our lips sealed together.

"Holy fuck. I told you we should have knocked louder."

Lo and I opened our eyes, and we knew that Gravel and Ethel were standing in my kitchen while Lo had his hands up my shirt and I was two seconds away from being topless.

"Well, how was I supposed to know they would be on the kitchen floor? Cyn told me Meg was a damn runaway bride."

"Well, it looks like King managed to talk some sense into her."

"You do know that we can hear you, right?" Lo asked.

"Well I would fucking hope so," Gravel chuckled.

"I bet this was some harebrained idea you two cooked up so you could see her before the wedding, isn't it, Lo?" Ethel questioned.

I sat up and rolled off Lo. "Um, I wish I could say that was true, but I actually did run."

"Well, I assume since you two were just about to screw on the floor that everything is under control. Let's get out of here, darlin'." Gravel reached for Ethel's hand, but she sidestepped him, shooing her hand at him.

"Nonsense. I'll ride with Meg back to Gwen's, and you two can ride back in my car. Besides, the less these two see each other, the better."

"Ma. I think all that bad luck shit is just that, shit. Meg and I can ride back together." Lo stood up and wrapped his arm around my waist. "We'll be there in an hour." Even after being busted by his mom, Lo still had plans for us. I liked the way he was thinking.

Ethel grabbed my hand and pulled me out of Lo's arms. "Nope. Not happening. Meg needs to get ready and so do you. Gwen is all set up at the clubhouse to do your hair. I called her as soon as we saw that you and Lo were here."

"But… Ethel… I want to…" She dragged me to the door and grabbed my coat off of the floor.

"No buts. Keep it in your pants until after the wedding, Lo," Ethel scolded. She threw open the door, her hand still grasping my arm and pulled me out the door and down the stairs.

I glanced up the stairs to see Lo and Gravel standing at the top of the stairs, both of them smirking. "Ethel, at least let the girl put her coat on," Gravel called.

"I'll crank the heat up in the truck. She'll be fine." She opened up the driver's door of my truck, pushing me in and slammed the door shut as soon as my butt was in the door. I couldn't see Lo anymore, but I'm sure he was laughing his ass off. Who would have thought on my wedding day I would be busted making out with my groom by my future mother-in-law who then drags me out of my house like a naughty child.

"Start it up. Let's go," Ethel ordered as she slid into the passenger seat.

"I don't have keys, Ethel. You dragged me out of the house so fast, I didn't have time to think much less grab my purse," I said, looking over at her.

A smile spread across her lips, and she pointed over my shoulder. I looked out my side window to see Lo standing there, my keys dangling from his fingertips. I cranked down the window and reached for my keys.

He snatched them away before I could grasp them. "Only if you promise not to run again. I planned on making you dazed, and compliant before my Mom showed up. Now I have to rely on your word that you'll be walking down the aisle."

"I promise." I reached for keys, sticking half of my body out of the window, but he still wouldn't give them to me. He leaned forward, his lips brushing against mine.

"Lo, give her the damn keys. I'll make sure she's there." I felt Ethel lean over the seat, and she flailed her hand out my window at Lo, shooing him away.

"Alright, alright," Lo laughed, handing me my keys. I grabbed the keys, sticking them in the ignition and cranking up the truck. "Make sure she gets there, Ma. No detours," Lo called as he stepped back from the truck and crossed his arms over his chest.

"Straight to the clubhouse. That's it," Ethel promised. I rolled up the window, giving Lo a little finger wave. I shifted the truck into reverse, backing out of the driveway and headed to the clubhouse.

"Still can't believe you ran, hun. I thought for sure Cyn was losing her mind when she called me," Ethel mumbled.

"I was stupid. I wasn't thinking clearly. I'm good now, though," I promised. And I was.

Lo was right. I had changed, but it was for the better. Sure, I didn't read anymore, but the main reason I did read was to escape my crap life. When I was with Hunter, I would devour at least seven books a week, if not more. Now, I didn't need that escape. Now I had Lo.

"Well, I'm not letting you run away again," Ethel mumbled.

I could have argued with her, telling her she didn't need to watch guard over me, but I just let her keep talking.

I knew that nothing was going to keep me from walking down the aisle to Lo and starting our lives together.

In less than two hours, I was about to become Mrs. Birch, and there wasn't a damn thing in this world that was going to stop me.

———————

Chapter 26
Lo

"Pussy whipped."

"Definitely."

Demon and Rigid were standing in the office of the shop, looking at each other and shaking their heads. After forty-five minutes of bitching and moaning about wearing a tux, we were ready to get this wedding on the road.

"You only have to wear it for the ceremony, and then I don't care what the fuck you wear." I straightened my tie and grabbed my cuff links off the stack of papers on the desk. "How the fuck do I put these on?" I was beginning to get a little fed up with this tux, too.

"Give 'em here," Gravel grumbled, pushing off the wall and holding his hand out to me. I dropped them in his hand and held my arm out as he worked magic.

"Y'all should see Slider. He just rolled up with Fayth, and he looks like he got kicked in the nuts. Bastard looks fucking miserable," Gambler chuckled, leaning against the door frame.

"He's miserable because he hasn't been able to get his dick wet since King put him on Fayth duty." Demon straightened his tie and sat down in the chair behind my desk. "You're torturing the guy."

I shrugged my shoulders, not caring. "Someone had to watch Fayth. He can suck it up and take one for the club." Gravel finished with one arm and grabbed the other. "Besides, Leo will be in town for at least a week, so Slider will have a break from her for a bit."

"Fucking talking about me?" Slider growled. I glanced behind Gambler and saw Slider with a cigarette hanging from his mouth and a grimace from hell on his face.

"Yeah. I was saying you can cheer the fuck up because, with Leo back in town, you're a free man for the next week."

"What the fuck ever. After that, I'll be right back to keeping an eye on the fucking princess." He took a long drag off his cigarette and blew smoke at Gambler's head.

"Dude, knock it the fuck off. I'm trying to quit fucking smoking. Now Gwen is going to smell that shit all over me." Gambler spun around waving his arms in the air and pushed Slider back out the front door.

"It's like a three-ring circus in here," Gravel grumbled, dropping my hand. "You're done. Try not to fuck it up before Meg sees you. Your mother about had a bird when I told her I had to come back here and make sure you fools look good."

"As long as she doesn't tell Meg about the tux, I don't care."

"Okay, let's get this fucking show on the road." Gravel herded everyone out of the office, but Demon and I lingered behind.

"You fucking sure about this? You and I could grab our bikes and be out of here before anyone even knows." Demon hitched his thumb over his shoulder, backing up a step towards the shop. "Just say the word."

"I'm not fucking going anywhere besides out to the common room and waiting for Meg."

"Just thought I'd ask. It's just one of the jobs of the best man."

"Oh, yeah, and what are the other jobs of the best man?"

Demon walked behind the desk and pulled a bottle of Jameson out of the drawer. "To get you slightly buzzed before you walk down the aisle." He grabbed two shot glasses off the filing cabinet and sloshed each glass full.

"So are those your only jobs?" I laughed, grabbing the glass from him.

He held his glass high, "To possibly making the biggest mistake of your life." He clinked his glass against mine, and we both tossed them back. The Jameson burned down my throat as I slammed my glass down on the desk and he refilled them.

"You gonna be an ass my whole wedding day or are you going to snap the fuck out of it and just be fucking happy for me?" Ever since Meg had said yes to me, Demon had been a prick about anything that had to do with the wedding. He tossed back his second shot and immediately refilled his glass. He held it up, motioning for me to drink mine, but I set my glass down. "Answer the fucking question."

He tossed his back and slammed his glass down. "I'm not a fucking ass."

"Then tell me what the hell you are then because it sure as hell isn't my best man supporting me."

Demon ran his hands through his hair and paced back and forth. "Look, it's nothing. Just shit from my past that got dredged up. There was a chick who, um, took something that was mine and didn't care. I was going to ask her to marry me before shit went sideways. That's all. I'm over it."

Yeah, sure Demon was over it. I shook my head and tossed back the shot. "You still talk to the girl?"

"No. I haven't seen her in eight years."

"What did she take that was yours?"

"I don't wanna fucking talk about it. I'm over her, and I'm over the damn conversation. Let's go get you married so I can get the fuck out of this monkey suit."

I clapped him on the back, and we walked out the door. "It may be a fucking monkey suit, but it's going to fucking help me get laid tonight."

We stopped in front of the door to the common room, and I took a deep breath.

"She's the one," Demon mumbled.

I glanced over at him, and a smile spread across my lips. "Fuck yeah, she's the one."

"You're sure."

"Yes, I'm fucking sure. Let's do this."

Meg

"I'm not sure I can fucking do this." I fanned myself with my hand and bent over, shoving my head between my knees. "I think I'm going to pass out."

"We should get the wheelbarrow. We'll just roll her down the aisle and dump her at King's feet."

"You really think he'd appreciate us dumping his bride in a wheelbarrow and wheeling her down the aisle?"

"I think he would appreciate the fact that we wouldn't let his bride run for a second time."

"I'm down with the wheelbarrow."

"I second the wheelbarrow. Or would it be I third the wheelbarrow?"

My head was swimming, and all I wanted to do was lay down and not get up. I was nervous. I was scared. I was more than likely going to puke. "I can't do this," I mumbled again.

"You think she knows that we can't understand a word she's saying?"

I whipped my head back and pushed my hair out of my face so I could tell who the hell was talking. With my head between my legs, they all sounded the same. Cyn, Jackie, Gwen and Marley were lined up in front of me, all of them with their hands on their hips smirking at me. "Get your ass up or I'm getting the wheelbarrow," Cyn ordered.

"You can't do that to me. You're my best friend and maid of honor. You're supposed to be the one with the car running out back so we can make our get away like Thelma and Louise." How all four of them were siding against me was beyond me.

"Maids of honor only do that when they know the bride is marrying a douchebag. You are not marrying a douchebag. You're marrying King, and in less than twenty minutes, the nice preacher you have out front is going to make you King's Queen." Cyn had been saying that all morning that I was going to be King's Queen. I had been telling her that was corny, but secretly I loved it.

"I need a drink." Yeah, maybe a drink would help. Sooth my nerves.

"You've already had three old fashions," Gwen mumbled.

"And two wine coolers. I think you might need to just chill. We've only got five minutes." Jackie glanced over her shoulder at the clock, "Make that four minutes."

"Oh my God, oh my God," I chanted over and over.

"Either this wedding is going to be fucking beautiful, or it's going to be a shit show with Meg running down the aisle and straight out the door." Marley flopped down on the bed next to me and rubbed my back. "Meg. Chill out. You're acting like you're walking down the aisle to the devil, not King."

Cyn grabbed the desk chair, rolled it in front of me and sat down. Jackie and Gwen stood on each side of her, and I knew I was about to have a come to Jesus moment. "Do you love him?" Cyn fired off.

"Yes."

"Does Remy like him?"

"Yes." At least I think he did.

"Do you like having hot, sweaty, monkey sex with him?"

"Oh, Jesus Christ! She's my sister. I don't need to hear the details," Jackie whined.

"Shush," Cyn said, elbowing Jackie. "Answer the question, Meg."

"Cyn, I don't know what this has to do with me marrying Lo." She crossed her arms over her chest, resting them on her tiny baby bump and glared at me. "Okay, yes. Of course, I like it."

"Then stand your ass up and marry the man. I can tell you right now, us five in this room have the best men. Marry him and make him yours."

I looked at my girls, all of them shaking their heads agreeing with Cyn. She was right. "I love him," I whispered.

"Alright! Good pep talk. Let's get this show on the road." Marley jumped up from the bed, grabbing her flowers off of the dresser and threw the bedroom door open.

"Wait," I called before they filed out of the room. "I just want to thank each of you for being here today and well, just thank you for putting up with my crazy ass." My vision blurred as we all hugged. Marley, Gwen, and Jackie filed out the door, and Cyn threaded her arm through mine.

"Ready to do this?" She asked.

"Just one more drink," I pleaded reaching for the half empty bottle of Southern Comfort.

"No," she said clamping down on my arm. "The rest of your life starts right now, Meg. Are you ready?"

I looked down at my dress, and she handed me my flowers. I was ready. I had my purple chucks on, my beautiful dress that I had dreamed of all my life and my hair and makeup were flawless. The only thing missing was my groom.

"I'm ready."

———————

Chapter 27
Meg

"You sure about this?"

I glanced over at my dad and a huge grin spread across my lips. "I've tried to run twice today, Dad, and I'm still standing here. I'm sure."

"Well, if you're sure," he huffed. "But if you're not, all I need to do is signal your mother and she'll hightail it out of here and pull the car around the front, and we'll be out of here lickety split."

My dad was reaching to itch his nose, and I knew that was the signal. I grabbed his arm and threaded my arm through it. "I'm good, Dad. I promise."

"Marley just walked down the aisle. Jackie goes and then I do. Are you ready?" Cyn whispered to me.

I squeezed my Dad's hand and nodded my head. I was ready. I. Was. Ready. Cyn nodded to me over her shoulder then turned the corner in the hallway. This was it. As soon as I turned the corner down the hall, there would be no turning back.

I waited until I heard the opening chords of 'Give In To Me' by Rose Falcon and my feet started moving without even thinking. I knew in my heart that this was right. Walking down the aisle to Lo was the best decision I had ever made.

My breath caught when I reached the end of the hallway that opened into the common room, and my eyes went directly to Lo. All I could see was him, standing there waiting for me in a tux. Logan Birch, the sexiest man on all of the earth, was wearing a tux. My heart sped up as my eyes traveled over his body, taking in every detail that I possibly could.

His tux was pitch black with a dark gray vest with a pressed white shirt underneath, and he had managed to get a tie that matched the flowers and the bridesmaid's dresses. He looked so different and handsome, but he was still my Lo.

We walked down the aisle that parted the room full of guests who were all camped out on chairs watching me, but I only had eyes for Lo. Dad and I made it to the end of the aisle, Lo only mere feet away from me. Dad hugged me, whispering in my ear, "You're beautiful. I love you." And I felt the tears begin to fall. He wrapped me up in his arms, holding me tight and then he handed me off to Lo.

He grabbed my hand, pulling me close and buried his face in my neck. "Babe."

One word and it felt like my heart was going to burst. One word and I knew exactly what he was feeling and thinking. "I love you."

He crushed me in his arms, and I wrapped my arms around his neck. This was right. This was what I had always been missing in my life. Lo.

"You think we can let the preacher man get through his spiel before you go all caveman on her ass?" Demon whispered.

Everyone chuckled under their breath, but Lo still held me close. "You're mine," he whispered in my ear.

"Always." He finally let me go, well, not exactly let me go. He pulled away from me, but he grabbed my bouquet out of my hands, tossed it to Cyn then threaded his fingers through mine.

"We're good now," he mumbled to the preacher.

I turned my head and looked at the 'preacher'. I kept calling him that because I had no idea what else to call him. Lo had sprung the idea on me a couple of weeks ago that we should let his old club president marry us. I couldn't really argue with the idea because I was stumped on who I was going to have ordain the ceremony. Lo's old friend and ex-club president seemed perfect. Looking at him now, I might have rethought how perfect he was.

While Lo and I were dressed up, Blade was, well, dressed how Lo normally is. I guess Blade didn't get the memo that this was a wedding, but from the rough around the edges look of him, I wasn't going to be the one to tell him.

Blade's voice boomed as he addressed the crowd, welcoming them to our wedding and this was when I took the time to look around. I paid attention to his words, but I quickly sneaked a peek at my bridesmaids, all lined up perfectly and looking gorgeous. Then I looked behind Lo, smiling as I saw Demon, Rigid, Gambler, and Troy were each wearing tuxes also. They each looked handsome, but Lo definitely stole the show.

Ethel and Gravel sat in the front row surrounded by the rest of the club and who I had to assume were members of the Collinsworth club that Lo had once belonged to. My Mom and Dad sat behind me, and I knew they were surrounded by my sister's family and multiple aunts and uncles who had made the trip.

Everyone we both loved was here, and I couldn't ask for anything else.

"Meg and Lo both decided to write their own vows. Meg." Blade nodded at me, and I knew it was show time.

Lo's hands squeezed my fingers, and I cleared my throat. "Lo, Logan Birch." I paused, trying to gather my thoughts. I had planned on writing my vows but decided to wing it and just say what was ever in my heart. "From the day I met you, I knew you were unlike anyone I had ever met. You see me for who I am, and you never want to change that. You've accepted not only my weird and strange ways, but you've also accepted my son. Remy has had my heart since the day he was born, and I never wanted to share my heart with anyone but him until the day I met you. You give me things I never knew I was worthy of. You make my heart full and my life complete."

"Oh my God, don't do it," Cyn whispered from behind me.

A smile spread across my lips. "You complete me." Cyn and all my girls giggled behind me, and the whole crowd groaned. Lo threw his head back laughing and wrapped me up in his arms. I guess that was what happened when I went total improv, Jerry Maguire came out of my mouth. But it was true, though.

"You're Goddamn crazy, and I love it," he whispered. He pressed a kiss to the side of my head and stepped back, our hands still connected.

"Lo," Blade nodded.

Lo cleared his throat and closed his eyes. I couldn't tell if he was nervous or just trying to collect his thoughts. I assumed he was doing what I did and just winging it. He opened his beautiful green eyes and stole my breath with every word that came out of his mouth. "I don't even know where to start, babe. I knew the day I met you that I wasn't going to let you go. The love that you have for your family and friends amazes me and the joy and laughter that you bring into my life day in and out is more than I ever could have asked for. I'll do anything to keep you, even buy you ten more big ass beds that you break as long as it means you'll be in them with me. I love you, and I'll always be yours for as long as you'll have me."

Tears streamed down my cheeks, and all I could do was nod my head. God dammit, I loved this man.

"May I have the rings?" Demon stepped forward, reaching into his pocket and dropped the rings into Blade's hand. "Meg, take this ring and place it on Logan's left ring finger."

I grabbed the black tungsten ring and put it on his finger. Blade continued to talk, telling me what I need to say, but everything just went by in a blur. All I can remember is Lo putting the beautiful ring on my finger, and my tears multiplied.

This was it. I had found my happily ever after.

———————

Lo

"You may kiss the bride."

Those were the words that I had been waiting for. This was the moment I had waited for my whole life. I wrapped my arms around Meg, her body melting into mine, and I kissed her like she was the last woman on earth. I kissed her like she was mine. Always and forever.

I was keeping her, and there was no going back.

———————

Chapter 28
Meg

"It's five minutes to midnight. Are you ready to ring in a new year with me?"

"I'm ready to spend the rest of my life with you."

"So that's a yes on ringing in the new year with me?" I laughed. Lo danced me around the area of the clubhouse we had cleared as the dance floor and shook his head at me.

"Yeah, babe. No one else I'd rather spend it with," he growled, leaning down to kiss me on the lips.

I dodged his mouth and tsked at him. "Not until midnight."

"I'll kiss you at midnight, too."

"You can wait four minutes," I scolded. His arms flexed around me as he pulled me close, and I buried my face in his chest. Fleetwood Mac was pouring out of the huge speakers on the sides of the dance floor, and I hummed along to 'You Make Loving Fun' as I snuggled into Lo.

"In those four minutes, I could have you back in our room, and we could ring in the new year a whole different way."

"Hmm, twirl me around a couple more times and it'll be the new year before you know it and then you can officially make me your wife in every sense of the word." I leaned my head back, a small smile on my lips.

Someone turned the music down, the sounds of Fleetwood Mac fleeting and the voice of Ryan Seacrest getting louder. "Promise me we'll spend every new year like this."

"You expect me to marry you every new year?" That seemed a bit crazy. I had heard of people renewing their vows but doing it every year seemed a bit over the top.

"No. Every year, you and I ringing out the old and welcoming the new together."

"I think I can manage that," I whispered.

"One minute!" Marley yelled as her, and Troy danced past us, headed for the TV. The dance floor had mostly cleared off, and everyone was gathered around the huge TV ready to countdown to the new year.

"Demon still seems to be in a mood," I mused as my eyes fell on Demon, who was leaning against the bar looking like he was sulking.

"He's dealing with his own shit, babe. His attitude doesn't have anything to do with you."

"Maybe we should try to set him up with someone."

"Nah, not happening, Meg. Get that shit out of your head."

"But this is the good kind of shit, Lo," I pleaded.

Lo threw his head back laughing, and I socked him in the shoulder. "Did you not just hear what you said."

I played back in my head what I had said and had to agree it was pretty funny. "You know what I meant."

"I did, and I still say no."

"Fine," I pouted.

"Ready?" I heard Marley shout. "Ten, nine…" Lo grabbed my hand and dragged me off to a dark corner and pinned me up against the wall. "Three, two, one. Happy New Year!"

"Happy New Year," Lo growled low, his lips hovering over my mouth. "Can I kiss you now?" He smirked.

"You can kiss me forever," I whispered.

"Thank God." His lips devoured my mouth, and his tongue swooped in, claiming me as his hands delved into my hair, tilting my head back.

I wrapped my arms around his waist, leaning into him, knowing with everything that I had that this was right where I was supposed to be.

Right here in Lo's arms.

———————

Chapter 29
Paige

I was ready to go home. I mean *beyond* ready to go.

Gwen had somehow meddled and set me up with Princeton, who by the way, was a nice guy but he just wasn't my type. He was serious and barely talked, so when thrown together with me, who never talked, you can imagine the stimulating conversation we'd had.

"You want another drink?"

I shook my head no, realizing that three cosmos I had already had was more than enough. Usually, I stuck to only one drink when I was out with a new guy, but the first one went down so smooth that I figured what the hell and had two more.

Princeton made his way to the bar, and I had to admit he was a good looking guy. His body was stacked like a brick house, and his face was chiseled to perfection, but I just didn't feel any connection with him.

"Hey, how's it going?" Gwen sang as she walked over to the table I was sitting at.

"I'm ready to go," I yawned. Princeton and I hadn't made it to the wedding until after the ceremony, and although we had only been here a couple of hours, I was exhausted.

"Oh, you're such a party pooper. It's only a little after midnight."

Trust me, I fully know what time it was. I had sat at this table in an awkward silence with Princeton as everyone in the clubhouse had basically made out. Talk about awkward. "I normally turn into a pumpkin after midnight," I laughed.

"Are you at least having fun with Princeton?" Gwen babbled.

"He's nice, Gwen, but there's nothing there."

"You hardly gave him a chan–"

"Gwen!" Meg yelled as the opening chords of Journey's 'Don't Stop Believing' started playing. "Get your ass out here!"

"Shit, I gotta go. Text me when you get home, and I'll call you in the morning." Gwen danced off in the direction of Meg, and I had to laugh when Gwen, Cyn, and Meg all started belting out the lyrics.

I was glad Gwen had found such good friends. After the whole Matt debacle, I was worried she would never get back to the wonderful person I knew she was.

Thankfully she had met Gambler, and her life seemed to be exactly what she deserved.

I grabbed my purse and pulled my shawl over my shoulders and made my way over to the bar where Princeton was standing talking to Creed, his partner from what I had gathered. I elbowed my way to bar but managed to trip over a pair of legs that were lounging in front of the bar.

A pair of arms managed to grab me around my waist and twirl me around before I fell face first on the floor.

I pushed my hair out of my face, ready to thank whoever who had just saved me from possibly making a fool of myself when all the blood rushed from my face, and I saw a ghost from my past I never thought I would see again. "Demon," I gasped.

———

Demon

"What the fuck?"

The End
(For Now)

Fighting Demon
Devil's Knights Series
Book 7

Winter Travers

Chapter 1

Demon

She was here.

Paige was fucking here.

What the ever-living fuck was going on?

"You're hurting me," she mumbled, her eyes huge as she looked up at me trying to wiggle out of my grasp. My fingers dug into her arm, holding her up as I tried to wrap my head around the fact that Paige fucking Lawson was standing in front of me. "Demon," she whispered, throwing me back to a time where she would whisper my name and bury her face in my neck right before she came.

I loosened my grip on her arm but didn't let her go. "What are you doing here?" How the hell did she know King and Meg? Was she here as someone's date?

"I'm here for the wedding. We were just about to leave." She tilted her head back and looked up at me. "Please let me go."

"No. Not until you tell me what the hell you're doing in my clubhouse. I haven't seen you in over seven years. You just fucking disappeared."

"Because I didn't want to be found, but I didn't expect you to look for me. You made it perfectly clear what you thought of me, Demon. I wasn't going to hang around."

"Because I thought you didn't take care of what was mine," I growled.

"It wasn't just yours, Demon."

"Why are you here after seven years? What the hell do you want from me?"

"I don't want anything from you, Demon. If I had known that this was your clubhouse and hell, if I had known that Gwen knew you, I never would have agreed to move here." She ripped her arm out of my grasp and took a step back.

"Gwen?" I was confused as hell what Gwen had to do with Paige.

"She's my sister, Demon."

Fucking hell. I had known that Gwen's sister's name was Paige, but I never figured her Paige and my Paige were the same person. "Fuck."

She spun around, ready to take off. I grabbed her by the arm again. "Demon, let me go," she insisted as I spun her back around. "I just want to go home."

"How the hell are you getting home? I can tell you've been drinking."

"The same way I got here, in Princeton's car."

My blood boiled at that pricks name. Leo's latest two men who rolled into town had been butting heads with everyone in the club. Well, at least with Slider and I. "You're fucking dating Princeton?"

"What does it matter to you," she hissed. "The last I heard from you was that I was nothing. Who I date should also be nothing to you." She tried twisting out of my grasp, but instead of letting her go, I pulled her close and wrapped my arms around her.

"I never thought I'd see you again." One week after everything had happened, I walked out of Paige's apartment telling myself things would never be the same. So much had changed from just one phone call. The panic in Paige's voice as she told me she was on the way to the hospital was something I'd never be able to forget. At the time, I blamed her for everything that happened, but after I left and had time to think about it, I knew it wasn't anyone's fault. I should have gone back to her, but I didn't. I was too stupid and bullheaded to listen to reason.

"Well, I hoped to never see you again, so just please let me go." She looked up at me, panic in her eyes, but I also saw the Paige that I had once loved and wanted to spend the rest of my life with.

"Is there a problem here?"

I looked over Paige's shoulder and saw Princeton leaning against the bar, a glass dangling from his fingertips. "That better be fucking water you're drinking if you're driving Paige home," I barked.

"Last I checked I didn't fucking answer to you." Princeton drained his glass and set it on the bar. "And for the record, I'm fucking working. Not that you would know anything about that."

"Guess that answers my question if you're dating this asshole." I glanced down at Paige, smirking, and she rolled her eyes. "Not that you fucking deserve her." I looked back up at Princeton who just shrugged his shoulders. What in the hell was Paige doing with this asshole?

"Please, just let me go home," she pleaded. She pressed her hand against my chest, trying to pull away. "I'm tired, Demon."

My eyes fell on her sweet and innocent face, and all I wanted to do was lay her out on the bar and remember every curve and inch of her sweet body that I used to worship. "This isn't over, Paige," I whispered. I let her go, took a step back and watched her stunned face at what I said sink in.

She got a grip, finally tearing her eyes off of me and stepped back into Princeton. "I'm ready," she mumbled, looking over her shoulder at him. He grunted in reply and slid his arm around her waist and pulled her into his side. She stiffened at his touch but didn't pull away like when I had touched her.

"I'll take good care of her, Demon. Don't worry." Princeton winked at me and they disappeared into the crowd and out the door. I counted to ten, trying to get a grip but it wasn't working.

Seeing Paige was a sucker punch to the gut, but then having to see her leave with that douchebag fucking enraged me. I glanced around the clubhouse, seeing if anyone had just witnessed Paige and me together.

Lo was standing ten feet away, with his eyes trained on me.

"Son of a bitch," I mumbled under my breath.

I reached over the bar and grabbed the closest bottle to me. I thought about grabbing a shot glass but figured that would only slow me down from getting annihilated.

"Yo, that's the last bottle of vodka," Turtle called from behind the bar.

I shrugged my shoulders and made my way past the bar and down the hallway to my room. I didn't fucking care if it was the last bottle of booze in the clubhouse.

Shit was coming back that I never thought I would have to think about again, and my plan was drowning those memories as best as I could tonight.

———————

Chapter 2

Paige

"You sure you're OK?"

I glanced over at Princeton, and all I could do was nod my head. I was so close to losing it, and all I had left to do was get out of the car and then I could fall apart in my apartment.

"I'll walk you to your door." He reached over to unbuckle his seatbelt, but I put a hand on his arm to stop him.

"Please don't. I'm all right." My voice cracked, and I prayed that Princeton would ignore it.

He looked at me, his eyes seeing more than I wanted him to see. "I'll wait till you're inside before I leave."

I said a silent thank you, grateful that he could tell that I just needed to be alone. I slid out of the car, not whispering a goodbye. My voice had already betrayed me once; I wasn't going to risk it again when I was so close to making my escape.

I scurried up the stairs, trying to unlock the door through tears and collapsed on the floor when I finally got the door open. I pushed the door closed and reached up, flipping the lock.

Sobs racked my body as the past came flooding over me.

Over Seven Years Ago

"Paige, open the damn door and tell me what the hell the damn stick says." Dustin pounded on the door, and all I could do was giggle as I looked down at the pregnancy test in my hand and stare at the two pink lines.

Dustin pounded on the door harder, and I flipped open the lock afraid he was going to break the door down. "It's about damn time, woman. I ain't never had to take a pregnancy test before, but I know it doesn't take fifteen minutes."

"Well," I said, holding up the test. "You're gonna have to wait about nine months before we have to take another one."

"Nine months," he whispered, grabbing the test from my hand.

"Dustin, I peed on that. Like, all over that." I reached to grab it out of his hand, but he pushed my hand away and walked out of the bathroom. I swatted off the light and followed his retreating back down the hallway. "Would you stop waving it around."

Dustin walked into the kitchen of my tiny apartment and turned on the light. He held the stick up to the light and squinted. "Are we sure this is right? How accurate are these things? I think you should go to the doctor right now before anything happens."

"Happens," I laughed. "I'm pretty sure nothing is going to happen for at least eight months."

"Eight months? You really think you're that far along? That's a whole month that you didn't know you were pregnant." He threw the test in the sink and pulled me into his arms, burying his nose in my hair.

"I don't know how far along I am. I've only missed one period."

He pushed me back, holding me at arm's length. "We need to go to the doctor right now, make sure everything is alright."

"Dustin, people get pregnant every day and don't run to the hospital. I'll call in the morning and make an appointment."

"Baby, you're having my baby." A huge grin spread across his lips, and he pulled me back into his arms. "Our baby," he whispered into my hair.

Yup, we were having a baby.

The sound of P!nk blaring from my phone brought me out of my daydream, and I opened my eyes. I fished my cell out of my purse and hit the talk button. "Hello?"

"Paige? Are you okay? You didn't tell me you were leaving."

I fell back onto my butt and leaned against the door. "I just got tired. I saw you were having fun and didn't want to interrupt."

"Are you sure? Meg and the girls said they saw you leave, and you seemed shaken up."

Ha, shaken up was an understatement, but Gwen wasn't going to know that. Gwen didn't even know that Demon and I were once a thing, let alone about the baby. "Oh, that? I bumped into someone and spilled their drink. It was nothing."

"Really? Meg said it looked like you two knew each other."

"Nope," I sang out, "Unless you call the minute I talked to him as knowing him." I had to get her to stop talking about Demon. Gwen was never going to find out what happened between Demon and I. It was in the past, and that was exactly where I planned on keeping it buried. "Are you still at the party?" I was surprised at how quiet Gwen's side of the call was.

"No, well, yes, but not right now. I had to run to the bathroom and decided to call you. Are you sure you're okay?"

God dammit, she wasn't going to let this go. "Yes, little sister. I promise that everything is okay. I had a long day at work today, and I'm not used to staying out so late." I faked a yawn hoping she would believe me even though I was wired right now and had no idea when I would be able to sleep.

"Okay, I was just checking on you." I heard Gambler in the background, and I thanked God that he was so attached to Gwen. Hopefully, he would help to distract her from bugging me about Demon anymore.

"I'll let you go, Paige. Call me tomorrow or when you get off of work on Monday,"

"Okay, but you know you can call me whenever you want."

Gwen bugged me all the time that she was the one who was always calling me, and I needed to learn how to pick up the phone every now and then. "I know, Gwen. But you know I don't call unless I have something to say." I was quiet and, shall we say, Gwen is not.

"Gambler, I'm coming." She put her hand on the phone and yelled at Gambler to keep his pants on. "I'll call you in the morning, P. Love you." Gwen hung up before I could even get the b in bye out of my mouth. I tossed my phone on the chair by the door and tilted my head back.

I loved Gwen, but I wasn't going to tell her about Demon. It happened such a long time ago when I was a different person from whom I was today. I piled my long brown hair on top of my head and looked around my tiny apartment. At the time, I thought finding this apartment so quickly was a sign that this was where I was supposed to be, but now I knew how wrong that was. Demon was here, and I had no idea how the hell I was going to be able to live in the same town as him.

Gah, what the hell was going on. I thought I was over Demon. Hell, I figured I was *long* over Demon. It had been over seven years since he had walked out of my life, but now it felt like it happened yesterday. Seeing him turned me back into that naive twenty-one-year-old who thought her whole world hung on the shoulders of one tall, handsome, dirty talking biker who loved her.

I laughed and shook my head. You can see how well that worked out for me. Now I needed to figure out what the hell I was going to do.

I was here for Aunt Rose, not Demon, and I didn't have anywhere else to go. Gwen had lived in Rockton for a year before she had convinced me to move up here and stupidly I had come. Now, I felt the urge to run, but I didn't have a place to run to.

How had I lived here over two months and never ran into Demon? Especially with Gwen dating Gambler who was part of the same damn club. Seriously, how in the hell do I get myself into situations like this?

I yawned loud, taking my hands off of my head and my hair cascaded around my shoulders. I was trapped. Trapped like a rat and I had no idea what the hell I was going to do.

How had I avoided him for this long? And then it hit me. All I had been doing for the past two months, was working, taking care of Aunt Rose and that was it. Tonight was the first time I had actually left my apartment for something that wasn't work or taking care of Rose.

So, I knew what that meant. I had just figured out the way that I was going to avoid Demon.

No more going to the Clubhouse.

No more hanging out with Gwen if she was with any of the guys from the clubhouse. (Besides Gambler.)

I was only going to work, Rose's and the grocery store. Three places I was guaranteed to not see Demon.

So, from now on, I was going to be a hermit.

Oh, Jesus, this was going to be ridiculous.

———————

Chapter 3

Demon

"You wanna tell him he's not in his room, or should we just let him sleep?"

I cracked one eye open, trying to figure out who the hell was talking to me. I looked around the room and realized I had no idea where the fuck I was.

"Does he do this often?"

My head was pounding, and it felt like I was laying on a brick wall. Where in the fuck was I?

"This would have to be a first, babe." King, I knew that was King's voice, and I had to assume he was talking to Meg.

"Laying on that table has to be uncomfortable. I mean, Demon is older than I am, and I know I couldn't sleep on a table like that all night."

"I'm thirty-five," I mumbled. I rolled to the right a little, careful not to roll off the table and pulled my arm out from under me that was pinned to the table.

"What?!" Meg gasped. "How in the hell am I older than all of you?"

"Babe, does it matter?"

"No, well, yes, I mean no," Meg sputtered.

I opened both eyes, taking a good look around and realized I was in church, laid out on the big ass table we sat around. How in the fuck did I get here? I reached out, grasping for the edge of the table and managed to roll over without throwing myself over the ledge of the table. Meg and King were standing at the head of the table looking down at me. "You're not older than all of the guys."

"Don't do it," King warned.

He knew exactly what I was thinking, and I was too hungover to realize that saying it was not the best idea. "I don't believe that you're older than Gravel."

Meg gasped, threw her hands up in the air and stormed out of the room, but not before she walked by me and slugged me in the shoulder. "Ass," she hissed.

I closed my eyes and ran my fingers through my hair. "What the hell time is it?" The last I could remember was falling into bed after finishing the bottle of vodka. Which again led me to the question, what in the hell was I doing on the table?

"Half past twelve. Meg and I were headed out for our little honeymoon when she spotted you in here. I figured I should make sure you weren't dead." King pulled the chair at the head of the table and sat down. "You mind telling my why the hell you're in here and not in your room?"

"I don't have a fucking clue how the hell I got in here. The last I remember; I was in my room."

"How fucking drunk did you get last night?" King laughed.

"Apparently too drunk." I slowly sat up and felt my head swimming and the room slowly spun.

"You getting wasted wouldn't have anything to do with Paige, would it?"

Fucking King. I knew when I had spotted him last night after talking to Paige that he had seen shit he shouldn't have. "Who the hell is Paige?" I was going to play stupid, because honestly, I was too hungover to do anything but.

"Something tells me you know exactly who Paige is, but since I've known you ten years, Demon, I'm going to let you wallow in your own self-pity for a bit longer." King stood up and pushed the chair back under the table. "I'm taking Meg away for a couple of days. Sober the fuck up and then maybe you'll tell me what the hell is going on when we get back."

"Not likely," I mumbled.

"We'll see about that. You're in charge, you already fucking know that. Call me if you have any problems. We'll only be an hour away." King walked out the door, and I was left alone with the pounding in my head.

I swung my legs over the side of the table and looked down at the floor, willing it to stop spinning before I stood up. It had only taken me twenty minutes to finish that bottle of vodka, and that was the last thing I remembered.

"Well, if it isn't sleeping beauty."

Ugh, fucking Rigid and Gambler. The last two assholes I wanted to talk to right now. All I wanted to do was find a gallon of coffee and crawl into the shower. "Fuck off," I growled. I stood up and closed my eyes as the spinning of the room picked up.

"I think he's more like Goldilocks, Rigid. I think he came into my bedroom first, trying to crawl into bed with Gwen before I kicked his ass out and then he wandered into your room." I opened my eyes as Gambler leaned against the wall by the door and crossed his arms over his chest.

"Ah, so it was you who gave him the black eye."

I reached up, touching my eye that I had noticed was throbbing but figured it was from the roaring headache I had. "You fucking punched me?"

Gambler shrugged his shoulders. "You climbed into bed with Gwen while I was in the bathroom."

"Now see, I have to believe that he really didn't know what the hell he was doing because when he came into my room, Cyn was standing in front of the TV trying to find a movie to watch when he climbed into bed with me and tried to fucking spoon me."

"He spooned you?" Gambler wailed. He busted out laughing while Rigid flipped him off and sat down in the chair next to the one King had just sat in.

"Are you fuckers done?" I was always up for a good ribbing except when I was the one taking it. "I don't even remember what the fuck happened last night, assholes, so yuck it up and leave me the hell alone."

"Oh, but where would be the fun in that, Demon. You give us shit all the time, it's time the tables have turned." Rigid leaned back, propping his feet up on the table. "Plus, we came in here to find out what the hell was going on with you and Paige last night."

"I don't know who the hell you're talking about." Time to act stupid again.

"See, now that is where I think you actually are lying. Now, I know that you think Rigid and I get all of our info from Meg and the girls, but when in reality, everything we heard came straight from your mouth. Paige's too, although she does speak rather quiet so we had to fill in the blanks in some parts." Gambler pushed off the wall and stood in front of me. "You forgot to look at who was behind you, brother."

Son of a bitch. I didn't even think that these two assholes would hear everything that Paige and I said. "It's nothing, and you'd do best to forget about everything you heard."

"I don't think you're right, Demon. I think what we heard is a whole lot more than nothing." Gambler crossed his arms over his chest and glanced at Rigid, a smirk on his lips. "I'm pretty sure if I let it slip to Gwen that you know Paige, I'd find out real quick what exactly what it is you're hiding."

I scrubbed my hand down my face. "I thought we were fucking brothers, Gambler."

"Oh, we are. I have no intention of telling Gwen because I know she would fillet you like a fish. I'm just interested in one thing."

Lord knew what the hell Gambler wanted to know. Fuck, Paige and I had nothing to do with him. When I was with Paige, I was still only a prospect. Paige barely even knew the name of the club when she and I were dating. "Spit it the fuck out, and if you're lucky, I'll tell you what you want to know."

Gambler eyed me up and down. "Is she the one you always talk about? The one you let get away?"

I glanced at Rigid who looked as eager as Gambler to hear my answer. Paige was definitely the one who got away. "Yes," I bit off.

Gambler reached out, resting his hand on my shoulder. "In that case, Rigid and I are here to help you get her back."

Oh fuck me.

Chapter 4

Paige

"Do you want to tell me why you've been avoiding me like the plague since Meg and King's wedding?"

I was at work on my lunch break, my phone pressed to my ear while Gwen scolded me for barely talking to her for the past two weeks. I had been doing an impressive job of avoiding anything that would bring me into contact with Demon, but I was utterly exhausted from constantly worrying about running into him. "I'm not avoiding you. We just got a new shipment of books in and I've been helping Rose put together a new puzzle." Jesus, even my excuse sounded lame to me.

"Books and a puzzle are the reason you can't talk to your sister?"

I shoved the last bite of my sandwich into my mouth and crumpled up the empty brown paper lunch bag. I was going to gain fifty pounds if I continued to get lunch from the deli down the street every day. One had to think that having a huge roast beef sandwich every day wasn't good for my waistline. "Yes and no."

"I don't care what you say, Paige. Gambler and I are coming over tonight."

Shit. Although I had to admit, Gwen and Gambler coming over was better than all the other things she had suggested. First, she wanted me to come over to the clubhouse and watch a movie with her, and you better believe I shot that one down right away. "Fine. I'll grab something on the way home for dinner."

"No, I'll bring something. Gambler and I won't be over until six, and you get off of work at five. It'll be cold by the time we get there."

"I need to stop at the store anyway, Gwen. I'll just pick up a rotisserie chicken and some salads from the deli." From the weather reports I had been hearing, there was a huge storm blowing in that was supposed to dump over sixteen inches of snow over the next three days.

"Fine, but probably get two chickens. Gambler can finish one off by himself."

I couldn't help but laugh. "Well, he is a growing boy."

"Yeah, a growing boy at the age of thirty-three. We'll be over at six." She hung up before I could protest again and I set my phone on the small table in the break room.

I ended up getting a job at the bookstore that was only four blocks away from my apartment. Finding this job was another thing that made me feel like moving here was the right thing to do. The only thing that didn't scream that was Demon.

"All done with your break already?" Marg, the owner of the bookstore and an all-around awesome lady, walked into the break room and opened the fridge. "I brought lunch from home, trying to make sure I didn't go to the deli but wouldn't you know their tuna on rye is calling to me." She slammed the door shut and looked down at the crumpled paper bag in my hand. "Looks like I'm not the only one who can't stay away from there."

I couldn't help but smile. Marg talked a mile a minute and typically I just tried to keep up. "The roast beef is going to be the death of me. It's addictive."

"Same with the tuna." Marg sat down in the chair next to me and kicked her feet out in front of her. "Any plans for the weekend?"

Thankfully today was Thursday, and I was fortunate to have the whole weekend off. "Nope. I just need to run over to Rose's house, check up on her before the storm hits and then I plan on being snowed in." Yes, I was one of those freaks who absolutely loved winter and snow. If it would snow every day, I would be happy.

"Hmmm, sounds good except I think you need a man to be snowed in with. I can still remember the first time Rod and I were snowed in together." Marg got a dazed look on her face, and I could only imagine what she was thinking about.

I stood up and tossed my trash in the garbage. "Well, from the sounds of the weather report, you and Rod can relive that memory this weekend. Are you heading out to get lunch?"

"Yeah, I think I'll text Rod and see if he can sneak out for a nooner." Marg pulled her phone out of her pocket and sent a message off to her husband.

A month ago, I would have been shocked by what Marg had just said, but now that I've been around her and know that there isn't a filter from her brain to mouth, all I could do was giggle and head back to the front counter.

I looked up and down the aisles, making sure there weren't any customers who needed help, and then plopped on the stool behind the counter and picked up the book I had been reading. Working at Read Your Ass Off definitely had its perks.

Marg ran a traditional bookstore, but where she actually made money was in her online store where she catered to any and every book request that was thrown at her. Generally, only a handful of people came into the store every day, and the rest was all over the good ole' internet which was what Marg took care of. Before I moved to town, she took care of both ends of the business and was burning out quickly.

Now that I was here taking care of the actual customers that came in, most of the time she spent her time in back or some days she didn't even come in, working from home. I glanced on the wall on the clock, seeing I had over four hours of work left and opened my book.

At least I'd have good company until it was time to go home.

———————

"That'll be twenty-seven fifty-two, ma'am." I fished my money out of my wallet and handed it over to the cashier.

Two chickens, a pound of pasta salad, garlic rolls, and an angel food cake later, I was ready to get home and relax. I hadn't done a lot at work today besides read and do a quick inventory, but I was completely exhausted. I had tried calling Gwen to tell her I was too tired for her and Gambler to come over tonight, but she didn't answer her phone or the five text messages I had sent her.

"Hey, beautiful, Paige is here." Rigid and Cyn walked through the doors of the store, and I couldn't help but cringe a little at the fact that I wasn't going to be home as soon as I had hoped.

"Hey," Cyn chirped. I had never seen a more beautiful and happy pregnant woman in my life before. Add in Rigid who was always fawning over and watching her, I was a tad bit jealous.

"Hey, guys!" I grabbed my change from the cashier, shoving it into my wallet then picked up the two bags.

"Whoa, two chickens?" Cyn laughed as she looked into my bags.

"Gambler and Gwen are coming over tonight. I was advised that Gambler had the appetite of a growing teenager."

"So does this one," Rigid laughed, pointing at Cyn.

"Hey," Cyn whined, smacking Rigid. "I'm growing your damn baby right now."

"Yeah, apparently growing babies need Caesar salad, pickle flavored sunflower seeds, and lemon bars."

Pickle flavored sunflower seeds? I couldn't help but cringe at that combination. "That sounds interesting."

"Speaking of lemon bars," Cyn said, rubbing her belly. "Meg told me she'll be over in twenty minutes with a pan fresh from the oven. We better grab the salad and seeds and get home." Cyn grabbed one of the red shopping baskets, put it over her arm and grabbed Rigid's hand.

Rigid nodded to me as he pulled his phone out of his pocket and they headed into the depths of the store. "I'll talk to you later, Paige," Cyn hollered over her shoulder.

I walked out of the store, thankful Cyn was too occupied with her cravings to want to talk much and headed down the street to my apartment.

Now I only hope Gambler and Gwen didn't want to stay long and then I could pass out.

———————

Chapter 5

Demon

"You think you could not look at your phone right now and help me pull this God damn engine out?"

I shoved my phone back in my pocket and cranked on the hoist to raise the motor out of the Buick Gravel and I were working on. Rigid had just texted me saying he had just seen Paige at the grocery store. I couldn't shake the feeling that I was jealous as hell that Rigid had just seen Paige.

It had been over two weeks since I had seen her at the wedding, but it felt like years. "Cool your jets, old man. This car doesn't have to be done for another three days." This morning King had a meeting with all the shop employees telling us with the storm coming we needed to get all of the work done as soon as possible. Gravel must have taken his words to heart because he had been working his ass off all day.

"The way I see it, we get this done, and we ain't gotta work until Tuesday." Gravel guided the engine out of the car, and I lowered it down to the floor.

"Yeah right. We get this done today, and King will give us two other things to work on Monday." I grabbed a rag out of my back pocket and wiped my hands. "It's almost six o'clock. Can't we finish this shit tomorrow?"

"Yeah, I suppose. But your ass better be here bright and fucking early." Gravel walked out of the shop grumbling under his breath about God knows what.

I leaned up against the car and crossed my arms over my chest.

Paige. Fucking Paige Lawson. Just seeing her had brought back so many fucking feelings. Feelings that I had no idea what to do with. When I had left her, I hated her. In my own grief, I blamed her for everything that had happened. But it also brought back feelings I never thought I would have about her again.

I knew now that everything that had happened wasn't Paige's fault, that we just weren't meant to be parents then. But it was what had happened after that I was afraid that we weren't going to be able to come back from.

"Where are you?" I barked into the phone. I was sitting outside of Paige's apartment wondering why the hell her door was locked to her room, and she wasn't anywhere to be found.

"I'm at the library studying for my finals next week."

328

"Fucking bullshit," I mumbled into the phone. This, this right here was what Paige was doing after losing my baby a week ago. "I thought we were going to have dinner tonight."

"I forgot. I'm leaving right now. I'll be home in twenty minutes." I could hear her frantically shoving books and shit into her bag.

"Fucking forget about it, Paige. I'll find someone else who wants to spend time with me."

"And what is that supposed to mean?" She trembled into the phone.

"It means if you don't want to spend time with me, I'll just go pick one of the girls out at the club who love to fucking eat dinner with me." All I had to do was walk in the clubhouse, and I would have bitches hanging all over me.

"You don't mean that, Dustin."

"You know what, I think for the first time, I might actually mean it. When was the last time you spent any time with me, Paige?"

"I was in the hospital for a couple days, Dustin, and now I'm trying to get caught up on my schoolwork."

"I thought you were going to take off the next semester?"

"There isn't a reason for me to miss school anymore."

She was right. Now without a baby on the way, she could go back to school and everything would go back to normal except things weren't normal anymore. Our baby was gone, and Paige was going back to her regularly scheduled life while I didn't know what the fuck I was going to do.

"I'm taking off for a couple of days, Paige, I'll talk to you when I get back."

"Dustin, just wai—" I ended the call before I could listen to all the reasons she had for why I shouldn't leave.

I needed to get out of town and try to figure out what the hell I was going to do next.

I did something I never should have done that night. Something I've regretted ever since.

———————

Chapter 6

Paige

"Well, shit." When I had left the house this morning, I had walked because I didn't really see the point in driving my car to the store that was only two blocks away. Except I hadn't figured in the snow that had started falling as soon as I had walked into the store and had been falling heavy since.

The whole reason I had gone to the store last night was to get dinner and then a few things I would need for the weekend so I could be snowed in with all of the necessities. I, of course, only bought dinner because my brain was so fried last night. Gambler and Gwen had only stayed for an hour before I started to nod off on the couch and they took the hint that I really was tired and wasn't just trying to get out of hanging out with them.

This morning I had run over to Rose's to make sure she was ready for the storm and stayed for a couple of hours helping her do a puzzle, and then I had headed out. I had parked my car behind my apartment and then walked to the store for wine, chocolate ice cream, and Swiss roll cakes. Only the necessities.

I stood at the door watching the snowfall and knew I had miscalculated when the snow was going to start falling, and now I needed to walk home in a snowstorm.

"Oh well," I mumbled. I pulled my coat tight around me, pulled my hat firmly down over my ears and slid my gloves on. If I was going to make a run for it, it was now or never.

The snow was falling so heavily that I could barely see across the street, and the two blocks back to my apartment had never seemed longer. I glanced over my shoulder and saw an old truck slowly following me down the street. "What the hell?" I whispered.

The truck pulled up next to me, and they rolled down their window. "Paige, get in the truck." Shit, it was Demon. I had done so good these past weeks not seeing him, and now here he was.

"I'm fine," I hollered. I swung my arms, walking faster. Demon sped up the truck and turned down the next street and stopped in front of the sidewalk, blocking me.

"Demon, just please leave me alone." I pleaded.

He leaned over, opening the passenger door and pushed it open. "Just a ride, Paige. It's a fucking blizzard out here."

The snow seemed to get heavier with his words, and my fingers were already numb. Damn him. Why did he have to show up when I actually needed him? I stood there staring at his truck deciding if I was going to be stubborn and get frostbite on my fingers or just get in the truck. "Just a ride."

Demon held up his hands and moved back over to his side of the truck. I cautiously stepped to the truck and put my bags on the floor. I slid in, careful not to get too close to Demon and slammed the door shut. "That storm sure did come out of nowhere." Demon pulled away from the curb, turning the truck around and headed down the street.

"Do you know where I live?" I pulled my gloves off and held my fingers up to my mouth and blew on them. It had to be below zero out there right now and with the gusting wind, it was probably colder than that.

"No, as much as you'd like to think I was stalking you, I wasn't. I had to run and pick up a part from the parts store only to see that they had closed because of the storm blowing in.

"Oh. Well, I live over the pet store." Demon slowly crept down the road, leaning into the windshield, trying to see where we were going.

"That place can't be very big."

"It's big enough for me. All I need is a place to sleep, eat and watch a little TV at night."

"And room enough for all of your cows." Demon glanced over at me, a smirk on his lips.

I ducked my head and looked out the side window. "Yes, I guess that, too."

Demon pulled up in front of my apartment and thought how ridiculous I was that I couldn't walk the rest of the way home. I pulled my gloves back on and grabbed the bags from between my legs. Demon had opened his door and jogged around the front of the truck and opened my door before I had a chance to put my hand on the handle. The air blew in bringing the huge snowflakes with it, and I remembered why I chickened out and took the ride that Demon offered. "Oh, buckets," I mumbled as I stepped out of the truck.

"What did you say?" Demon asked as he shut the door behind me and moved to grab the bags out of my hands.

"Huh? What?"

"Did you say 'Oh, buckets'?" Demon laughed. "You always did say the weirdest shit when you didn't want to cuss."

I batted at his hands as he tried to take the bags, but he didn't care and still grabbed them. "I can carry my own bags, Demon. I don't need any more help from you."

"I'll walk you to your door, Paige." He looked down at me, and his tone took me back seven years ago. When I knew if he would say something with that matter of fact tone, I knew that there was no arguing. I generally didn't argue with him, though, because I usually agreed with whatever he said. Except for this time, I didn't. Things were different, and that one huge difference from now to then, was that I wasn't Demon's anymore.

"Thank you, but no thank you." I lunged for the bags, but he spun away as they slipped through my fingers and he stepped to the left. I stumbled forward, barely catching my balance before I went ass over tea kettle into the bench that was in front of the pet store. "Darn it, Demon. Give me the bags."

"I will, as soon as you let me walk you to your door. And why are you calling me Demon? You never used to do that."

"Correction, I only called you Demon when I was mad and upset at you." I stomped my foot and lunged at him again. At the last second, he saw me coming and jumped backward into the street. I wasn't as lucky as the last time and tripped on the curb and face planted in the fresh snow.

Demon roared with laughter above me, and I glanced up to see him bent over, his hands on his knees trying to catch his breath. I rolled over, completely aware of the fact that I was laying on the side of the road in a snowstorm with a crazy man laughing like a loon at me. "I see your gentlemanly manners disappeared after all of these years."

"Baby, I can't help but laugh when you're so insistent that you don't want my help that you'd dive into the snow just to get rid of me."

"I didn't *dive* into the snow." I managed to pull myself off of the road and tried to brush all of the snow off of me. "I was trying to get my bags from you that you *stole* from me."

"I stole from you! I'm trying to help you, Paige. The last I checked the definition of stealing had nothing to do with helping." He crouched down in front of me and worked on brushing all of the snow off of my legs. "We need to get you inside. Once this snow starts melting on you, you're going to get cold fast." He stood and grabbed my hand and tugged me over to the side entrance of the pet shop and opened the door. "Why in the hell isn't this door locked?" He asked as he pulled me in behind him and shut the door.

"I never lock it. The one at the top of the stairs is locked most of the time. There's no point in having both of them locked. I'm the only one who lives here." I stomped up the stairs, snow falling off of my legs and body with each stomp of my feet. I reached the top of the landing and turned around to look down at Demon who was two stairs down from me. "Just leave the bags here. Thank you." I turned back around to the door, hoping that he would get the point and leave. I fished around in my purse for the key, stabbed it into the lock and threw the door open. I turned back around to grab the bags Demon should have set down, but he was still standing there looking up at me.

"I'm not leaving until you get warmed up and you damn sure better lock both of these doors from now on." He moved up a step and my jaw dropped, speechless. He pushed past me and walked into my apartment like he lived there. "Get in here, Paige, before you catch a cold."

I looked down at the keys in my hand and wondered when in the heck I had stepped into the twilight zone.

———————

Demon

Paige eyed me up and down but didn't budge from the steps. The snow that was covering her was melting, and she shivered. "Get your ass in this apartment, Paige, before I *make* you get in here."

She narrowed her eyes at me, but she skirted around me into the apartment, and I slammed the door shut. She was crazy to think that I was going to just drop her on her doorstep without making sure she was okay.

"I don't understand why you are here, Demon. You were my knight in shining armor and delivered me home. Now you can go." She pointed to the door and grabbed the bags out of my hands.

"Because you obviously need someone to look out for you since you were outside traipsing around in a fucking blizzard." I took the bags back from her and headed into her small kitchen. "This place is fucking tiny."

"It suits me just fine. It's only me who lives here." As soon as I had the bag empty, Paige ripped it from my hands and shoved it under the sink.

"I see some things never change. You remember that one time you had so many bags under your sink that you broke the damn pipe off and had water gushing out of the cabinet?" There were so many memories I had with Paige, that it was hard to remember them all. We had only been together for a year, but it had felt like we had known each other forever.

"I learned my lesson. I only put a handful under there and toss the rest in the pantry." She crossed her arms over her chest and leaned against the sink. "You can go now, Demon. I plan on changing and then just reading for the rest of the day."

"Still a bookworm, too, I see." I picked up the huge container of cocoa she had bought and stepped towards the cabinet. "How about I put–" My words died as the lights flickered and then the apartment went completely dark.

"Oh hell," Paige cursed.

"That was a heavy snow coming down, but I didn't think the power would go off this soon." I walked over to the window in the living room and looked up and down the street. Just as I stepped back, a squad car came streaking down the street with his siren blaring and his lights flashing. "Must be an accident somewhere for him to be going so fast."

"You think that's why the power went out?" Paige wrapped her arms around herself and looked around.

I opened all the curtains on the windows, letting in any light possible. "More than likely. Does that fireplace work?" I crouched down in front of the old fireplace she had in the corner of the living room and opened the glass doors.

"As far as I know it works. The landlord said it did, but I haven't used it yet."

I opened the flue and peaked my head into the chimney to make sure it was clear. Thankfully no birds or anything was obstructing it so now all I had to do was light a fire. "You know if he had any wood downstairs?"

"Um, I think by the back door he does."

"I'll run down and grab an armful. Who the hell knows how long the power will be out for. This place is going to cool down real quick with no heat pumping into it." I stood up and brushed my hands on my jeans.

"You don't have to do that; I can go get some when I need it."

"You need it now, Paige. If you wait too long, you'll be too cold. I'll grab some and get the fire going. Why don't you put on some coffee or, hell, even some of that cocoa going?" I slipped out the door before Paige could protest and jogged down the stairs.

I don't know how we had both missed the pile of wood at the bottom of the stairs, but we had. I stacked the wood into my arms trying to grab smaller pieces that would be good for kindling and headed back up the stairs.

Paige was standing at the sink filling a teapot as I walked by and kneeled back in front of the fireplace. "You still drink that tea crap I see."

Paige sighed and slammed the teapot down on the stove. "If you don't like my *crap,* you are more than welcome to leave. The last I checked, I didn't need to put up with your shit attitude."

"Just make me some damn coffee, woman, and we'll be good." I grabbed a newspaper she had laying on one of the side tables and ripped it apart.

"I had planned on it, Demon." She reached up into the cabinet and pulled down a canister of coffee.

"You wanna tell me why the hell you call me Demon now? I remember correctly you only knew my road name was Demon for about ten seconds before you split."

She set the coffee down and turned around to look at me. She propped her hands on her hips and cocked her head at me. "You really can't figure out why the hell I'm calling you Demon and not Dustin?"

"Well, I mean, I think I know why, but thought I'd rather hear it straight from you why you're calling me my road name that you swore before I even got it that you would never call me."

"Because the man who is in my apartment right now is a stranger." She stared me down and crossed her arms over her chest. "We're both different people now, Demon. The Paige you knew is gone, just like the Dustin I knew is gone."

"They're not gone, baby. Just different."

"You're wrong, Demon. That young, naive, stupid girl is long gone. Just like our baby. Neither one is coming back. Please," she whispered, "just leave." She fled down the hallway and slammed the door behind her.

I fell down to my knees and bowed my head. Son of a bitch, that was not how I had seen this going. I didn't want to hurt Paige anymore. That was the last thing I wanted to do. We had both been through so much back then, and I could tell that even now, years later, Paige still wasn't over it. I had royally fucked up that day when I had left her apartment, and it looked like there was no coming back from that.

I had lost Paige before, and there wasn't a chance in hell that I was ever going to get her back. No matter how much I still loved her, I couldn't take back the things and words that I had said to her.

Fuck.

Chapter 7

Paige

I had no idea where the hell Dustin was. I had looked for him all over and called him fifteen times, but he never answered. There was one last place to look, and I was terrified to go there. I was parked outside of the crowded clubhouse, my hands gripping the steering wheel trying to work up enough courage to walk through the door and find Dustin.

Dustin had invited me to the clubhouse many times before, but I had never taken him up on it because the timing never seemed to work out. Now I wished that I had made the time to come before. There were groups of people lingering by the door, and I could hear the music from the too loud stereo pouring out into the quiet night.

I hated the way Dustin and I had ended our phone call, but I didn't know what to do anymore. I felt like I was drowning and there was no one there to save me. Dustin and I never had the chance to really talk about losing the baby, and I didn't have any friends I could talk to who could relate to what I was feeling inside. I was alone, and the one person who should be there for me was blaming me for what had happened.

The doctor had told me till he was blue in the face that there was nothing I could have done differently to have helped the baby live. It wasn't meant to be, and I just had to learn how to accept that. Except I didn't know how to do that, especially with the way Dustin was acting.

I opened my door, stepped out of my car and slowly made my way to the front door, praying that I would find Dustin right away. I knew that he lived a life that I wasn't sure I was ready to be a part of with the club but knew that I wanted to be with him. This was my opportunity to see what this part of his life was like. He was still only a prospect, and he eagerly talked about getting his road name and becoming one of the brothers.

The door burst open before me, and two girls drunkenly stumbled out, and I managed to grab the door before it slammed shut. I slipped inside, my eyes scanning the vast room, hoping to see Dustin right away. The music was so loud I could barely see straight, and there was such a cloud of smoke in the room that I rubbed my eyes trying to make out the people who were walking past me.

This was the kind of party Dustin had been trying to get me to come to. He said if I ever came to the clubhouse, I would need to be with him, especially on party nights. The girls walking by me were barely dressed, and some had two or three men trailing after them trying to get their attention.

I had no idea where to look for Dustin. I knew that he had a room that was his, but again, I had never been here before, so I was completely lost. I shuffled my way over to the bar, dodging half naked bodies and grabby hands. It was like I was at a frat party but ten times worse. I set my purse down on the bar and pulled my phone out, hoping that when I called Dustin, this time, he would answer.

"What can I get you to drink?" I looked up from my phone into the eyes of a well-built man behind the bar and put my cell to my ear.

"Um, just water." The phone rang and then went to Dustin's voicemail.

"You sure I can't get you something stronger?" The man asked me as he wiped his hands on a white towel.

"No, this is good." I took a tentative sip and held the glass in my hand. "You wouldn't happen to know where Dustin is, would you?"

"You mean Demon?"

"Um, no, I mean Dustin."

"It's Demon now, babe. Last I saw he was headed to his room. Down the hall, to the left and he's the third door."

I set my glass down on the bar and wiped my hands down my pants. "Um, thanks," I mumbled.

Three men bellied up to the bar next to me and started haggling the guy behind the bar. "Yo, King. You gonna pour some fucking drinks tonight or just pick up chicks all night?"

I backed away from the bar, hitching my purse over my shoulder and waved to King who winked at me. These guys maybe a bit rough around the edges but they seemed to be nice, at least King was.

I headed down the hallway, passing couples making out in the hallway and open doorways that were crowded with people who were watching what I could only imagine was going on in the rooms. I turned the corner, and the noise from the party quieted, and there were fewer people.

I made it to the third door that was partially closed, and I could hear AC/DC pouring from a radio inside. After looking up and down the hall and gathering my courage, I knocked on the door.

"Doors fucking open!" That sounded like Dustin, but he sounded different.

I cautiously pushed the door open, and the strong smell of weed hit me, but I was completely unprepared for the sight that met my eyes.

Dustin was sitting on the bed, his back against the headboard with his pants unzipped. His hand was stroking his cock while his eyes watched every move two naked women were making while they made out with each other at the end of the bed. I stopped, my breath caught in my throat and I didn't know what to do.

My boyfriend, the man who I was going to have a baby with not even three weeks ago, was watching two women make out while he jacked off to it. My heart felt like it was repeatedly being stabbed over and over as I stood there watching.

My whole body went numb and my phone that I was holding slipped through my fingertips and crashed onto the floor. Dustin's eyes finally fell on me, and he just stared at me. His hand in mid stroke on his dick and a shocked expression on his face.

I couldn't rip my eyes off of Dustin. Even though every part of me screamed to get the hell out of there, I couldn't. I needed to see this, I needed to remember that this was what Dustin was doing when I felt like I was dying inside.

"Paige."

I shook my head violently, knowing whatever he had to say wasn't going to make this better. Nothing could make this better. "No, please don't." I held my hand up as Dustin scrambled to get up from the bed. I couldn't do this. I had seen enough. "Please don't." I didn't know what I was pleading for him not to do, but that was all that would come out of my mouth.

I backed up, bumping into the frame of the door and whacked my head against the wood. "Paige, just stop." Dustin struggled to zip up his pants, and I darted out the door before I had to watch anymore.

Tears clouded my eyes as I blindly ran down the hallway, pushing past people. The crowd in the main room and by the bar seemed to have doubled, and it took everything I had to push my way through the massive crush of bodies.

I stumbled out the door, the brisk night air hitting me. I heard Dustin call my name before the door slammed shut and I knew I needed to get to my car. The parking lot was pitch black with more groups of people scattered all over as I dodge them all, running towards my car.

"Paige, fucking stop!" I glanced over my shoulder as Dustin gained on me and everyone turned to watch whatever the hell was going on.

I was mere feet away from my car when Dustin grabbed my arm and spun me around. "Don't touch me!" I shrieked as I struggled to pull out of his grasp.

"Just fucking stop for a Goddamn minute," he bellowed. He tightened his grip on my arms and pushed me against my car.

"Take your hands off of me," I whispered. I didn't know what had happened before I walked into that room and just the thought of Dustin's hands on me made me want to shower for days. I used to love whenever he touched me, be it a brush of his fingertips or wrapping me up into a big hug, I had loved it. Now, it felt like a stranger was touching me.

"What the hell are you doing here?" He demanded like I was the one doing something wrong. What a fucking joke.

"I was trying to find you."

"You should have fucking called me."

"Why so you could have put your dick back in your pants before I came over, or so you could have finished quicker?" I sneered.

"Knock it the fuck off, Paige."

I reared back, not believing that he was trying to tell me to calm down. "Knock it off? I just saw my fucking boyfriend jacking off to two women making out! How in the hell am I supposed to calm down?! You were cheating on me!"

"I wasn't fucking cheating on you!"

"What? You weren't cheating on me? Have you lost your mind, Dustin?" A crowd was slowly gathering around us, everyone interested in what we were yelling about.

"I wasn't going to touch them," he gritted out through clenched teeth.

"So that makes is better?" I leaned into him, pushing him back. "Let. Me. Go. I don't want to even think about you right now!"

"So it won't be any different from the past two weeks then."

"What? What the hell is that supposed to me?"

"It means, Paige, that ever since you got out of the damn hospital, you haven't said ten words to me. We were supposed to go out that night and instead you go to the fucking library."

"I told you I forgot, and you haven't talked to me! You act like you are the only one this affected."

"That's because you act like nothing happened and you can go back to your normally scheduled life now!"

I wrenched my arms out of his grasp and pushed against his chest. "You think this didn't bother me? You think you are the only one that who is upset? I cry myself to sleep every fucking night, Dustin! All I want is to have my baby back, but I know that won't happen. But you know what I want more than anything? I want you! I wanted you so bad, and you weren't there," I gasped as my sobs took over my body. "I just needed you to be there and tell me that we were going to be okay, and you weren't. All I've felt from you is blame and fucking hate! The one person who should be there for me isn't!"

"I didn't know what to fucking do!" He bellowed at me.

"So this," I swung out my arm, motioning around. "This was the best thing you could think of to do? Leave me and find two sluts to occupy your time? That was going to make everything better? I fucking loved you with everything I had, Dustin. I wanted that baby more than I wanted to breath. But since you didn't see me physically grieving, you thought I was some heartless bitch who didn't want my baby. Is that what you thought of me?"

340

"That's not what I thought," he growled.

"Then tell me what you thought, Dustin."

His eyes bore into me, but he didn't say a word.

Here we both stood, both hurting in the same way, but we didn't know what to do with it. We didn't know how to make it better. "I'm leaving, Dustin. I can't… I can't do this anymore. I'm hurt enough. I can't stand by and watch you mess around on me."

"That wasn't what I was doing."

I shook my head and ran my fingers through my hair. "I don't know what to do."

"I wanted my baby, Paige."

I laughed. I fucking laughed. "And I didn't?"

"You didn't…"

"I didn't what, Dustin? What didn't I do? Say it, say what you have been dying to say." I looked around, a crowd circled around us. "I killed your baby, right, Dustin? That is what you've wanted to say, right? I killed your baby, it was all my fault. Deny it, tell me to my face that you don't think that."

Dustin growled low, but he again didn't say anything.

I hung my head and knew this was it. His silence told me everything I needed to know. "I loved you with everything I had, Dustin, and I wanted that baby so much. But you'll never see that. All you'll see when you look at me is someone who killed your baby, and I can't live with that." I pulled my keys out of my pocket, turned my back to Dustin, and blindly stabbed my key into the lock realizing not only had I lost my baby, now I was losing the one man I would only love.

I waited a second, hoping and praying that Dustin would stop me, wrap me in his arms and finally tell me that everything would be okay, but he didn't. I felt my heart break in that moment and knew that I would never love another man again. I opened the door and slid into the seat. I numbly put the key in the ignition, trying hard not to look at Dustin and shifted the car into drive. The crowd that had surrounded my car parted letting me slowly pull out of my parking spot.

I couldn't help but look back one last time at Dustin, a little spark of hope that he would do something to keep me from leaving but he didn't. He was still standing where I had left him, his back to me and I did the only thing I could do.

I left and felt my heart shatter.

I hadn't thought about that night in years. Every time I used to think about it, my heart would break again. Demon and I both loved each other, but we somehow couldn't get past our grief to be together.

I closed my eyes, my head resting on my pillow and tried to listen to the sounds of my apartment, wondering if Demon had left. His footsteps sounded on the wood floor of the kitchen, and I could only assume he was putting away the rest of groceries and then I heard the front door close.

I waited fifteen minutes, wondering if he would come back, but he didn't.

He was gone again, and it felt like my heart had been shattered all over again. He still had the power to hurt me and that made me hate him even more because I realized something I had denied for so long.

I still loved him.

———————

Chapter 8

Demon

It had been a week since I had seen Paige, and I was climbing the walls like a caged animal wanting to go to her. After I had crawled back home to the clubhouse during the snowstorm, all I could think about was Paige and how I needed to find a way to make things up to her. I needed a woman's perspective on things because I had no idea where to start with Paige. I knew saying I'm sorry wasn't going to be enough.

I was standing in front of King's bedroom door at the clubhouse, trying to talk myself into knocking on the door. I knew I couldn't ask Gwen for help because she would probably castrate me if she knew that I had hurt Paige, although I thought I might run into that problem with any of the girls I decided to tell.

I raised my hand to knock, but the door opened before I made contact with the door and instead almost knocked on King's head. "Jesus Christ," I mumbled, dropping my arm.

"What the hell?" King asked.

"I was just about to knock, brother. I was hoping I could talk to Meg for a second."

"And I was just about to head to the shop, but I think I can delay those plans until you're done talking with my woman." King stepped back, opening the door wide and motioned for me to come in.

I couldn't really blame King for not wanting to leave me alone with Meg. Not that I would try anything with her, it was just the principal of it.

"Babe, Demon wants to talk to you," King called as he shut the door and leaned against it. "Sit down. She was just finishing up when I told her I was leaving."

I glanced around the room seeing my only options of sitting were on their bed or in a ratty old recliner that was in the corner. "If she's busy, I can always come back another time." King shook his head and motioned for me to sit down.

"Hey, I was just headed over to Cyn's house." Meg walked out of the bathroom and flopped down on the bed. "What are you still doing here, handsome?" Meg asked King, surprised to see him.

"Just interested in what Demon has to say is all." King crossed his arms over his chest and stared me down.

"So, what's crackin'?" Meg crossed her legs underneath her Indian style and propped her head on her hand.

Fuck. Where the hell to start? No one had a clue that there was history between Paige and I. "Uh, I was wondering if you might help me out with a problem."

"Sure, although I'm curious as to what problem you could have that you would need my help with."

"It's more that I need some advice. It's about a chick."

Meg rubbed her hands together and a smile spread across her lips. "It's about time Demon. I've been waiting for this. Who is it?"

"Well, it's someone you know."

"I fucking knew it. It's fucking Paige, isn't it?" Lo crossed his arms over his chest and smirked at me like he had just cracked the Da Vinci code.

"What?" Meg screeched, outraged. "How in the hell did you know that and I didn't? You're supposed to tell me everything!"

"Just a hunch I had, babe. I knew when he said you knew her that it was Paige. I saw them together at the wedding."

"You were with her at the wedding?" Meg eyed me up and crossed her arms over her chest. "Why didn't I know any of this?"

"I only talked to her for a minute. We were both shocked as hell to see each other."

"Babe, you were three sheets to the wind by ten o'clock. You wouldn't have noticed a pink elephant walk through the room."

Meg grabbed a pillow from off the bed and launched it at King. "Pretty sure you weren't too upset by my drunkenness when we made it back to our room."

King shrugged his shoulders and tucked the pillow under his arm. "You'll pay for that later."

Meg rolled her eyes and turned back to me. "I'll probably like it," she smirked.

King chuckled under his breath. "We'll discuss that later," he mumbled to Meg.

King and Meg both stared at me, and I figured it was my turn to talk. "Uh, well, it is Paige. We knew each other a few years back."

"How long are we talking here?" Meg asked.

"7 years. Give or take a couple of months."

"And how exactly did you two know each other? Like friends or *friends?*" Meg wiggled her eyebrows, and a sly smile spread across her lips.

"We dated. Well, more than dated, but we broke up."

"Who broke up with who?"

I ran my hands through my hair and shrugged my shoulders. It felt like I was in front of a firing squad. "It was mutual, I guess."

Meg rolled her eyes and looked at King. "He broke up with her, or he did something stupid that made her break up with him." She turned back to me and crossed her arms over her chest. "What did you do?"

Shit. Did I really have to tell her what I did? I was a fucking idiot back then. Just thinking about Paige walking in on me and those two chicks made me cringe. I didn't want to say it out loud. "You really think you need to know what happened to help me apologize to her?"

"Hmm, I want to know, but I'm sure I don't need all of the dirty details. How about we rate it and then I'll try to help. Or, if it's bad enough, I might go help Paige."

Definitely did not want to tell Meg what happened. There would be no way in hell that she would help me then. "I'm good with rating it."

"Ok, on a scale of eating the last of the ice cream or running over her dog, where are you?"

Well, watching two girls make out while I beat it probably wasn't like eating the last of the ice cream. "Closer to the dead dog."

"You didn't kill her dog, did you?" Meg asked, shocked. She looked over the edge of the bed at Blue and then looked up at me, suddenly afraid I was going to hurt her dog.

"I didn't kill anyone or anything. Jesus Christ" This conversation was going sideways fast. "I cheated on her but not really. I didn't touch, okay?" That's all she was going to get from me.

"You're an ass!" Meg shouted as she threw a pillow at me.

"Babe," King laughed. "You're supposed to be helping him, not calling him names and throwing pillows at him."

"But he cheated on Paige!"

"Babe, he cheated on Paige, not you. Bring it down a notch."

Meg glared at King but didn't say any more.

"I made a mistake, and I don't know how to fucking fix it. I should have fixed it back then, but I was fucking stupid and blamed her for everything that happened."

"You cheated! How the hell did you blame her for that?"

It was like I was talking to Paige right now. "I meant, I stupidly blamed her for something and cheated on her because well, I was stupid."

"Stupid isn't the right word," Meg growled.

"You think you can calm your wife down before she tries to scratch my eyes out?" I asked King.

"You think you could manage to keep it in your pants while you're trying to get Paige back?" Meg snapped.

"This is fucking pointless. I could have this same conversation with Paige over and over. I'm trying to avoid that." I stood up, nodded to King and headed out of the room. I knew I had fucked up, but I was trying to fix it now.

"Wait," Meg called. "I'll help you, but only on one condition."

"Oh, this ought to be good," King chuckled.

"I'll do whatever you want me to do as long as I get Paige back."

"Now that's the kind of attitude I like to hear." Meg clasped her hands together and gave an evil chuckle. "I won't make you pay up until you and Paige are back together. I'm trying to be fair. After all, when you think about it, getting Paige back with you will be *way* easier than what I'm going to have you do."

"You just made a deal with the devil, brother. I would not want to be you right now," King smirked.

"Whatever it takes to get Paige back, I'll do it."

"I have a plan for our first plan of attack. There's a winter festival next weekend. The girls and I are going, and we plan on dragging the guys with us. I'll have Gwen ask Paige to come."

"She won't come if she knows that I'm going to be there."

"That's why she won't know that you'll be there. Gwen will tell her it's just a girl thing, and she'll come, guaranteed. Don't worry Demon, I'll get her there so you can grovel for all of your past sins," Meg winked. "Plus, I might make you grovel some too just for good measure."

"Just tell me where and when and I'll be there." I ran my hands through my hair and headed out the door. I would do anything to get Paige back, even enlist the help of Meg and her girl posse. The brothers and I all knew that if you had Meg, Cyn, Marley or Gwen plotting against you, you didn't stand a chance.

Poor Paige didn't know what was about to hit her.

———————

Chapter 9

Paige

I had three missed calls from Gwen and multiple text messages from Cyn and Meg on my phone. They were all begging me to come to the Snowflake Festival this weekend, and I had yet to reply to any of them.

"Hey, Hun, can you grab that new shipment of books and start putting them on the shelves. I know we close in half an hour, but I figure we could start getting some of them out."

I shoved my phone in my pocket and headed into the backroom. I could think about the Snowflake Festival after work. I had never really hung out with everyone and was hesitant about Demon being there. It had been over a week since I had last seen him and I wasn't eager to see him again.

I grabbed the cart that was loaded full of all of the latest indie books and headed over to the display by the front door. Just as I opened the first box, Gwen and Meg walked through the front door. It appeared since I didn't answer their numerous messages, that they had come for an answer in person.

"Hey, girl," Gwen sang as she shut the door behind her. "You get my messages today?"

"Yeah, I just saw them. I was going to call you after work."

"Holy hell, you have a whole wall dedicated to the greatness that is Kristen Ashley," Meg gasped. "I have all of her books on my Nook, but I've never held all of the Rock Chick awesomeness in my hands before." Meg grabbed a book off of the wall and slowly paged through it. "I know what I'm buying with the gift card Lo got me for my wedding gift."

"I thought you just said you have all of her books?" Gwen asked.

"Holding this in my hand, I now realize I need a bookshelf and it needs to be filled with all of my favorite books, including all of these." Meg put the book back on the shelf and stepped back, her eyes roaming over all of the books.

"How much is your gift card for?" Marg asked as she pushed the other full cart of books from the back room.

"Oh, it's not for here. It's for Barnes and Noble." Meg replied.

"How much is it? I'll honor it for here." Marg leaned against the cart and smiled. I had seen Marg do this before. She accepted gift cards from Amazon and Barnes and Noble in the store. She just bought them from the store and used them for her own personal use. She just liked people coming to the store and buying actual books. Plus, Meg was drooling over her shrine to Kristen Ashley, Marg always appreciated that.

"Five hundred. Well, it's probably more like four fifty. I bought a couple of books last night."

"Holy hell, your man bought you a five-hundred-dollar gift card for books!" Gwen gasped.

Meg shrugged her shoulders and blushed. "He might have gone a little overboard when I said I never had time to read. Now, he basically banishes me from our room for an hour so I can read. I've finally convinced him that I can read with him next to me."

"That is the weirdest, but sweetest thing I've ever heard," I swooned.

"Well, I was going to say I'd buy it from you, and you could have your choice of books, but I doubt you need four hundred dollars' worth of books," Marg laughed.

"Yeah, Lo might kill me if I come home with a truckload of books. I'll just take these." Meg grabbed all of the Rock Chick series books and set them on the counter. "I'll be back later for the others."

"Um, Earth to Meg, Earth to Meg. Can we get back to the reason why we're here?" Gwen asked.

Meg pulled her credit card out of her purse and set it on top of the pile of books. "Lo is going to kill me," she giggled.

"I'm glad to see that isn't stopping you, though," Marg winked.

"Oh, Lord, if I knew she was going to be like this in a bookstore I wouldn't have brought her with." Gwen waved her hand at Meg, realizing she was a lost cause for any help that Gwen was looking for from her. "You're coming this weekend with us. Meg, Cyn, Marley and I are going, and I've decided that you need to get out more."

"I really don't think I can make it. I have to work Saturday."

"Nonsense, you can have the day off. I'll make Rod come in and man the counter. It can be like old days when I pretended to be the lost book nerd looking for the right book. Oh, the memories we have on that counter," Marg said dreamily.

"You, you I like," Meg laughed. "We should so invite her over to the clubhouse. Lo would have an aneurysm."

"I don't want to make Rod work for me." Dammit, working was the only reason I had for not going to the festival. Now I was either going to have to go or come up with some crazy reason why I couldn't go.

"You should go. The Snowflake Festival is fun. Snowmobile rides, outhouse races, chili cook-off, and fireworks. You have to at least go once, Paige. Rod and I will be there after the store closes." Marg bagged up Meg's books, set them on the counter and handed her credit card back.

"There, problem solved. You're coming with." Gwen put her arm around my shoulders and gave me a quick hug. "It'll be fun."

"Make sure you dress warm; I think it's supposed to snow in the afternoon." Meg shoved her credit card back into her purse and grabbed her books. "We'll pick you up around noon. We'll wander and stuff ourselves until the fireworks at eight."

"We're going to be there for eight hours?" That seemed like a mighty long time to wander around.

"Around there. It'll be fun, I promise." Meg tucked her bag under her arm and waved bye to Marg. "We need to leave before I buy every book in here." Meg grabbed Gwen by the arm and hauled her out the door.

"Noon. Saturday. Be ready Paige, or I'm throwing you over my shoulder and dragging you out of the house," Gwen threatened. She slipped out the door but not before she pointed her finger at me and glared.

The door slammed, the tiny bell ringing in their wake. "Next time, don't be so helpful." I grabbed a stack of books off of the cart and started stacking them as I turned my back to Marg.

"Oh, come one, Paige. You've been in town for how long, and you've done nothing other than work and read."

"Hey, I went to King and Meg's wedding."

"Ah yes, the night with the mysterious mafia man. You never did really tell me much about that." Marg rolled her cart over by me and started to unload the books onto the shelf.

"I did tell you everything. He barely spoke twenty words to me and then he took me home."

"Girl, you have all this opportunity to live out one of your favorite romance novels. A night with a suspected guy connected to the mafia and now going to hang out with a bunch of ol' ladies from an MC. Live it up, have some fun. Find a biker and ride him till your legs give out."

Been there, done that. I thought to myself. "I'm not one to go out and party or just hang out. I like being in my own company just fine."

Marg reached over and took the stack of books out of my hand. She set the books down and put her hand on my shoulder. "Paige. How old are you?"

"Thirty-one." Marg knew how old I was. It was on my application when I had applied for my job.

"No, I seriously think that you are a ninety-year-old stuck in a banging body that you have no idea what to do with." Marg eyes me up and down, and I crossed my arms over my chest.

"Um, well, thanks, Marg. But I'm not ninety. I just act more mature for my age." I had always acted older than I was. Growing up, I always felt that I needed to take care of Gwen, and I guess that just translated over to everything in my life. I needed to be the serious one who always had a plan.

"Sweetie, you are the best employee I have ever had and also the youngest. When you walked through that door, I knew that there was more to you then what you put out, but you hide it away because you think having fun or letting loose will somehow hurt you."

"I don't believe that entirely. I believe that you can have a good time without getting hurt." Like reading. Reading was fun and safe. It's when you added in other people into that fun was when things got out of hand, and people got hurt.

"What happened, Paige? What made you what you are today. I'm not letting you leave until you tell me. Hell, I'll even get the tequila out, get you rip roaring drunk and drag it out of you." Marg crossed her arms over her chest, and I knew that she meant business.

"It's nothing, Marg. Haven't you met some people that are just more serious than others?" Hell, half of the people who came into the store were straight-laced and quiet. Although it always seemed it was the quiet ones who bought erotica by the handful.

"Yes, and there is always something that made them that way." Marg picked up the stack of books and handed them back to me. "And you, my dear, are the way you are because a man screwed you over."

My jaw dropped, and I grabbed the books. How in the hell did she know? I had never mentioned anything to her before about any guy, especially Demon. I kept my eyes glued to the shelf in front of me and lined up the books.

"He cheat on you?" She asked. "Eat the last of the chocolate? Hit on one of your friends?"

"I'm not sure if eating the last of the chocolate is the same as being cheated on."

Marg shrugged her shoulders and kept stacking books. "I'm serious, girl. I'll call Rod and tell him I'm not going to be home till late. I'm not leaving until I know why there's a stick shoved up your butt."

"Marg!" I gasped.

"Oh, you know I love you. I just mean, well, you know, you got a stick up your butt."

"You should actually write a book, Marg. Your words are so eloquent."

Marg scoffed and crouched down, filling the bottom. "I tried it once. I got to a sex scene and about peed my pants when I read it out loud. Worst shit I've ever read in my life." She plopped down on her butt and crossed her legs Indian style. "Pull up a patch of rug and tell Auntie Marg everything."

I looked down at her and knew I wasn't going to be able to get out of this. I finished putting the books on the shelf and sat down next to her. If anyone walked through the door, they were going to think we were a bunch of weirdos. "There's not much to tell, Marg."

"I'll be the judge of that. Start from the beginning and don't leave any of the good stuff out." She leaned back against the bookshelf and waited.

Where the hell to start and how much do I tell her? No one, and I mean *no one* knew anything. Gwen, my damn sister, had no clue of the things I was about to tell Marg. "He cheated, but he says he didn't technically cheat."

"Hmm, sounds like a man. What'd he do?"

"Well, he's not completely to blame."

Marg scoffed and crossed her arms over her chest. "Please do not tell me you are going to defend him."

"No, at least not about the cheating. We were going through some really heavy things, and I was pushing him away because I thought I knew what he was thinking, but I really didn't. It was seven years ago while I was in college."

"I'm going to need more details than that."

"Jesus, can't I be vague, and you just go along with it?"

"No. You're spilling right now, and then I'm going to help you get over what this asshole did to you."

I took a deep breath and told Marg everything that had happened seven years ago, all the way up to seeing Demon three weeks ago.

"Holy mother of God, you *are* living a fucking romance novel."

"Hardly, Marg," I laughed. "It's just my messed-up life. Now you know why I don't want to go out with Gwen and the girls. I know for eight hours they are not going to stay away from their boyfriends. I know Gwen has no idea that there is anything between Demon and me, and that is the way that I would like it to stay."

"Well, I have to say in Demon's defense, he didn't cheat. At least not from what you tell me. It sounded more like he was watching live porn."

"Would you let Rod watch "live porn" the way Demon was?" I was a rational person, I prided myself on it, but it was so hard not to want to kill Demon for what he had done.

"If I was there with him, yes. We go to the strip club together, and that's basically the same thing, except, you know, Rod can't pull his wang out."

"So I shouldn't be mad at Demon for what he did?"

"No, no, no. That is not what I meant. If Rod did that without me being there, I'd tie him up, hang him from a tree, and beat him like a piñata. You did the right thing by breaking up with his punk ass. The problem is now."

"What do you mean? I'm not going to ever see Demon again, problem solved." I folded my hands in my lap and acted like I had just solved world hunger. I was so delusional, Marg rolled her eyes at me.

"This is a small town, Paige, and there is no way in hell that you can avoid that man. Especially with your sister dating one of the club members. Unavoidable."

"So what in the hell am I supposed to do?"

"First I need to go back to one thing." She reached over and grabbed my hand and squeezed it tight. "I'm so sorry you had to go through losing your baby, hunny. Young, old, single, or married that is never an easy thing to do." Tears clouded Marg's eyes, and I had to look away before I lost it. I had never had someone say that to me before. I knew that I wasn't the only one to have lost their baby before, but at the time, I had felt so alone that I didn't think anyone knew what I was feeling. "Rod and I lost a baby the first year we were married. I know what you went through."

"I'm sorry, Marg," I whispered.

"Thank you, hunny. Rod and I wanted that baby something fierce, but God didn't want us to have him. Lord knows what kind of parents Rod and I would have been anyway. We're too crazy for our own good half of the time," she laughed. She wiped her tears away with the back of her hand and sat back. "Now back to the problem at hand. Demon."

"Demon is a definite problem."

"So, you know what I'm going to ask you next, right?" I shook my head no and stretch out my legs. "Do you still love him?"

I stared down blankly at the toes of my shoes and took a deep breath. "Do I have to be honest about this?" I laughed.

"Well, just from what you've told me, hun, I know you're not over him. No matter how badly he messed up back then, the fact that he's back and trying to talk to you shows that he still loves you, too. I know this is a hard pill to swallow, but he didn't cheat on you, Paige. He was just an enormous fucking idiot that didn't know how to deal with what he was feeling. And from the sounds of it, you were struggling with how you felt back then, too."

"But I never would have done that to him, Marg. Why would he do that to me?" Tears fell down my cheeks, and they dropped onto my jeans.

"That's something you're going to have to ask him. You're going to have to look past your pain and hurt and talk to him. Maybe if he gives you the answers you need, you two can move on. Of course, you're going to have to make him grovel. A lot."

"You really think that I can forgive and forget?"

"I think for your own good, you need to, hun. You thought you were going to spend the rest of your life with that man and grow a family with him. You're both different now, and I think you both need to sit down and see each other for who you are now." Marg stood up and brushed off her pants. "Now, I'm gonna go grab the vacuum, because I just realized I can't remember when I cleaned these floors last," Marg laughed.

She headed into the back room, and I leaned against the shelf behind me.

I had loved Demon back then, and if he hadn't been an idiot that night, I would still be with him today. I had gone to the clubhouse that night, hopeful that we would finally talk and get back to the way we were, but that wasn't what happened.

I leaned my head back and closed my eyes. I loved Demon with everything I had back then, and now I needed to figure out if I still loved him.

Demon and I needed to talk, and I hoped that I got the answers I wanted.

The problem was I didn't know the answers I wanted to hear.

————————

Chapter 10

Demon

"You're fucking pussy whipped now, too?" Slider sat down opposite of me and set down the two beers in one hand and took a sip from the glass of whiskey in his other hand. "You don't even have a fucking drink in front of you."

It was Friday night, and everyone was spread out in the common room mowing down on pizza and chicken wings. I had finished my plate of food and was just drinking soda. Tomorrow was the festival and from the sounds of Meg's plan, I needed to be on my game tomorrow and not hungover. "I'm good, brother. You can drink mine for me."

"I didn't ask if I could drink one for you, I wanted to know why the hell you aren't drinking." Slider finished his glass of whiskey and then chased it with a swallow of beer. "This is the one night I don't need to be at Fayth's, and everyone is boring as hell. What the hell happened to this club?"

Slider did have a point that the way the club was now was entirely different from only a year ago. King, Rigid, and Gambler were all sitting by their girlfriends, or wife in King's case, just talking among themselves and Gravel wasn't even here tonight. With Ethel going through chemo for cancer, which she was kicking its ass at the moment, the clubhouse was pretty tame. "Priorities change, brother. I guess we're all growing up and finding out what life is really about."

"I knew these fuckers were whipped, but I didn't even know you were chasing some skirt. I know I'm not around the clubhouse more since I got put on babysitting duty, but I figured you would tell me when you strapped on your ball and chain."

"I haven't done it yet. First I need to convince her to even be in the same room as me."

"Oh fuck me, you're the worst one out of the bunch. Chasing women. There was a time that all we had to do was sit back, and the bitches would be crawling all over us." Slider finished his beer and crushed it in his hand.

"You don't ever get sick of that, though, Slider? I mean, don't you want someone that is just with you and not ten other guys?" I had grown tired of that life a long time ago. After Paige and I had broken up, I dove into the stereotypical biker lifestyle, enjoying it for years, but I always knew that there was something better.

Something I had, and then threw away like a fucking idiot. I would trade all of those years of partying and sleeping around for just one more day of Paige loving me.

"I haven't met one chick yet that is worth giving everything up for. I'll keep my nameless lays and drunken nights." Slider chugged his other beer, stood up, the chair skidded across the floor and walked back over to the bar.

I had sounded like Slider at one point. When I still thought, Paige was to blame for everything and thought that all women were trouble. Now, all I wanted was Paige, and starting tomorrow, I was going to do everything I could do to get her back.

———————

Paige

It was nine o'clock, and I had just got off the phone with Gwen. I had no idea what to wear tomorrow, and she really hadn't helped. Her style was so different from mine that all of her suggestions were so far out of my comfort zone that it was ridiculous.

Half the time when I work, I wear flowy skirts, and I know that was the last thing I wanted to wear tomorrow. The weatherman was predicting a high of only twelve and a seventy percent chance of snow. Have my legs covered and probably wearing at least two layers of clothes was a must. It looked like I was going to go for warmth overlooking fashionable.

My phone rang from the kitchen where I had left it after talking to Gwen, and I could only imagine that it was her calling with more ideas.

"Hello?" I had looked at the caller ID, but I didn't know who the number was.

"You're not backing out on us tomorrow because you can't find anything to wear, are you?" Meg. I could only imagine Gwen calling Meg after she got off of the phone with me and told her that I was freaking out over what to wear.

"No, but I hope jeans, snow boots and a big ass puffy coat are acceptable."

"You'll blend right in. That's the basic attire around here in the wintertime."

"Well, that's good to know." I opened the fridge, realizing in my search for clothes to wear tomorrow I hadn't eaten dinner. I had gotten home from the bookstore at seven and went directly to my closet and tore it apart looking for something to wear.

"I told Lo about the bookstore. He thinks I'm crazy because I now demanded a bookshelf to be made that spans the whole wall in the living room."

"Holy hell, you have a house big enough for that?" I glanced around my apartment wishing I had a room for even a second bookshelf, but I barely had enough room for the one I had. Granted, half of it was filled with Mary Moo Moos.

"No, not really, but he said that he could make it work or that he could always add onto the house," she giggled.

"I think you have a keeper there, Meg." I couldn't help but be a little jealous of the relationship that Meg and King had. I had never seen a man love his wife like the way he did.

"Yeah, I think we might still be in the honeymoon stage, and neither of us knows how I'm going to be when I go through menopause." Meg cackled into the phone, and I could imagine her throwing her head back, laughing. "Lord knows Lo barely keeps a grip on me now."

"It's good to keep him on his toes, too," I giggled.

"Amen, sister. I better go before he starts yelling at me for not reading again," she laughed. "I was just checking in to make sure you were still coming tomorrow."

"I'll be ready at noon. Promise." As much as I wanted to back out, I knew that it was going to be fun. I mean, could you really have a bad time with Meg, Cyn, Gwen, and Marley? I think that was impossible. I had heard stories of coffee pots and broken beds, so I was a bit curious to see what kind of craziness they would get into tomorrow.

I hung up with Meg and headed back to the fridge, pulling out a jar of jelly and decided PB&J was what was for dinner.

I leaned against the counter, munching on my sandwich and mentally picked out what I was going to wear. Now that I knew that tomorrow wasn't a beauty contest, I was breathing a bit easier.

After I had wiped my hands on my pants, I turned off all the lights, and headed into the bedroom and put all my clothes back in the closet, leaving out my favorite pair of jeans and a red and black button down flannel shirt. Lumberjack chic at its best.

I fell into bed with my Kindle, the lights turned out, prepared to fall into the world of rock chicks and alpha males. Except I couldn't get into the story that I had read over and over because there was one thing that was taking over my mind again and I hated it.

I couldn't stop thinking about Demon. Bastard.

———————

Chapter 11

Paige

"Oh, sweet Jesus, who in the hell let me eat the beer battered cheese curds and the big ass plate of nachos." Meg leaned back from the picnic table we were sitting at and patted her stomach. "I think I have a food baby."

Cyn snorted and reached over, rubbing Meg's stomach. "I'd have to say you're at least two months along."

"You're an ass," Meg laughed, swatting her hand away. "How in the hell did I eat more than you?"

Cyn shrugged her shoulders and crumbled up her napkin. "It could be the huge plate of scrambled eggs, sausage, and toast that Rigid made for me this morning." Cyn winked at Meg and collected everyone's garbage and headed to the trash can.

"Well, now that we've eaten everything the festival has to offer, how about we go check out the outhouse races and then the dog sled races are after that." Gwen pulled the flyer they were handing out at the entrance to the festival and looked it over. "The chili cook-off is in three hours, too."

"Ugh, please don't mention food," Meg moaned, laying her head on the table. "I've made a very bad decision," she grumbled.

"Suck it up, buttercup, and let's go watch these shitters shoot across the ice." Marley stood up and dusted off her butt. "You know, that's a sentence I never thought would come out of my mouth, but yet, here we are, watching shitters race across the ice."

I had to admit that it was rather weird, and I didn't entirely understand what was about to happen, although Gwen and Cyn seemed to be pretty excited about it.

"So, what exactly is an outhouse race?" I asked as we all trudged past the dozen food wagons and headed to the ice where there was a crowd gathered.

"It's basically an outhouse on skis that two people push, and one person sits inside on a toilet, and they race across the lake," Meg explained.

"And what exactly is the point?" I couldn't help but question what was going on.

"Well, I think it all started when a bunch of guys had too much to drink and were trying to stay warm." Meg cupped her hands together and held them to her lips, blowing hot air on them. "I mean, in Wisconsin, that's where all the good ideas come from, 'Here, hold my beer and watch this,'" she giggled.

"This sounds like just the kind of fun I bargained for today." Cyn rubbed her hands together like Meg, but hers was in a menacing way.

"Oh, Lord, help us," Gwen laughed.

We joined the crowd that was growing bigger and stood on the side of the, well, I guess you would call it track.

"Alright, ladies. I think it's time we place a little bet."

"Oh, hell, she's been with Gambler too long. Every time we do anything, she has to place a bet." Marley rolled her eyes and huddled closer to me. It really was cold today, and I was barely able to keep my teeth from chattering.

"Okay, what's the bet?" Meg asked.

Gwen looked at us, eyeing us up and nodded to the outhouses at the start line. "Whichever one of us can convince one of these guys to sit in their shitters gets a free cut, dye, and style. The works, on me."

"I can convince you to give me that anyway," Meg scoffed.

"Annnd," Gwen drawled. "Two tickets to the Adele concert next month."

"Holy mother of God. You have tickets to see Adele?" Marley grabbed Gwen's arm and shook her. "How in the hell did you get them?"

"I managed to get my hands on a pair, that's all you need to know." Gwen backed up, and we all turned around to look at her. "Now, who's in?"

"Hell, I'll sit in any man's shitter for a shot at Adele tickets," Cyn replied.

"Eh, when I win, I'd have to convince Lo to come with me, and I know that would never happen. I'll let you ladies duke this one out." Meg crossed her arms over her chest and smirked.

"Ha, when you win. You're so cute, Meg. It's a good thing you're not going in on the bet, you would so lose," Marley sassed.

Meg waved her hand at her and laughed. "They're all yours, Marley. That is if you can beat Cyn and Paige."

"Oh, me?" I held my hands up and shook my head. "I'm not looking to sit in a random guy's shitter." I was too shy for this. Walking up to a stranger and asking if I could sit in his outhouse was more than out of my comfort zone.

"Nonsense. You three are in the running for them." Gwen looked at her watch and shook her head. "The races start in twenty minutes so you ladies better get your asses in gear if you want to see Adele next month."

Cyn and Marley took off to the start line. "Which one of these guys will let me sit in their shitter?" I heard Cyn muse. Marley bumped her with her hip and took off running.

"You did not just bump a pregnant woman!" Cyn screeched.

"It's all in the name of Adele!" Marley called over her shoulder. Cyn waddled after her, waving her arms in the air and ranting about womb abuse.

"Come on, Paige. I bet you could beat Preggers and Blondie," Meg winked at me.

"No, I don't "

"Move, now," Gwen ordered, pushing me towards the start line. "This is your day to have fun, and this is exactly how you are going to loosen up. Maybe one of these guys are single and will let you sit on their shitter."

"I feel like we are entirely overusing the word shitter," I scoffed, digging my feet into the snow.

"Nonsense, that's impossible. Shitter, shitter, shitter," Meg chanted. "You never know, you might be able to tell your kids one day you fell in love with their daddy on a shitter," she laughed.

"Paige, go have fun." Gwen gave me one last push, and I gave in.

What did I have to lose? Marley or Cyn were probably already sitting in an outhouse, and I wouldn't have to make a fool of myself. Although, Adele tickets were pretty damn tempting.

I shoved my hands into my pockets and eyed up the crowd. I guess it was time to find my prince and his perfect shitter. I strangely felt like Goldilocks looking for the perfect bed, except you know, I was looking for the perfect shitter.

I had to laugh and shake my head. I was right when I had thought that hanging out with these girls craziness would ensue.

Little had I known that I would be thrown into the middle of it. It was time to live a little.

———

Demon

362

"This, this was your wife's bright idea for me to get Paige back?"

King shrugged his shoulders, a smug look on his face and headed to the back of the outhouse.

I was presently sitting on a toilet in an outhouse on Crystal Lake, freezing my balls off. Sitting on a porcelain toilet wasn't exactly warm, and I had been cursing Meg all morning.

King hadn't told me the plan until he texted me this morning and told me to meet him in the body shop. When I had walked through the door, I hadn't planned on seeing an outhouse sitting in one of the bays.

After King had given me the run down what outhouse racing was, we had torn off the door of the shitter, screwed in a toilet and painted the name of our racing team that Meg had given us.

We were Stool Runnings. Even I couldn't keep a straight face after King had stenciled it on the back wall of the outhouse. "I do have to give creativity points on the name," Hammer had laughed.

But I hadn't even discovered the best part of it yet. My two teammates were Hammer and Turtle. I was convinced right then and there we were going to go down in flames, and Paige was going to think I was a fool.

"Okay, Marley and Cyn are headed this way. I'm gonna head over to where Demon, Troy, and Rigid are standing." Meg said Marley and Cyn were going to throw the bet so Paige should be a shoe in." King pulled his leather jacket tight around him and pulled a wool hat out of his pocket. He pulled it over his head, and I couldn't help but laugh at him. "Shut the hell up," he grumbled. "It's fucking cold out here." King trudged off into the crowd, and I was left with Hammer and Turtle as my wingmen. I was utterly doomed.

"You know, I never in my life thought I would be pushing Demon in an outhouse on a frozen lake," Hammer pondered. He had a half-eaten bag of popcorn in one hand and a chili dog in the other.

"You're not the only one," I mumbled. I looked around, trying to catch a glimpse of Paige, but didn't see her. The thing of it was, I don't understand how Meg thought Paige was going to talk to me once she saw me. She was pretty clear the last time I had seen her that she was done with me.

My phone dinged with a text, and I pulled it out.

Hello, Demon. Meg here, your trusty matchmaker. I've sent Paige unsuspecting towards you. Try not to blow it.

I shook my head, and my fingers pecked away at the letters. Texting was not something I enjoyed. My fingers were too damn big for the fucking tiny letters. *This isn't going to work. The first guy she asks is going to say yes.* A guy would have to be stupid to say no to Paige. She was the perfect combination of sexy and innocent. I was amazed when I had run into her and found out she wasn't married.

It'll work. I've planned for that contingency.

What in the hell are you talking about? Even in text message, Meg came across as a nut.

It means Lo told all the guys if they say yes, he'll beat the hell out of them and steal their wives.

Bullshit. I doubt Meg would let King threaten to steal wives.

Okay. I lied. But just don't worry about it. She should be to your shitter any minute. Try not to be a dick.

I shoved my phone back into my pocket and shook my head. This is what I get for enlisting the help of Meg. Out in the middle of a frozen lake sitting on a toilet.

"There goes Cyn and Marley," Turtle called. Cyn and Marley strutted by, waving as they went but didn't stop to talk.

"Who are we waiting for again?" Hammer asked. I swear to Christ, it was like I was stuck with dumb and dumber on this mission.

"Paige, you idiot." I scanned the crowd again and finally saw Paige talking to another team. The guy thankfully shook his head no. Otherwise, I was going to have to smash his skull in if he had said yes.

She had asked two more teams before she was right at our shitter and I prayed to God that she didn't run when she saw me.

"Um, I have this bet going with my friends, do you think that I could just sit in yours for a second?" she mumbled. Her voice was timid, and I could tell how nervous she was.

"You'll have to ask King shitter. He's on his throne right now." Turtle laughed at his joke, and I couldn't help but give a smile. Fucker may be slow, but he was funny.

I heard Paige shuffle around to the front of the shitter, and she looked like I killed her dog when she saw it was me. "Shit," she mumbled. "I thought those two guys looked familiar."

"Hello, Paige."

"I can't believe I fell for this. I mean, who actually would bet people if they would sit in someone's outhouse." Her face turned bright red, and she dropped her eyes to the ground.

"It's really not that far-fetched if you are hanging out with those four. Crazy is their middle names."

"OK, well, I'm just going to go home."

She turned on her heel, but I grabbed her arm and spun her back around. "Paige, don't leave just because I'm here."

"Demon, why are you here?"

"Thought I'd take my shitter for a ride. See how she runs wide open." I leaned back, my elbows resting on the tank of the toilet and stretched out my legs. For an outhouse, this thing was pretty spacious.

Paige shook her head and looked down the track. "I'm assuming you can hit what, two, three miles an hour?"

I threw my head back laughing. "On a good day." I forgot what an excellent sense of humor Paige had. She had a dry and sarcastic way about her that if you weren't paying attention, you wouldn't know that she had made a joke.

"I suppose there aren't any Adele tickets up for grabs, are there?" she pondered as she crossed her arms.

"I'm not for sure, but I'm pretty sure that was just a ploy to get you to come over here."

"I was completely played, wasn't I?"

"Just a bit, baby, but I have to say in your defense that with Meg scheming against you, you didn't stand a chance."

"I should have known Adele tickets were too good to be true. I tried to get some when they went on sale, and they were sold out before I could even log in." Paige pulled her coat tight around her and ran her hand through her hair. "I'm gonna go find Meg and Gwen, so I can kill them."

"That mean you're going to stick around and actually watch me race?"

"You're actually planning on racing this thing?" She laughed.

"Might as well. King and I put all the work in, might as well at least give ol' Stool Runnings one race."

Paige scoffed and shook her head. "I have to give you credit for a creative name, although I did see some other good names, too. Can Doo, Party Pooper, and Poop Coupe were in my top three until Stool Runnings crossed my path."

"Well, I wish I could take credit for it, but that was also Meg." I wished I could take credit for the name. I was desperate to do anything that would impress Paige.

"Hmm, well, I'll see you around, Demon." Paige headed into the crowd, and I panicked. She was leaving, and I had no idea how to get her to stay.

"Paige," I called. She turned back around and propped her hands on her hips. "I'll see you at the finish line?"

"We'll see." She shrugged her shoulders and slipped into the crowd.

"I thought she was supposed to sit on the toilet?" Hammer asked.

I shook my head and leaned back. That hadn't gone exactly how I had hoped it would, but it definitely wasn't a crash and burn. Paige had talked to me, and although she had left, it wasn't like she was dying to get away from me.

I was making progress, and I hoped when I crossed that finish line she would be there. If she were, I would know that there was still hope for us. If she weren't, I would just have to step my game up even more.

Either way, I wasn't letting Paige go again.

———

Chapter 12

Paige

"I'm not speaking to any of you." We were all crowded around the finish line, and I was ready to run for the hills. I had been set up, and I didn't appreciate it at all.

I was now the odd man out as King, Troy, Rigid, and Gambler were hanging out with us now, too. So much for a girls only day. Meg was curled under King's arm, and she grimaced. "I'm sorry, Paige. Demon asked for help, and this seemed like a brilliant idea at the time."

"We're all sorry, Paige, but you can't even imagine how I felt when Meg told me that you and Demon used to date." Gwen put her arm over my shoulders and rested her head on my shoulder.

"Don't you think you should have talked to me about this before you plotted against me."

"Don't you think you should have told me about Demon?"

"There wasn't anything to tell." Lie, lie, lie, but I didn't want to tell Gwen anything at all. Demon and I were in the past, and that was where we were going to stay.

"Hmm, you'll tell me."

"Here come the shitters!" Cyn called. She leaned over the barrier and pointed down to the start line.

They were doing races two people at a time and Gwen had said that Demon was in the second race against Shitters Full. I couldn't help but giggle at the *Christmas Vacation* reference.

It was a hundred-yard dash down the track, and whoever won went into the semi-finals. Sixteen teams were racing with the final race right before the fireworks started.

"I could so do this if I were the guy sitting in the shitter," Marley mused.

Troy wrapped his arms around her from behind and pressed a kiss to the side of her head. "I better not see you in any man's shitter besides mine."

Marley looked over her shoulder at him and rolled her eyes. "You're such a charmer, Troy. I promise to never step foot in another man's shitter," she giggled.

"Well, these guys aren't going very fast. I bet Demon will at least make it to the semi-finals as long as the shitter King and Demon made doesn't fall apart." Rigid chuckled under his breath and Cyn elbowed him in the side.

"His shitter falls apart, you better go out there and help him cross the finish line," she threatened.

"Beautiful, no way in hell will you catch me pushing a shitter across the snow."

"Hmm, we'll see about that. I already signed you, Slider, and King up to race next year."

"Bullshit," Rigid muttered.

"Ha, y'all fuckers got thrown under the bus. At least my ol' lady didn't sign me up for shitter races," Gambler taunted.

"I may not have signed you up for the outhouse races," Gwen said, "but I did sign you up to go on a dog sled ride with me."

"What? A dog sled? Have you lost your mind, doll?"

Gwen cuddled into his side and looked up at him. "Please?" she pleaded.

Gambler shook his head no, but we all knew his ass would be on that dog sled even if he didn't want to be there.

The first two teams crossed the finish line, one almost tipping over, but they made it. Holy Poopers had made it to the semifinals while Shit Shack was out.

"Okay, I bet Stool Runnings wins by ten shitter lengths." Gambler pulled a twenty out of his pocket and held it up. "Who's in?"

"I'm surprised you're actually betting in Demon's favor," King laughed as he pulled out a twenty and handed it to Gambler. "I'm not betting against Demon."

Everyone put a twenty in, with Rigid the only one betting against Demon.

The flare gun went off on the other end, and Stool Runnings took off in the lead with Shitters Full trailing behind. Hammer tripped, almost going ass over tea kettle but managed to keep it together.

Demon was yelling from inside the outhouse for Hammer and Turtle to run faster. Hammer and Turtle were huffing and panting when they slid by, and they were beating Shitters Full by a good twenty feet.

They crossed the finish line, Turtle tripping over his own feet, falling into the outhouse and almost knocking it over with Demon inside.

The crowd cheered and laughed as Turtle stood up and took a bow. "Never a dull moment when Hammer and Turtle are around," King chuckled.

"Come on!" Gwen called. She grabbed me by the hand, tugging me over to the finish line. I dug my feet in, trying to stop her, but she was more than determined to get me over to Demon. "Just tell him good race, Paige, and then I'll buy you cotton candy."

I rolled my eyes and silently decided she was going to have to buy me a hell of a lot more than cotton candy to make up for today.

Demon was standing next to the outhouse that had been pushed off to the side to make room for the next race.

"So you didn't leave," he said.

"Gwen and Meg refused to let me. Going up against those two is impossible to win against. I'm waiting for them to get distracted by King and Gambler so I can make a break for it."

"Well, while you wait for that break, how about we head over to the bar and get a drink."

"Um, hot chocolate sounds better right now." I wrapped my arms around myself and ran my hands up and down my arms.

"I think I know what would be perfect for you right now. Just one drink with me, Paige, and then I'll personally drive you home." Demon held his hand out to me and winked. "One drink won't hurt, baby."

I hesitantly reached out, his fingers lacing through my fingers. "I can't afford to trust you, Demon."

His eyes connected with mine. "And I can't afford to lose you again, Paige. I'm going as slow as I can with you. One drink, that's all I'm asking for right now."

I nodded my head slightly, and he tugged me to his side. "One drink," I whispered.

We all headed over to the bar that was on the shore and Demon, and I brought up the rear. "I'm a different man than I was back then."

"And I'm a different person, too."

"Then I guess we should get to know each other again, don't you think so?"

He glanced over at me, and I couldn't help but feel the same tingle deep in my stomach that I used to get when he looked at me. I quickly beat the feeling down, knowing that what happened between Demon and I wasn't going to be fixed over one drink and everything would go back to the way it was seven years ago.

It was never going to be the way it was, and now it was time to find out if the person that I was is ready to be with Demon again. Because the girl Demon hurt back then, was yelling at me to run away as fast as I could.

It was time to see who won, old Paige, or grown up Paige.

————————

Chapter 13

Demon

"Just try it. I promise it's not that bad."

Paige lifted it up, taking a sniff and wrinkled her nose. "I have to say that a hot chocolate smells much better than this."

"Come on. You live in Wisconsin you have to try a Tom & Jerry or a Hot Toddy at least once. It'll help keep you warm when we go back outside."

"I thought you were taking me home after this?"

We were all gathered around the bar, taking up three-quarters of the area. Paige was sitting next to me, her ass perched on the edge of her stool as she gently swirled the liquid in the glass. I had ordered her a Tom & Jerry, and she had yet to take a sip. I figured eggnog and brandy were a safe bet. Evidently, I was wrong. "First, you have to have a drink with me. All you've done is smell it and give it the evil eye."

"I've never had a warm drink with alcohol in it before."

"You've never spiked your coffee with Bailey's in the morning?"

Paige's eyes bugged out, and she shook her head. "Are you crazy? I'm pretty sure if I drank before noon, I'd barf."

"After you live up north for a while, you'd be surprised at the things you'll do to stay warm. Drink up. I've got another race to win."

She hesitantly took a sip, and she looked up at me, surprised. "That's pretty good." She took another sip and set it down on the bar. "You can't even tell there is alcohol in there." She eagerly picked it up again and took a long drink.

"Okay, baby. Maybe not so fast." I figured from the way Paige talked, she wasn't a big drinker. "It's this kind of drink you need to watch out for. They sneak up on you fast and knock you on your ass quick."

She waved her hand at me then motioned to the bartender. "Can I get another one of these but in a to-go cup."

"Now that's my kind of girl," Meg called. "Asks for a to-go cup in a bar." Meg high fived Cyn and motioned to Lo that she needed her own to-go cup.

"Drink up, baby. I think you just got the official seal of approval from Meg."

"This is the best thing I got for a to-go cup." The bartender set down a Styrofoam soup bowl with a lid in front of Paige, and I laughed.

Paige looked it over and nodded her head. "It'll work."

The bartender shook his head and started working on filling the large soup bowl. "Make that four," Meg called.

"Can I ask how you are going to drink out of a soup bowl without spilling it all over yourself?"

Paige finished off her first drink and set it down. She grabbed her purse, fished out a pair of nail scissors and grabbed the lid to the soup bowl. She made the small cuts in the lip then grabbed a straw and stuck it through the lid. "Like this." She held up the makeshift lid with the straw in it, and I couldn't help but laugh.

"You always were an inventive one."

Meg ran over, plucked the lid out of Paige's hand and climbed into King's lap. "This is mine!" she called. "We need to take her drinking with us more often, Lo. I was just going to slurp the damn drink out of the bowl like Blue." Meg spun the lid around the straw and smiled at King.

Paige grabbed three more lids and cut holes in them, making room for the straws.

By the time the bartender had all four drinks made, the girls had snapped the lids onto their bowls and we all bundled up to head back outside. Paige stood up from her stool and stumbled into me. "Easy," I mumbled as I steadied her.

"Maybe this second drink isn't a good idea," she giggled as she took a sip from the straw.

"Once we get outside you'll be fine. You need the booze to keep you warm. Just hold on to me."

She wrapped her arm around mine, leaning a bit into me and we headed out the door, once again bringing up the rear.

"You know, I guess I never realized how cold it got here. This is fun, but what else do you do when it's this cold. I don't think I could hang out all day outside drinking without a toe or two falling off."

"There's other things to do. Like, drinking inside."

Paige giggled and shook her head. "Is there anything that doesn't involve drinking?"

"Well, you did move to Wisconsin, where we consume 40% of the national average of Korbel."

"What's Korbel?"

Proof that Paige was not a drinker. I could only imagine the headache she was going to wake up with tomorrow. "Brandy, baby. That's what is in your drink."

"Oh. Wow, 40%? That's a lot."

"That's Wisconsin."

Paige slipped on a patch of ice and clung to my arm. Thankfully she had a lid on her drink, so she didn't spill as her cup went sideways and her arm flew into the air. "I guess I still haven't gotten used to walking in snow yet," she laughed. "Now, I'm going to need more examples of what to do in the winter here, or I'm going to become a raging alcoholic in no time."

"Well, I work on my bike. Get it ready for the spring."

"You're telling me that every person here works on their bike in the winter and drinks. That's it? You go out on a date, and you drink and work on your bike. There had to be something else to do." Paige stopped walking and put her hands on her hips.

I ran my hand through my hair and shrugged my shoulders. "Well, baby. There is a lot of other things you do in the wintertime."

"Well tell me. I'm going to blow through my TBR pile in no time if all I have to do is read and work."

"What the hell is a TBR pile?" She was talking fast and now abbreviating her words.

"To be read. I've got a shit ton of books I want to read."

"Oh." I looked around trying to think of what there was to do around here, but the only thing I could think to do during the winter was the thing that led to so many babies being born in the summer. Sex. Lots of sex.

"Hey, are you guys coming?" Gwen called. She was standing at the finish line of the track next to Gambler. "You're up next, and you still need to push your shitter to the other end of the track."

I looked at Paige, and she shrugged her shoulders but pointed a finger at me. "You're not off the hook on this one, Demon. I want a detailed list of the things I can do during the winter here, or I seriously might consider vacationing to Florida November through April."

"Did anyone ever tell you that you get feisty when you drink?"

"I would have to have been drunk more than two times in my life for someone to tell me that." She put the straw to her lips and took a long drink. "This makes three."

"Well, baby. You are definitely feisty when you drink."

"Feisty is good, right?"

"On you it is." I reached up and cupped her cheek. "Stay with the girls and I'll take you home after the race, okay?"

"No."

"No?"

"No. Meg said that there were fireworks tonight. I haven't seen fireworks in person for at least ten years. I want fireworks." She stomped her foot and took another drink.

She was going to have that bowl of Tom & Jerry gone in no time. Hopefully, she wouldn't want another one. I would walk across town to get her a damn hot chocolate if she wanted it because I knew any more booze and she would end up on the ground. "All right, baby. How about I win this shitter race and then we can hit up the fireworks?"

Paige held up her glass and looked at it. "Demon, I just stomped my foot like a little kid. What in the hell is in this cup?"

"Booze. Lots of it, especially when you're not used to drinking."

Her eyes grew huge, and she looked at me. "I'm drunk. I got drunk, and I'm being nice to you. I told myself when I saw you in your shitter that I couldn't do this. I couldn't be with you again, but here I am, drunk and demanding to see the fireworks. I'm a hussy. A complete and utter hussy who gets one drink in her and forgets everything."

I grabbed the bowl from her and tossed it in a nearby garbage. "Calm down, Paige. It's not like you've slept with me or we got married. All we've been doing is talking."

"I know, but I vowed to myself that I would never speak to you after what you did to me. You hurt me and acted like you didn't do anything wrong."

"You're right, I did do that back then, but now, now I know what a complete dick head I was, and now I want to make it up to you."

"You can't change it."

"I can't, but I can make up for it."

"How?" Paige slurred. I hadn't taken her drink away from her soon enough.

"Take you to the fireworks tonight."

"It's gonna take a whole lot more than fireworks to make up for jerking off to two girls."

I cringed at her words. I fucking hated remembering that. "It'll probably take my whole life to make it up to you, Paige. So, why not let me start right now. I win this race, I give you my beer can trophy and then we watch fireworks from the back of my truck."

"You're not playing fair. I'm drunk, you're still hot, and I want to see fireworks." Paige sidestepped, stumbling a bit and I grabbed her arm. How in the hell was she getting drunker? Apparently, the full effect of the booze was kicking in.

"I'm playing as fair as I can. You're still beautiful, and I want to spend as much time with you as I can."

Paige leaned forward and stuck her finger out, pointing at me. "That, right there, is shit from one of the books I read that would make me swoon and throw my clothes off."

"You take your clothes off when you read?" I definitely had to interrupt Paige when she was reading if that were the case.

"No, you dope." She slapped my shoulder and stumbled into my arms. "Meta… metafor…" she ran her fingers through her hair and stood up straight. "Metaforkaly." I smothered a laugh with the back of my hand and turned my head away. "Shit, there shouldn't be a fork in there," she mumbled.

"Yo, Rigid," I called over Paige's shoulder. "Can you run and get Paige a coffee for me?" Rigid eyed me up, ready to tell me off when he saw Paige stumble to the left and figured out why I needed him to get coffee. It was either he needed to hold Paige up or go get coffee.

"Be right back." Rigid grabbed Cyn's hand and headed to the mobile coffee cart that was on the other side of the track.

"Drink a cup of coffee while I race. It'll help you feel better." I wrapped her arm around my waist and pulled her to me as we walked over to Gwen who was glaring at me.

"How many drinks did you give her?" Gwen demanded. Gwen put her arm around Paige and pulled her out of my arms.

"Two. She's a lightweight apparently."

"Two, seriously?" Meg asked, shocked. "Hey, what happened to your to-go cup?"

Paige reached out, patting Meg on the shoulder and shook her head. "It's for the best, Meg. I should stick to wine. Tag-teaming with Tom and Jerry was not a good idea."

Meg's eyes bugged out, and Gwen put a hand over her mouth, smothering a laugh. "Ugh, yeah. I hate being tag-teamed," Meg laughed.

King walked over and put his arm over Meg's shoulders and shook his head. "Meg got drunk on our first date, too, Paige."

"Hey," Meg protested. "I'll have you know that I am not a lightweight. Cyn and I each had over eight drinks that night." Meg elbowed King and a smirk spread across her lips.

"Best eight drinks I've ever bought. Although, it should have taken only five drinks to get you to let me go back to your room with you."

Meg shrugged her shoulders and grinned. "I'm born and raised from Wisconsin. If it only took me five drinks to get me rip-roaring drunk, I would be a disgrace to the state."

"She's right," Cyn called.

"Now I really feel like a lightweight." Paige closed her eyes and rested her head on Gwen's shoulder.

"Don't worry, hun. Not everyone can drink like a sailor, or like Meg." Gwen patted Paige's head and giggled.

"I'm pretty sure Meg could drink a pirate under the table," King mumbled.

"Here's your water." I walked past Hammer and Turtle. "They're waiting for you."

I handed the bottle to Gwen and looked over Paige. "You sure you're okay?"

Paige nodded her head and opened her eyes. "I'm fine. The water will help." She waved her hand at me. "Go race your shitter, I'll be here, leaning on Gwen." She took a sip of water and gave me a small smile. "I'm good, I promise." She looked pale and tired, but she was at least standing without falling over.

I nodded my head and headed down the track to where Turtle and Hammer were waiting for me.

"It's about damn time you decided to make your way down here. They were five minutes away from disqualifying us. You can't run a shitter with only two people." Turtle crossed his arms over his chest and tried to look like he actually cared about what he was saying. "Hell, I was hoping you'd stay down there, and we wouldn't have to push the shitter anymore." Hammer leaned against the outhouse and took a drink from the beer in his hand.

"Three more races, boys, and then that trophy is ours."

"Come on, can't we just throw this next race and call it a day? Pushing a shitter up and down the ice was not how I pictured my day going."

"Well, things change, Hammer, and it looks like it's your lucky day to push a shitter up and down the ice."

Turtle and Hammer both grumbled, but they took their places on either side of the outhouse, and I sat down on the toilet inside. I heard Turtle and Hammer mumbling that this was one of the stupidest things they had ever done, and I knew right then that they were right.

I had to get out of my comfort zone to show Paige that I had changed and the man she had known back there was gone, replaced by the guy who was going to make her fall in love with me again.

I was going to make Paige mine again, and the first step to getting her back was to win this damn shitter race. I was going to win, even if that meant I would have to get out and help these two fuckers push.

Nothing was going to keep me away from Paige.

———

Chapter 14

Paige

"You know you're going to have to tell me what the hell went on between you and Demon. When Meg said we were trying to get you to come to the festival to meet Demon, I was speechless."

I rolled my eyes and cupped my hands in front of my mouth and blew into them. "Well, that doesn't happen often."

Gwen bumped me with her hip and laughed. "I know, right? Gambler couldn't believe how quiet I was."

"Wait, Gambler knows about, well, me and Demon?" Gwen and I were standing by the hot chocolate booth waiting for everyone. Demon and his team had won the outhouse race, and they were loading up the championship winning shitter right now.

"Gambler knew before I did. I swear, Gambler and all the guys are worse than women when it comes to gossip. Although, with them, it's not really gossip. They more like say what their problem is and then they all figure out how to fix it."

"Wait. I'm a problem?" This was going from bad to worse. Not only did everyone know that Demon and I used to date, they thought that I was a problem.

"No, I didn't mean it like that. They just talk about shit."

I crossed my arms over my chest and shook my head. "That really doesn't make it any better."

"Knock it off. We're not talking about the guys, we are talking about the fact that you dated a guy in a motorcycle club, and you never told me."

"I was away at college, Gwen. I did have somewhat of a life." Honestly, the time I was with Demon was the extent of the life I had. After I had finished that last semester, I had moved back home and began living my hermit ways. You never got hurt if you didn't put yourself out there.

"So, why did you two break up?"

"Things happened, we changed."

"That's not what Meg said. She said that Demon cheated on you."

I didn't know what to say. I used to think that he had cheated, but ever since I had talked to Marg, I wasn't so sure. Yes, he did something that was way wrong, but he didn't actually cheat. He claimed he was never going to touch them, and a part of me believed him. But there was still a part of me that was too hurt to see past anything. Plus, that was just the cherry on top of the fucked up sundae that was our relationship. We had way more problems than Demon watching 'live porn', as Marg liked to call it. "I really don't want to talk about this, Gwen."

"Well, obviously since you dated him years ago and this is the first I'm hearing about it."

I shoved my hands in my pockets and looked at Gwen. "A lot happened, Gwen. A lot that I never want to think about. Demon and I have a messy history that honestly, I never can get sorted out. We both hurt each other because we were too young to know our asses from our elbows, let alone navigate the kind of relationship we had."

Gwen looked me up and down and put her hand on my shoulder. "What happened, Paige?"

I wasn't going to tell her. Especially not standing next to a hot chocolate booth. "Too much, Gwen."

Gwen pursed her lips and nodded her head. "It's never too much if you love each other, Paige. Just remember that. I get that you don't want to tell me, but maybe now that you're both older and know more of who you are, maybe things can be different. I know if I had met Gambler seven years ago, we never would be where we are right now."

"Well, the difference between you two and me and Demon is that we did meet all those years ago, and we messed it up royally."

Gwen wrapped her arms around her middle and took a step back. "Just give him a chance, Paige. I don't know Demon extremely well, but he doesn't seem like the kind of guy to ask for help, let alone from Meg and I. I think he knows what he did, and he wants to make it right. Whatever it is since you won't even tell your own flesh and blood what happened." Gwen pouted and pulled her hat down over her ears. "Here comes everyone. You don't need to decide right now what you are going to do, but I do think that you need to give Demon a chance. Everyone deserves a second chance, Paige."

I turned away, looking down the row of food booths and vendors and felt the tears coming. Gwen was right, but I didn't know how to give Demon a second chance without remembering everything that happened. I was becoming one of those whiny girls in the books I read that I hated who couldn't make up her mind of what she wanted.

"I don't know what you're thinking right now, Paige. But I do now that if you didn't care about Demon anymore, you wouldn't look like you were ready to cry. Maybe you two aren't as over as you thought."

For once Gwen was absolutely right.

I still loved Demon, and I had no idea what to do next.

Demon

"I'm telling you, the only way to watch fireworks is laying in the back of a truck."

"We can't all fit in the back of one truck, babe. Why the hell can't we, just stand up or use the damn chairs I loaded up before we left?" King had a smirk on his face, and I could tell he was doing everything he could to keep it together while Meg went on a tirade of how to watch fireworks.

"We each have our own truck, so we can just park them next to each other and watch them that way."

Paige raised her hand. "Um, I don't have a truck. I'll just take a chair."

"Nope, not happening. To get the full effect of the Snowflake Festival fireworks, you need to be laying down in the back of a truck," Meg insisted.

"Well, then I guess I'm going home since I don't have a truck," Paige laughed.

"Nonsense, Demon drove his truck here. You can watch them in his truck." Meg clapped her hands, a look of satisfaction on her face like she had just solved world hunger and headed in the direction of her truck with everyone following behind her. They were all smart, knowing that Paige was about to have an aneurysm about the fact she was going to have to watch the fireworks in my truck.

She turned towards me, her arms crossed across her chest. "So, is this another part of the throw Paige and Demon together plan?"

"Baby, I have no idea, but I'm going to assume that this is Meg's not so subtle way of getting you to talk to me."

"I'm tired, Demon. All I want to do is watch these fireworks and then go home. So if that means I'm going to have to watch them with you, then let's do it. Which way is your truck?"

It was half an hour to the fireworks, and everyone was clearing out, heading to the big field that they plowed where the parking was. "I can take you home now if you're tired, Paige." I didn't want her to feel forced into spending time with me. Yeah, I had wanted Meg to get Paige here, but I didn't want to make her resent me for wanting to be with her.

"It's fine, Demon. I think you and I can handle being by each other for half an hour with no one around." Paige shoved her hands in her pockets and looked up and down the road.

"This way," I motioned to the left, and we headed in the opposite direction everyone else headed. "So you like working at the bookstore?"

Paige shrugged her shoulders and huddled into her jacket. "I do. I actually love it, although might have to do with my boss more than my actual job."

"I'm surprised you're not doing something with your degree."

Paige looked away and brushed her hair out of her face. "I don't have a degree."

"What?" Paige had been going to school for her nursing degree when we had been dating and had planned on graduating in a couple of years. She had planned on putting school on hold after the baby was born, but she was adamant about going back and finishing school.

"I don't have a degree," she repeated.

"I heard you the first time. What I don't get is why the hell you didn't finish school?"

"It wasn't for me."

I grabbed her arm and spun her around to look at me. "That's bullshit. You were making the damn dean's list when we were dating."

"Things changed, Demon. I finished up my semester and then I moved back home."

"You only had three semesters left after that one. You were so close to finishing."

"Not close enough, Demon, and I wasn't on the dean's list for much longer. It was the best choice for me to quit and just go home."

"Why? Why did you leave? Becoming a nurse was the one thing you talked about all the time, and you always said you couldn't wait to be able to help people. Why did you quit?" I was fucking pissed. I couldn't believe that Paige had left.

She looked up at me, tears in her eyes but an angry scowl on her lips. "I couldn't be there anymore. I couldn't walk around like everything was okay when inside I was dying. Everywhere I looked, I saw you. Or I saw you and our baby. I kept seeing the life we talked about all the time, and I couldn't take it anymore. I was failing half of my classes, and all I wanted to do was die or sleep. Every day that went by, dying looked more and more appealing until one day I woke up, and realized I needed to leave."

Each word she spoke slapped me across the face. Paige quit school because of me and losing the baby? When we were together, after we lost the baby, she acted like everything just went back to normal. I had no idea that she was so upset. I reached up and cupped her cheek. "I'm sorry," I whispered as I wiped away the tears that were sliding down her cheek. "I had no idea."

"No one did, Demon. I just went home and told my aunt that I was homesick. She knew something more was wrong, but I refused to tell her. Thankfully Gwen was too much into herself back then that she never noticed anything out of the normal."

"You should have come to me, Paige. We were both so messed up after we lost the baby."

Paige looked around and wiped her eyes with the back of her hand. "I don't want to talk about this here, Demon. What happened in the past needs to stay there?"

"No, we need to talk about this, Paige."

She stepped away from me and shook her head. "I changed my mind, I just want to go home now."

"Wait," I grabbed her arm as she turned away and pulled her to me. "I can take you home, Paige."

"No." She tried to twist her arm out of my grasp and shook her head. "I only live five blocks away. I can walk. Please, just let me go."

"No, I did that once. I'm not letting you go again."

"Demon, please," she pleaded.

I knew if I let her go now, she would never talk to me again. "Come with me."

"No, I want to go home. I just want this day to be over."

"Just please come with me, Paige." I was desperate. I knew by the way she looked, she was done with me, but I couldn't let that happen. She hadn't given me a chance to explain and make up for all the shit that had happened. "One week."

"One week for what, Demon?"

"Give me one week. No interruptions, just you and me. No one else interfering, trying to throw us together, one week." I was flying by the seat of my pants right now, not exactly sure what I was going to do, but I knew I needed to do something. If Paige and I kept going the way we were, we wouldn't be talking within a day.

"Demon, I have no idea what you are trying to say."

"Come with me." I grabbed both of her hands and pulled her to me. "Come with me for one week. There is so much between us and no way to talk about it here."

"I know, that's why I want to go home."

"No, you don't get it, Paige. Come away with me for seven days, just us. Talking and finding out if we can get back to the way we were."

"I can't just run away with you, Demon. I have a job and responsibilities here. I have a life that has nothing to do with you." She crossed her arms over her chest and scowled. "I have my aunt to look after. She's the whole reason I moved here."

"You have vacation time, and you have Gwen who can help your aunt for a week. You don't have pets or any other pressing matters that need to be taken care of. Call your boss, ask her for the week off, then text Gwen and tell her this week she's checking in on your aunt."

"It's not that easy, Demon."

"Yes, it is, Paige. Life is only as hard as you make it. I'm not asking for a month or a year. I just want seven days with you. I'm not going to force you to do anything you don't want to."

"You're forcing me to go away with you."

"Well, after this, I won't make you do anything you don't want to. Just come with me and then everything is up to you."

"This is kidnapping, you know that, right?" Paige crossed her arms over her chest and tapped her foot. "Seven days isn't going to fix us, Demon."

"Talking and discovering who we both are now is going to fix us. Just say yes. You used to trust me, Paige. Trust me again. Please." I was not above begging. The more I thought about this, the more it made sense.

"I don't know if I want to be with you for seven days straight, Demon. Right now, all I want to do is punch you in the balls and go home."

"Well, why don't we skip the ball punching, for now, head to your house, pack some clothes, then swing by the clubhouse so I can pack a bag and then we can get out of here."

"Why do you even think that I'll agree to this?" she asked.

"Because I know deep down, you want to know why. You want to know why things happened the way they did back then, same as me. We loved each other, Paige. Even before you got pregnant, I knew that I wanted to spend the rest of my life with you, but then all hell broke loose, and we lost each other."

"I didn't do any of the losing, Demon. That was all you and your 'live porn'," Paige held her fingers up in quotation marks and wrinkled her nose.

"What in the hell is live porn?"

"What you were doing that night in your room when I walked in on you."

"I fucked up, Paige and I will tell you every day until I die, that night has been my number one regret for the past seven years."

"Your regret doesn't make me feel any better."

"Then come away–"

Paige's ringtone started blaring, and she pulled her phone out of her pocket. "It's Gwen."

"Good. Tell her she needs to hang with your aunt this week."

"I can't,"

"You can."

"I can't just run away and expect someone else to take care of everything I should be doing." The phone stopped ringing but not even ten seconds later it was ringing again.

"Please, Paige. We both need this. After this week, if you never want to see me again, I'll disappear forever. I promise.

Paige's finger hovered over the accept button on her phone, and she closed her eyes. "Son of a bitch," she mumbled as she swiped her finger left. "Hey, Gwen," she chirped into the phone.

I heard Gwen demand to know where Paige was and if she needed to come and kick my ass. I rolled my eyes and prayed that Paige wasn't going to tell her to come beat the shit out of me. "Um, we're actually headed to Demon's truck." Paige cleared her throat and shuffled her feet in the snow. "So, do you have any plans this week?" I couldn't hear what Gwen said, but Paige closed her eyes and dropped her head as Gwen talked. "Do you think that you could go over to Aunt Rose's house this week and do her shopping for her. I had something come up that is going to take me out of town for seven days." Paige turned around, and I heard Gwen fire off fifty questions wanting to know what Paige was going to be doing for seven days. "Just check on Rose, and I'll be back next Sunday." Gwen screeched into the phone, and Paige listened for ten seconds before she ended the call and shoved the phone back into her pocket.

She turned back around to me and propped her hands on her hips. "Seven days and if I never want to talk to you again after, you do what I ask and leave me alone." She held her hand out to me, and I looked her in the eye.

"Seven days, Paige. Seven days to make you fall in love with me again." I grabbed her hand, shaking it firmly as she rolled her eyes at my words.

"Fine. Have at it, but if you even want a remote chance at that happening, we need to leave now, because I know that Gwen will be hunting us down in minutes."

I didn't need to be told twice. I grabbed Paige's hand, tugging her in the direction of my truck and looked over my shoulder to make sure Gwen was not behind us.

I had seven days to make Paige fall in love with me again, and I knew I was going to need every second of them.

Game on.

———————

Chapter 15

Paige

I needed to be institutionalized. I was absolutely crazy to agree to seven days alone with Demon. We had been driving for two hours and had just stopped at a huge truck stop for gas but mostly because I had to pee for the last thirty minutes.

"Head on in, I'll be in after." Demon motioned to me, and I didn't need to be told twice. The Tom & Jerry's and the hot chocolate from before had caught up with me, and a bathroom was my number one concern.

Thankfully, Demon had picked a nicer truck stop with a well-lit parking lot, three restaurants attached to it and best of all, clean bathrooms.

After I had hit the bathroom, I was wondering around, gathering snacks in my arms when I remembered that I still needed to call Marg. I had the day off tomorrow so the worst that would happen if she said no was that Demon would have to take me home before Monday.

It was after ten o'clock, but I knew that Marg would still be awake. I set down my bevy of snacks on the counter next to the soda machine and pulled out my phone. I had turned it off ten minutes after we had left because Gwen, Meg, and Cyn wouldn't stop calling me. I had only talked to Gwen once, listening to her rant for thirty seconds on why I was making the worst decision of my life and then had turned my phone off.

After I had powered it back on, I saw that I had four more missed calls, all from Gwen, and numerous text messages from Meg and Cyn. Apparently, everyone thought they knew what was best for me. Hell, I didn't even know what was best for me.

I cleared out all the messages and calls, not looking at any of them, and swiped left on Marg's name and put the phone to my ear.

"Either you're calling because you want to kill motorcycle man, or you need a condom because you're ready to rip his clothes off, and you want to be prepared."

I shook my head and leaned against the counter. "That would be a no to both," I laughed.

"Well, I guess that's good, except I don't know why the hell you're calling then."

"Um… I was hoping I could have next week off. All of it."

"What? Did something happen, hunny?" Marg's voice was filled with concern, and I could only imagine what she was thinking. She probably thought someone had died, but when in reality, I had just shoved all of my responsibilities aside and ran away with Demon.

"No, no. Everything is fine. I'm just going to be out of town until Sunday."

"Oh, I didn't know you had a trip planned."

"I didn't. I'm with… Demon." I swear I could hear Marg's jaw drop when I said Demon's name.

"Holy mother of God. Rod, get me my inhaler," Marg mumbled into the phone. "Paige ran off with that motorcycle man I was telling you about." Great, Marg had told Rod about Demon. How had I gone from no one in the whole world knowing about Demon and I, to now everyone I talked to knew?

"I didn't run off. I do plan on coming back. Next Sunday, as a matter of fact." I held the phone up with my shoulder and crossed my arms over my chest. "I'm really not sure what I'm doing, Marg," I whispered.

"Oh, hunny," Marg cooed. "You're finally listening to your heart and not your head."

"But my head won't shut up, Marg. Everything is telling me to run, but yet here I am, standing in a gas station, lord knows where, with a man that broke my heart and left me with nothing."

"No, hunny. You're with a man who knows he messed up and will do anything to get you back."

"But I'm not sure if I want him back," I whispered so quietly that I didn't even think Marg heard me.

"You've already answered that question by agreeing to go away with him. You want him back, Paige."

"But what if–"

"But nothing. Stop lying to yourself. He hurt you, hunny, there is no denying that, but now you need to move past it and get that happy ending you wanted."

"You make it sound so easy, Marg."

"It is easy if it's meant to be, Paige. Trust me, and trust your heart." The phone clicked in my ear, and Marg was gone. She had never agreed to me having the week off, but I had to assume she was okay with it if she was telling me to follow my heart.

"Everything okay?" Demon asked, walking up next to me. He had two bottles of soda in one hand and a giant cup of coffee in the other.

"Yeah," I mumbled, shoving my phone into my pocket. "I just called Marg to let her know that I won't be in next week."

Demon juggled his drinks in his hand and helped pick up all of the snacks I had gathered earlier. "You think you got a big enough peppermint patty?" Demon asked, holding up the half pound round package.

I shrugged my shoulders and grabbed it from him. "I had no idea they made them so big. I'm not going to eat the whole thing." Demon shook his head, not believing me and headed to the cash register. He apparently remembered my love affair with peppermint patties. I could eat twenty of them in one sitting and still want more. "You think you got enough caffeinated beverages?" I asked, mocking his question about my peppermint patty.

"We've got another three hours on the road before we get to where we are going, and I don't plan on stopping until we get there."

"Where are we going?" I asked as I watched the cashier ring up all my junk food.

"You'll see once we get there."

"Well, I'm assuming we're not in Wisconsin anymore, Toto," I giggled.

"You're right about that one, Dorothy," Demon smirked, grabbed the bag full of goodies and we headed back to the truck.

"So, you're really not going to tell me where we are going?" I slid into the truck, clicked my buckle into place and looked at Demon who was standing outside my door.

"Nope, you're just going to have to wonder until we get there." He handed me the bag and slammed the door shut.

I ripped into my huge peppermint patty, gnawing off a huge bit as Demon slid in next to me. "I see you lasted a whole five seconds before you had to open that. I remember every time we went to the store you would always buy one and have it gone before we even made it to the checkout. You always made me hand them the empty wrapper, making them think I was the one who ate it."

I shrugged my shoulders and couldn't deny it. What could I say, peppermint patties were my weakness. "You're not supposed to remember that." I broke off a chunk and wrapped the rest up and stuck it in the bag.

"I remember everything that you and I did." Demon looked over at me, his eyes warm and a small smile on his lips. "You're not easy to forget."

"Neither are you," I whispered.

He put his arm across the back of the seat and brushed my hair off of my shoulder. "I'm glad that we can agree on that."

"I think we can also agree that there are some things we wish we didn't remember." His hand cupped my cheek, and I leaned into his touch, His thumb stroked my cheek, and it felt like all the years we were apart disappeared.

"There were one hundred times more good things than bad things, baby. I made mistakes back then, but now I'm going to fix them."

I sighed deep and leaned away from his hand. "Well, let's get this truck back on the road and get this makeshift kidnap back underway."

Demon chuckled and stuck the key in the ignition. "It's hardly a kidnapping if you voluntarily get in the truck."

I shrugged my shoulders and took another bite of my candy. Demon pulled out of the gas station and headed west, or at least I thought we were headed west.

Demon reached over, broke off a chunk from my peppermint and popped it in his mouth. "Hey," I scolded him. "You should have bought your own if you wanted some." I shoved the rest in my mouth and struggled to chew it.

"You never were good at sharing, were you, baby?"

I glared at him as I managed to swallow some of it down and wiped my mouth with the back of my hand. "Next time we stop you're buying your own."

"I'm hoping not to stop at all until we get there."

I leaned back in my seat and tried to think of what was five hours away from home. I pulled my coat tight around me and rested my head on the back of the seat. "Well, I hope you're not thinking I'm going to help keep you awake. It's past my regular bedtime and today's activities wore me out."

"I suppose getting drunk at four in the afternoon really takes it out of you," Demon laughed.

"Whatever," I muttered. I curled up in the seat, tucking my legs up on the seat and closed my eyes.

"Just sleep," Demon mumbled. He turned the radio on, keeping the volume low and I heard him humming along to the song that was playing.

"Wake me up if you need me," I whispered, already half asleep.

Demon reached over and brushed my hair off of my forehead and ran his fingers through my hair. "I'll wake you when we get there."

I drifted asleep, on the road to somewhere I didn't know, next to a man I never thought I would see again, let alone give him a second chance.

I had no idea what I was doing, but it felt right.

———————

Chapter 16

Demon

"Baby, time to wake up." I gently shook Paige, but she didn't move. This was another thing I remembered from when we dated, she hated waking up. "Baby, the trucks on fire." She mumbled in her sleep, but still didn't budge.

This was starting to look like it always did when Paige used to fall asleep in the car; I was going to have to carry her. I managed to slide my arm behind her back, scooped her up into my arms and bumped the door shut with my hip. She wrapped her arms around my neck, held on tight, and I headed down the cobblestone walk, careful of my step. It had been years since I had been here, and back then this sidewalk had been hazardous.

"Hmm, are we there yet?" She mumbled into my neck.

"We're here, although right now all I want to do is sleep. I forgot how long of a boring ride that is." All she did was whimper and try to burrow even further into my arms.

I managed to unlock the door with Paige still wrapped up in my arms and headed straight to the bedroom. I opened the bedroom door, the moonlight offering enough light that I didn't need to turn on any lights and laid Paige down on the bed.

"Where are you going?" She asked, not letting go of my neck.

"I just gotta lock the door quick, and I'll be right back." My words pacified her enough that she let me go and laid her head down on the pillow.

"Two minutes, Demon." She scurried under the blankets with her coat still on and burrowed into the warmth of the thick comforter.

I made my way back down the hallway, actually looking around and saw that this place was exactly how it had been the last time Paige and I were here. The only difference was the fresh blanket of snow on the ground outside.

After I had stoked the fire in the wood burning furnace, I locked the front door and sent off a quick message to Stan who had gotten the cabin ready for us and told him we had made it.

"You do know it has been way longer than two minutes, right?" Paige grumbled when I walked back into the bedroom. Her coat was thrown on the floor, and she was laying on her side, watching me. "I have no idea where I am."

"Yes, you do know where you are, baby. Merkmeir Lake."

"No, we're not. It used to take us forever to get here."

"It used to take eight hours, but now that we live in Rockton, we're only five hours away."

"Hmm, funny how that works," she giggled. "You do realize that I'm somewhat awake now, and it won't be so easy to sleep in the same bed as me now."

I pulled my shirt over my head and tossed it in the corner. "Well, I'm telling you right now. You are laying in the only bed in this house and that so happens to be the same bed that I'm going to be laying in about thirty seconds."

"The couch pulls out into a bed, Demon. You can sleep out there."

"The couch used to pull out into a bed until I got rid of it and bought a new one." I bent over, untied my boots and toed them off. "Now it's just a couch."

"Why would you get rid of that couch? It was a classic."

"No, baby. It was a classic seven years ago. Now, it's rotting away in a landfill."

"Well, I bet you're regretting throwing it away now because you're going to have to crash on the 'just a couch' for the next seven nights." Paige rolled over, tucked the pillow under her head and sprawled out in the middle of the bed.

"It's a big bed, Paige. If you scoot over to one side, I can lay on the other side, and we won't even touch."

"That would be fine and dandy if I didn't sleep the way I do."

I smirked and tugged on the blanket, pulling it down her body. It was hard to forget how Paige slept. She could fall asleep straddling the edge of the bed, and I'd wake up with her wrapped around me, every inch of her lush body touching me. "You just gotta control yourself, Paige. It really shouldn't be my fault that you can't seem to keep your hands off of me."

Paige grabbed the pillow out from under her head and threw it at me. It bounced off my chest and landed at my feet. "Move over, before I make you move over." I grabbed the pillow and threw it at the head of the bed. "You got ten seconds to move."

Paige shook her head and crossed her arms over her chest.

I counted down from ten, and when I got to two and pulled the blanket all the way off, she finally realized that I wasn't joking. She rolled over, her back to me and huffed under her breath. "You're not playing fair, Demon."

I slipped into the bed, pulling the blanket over us and threw my arm over my head. "I'm not playing a game, Paige."

"You could have fooled me," she whispered.

"I want you, Paige. I want all of you again, including your heart."

Paige huddled even closer to the edge of the bed, and she lightly sighed. "You never lost me."

———————

Chapter 17

Paige

I was on my third cup of coffee and Demon still wasn't back from wherever the hell he had gone this morning. I had woken up to an empty bed, Demon's pillow wrapped up in my arms and a note on the side of the bed from Demon. All it had said was he had to run to town and would be back soon.

Well, that had been over an hour ago, and I was running out of things to do. I had discovered that winter at the cabin was a bit different than summer at the cabin. Demon and I went hiking and swimming all the time when we used to come here, but with over a foot of snow on the ground, both of those options were out of the question.

There was barely any food in the fridge so to keep my mind off of my grumbling stomach, I snooped around the cabin, discovering that although everything was updated, it was still very much the same. It was only a one-bedroom cabin with one full bath and one huge room at the front of the cabin that was the living room and the kitchen. It was small, but I had always loved coming here. It was a little vacation without having to go too far.

I was perched on the stool in front of the kitchen island when Demon finally came through the front door with six grocery bags filled full hanging from his arms. "You're awake," he said, surprised.

"It's almost ten, Demon."

"I know, but I figured you would sleep in."

I shrugged my shoulders and drank the last of my coffee. "I normally wake up at seven each morning. Sleeping until nine was definitely sleeping in."

"Well, I ran to town and got breakfast and groceries to last us a couple of days." He plopped the bags down on the counter and rummaged through them. "Did you get a chance to look around at all?"

I grabbed one of the bags from him and emptied it out onto the counter. "As much as I could without having to put my boots on. The inside basically looks the same besides obvious updates you did."

"Yeah, I didn't come up here for a couple of years, and the place went to shit. Updating was more of necessity, not an option."

I grabbed the pound of bacon and dozen of eggs and set them by the stove. I need more sustenance than coffee. "You used to love coming up here, why did you stop?" Every time Demon and I would make the trip to the cabin, it was like he was transported to a different world and he was so laid back. We had only come here four times together, but each time together was fantastic.

"I don't know," he said as he shrugged his shoulders. "I guess it just didn't feel the same. I hired Stan a couple of years ago to get the place in shape and look after it, but this is the first time I've been here since."

"What? You updated the cabin without actually being here? How in the hell did that work?" I couldn't imagine having someone remodeling a place that was mine without me being there telling them what to do.

"Picture message. It's a beautiful thing."

I shook my head at him and grabbed a frying pan out of the cabinet. "You're crazy."

"Yeah, but a good crazy. Thankfully everything turned out good." Demon finished putting away all of the groceries while I scrambled some eggs and fried the bacon.

I slid the bacon onto a paper plate and set it on the island where Demon was sitting, drinking a cup of coffee. "So, what is the plan, Demon?"

"Don't really have one, baby."

"Hmm, I can see you're still the same as you were before. Always going with the flow but never really having a plan."

Demon shrugged his shoulders and picked up a piece of bacon. "It hasn't failed yet," he winked.

This was where Demon and I were as different as night and day. While I liked to know what was going on and know the plan, Demon just sat back and went with it. No matter what it was, Demon dealt with it. If that meant going with it, or leaving if he didn't like it, he did. "I should have known you didn't have a plan. I bet you thought of coming up to the cabin only seconds before you asked me to come with you."

A smirk spread across Demon's lips, and he popped the piece of bacon into his mouth. "Somethings don't change. If it ain't broke, don't fix it."

I grabbed the platter of eggs and two plates and sat down next to Demon. "You know having a plan isn't a bad thing," I mumbled.

"I know, baby, but what happens when you're in the middle of a plan, and something better comes along. Something that blows all of your plans out of the water?"

"You adjust your plan, but still, have a plan."

Demon shook his head and filled his plate. "Well, if that's the case, I just came up with a plan."

"It's not really a plan if you haven't planned it."

"Well, now that is where you might be wrong about this plan."

"Do you think we've said the word plan enough?" I asked, looking at him.

"Maybe just a couple more times." He winked at me, grabbed both of our cups and headed over to the coffee pot. "You already know what my huge plan is." I ducked my head and scooped a pile of eggs onto my plate. "I want you back, Paige. I'm not playing this with my cards close to my chest."

I swallowed hard on the small bite of bacon I had just chewed. "You never were one to beat around the bush, either," I whispered.

"I think we need to get something straight, Paige." Demon set the cups down in front of the coffee pot and turned around to look at me. "Seven years ago, I made the biggest mistake of my life letting you walk away. There isn't a damn day that goes by that I don't think about you and what we had. We went through some hard shit that neither of us knew how to deal with. You pushed me away, and I fucked up royally."

"You can say that again," I mumbled.

"I fucked up royally, Paige. I will tell you every day until I die. You want me to tell you every day when we wake up, I will. I'm not ashamed to tell you that I was a fucking idiot who threw away the best thing he's ever had, and I will do everything on this earth to get back into your heart and your ass in my bed."

"I just wish things could be different."

"They can be, Paige. Look," Demon rounded the counter and pulled out the stool next to me. "I know it's hard, but we both need to let go of the past."

"But what if I hadn't walked in on you that night, Demon? Would that have gone further, to the point where we can't wax over it and say technically you didn't cheat?"

"If you wouldn't have walked in, it wouldn't have gone any further. I know it sounds ridiculous to you, but I was yours Paige and no one else was going to have me."

I pushed my plate away and turned to look Demon in the eye. "Do you know how ridiculous that sounds, but for some reason, I believe you. How in the hell does that work?" I wanted to believe every word he said, but I couldn't. I knew before, when things were good with us that Demon would never hurt me, especially wouldn't cheat on me. It was something I always felt.

"I never hid the way I felt about you, Paige. I knew that first night together that you were mine. I didn't want anyone else, even that night with those two girls, I knew I belonged to you."

"Then why in the hell did you do it, Demon? Why would you go into that room with those two girls and… and… touch yourself while they, well, did whatever the hell they were doing?" I was flustered, trying to get everything out that I had wanted to say for the past years. I had so many questions, and I needed an answer to all of them before I let Demon back in.

Demon ran his hands through his hair and shook his head. "Honestly, Paige? I was fucking mad at you. It felt like when the baby died, we died, too, and I had no fucking clue how to handle it. I wanted to be with you, but it was like you always had fifty things you needed to do that didn't have anything to do with me."

"That's not true. I felt like I had failed you and you blamed me for losing the baby." I had struggled for so long thinking that if I had done just one thing differently that the baby would have been fine and so would Demon and me.

"I didn't blame you for losing the baby. At least I didn't mean to make you feel that way, Paige. I still sometimes can't figure out what I feel, but I know that you weren't to blame for losing the baby. We both wanted that baby more than anything, and when things went bad, we didn't know how to deal with it."

"You hurt me, Demon."

"I know, Paige."

I clasped my hands in my lap and bowed my head. We needed to move past this, or stop trying. I loved Demon. If I let myself go, and didn't think about anything but Demon, I loved him. "You can't hurt me again. I can't take anymore. You almost broke me last time."

"I will die before I hurt you again, Paige," Demon vowed.

I closed my eyes, and a small tear slid down my cheek. I was going to do it. I was going to give this man my heart again even though I knew that he might hurt me, I was going to do it. Because I had to admit, the pain was worth it. "Okay. Starting right now, Demon, let's see what happens. There's just one thing, though."

"What's that?" Demon asked.

"You don't have to earn my love because you already have it. You have to prove you're worthy of it. That man seven years ago didn't deserve it."

Demon caressed my cheek and tilted my head back. My eyes connected with his and his thumb brushed my lips. "I'm yours, Paige, and I'll do everything to prove that I deserve your love, because without it, I can't live any longer."

———————

Chapter 18

Demon

"I can't remember the last time I did anything like this." Paige stared down at me, a small smile on her lips.

"Probably that time we went tubing down the river. I swear you screamed whenever something touched you." I held my hand out to her. "Sit down, I won't let anything happen to you." I was freezing my ass off, sitting on a bright blue sled that we had just bought from the store an hour ago, trying to convince Paige to sit down in between my legs.

"This is a perfect example of what crazy things you come up with if you don't have a plan. Who goes sledding?"

"We do. Now sit your ass down and let's go."

She grabbed my hand, gripping the whole time while she cautiously sat down in between my legs. She wrapped her arms around my knees and held on for dear life. "It's just a sled going down a small hill, Paige. No need to cut the circulation off to my legs."

She didn't loosen her grip and looked at me over her shoulder. "If I die, Gwen gets all my Mary Moo Moo's."

I busted out laughing at the seriousness in her voice. "Okay, baby, I'll remember that, but if you die, the odds are good that I'll die right along with you."

"Hardly," she huffed. "You're invincible." She leaned forward and looked down the hill. "I don't know how you can say that this is a small hill, it's ginormous."

I grabbed the rope from each side of the sled and wrapped it around my hands. "It just looks big because you're scared. Once you get to the bottom, you'll see it's not big."

I moved my legs, setting my feet in the snow to push off and Paige dug her nails into my calves. "What are you doing?" she screeched.

"Paige, calm down. I think we should have stopped at the bar before we came up here. A beer or two might have loosened you up a bit."

"No, the last time I loosened up a bit I ended up in your truck headed to some place. Me loosening up with you around isn't a good idea." I moved my left foot, and she gave a yelp. "Why are you moving?"

I shook my head and wrapped my arms around Paige. "I think it might be best if you just closed your eyes."

"What, why?" She asked. I ground my feet into the snow, getting as much traction as possible and moved the sled back and forth, smoothing down the snow. "Stop moving!" she demanded.

"I promise to stop moving, as soon as we get to the bottom."

"Demon, no!" she yelled.

I pushed off, shoving us over the edge of the hill. Paige leaned back into me, her mouth wide open as she screamed bloody murder. We hit a bump that launched us into the air which I thought was awesome, but Paige's yelp of shock and her arms wrapping around herself and her fingers digging into my arms showed that she didn't think it was as awesome as I did.

The sled veered to the left, throwing us off course to a clearing of trees at the bottom. I put my right foot in the snow, skidding us to the right as a large cloud of snow surrounded us. Paige waved her arms frantically trying to fan out the snow as I managed to steer us to the clearing.

We were halfway down the hill by the time Paige stopped screaming, and she realized that we weren't going to die. "Demon!" she squealed as a tree whizzed by us.

I had to admit I judged the hill wrong, because going down it, it did seem pretty fucking big now that we were sliding down it on our asses. "Hold on," I hollered as we neared the bottom. I put both of my feet down in the snow, trying to slow us down. It was working pretty well until my right boot hit a root, jerking my leg back and my knee almost whacked Paige in the face. I gripped the sides of the sled, trying to steer and put my boot back in the snow when my other foot hit a bump in the snow. I felt the side of the sled lift up, knowing that this was not going to end well.

I wrapped my arms around Paige, pulling her close to me, and rolled off the sled before it threw us off into the trees. I managed to stay on my back, Paige on top of me, and we came to a sliding stop. Paige was sprawled out on top of me, a huge grin on her face. "That was incredible!" she giggled.

I glanced to my left, seeing the trunk of a tree not even three feet away and knew that the amazing ride Paige just had could have ended completely differently. My head plopped down in the snow, and I closed my eyes. Thank fuck we didn't hit that tree.

"Do you think we can do that again?"

I opened my eyes and was face to face with Paige who was beaming down at me, a huge smile on her face, and her cheeks flush. "I thought you didn't want to go sledding, now you want to go again?" I wasn't sure if my heart could take another ride like that. Although the beginning of it wasn't bad, the ending almost killed me.

"That was before I knew how fun it was." She moved to push off of me, but I wrapped my arms around her.

"Paige, let me catch my breath."

"Come on, you can't tell me that wasn't fun. Granted the landing could have been a bit more graceful," she giggled.

"Oh, really," I laughed. "You think the landing needs improvement?"

"Yup, that's why we should go again and this time, you can get it right." She pulled out of my arms and ran over to the sled that was twenty feet away and wedged between two trees. I sat up and brushed the snow off of my gloves. Paige trudged back over, the sled gliding behind her, and I couldn't help but notice the huge, glowing smile that was on her face. Her dark brown hair had started tucked under her hat but was now flowing behind her, and her hat was on crooked. "Come on, old man. If you don't get up that hill with me, I'll make you run back to the store and get two sleds so we can race each other down the hill."

Like hell, that was going to happen. I could only imagine Paige going down the hill by herself. I quickly stood up, brushing the snow off of my pants and followed the skid mark my body had left in the snow and grabbed the sled from her. "I'll be doing the driving, baby. You need to just hold on."

"Humph." She threaded her arm through mine and held onto my arm. "I see how well that worked last time."

I threaded my fingers through hers and pulled her close. "You do know I'm going to be sore as hell tomorrow," I chuckled.

"I have no sympathy for you. This was all your idea." She strutted off in front of me, her hips swaying back and forth. "Besides," she said over her shoulder, "it wouldn't be the first time you're sore after an afternoon with me." She winked at me and then hightailed it up the hill, leaving me behind.

I stood still, watching her. This was the Paige I had known seven years ago. Her playful banter mixed with her straight-laced ways was the reason I had fallen in love with her. You never knew what was going to come out of her mouth, but that was all part of her charm.

She was giving me a chance, and you can bet your ass I was going to take it.

Chapter 19

Paige

"How is it I've lived thirty-one years and never sat in front of a fireplace drinking hot chocolate?" I was perched in front of the huge fireplace, pillows surrounding me with Demon laying on his side next to me. I had a steaming cup of hot chocolate in my hands, and Demon had a cup of coffee in front of him.

"Hmm, I'm not sure. I'm glad I get to be your first, though," Demon winked at me and took a sip of his coffee.

Every time the damn man winked at me, butterflies attacked my stomach, and it took all my willpower not to jump into his arms and let him have his way with me. "How does your butt feel?"

Demon shook his head and grabbed one of the pillows from around me and shoved it under his head. "It felt better before I skidded down the hill on it."

Demon had lost his footing the last time we had hiked up the hill and had proceeded to slide down the hill on his butt, backward. I giggled under my breath and took a small sip of my cocoa. "That's what happens in your old age apparently, huh?"

"My age has nothing to do with the fact that the hill was slick as shit."

"Excuses, excuses," I mumbled. "I'm gonna pop some popcorn, do you want any?"

"How can you be hungry after all the food we just ate?" We had stopped at the local pub down the hill before heading back to the house, and I had gorged on greasy, yummy bar food.

"I only had a burger and fries. And cheese curds. And deep fried pickles." I propped my hands on my hips and looked down at Demon. "OK, I had a lot of food then, but I'm hungry for popcorn now."

"Well, I guess I can't argue with that logic. Pop that popcorn and bring your ass back here." Demon patted the floor next to him and wouldn't you know, he fucking winked at me. Initiate butterflies in my stomach in 3...2...1...

"You need to stop doing that," I huffed and headed into the kitchen.

"What exactly is it that I need to stop doing?" Demon asked.

I opened the cupboard and grabbed down the box of popcorn. I ignored Demon's question. There was no way in hell that I was about to tell him that his wink gave me butterflies and made me feel things in places I shouldn't be feeling things.

I was leaning against the counter, watching the bag of popcorn go around in the microwave when Demon's arms wrapped around me from the back, and he pulled me to his chest. "How am I supposed to stop something, when you don't tell me what it is that I need to stop," he growled into my ear. His hand spanned my stomach, holding me in place. "You need to tell me, baby."

I shook my head no, and closed my eyes. "It's nothing."

"If it was nothing, you wouldn't have said anything," he countered.

"Just forget I said anything."

"Not likely. Tell me what I need to stop doing. From where I'm standing, basically, the only thing I was doing was breathing."

"You did more than that," I whispered.

"Tell me what I did," he said, low and gruff. His lips grazed my ear, and a tremor rocked my body.

I was going to combust right then and there if Demon kept teasing me the way he was. He knew exactly what he was doing, and no matter how much I wanted to not react to it, I couldn't. "Please," I whimpered.

"Please, what? You need to tell me."

"Please don't... don't..."

His hand slipped under the hem of my shirt, and the touch of his hand scorched my skin. "I'm going to keep touching you until you tell me what it is you want me to stop."

"Everything," I gasped when he pressed a kiss behind my ear. He brushed aside my hair, giving him access to my neck. "Demon, please."

He spun me around in his arms and looked down at me. "Please what, Paige?"

I closed my eyes and took a breath. "Please stop winking at me and acting like the man who stole my heart, who has yet to give it back to me even after all of these years."

"That man who had your heart isn't going anywhere. He was a fucking idiot to leave you before and the only way he'll leave you again is when he's six feet in the ground."

My heart squeezed at his words, knowing that he meant each and every one of them, but he had promised the same thing before. "You'll be there to hold me up when I can't stand? Because of last time, that man who had stolen my heart also left me."

"Paige, stop fighting me. Every time you give me an inch, you back up twenty feet."

"I'm not fighting you, Demon, I'm just... worried. It all sounds good coming out of your mouth, but it's different actually doing it. It's harder."

"Nothing is easy, Paige. But I know you coming back into my life tells me that you and I are meant to be, no matter what happened in the past."

I shook my head, and a tear streaked down my cheek. "You make it sound so easy."

"It's not, but I'll be damned if we don't give this another shot." His hand cupped my cheek, and his thumb brushed my lips. "Stop fighting, and just feel."

"I just don't know—"

"Fuck it." Demon pressed me against the counter, his hips pinned me in place, and his fingers delved into my hair. "I'll just have to show you how I feel." His lips connected with mine, and it instantly felt like I was home. That everything in my life that had seemed off was now right, and nothing else mattered besides the man in front of me.

His lips moved against mine, giving me everything that I had been missing and promising me so much more. "Feel it, Paige," he growled against my lips.

I whimpered at his words and wrapped my arms around his waist. My fingers pulled up the hem of his shirt, my need to feel his skin under my fingers overwhelming. "Please," I mumbled against his lips. Everything that had been holding me back was gone, and all that was left was Demon and me.

His hands skimmed down my neck, shivers running over my body. In the wake of his touch, he lit my body on fire, and I knew no matter what happened next, I was Demon's. I had been before, and even seven years later, nothing had changed. This man could turn me on in seconds and keep me hot and bothered from one single touch.

His hands traveled down my body, and I wrapped my arms around Demon's neck. His hands grazed my ass, and I deepened the kiss, opening my mouth to give him what both of us had been wanting. He grabbed my ass, lifting me up and set me on the counter. I spread my legs, and Demon stepped between them. "This is what I've missed every night," he whispered against my lips.

I delved my fingers into his hair and wrapped my legs around Demon. I had missed this, too, but I hadn't let myself think about it until now. I used to love the quiet moments Demon and I would have together when no one was around but us. I don't know if it was because we were so young, but we would just lounge around for hours, teasing and kissing each other. "I missed you," I whispered against his lips.

I grabbed the hem of his shirt, working it up his body and pulled it over his head. My eyes traveled over his chiseled chest taking in all the tattoos that now covered it. "Looks like you've had quite a bit of work done." My fingers grazed his arm where he had an angel tattooed.

He looked down where my fingers had touched and pulled me close. "I had that done a couple of weeks after you left."

"Really? Why an angel?" I asked.

"It's for our baby. Even though we never got to meet him, I'll never forget him."

"You got a tattoo to remember our baby," I croaked out, tears threatening.

"Yeah, each and every one of my tattoos means something important to me. The angel is one of my favorites."

"What's another one that is your favorite?" I whispered, looking him in the eye.

The microwave beeped and the smell of popcorn wafted through the air as Demon opened the door, letting the popcorn cool. "Why don't we grab the popcorn and some drinks and we can discuss this back in front of the fire." Demon looked down at me and took a step back.

My arms dropped to my sides, and I suddenly felt far away from him when he was only a foot from me. "Sounds like a plan," I mumbled. I turned around, grabbed a big bowl down from the cabinet and set it on the counter.

Demon grabbed the popcorn and dumped it into the bowl as I refilled my cup with cocoa and grabbed the coffee pot. "Splash some whiskey into that, baby." I cringed at the suggestion but reached up into the cabinet and pulled the bottle down.

"The thought of alcohol makes my stomach roll," I laughed as I poured in a finger of whiskey and twisted the cap back on the bottle.

"Well, you did down those drinks last night pretty quick. I think you need to slow it down a bit the next time you drink." Demon grabbed the bowl of popcorn and headed into the living room.

I switched off the lights in the kitchen and followed Demon with both cups. "I think I should just give up drinking altogether. I think I'm one of those people who can't hold their liquor." I sat down on the pile of pillows, set our drinks down in between us and pulled a blanket across my lap. "So, back to what we were talking about before. I want to know the story of all of these tattoos. When we were together, you only had three."

"We were just babies when you and I were together."

"Yeah, we definitely were." I took a sip of my cocoa and grabbed a handful of popcorn. "Spill, Demon."

"Well, why don't we do it this way." He laid down and folded his arms under his head. "You tell me which ones you want to know about."

My eyes traveled all over his body, not knowing where to start. "Okay, how about your back. It looked like a pretty big piece." I had only seen it for a second before Demon had sat down.

Demon rolled over on his stomach and looked over at me. "That is for the club. Most everyone in the club has a tattoo like mine. Although I think mine is probably the biggest." I had to agree that it was huge. The skeleton riding a motorcycle wearing knight armor was in the center of his back with the words, Devil's Knights, stretched across his shoulder blades.

"That had to have taken forever."

"Eh, it wasn't too bad. Only a couple of sessions." Demon rolled back over and grabbed one of the pillows I had around me.

"So, how about the butterfly?" It was rather weird to see a man with a butterfly tattoo. I thought those were reserved for drunk college girls.

"It's a moth."

Oh, well, I guess that was more manly than a butterfly. "Okay, so why a moth?"

"Moths are nocturnal and are adept to see well in the dark. I got it to represent that I'm determined to find my way through life, even when passing through dark times."

"Well, damn. That's pretty impressive when you explain it." Demon chuckled and sat up. He grabbed his coffee and took a long drink.

"I told you they all have meaning, baby."

"Okay, one more." I looked all over his body, trying to find one that stood out to me. "Alright, now about the roses over your heart." Demon had a cluster of roses colored red and purple over his heart.

Demon laid back down and looked at me. "You really don't know what those mean?"

"Well, normally red roses are for love, but I don't know what purple flowers for."

"Purple flowers represent love at first sight."

"Oh," I mumbled. I wasn't quite sure what to say. He had red roses for love and purple roses for love at first sight.

"Those are your flowers. I got them a week after you left. Even though we weren't together anymore, I still loved you."

"But, love at first sight?" I whispered. I had no idea what to say. Demon had never told me that he fell in love with me at first sight.

"That first time I saw you, baby, I knew that you were mine. There wasn't a doubt in my mind that you and I were going to be together."

"But, we broke up. I left."

Demon shrugged his shoulders and rolled over on his side. He propped his head up with his hand and smirked. "That didn't change the fact that I still loved you."

"But, Demon, what if you and I never... I mean, what if you never saw me again?"

"I got it because I thought I never would see you again. No matter what happened, you were always going to be the one who had my heart, whether I ever saw you again or not." He reached, grabbing my hand and laced his fingers through mine. "I know it's hard to believe, Paige. But I loved you with all of my heart back then, and I still do."

I set my cup down, threw a pillow next to Demon and laid down. "This all could have been different if you just would have kept your pants on," I laughed.

"Yeah," Demon agreed. He turned over on his back and laid his head next to mine. "I bet Bill Clinton says the same thing all the time."

"You're comparing yourself to Bill Clinton now?"

"It was the best comparison I could come up with," Demon shrugged.

"I seriously don't know how to argue with that," I laughed.

Demon turned his head and reached up with his hand to touch my cheek. "I've missed this. Just being with you."

I leaned into his touch and closed my eyes. "Me, too," I whispered. It was so close to being the way things used to be. Demon and I together, just enjoying each other. "I want it back, Demon."

"Then just let go, Paige. I'm here now, and I'm not going anywhere." He wrapped me up in his arms and pulled me close. "I know we can't change what happened in the past, but we can make a new future and start over."

I tilted my head back and looked up at him. "Okay. I'm terrified to death, but I want this more than I'm afraid of being with you."

"I gotta admit. I thought it would take every single second of these seven days to convince you to give me a second chance."

"What can I say, you have a way with words," I laughed.

"Really, because I thought for sure it was that kiss five minutes ago."

"Ya think? I can't even remember that kiss. You might have to refresh my memory."

"Refresh your memory, huh, baby? I think I might more than refresh your memory. I think we need to make new memories." Demon rolled me on top of him, my knees straddling his hips, and our bodies pressed together.

"New memories, huh?" I purred. "As good as that sounds, how about we just keep it to kissing tonight, and we'll see where tomorrow takes us." I had said yes to giving Demon and I a second chance, but I didn't want to jump too quick. I wasn't worried about whether or not that Demon and I were compatible in bed, I knew that when we were together in bed, it was explosive. I was more concerned how we were going to be out of bed.

"Whatever you want," Demon growled. His hands roamed over my back, lifting the hem of my shirt as I leaned down and stole a kiss.

"You're rather agreeable," I said against his lips.

"As long as I have you laying on top of me, I'll agree with anything you say, baby."

"Hmm, that could be dangerous for you. I could suggest that we go sledding again tomorrow."

"I'll agree to anything but that. I know I'm going to be sore as shit tomorrow. Besides, I already have plans for us tomorrow."

"Really? Demon, big bad motorcycle man who flies by the seat of his pants, has made plans for us tomorrow?"

"Don't act too impressed. I thought of it today and tried to get it lined up, but the guy said he was booked for today. Although it does involve another sled, so I'm not too sure of it after today."

"Hmm, now you have me intrigued."

"I know you love surprises, so you'll have to wait and see until tomorrow. He's picking us up at three, and we need to have a picnic packed to take with us."

"Demon, if I didn't know any better, it sounds like you're trying to woo me."

"Woo you?" he asked.

"Yes, woo me."

He shook his head and pressed a kiss to my lips. "Call it whatever you want, baby. I'm just trying to make you mine."

"Definite woo," I laughed.

"Is that from all those books you read?"

"No, well, yes. I mean, doesn't every girl want to be wooed?"

"If wooing is what you want, wooing is what you'll get."

"Do you think we could say woo anymore?" I giggled.

"I hope not," he smirked.

"How about you woo me a little bit more and then we head to bed?" I wiggled my eyebrows at him, and he wrapped his arms around me and rolled us over.

"Oh, baby, you haven't seen nothing yet. I plan on being the king of woo when I'm done with you."

"Promises, promises," I whispered against his lips.

"A promise I plan to keep."

"We'll see."

His lips moved against mine, giving me everything we had both been missing.

Let the wooing begin. I was ready.

————————

Chapter 20

Demon

"He's here? How is he here? I didn't even hear a car pull up." Paige walked out of the bathroom and grabbed her coat that she had tossed over the back of the couch.

"Because he's not driving a car." I grabbed the picnic basket off of the counter and grabbed the chilled bottle of wine out of the fridge. "Can you grab the two blankets?"

Paige buttoned up her jacket and looked at me like I was crazy. "Demon, it's like fifty million degrees below zero. These two blankets aren't going to keep us warm."

It was cold out today, but it wasn't as bad as Paige thought. Saul had assured me that he had two small space heaters that would keep us plenty warm, but he had advised also bringing a couple of blankets along. "Just trust me. Grab the blankets, and I'll grab the basket."

"Sounds like a plan to me. I know how much food is in that basket, and you can bet these two blankets don't weigh as much."

Paige and I had gone shopping this morning then spent the early afternoon, making dinner for the basket and just hanging out with each other. We so easily slipped back into the way we used to be, it was almost as if we had never been apart.

"You're going to have to close your eyes."

"What?" she squawked. "How am I supposed to walk with my eyes closed?"

"Very carefully," I laughed. I stood in front of her and looked over my shoulder. "Grab onto my shoulder and close your eyes. I'll guide you outside."

Paige shook her head but put her hand on my shoulder. "Demon, this is the weirdest thing you have ever made me do."

"Close your eyes."

She pursed her lips at me but closed her eyes. "If I fall, I'm taking you down with me."

"I know how graceful you are, baby. I will heed that warning carefully." Paige put her hand on my shoulder, and I couldn't help but laugh at the annoyance that was written all over her face.

"Hey, who was the one who slid down the hill on their ass yesterday? It sure wasn't me," Paige sang out.

We slowly made our way to the door with Paige only tripping over her feet twice by the time I had the door open. "Step down, and then you can open your eyes."

I stepped to the side of the door and helped Paige down the step and held my breath as she opened her eyes. I hoped to hell that she liked the surprise I had.

"Pinch me."

"What?"

"Pinch me right now, seriously." Paige grabbed onto my arm and turned to look at me. "There is a massive Clydesdale with a sleigh hooked to it in the driveway. Pinch. Me. Now."

A smile spread across my lips, and I knew that Paige liked my surprise. "I'd much rather go for a ride with you, baby. I promise to pinch you later," I winked, swatting her on the ass.

"Hey," Paige squealed. "Just for that you get to carry the blankets now, I'm going to pet the horse." Paige piled the blankets on top of the picnic basket and scurried over to the horse and Saul, who was climbing down from the top of the sleigh.

Well, I guess I could mark this down in the win column. Paige was happy, and I was to thank for it.

Score one for Demon.

Now, I just needed to not fuck it up.

———

Paige

"Where are we headed?"

"Not really sure," Demon laughed. "Saul just said the ride can last for however long we would want, really. I said two hours and he said no problem."

"Here comes that brilliant planning of yours again."

Demon shrugged his shoulders and put his arm around me, pulling me close. "You have to admit, my ability to not plan, but still plan is what attracts you to me."

412

"Um, that would be a negative," I giggled. I really was a girl who loved to have a plan no matter what it was, and Demon just loved to drive me crazy by never planning.

"You ready to eat? Saul said to give a holler when we were ready to pull over for a bit."

We had been driving around for over an hour, and I had to admit I was growing hungry. "I could eat."

Demon nodded his head, pressed a kiss to the side of my head and gave a shout to Saul that we were ready to stop for a bit.

Saul pulled over to the side of a trail we were on and hopped down. "I'll go take a walk for half an hour. Kong needs a drink, and there's a stream just down the way." Saul unhooked the horse, and I felt bad that he was going to leave while Demon and I ate.

"Do you want a coffee and a sandwich to take with you?" We had only brought two cups for the coffee, but I could drink out of Demon's.

"You don't have to do that," Saul called.

"I insist." I fished out one of the sandwiches while Demon poured a cup of coffee. "And, you really don't have to wander off, we're just going to eat." I didn't want this guy to think he needed to disappear so Demon and I could be alone.

"Kong needs a drink, and I'll take him for a walk." He winked at me, then nodded his head at Demon and disappeared down a trail I hadn't seen with his sandwich and coffee.

"He totally thinks we're going to make out or something."

Demon threw his head back laughing and kicked back in the seat, a cup of coffee dangling from his fingertips. "I don't think this is his first romantic sleigh ride he's ever done, Paige. Ninety-nine percent of guys who take their women on a sleigh ride are looking to get laid."

"Is that a proven statistic?"

Demon shrugged his shoulders and took a sip of his coffee. "Ask me tomorrow, and I'll let you know."

I rolled my eyes and shifted through the cooler, looking for the bowl of fruit we had packed. "You do know you need to share your cup with me now, right?"

"I'll share anything with you."

"Hmm," I hummed. "What did you want to eat?"

"A sandwich and some fruit will be good."

I found the bowl of fruit and two more sandwiches and closed the lid on the basket. I sat back, throwing the blanket back over our legs and handed Demon his sandwich. "So, why don't you tell me how you got the name Demon." When Demon and I had been dating, he had been itching to get his official road name but didn't know when it would happen.

"It's really a stupid story," Demon mumbled, as he unwrapped his sandwich.

"Oh man, now I really want to know," I laughed.

Demon shook his head and took a bite of his sandwich. "I'd much rather you call me my other name. You never even knew me as Demon, I don't understand why you call me it now."

"I don't know. I guess when I heard that you were now called Demon, it made it seem like even more that the man I knew was gone."

"That man isn't gone, Paige."

"So I'm coming to see," I mumbled. I unwrapped my sandwich and tossed the wrapper into the basket. "Now, tell me where Demon came from."

"Jesus, you're not going to let this go, are you?" I shook my head no and batted my eyelashes at him. "I'll tell you, but then you gotta tell me something."

"I'm an open book."

"Yeah, we'll see about that." Demon finished his sandwich in two bites and tossed his wrapper into the basket. "King and I were shooting the shit one night. Neither one of us had gotten our road names yet, and we were both eager to get them." This was something I had known. "So, we got drunk. I'm talking, we were falling off of our bar stools, drunk. Prez came over, wanting to know what King and I were talking about. King and I were both drunk enough to tell him that we were trying to think of tough road names."

"Oh, my. I think I know where this is going." I had seen Demon drunk before, he was quite the talker.

"Prez humored us as we rattled off all of the names we were coming up with and he continued to feed us shots of whiskey. Everything was going fine until I got up on the bar and announced to the whole club that I wanted to be called Demon."

"Wait, you got the name Demon because you asked to be called that? How in the hell does that work? I thought you had to earn that? I call bullshit." I eyed Demon up, knowing he wasn't telling the truth.

"I swear. That's how it went down."

"Wait, is that how King got his name too? He asked to be called that? Because if it is, please don't tell me, because you'll just ruin the MC fantasy I have."

"No, babe. That's not how King got his name."

"Dammit, Demon. I wanted some kick ass story why you were called Demon." I waved my hand in my face and frowned. "Color me disappointed."

"Sorry, baby. I can tell you with the condition of the club calling me Demon, I had to live up to the name."

"Oh, now that is more interesting. So, what did you do to live up to the name?"

"Nope, not happening. I answered your question. Now, I get to ask you one." Demon grabbed my hand and pulled me close. "Put your leg over me, baby."

"That's not a question, Demon," I mumbled. Demon ran his hand down my body and cupped my knee, and pulled my leg over him so I was straddling his lap.

"You know you talk too much sometimes?" He growled into my ear.

A tremor rocked my body as his lips grazed the lobe of my ear, and I couldn't fight the rush of desire I felt. "I do not," I protested, trying to act like the mere touch of his lips wasn't my undoing.

"Just sometimes. Only when all I want to do is kiss you until we lose ourselves in each other."

"Sometimes I just have something I need to say."

"Baby." One word. One word this man says and he has my full attention. "You're doing it right now."

"Oh, sorry," I mumbled.

"Can I ask my question now?" He asked. I nodded my head, knowing that if I opened my mouth, I was going to start babbling. Demon reached up, his hand cupping my cheek. "Can I kiss you?"

Wait, that was his question? I thought for sure it was going to be some soul searching question, trying to find out what I was thinking, and all he asked was if he could kiss me? "Um…" and I was speechless.

"Baby, I'm taking that as yes since your hot body is still in my lap. Wrap your arms around my neck." Demon was full of demands, and I was more than willing to follow whatever he wanted. My arms mindlessly wound around his neck, and I leaned in, eager to feel his lips on mine again. "So fucking perfect," he mumbled right before his lips brushed mine. My fingers delved into his hair, deepening the kiss, needing more. Demon's tongue invaded my mouth, melding our bodies together while his hands roamed over my body.

"Demon," I moaned as his lips traveled down my neck, sucking and nibbling. "Please, I need more."

"Tell me," he demanded. "Tell me what you want." His hands went to the waist of my jeans, trying to tug them down. His fingers slipped between the fabric and my skin, kneading my butt.

"I… I need…" I needed to get a grip, but with Demon's hands on me, I lost every reasonable thought.

"You need this?" he asked as his lips stayed on my neck, but his hands moved around to the front of my body, and I felt the button of my jeans pop open. His hands deftly parted my jeans and tugged them down my hips a bit.

"Please, yes," I moaned, grinding my hips into him. The cold air hit my bare skin, but the heat from Demon's touch warmed me instantly. "Are we really going to have sex in the sleigh?" I had to say, I wasn't completely opposed to it.

"No, baby. I am going to make you cum all over my hand, though," he growled. "Reach over and grab the blanket. I don't want you getting cold." I blindly reached over, not wanting to move away from Demon's lips and pulled the blanket over my shoulders. "Good girl," he murmured, "Now get ready to feel, and try not to moan so loud that Saul hears you."

Demon's lips attacked my mouth as his hand slipped into the front of my panties and his fingers parted the lips of my pussy. "Demon, please," I begged. He was barely touching me, and I was ready to bust apart at the seams.

"I'll give it to you. You were always my greedy girl." I preened at his words, relishing in the fact that Demon remembers what I liked. His finger swirled around my clit, teasing me and making me squirm against his hand. "You know I'm not going to give it to you, baby, until I'm ready to."

My dirty talking biker was back and with each word he spoke, I crept closer to the edge of ecstasy. "Demon," I moaned.

"First, you need to give me something."

"Anything," I gasped as his finger grazed my clit, giving me a taste of what I wanted, but not enough.

"Say my name," he growled into my ear.

"Demon."

"No. I said say my name."

I knew what he wanted, but I wasn't sure if I wanted to give that to him yet. "Please, I need…"

"You need to say my name, and then I'll give you everything you need right now, and then I'm going to take you back to the cabin and fuck you so hard you won't be able to walk for days. Say. My. Name." Demon nipped my neck and didn't move.

I knew that we were at a big step into getting back to the Demon and Paige we were. "I… I just don't…"

"Stop thinking and just do what you want to, Paige. Don't overthink or overanalyze. Do what feels right."

I took a deep breath and closed my eyes. "I need you, Dustin." Demon growled low at my words. He buried his head into my hair, as his finger attacked my pussy, giving me what I had been wanting.

"Say it again," he demanded.

"Dustin, Dustin…" I trailed off as his lips worked their way up to my mouth. He thrust his tongue into my mouth, mimicking the movements of his finger. He flicked my clit over and over, my release building with each touch.

"God dammit, I missed this, baby. Your tight pussy needing only me."

I opened my eyes as he moved backward and I wrapped my arms around his neck. "Dustin, please." He was still teasing me. He still knew exactly how to work my body like no one else. "You're driving me crazy."

"No. I'm giving us everything that we've been missing." He slammed his lips down on mine, and I buried my fingers into his hair. I could have sworn that Demon had mumbled something against my lips, but I was so close to tipping over the edge of my desire that I barely heard him.

"Cum for me. Cum." I leaned back from Demon, arching my back and slammed my eyes shut as my orgasm rocked my body. "Yes, yes. So fucking beautiful," Demon whispered. His hand still worked me over, milking every last drop of my desire out of my body. "Holy fuck," Demon murmured.

I cracked one eye open and looked down at him. "I think I should be the one saying that."

"Baby, you have no idea what that was like watching you."

"I'm sure it looked like I was trying to exorcise a demon out of me."

Demon reached up, snaking his hand around my neck and pulled me to him. "No, that was the most beautiful thing I have ever seen, and it took all my willpower not to rip off both of our pants and drive into you, taking what's mine."

My body shivered at his words, wanting more of what he just gave me. "How much time do we have until Saul comes back?" I purred.

"Not enough to let me take you the way I need." Demon worked the zipper up on my pants and buttoned them up. "Tonight. You're all mine." Demon pressed a quick kiss to my lips and sat back. "Now, you need to be a good girl and sit in your seat before you completely destroy my willpower, and I take you right now, Saul be damned."

I leaned forward, wrapping my arms around his neck and pressed my lips to his ear. "There's my dirty talking biker I've missed all these years."

Demon growled low and grabbed my ass. "There's more where that came from, baby. Just wait."

The butterflies in my stomach were in full effect at his words, and I was counting the seconds till we were back at the cabin.

I was ready to be Demon's again.

Chapter 21

Demon

I was going to kill Saul. All it would take is grabbing the shovel that was next to the front door and smash him over the head. Paige was inside the cabin, and I was standing outside in the falling snow with Saul as I listened to him drone on about all he had done on the cabin. I wanted to tell him I knew what he had done since I paid all of the bills, but I really did owe him for taking care of the place for me.

"The tub leak at all?"

"Um, no, not that I noticed. Paige and I have only showered, but it seemed good." I knew Paige was using the damn shower right now, and it was killing me knowing she was standing under the shower head with the water streaming down her lush body, and I wasn't there to watch.

"Well, you let me know if it leaks. I had a hell of a time getting that new tub in there, but I have to say when it was all said and done, it turned out damn good."

Saul was right. The tub that had been in the bathroom before was falling apart seven years ago, and I could only imagine what it had looked like before Saul had ripped it out. Now there was an oversized claw-foot tub that sat in the middle of the room that was the centerpiece. "The whole cabin looks good, Saul. I can't thank you enough for all you did."

"Not a problem. It gave this old man something to do. I'll let you get to your lady." Saul gave me a wink and lumbered over to the sled.

"We'll be here until Sunday," I called.

"I'll make sure to call before I come over." Saul looked over his shoulder at me, a knowing look on his face, and I couldn't help but laugh. I guess Paige and I weren't as subtle as we thought on the ride back to the cabin. At one point Paige had climbed back into my lap, her hands roaming all over my body when Saul had hit a bump and almost bounced her right out of the sled.

Things had changed too quickly with Paige, that I was worried it wasn't going to last. I felt like being up here at the cabin, we weren't really living and that when we went back to Rockton, things were going to change, and not for the good.

My phone buzzed in my pocket, and I pulled it out to see that King had texted.

Shit is going down. Keep close to your phone.

Son of a bitch. *You need me to come back?*

No. Just stay by your phone. Things might change quickly.

I shoved my phone back into my pocket and crossed my arms over my chest. I should have fucking known. Things had been too quiet with Big A, and I had a feeling things were about to blow up at the shittiest time possible. "You coming in, or just plan on standing outside all night?"

I turned around and saw Paige leaning against the open door of the cabin with her arms crossed over her chest. She had changed out of the warm clothes she had worn on the sleigh ride and had changed into something much more comfortable. "You think it's little cold out here?" She was wearing yellow short shorts and tight, white tank top that was molded to her lush breasts, and I was ninety percent sure she wasn't wearing a bra.

"Hmm, you're probably right." She shrugged her shoulders and stepped back into the house. "Why don't you come and keep me warm?" she purred and shut the door.

I pulled my phone out of my pocket, making sure King hadn't texted me again and turned the volume up all the way. King may not need me now, but if he did, I'd be ready. Until then, I had Paige to keep warm.

I headed into the cabin, shutting the door behind me and stomped my feet on the rug. Paige was in the kitchen, leaning against the counter with her arms at her side. "Was Saul telling you his life story?" Paige laughed.

"It sure as shit felt like it, baby. I never thought he would leave." I shrugged my coat off, threw it on the coat rack and toed my boots off. "You heard from your sister at all?" I highly doubted that Gwen would tell Paige anything that was going on, but I needed to know for sure.

"Only three times a day. I haven't answered or listened to any of the messages she's left, though."

"You should probably touch base with her. At least at some point."

"I'll call her tomorrow. Or, I'm sure she'll be calling within the hour."

"You shower without me?" Her dark brown hair was piled on top of her head, and she had a small smirk playing on her lips.

"I might have, although I'm always open to getting dirty again."

"Game on, baby." I pulled my shirt over my head and tossed it on the couch. "Getting you dirty was always my favorite thing to do. You were my prim and proper I got to get dirty every night."

"I wasn't prim and proper, I just… was conservative."

I popped open the button on my jeans and watched Paige rub her legs together and run her eyes over my body. "You were exactly what I wanted. I just could never figure out what you saw in me, though."

"Um…" She took two steps towards me and hooked her thumbs into the waistband of her shorts. "You were my dirty talking biker who treated me like a queen. Everything I didn't know I wanted but needed."

"You remember that first night we were together, baby?" I asked as I watched her walk towards me.

"Hmm, that is definitely one night I could never forget," she purred.

"I was absolutely terrified you were going to turn tail and run."

Paige shrugged her shoulders and slowly pulled her shorts down. "The way you acted was the reason I didn't run that night. You were so gentle and caring with me that I would have had to have been insane to run."

My eyes watched as she bent over, giving me a view straight down her tank top, confirming she wasn't wearing a bra. "That's called being scared shitless. I knew you were something special." She slowly stood up, and I couldn't help but stare at the lips of her pussy that were glistening with her desire.

"You could have fooled me." She ran her hands up her body, pulling her shirt up, exposing the bottom swell of her breasts. "I knew after that night; I wouldn't want anyone but you. It's been a long seven years."

My world rocked at her words and my mouth dropped. "What the hell do you mean that it's been a long seven years?" She couldn't mean what I thought she meant.

"It means I haven't been with anyone since you." She pulled her shirt over her head and tossed it on the floor. "You ruined me, Dustin. All these years, after everything that happened to us, and you still had me."

"Baby, I… I don't know…" Son of a bitch. All these years, and I had still been the only one to touch Paige. Guilt washed over me, knowing that the same couldn't be said about me. I was no saint the years Paige and I had been apart. I had still loved her, but I knew that I had fucked things up too much to ever get her back.

She closed the gap between us and pressed her finger to my lips. "Stop. I don't expect the same from you, Demon. My prolonged abstinence wasn't intentional, I just never found the right person."

I still felt like an ass. "Paige, I don't deserve you."

She wrapped her arms around my neck and pressed her warm tits into my chest. "You do. Just like I deserve you."

"But I didn't… well, I wasn't…" Fucking hell. Telling Paige that I had been with numerous women since her was not how I had seen this night going.

"Stop, please. Whatever it is you're thinking or feel you have to tell me, you don't. Everything is in the past, Dustin."

I wrapped my arms around her, spun her around and pushed her against the wall. "You. You're the only one who has meant anything. It was always you, Paige. I just thought I had hurt you too much to ever get you back." I slammed my lips down on her mouth, and she delved her fingers into my hair.

She moaned and whimpered as our tongues danced, and I tried to make up for every kiss I had missed these past years. My hands roamed over her naked body, feeling like I was finally home. "Dustin, you have too many clothes on," she moaned. Her hands urgently tugged and pulled on my pants, working them down my legs.

I reached in the back pocket of my jeans and pulled out a condom before she completely ripped them off. "I'm on birth control," she mumbled against my lips as she grabbed the condom out of my hand and tossed it over my shoulder.

"What the hell are you on birth control for?"

"Girl stuff," she mumbled, her cheeks blushing pink.

"Well, thank God for girl stuff," I laughed. "Wrap your legs around me, and hold on." I grabbed her ass and hoisted her up in my arms as she wrapped her body around me. "You were made for me."

"Hmm," she hummed into my ear. "I'm not going to argue with that." I turned around and headed down the hallway to the bathroom, kicking the door open and fell onto the bed with Paige on top of me. "I see you still don't wear underwear," Paige purred as she rubbed her soft body against me.

"When you're around, no, I don't."

"I think we should just forget clothes altogether."

"For the next twenty-four hours, that's my plan."

Paige leaned back on her heels, her body on display above me and all I could do was stare. She cupped her breasts in her hands, squeezing her tight, budded nipples with her fingertips. "You have no idea how many times I've touched myself and wished it was you."

Jesus Christ. Jesus fucking Christ. Her words were like music to my ears, knowing that she had wanted me all these years. "Show me. Show me what you've been wanting."

She bit her bottom lip and hesitantly moved her hands down her body. "I'd much rather you touch me."

"We have plenty of time for that, baby. I want to see how my girl makes herself feel good." I grabbed a pillow and shoved it under my head. This was one show I did not want to miss one minute of.

Her fingers parted the wet lips of her pussy and the tight bud of her clit called out to be touched and teased. "Dustin, please." She was looking down at me, hesitant of what to do next.

"Trust me. No matter what you do next, trust me."

She licked her lips, doubt still in her eyes, but something changed. I could feel her confidence grow, knowing that I loved her no matter what she did. She raised up on her knees her eyes never leaving mine and her finger slid up and down on her clit, a surprised moan escaping from her lips.

My dick grew harder and harder with each moan and quick intake of air that escaped her mouth. Her finger moved quickly, flicking her clit and I could see her orgasm approaching quickly. "Slow, baby."

She shook her head and closed her eyes as she leaned forward pressing a hand to my chest to hold her up. Her hand was buried in her sweet pussy, and her body trembled above me. My hands gripped the sheets, needing to touch her, but the need to watch her tip over the edge by herself was greater.

"Dustin," she gasped, her nails digging into my chest.

"Yes, reach it, baby."

Her eyes snapped open, and strangled cry ripped from her lips as she fell over the edge and let her orgasm wash over her. She collapsed on top of me, her breathing shallow and her eyes closed. "That was quick," she panted.

"It was fucking perfect. Each time I watch you cum is better than the last."

She wrapped her arms around me and rested her head on my chest. "Twenty-four hours of this, and I'm going to need a nap for twenty-four hours."

"Why do you think we're at the cabin far away from everyone? My ultimate goal is to keep you naked and wet the next four days." My hands traveled down her body, cupping her ass and giving it a squeeze. "I think we're making a pretty good start of it."

She tipped her head back, a lazy smile on her lips. "We start the napping now?"

"Not even close, baby." I rolled her over, tucking her under my body, and caged her in with my arms. My dick throbbed in between us, and all I wanted to do was bury myself in her and never come up for air.

She ran her fingers up and down my back and leaned up to brush her lips against mine. "I suppose I'm okay with waiting for my nap, as long as you can keep me awake." She batted her eyes at me and a sly smile spread across her lips.

"I'll try my hardest."

Her hand trailed around my body, and she wrapped her fingers around my hard cock. "I think you're doing good in the hard department." She stroked my dick up and down, and I groaned low as I watched her lick her lips, wishing she was wrapping those lips around my cock. "I love touching you."

"And I fucking love when you touch me." Paige's hands on me was heaven on earth. "Are you ready for me?" If Paige stroked me for one minute longer, I was going to cum all over her hand.

"Always," she whispered. She spread her legs, cocking them open and I slipped between them. Paige and I fit perfectly together, and I slowly sunk into her, her tight, warmness wrapping around me.

"This, this is what I've been missing," I whispered against her lips. I slowly pulled out of her warmth, relishing in the fact that her pussy was like a tight vise. "Home, you're fucking home to me, Paige."

She leaned up, slamming her lips on mine and stole my words out of my mouth, and all I could do was feel. I pounded into her, our lips and bodies connected as nails dug into my back. "Dustin, please," she pleaded.

"You're mine, Paige. All. Mine," I growled against her lips.

"Yes," she moaned. Her body melted into me with each thrust of my hips, and her breathing became shallow and short.

I was so close to cumming inside her sweet body, but I knew that Paige wasn't there yet. I knew she would need more time since she had already come twice. My hand reached down, searching out her clit as my hips rocked into her.

"I need you to cum for me, baby. I want to feel your body shatter underneath me." She moaned low, and the walls of her pussy contracted around me and with every thrust, I knew she was getting closer.

"Dustin, I need you. I just need…" Words that I had waited seven long years for washed over me and I knew that Paige was mine. Nothing was going to tear us apart again.

"I'm here. I'm always going to be here."

She grabbed onto me desperately, almost trying to climb into my skin. "I'm so close," she panted, her eyes boring into me, showing me everything she was giving me.

My hips pounded into her, her tight pussy milking me as her orgasm washed over her body, and a tremor rocked my body as with one final thrust I filled her sweet pussy with my hot cum. "Mine. All fucking mine," I growled. It had taken me seven long years to get back to this, and you could bet your fucking as I was never going to let it go again.

"I love you," she whispered into my ear. Her arms were wrapped around my neck, and her face was buried in my neck.

I didn't know what to say. After all of these years, I had finally heard those sweet words come out of her mouth again, and I was fucking speechless. "Baby," I choked out. "You don't have to say that."

"Hmm, I know I don't. But it wasn't like I ever stopped loving you."

I grabbed her chin and tilted her head back. "You're fucking destroying me, Paige. I never thought I would ever see you again, and now you're in my bed, and my life and I don't know what the fuck to do."

She rolled over on her stomach, looked up at me and wiggled her eyebrows. "I think I might have an idea of what you can do."

I threw my head back laughing and said the only thing I could. "I fucking love you, Paige." And then I fucked the hell out of her. Again.

————

Chapter 22

Paige

"I need food." I was sitting in between Demon's legs in the giant bathtub with my head tilted back and staring up at the ceiling. "That cheese sandwich we had two hours ago isn't cutting it anymore. I wish the deli by the bookstore was here."

"Halverson's?" Demon asked.

"You know Halverson's?" I thought I was part of a secret club that knew of the holy grail deli.

"Baby, everyone knows Halvies."

I turned around, water splashing over the edge of the tub and looked at Demon, shocked. "Halvies? They go by Halvies?" I thought I knew everything there was to know about my favorite deli.

"That's what the locals call it. Sam is from New York. He moved here five years ago and opened the deli when he couldn't find a good sandwich."

"Well, I feel like I'm not part of the cool kids since I didn't know that they are called Halvies."

"Just by the locals."

"How long do you think I need to live in Rockton before I'm a local and can call them Halvies?"

"I don't know, but I can't figure out why this is a big deal to you? I'm sure they don't care what the hell you call them as long as you pay 'em."

I crossed my arms over my chest and huffed. "I suppose you're right, although it felt like I had found a diamond in the rough that only I knew about."

"Paige, you're a nut sometimes, you know that?"

I shrugged my shoulders and turned back around, snuggling back into his lap and the warm water. "Eh, it's part of my charm. Or, my geekiness. I try not to think about it."

"So, back to me feeding you. What are you hungry for, baby?" Demon asked.

"I'm not picky. Is there anything open now, or are we going to have to make something?"

"It's only seven thirty. I know we're kind of in the middle of nowhere, but I'm pretty sure the pizza place is open until ten."

"Pizza sounds good. Make sure you get cheese bread and I want all the veggies on my pizza." I laid my head back on Demon's chest and closed my eyes.

"You still into that veggie pizza shit I see."

I shrugged my shoulders. We were going to have to order two pizzas because I knew that Demon was going to want every meat they had, and I was into veggies on my pizza. "Order two, and then we can have pizza for breakfast."

"How about if we get veggie pizza with a shit ton of meat."

"Then it's really not a veggie pizza, Demon," I laughed.

"Yeah, but it'll be fucking delicious, though."

"You do know this is the same fight we always used to have?"

"I know, and that's why I love it." Demon leaned down and pressed a kiss to the side of my head. "I'll order the pizzas while you dry off. Sound like a deal?"

"Yeah," I mumbled and stood up, water streaming down my body.

Demon grabbed my hand, and I bent over to kiss him on the lips. "You okay?" he asked.

"Yeah. I'm good. I'll be even better when you feed me," I whispered against his lips. I grabbed the towel off the rack and wrapped it around my body.

"Clothes are optional by the way, baby. I think you're already wearing too much with this towel on." Demon tugged on the end of the towel, but I managed to step out of the tub before he yanked it off.

"I think eating pizza naked might be dangerous," I giggled as I slipped out of the bathroom and into the bedroom. My towel fell to the floor, and I grabbed a pair of panties from my suitcase.

"I hear clothes," Demon called from the bathroom.

"How can you hear clothes?" I laughed and grabbed Demon's shirt he had been wearing earlier and pulled it over my head. "Did you hear that?"

"Yeah, it sounded like your sexy body has clothes on it." Demon walked out of the bathroom buck naked and wrapped me up in his arms. "I was right." He grabbed the hem of my shirt, pulled it up and grabbed my ass. "We still have twenty hours of no clothes."

"Half an hour break? Plus," I whispered, "you still have easy access." My hands trailed down his back, and I couldn't help but laugh. "Although I have open access to you like this."

Demon pressed a kiss to the side of my neck and pulled away. "Nope, you get clothes, so do I. At least boxers." Demon bent over and looked under the bed. "As soon as I figure out where they are."

"I think they're by the front door. You want me to run and get them?"

"Yeah, I don't think you want me wearing yours." Demon grabbed a pair of my panties off the floor and held them up. "Plus, I don't really think yellow is my color."

"I'd have to agree with you on that one." I jogged down the hallway and grabbed his boxers and tossed them down the hallway. "Put those on and order my pizza," I called.

I headed into the kitchen as I heard Demon mumbling about hangry women and veggies.

"Do you want coffee or beer?"

"Baby, we're eating pizza. Beer all the way." Demon grabbed his phone out of his pocket and headed back into the bedroom. "You wouldn't go wrong with whiskey either," he said over his shoulder.

"Whiskey with a beer chaser it is," I mumbled as I opened the liquor cabinet and grabbed the bottle of whiskey. I grabbed two beers from the fridge, popping the top on mine and took a small sip.

I looked around, seeing our discarded clothes on the floor and couldn't help but smile. I had finally stopped thinking and just felt. I knew I had loved Demon all these years, but I was never able to move past what had happened. Now, being back with Demon, and knowing that I loved him more than anything that had happened in the past, this was where I was always meant to be.

"Pizza ordered." Demon walked into the kitchen and grabbed the beer I had set out for him. "Your phone was buzzing when I went by."

It was probably Gwen calling again. I wasn't sure what I was going to say to her when I talked to her finally. I know she was chomping at the bit wanting to know what was going on with Demon and me, but I wasn't sure I was ready to share. Things were complicated with Demon and me, and we had just figured everything out. I didn't really want to revisit the past anymore. "I'll check it before I head to bed."

Demon shook his head, knowing that I really didn't want to see who had called me and thankfully didn't say anything about it.

"So, what happens when we get home?" I asked.

"What do you mean, baby?"

"I mean, what if we get back, and we mess this up? Right now we're good, but we're alone. I'm just scared." More like terrified, but I wasn't about to say that. "We messed this up royally last time."

Demon set his beer down and crossed his arms over his chest. "Baby, not to be a dick, but we were fucking dumb and stupid back then. Neither of us knew how to talk to each other. We were both hurting, and we should have leaned on each other instead of self-imploding like we did."

"You did the ultimate implode," I laughed, poking him in the chest.

"I sure did, and I've paid for it the past seven years."

I leaned into him, rested my head on his shoulder and sighed. "We both paid for it because we both messed up." He wrapped his arm around me and pulled me close.

"But we're moving on, baby. I've loved you for so long, and there's no way in hell that I'm going to fuck this up again."

"I love—"

Demon's phone cut me off as it started ringing. Five seconds later I heard my phone ringing from by the fireplace. Demon looked at the screen on his phone. "It's King. Go check who's calling you."

I pulled out of his arms as Demon put the phone to his ear and rumbled a hello to King. I grabbed my phone and saw that it was Meg calling me.

"Incoming!" she yelled when I answered.

"Meg? What?"

"I felt like I was part of an army brigade for a second," she giggled.

"Okay…"

"Did you talk to Gwen?" she asked.

"No. Not since Sunday."

"Well, you probably should have answered the phone the last time she called. Slider and Fayth are headed your way with Remy, and I close behind."

"Wait, what? Why?" Why in the hell would Meg and her son be coming up here with Slider and Fayth? And who was Fayth?

"Lo has banished me. Well, he's banished basically all women and children. Silly man. It's really cute how he goes all hardass biker giving orders and thinking he can tell me what to do." Meg laughed, and I was even more lost than before.

"Meg, slow down. I have no idea what you are talking about. Why are you banished?"

"Big A. Crazy fucker is trying to start shit. Well, I guess he's technically trying to finish it since Lo, and the boys started it."

Her explanation was making everything clear as mud. "You think you could start at the beginning?"

"No time for that. GPS says I'll be to the cabin in five minutes. I'll tell you everything when we get there. Slider is probably pulling up right now." Meg disconnected the call, and she was gone as fast as she was there.

"Baby, go put some pants on. We've got company coming."

I held my phone up dumbly and pointed at it. "That was about the only thing I understood from the strange phone call from Meg. Except, I still don't understand why."

"Pants, and then I'll try to explain as much as I can to you."

As much as he could? He better explain everything to me. I heard a car door slam and knew I had only seconds before Slider and whoever Fayth was, would see me in Demon's shirt and basically nothing else.

I scurried down the hall and shut the door just as I heard the front door open. I dived into my suitcase trying to find a bra and something that would cover my ass. There went any plans that Demon and I had for tonight, although the night was almost over. I glanced at the bedside clock and saw that it was edging in on eight thirty.

I managed to find a pair of pajama bottoms and an oversized sweatshirt that would hopefully hide the fact that I wasn't wearing a bra. I swept my hair up into a messy bun and headed back into the kitchen to find out what in the hell was going on.

"Where in the hell are you all going to sleep? It's a one fucking bedroom cabin," Demon growled at Slider.

"Aren't there some fucking cabins for rent around here? It's the middle of the god damn week. I'm sure there has to be," Slider replied.

"I'll google it. Maybe we can find a place with a hot tub," Meg mumbled as she pulled her phone out of her pocket and plopped down on the couch. Remy, her rather handsome son, sat down next to her and pulled his phone out too.

"I saw a couple of cabin rentals we passed." My eyes landed on a woman who was standing by the front door. She had a white, puffy vest on over a long sleeve purple henley and the most perfect fitting pair of jeans ever. She looked like she had just walked off the ski slopes. Her pitch black hair was pulled back in a low ponytail, and I couldn't help but notice how stunning she was.

"That would have been something to say as we passed them, Fayth," Slider grumbled.

"How was I supposed to know what we were doing? You herded me out of the house so fast I barely had time to grab clothes and my toothbrush," she snapped back.

It was a little comforting to know that I wasn't the only one in the room that didn't know what in the hell was going on. Five minutes ago Demon and I were the only ones here, and suddenly we had turned into a group of six in a one-bedroom cabin.

Slider growled low and headed back out the front door.

"He sure is feisty," Meg laughed. "Lo was telling me you've been giving him a run for his money, Fayth, but it's nice to see it in person."

"I'm not trying to give him a run for his money, but he is the hardest headed man I have ever met. Just one wrong word can set him off." Fayth pulled her vest tight around her and gazed out the window next to the front door. "I never know what he's thinking," she mumbled as she watched Slider pace back and forth.

I looked at Demon who had his phone in his hand and was busily typing. "Welcome to the mystery that is Slider, darling. You never know what kind of mood the fucker is going to be in."

"Oh! I found a three-bedroom cottage on the lake that has availability." Meg held her phone over her head, and Demon walked over and looked at the cabin she had found.

"Where's it located? King said he wanted us to stay close."

Meg pulled her phone back down and scrolled down. "GPS says it's one mile from here."

"Really? I wonder where."

"It's probably one of those driveways that snake back into the woods, and you can't see the house from the road," I mumbled. I had always wanted to just drive down one of those driveways to see if there was a shack or a mansion at the end.

"You want me to call and see if it's actually available?" Meg asked.

"Yeah. There's no way you guys are going to be able to stay here."

"If you wouldn't have gotten rid of the sofa sleeper they might have been able to," I teased.

Demon just shook his head and pulled me into his arms. "If I hadn't gotten rid of that old couch, I never would have gotten you into my bed Sunday," he rumbled into my ear. He pressed a kiss to the side of my neck and a shiver coursed through my body. Damn, this man was sexy as hell. "I should send Saul a bottle of scotch for getting rid of the damn thing."

"Can you guys turn to look at me?" I peeked over Demon's shoulder and saw Meg holding her phone up as she took a picture of us. "Gwen is going to shit a brick when she sees this. She's been freaking out since Demon pulled a caveman and kidnapped you."

"I did not fucking kidnap her. I asked."

"Mmhmm. That's not what I heard, but whatever." Meg flipped back around on the couch, and I assumed sent the picture to Gwen.

"How about you find a place to sleep for the night instead of taking pictures," Demon growled.

"So grumpy," Meg teased. "Maybe you should go cool down with Slider outside."

"Sounds like a good idea. I need to talk to him anyway." Demon pressed a kiss to the side of my head and walked into the bedroom.

"Score! They have a hot tub, too. Good thing I packed my swimming suit." Meg put the phone to her ear and gave Fayth a thumbs up.

"Well, you can count me out of hot tubbing. I'd be surprised if I remembered to grab underwear and pants. Slider rushed me out the door so fast you would have thought the house was on fire." Fayth sat down next to Meg and kicked her feet up on the coffee table. "Thankfully Manny is with his uncle right now. Those two were butting heads so badly, I was ready to bang my head on the wall."

"Um," I mumbled as I walked around the couch and held my hand out to Fayth. "I'm Paige. I figure you must be Fayth."

"Yup, that would be me." She grabbed my hand and gave it a quick, but firm shake. "I'm Leo's sister."

"That doesn't help her. She has no idea who Leo is," Meg laughed.

"Oh, well, I thought everyone around here knew who Leo was," Fayth laughed. "It's kind of nice to have someone who hasn't heard of my family or me before they meet me."

"Now that right there just made you even more intriguing to me than you were before." I sat down in front of the fireplace and pulled my legs to my chest and crossed my legs at the ankles.

Meg got up and headed down the small hallway as she talked to the person about the cabin for rent.

"So, you really don't know what's going on?" I asked her.

"If mom asks, tell her I went outside," Remy mumbled as he stood up and walked out the front door. I gave him a finger salute and turned back to Fayth.

"I am so clueless. I think the problems you guys are having are entirely different than the ones I was having before we moved here."

"Oh, really? I'm pretty sure we are equally clueless then," I laughed. "Demon said he would tell me what was going on, but here I am, still clueless."

"Well, hopefully, we find out what's going on before it's too late."

"All booked. Thankfully they had a last minute cancellation so they were able to fit us in. Three bedrooms with a futon in the living room. Plenty of room for all of us." Meg shoved her phone back in her pocket and walked into the kitchen. "Gwen texted me back, by the way. I'm supposed to get all the details of what is going on with you and Demon."

I rolled my eyes at Fayth and leaned back. "We're together." That was the short and simple explanation.

"Well, a blind person could see you two are together. I think she, and by she I mean all the girls and me, want to know all the dirty details." Meg opened the fridge and wrinkled her nose. "How do you have barely any food in the fridge? You're on vacation. This thing should be filled with every junk food known to man."

"Um, we have been distracted."

"Ah," Meg said, closing the door. "There are those juicy details I've been wanting. Too distracted to even worry about eating." Meg crossed her arms over her chest and leaned against the counter.

"That is the only detail you are going to get out of me."

"That's fine. I've got a good imagination and an extensive backlog of steamy books I've read that can fill in the blanks," Meg smirked.

"Well, I don't have that good of imagination and my love life has more than been lacking these past years. I'm gonna need details," Fayth laughed. "All you girls involved with the Devil's Knights seem to not be wanting at all in the passion department."

"I can confirm that," Meg said, raising her hand. "Lo sure knows how to show this girl heaven. Total *Lo Daze*," she said dreamily.

"I don't know about the whole *Lo Daze* thing," I laughed, "but I can say that Demon has always known what he's doing."

"See, this is the story we all want to know. How did you and Demon become something so long ago and no one knew about it?" Meg asked.

I shrugged my shoulders and wrinkled my nose. "I don't know. We had met at a party, and we just clicked. He was just starting with the club. I think he was what you call a prospect."

"How long did you two date for?"

"Um, a year or so." I could have told her exactly how long, but I didn't want her to try to dig any deeper.

"Hmm, fascinating." Meg tapped her finger on her chin and studied me carefully. "There's more to that story, but I can tell you aren't going to let that cat out of the bag." Meg pushed off the counter and headed to the front door. "I'm gonna call Lo and let him know where we are staying."

She slipped out the door, leaving me alone with Fayth again. "Have you spent much time with Meg and all the girls?" Fayth asked as she crossed her legs.

"Um, well, Gwen is my sister, so, yeah, I have spent quite a bit time with them."

Fayth nodded her head and tucked her pitch black hair behind her ear. "I've just never really met such a tight knit group of women before. Typically the women I've met treat each other like competition, and it's everyone for themselves."

"That doesn't seem like much fun."

"Well, I'm sure that partly has to do with who my family it. Being Fayth Banachi hasn't been easy the past twenty-nine years."

"I'm sorry." I still had no idea who she was. I had never heard of anyone with the last name Banachi.

"You still are clueless as to who I am, aren't you?" she laughed.

I threw my head back laughing, "Ding, ding, ding. You are correct."

"You have no idea how refreshing that is. My brother is Leo Banachi who has recently taken over the family business in Chicago. I'm sure the reason you've never heard of my family is because you've probably never had the need to contract a man of his business dealings. Leo and the family are all good men, but they are on the other side of the law."

A light bulb went off in my head, and I realized that Fayth was saying her family was mafia related or something like that. She was right saying they ran in circles that I didn't even know existed.

"Oh, well, that's cool." I wasn't exactly sure what to say when someone tells you that their family is part of the mafia.

Fayth laughed and shook her head. "You don't need to look so terrified, Paige. I promise not to put a hit out on you. I leave that all up to Leo." Fayth winked.

"Well, I guess that's good to know."

"Pizza is here," Demon called as he walked through the front door with the two boxes with a bag on top in his arms.

"Thank God. I was starving," Slider muttered as he followed Demon.

"You? I looked in the fridge thinking I could make something to eat for all of us, and all I was greeted with was a half brick of cheese and a can of cool whip. I didn't even want to think about all the kinky things going on with only those things in the fridge," Meg mumbled.

"Do you think for one conversation you could not embarrass me, Ma?" Remy said as he plopped back onto the couch. "I do not want to hear my mom using the word kinky. Ever."

"Oh, my dear boy. I thought by now you would have realized the only reason I'm on this earth is to embarrass the hell out of you."

Remy threw his arm over his eyes, and you couldn't help but feel a little bit sorry for the kid. Meg had no filter and said whatever came to mind. I could only imagine what it would be like having her for a mom.

I crawled off the floor and made my way into the kitchen and grabbed plates while Demon opened the boxes. "I call at least three pieces of the veggie."

"Veggie?" Slider sneered as he grabbed a slice loaded with meat and shoved half of it into his mouth. "Who the hell eats veggie pizza?" he asked around a mouthful.

"I'm so hungry I would eat anything." Remy grabbed a slice of veggie and folded it in half and bit off a chunk.

"Baby, you better grab you a slice before Remy eats it all," Demon laughed. He had a slice loaded full of meat held up to his mouth and winked at me before he ripped off a huge mouthful.

I grabbed two pieces of veggie as Meg and Fayth both grabbed some for themselves. We all camped out in various spots in the living room and kitchen, sitting wherever we could find room. This cabin was definitely only made for two people.

"I booked the cabin just down the road for the next three nights. I told the lady I didn't know exactly how long we were going to be here." Meg said.

Slider nodded his head at her. "You let King know?" Meg nodded her head, and Slider walked to the fridge and pulled out a beer. "Three days is good to start with until we figure out what we're dealing with."

"And what are we dealing with?" Meg asked.

"Talk to your ol' man. He'll tell you what you need to know," Slider gruffed. Meg rolled her eyes but didn't try pressing Slider for more information. "What time can we get into the cabin?"

"Anytime. She lives in the cabin next door and will be waiting for us."

"Good. Eat up and then we'll head over there. King wants us settled in."

"Hmm, I thought Lo going all bossy biker was sexy, but I'm beginning to see the drawbacks of it," Meg pouted.

"I call my own room," Remy called from the couch.

"I'll sleep in the living room. I need to keep a watch out anyway." Slider grabbed one more piece of pizza and headed out the front door again.

I moved over to Demon and leaned into him. "You do know that as soon as they leave, you are going to tell me everything that is going on."

Demon shook his head, a smirk on his lips and tossed his arm around me. "I'll tell you everything I can."

I rested my head on his shoulder and could only think that Demon wasn't going to tell me everything, and I wasn't sure how well I liked that.

————

Chapter 23

Demon

"Is that how Meg is all the time?" Paige was peeling back the blanket on the bed while I was undressing in the bathroom.

"You mean how she says whatever she's thinking?"

"Um, yeah. It's kind of refreshing but hilarious at the same time."

I flipped off the light in the bathroom and headed to the bedroom. "Yeah, that is Meg one hundred percent. She doesn't really know when to stop." I slid under the covers and pulled Paige into my arms.

"You forgot to turn the light off," she mumbled into my chest.

"Just close your eyes and you won't even know that it is still on," I joked.

"Oh, is that how that works?" she laughed.

"If I turn it off, do we have to talk about whatever has been bothering you all night?" Paige stiffened in my arms, and I knew the answer was no. I tossed the covers back, turned off the light and pulled Paige back in my arms. "Ask whatever questions you got, baby."

She sighed and tilted her head back to look at me. "I'm really not sure what question to ask first."

"Just pick one. I'm sure you'll get around to asking them all."

She tapped her finger on her chin, and I couldn't help but notice how fucking cute she was. "

"Who is Big A?"

Jesus Christ. She went straight to the gut shot. "Big A is a cockroach that won't go away."

"I assumed he wasn't one of the club, and I'm going to need more details than that." Paige poked me in the chest, and I knew she wasn't going to let this go.

"I'll tell you what I can, baby." She settled into me, ready to hear the fucked up story of the Devil's Knights and the Assassins. "Cyn used to date this guy. Hell, I can't even remember his fucking name anymore, but he was an asshole. I only know the bare details, but Cyn told the fucker she was pregnant, and he beat the hell out her."

Paige gasped and sat up. "He beat her up?"

437

"Yeah. Cyn lost the baby and Rigid lost his shit."

"But what does this have to do with Big A?"

"Asshat and Big A were cousins."

"Oh…" Paige gasped.

"Yeah, and when Asshat well, um, disappeared, Big A pointed his finger at us as the ones who were responsible."

"You guys didn't, I mean, you weren't…" Paige trailed off unable to say what she wanted to.

"He wasn't a good guy, Paige and he got what he deserved. That's all you need to know about him."

"So what is Big A trying to do now?"

"Big A was the head of the Assassins, a gang that ran drugs and whatever they could get their hands on. We didn't start out on the right foot with them when we moved to Rockton, and then when all the bullshit with Asshat went down, Big A and the Assassins vowed revenge on us. Thankfully they haven't been successful, but now they are getting desperate. Big A especially."

Paige sat back on her butt and crossed her legs under her Indian style. "Did something happen back in Rockton?"

I rubbed my hand down my face, deciding if I could tell Paige what I knew. King had said that it was up to me on how much I told her. I just didn't know how much she could handle. "There's some things going on."

Paige rolled her eyes and rested her hand on my stomach. "What about Fayth? Where does she fit in all of this? And by the way, you're not off the hook on the last question," she winked at me.

I really didn't think she was going to let me off that easy. "Fayth is the sister to Leo Banachi. Infamous mob boss and all around bad guy." I gathered Paige in my arms and pulled her on top of me. "You're too far away," I whispered against her lips.

"Stop," she said, pressing a finger to my lips. "Finish the story, and don't leave out any details."

"It's a damn good thing I love you, baby," I growled. I pressed a hard kiss against her lips and wrapped my arms around her.

"I love you, too," she whispered. "Now back to Fayth."

I laid my head back down, and Paige kept her eyes trained on me, waiting. "So, while Big A was trying to seek revenge, he enlisted the help of Leo Banachi, and it would have worked if Big A hadn't screwed over Leo."

"This is like a soap opera," Paige gasped.

"So Leo decided that helping the Assassins and Big A were not in his best interest and realized that King and the Knights were more the type of people he wanted to deal with. Leo asked a favor of us to keep an eye on his sister and nephew. The nephew was causing problems in Chicago, so Leo thought Rockton would be a good place for them until all the shit that the kid had kicked up, settled down."

"So why is Slider always with her?"

"King put Slider on her to keep her safe. Everyone that is connected to us isn't safe against Big A. Although, Big A would have to be the biggest idiot if he decides to mess with Leo's sister."

"So, back to my question from earlier. What happened that Meg and Fayth had to come here?"

"Baby, you need to understand that there are somethings that I'm not going to be able to tell you. What's going on is club business, and you just need to know that the club and I are going to do everything we can to keep you safe."

Paige tilted her head back and looked at me. "I don't like that answer, Demon."

"That's an answer you're going to have to get used to if you want to be with me. You know I'll tell you anything, but it if has to do with the club, I can't tell you."

"You do know you just totally contradicted yourself, right?"

"It is what it is."

"Does Meg know what's going on?" she asked.

"I highly doubt that Meg knows more than you do. King and all the guys know that whatever is going on with the club, needs to stay with the club."

Paige laid her head down and sighed. "You have to know that I don't like that, Demon. I really don't think that you having secrets from me is going to help our relationship."

"Paige, I'm not keeping secrets from you. Just think of it as my job. Would you expect to know everything that happens when I'm at work?"

"Well, no. But this is different. It's way more than a job. It's your life, Demon."

"And you're ninety-nine point nine percent of my life. I'll tell you most things that happen in the club, but there will be times where I can't tell you what is going on."

"Like now," she mumbled.

"Yes, baby. Like now."

She wrapped her arms around me, and I waited to see if she was going to keep arguing. "I love you, Demon, and I hate the fact that you have secrets from me, but as long as you promise that those secrets won't hurt me or upset me, I guess I'll have to be okay with it."

"Baby, I promise to tell you everything I can."

"Hmm, I guess I'm okay with that." She yawned loudly, and her body relaxed into me. "I'll just have to find a secret to keep from you so we're even," she teased.

"So that's how it's going to be, huh?"

"I guess you'll just have to wait and see. Now let me sleep, Demon. Someone wore me out earlier."

I chuckled under my breath and closed my eyes. "I love you, Paige. And whoever got to wear you out earlier is one lucky son of a bitch."

"We both are," she whispered.

I had to agree. We were both fucking lucky to have found our way back to each other.

———

Chapter 24

Paige

"Holy hell, now this is a cabin."

"I know, right? I called Lo this morning and told him I was never coming home. This place is the bomb dot com."

Fayth choked on her coffee and slammed her cup down on the counter. "You did not just say bomb dot com. Did we just flashback to the nineties?" she asked.

"Sure did." Meg winked at Fayth and refilled her cup. "And FYI, Lo said no to moving here. He went on and on about all the things we would miss about Rockton because he didn't realize I was joking. At least a little bit," Meg giggled.

"So, did either of you find out what in the hell is going on?" Fayth asked.

"No, Demon said he can't tell me," I pouted.

"Same here, Lo's lips are sealed for the time being. He just kept telling me that it was for the best."

"Ugh, you two are no help. I'll have to call Leo and see if he'll tell me anything." Fayth grabbed her phone and headed out onto the front porch, and I grabbed a cup down from the cabinet.

I had tried this morning to get more info out of Demon, but that man was locked down like Fort Knox. I had even woken him up with a way he used to love and still nothing. I wondered if my blow skills had wavered in the past seven years. Although Demon's growling and moaning had me thinking that wasn't the case.

"You talk to Gwen yet?" Meg asked as she pulled the stool out from under the island and plopped down on it.

I held my cup up to my mouth and blew on the hot chocolate. "No. Demon said I needed to call her, but I don't know if I'm ready for that. I know she has a million and one questions, and she has every right to have those questions, but I don't think I'm up to answering them."

"You can't blame her, Paige. I mean we were all blown away when we found out that you and Demon were once a thing. I swear Gwen shit a brick when she found out."

I pushed off the counter and wandered over to the big patio door. "It was something in my past that I thought was going to firmly stay there. Hell, when I had first seen Demon again, I prayed that the past would stay there and not come back."

"But now you're happy that he's back, right?"

A smile spread across my lips, and I couldn't help the laugh that bubbled out of me. "I think happy might be an understatement."

"Alright, now that's what I'm talking about," Meg laughed.

"But…"

"Uh oh. A but is never good unless, ya know, it's Lo's naked ass."

I looked over my shoulder at her and shook my head. "You really are a trip, Meg."

"I know. Gotta have fun," she winked. "Now, tell me what this but is all about."

I sighed and leaned against the cold glass. "He's not telling me anything about what is going on. I feel like I'm wandering around, knowing that something bad is happening, but I don't know what it is."

"Girl, I felt the same way right before Lo and I got married. He's so secretive with everything with the club that it scared me that he was keeping everything from me."

I sighed and turned around to look at Meg. "That's exactly how I feel, and with us just getting back together and having to get over all the things that happened before, I just don't know if I can handle this."

"Paige, there really isn't a lot I can say. The only person that made me feel better was Lo. I believe and trust in him, and that means I have to blindly believe that he is doing everything he can to keep me safe."

"But, Meg, I plan everything. I thrive on knowing what is going on and structure. I know being with Demon means he doesn't plan, and he flies by the seat of his pants. I remember from when we were together before that is how he operates. But now I feel like I have the club making decisions for me, and I have no idea what is going on. I feel like I'm one breath away from having a panic attack and heading for the hills."

"I know this seems like a lot, but you have to just trust him, Paige. There is so much going on that it is for the best that we don't know. Did Demon tell you anything?" Meg asked.

"He told me about Big A, the Assassins, and everything that happened with Cyn. Which by the way, I need to make sure I give her a big ol' hug the next time I see her."

"Then you basically know everything I do. And, you'll have to get around Rigid to give her a hug," Meg tsked. "With each passing day, that man gets more and more protective of her and the baby."

"How far along is she?"

"Six months."

"Only three months to go. Do they know what they are having?"

Meg rolled her eyes and kicked her feet up on the stool next to her. "No. They both decided they want to wait till the baby comes to know, but they are driving me insane. Cyn wants a boy and Rigid wants a girl. I swear I hear at least three times a day them arguing about what the baby is. I tried telling them if they would just find out, they could put a sock in it."

"I think I would want it to be a surprise, too."

Meg rolled her eyes and held her cup out to me. "You're just as crazy as her. Fill me up?"

I grabbed the pot of coffee and topped off her mug. "Eh, I say that now, but when I get pregnant again, I might change my mind."

Meg's eyes bugged out, and she slapped her hand over her mouth. "Again?! You were pregnant before?" she gasped.

Shit. Double shit. How in the hell was I going to talk my way out of this one? "Uh…" Jesus, I sound like a regular genius. "I was… we were… Demon and…"

I didn't think it was possible, but Meg's eyes bugged out even more. "Demon," she gasped.

I think we were up to triple shit now. Why the hell did I say Demon's name? I could have played it off that it was, I don't know, a one night stand or something and lead her off the trail of Demon and I. But no, I was an idiot. "You can't tell anyone," I ordered as I pointed my finger at her.

"Oh my God! Gwen doesn't know, does she? Holy hell, she is going to flip when she finds out!" Meg reached for her phone, but I snatched it out of her hand as I dove at the counter.

"You will not tell anyone this, Meg. You have to swear on King's life."

"Paige, this is huge. Why the hell wouldn't you want your sister to know?"

I shoved her phone in my pocket and leaned against the counter. "Because it was a long time ago, Meg. Demon and I are both trying to move on and telling everyone won't really help."

"But, Paige, that must have been awful. Is that why you and Demon broke up? Did he really cheat on you or was that all a cover?"

"He didn't cheat on me really…"

"What the hell does that mean?"

I ran my fingers through my hair and closed my eyes. Jesus, I was going to have to tell her everything. "It means I was pregnant, and Demon and I were so happy that we were walking on air. I lost the baby three weeks later, and Demon and I lost each other not much longer after that. We both stopped talking to each other, Demon blaming me for losing the baby, and I felt like he didn't want me anymore. We had a big fight, Demon went to the clubhouse, and I walked in on him with two girls. He wasn't touching, just watching, but it still hurt like hell." I opened my eyes and looked at Meg. "I can't believe I told you all that."

"I… I don't…" She shook her head and planted her hands on the counter. "How in the hell did you just condense that down to six sentences? That is like a damn soap opera right there," Meg laughed. "But for the record, if that was King, and I walked in on him whacking his tallywacker to two chicks, I can tell you he wouldn't have a tallywacker to whack anymore."

"Yeah, well, that is the *really* condensed version and believe me, it took all my willpower not to snatch his tallywacker off," I laughed. "So, do you now see why I don't want to tell Gwen? It's a whole lot of drama that is over, and I don't want to talk about anymore."

"I get it, but, wow, that is a lot, Paige. Are you sure you're even over what happened back then? Losing a baby is hard, but losing a baby and then losing the one person you love on top of that is crazy. I don't know how you made it through that without telling anyone."

"Trust me, it wasn't easy. I moved back home, and it tore me apart, but I just couldn't tell Gwen or my aunt."

"And now you really don't want to tell Gwen, because you know she'll kill Demon and get Gambler to help hide the body."

"There could be that, too," I mumbled.

Meg threw her head back, laughing. "I don't envy you at all. Gwen is going to be all over you like white on rice wanting to know what is going on with you and Demon."

"And I'll tell her. Parts of it. At least what has happened in the past month or so. Look, Demon and I have moved on from that and are trying to just look at the future."

"Well," Meg said as she raised her mug. "I wish you luck because you are going to need it. Not with Demon, but with Gwen."

I clinked my glass against hers, and I couldn't help but agree. "Well, how long do you think it's going to take for the guys to come back with wood for the fireplace?"

"At least a little bit longer. They took Remy along so he could be the muscle," Meg laughed. "I swear he's growing like a damn weed lately. He's going to be taller than Lo soon."

"You definitely have your hands full with him. What, he's only seventeen, right?"

"Soon to be eighteen and off to college. He was planning on going to the local tech school, but now he's thinking about going out of state. I'm trying to not have a panic attack just thinking about it."

"He'll be fine. I went to school out of state."

"You do know you just told me a story of how you got pregnant, lost the baby, and then went home, right?" Meg laughed.

Whoops. "Uh, yeah. But that won't happen to Remy. He's got a good head on his shoulders."

Meg rolled her eyes and took a sip from her mug. "You think Fayth is going to get any info from Leo?"

"I don't know. I barely know her, but she seems to have an edge to her that I don't want to cross."

"That's probably the mafia coming out of her. She seems real nice, but I have a feeling that Fayth has seen some things that have made her into who she is."

"You're right about that."

"You think I can have my phone back now?" Meg reached her hand out. "Gimme, gimme."

"Only if you promise not to tell Gwen."

Meg rolled her eyes but held her hand to her heart. "Scouts honor. I promise not to tell Gwen what you should tell Gwen."

I reached into my pocket and set it in her hand. "I think I agree," I laughed.

"I'm gonna call Lo and see if I can bribe him into telling me what's going on with daily bj's for the rest of the year." Meg winked and headed up the stairs.

I folded my arms over my chest and gazed out the patio door. Demon, Slider, and Remy were headed around the side of the house, each of them with their arms full of wood.

I couldn't believe that I had opened my mouth and told Meg, well, everything. "Gah, stupid," I whispered. Now I had to tell Demon that I had opened my big mouth because when you talked to Meg, you felt like you could tell her anything. Damn her trusting ways.

"Hey, baby," Demon called as he peeked his head in the door. "You think you can get a fresh pot of coffee going for us?"

"Um, sure. No problem." I grabbed the carafe and stuck it under the faucet.

"You okay?" he asked.

"Yeah, just a bit tired."

"Better get your energy up. I plan on wearing you out again tonight," Demon winked and closed the door.

I set the coffee pot under the coffee maker and banged my head against the cabinet. Now I had to figure out if I wanted to tell him that Meg knew about the baby, before or after I let him have his way with me.

Definitely after.

———————

Chapter 25

Demon

"Head on in and let your mom know that we're back, Remy." Remy nodded his head at my words and climbed the steps of the front porch and headed into the house.

"So you think you can finally tell me what the hell you know?" Slider asked as he pulled a cigarette out of his pocket and popped it into the corner of his mouth.

"Well, apparently Big A has taken a shine to sending letters to King. Every day for the past two weeks. At first, King brushed them off, but in the past couple of days, Big A has upped his threats big time."

"Jesus Christ," Slider said with the cigarette hanging out of his mouth. "You think this fucking clown would get a goddamn clue and just fucking disappear." I held out my light to him, but he shook his head. "I don't light it."

"Then what the hell do you have the damn thing in your mouth for?" I asked.

Slider ripped it out of his mouth and threw it on the ground. "Fucking Fayth," he growled. "Damn woman had me doing shit I never thought I'd do."

"Hold on, Fayth has you chewing on an unlit cigarette?" I laughed.

"Shut the fuck up, would you? I'm not whipped like you are."

"Yeah, well, I may be whipped, but I'm at least getting something out of it. Last I knew, you and Fayth couldn't fucking stand each other."

"We can't. Or at least we used to not." Slider threw his hands up in the air and paced the length of the porch. "I can't stand her. She's always telling me this and asking me to do that. I don't know what the hell is going on anymore. She told me she doesn't like me smoking around her, but I always have to be around her, so I had to figure out something to do to smoke."

"But you're not really smoking, you know that, right?"

"Well, having the damn thing in my mouth is better than not."

"You do know how fucking insane you sound, right?"

"I'm well aware of the fact that a woman who is not even warming my bed has somehow affected my whole life." Slider grabbed another cigarette and shoved it in his mouth. "One fucking word out of you and I'll pound your face in." He pointed a finger at me and spun around, continuing his pacing.

"Hey, I know how it is, brother. Paige has got me all wound up that I don't know which way is up anymore." I leaned against the porch railing and crossed my arms over my chest.

"I repeat, that woman," Slider waved his hands in the direction of the woods where Fayth had just disappeared too, "has no hold on me. I'm just nice to her until King stops sucking Leo's ass."

"He's just keeping up relations, brother. You know Leo has been helping us out big time with the whole Assassins bullshit and keeping an eye on his sister isn't that big of a deal."

"It is when it's not only her but her son that when he opens his eyes every morning, he instantly falls into trouble. You know, I can appreciate a kid that's in trouble because I was the same way growing up, but this kid is fifteen years old and has a longer rap sheet than I do." Slider pulled the cigarette out of his mouth, tossed it on the ground and pulled out another. "I'm going crazy between that woman and her son."

"Once we get this whole Big A thing squared away, I'm sure you'll be off Fayth duty." I couldn't help but notice that Slider was affected way more by Fayth than he should be.

"So do we know what we're dealing with? Has Big A completely fallen off his rocker?"

I pulled my phone out of my pocket and showed Slider the messages that Big A had been sending King. "Hide your children. Hide your women." Slider looked up at me, shocked. "Is this guy fucking serious? I'm assuming these are the messages that split us apart trying to throw off Big A."

"Yeah, these were the last messages King got. Big A is focusing on our ol' ladies and kids now." I scrolled over to another message, and I held it up to Slider. "This all goes back to that fucking idiot that hurt Cyn."

"'You took my family, so now I take yours.' This guy is fucking whacked."

"Yeah, he is. King and Leo are trying to find him, but every rock they overturn he's dodged them by seconds."

"So we are just supposed to be here like sitting ducks, waiting for Big A's next move?"

I shrugged my shoulders and glimpsed Paige through the window of the cabin. "Honestly, I don't know what the hell we are supposed to do, but I have to admit being in a secluded cabin with Paige is okay with me."

"Yeah, I'm sure it fucking is since you're not trapped in that damn cabin with Meg, her kid, and Fayth."

"Aw, come on. The kid isn't bad at all," I joked.

"Yeah, he is the only one I don't have to worry about. Meg is just fucking insane, and Fayth, well, I don't fucking know what to say about Fayth." Slider ran his fingers through his hair, leaned against the railing of the porch, gazing into the woods that Fayth had disappeared into. "You think I should go look for her? She shouldn't be out there wandering around by herself."

"She said she would just be on the edge of the woods." I cupped my hands around my mouth and yelled for Fayth.

"I'm on the phone," she hollered back. She peeked her head out from behind a tree and waved a gloved hand at us.

"There ya go. I don't think you have anything to worry about with her. She seems to have a pretty good head on her shoulders." I grabbed my empty coffee cup off the railing and headed into the house. "You think anyone followed you up here? To me splitting up the way we did was the best thing to do." I turned around, my hand on the doorknob and looked at Slider.

"From what I could tell, no one knows we are here except for the club."

I nodded my head. "Good. I'm gonna see what trouble Meg is getting Paige into. Corruption is Meg's middle name."

"Good luck," Slider laughed as he walked down the porch steps and headed in the direction of Fayth.

I watched him walk away, and I couldn't help but think he was going to need luck too if he thought he had a chance in hell of not falling for Fayth. From what I had seen, Fayth was just what Slider needed, now he just had to figure it out for himself.

I pushed the door open, the smell of warm apple pie hitting my nose as I spotted Meg and Paige in the kitchen. Paige was leaning against the counter, a coffee cup in her hands while Meg pulled a pie from the over. Paige's eyes fell on me, warm and inviting, and I couldn't help but think that even though things were going sideways with Big A, I at least had Paige to come home to.

Nothing and no one was going to take that away from me.

————

"Shopping, really?"

"Yes, really. I've googled it. There are a couple of shops that are only twenty minutes north. We could make an afternoon of it." Meg clapped her hands, excited that she had thought of a brilliant idea.

"Mom, do we really have to shop? Isn't there something else we could do? You can shop at home all of the time," Remy grunted. I tilted my head to the side, realizing that Remy fit in well with all the grunting and growling all the guys of the club did. Meg was raising her own alpha.

"Yes, Remy. You're still only seventeen, so you do what I say." Meg propped her hands on her hips and stared down Remy. "I'll buy ya an ice cream cone if you're good."

"I swear; she treats me like I'm ten." Remy grabbed his coat and headed to the door. "I'll be in the truck waiting like a good boy."

"Love you," Meg called as he slammed the door. "I swear; he could be a little bit more thankful to me for bringing his broody butt into this world. So," she asked, looking around, "you guys ready?"

"I'm down with shopping. I'll grab my purse." Fayth jogged up the stairs, and Meg cleared her throat, looking at me. "What about you? Up for some retail therapy?"

"Um…" No, I really wasn't, but I had no idea how to tell Meg no without her railroading me and throwing me into the truck.

"I think we'll just stay here. We'll make dinner while you're gone," Demon replied for me.

"Aw shit, you're fucking kidding me. Now that means I have to fucking go. I was hoping Paige would go, and then you would follow like a good puppy," Slider growled.

"Sorry, brother. Looks like you're the chaperone of this field trip," Demon laughed.

"We ready?" Fayth asked as she bounded down the steps, and waited by the door.

"You owe me," Slider growled. He grabbed the keys to the SUV and moved to the door. "I drive, everyone shuts up, and that's it," he ordered as he brushed past Fayth and stormed at the door.

"Well, this should be interesting," Fayth laughed as she followed Slider.

"I'm pretty sure that's an understatement," Meg laughed as she grabbed her purse and hitched it over her shoulder. "You two have fun," Meg called. She slipped out the door but popped her head back in. "No sex in my bed," she winked and closed the door as she laughed her ass off.

"Did she really just say that?"

"Yeah. She sure as shit did." Demon leaned against the counter, and his eyes devoured me.

"So, um," I stuttered. "What did you think we could make for dinner?"

He rested his palms on the counter behind him. "Come here," he growled.

"Demon, you said we'd make dinner," I reminded him, even though dinner was the last thing on my mind.

"Paige, come here now," he ordered again.

I shuffled my way over to him and stood between his spread legs. "I'm here," I whispered.

"But not close enough." He grabbed me behind the neck and pulled me close. His other arm wrapped around my waist and he buried his face in my hair. "How in the hell did I miss you when we were together the whole day?"

"Um, I don't know," I said dumbly because I felt the same way and I didn't know why.

His hand roamed under my shirt and up my back where he found the clasp of my bra. Before I knew what he was doing my bra was unhooked, and I gasped. "Demon, what are you doing?"

"Taking what's mine," he growled in my ear. "I don't know what you're doing to me, but I fucking like it."

"Demon, we can't do this here," I protested.

"Like hell we can't."

"There aren't any beds open, we have to go back to our cabin."

Demon shook his head no and pressed a kiss behind my ear. "There may be no beds, but there is one place I've imagined you all day."

My mind raced trying to figure out what he meant. "Couch."

"No. Where I want to sink into your warm body, we can't have any clothes on."

"Hmm, shower," I hummed as he trailed kisses down my neck.

"Closer, but not exactly what I had in mind."

"Just tell me," I purred. Demon wrapped his arms around me and hoisted me up. I wrapped my legs around him, and he headed out the back door. "Demon, where are you taking me?" I shrieked. He opened the door, and the cold burst of air hit me, sending a shiver down my body.

Demon nodded over my shoulder. "Right there, baby."

I glanced behind me and saw the hot tub on the edge of the deck. "What? It's absolutely freezing out here."

"Then I guess you better quickly get your clothes off and meet me in there." Demon set me down and toed off his boot while he pulled his shirt over his head.

"I don't have a swimming suit," I huffed while he unzipped his pants and worked them down his legs.

"Good, because swimming suits aren't allowed in there when I'm with you." Demon peeled his socks and boxers off and made his way over to the hot tube. He lifted the cover off, and hot steam bellowed. "You got one minute to get your ass in here, or I'm tossing you in with your clothes on." Demon stepped into the tub and sunk into the steaming water.

"Aren't you cold?" I asked, contemplating making a run for it before Demon could get his shorts on and chase me down.

"No, baby. The water is a balmy ninety-eight degrees," he smirked as he sat down and rested his arms on the side of the hot tub. "You're down to forty-eight seconds."

"You're going to make me do this, aren't you?" Demon smirked at me and only nodded his head. I looked around, making sure we were surrounded by trees and the neighbors couldn't see.

"Thirty seconds," Demon called.

Shit. There was no way I was going to be able to get out of this. I grabbed the hem of my shirt and pulled it over my head, and my bra came with, thanks to Demon's eager fingers. The cold air hit my skin prompting me to quickly strip off my jeans and boots. "I can't believe you're making me do this." I hooked my thumbs in my panties, pulled them down my legs and then I was standing naked for Demon and all of nature to see.

"Ten seconds," Demon drawled.

"You're an ass," I scoffed as I lifted one leg over the ledge and dipped my toes in the water. "Holy hell that is hot," I wailed.

"Baby, you were just worried about being cold, and now you think the waters too hot? You sound like one of the three little bears."

"I do not," I pouted. I did, but I wasn't going to admit that to Demon.

"Zero," Demon called out.

"Huh?" I looked up at Demon just in time to see him reach out and grab both of my arms and drag me into the tub. My hand slipped on the seat, trying to keep me from drowning, and the next thing I knew I was completely submerged and gasping for air as I sputtered to the top. "What the hell?" I screeched. My hair was matted to my face, and I was gasping for air while I listened to Demon laugh his ass off. "You are an ass," I muttered as I wiped my hair out of my face.

"Baby," he started but didn't finish, because he was still too busy laughing.

I leaned back, dipping my hair in the water and smoothed it back. "And now you think you're going to get laid. You're insane." I sat in the opposite corner from him, brooding and pissed off.

Demon wiped the smirk off his face and leaned back, resting his arms once again on the sides. "Don't be mad at me. I warned you that you only had one minute."

"I was getting in the damn hot tub. Have some patience, man," I scolded.

Demon held his hands up. "Alright, alright. I'm sorry."

I crossed my arms over my chest and glared at him. "You almost drowned me."

"You weren't going to drown." He rolled his eyes at me and flicked his hand in the water, splashing water at me. "I see my serious Paige got in the hot tub."

"Ha, more like your pissed off Paige."

"I'm okay with that, though. You wanna know why?" I shrugged my shoulders, wanting to know, but I didn't want him to know. "Because whoever I have, broody, pissed, happy, sad, quiet, or sexy, you're my Paige. No matter what mood you're in, you're mine."

It was my time to roll my eyes and shifted in my seat and tried to turn my back to him. He wasn't going to know that what he had just said melted my heart. I was his no matter what. I was just going to make him sweat it out for a bit. "If that's what you think."

I heard him move in the water and closed my eyes. The damn man was moving towards me, and I held my breath, waiting to see what he was going to do.

"It's not what I think," he growled, "it's what I know," he growled right before he wrapped his arms around me and pulled me into his lap so my legs were straddling his hips. "You love me, Paige, and a little dunk under the water isn't going to change that."

"I was getting in, why the hell did you have to pull me in?" I demanded.

"Because I needed you, and you were taking your sweet ass time."

"Well, maybe I needed to take my sweet ass time. You ever think of that? We're sitting in Satan's bathwater right now. It's hotter than a witch's tit."

Demon reached up and cupped my breast. "This is the only tit I'm worried about right now." He leaned down, his mouth sucking on my nipple and I couldn't fight the tremor that rocked my body. His tongue swirled and licked as I wrapped my arms around his neck.

"You don't play fair," I moaned.

"I told you I don't play. You're mine, end of story."

"Well, caveman. The same goes for you, too. You're mine, end of story," I mimicked.

"Damn straight," he growled right before his lips found my mouth and he gave me the sweetest yet possessive kiss ever. "You're the only one I've ever wanted," he mumbled in between kisses. "And I know since I'm the only one who has had you, I'm all you want."

"That's a pretty big assumption. Maybe the pickings were slim these past years." Lie, lie, lie, Paige.

Demon smoothed his hands down my hair and rested his hands on my shoulders. "They weren't. You loved me even after I fucked up, and I know I don't deserve the kind of love you have for me."

"You deserve everything in life, Demon. Including me."

"Do I deserve you calling me Dustin?" he asked.

"Yes," I said automatically.

"Then why the hell do you call me Demon?"

"Oh." Shit. I really had no idea why I called him that. "I guess it fits you better than Dustin now."

"I want to be your Dustin again, Paige. I want to be the guy you fell in love with back then and hung all of your hopes and dreams on."

I shook my head and gave a little laugh. "But you're not him. That Dustin back then is the watered down version of the man I see today. Everything you were back then, you're that now, but times ten."

"But you're the Paige I remember."

I shook my head and ran my thumb over his bottom lip. "I am, but I'm not. I'm not the same naive girl I was back then. I've grown up and grown into the person I needed to be to survive."

Demon leaned forward and rested his forehead against mine. "You changed because I fucked up." His voice was low and gruff.

"Demon." He growled at me calling him that, but I didn't think I would ever call him Dustin like I used to. "I changed because I needed to, just like you needed to change, too. You fucked up, and looking back if you wouldn't have done what you did, one of us would have screwed up in a different way. We were both too young to deal with what we were going through, and we were going to self-implode no matter what."

"Because I didn't deserve you," he whispered.

I sighed and pushed his head back. "No, because we weren't meant to make it. Not then. But now, now things are different. Don't you feel different being with me? I know I do."

"I do, baby. But I'm afraid that it's too different from the way we were."

"The way we were didn't work before. This, right here, right now, feels so perfect that I want the world to stop spinning and just spend the rest of my life in your arms." A lone tear streaked down my cheek. "I love you so much, Demon. I loved the man back then, but the man here with me right now has my heart, and he's the one I want. I want the future, not the past."

"Son of a bitch," Demon swore. "I'm the luckiest fucker in the world." He buried his face in my neck, and he just held on. "I don't deserve you, Paige, but I'm too greedy of a fucker to let you go, so I'm going to take everything you have to give and die knowing that you'll forever be mine."

A sob escaped my lips as his words, and everything was right. No matter what happened in our lives, I knew that as long as I had Demon with me, everything was going to be perfect. "I need you to kiss me," I whispered.

Demon growled and leaned back, his hand cupping my cheek. "I love you."

"I love you, too."

He slammed his lips down on mine, taking and giving with each stroke and thrust of his tongue. My hands roamed over his body, feeling every soft and hard plain of his wet, slick skin.

I ground my hips into his rock hard dick, needing to feel him buried deep inside me. His hands traveled down my body, grabbing my ass and he squeezed hard making a moan escape from my lips. "Tell me," he growled low.

I leaned back, taking in the man before me. "I've loved you for seven years, Demon. I never stopped."

"All mine," he bragged. He threaded his fingers through my hair and gently pulled my head down to him. "It's always been you, Paige. No matter what you think, it was always you." His hips bucked underneath me, and I lifted up on my knees and reached down into the water. My hand connected with his cock, and I gently stroked him up and down.

"I thought about you all the time. Even when I shouldn't have, my thoughts always came back to you."

"Me too. Every hour of the day I wondered where you were, what you were doing and who you were with. We missed so much, but now I get to make up for those years for the rest of my life." His words wrapped around me and I felt like I was home again. I was finally where I should be.

I lifted up a little higher and scooted closer to him. "Good, now make me yours, Demon." His dick throbbed in my hand, and I knew he needed this as much as I did. I slowly slid down on him, his cock stretching me open and I closed my eyes. "Yes," I gasped.

Demon's hands traveled down my body, grazing my breasts and land on the curve of my hips. "You ready to ride me, baby?"

I nodded my head, unable to speak. I felt so full, feeling Demon in me all the way to the root of his cock. His hands grasped my hips and slowly pulled me up and down. The water swirled around us, and I rested my hands on his shoulders as I felt everything he was giving me.

"So fucking tight," he grunted as he picked up the pace, his hips slapping against me with every thrust. "You like that?" he snarled.

I arched my back, thrusting my breast into him and his mouth clamped down on my nipple. "Yes, God yes," I called. His teeth nipped at me, sending shivers down my spine. "Please," I called over and over. My nails dug into his back as I felt the edge come closer, knowing it was only a matter of time before I shattered.

"Take it, baby. Take all of me." I shivered at his words, knowing that I finally had my dirty talking biker back.

He slammed into me over and over, his lips on my neck when I fell apart in his arms, and I knew that he would put every piece back together just so we could do it all over again. I collapsed into his arms as his grunts and groans of pleasure surrounded me knowing that I was the one to give that to him.

The jets of the hot tub turned off, and the sound of our heavy breathing mingled with sounds of nature. "Hot tub sex. Can check that one off the list," I laughed.

"I can tell you one thing, baby, that won't be the last time."

"How come the jets turned off?" I asked as I twirled my hand in the water.

"Timer. They'll kick back on in a little bit."

"Hmm," I hummed. "You were amazing, by the way."

"So were you, Paige. I could never get tired of being with you." He pressed a kiss to the side of my head and his hands gently rubbed my back.

Snowflakes started falling from the sky, adding an extra coat of flakes to the ground. "Were you always this romantic?" I asked, leaning back. "I mean, sledding, a horse-drawn sleigh ride, and now sexy time in the hot tub. Your woo game is strong," I laughed.

"I think it was always there, I've just refined it over the years. I used to bring you flowers all the time. Now it's a romantic kidnapping."

I snorted and slapped my hand over my nose but couldn't stop laughing. "No one has ever had a more romantic kidnapping," I agreed. I laid my head down on his shoulders and sighed. "I love you, Demon."

"I love yo-"

"Oh my God! Not the hot tub!" Meg screeched. "I'm blind!" Demon wrapped his arms around me, turned me around pressed me into the side of the tub, shielding me from anyone seeing me. "Ah, now I can see your ass!"

"Then close your damn eyes," Demon growled.

A laugh bubbled out of me, and I buried my face in Demon's neck. "I have my hands over my eyes, but you should have warned me that you were going to twirl around and show me your lily-white ass."

"I don't fucking twirl," Demon grunted back.

"That was a twirl, definitely. Ow, shit." Something rattled on the deck, and it sounded like Meg stumbled.

"What the hell are you doing?" Demon demanded. "Just go in the house."

"I'm trying, but I don't want to open my eyes. I knew I should have brought Blue with me even though he wanted to stay with Lo. He would have guided me out of this horrible situation. Why am I the one who always walks in on people bumping uglies?" Meg gripped. "Like I haven't been punished enough seeing Troy's ass, now I have Demon's to add to my memory bank of traumatic shit. Nightmares, all of them," Meg rambled.

"Slider," Demon hollered. "Get this crazy woman out of here!"

I heard another set of footsteps but was too embarrassed to look. "Woman, I told you to leave them alone," Slider barked.

"How was I supposed to know that they were naked playing hide the sausage? Give me your hand and guide me. I've been blinded by Demon's white ass."

"I swear to Christ, it wasn't bad enough babysitting Fayth, now I've got your crazy ass to deal with," Slider snarled.

"There, just pull me along and tell me when there's a step." I peeked over Demon's shoulder and saw Meg with her arm stretched out, and Slider tugged her back into the house. "Oh, and Demon, you're an ass," she snapped. "If you're going to talk about my ass, as least say I have a sexy, crazy ass, it lessens the blow."

Slider shook his head. "Step," he growled. Meg lifted her foot but not high enough and fell into Slider.

"Good God man. Have you never guided someone blinded by ass before? Give a girl some warning, would you?" Meg scolded. She tried again and managed to make the step this time into the house, and Slider slid the patio door shut.

"They gone?" Demon growled.

"Yeah, at least for now. We should probably get out before Meg comes out with disinfectant for the hot tub," I laughed. "We forgot towels," I shivered, looking around at our clothes that were scattered all over the deck. Thankfully Slider and Demon had shoveled it off earlier, and they were sitting in a pile of snow.

"There's towels in a cubby on the side. Fucking thing is heated." Demon set me down in one of the seats, and he moved to the other end if the tub where he leaned over and pulled out two towels.

I stood up, wrapped it around me. "It's almost like you have this planned."

"I did, baby. You're wearing off on me," he winked as he stood up and wiped down his body. He slid out of the hot tub and gathered our clothes. "Let me get dressed first, and then I'll help you." He made quick work of pulling clothes on, and I just watched.

"Did you just admit to planning this?" How strange was it that the thought of Demon planning something made me want to pull him back in the hot tub and show him my appreciation?

Demon helped me out of the tub and wrapped me up in another warm towel. "You'll never hear me admit it again, baby, but, yeah, when I was out here shoveling the deck, I scoped out the tub and knew I needed to get you out here."

I used the towel he had given me before and dried my hair. "I promise not to tell anyone," I laughed.

Demon wrapped his arms around me and pulled me close. "I think Meg interrupted me before from something very important that I was going to tell you."

"Oh really?" I said as I batted my eyelashes at him. "And what would that be?"

"I love you with everything I am, Paige Lawson, and I'll never let you go." Demon's eyes were warm and showed me everything I needed to see to know that this time, Demon and I were going to make it, and nothing was going to stand in our way. The past was where it belonged, in the past, and Demon and I were right where we were supposed to be.

"I've never wanted anyone but you, Demon. I love you, too." He kissed me long and hard, and I knew that this was right where I was meant to be.

I was Demon's, and he was mine.

—————

Chapter 26

Slider

"I need to make a phone call." Fayth stood up from the couch and headed to the front door.

"You really need to go outside? I just got comfortable, and now I need to follow your ass outside?" I asked, annoyed as fuck. All I wanted was just a quiet night. Demon and Paige had headed back to their cabin after their escapade in the hot tub, and now we were waiting for the pizza Meg had ordered to be delivered.

Remy was camped out in his room, and Meg was in the kitchen making something.

"I'll be fine. I won't lose sight of the cabin. I just want a little privacy. You know, that thing I haven't had since I moved to Rockton," Fayth bit off.

She acted like everything that was going on was my fault, and I was at my wits end trying to not tell her we were all put out by all the shit going on, but I held it together. For now, at least. "Five minutes, and if you're not back by then, and I have to find you, you're going to have a sore ass."

Fayth saluted me with her middle finger and headed out the front door. I knew I was going to have to find her because she was just going to spite me and not come back.

"You do realize that you told her she was going to have a sore ass after you were done with her, right?" Meg laughed from the kitchen. "Those words can be taken in so many ways."

"Yeah, well, I can guarantee they're not meant the way you're thinking." I peeked out the window and saw Fayth by the tree line with her phone to her ear, and it looked like she was yelling to whoever was on the other end. "That woman is going to drive me fucking insane before all of this bullshit is over."

"When I talked to Lo this afternoon he said hopefully soon they'll have Big A."

All I could do was grunt because King might think that, but none of them knew when this was all going to be over. The mother fucker had been running from us for a long time, and I didn't see the end in sight. Especially after the shit he had been pulling lately. Sending a fucking morbid message that we better hide the women and children did not seem like he was going to go down easy.

"Fayth is going through a lot more than we are. We at least weren't ripped from our homes and thrown into this mess." Meg pointed her finger at me. "You need to cut her some slack and not give her such a hard time. I was talking to her today when we were shopping, and she seems pretty amazing, Slider."

I again grunted because honestly, Meg was fucking right, but there was no way in hell I was going to admit that to her. I had been with Fayth for over a month, and there were times when she thought I wasn't watching, and I saw a completely different person from the front that she put on. The woman was a mystery that I was way too curious to figure out.

My phone that was on the island started ringing, and Meg tossed it to me as she grabbed a cup of coffee off the counter and made her way to the couch.

"Sup," I grunted as I put the phone to my ear.

"Something's happening, but I have no idea where. Get everyone and stay alert."

I sat up and slammed my cup down on the coffee table. "What the fuck does that mean?"

"It means I just got another message from Big A."

"What does it say?"

"One down, seven to go."

The blood drained from my face, and I knew exactly what that meant. "I'll get everyone together. You get headcounts from everyone else?" I stood up and headed to the front door.

"Yeah, just waiting on you."

"I've got Meg and Remy with me, and Demon and Paige just left."

"What about Fayth?"

"She's outside. You really think Big A is dumb enough to go after Leo's sister?" Fucking with a notorious mafia boss's sister was not something I would do.

"I wouldn't think so, but Big A has already shown that he's not playing with a full deck. Get Fayth and report back to me."

I shoved my phone back into my pocket and grabbed my coat. "You and Remy need to come with me. I'm not letting either of you out of my sight."

"What? Why?" Meg asked as she stood up.

"That was King. Something is going on. I just need to keep you two with me. Run up and get Remy. Quick."

Meg nodded her head, knowing that something wasn't right, and headed up the stairs. "Wait, Meg. Who was on the phone before?"

"I don't know. It said unavailable, and all I could hear was someone breathing."

A chill ran down my spine, and I knew it wasn't a coincidence that Meg got that phone call. I nodded my head and shoved my feet into my boots. I heard Meg telling Remy to get up and head downstairs.

I headed to the closet next to the door and pulled down my Glock that I had on the top shelf. I checked to make sure it was loaded and put it in the waistband of my jeans.

Someone was going to get hurt tonight, that much I knew for sure. I just didn't know who.

———————

Fayth

"God dammit," I cussed as I shoved my phone back into my pocket. Leo still wasn't telling me what was going on, and I was ready to go crazy being stuck in that cabin with Slider.

Something was going to have to give between us, and I was worried that something was going to end up with both of us in the same bed. I looked around realizing while I was talking to Leo, I had wandered away from the cabin, and now I had no idea which way to go.

I pulled my phone out again hoping that I could pull up my GPS or something, and that would help me figure out how to get back. I couldn't help but laugh at the situation I had gotten myself into. Who got lost in the middle of nowhere because they were too busy yelling at their brother. That would be me, Fayth Banachi.

"How in the hell did I manage to find the one spot in the woods that does not have reception." I held my phone up to the sky, praying to the gods of reception that my Google would connect, and I could find my way back to the cabin.

I heard a branch break to my left and froze. Someone or something was close by. It was more than likely Slider who had followed me, but a shiver ran down my spine when a branch broke to my right.

What the hell was going on? "Slider?" I called out, hoping that he was to the right of Bambi and me was to the left of me.

"No Devil's Knights here to save you, Chiquita," I heard from my left.

Oh, fuck. I took a step back trying to figure out what to do. I cursed my choice of style over sensible shoes and knew I wouldn't be able to run fast. "Shit," I whispered.

"I've been waiting for you. I watch all the other women with their men, and I knew you were going to be the one who would be my first." First? First for fucking what? "You know the most ironic thing about this?" A man finally stepped out from behind a tree to my left, and I felt the blood drain from my face. Big A. "You're not even with one of those Knights, but I'm still going to kill you."

"Wh... why?" I stuttered.

"Because they took my family from me, and now I'm going to take everything they care about. Including you. You know war, Chiquita, there are always innocent people who die. But I think this is for the best. It sends the best message. I'M NOT FUCKING AROUND ANYMORE!" he screamed.

I jumped at his words, and he lifted his arm and pointed a gun at me. "Say hello to Nick for me, and tell him I'll kill every one of those Knights, just for him." I heard the gun click as he cocked the trigger and I screamed the only name that I could think of that I knew would save me.

"Slider!" I yelled at the top of my lungs. The world slowed down as I saw Slider barreling down on Big A, but he was too late. The gun exploded in Big A's hand, and I fell to the ground, my head shattering with pain. I felt warm, sticky blood trickle down my cheek, and my world went dark.

The End
(For Now)

Unraveling Fayth
Devil's Knights Series
Book 8

Winter Travers

Chapter 1

Slider

"How long does this normally take?"

"I don't know, man. I've never done this before."

"Well, why don't you ask Meg? She's done this at least once."

King shook his head and sat down in the chair next to me. "I really don't think I should barge in there and demand to know how much longer they are going to be."

"Why the hell not? If it's going to be hours, we could grab something to eat without them even knowing that we were gone."

"Thinking with your stomach again, huh, Turtle?" I kicked my feet out and stretched out my legs. We had been at the hospital for five hours already, and we hadn't heard what was going on other than Cyn was going to have the baby, eventually.

"Shut the hell up." He rubbed his stomach and flipped me off. "I'm a growing boy."

King shook his head and leaned back on the wall. "Take a walk, Turtle. I'll talk to Meg in a little bit. I don't think having a baby happens instantly. We're in for a long wait."

Turtle grabbed his leather jacket off the back of my chair and headed down the hallway. "I'll be around," he called.

"Jesus," King swore. "It's like herding cats with you fuckers."

"Hey, don't group me in with that asshat." I pulled my phone out of my pocket, checking for the fiftieth time to see if I had missed her phone call.

"She call you yet?" King asked.

I shook my head no and shoved my phone in my pocket. I hadn't heard from Fayth in over two months, and I was going fucking crazy waiting. "You talk to Leo lately?" Updates from Leo were the only thing that was keeping me in Rockton and not hopping on my bike headed to Chicago.

"He said she's doing good. Not much has changed, though."

I nodded and gritted my teeth. No change was all I've heard for the past two fucking months. "I need to go see her, King."

"Leo doesn't think that's a good idea."

"I don't give a flying fuck if Leo thinks it's a good idea or not. I've waited long enough. I didn't even get to say goodbye when he swooped in and took her back to Chicago." I was still pissed as hell. It had been a week after the shooting, and I had left the hospital for half an hour to grab a shower and something to eat. By the time I had gotten back, Fayth was gone, and the only person who was there was one of Leo's henchmen, Apollo.

Two and a half months ago

"Where the fuck is she?" I demanded.

Apollo sized me up and crossed his arms over his chest. "He took her home."

"What the fuck for?" This was fucking bullshit. Fayth was in one of the best hospitals in Wisconsin. She was receiving all the help and attention she needed. I was making sure of that.

"Leo has some things going on back home that he is dealing with, and it's in Fayth's best interest not to be far away."

"You always talk like you got a stick up your ass?" Apollo growled but didn't say anything. "She was fine here. I was looking after her."

"Just like you were looking after her when she got shot in the head?"

I ran my fingers through my hair and sat on the edge of the bed. Apollo was the only one who had the balls to say what everyone else was thinking. "I didn't think Big A was going to go after Fayth. Hell, she doesn't have anything to do with all the shit going on."

Apollo shrugged. "He did and now she's back in Chicago. Tell King that Leo will be in touch." Apollo ducked out the door and I was left in an empty hospital room wondering what the fuck I was going to do next.

King stood and started pacing the hallway. "Give her more time, Slider."

"You telling me that you would be able to stay away from Meg that long?"

"Hell no, but that's because I'm married to her and plan on spending the rest of my life with her. You don't know what you want from Fayth. Part of me thinks that you just feel guilty because you didn't protect her."

I stood and glared at King. "I didn't protect her, and nothing will ever make up for that. If you could not throw it in my fucking face, that'd be great."

"I'm not throwing it in your face. All I'm saying is that if you want to see her, make sure it's for the right reasons, and not just to sooth your own pride." King stood in front of me and put his hand on my shoulder. "You've changed since that night,

Slider. So did Fayth. Just know what you want before you see her. She deserves that much."

King wandered down the hallway and disappeared around a corner.

I sank back down into the chair and put my head in my hands.

I had no fucking clue what I wanted, but I knew I wasn't going to figure it out here. Two more weeks was all I was going to wait, then I was headed to Chicago, whether I was wanted there or not.

****

Chapter 2

Slider

Meg ran to the front door and shouted, "They're here!"

"Jesus, Meg. You're acting like you haven't seen Cyn in months. It's been a couple of hours." King shook his head and sat down next to me at the poker table.

"She's got baby fever," I chuckled.

"Yeah, well she can work out that baby fever with Cyn and Rigid's kid. She can spoil Micha rotten and then give him back," King grumbled. "I'm not into sharing Meg with more than Remy. I'm a selfish bastard when it comes to her."

Rigid came through the front door, the baby carrier over one arm and a blue diaper bag slung over his shoulder. Meg had stepped off to the side and was *oohing* and *ahhing* over the baby as soon as Rigid set the carrier down.

"Stop," Cyn called. "Did you wash your hands?" she asked Meg who was hunched over the carrier, her hands poised to lift Micha out of the seat.

"Really?" Meg scoffed. "You're going to get over that new paranoid parent thing real quick," she said laughing while she unbuckled the straps and gently lifted Micha into her arms.

"So, are we going to be calling you daddy soon?" Hammer asked when he sat down at the table with us.

King, Turtle, and I looked at Hammer and shook our heads. "Sorry, Hammer. But that's really not a kink I'm into." King smirked.

"Oh, fuck you," Hammer said. "You know what the hell I meant."

Meg sat down on the couch and scolded Hammer. "Language."

"Babe, the kid doesn't even know his name. I'm pretty sure he's not going to know what fuck means." King stood and made his way over to the bar.

"He may not know what it means now, but he will eventually. It's better if you start curbing your cursing now."

"Babe, you cuss just as much as I do." King grabbed four beers and a bottle of Jack. "You're supposed to be the cool aunt, not the one with a stick up their ass."

"I do not have a stick up my ass," Meg growled. "We just don't need to corrupt the kid not even an hour out of the hospital."

Cyn sat down next to Meg and watched every move she made. "Make sure you're supporting his neck."

Meg shook her head and smiled down at Micha. "Your mama needs to take a chill pill, yes she does," she cooed.

"I do not need to take a chill pill," Cyn muttered and crossed her arms over her chest and leaned back in the couch. "I need a nap and a hot bath. Everything feels stretched out and saggy. How come no one ever tells you about this part of having a baby?"

"Because then no one would *want* to get pregnant, that's why. My body hasn't been the same since I had Remy."

Cyn's eyes got huge and her jaw dropped. "Meg, Remy is almost eighteen years old."

Meg laughed and cradled Micha in her arms. "Yup. He most definitely is."

"Oh, my God," Cyn gasped. "I'm destined to be stretchy and saggy for the rest of my life," she moaned.

"Hey, could you not terrify Cyn right now, Meg?" Rigid called from the kitchen. "She's hot as fuck and nothing is going to change that. Even pushing an eight-pound baby out of her who-ha."

"Who-ha?" King chuckled.

"Can't really call it a pussy when I'm talking about the boy." Rigid strutted out of the kitchen with two bottles of water in his hand and a bag of chips in the other.

"Words!" Meg yelled.

"Aw hell, we can't even say pussy anymore?" Hammer grumbled.

"Not in front of Micha. I swear y'all are trying to turn him into a dirty-talking biker and he's barely been out of the womb for four days." Meg stood and paced back and forth, rocking Micha in her arms.

"His father is one of those dirty-talking bikers, so I don't really think it's that far of a stretch that the apple isn't going to fall far from the tree." Rigid shrugged and moved over to Cyn. "You wanna go lay down for a bit," he asked and handed her a bottle of water.

She twisted the cap open and took a small sip. "A nap sounds heavenly but I doubt Micha is going to cooperate."

Meg waved her hand at Cyn. "Nonsense. I can watch Micha while you take a nap. That's was kick-ass aunts are for."

"   Hey! She just said ass. How the hell does that work?" Turtle asked.

"It works because she's my wife, and she has no logic to her reasoning. Just go with it, Turtle. You'll be better off that way." King tilted his head at Turtle and winked. "At least, that's what I tell myself every night."

"I'll pass on that shit," Hammer muttered under his breath.

"Anyway," Meg said rolling her eyes. "Take a nap. I'll be here."

Cyn stood and looked over at Meg. "Are you sure?"

"Yes. Go now, before I change my mind."

Rigid grabbed Cyn's hand and dragged her down the hallway to his room.

"I give her twenty minutes before she's out here checking on Micha," I chuckled.

"Hopefully, she lasts longer than that." Meg glided over to King and sat down in his lap. "She's going to have a lot of sleepless nights coming up."

King looked down at the baby in Meg's arms and wrapped an arm around her waist. "You look pretty good with a baby in your arms, babe."

Meg laughed. "It may be more than sixteen years since I've actually held a baby, but it all seems to come back to ya real quick."

"Well, you can get your baby fix with Micha and then give him back."

Meg pressed a kiss to the side of King's head. "That's the plan, handsome. Besides, I am way past my baby-having days."

"Good. Keep it that way," King ordered.

Meg looked around the table at us with a small smile on her lips. "Have you heard anything new about Fayth?" she asked me.

I shook my head and took a long pull from my beer. "Nope. I hear the same thing every day. She's doing fine."

"Are you planning—"

"Meg," King cut her off. "Let it be, babe," he ordered, shaking his head.

"But, why can't I?"

"Because you're not going to say anything Slider hasn't thought or been asked fifty times."

"But he can—" King cut her off with a stern look and Meg snapped her mouth shut. "Fine," she muttered.

I could only imagine the fifty questions Meg was going to fire off at me. They weren't going to be any different than the ones I had been asking myself. "You'll be the first to know if anything happens, Meg. Although, I doubt that is going to happen anytime soon."

"Who are we talking about?" Hammer asked.

"Oh, sweet Jesus," Meg whispered.

"Fayth, jackass," King growled.

"Leo's sister?"

"Were you dropped on your head as a baby, Hammer?" Turtle asked.

"No. At least, not that I know of," Hammer replied and scratched his head.

"I think you need to have an entry-level test that all prospects have to take if they want to be part of the club," Meg laughed.

"Then I wouldn't have anyone in the fucking club," King chuckled.

"But he'd have me," Meg cooed down at Micha. "I'm gonna go to our room and play with Micha."

"He's a baby. How in the hell are you going to play with him?" King asked, as Meg stood and headed down the hallway.

"Come with me and find out," she called. "Oh, and bring his bag."

"Walked right into that one, didn't I?" King grumbled and grabbed the diaper bag from next to the couch and followed Meg.

"Sure did, brother," I chuckled.

Hammer looked between Turtle and me. "Now, what the hell are we going to do tonight?"

"Pizza and poker?" Turtle suggested.

"Works for me," I said, as I shrugged. It wasn't like I had my own ol' lady to hideaway in my room with like most of the fuckers in the club did.

"You think we could get Gambler to play?" Turtle asked and walked behind the bar.

I pulled my phone out and fired off a couple of messages to Gambler, Demon, and Troy. I doubted any of them would come, but what did it hurt to ask? "I asked him. We'll see. If anything, he'll bring Gwen with him so she can fawn over the baby and then maybe he can play a couple of hands with us." I kicked my feet out, stretching my legs and looked around the clubhouse.

Things had sure changed from a year ago. Normally on Friday night, the common room would have been overflowing with people partying, celebrating the end of another week with a twelve-pack and ten bottles of booze. Now here we were, me with these two fuckers playing a pathetic game of poker begging Gambler and Demon to leave their ol' ladies for a couple of hours.

"I bet if you text Troy and have him tell Marley that we're ordering pizza, they'll be over before it even gets delivered." Turtle grabbed the half-empty bottle of whiskey, a couple of shot glasses, and the deck of cards.

"I texted Troy, Gambler, and Demon. We'll see if any of them come." I grabbed the deck of cards from Turtle and shuffled them.

I dealt and sat back in my chair while I waited for Hammer and Turtle to finish pouring their drinks.

This was not how I had expected to spend my night, but the one person I wanted to be with, I couldn't.

Life sucked, and I had no fucking clue how to fix it.

****

Chapter 3

Fayth

"Did she say anything today?"

"No. Same as the past weeks. She wakes up, gets dressed, then sits in the chair by the window all day."

They were talking about me like I wasn't even in the room. I stared blankly out the window and wondered what the hell was going on.

I wanted to talk. I wanted to tell everyone to shut the hell up and leave me alone, but I couldn't. The words I yearned to speak wouldn't leave my throat.

"Are there any more tests we can run? Are you sure there isn't something going on that we can't see?" Leo's voice drifted over to me, and I shook my head. It was like he was hoping there was a problem because without a problem to fix, there was nothing for him to do.

"There isn't much more that we can do. Considering what she has been through, she's doing miraculously well."

"But she's not fucking talking!" Leo thundered.

"She acknowledges people when they talk to her, and there are no signs that there was any brain damage. Her muteness is more than likely the way she is dealing with the trauma." I heard the doctor's footsteps lightly tread out of the room.

Leo sighed heavily. "Just one word, Fay, that's all that I want." He sounded exhausted.

One word? Hell, I had a hundred fucking words to say, but I just couldn't get them out.

"I don't know what it's going to take for you to talk." Leo fell into the chair across from me and crossed his legs. He glanced at the table next to me and sighed. "I don't know why you refuse to use the pen and paper to communicate."

I rolled my eyes and looked back out the window. I didn't need the pen and paper. I woke up in the morning, the nurse helped me shower, and then I moved to the chair by the window. I didn't have anything to tell anyone, and I wouldn't have anything to say until I was able to talk.

Out of the corner of my eye, I saw Leo shift in his chair and lean his head back. "They set the court date for next Monday. Did you want to go?"

Did I want to go to court and see the guy who had tried to kill me? No, thank you. I had seen that asshole one too many times.

"I'll take your silence as no. Apollo and I will be there. I'm going to make sure that bastard never sees the light of day again."

I didn't want to think of Big A ever again, let alone know what happened to him.

"Greer come by to see you today?" Leo asked. I didn't answer, because he already knew the answer. There was rarely ever an answer Leo didn't know. He made it his prerogative to know the answer before he asked the question. "She just wants to see you, Fay. You and Greer used to be good friends."

Yeah, we were great friends before I got shot in the head and went mute.

"I went out to lunch with her and Apollo today. It's still hard to believe that those two are together. It's a miracle Kane didn't blow a gasket when he found out about those two in Vegas."

That was an understatement. Greer was Kane's younger sister who had gone to Vegas over New Year's, and when she had come back, she was with Apollo, Leo's right hand man and Kane's best friend. I had known Greer for years and knew she had a thing for Apollo, but never imagined she would actually do anything about it. But if you hear Apollo talk about Greer, you would figure out Greer hadn't been the one to do the pursuing. Apollo had wanted Greer, and he didn't give her room to say no.

"I think Greer is going to be good for him. She gives him a different perspective that he never had before." Leo sighed heavily, and I looked over at him. He looked tired and worn down, like he hadn't slept in weeks. I quirked my eyebrow at him, and he knew I was waiting to hear whatever he had to say.

"I don't know what to do anymore, Fayth. I've exhausted every avenue I can go down to help you. I'm at a loss and I fucking hate it." He scowled.

Leo Banachi at a loss. Now, that was something I never thought I would see. Leo was in the position that he was because he never took no for an answer, and if there was anything standing in his way, he bulldozed through it. I never would have thought I would be the person to break him.

"I need you to tell me what to do, Fay. You've always been there telling me what you think I should do even when I'm not asking you."

I cocked my head to the side. Did he really think this was what I wanted? I felt like I was suffocating in my own body with no chance of catching my breath anywhere.

"Marco fucking needs you, Fayth. If this is how you are going to be from now on, we need to get back to living, and we'll figure out how to deal with this."

Marco. I was being a shit mom, but I couldn't help but think he was better off without me. We had temporarily moved to Rockton because Marco had decided he was going to take after Leo and was doing shit no fifteen-year-old should know how to do, let alone be doing them. But in the end, all moving to Rockton had done was get me shot, mute, and Marco hating me even more.

Leo's phone rang, and he shook his head. "Mother fuckers, can't leave me alone for more than ten minutes." He pulled his phone out of his pocket and scowled. "I need to take care of this. We'll finish this conversation later. Just try harder, Fay."

He pressed a kiss to the side of my head and then disappeared from the room.

I looked back out the window and sighed. Try harder? Was that even possible?

I opened my mouth, praying the simple word, "hi," would fall from my lips, but nothing came out. The room was silent, and I was going crazy in the prison my body had become.

****

Slider

"I'm coming to see her," I barked into the phone.

"No. you can't."

"She's fucking thirty-one years old. I'm pretty damn sure I don't need your fucking permission to see her."

"You're right, but she's going through enough right now without you pulling into town and fucking up her life even more than you already have."

I wanted to reach through the phone and punch the fucking shit out of Leo. I knew I was the reason Fayth had gotten shot and now couldn't speak. I was supposed to be the one to protect her, and I had let her wander off without taking notice of what she was doing. Every damn day I woke up blaming myself. "Once. I just need to see her one time to let her know that I fucked up."

"We all know you fucked up, Slider. I'm reminded of your fuck up every time I talk to her, expecting a response, and all I get is silence."

I gritted my teeth and growled. "Let me see her."

"No. I've told you every day that I will be the one to let you know when you can see her, but still you insist on calling every day."

"You can't keep me from her. Not forever, Leo."

"You'd be surprised at the things I'm capable of, Slider. Lose my number." The line went dead in my ear, and I gripped the phone in my hand, trying to crush it.

This wasn't fucking fair. I hadn't known back then that Big A was going to go after Fayth. The guy was a complete psychopath and had stopped making sense months ago when he had gone off the deep end.

"And that is why you should have kept Fayth close," I said to my empty bedroom. Leo was right, this was all of my fault.

I had pushed Fayth away, trying to convince myself she was some stuck-up woman who was a pain in my ass who I didn't care about. Deep down, I knew she was unlike any woman I had ever met, and that terrified the hell out of me.

I tossed my phone on the bed and ran my fingers through my hair. The only noise in the room was the quiet tick of the alarm clock I had next to the bed, and I saw it was only six o'clock. Every day dragged by, an hour feeling like four, and a day feeling like ten. I was going crazy waiting for the chance to see Fayth again.

Calling Leo was the only glimmer of hope I had each day, praying today would be the day he would let me know Fayth had spoken or that I could come visit. But today was like all the other days. No change and there was no way in hell I could come down there.

"Yo, Slider," King called and banged on my door.

"What?" I growled.

"We're heading out to eat. You wanna come with?"

Hang out with King and Meg, along with probably all of the other brothers and their ol' ladies? No fucking thanks. "I'm good. I'm just grab something from the kitchen."

"There ain't a lot to fucking eat. That's why we're headed out."

"I'm good." Not only did I not want to go out, I knew I wasn't good company. Hell, I hadn't been good company for the past two months.

I heard King tread back down the hallway, and I grabbed my phone off the bed. I had one more phone call to make. It was the same phone call I always made right after I talked to Leo, and I knew I would get the same result I always did.

My thumb swiped over Fayth's name, and I put the phone to my ear.

Hi, you've reached Fayth. I can't get to the phone right now because I probably screened your phone call and don't want to talk to you. Leave a message that I'll never check, or just hang up. Have a good day!

I tossed my phone back on the bed and ran my fingers through my hair. Same as every day. Her phone was off, but I still listened to her message to the end because that might be the last time I hear her voice.

Listening to her message was better than replaying her screaming my name and that awful, blood-curdling scream that came right after it. I didn't think I could ever forget that day. The way her body jarred back and then crumpled to the ground in the next second was burned into my brain.

I fell back onto the bed and closed my eyes. I replayed it over in my head, knowing this would be my punishment for the rest of my life. I was supposed to keep Fayth safe, and I had failed her.

Now, I get to relive that hellish day forever.

Three months ago…

I didn't get to her fast enough.

In the time King had called, telling us to make sure everyone was accounted for, Big A had already grabbed her.

She was lying on the ground, blood oozing from her head and her body limp.

"Slider!" I heard Demon call.

I knew he had heard the gunshot, and I prayed like hell for him to hurry up and get here so I could go to Fayth.

Big A struggled underneath me, gasping for air as my knee dug into his throat, pinning him in place.

The barrel of my gun pressed to the side of his head and my finger was poised on the trigger as I watched the realization of what was going on wash over his eyes. "You're fucking dead, asshole," I growled.

Footsteps sounded behind me, and I cocked the hammer back.

"Is she dead?"

I looked over my shoulder and saw Demon and Remy standing there. "No," I growled low.

"Remy, call nine-one-one and head back to the house. Stay with your mom and Paige," Demon ordered.

"Are you going to kill him?" Remy asked, his eyes glued to the man beneath me who was still trying to wrestle his way out from under me.

"Go back to the house now, Remy," Demon barked.

Demon knew what I was about to do. A man like me didn't let a piece of shit like this live after he had terrorized the people I called my family. "He doesn't deserve to live."

"Demon?"

"Son of a bitch." Demon spun around, and I saw Meg and Paige traipsing through the woods.

"Mother fucker," I cussed. There was no way in hell I could do what I needed to do now with Meg and Paige here. "Demon, hold this piece of shit." I hauled Big A off of the ground, twisted his arms behind his back, and marched him over to Demon.

"We called the police when we heard the gunshots," Meg said, her voice quaking.

Demon grabbed Big A and I flew over to Fayth, falling on my knees beside her. I brushed aside her hair and pressed my hand to the wound on the side of her head. As far as I could tell, it looked like the bullet had just grazed her, but it was still bleeding like a son of a bitch.

I had tried to get a shot off at Big A when he had fired at Fayth, but I wasn't as lucky as he had been. "I need something to tie around her head," I barked.

"Here," Remy called. He thrust a sweatshirt into my hand and kneeled next to me. "Just tell me what you need me to do."

"Hold her head still while I try to tie this to help stop the bleeding." Remy cradled her head and I gently slid the shirt under her head and tied it tightly around it. "How long did they say it would take the ambulance to get here, Meg?"

"Ten minutes, but that was more than five minutes ago. They should be here anytime," she chattered.

"Should we move her?" Remy asked.

"I don't fucking know." I had no idea what the hell to do. I wanted to scoop her up, take her to my truck, and drive to the hospital myself, but I had no idea if that would hurt her even more.

"I hear sirens," Paige called.

"I'll run to the road and flag them down," Meg said.

"Paige, go with her. I'll be right behind with this asshole," Demon ordered. "You okay with her? Is she still breathing?" Demon asked me.

Fayth's chest was gently rising up and down, and she moved slightly on my arms. "Yeah, for now. I have no idea how bad he got her."

"We need to move her. I don't think they'll be able to get back here to grab her."

I had already fucked up royally, I didn't need to hurt her even more. "Demon, I don't—"

"Slider, pick her up and bring her to the cabin now." Demon marched toward the cabin, leaving me no choice on what my next move would be.

Remy stood up. "I'll help you."

I gathered Fayth into my arms; a small groan fell from her lips. Her eyes were still shut as I gently lifted her up and rested her head on my shoulder. "Run ahead, Remy. Make sure they are ready for her."

Remy sprinted off, jumping brush and fallen branches. I followed behind slowly, careful not to jar her head. Each step I took, I felt the weight of what had just happened settle on me.

We had finally stopped Big A, but now Fayth was hurt, and it was all my fault.

****

479

Chapter 4

Fayth

"Mom."

I looked away from the window and saw Marco standing in the doorway. I attempted a small smile at the sight of him. He was becoming a man with each passing day, and it felt like I was missing it. He looked so much like his Uncle Leo that he had been mistaken many times for being Leo's son rather than mine.

"Did you want to watch a movie with me downstairs?" he asked. "We can even watch one of those girly movies you like." He shoved his hands in his pocket and shifted his weight from foot to foot.

I opened my mouth to say yes, but nothing came out. Disappointment washed over me, and I again wished like hell I could say one simple word. Every day, Marco came to my room, asking me to do something with him, and each day, I said no because I had been wallowing in my own self-pity. He ate breakfast with me each morning, filling the silence between us with mindless chatter about his day.

"I can pop some popcorn for us," he said, hope filling his voice.

I nodded once, knowing I couldn't keep going the way that I was. I was still a mother even though I couldn't talk.

"I'll get the movie ready and pop the popcorn." Marco sprinted down the hallway, and I couldn't help but notice how happy I had made him just by agreeing to watch a movie with him. Baby steps.

I rose from my chair and glanced in the mirror over my dresser. I looked the same, but I didn't feel like it. Everything had changed, but yet, it hadn't. It was like I had stepped into a time machine and come out six months earlier—before Marco had started acting up, and we had moved to Rockton. One move had changed our lives, and, at the time, I thought that change would be for the better, but now, I couldn't help but regret picking up and moving.

"Marco said you were going to watch a movie with him?" Leo asked. I saw his reflection in the mirror as he crossed his arms over his chest and leaned against the doorjamb.

I nodded and grabbed my brush. I gingerly pulled it through my hair, careful of the six-inch scar on the right side of my head. They had shaved around the wound in the hospital so they were able to stitch it up, and the hair had finally started to grow back. Thankfully, if I wore my hair down, you were barely able to tell I had a massive bald spot.

"You think I could watch with you guys, too?"

I shrugged. It was up to Leo if he wanted to hang out with us. It wasn't like I could tell him no.

"It's going to get better, Fayth," he said quietly.

Was it? It didn't feel like it was. I sat in my chair, day in and day out, and only got up for Marco. If I had it my way, I wouldn't get out of bed most days.

"I'll meet you downstairs." Leo disappeared down the hall, and I focused on my image in the mirror.

Everything looks the same—my slightly curly black hair, my striking and a bit exotic face, my body, although it was a bit thinner given my lack of appetite these days. How could everything be unchanged on the outside, but be so completely different on the inside? It was driving me crazy.

Getting my nails done and hitting the latest Coach sale at the mall no longer mattered to me. Hell, if I was honest, nothing mattered to me anymore.

Today had been the first day I had actually taken Marco's feelings into account.

"Mom, the popcorn is ready!" he called up the stairs.

I took one last glance in the mirror and sighed.

Time to fake being the person I was, until I could come back to my room and fall apart all over again.

****

Chapter 5

Slider

"Have you seen Demon?"

I looked up from the TV I was blankly staring at and found Paige looking down at me. I hadn't even noticed her walk in front of the TV. "Ah, I think he's out in the shop." King and Demon were working on getting their bikes ready for the first warm day of spring that would be here any day now.

Paige cocked her head to the side. "You're not getting your bike ready?"

Honestly, I didn't give a fuck about my bike. Hell, I didn't give a flying fuck about anything. "I'll work on it next week."

She flopped down on the couch next to me. "I thought all of you were motorcycle die-hards who wait for the first thaw and you were out on your bikes even if it was only forty degrees."

She was right. At least, she was right about how I used to be. "I've got time," I mumbled.

Paige sighed and crossed her arms over her chest. "Have you heard anything new about Fayth?"

"No."

"Is she still not talking?"

"Yes."

"Did Leo say when we can go and visit her?"

"No."

"Am I going to get an answer that is more than one word out of you?" She didn't bother to try to hide her annoyance at my shortness.

"Not today."

"You haven't said more than ten words to anyone all week, Slider."

I shrugged and picked up the remote. I didn't want to have this conversation. It had been a week since I had last spoken to Leo. I couldn't keep torturing myself, calling him each day and getting the same answer. I was in a shit mood, and I had no plans of shaking it. "I ain't got nothing to say, Paige." I turned the volume up on the TV and started flipping through the channels.

"Good. You can sit here and listen to what I have to say then."

I turned the volume up even louder but Paige snatched the remote out of my hand, turned down the volume, and shoved the remote under her ass. "What the hell?"

"Be glad I didn't put it down my shirt."

"I'm pretty sure that's the same as shoving it under your ass."

Paige rolled her eyes and crossed her arms over her chest. "Are you ready to listen?"

"I don't really have much of a choice. I'm shit at reading lips, so the TV is useless until you give me back the damn remote." I crossed my arms over my chest and waited to hear what Paige had to preach at me.

Paige smirked, pleased with herself. "Why won't you just go see Fayth?"

"Because I'm pretty sure Leo would kill me if I showed up. He's threatened bodily harm if I drive down there without letting him know."

Paige rolled her eyes. "And why is that stopping you?"

"Paige, I'm going to assume that you have no idea who Leo Banachi is."

"Demon told me who he is, and I still don't understand why you're here, when you clearly want to be there."

"Even if Leo wasn't threatening to kill me, I'm not entirely sure that Fayth would even want me there."

Paige grabbed the remote from under her ass and stood up. "Why wouldn't she want you there? You saved her life, Slider."

"No, I didn't. I fucked up and let her traipse around the woods and couldn't manage to find her before Big A put a bullet in her." If I would have been five seconds longer, Fayth wouldn't be here at all.

"Oh Jesus. Now I see what's going on. You feel guilty that she got hurt."

I looked up at Paige. "I liked you a lot more when I thought you were some quiet and shy chick with her nose in a book."

Paige shrugged. "I am shy and quiet."

"You sure aren't acting like it right now."

"I'm only saying something because all those books I've had my nose in help me see what is going on with you and Fayth."

"Oh geez, this is going to be good. Why don't you tell me what is going on with Fayth and me? I'd love to hear what you think you know."

Paige grinned and laid into me, "I think you're terrified of Fayth, because she represents everything you want but don't think you can have."

"I take whatever I want, Paige."

"Normally, but not when it comes to Fayth. I know you say that you don't want to go there because of Leo, but I think that's just an excuse. I think if you go there, you have to face all the emotions and feelings that you don't want to have to deal with."

I scoffed. "I don't have feelings or emotions when it comes to Fayth."

"Then, why are you walking around like a grumpy bear who can't find his picnic basket?"

"Picnic basket?" I asked, confused as hell.

"Sorry, Meg was watching Yogi Bear in her room when I walked by. I digress," Paige said, waving her hand. "If you don't have feelings for Fayth, then why are you so pissed off?"

"Because I didn't do the job that King asked me to do."

"Has he yelled at you? Asked you what the hell you were thinking letting Fayth go out alone?"

"No." King has surprisingly said nothing about it.

She pointed the remote in my face. "Then, why are you beating yourself up about it."

I didn't have an answer to that. I just knew that I had fucked up and it was driving me crazy. "Are you done, Paige?"

"No. Not yet. I think the reason you are beating yourself up about it is because you have feelings for Fayth that you can't and won't admit to."

"I don't hav—"

Paige wagged the remote in my face. "You're lying to yourself, Slider. If you didn't have feelings, you should have been over this two months ago."

"There isn't anything to get over," I growled.

Paige rolled her eyes. "Then, stop being so pissed. Man up and go see Fayth, or get the hell over it and stop biting people's heads off."

"And what if I don't?"

Paige tossed the remote on the couch, walked to the door that lead to the shop, and turned to look at me. "Then, all you're doing is screwing yourself over, Slider." She opened the door and slammed it behind her.

I grabbed the remote and threw it against the wall. It shattered with the batteries flying all over. "Son of a bitch," I roared.

I didn't have feelings for Fayth. I couldn't.

Being with one woman was not the life I wanted. I saw first-hand how each and every one of these fuckers settle down with one woman and put a collar around their necks so their ol' ladies could drag them around. I didn't fucking want that.

I felt guilty she had been hurt because it had been my job to protect her and I hadn't. There wasn't any other reason behind it. Paige wanted to sit there and paint some romantic bullshit that deep down I cared for Fayth, but she was wrong.

Fayth Banachi was not the type of woman I wanted.

I didn't want any woman, and that's the way it was going to fucking be.

****

Fayth

"Night, mom," Marco called and closed the door to his room.

I quietly made my way down the end of the hall and slipped into my room.

Marco, Leo, and I had watched two movies and managed to eat four bags of popcorn between the three of us. It had been nice to do something normal, but the fact that I couldn't speak was still the pink elephant in the corner. Hell, I couldn't even laugh when something funny happened. All I would do was open my mouth, rock back and forth, and clap my hands like a seal. Whenever I did that, it sent Leo and Marco into a fit a laughter.

Somehow, my muteness had turned into a joke. It was a good thing I loved both of them and knew they weren't being mean.

I piled my hair on top of my head, tied it into a knot, and headed into the bathroom where I turned on the water and waited for it to warm up. My reflection stared back at me, and I was once again looking myself over, wondering if I actually knew the woman staring back at me anymore.

I turned my head, looking at the scar, and thought about the one man I told myself I shouldn't think about. He hadn't called, visited, or anything, and yet, I thought of him more than not.

Slider had been the one man in my life who gave it to me straight and didn't try to tell me what I wanted to hear. I had hated him those first couple of months. He acted like he wanted to be anywhere but in my house with Marco and me, and we would butt heads at every corner. But things had slowly started to change. Slider and I still disagreed on most things, but it was like we had come to an understanding that we were completely different people, but we could still appreciate each other for what we were.

That day at the cabin, everything had been irritating me, the main thing being Leo. I was sick of being told what to do all of the time, and I was at the end of my rope that day. Marco and I had finally started to settle into Rockton when Leo had called to tell me to pack a bag and that he didn't know when we would be back in Rockton again.

I shouldn't have wandered from the cabin, but I hadn't realized how far away I was until it was too late and Big A was there. Slider had saved my life that day, and I hadn't seen him since.

I wanted to call him, but what would be the point? It wasn't like I could talk to him.

The cold sheets greeted me as I slipped into bed and my head touched the pillow. I closed my eyes and reminded myself that I need to forget about Slider. Things had changed once again, and I was right where I had started out, and apparently, this wasn't where Slider wanted to be.

I still missed him even though I knew I shouldn't.

Slider was the one man I just couldn't seem to get off of my mind.

****

Chapter 6

Fayth

I was falling, and I couldn't catch myself. My body thudded onto the ground, and my head felt like it had been run over by a freight train. The wet earth beneath me soaked through my coat, and I tried to roll over but my body wouldn't cooperate.

Two gunshots sounded, and I prayed for my eyes to open so I could see if Slider was okay. I tried one last time to open my eyes, but the pain in my head was clouding my mind. I heard Slider and Big A wrestle on the ground, but the darkness that was falling over me settled around me and all I could do was scream "Slider" over and over.

His name ripped from my throat, "Slider!" I jarred awake and screamed his name again. "Slider!" I chanted his name over and over, unable to say anything else.

"Fayth?" Leo called and came skidding into my room. "Fayth, what's wrong?"

He turned on the light and all I could say was "Slider."

"Is that Mom?" I heard Marco ask sleepily.

Leo sat on the end of my bed. "Fayth, calm down. What happened?"

"Slider," I whispered.

"Holy hell, she's talking," Marco said, amazed while he rubbed the sleep out of his eye.

"Yeah, but all she's saying is Slider," Leo replied. He rested a hand on my arm and looked me in the eye. "What happened, Fayth? Did you have a nightmare or something?"

I nodded and opened my mouth to answer but nothing came out.

"Fayth, you just talked. Say something," Leo demanded.

I tried. I really fucking tried but nothing came out.

"What did she say before? Just Slider?" Marco asked.

"Yeah, that's all I've heard her say."

I looked from Leo to Marco and shook my head. I felt like I was about to crawl out of my skin. The words were right on the tip of my tongue, but they wouldn't come out.

"What are you doing?" Marco asked Leo when he started punching buttons on his phone.

"Making a phone call that's been a long time coming."

****

Slider

"I fold."

"Fucking pussy. Nobody fucking bets against me anymore." Gambler reached across the table and grabbed the pile of money.

"Deal again," I said, nodding at King. "I think Gambler's luck is about to run out."

"Yeah, yeah. You fuckers always think you can beat me." Gambler shook head and leaned back in his chair. "Even Gwen can't beat me. Although, she sure does like to try."

"I heard that," Gwen called from over by the bar. "Don't be so cocky. One day, you'll lose, and I'll be there to collect my winnings."

Everyone was gathered at the clubhouse tonight, the guys playing poker and all the chicks were gathered around the bar, looking at some kind of bags while drinking wine.

"Is this what we've come to?" Hammer asked. "Poker while the chicks cackle over by the bar? I wouldn't fucking mind if one of those chicks belonged to me, but they don't, so this sucks."

King patted him on the back and picked up the cards Rigid had dealt. "One day, you'll understand it, Ham. You just gotta find the right chick to trade in one-night stands and drunken nights for."

"Hey. Don't knock one-night stands," Troy said, tipping his beer at King. "My one-night stand is standing next to your wife."

"True that, brother." King tapped his bottle against Troy's beer.

"So, the moral of the story, Hammer, is keep up the one-night stands, one of them will pan out eventually," I said, laughing.

Troy flipped me off and chugged the rest of his beer.

"Hey!" Meg called. "Someone's phone if going off under the bar." Meg held up my phone and waved it in the air. "My mom always said a phone call after midnight is never a good one."

"Not in the life of a biker, babe," King replied.

"Mine." I walked over to the bar and grabbed the phone out of her hand. The ringing had stopped before I had been able to answer it.

Within seconds, it was ringing again, and Leo's name flashed on the screen. "Oh shit." I swiped right and put the phone to my ear. "Leo?"

"Slider."

"What's going on? Is Fayth okay?"

"I don't know. You need to get here. Now."

"What the hell does that mean?" She was fine the last time I talked to him. How the hell had things changed? I knew with it being in the middle of the night, it couldn't be good.

"It means you need to be here right away in the morning. Things have changed, and you need to be here."

I looked up at King who had his eyes trained on me. I was going to have to clear it with him before I could go running of to Chicago for God knows what. "I'll be there by eight." I still didn't know what the hell I was going to do when I saw Fayth again, but I knew this was going to be my only chance to see her.

"Make it seven." Leo hung up, and I shoved my phone in my pocket.

"Everything okay?" Meg asked.

I huge smile spread across my face. I may not know what the hell was going on, but I knew this time tomorrow, I would see Fayth, and all the shit swirling around in my head should be figured out. "Never better."

****

Chapter 7

Fayth

I didn't sleep the rest of the night. I couldn't.

I had finally spoken, but it was only one damn word. "Slider," I whispered to my empty room.

It still worked.

Dog. I opened my mouth to say the word, but nothing came out. Son of a bitch.

I was lying flat on my back, looking up at the ceiling, trying to say any word besides *Slider.*

No luck.

The last time I had looked at the bedside clock, it was only five forty-five and I knew the minutes were sliding by like molasses.

"Slider," I whispered again. As much as I hated the fact it was the only word I could say, I still said it so I wouldn't lose it.

"Mom?"

I turned my head and saw Marco standing in the doorway. I sat up and turned on the lamp.

"He's been sitting out there for an hour. Should I let him in?"

He? Who was he? Was it Slider? I looked at the clock as saw that it was six-thirty. He was early. Leo had told me Slider was coming, but that he wouldn't arrive until late morning. I grabbed the pad of paper that had been sitting beside my bed for a week. I hadn't ever used it, but now I needed to ask a question, and this was the only way for me to get my answer.

Who is it? I scribbled down. I knew it was Slider, but I was back to not wanting to say his name. I was a complete nutcase at this point. I held up the pad of paper to Marco, and he nodded.

"Yeah. He's sitting in his truck, just staring at the house."

Slider knowing where I lived also blew my mind. The house we shared with Leo was completely different from the two-bedroom bungalow Marco and I had lived in back in Rockton.

Tell your uncle, I wrote.

Marco nodded, read my words, and disappeared down the hallway to Leo's room.

I laid back down and closed my eyes. Slider was sitting in my driveway, and I had no idea what the hell was going to happen next.

****

Slider

Six forty-one. My hands were gripping the steering wheel, and I stared at the front door to Fayth's house.

The mother fucker was huge.

The thing wasn't even a house. It was more like a fucking mansion.

"What in the fuck am I doing here?"

No one answered because I was fucking talk to myself and even I didn't have the answer to that.

Six forty-three.

I should knock on the door, get it over with, and stop torturing myself wondering what had changed with Fayth. It couldn't be bad. It had to be something good. Maybe she was talking now. Maybe she had asked to see me.

"Maybe you should just get out of the truck and find out what the hell is going on, asshole," I murmured to myself.

Before I had the chance to get out, the front door opened, and Leo stepped outside. He closed the door behind him and headed over to my truck. "I see you can't tell time," Leo said through my open window.

"Couldn't really sleep after you called. I figured early was better than late."

"Normally, I would agree with that except when it interferes with my sleep."

I shrugged. I didn't give a fuck about Leo's sleep. "You wanna tell me why you suddenly decided that I need to some down here?"

"Inside. I put some coffee on before I came out. Marco woke me up when you got here."

Leo stepped back, and I opened my door. "I woke him up?" I asked as I stepped out and slammed the door shut.

"I guess no one slept well since I called you." Leo walked up the sidewalk to the front door and pushed it open. He motioned for me to walk in and stood back.

Class. That was the only word that came to mind as I took in the inside of Leo's house. Everywhere you looked, you could tell Leo had money and wasn't afraid to show it. When I'd been examining the exterior of the house—two stories, solid brick, with huge bay windows on either side of the front door—I had thought it was impressive. Now, seeing the interior, the outside seemed even more grand. "This is quite a house," I said with a low whistle.

Leo shrugged and headed down a hallway to the right. "I like to live comfortably."

Comfortable was an understatement. "I think you took comfortable and upped it about ten notches." We walked into a lavish kitchen with a huge center island that had plush stools pushed under the counter. "You actually cook in here?" The kitchen looked too perfect to dirty with cooking and baking.

"No, I don't, but Fayth does. Making coffee is the extent of what I do in here."

I nodded. That sounded about right for a man like Leo. I couldn't see him taking the time to cook being in the position he was in. "Is she awake yet?" I asked, as I pulled out a stool and planted my ass in it.

"Yeah. Marco told me she didn't sleep all night. I'm hoping she'll fall asleep for a bit." Leo grabbed two cups down from the cabinet and filled them. "Although, I think she has slept enough the past month that one night with only a couple of hours of sleep won't affect her." Leo set a cup in front of me and sat in the stool next to me.

I took a sip of the hot coffee and returned it to the counter. "You think you can tell me what's going on now? I haven't had any sleep all night either. Once I find out what you want from me, I plan on locating the nearest hotel and crashing."

"I don't think a hotel will be necessary." I turned to look at Leo. I wasn't sure what he meant by that. "You'll be staying here."

"Here?"

"Yes." Leo took a drink then clasped his hands in front of him. "She spoke last night."

"What?" I gasped.

"She woke up screaming and saying the same word over and over. In fact, it seems to be the only word she is able to say."

She spoke but only one word? What in the hell did that mean? "Well, what word did she say?"

"This is probabl—"

"Slider."

I spun around in my chair and saw the most beautiful woman in the world.

****

Chapter 8

Fayth

I couldn't stay in bed. The fact that Slider was in my house was enough motivation for me to get dressed and seek him out.

I heard Leo and Slider before I actually laid eyes on them. Slider's voice was one you never really forgot. It was rough and low and, if I were to be honest, sexy as hell.

Standing at the entrance to the kitchen, I couldn't keep it in. I had to say his name. "Slider."

He spun around on his stool, and he looked like he had seen a ghost. I knew I had been shot in the head, but I didn't think it was that touch and go that he would be surprised to see me alive. "Fayth." His voice cracked, and I watched his adam's apple bob while he swallowed. "You said my name," he said in awe.

"This shit is going to go straight to your fucking head, isn't it?" Leo said. He turned around and looked between Slider and me.

"More than likely," Slider replied, smirking.

There was that smirk—the one that drove me crazy, knowing he was a cocky son of a bitch, but also it made him fucking gorgeous. I stood there, not knowing what to say. Hell, I couldn't say anything. I clutched the pad of paper I had in my hand to my chest and took a deep breath.

"Come sit, Fayth. I made breakfast."

I rolled my eyes and scribbled on my notepad. *Coffee isn't breakfast.* I held up the pad and Leo crossed his arms over his chest.

"It is when I don't have anyone to cook for me."

I sighed and headed over to the fridge. I grabbed a dozen eggs and a pound of bacon from the drawer and bumped the fridge door shut with my hip.

"Wait, I'll get it," Slider said. He stood and rushed over to take the food from my arms. "You shouldn't be doing this," he scolded.

"She's fine, Slider. It's good for her to finally be out of her room and not staring out the window all day."

I flipped off Leo and turned around to grab a pan out of the cabinet. I would have loved to tell Leo to fuck off.

Slider set the eggs and bacon next to the stove and watched me. I motioned to the stove, letting him know he needed to move if he wanted me to make breakfast. He hastily backed up, leaned against the counter and looked completely out of place.

"Fuck," Leo cursed as his phone rang. "I need to get this. You okay, Fayth?"

I rolled my eyes and waved my hand at Leo. It was Slider—the same man who I had basically lived with for the past couple of months. I would be fine.

Leo walked down the hall to his office, barking into the phone the whole way.

"You don't need to make me breakfast, Fayth. That's not why I came here."

I quirked my eyebrow up at him, wondering what he was here for then. I set the frying pan on the stove and opened up the bacon. I spotted my pad of paper over by the fridge, knowing that was going to be the only way I could communicate with Slider.

"Got it," Slider mumbled and grabbed the paper and pen. "Is my name really the only word you can say?"

I nodded and took the paper out of his hand. He smirked and leaned next to the stove with his arms crossed.

Are you just going to stand there watching me?

"Yes," he said, looking over my shoulder.

Stop.

"No."

Yes.

"I could do this all day, Fayth, and I bet your hand is going to get tired before I do."

I tossed the pad of paper on the counter and flicked the pen at him. I was going to be nice and try to have a conversation with him, but he could live with my complete silence if he was going to be an ass.

"Did you want me to get you a cup of coffee?"

I nodded and went back to laying the bacon in the pan.

The bacon was gently sizzling when he set a cup of coffee next to me that was the perfect dark caramel color.

"I remember how you like your coffee," he mumbled.

I took a sip and confirmed he really did remember. It wasn't a big deal to remember how someone took their coffee, but it felt like one. I turned over the bacon then squatted down and grabbed a small fry pan out of the cabinet to start the eggs.

"Do you remember how I like my eggs?" he asked, as I set the pan on the stove then spooned a little bit of the bacon grease into it. I cracked three eggs into it, careful not to break the yolks.

I nodded and gently splashed some of the hot grease onto the eggs. He liked them over easy with a runny yolk. Just how I liked them.

"So, this is where you live?" Slider looked around, taking in the extravagant kitchen.

I shrugged and nodded.

"I guess I didn't realize you lived with your brother." He grabbed his cup of coffee and shuffled over to the sliding door that led to the backyard. "Although, the house is big enough that if you didn't want to see him, that wouldn't be a problem."

He was right. Especially with how much Leo worked and was away from home, there were times it felt like I did live alone. I reached up in the cabinet, pulled down some plates, and set them next to the stove.

"You like living here?"

I grabbed the pad of paper. *It's home.* I tapped on the counter to get his attention, and pointed at the paper as he turned around.

"You didn't answer my question."

Did I like living here? I guess I hadn't really known anything else. Even growing up, my parents had provided Leo and me a life that most kids dreamed about. I had gone from their huge, extravagant house right into Leo's when I found out I was pregnant. *It's what I know.*

"How in the hell did you manage to live in Rockton and not go crazy?"

I like Rockton.

"But Rockton is far from this, Fay. Your house could have its own zip code."

Now, that was an exaggeration. It was a large house, but it wasn't that big. I slid the eggs out of the pan onto a plate and put four pieces of bacon next to them. I glanced at the pad of paper but didn't pick it up because I didn't know how to explain to Slider that this wasn't my life anymore.

After I set his plate on the island, I worked on making eggs for Leo.

"I'll wait to eat until yours is ready."

I shrugged. If he wanted to eat cold food, that was up to him. I cracked three more eggs into the pan and spooned in some more grease. Leo liked his eggs sunny-side-up with crispy edges. I swear, I could be a short-order cook if it ever came to it.

No one around here wanted the same food, and I always found a way to make whatever they wanted.

Slider watched me, sipping on his coffee, but didn't say anything more. That was the one thing about not being able to talk. Conversations were short and no one seemed to really want to talk with someone who couldn't respond. I had the paper to write on, but even doing that was a hassle.

"Is that mine?" Leo asked, pointing to Slider's plate as he strode back into the kitchen.

I shook my head no and splashed more grease into the egg whites.

"It's mine," Slider piped up.

"Why the hell aren't you eating?"

"I was waiting for Fayth."

I slid Leo's eggs onto the plate and dropped some bacon next to it, then held out the plate to him. "Make yours and then we'll eat."

Since when did Leo care if I ate at the same time as him? Half the time I didn't eat until Leo and Marco were halfway done with their food.

I set his plate down next to Slider's and rolled my eyes while I grabbed the pad of paper. *I still have to make Marco's. Eat now.*

"Marco fell back asleep. Make your eggs so we can eat. I have a busy day ahead of me." Leo pulled his phone out of his pocket and sat down at the island.

"How's Marco been doing since you moved back?" Slider asked.

I really didn't know the answer to that. My zombie-like existence for the past few months proved I was being a shitty mom.

"He seems to be back on track. My men have been keeping an eye on him."

This was news to me, although it didn't surprise me. The reason we had moved to Rockton before was because Marco had been getting into trouble that had interfered with Leo's business.

"He's not trying to become the next Leo Banachi anymore?" Slider asked.

"Nah, I don't think that was ever his intention, although I wouldn't be surprised if he joins the family business one day."

I knew that was a possibility for Marco, but I wasn't sure I liked it. Leo was the king of the underworld and dealt with all of the lowlifes and all the shit the law turned a blind eye to. If there was ever an anti-hero, Leo and the Banachi family were it.

I cracked two eggs into the pan and grabbed my pad of paper. *Don't encourage him.*

"Is she talking to you or me?" Slider asked.

"Me. Fayth thinks my life isn't good enough for Marco."

I never said that.

"You didn't have to say it, Fayth. I know you." Leo set his phone on the counter and leaned back in his chair. He raised his arms over his head and stretched.

It's dangerous. That was the understatement of the century. Every time Leo stepped out the door, I worried if he would be coming home at all.

"It's only dangerous if you don't know what you are doing. What Marco was doing before was dumb and dangerous. He's damn lucky he didn't get himself killed."

I flipped over my eggs with the spatula in one hand and tossed the notepad on the counter. *He only does what he sees his uncle doing,* I scrawled out on the paper. I held it up as I slid my eggs out of the pan onto a plate.

"He doesn't see me do shit." Leo picked up his fork and nodded at me. "Are we good to eat now?" I could tell he was annoyed we were having this conversation in front of Slider, but it wasn't anything I hadn't told Leo before. Marco saw everything Leo had—the cars, houses, money, and women—and he wanted it too.

I waved my hand at him to eat.

"I need to head into the office today. I had planned on being home, but things are going a way that I didn't expect them to go."

I nodded and sat down on the stool next to Leo.

"I can stay with Fayth," Slider volunteered.

I rolled my eyes. I didn't need a babysitter, although Leo and Slider apparently disagreed.

"Good. I shouldn't be gone all day." Leo shoveled in a mouthful of food. "How long are you planning on staying?"

"However long I need to be here. I'm cleared with King to be here."

What did that mean? I wasn't sure why Slider was here to begin with, let alone why he would need to stay.

"Good. We'll talk tonight when I get back." Leo finished his eggs in two bites, then took his plate to the sink. "You have my number if you need me." Leo pressed a kiss to the side of my head and whispered, "I'll be back," before he disappeared down the hallway, and I was left alone with Slider.

I glanced over at him, and he leisurely drank his coffee. This was where things were going to get awkward. Slider was going to find out how it was to be with a person who couldn't talk. I spotted my pad of paper over by the stove and wished I had brought it over with me. "Don't look so scared, Fayth."

I looked scared? I was more unsure than scared. I had no idea what was going to happen next. Before I had gotten shot, Slider and I tolerated each other, knowing we were stuck. I never disliked him, I was just so lost in my own head, I couldn't process what Slider was to me. One day, I hated living in Rockton, and the next, I never wanted to leave. Leo had been going crazy trying to figure out what I wanted, and then, the day I had been shot, I was on the "get me the hell out of here," kick. Now, being back home, all wanted to do was go back to Rockton.

"You have any plans for today?"

I couldn't help but silently laugh, which just looked like a crazy smile on my face. I left my room today; that was a big accomplishment. I shook my head and cut up my eggs.

"Any friends you wanna go visit?"

Friends? That was another laugh. The only reason women were nice to me was to get closer to Leo. I had learned early on I was just a pawn to get to him. Now, I just kept to myself. I shook my head no.

Slider got up, grabbed my pad of paper, and slid it over to me. "This will make things a hell of a lot easier." He set the pen next to it and sat back down. "Now, what do you want to do today?"

Even with the pad of paper next to me, I still had no idea what I wanted to do. I shrugged and continued to eat. Slider was going to be bored as hell with me here all day.

"Well, I can't sit around the house all day, Fayth, so we need to find something to do."

Slider would be gone by tonight.

"What did you normally do when you were here?" he asked and sipped on his coffee. He had finished all his food and had pushed his plate back.

I grabbed the pad of paper. *Housework. Cook. Shop.* When put on paper, I had lived a shallow life.

"Well, all of that shit is off the table for today. I don't clean and cook, and the only shopping that I do is for Harley shit. We could go find the nearest Harley store."

I rolled my eyes. *No.*

"Well, then what do you suggest, Fayth?"

I tapped the pen against my chin. I thought of the one thing I always liked to do but hated doing it alone. *Movies?*

"Like the theater?"

I nodded, hopeful he would say yes.

"How about...Harley store, lunch, and then the movies?"

Lunch then movies? I had never been to the Harley store. I wasn't really someone you would see there.

"Nope. Harley store first. I need some new leathers."

I'll stay in the car.

Slider shook his head. "Not happening. Where I go, you go."

I thought it's where I go, you go.

"Same thing, Fay. I'm not making the same mistake twice. You wanna go somewhere, I'll be there with you. I wanna go somewhere, you're with me. Glue, Fay. Stuck together like fucking glue."

Mistake?

"I fucked up, Fay, and you can bet your ass that shit is never going to happen again." Slider grabbed his plate and dumped it in the sink. "I'm gonna grab my bag from the truck. Which way to the bathroom?"

I pointed down the hall then held up two fingers.

"Down there, second door?" he asked. I nodded. "See, we'll figure this shit out, Fay," he laughed. Slider headed down the hallway, and I heard the front door open and close.

I looked down at my plate and sighed. What in the hell was going on? I had spoken one word, and I was now suddenly thrown into a completely different path than the one I was destined to go down.

Slider was here, and according to him, we were stuck together like glue.

How long was that going to last, and did I really want it to end?

****

Chapter 9

Fayth

"Get out of the truck, Fay."

I shook my head no and hit the lock button again. Slider had made the mistake of getting out of the truck before I did, and now I was barricading myself inside, refusing to get out.

He hit the unlock button on his keys again, but I hit the lock button before he could get the door open.

He bared his teeth at me, frustration written all over his face. "Get. Out. Now," he barked.

I was playing with fire right now, but I didn't care. I was already out of my comfort zone leaving the house. Now, he wanted to throw me into the Harley store, a place I had never been before.

I shook my head no again and kept my finger hovering over the button.

He locked eyes with me, and I knew I had awakened a side of Slider I had never seen before. He pointed to the store, and my eyes followed his hand, wondering what he was doing.

The lock clicked open, and I didn't see it coming. Slider slung the door open, and I knew I was screwed.

****

Slider

A sick, twisted smile spread across my lips. "Get out, Fay." I was done playing this game with her.

She shook her head. "Slider."

Why the hell did the one word she could say have to be my goddamn name? She hadn't said my name but for the time in the kitchen and to hear her say it now brought me to my knees. "Fayth." She rolled her eyes and held her hand out to me. I pulled her from the truck and grabbed the pad of paper she had tossed on the dash.

"You're going to be the death of me, Fay. I've never met anyone as stubborn as you are." I slammed the door shut behind her and threaded my fingers through hers. "Glue," I mumbled as she looked up at me. I wasn't joking when I had said I wasn't going to let her out of my sight.

Fayth glanced around nervously, and her grip on my hand tightened.

"Is this the first time you've been out of the house?" I asked as we neared the front door.

She nodded and ducked into the door as I opened it. The smell of leather and freedom greeted me as the door shut behind us, and I felt at home. I looked around, taking in the motorcycles staged throughout the store and the merchandise staggered all over the spacious show room.

I hadn't realized Fayth hadn't left the house since she had been shot. I guess coming to a place she wasn't used to wasn't the best idea, but we were here now, and there wasn't any going back.

"I'm going to assume that you've never been to a place like this." She rolled her eyes and looked around. "It's just like any other store, just with motorcycles."

Obviously. She scribbled on her paper.

"Keep an open mind, Fay, you might be surprised." I looked down at her and smirked. "For the record, your feistiness comes across on paper, too." I winked at her and pulled her further into the store.

We wandered around, looking at each display, and I took notice of the things Fayth actually took time to examine. She had a thing for one of the Harley shirts, and I knew it would look hot as hell on her.

We were standing next to a new Dyna Glide, and Fayth was eyeing it warily. "What's wrong?"

Is this what your motorcycle looks like?

"For the most part. Less shiny and slightly older."

She nodded and brushed her hand over the handlebars. *Fast?* she scribbled.

"Plenty fast. I'll have to take you for a ride sometime."

Fayth shook her head and wandered back over to the shirt she had been admiring before. "Pick out your size, I'll buy you your first Harley shirt."

She shook her head and held up her purse. She pointed her thumb at her chest and mouthed the word "no." She folded the shirt over her arm and headed to the cashier.

I nabbed the shirt from her and dodged over to the leather chaps I had wanted. Fayth hit me on the back. "I have to say, the one nice thing about you not being able to talk is that you can't argue with me."

"Slider," she protested quietly.

I looked over my shoulder at her and shook my head. "Nope, not going to work this time."

She tugged on my coat, but I shook her off and set everything on the checkout. She furiously wrote on her pad of paper as I pulled out some cash and handed it to the cashier. "Writing a book there, Fay?" Instead of showing me the page, she just shook her head and tucked the note pad under her arm. "I don't get to see what you wrote?" I took the bag the cashier held up, grabbed Fayth's hand, and headed out the door.

"Give me the note pad," I said after we got in the truck. I held my hand out, and she slapped it down. She crossed her arms over her chest and glared at me.

"Your handwriting gets a little sloppy when you're feisty, Firecracker," I said, smirking.

She rolled her eyes and pointed at the paper. *Why did you buy me that? I don't want you to buy me anything. I'll pay you back when we get home. Don't do that again.*

I rolled my eyes and tossed her notebook on the dash. "That's a load of shit."

Fayth grabbed the paper and madly scribbled. *It's not shit.*

"It is. Now, where do you want to eat?" I started the truck and backed out of the parking stall.

Nowhere.

"Never heard of it. I saw a burger joint we passed."

I glanced over, and she held up the paper. *No. We can eat at the theater.*

"I'm not eating popcorn for lunch, Fay. I want real food." I pulled out of the parking lot and headed toward the burger place.

She thrust the notebook in my face. *Theater. Trust me.*

"Fayth, I don't thin—"

"Slider."

One word. Dammit.

We passed the burger place, and I headed to the theater.

"You better be right, Fay."

She tossed the notepad back on the dash and smirked.

I let her think she had won this round, but I had a few tricks up my sleeve.

****

504

Chapter 10

Fayth

How in the hell did this happen? Here I thought I had the upper hand by deciding to eat at the theater, but I realized it was a small victory now.

"Hand me the popcorn," Slider whispered.

I can't believe you got all of this junk food. We still have our meal coming, I wrote after I handed him the huge bucket of popcorn.

"You can't go to the movies and not load up on popcorn, candy, and soda."

I swear to Christ, you're a fourteen-year-old trapped inside a thirty-five-year-old body. He grabbed the notepad and held it close to his face.

"Once the movie starts, I'm not going to be able to read your feisty notes."

I grabbed the paper from him and rolled my eyes. I had never wanted to be able to talk more than I did right now. Not only had Slider bought-out the concession stand, he had also picked the movie we were seeing.

He had asked me at the ticket counter what movie I had wanted to see, but he had acted like he couldn't read my handwriting when he saw it was the latest chick flick. So, here we were, watching some crash and bash action movie.

"How long until they bring our food? You sure they know how to find us?"

I rolled my eyes. This was another new experience for Slider. Apparently, the theater back in Rockton hadn't joined the latest craze of the dining while you watch theater.

Soon. They will. They had taken our order in the seats we were sitting in, so I wasn't worried about them finding us, and it was like any restaurant when it came to how long the food would take.

"Well, thank God I bought popcorn. It'll hold me over until they decide to bring me my feast."

Feast was about right. Slider had ordered mozzarella sticks, spinach dip, a huge, half-pound burger with sweet potato fries, and a side of boneless chicken wings. I had ordered a BLT with fries.

I think you'll live.

"Feistiness coming though on paper again, Firecracker."

I saw the waitress coming towards our seats with a heavily laden down tray with our lunch. I poked Slider and motioned for him to swing his tray in front of him.

"Hell yes." He rubbed his hands together and watched the waitress fill his tray up.

"Um, can I put this on your tray?" she asked, holding up the spinach dip.

I nodded, and she crammed my tray with the dip and my sandwich.

The waitress disappeared down the aisle, rubbing her shoulder. "That chick was a beast for carrying all of this food," Slider said around a mouthful. "You can have some of this if you want, Firecracker."

I grabbed my pad of paper. *Why are you calling me that?*

"Feisty," was the only word of explanation he gave me before he took a huge bite of his burger.

The lights dimmed, and I focused on the screen, watching the previews as I started eating.

"I should have ordered the nachos," Slider mumbled.

I was at the movies with a fourteen-year-old man-child.

How did this happen?

****

Slider

"Where are you?"

"On the way back to the house."

"Where were you all day? I talked to Marco, and he said he hasn't seen either of you."

I didn't know I needed to report to Leo about my every move. "Out."

"Something has come up, and I need to go out of town. Get home as soon as you can."

I shoved my phone in my pocket and sighed. It was only half-past four, but Fayth was huddled in the corner of the seat, her hands under her head, and was lightly sleeping.

It had been a good day with Fayth, and now I had no idea what was going to happen.

Although she didn't say it, I knew she had a good time with me, which I knew she needed. She was so focused on not being able to talk that it was holding her back just letting the words come.

I liked Fayth, I had to accept that. There wasn't a man in this world who would leave in the middle of the night for a woman if he didn't care about her in the least.

I liked her. There, I fucking admit it, but that was it.

At least, for now.

****

Chapter 11

Fayth

"Fay. Fay, wake up."

I batted away the hand shaking me. I didn't want to wake up.

"Fayth, wake your ass up."

Grr. Why couldn't I just sleep?

"Come on, Firecracker. Leo is waiting for us. Something is up."

I perked up and wondered what was going on. I heard Slider's door slam, and seconds later, my door was opened.

"Come on, Fay. I want a nap just as bad as you do, but first, we'll talk to Leo." Slider held his hand out to me, and I surveyed him. He appeared exhausted and ready to fall over right there in the driveway.

I had forgotten he had driven here through the night and had zero sleep. I had at least managed a couple of hours before I had woken up saying his name. Although, that felt like days ago.

I grabbed his hand and let him lead me to the front door as I sleepily tried to keep up with him. I was in another situation where I wished I could just speak. All I wanted to do was stay sleeping where I didn't have to think. This mute shit was getting more annoying all the time.

As soon as Slider opened the door, Leo started barking orders. "Fay, head upstairs. The doctor is here to look you over. He needs to clear you for travel. Slider, come to my office. There are things we need to go over."

I grabbed Leo's hand and opened my mouth, praying the words I needed to say would come out.

"Fayth, go upstairs. Trust me." He shook off my hand and headed to his office.

Slider pressed a kiss to the side of my head. "Don't worry, Fayth," he whispered. He followed Leo, and I stood there, ready to scream. Things were happening around me, and I couldn't do anything because I couldn't get the words I needed to say out.

I stomped up the stairs, pissed off. My bedroom door was open, and Marco was leaning against the doorjamb.

"Did Uncle Leo talk to you?"

I growled and nodded.

"I'm going to assume it was more like he talked *at* you," he said, laughing.

Talking at me was a much better description. Talking to me would mean I actually had a say about what was going on and was not just being ordered around.

"The doc is in there. I was waiting for you to get back. That dude gives me a weird vibe, and I didn't want to leave him alone in your room. I gotta finish packing." Marco headed down the hallway and was in his room before what he had said registered. Pack? For what?

Ugh, so many questions with no answers. It was so much easier when I just sat in my room and no one really talked to me. Now they talked to me, and I couldn't say anything back unless I had my paper with me.

"Fayth, there you are. Leo called me and told me what has been going on."

I looked in my room and saw Dr. Stevens standing next to my bed with his arms crossed over his chest.

"Leo told me you have been speaking."

I wouldn't really say one word is speaking. I nodded and stepped into my room. Marco's words about the doctor giving him a weird vibe stuck with me. I had never really paid attention to Dr. Stevens before, but now that I was back to trying to participate in the real world, I needed to pay attention.

I nodded and looked around for a piece of paper.

"Can I ask what you've been saying? Leo was rather short on the phone with me."

"Slider." I found some paper on my dresser and now started the search for a pen.

"Oh. Um, what exactly does that mean?"

I found a pen on the floor and quickly scribbled. *Friend.*

"Okay, I'm assuming he must be a rather close friend for his name to be the first word you chose to speak. What other words are you able to say?"

I shook my head and dropped the paper.

"Just the one word? I'm not sure what that means. I'm not exactly a psychiatrist. That would probably be more in their field of expertise."

Then, what in the hell was he doing here? I needed someone to help me understand what in the hell was going on inside my head.

"Leo asked me to come over and make sure you are able to travel."

After a quick physical, the doctor left, letting me know there wasn't any reason I couldn't travel.

Now, I needed to figure out where the hell I was traveling to.

****

Slider

"Have a seat," Leo ordered when we ambled into his office. Everything was dark mahogany and expensive-looking. Much like the rest of the house.

"Everything okay?" I asked as I sat down in the leather chair in front of his desk, and he sank into the large, black leather chair behind it. Normally, I wouldn't be one to have someone to tell me to sit down, but I was in Leo's house and knew I needed to show him respect.

"No, things are far from okay, but that's not what we need to talk about." Leo picked up a glass half-full with a dark amber liquid and took a sip. "Like I said, I need to go out of town, and I don't want to leave Fayth alone."

"I can stay as long as you need me to."

"I'd rather you not."

Then, what in the hell did he want me to talk about? "I guess I'll just say goodbye to Fayth and head back to Rockton." I stood, pissed the hell off.

"No need to say goodbye. I want you to go back to Rockton, but I want you to take Fayth and Marco with you."

"Why? What's going on that you can't leave Fayth and Marco here?"

"I have some business associates who aren't seeing things the way they should, and I need to change their view. Having Fayth and Marco in Rockton is what's best."

"This isn't going to follow them?"

"I hope not, but I don't know. Having Fayth back in Rockton will help ease my mind."

I ran my fingers through my hair and paced the length of Leo's office. "You really think I can keep her safe? Hell, the last time I watched her, she got shot in the fucking head."

"She did."

"That's all you have to say?"

Leo shrugged and drained his glass. "There isn't much to say, Slider. You fucked up. Don't do it again."

"She's not going to trust me to keep her safe. Hell, I don't trust myself to keep her safe."

"She does. Did you not spend all day with her?"

"Well, yeah. But this is fucking different."

"It's not different. The threat that is possible now was there all day. Now, you just know about it."

"I can't do this, Leo." Fear took over my body at the thought of Fayth getting hurt or even dying.

"You can, and you will. You're the only person I trust with Fayth right now."

"What about one of your men? You had Princeton and Creed in Rockton. Why can't they watch her while you are gone?" I may have hated Princeton and Creed, but I knew they were damn good at what they did.

"Because I need my best men with me right now." Leo steepled his hands in front of him and looked me up and down. "You don't know yet, do you?"

Know what? I had no idea what the hell Leo was talking about. All I knew was I was not the man to keep Fayth safe. "What?"

"All of you Knights have a problem accepting the fact."

"What the fuck are you talking about?"

"Although, from what I hear, King and Rigid didn't put up much of a fight."

"You're speaking in fucking riddles, man. What in the fuck have I not accepted?"

Leo laughed and shook his head. "No, I'm not going to put you out of your misery. I'm going to let you figure it out on your own."

"What the hell ever, man. I'll figure out your goddamn riddle while you find someone else to watch over Fayth."

The smile fell from Leo's face and he stood. "No. I've already decided. You're not going to change my mind, Slider. You may doubt yourself, but I don't. A man like you won't let anything happen to Fayth a second time."

"She's not healthy enough to travel. She was shot two months ago."

Leo raised the hem of his shirt and pointed to a three-inch angry, red mark on his side. "I was grazed by a bullet two weeks ago and you didn't even know. Fayth is a fighter and more than healthy enough for a three-hour car ride. Try another excuse."

"You're making a mistake."

Leo smiled evilly. "A man like me does not make mistakes, Slider. We're done talking about this." He grabbed his suit jacket off the back of his chair and slid his arms into the sleeves. "You leave in the morning. I know you haven't slept. I would rather you not drive my nephew and sister in a sleepless stupor."

"She isn't going to like this. She hated living in Rockton."

Leo shook his head. "No, my sister actually enjoyed living in Rockton but was confused because she felt like she was leaving her family by being there. I'm doing this for her, as much as I'm doing it to keep her safe."

"She always told me she hated it."

"Because you were another reason why she was confused."

"You're speaking in riddles again."

"No, I'm not." Leo glanced at his watch and shook his head. "As much as I would love to continue this conversation with you, Slider. I need to be on a plane in half an hour."

"You're leaving now?" Panic climbed up my throat.

"Yes. As I said, I have something to take care of. Trust yourself and don't let Fayth run you over." Leo picked up a duffel bag he had sitting by the side of his desk. "I hope to be back soon, but I don't know for sure." He headed out the door and looked over his shoulder at me. "Will you die for her, Slider?"

"Ten times over." I didn't hesitate. I knew if it ever came down to Fayth or me, I would sacrifice myself every time.

Leo nodded. "Good. I'll say goodbye to Fayth and Marco, and then I'll be gone. Take care of my family, Slider. They are all I have."

I nodded, unable to talk. I was pleased Leo had enough faith in me to take care of Fayth and Marco, but I was also terrified he had made a horrible mistake.

There was only one thing for sure. I would die before anything ever happened to Fayth again. Nothing would touch her.

******

Chapter 12

Fayth

Do you think we could stop? I held the paper up to Slider and prayed he wasn't like a typical male who hated to stop during a trip.

He nodded once, and I sighed. Thank God. I had told Marco ten times to make sure to go to the bathroom before we had left this morning, but I hadn't taken my own advice.

"I see someone didn't go to the bathroom before we left," Marco teased.

I rolled my eyes and elbowed him in the side. Slider was driving, and I was wedged between him and Marco as we made our way back to Rockton.

"Yeah, I do remember her yelling at you to pee," Slider said while he chuckled.

Now, I elbowed him in the side. *Ass,* I wrote.

Slider shook his head and pointed down the road. "Two miles back I saw a sign for a big ol' truck stop. We can do a pit stop there and hopefully pick up some breakfast."

Breakfast was another reason why Slider was an ass. He had insisted I didn't need to make anything because we could just grab something on the way. Except, I didn't want to stop and grab *something.* I wanted actual sustenance. Not some half-warm breakfast sandwich from a warming table at a seedy truck stop.

"Uncurl your lip, Fayth. I promise to feed you something delicious."

I tossed my notepad on the dash and crossed my arms over my chest. I really doubted we were going to find anything good to eat at a gas station.

"Mom is a food snob. I bet you won't be able to find anything that she'll eat at a gas station."

"Yeah, I've kind of picked up on that." Slider laughed and ran his fingers through his hair.

I glared at Marco and grabbed the pad of paper. *Way to take your mother's side.*

Marco shrugged and put his headphones on.

Slider took the exit to the gas station, and I was surprised at the size of the building. *This thing is huge,* I wrote.

"That's what she said." Slider winked at me and grabbed my hand while he slid out of the truck.

I rolled my eyes and whacked him with my notepad.

"I'm gonna run to the bathroom," Marco called and headed into the gas station.

I moved to follow Marco, but Slider tugged me back and shook his head. "You don't leave my sight, Fayth."

I motioned to where Marco had disappeared into the building. What the hell was the difference from Marco to me?

"We're right behind him." Slider tugged me to the door. "I told Leo nothing would happen to you, and I intend to keep that promise."

As nice as that sounded, there was no way Slider could be with me all of the time.

I looked around once we strode through the door, and I was again taken aback by the sheer size of the gas station. The sweet smell of cinnamon hit my nose and I spotted the Cinnabon to the right of the door. My stomach rumbled and I knew that a cinnamon roll would be leaving with me.

Slider pulled me past the counter filled with those fluffy pillows of sweet dough and headed down a short hallway that led to the bathrooms. He crossed his arms over his chest and leaned against the wall as I walked in the bathroom, and he was in the same spot when I walked out.

"I gave Marco some money to get some cinnamon rolls." Slider grabbed my hand and tugged me further down the hallway. Silently, I was jumping up and down, happy as hell Slider had read my mind. "I told him to meet us at the restaurant."

I shook my head no and grabbed Slider's arm. I didn't want to eat at some fast food place. Marco was somewhat right when he had said I was a food snob.

"Just trust me, Firecracker."

We headed back the way we came, past the gas station cashier and then down another corridor where there were video games and those machines where you stuck a quarter in and got a toy or candy out. The smell of bacon wafted around us, and the hallway opened up to a restaurant with red booths and white tables.

"Just two?" a waitress asked while walking past with a tray overflowing with food.

"Make it three," Slider replied, holding up three fingers.

"Sit anywhere on the left. Lola called in sick and we're shorthanded," the waitress called.

Slider pulled me over to a booth in the corner, and I slid all the way in. Slider sat next to me and threw his arm over the back of the booth. "Eat up, Firecracker. I'm pretty sure you'll be eating your words soon."

I rolled my eyes and grabbed a menu. Anything you could possibly think of was listed, and my stomach growled reading all the different way they did waffles.

"Holy hell, this place could have its own zip code. I accidentally wandered down the wrong hallway and saw a Ping-Pong table, foosball, and a laundromat." Marco scooted into the booth across from us and set a plastic bag next to him.

"We're in the biggest truck stop in Illinois. It's right on the border to Wisconsin. I try to stop here whenever I'm nearby."

Marco grabbed a menu and opened it up. "Did you stop on the way down?"

"No. I just filled up the tank and headed straight down." Slider flipped over both of our cups for coffee and signaled for the waitress.

"All right, what can I get for you guys?" The waitress flipped open her notepad and clicked her pen.

"I'll have four eggs, sunny-side up, hash browns loaded, sausage, and sourdough toast," Marco said before setting down his menu.

He had looked at the menu for all of ten seconds. How in the hell had he decided that quickly?

"And you, ma'am?" The waitress looked down at me, her pen poised to write down my order.

"Slider."

"Sorry, Firecracker," he whispered in my ear and leaned over. "Point at what you want, Fay, and I'll tell her."

I pointed at the buttermilk waffles with strawberries. I held up one finger, letting him know I only wanted one. Lord knew my ass didn't need more than that.

"She'll have the strawberry waffles, full order, with a side of bacon," he told the waitress.

My jaw dropped, and I shook my head no.

Slider ignored me. "And I'll have the butter pecan waffles with a side of sausage and bacon. Coffee for both of us, too."

"I'll be right back with the coffee," the waitress said before she flounced off to the kitchen.

I can't eat all of that, I wrote and thrust it in Slider's face.

"Calm down, Firecracker. Whatever you can't eat, I'll finish."

That's not the point.

"Then, what is the point?" He grabbed my cup and put it next to his. The waitress came back to fill our coffee cups and set down three glasses of water.

I know what I want.

"I never said you didn't know what you want. I just figured I was hungry, but not enough for a double order of waffles. Eat what you can, and I'll finish off what you can't."

I crossed my arms over my chest. Well, I guess that was okay, although I still didn't like it. *Next time tell me that.*

Slider laughed and took a sip of his coffee. "Run everything by you, got it, Firecracker." He set down his cup and laughed, turning his attention to Marco. "Was your mom always this feisty?"

"Yeah, except you never really saw it. She's used to getting her way."

I balled up my napkin and tossed it at Marco. Where the hell was the loyalty to his mother?

"Hey," Marco protested. "I'm just telling the truth."

I rolled my eyes and grabbed Marco's napkin. He could use the one I had thrown at him.

"Are we staying in the same house?" Marco asked.

I nodded, but Slider shook his head no. *What?* I scribbled. Where in the hell were we staying then?

"I've got a place just outside of town. Not many people know about it." Slider pushed back his coffee cup and handed me mine. I hadn't even taken a drink of it yet.

"I thought maybe we were going to stay at the clubhouse. That would have been cool."

"Nah, there isn't enough room for all of us there. I have my room, but there aren't any extra rooms."

Wait. What happened to the house we were staying in?

Slider shook his head. "Leo let the lease go after he moved you back to Chicago. With such short notice, he wasn't able to find a new house."

But what about all of my stuff I left there? I had bought all new furniture when Marco and I had moved to Rockton. Furniture I was absolutely in love with.

"Leo had everything put into storage."

Well, that was relief, but I was still hesitant moving in with Slider. *Why can't we just stay in a hotel?*

"Because Leo doesn't know how long he'll be gone, and I can't keep you safe in a hotel. My house is better."

The waitress returned with a full tray, and I didn't have time to argue. I set my notepad on the seat next to me and watched all of the delicious-looking food she set down. Marco had a huge platter in front of him. He bugged his eyes out at it and immediately dug in.

Three huge waffles smothered with bright red berries were set in front of me, and I knew I wasn't going to be able to eat them all, but I would sure try.

"Try not to drool, Fay," Slider said as he laughed.

I elbowed him in the side and picked up my knife and fork. I wanted to tell him to shut it, but I didn't want to have to pick up my notebook. Having to write everything down was a pain in the ass sometimes. I was going to have to figure out another way to communicate. I sliced off a huge bite of waffles and moaned as I chewed. Holy hell, that was the best waffle I had ever eaten.

"I'll be expecting your apology after you're done eating," Slider replied, chuckling.

I rolled my eyes and spotted his plate of bacon and sausage when I looked over at him. I stealthy stabbed one of the links and moved it over to my plate. At least, I thought it was stealthy.

"Didn't you know you shouldn't touch a man's sausage without permission?" Slider asked, lowering his voice.

I choked on my waffle.

"Dude," Marco said, laughing. "I don't want to hear anything about your sausage and my mom."

"Then, she better ask next time," Slider said, smirking.

Oh Jesus. How in the hell did we get here? I took another bite, hoping if I just ignored Slider, he would shut up.

"I don't know, dude. If some chick wants to grab my sausage, I don't think she'll need to ask before."

I slammed my fork down and glared at Marco.

"There really is an advantage to you only being able to say one word," Marco said, laughing. "Thank God that word is Slider, and not no."

I picked up my butter knife and pointed it at him.

"Easy, Marco," Slider scolded. Thank God Slider was being an adult for two seconds. "You never know what your mom could do with that butter knife. You might not have a sausage left after she's done with it."

Marco busted out laughing.

"Slider."

"Oh, I know that tone," Marco said, shaking his head. "You're in trouble."

"I'll just take her notebook away."

I grabbed my notebook, shoved it under my butt and sat on it. He was not about to take my only way to communicate.

"You can't sit down forever, Firecracker."

I crossed my arms over my chest and sighed. There were other ways to communicate, but I didn't think giving Slider the bird in front of Marco was the most responsible thing to do.

Slider took pity on me and nodded at Marco. "Eat so we can get back on the road. We still have two hours of being crammed into my truck."

Marco ate, smirking and chuckling the whole time.

I needed to get my voice back sooner rather than later. How in the hell was I going to manage that?

****

Chapter 13

Slider

"This is it? This is where you live?" Marco asked, amazement in his voice.

Fayth's jaw was dropped and her eyes were bugged out taking in my house.

We were sitting in the truck, the motor off, while Fayth and Marco stared out the windshield. "Yeah. This is it."

"When you said you lived outside of town, this wasn't exactly what I had pictured. I was thinking more of a rundown trailer down by the river."

Fayth elbowed Marco and shrugged at me. She probably thought the same thing. "It was a foreclosure that I was able to snap up for cheap."

"Dude, it's like a brand new house."

"It's a year old."

Fayth grabbed her paper. *WOW!*

I chuckled and opened my door, then held my hand out to Fayth and pulled her across the seat. "Can you get the bags, Marco?"

Marco grabbed the four bags I had loaded into the back of the truck, and we headed up the walkway. I wasn't sure why Fayth and Marco were in awe of my house. Where they lived was three times as big. This was just a three-bedroom ranch with four-car garage. The attached garage was what made the house seem so big.

"I don't have a lot of furniture, but there is enough to get by." I unlocked the side door and reached in to open the garage door.

It slowly lifted and Marco dropped the bags when he saw the cars I had inside.

"Is that a Mustang?"

"Yup. '68."

"Wait. Hold up. How the hell do you have a Mustang, and a brand new fucking Corvette?" Marco sauntered over to the pitch black Corvette and trailed his fingers up the fender.

"Your uncle doesn't have nice cars?" I asked, avoiding the question about where I got mine. I wasn't exactly legal in everything I did.

"Yeah, but it's not like he'll let me touch them. Can I drive it?" he asked eagerly.

Fayth shook her head and stood in between Marco and me. She pretended she was driving a car with her hands out in front of her, then acted like she crashed and shook her whole body.

"One time!" Marco shouted.

"Huh?" What in the hell?

Fayth pointed at Marco and shook her head.

"One time I crashed Uncle Leo's car, and now Mom won't let me live it down."

"Wait, didn't you turn sixteen like a month ago?"

"Yeah," Marco replied sheepishly.

"So, how the hell did you crash your uncle's car if you just turned sixteen?"

Fayth smirked and crossed her arms over her chest.

"Because I might have borrowed it to go to the movies, and I might have hit the curb." Fayth grunted and held up her hand. "And a mailbox," Marco added. Fayth shook her head again. "And then the ditch," Marco finished. Or at least, I thought he finished. "Then a chicken coop." Fayth nodded and turned her eyes on me, then acted like she was driving again.

"Dude, how the hell do you hit the ditch *and* a chicken coop?" I laughed.

"Very carefully?" Marco shrugged.

"Yeah, you ain't touching my cars." I grabbed two of the bags Marco had dropped and headed to the door that led to the house. "Maybe when you are forty," I added over my shoulder.

"Forty, really? That's like twenty-four years. These things will be rusted-out and sitting in a junk yard by then."

Not if I had anything to do with it. These cars were in pristine condition now, and I planned on them staying that way.

"Why'd you have to tell him about the chicken coop?" Marco complained as he followed. "I was so close to him letting me drive his car."

I set the bags next to the kitchen island, and Fayth wandered around. The kitchen and living room were that open concept shit, where if you were in one, you could still see what was going on in other.

Marco stood in the middle of the living room. "Dude, you have no furniture."

He wasn't completely right. I did have furniture, there just wasn't a lot of it. "I don't have people over. A recliner, end table, and TV are more than what I need."

I didn't think I had ever used the end table. Hell, I could probably count on one hand how many times I had sat in the recliner.

For the past few months, if I wasn't over at Fayth's, I was at the clubhouse trying to catch up on shit I was missing.

"Am I at least going to have a bed?" Marco asked.

"Yeah, the spare bedroom had a twin bed. That can be your room."

"Sweet. Where is it?" he asked as he wandered down the hall.

"Second door on the right. The first door on the right is your bathroom." I turned to look at Fayth and crossed my arms over my chest. "Will it do?" There really wasn't a reason why she wouldn't like it here. Well, at least she didn't know of any reasons of why she shouldn't like it here. I was hoping she wouldn't find out until bedtime that I had only two beds, and Marco was already using one of them.

Fayth nodded and wandered over to the fridge. She opened it and I dove for the door, but missed. Fayth slapped her hand over her face and her skin went pale. She slammed the door shut and looked at me like I had just killed her cat.

"I haven't been here in over two weeks. I'm assuming the Chinese I brought home went bad." I shrugged. "I should probably clean that out."

Fayth gave me a thumbs up and backed away from the fridge. She grabbed her notepad. *I can bring some of my furniture over if you want. At least a couch.*

"You don't need to do that, Firecracker."

Yes, I do, if I want a place to sit.

I looked in the living room and eyed up the recliner. She was probably right. I didn't think we could all fit in the chair. "I'll call some of the guys and see if they're able to grab some stuff."

Fayth roamed around, opening cabinets and shaking her head while I called King.

"Yo, what's up, brother?" he answered.

"Not much. We just got back into town."

"Hell, you made good time. Where are you at?"

"The house."

"Wow, you actually took her to your house. I figured you were just going to stay at the clubhouse."

Fayth meandered down the short hallway and disappeared into the bathroom.

"Not enough room. We have Marco with us."

"You know he could have taken Roam's room. He's out in Kentucky doing Lord knows what right now."

I leaned against the counter. "Yeah, but I just thought this would be better for Fayth."

"She doing okay?" I had called King last night and given him the quick rundown of what was going on. All I had mentioned about Fayth was she was coming back with me.

"Yeah, still not speaking except for a word here or there. She's getting damn fast at writing out her words, though," I chuckled.

"Damn man, that fucking sucks. They know when she'll start talking again?"

"No. They said she'll talk when she's ready. Physically and mentally, she's fine. She just can't find her voice."

"It'll come, brother."

"I hope so." I heard the water turn on in the bathroom and knew Fayth would be back anytime. "I was calling wondering if you were able to get a couple of guys to go to Fayth's storage unit and bring some of her furniture over."

"Yeah, we can grab it today. You want it all?"

Now, this is where I was torn. I knew Fayth had two beds in storage, and if King brought the beds over, she wouldn't have to sleep in my room with me. "Just living room shit and probably kitchen stuff. Hell, stop at the store for groceries too," I laughed.

"I'm not sure about the groceries, but we can get the furniture to you. You gonna give me the address to that mansion you bought now?"

I wasn't kidding when I had said I don't have people over. King knew I had bought a house, but I never told him where. "I'll text it to you."

"All right, see you in a few."

I shoved my phone in my pocket just as Fayth flounced out of the bathroom. "Find everything okay?"

Fayth grabbed her pad of paper. *The toilet is hard to miss.*

I laughed and ran my fingers through my hair. I guess that was a stupid question to ask. "King said he would bring some of your furniture over. I asked him to bring groceries too, but we might be shit out of luck on that one."

Fayth gave me a thumbs up and yawned.

"Tired?" Fayth nodded, and I motioned towards the recliner. "Take a nap, Firecracker. I'll wake you up when your stuff gets here."

"Slider," she whispered.

Jesus. Did she even know what she did to me when she said that? "Yeah?"

She just looked at me, uncertainty written all over her face.

"Just go relax, Fayth. I see your mind running a hundred miles an hour. There's nothing for you to do right now. Trust me."

Fayth hesitated but finally made her way over to the chair. Before she sank into it and popped open the footrest, she grabbed the blanket that was tossed on the back and wrapped it around herself.

"I'll be in the garage, okay?"

Fayth nodded sleepily, and I knew it wouldn't take long for her to be knocked out.

I checked on Marco, who was camped out on the bed with his headphones on, listening to whatever shit he called music. I told him I would be in the garage if he needed me, and I couldn't help but notice how much he reminded me of his mom when he gave me a thumbs up.

I moved to the garage and hoped working under the hood of a car would help distract me from what I was feeling.

It felt damn good to have Fayth and Marco under my roof. What I always said I never wanted to do was happening to me, and I didn't even want to stop it.

Fayth was with me, and I never wanted her to leave.

****

Chapter 14

Fayth

"I brought five rotisserie chickens, two pounds of potato salad, two pounds of some noodle salad Lo likes, and about five different kinds of chips. I also grabbed some extras to throw into the fridge."

"I still think we should have gotten one more chicken."

"There are ten of us. I don't think half a chicken a person is enough."

I groggily opened my eyes and looked around the kitchen. My eyes fell on Cyn and Meg, who were arguing about chicken while they unloaded bags of groceries. When I had fallen asleep, I had thought only a couple of guys were going to drop off my furniture. Now, there were ten people here and a feast of rotisserie chicken was going to happen.

"Yeah, well, two of those people are growing teenagers who could probably eat a chicken a piece." Cyn balled up all of the plastic bags and shoved them into the garbage. "Not to mention the four grown men out there who can keep up with the teenagers when it comes to eating."

"Shit, you're right. Maybe we can have Turtle run and get two more chickens." Meg began popping open the containers of salads and then started searching in the cabinets. "Jesus, you can totally tell a bachelor lives here. I don't think he has anything that isn't plastic or paper for utensils."

"Maybe Fayth has something in all of those boxes that the guys are unloading," Cyn suggested.

"Slider told them to leave all of the boxes in the garage until Fayth and Marco go through them. I think they're only bringing in the furniture."

"Thank God for that. Hopefully, there is a kitchen table in there. I honestly don't know how Slider has lived here this long with nothing more than a recliner and a couple of beds." Cyn leaned against the counter and looked down by her feet. "I can't believe Micha is still sleeping. Do you think that I should wake him and make sure he is okay?"

Meg waved her arms and shook her head. "Hell to the no, girl. As long as that baby is sleeping, let him be."

Baby? Oh hell, Cyn had the baby while I was knocked out and then shipped off to Chicago. I tossed the blanket on the floor and sprung from the chair.

"Oh, you're awake," Meg cried as I bound into the kitchen.

I rounded the counter and saw Cyn rocking a dark blue baby carrier on the floor with her foot. "And she's as mesmerized with Micha as much as you are," Cyn laughed as I kneeled next to the carrier.

"Can you really blame her? He's damn cute."

Micha was sleeping peacefully, a light blue blanket tucked round him, and I had to fight the urge to unbuckle him and cradle him in my arms. It had been years since I had held a baby.

"Oh, I know that look. Just like I told Cyn, do not unbuckle that baby," Meg tsked. "Now that you're awake, you can run out to the garage and find some pots, pans, and plates. All Slider had was paper plates and a mountain of plastic forks."

I looked around for my pad of paper and spied it on the counter. I stood, holding up a finger to let Meg and Cyn know to hold on. *Hi,* I wrote in big, bold letters.

"Hi," Meg and Cyn chirped at the same time. They both looked at me expectantly.

How long have you been here?

"We got here a little bit ago. We were trying to help guide the boys on where to set stuff, but they sent us away when they couldn't handle us anymore," Meg laughed.

"Remy and Marco were listening to us, but it was the guys who were giving us a hard time. We started unpacking the boxes, but Slider insisted that you needed to unpack them."

That was nonsense. It wasn't like I had anything private in them. Opening a couple boxes of plates and cups that were mine wasn't exactly invading my privacy. *I'll look for some plates.*

"Perfect. I think the guys were about to start bringing in the furniture. They were trying to figure out which door to go through. That couch you have is enormous."

My sectional really was huge. When I had seen it in the local furniture store, I knew I had to have it. It had barely fit in the old living room, but I knew it was going to be perfect in Slider's living room.

"I heard Rigid threaten to saw it in half to make it in the door," Cyn said, with a giggle.

Oh, hell no. There is no way anyone was going to take a saw to that couch. *What?!?!* I scrawled out.

"Oh, don't worry. Slider told him there wasn't a chance in hell that they were going to do that. He said he used to sleep on it in your old house," Meg said reassuringly.

I headed out to the garage with Meg and Cyn following closely behind. "Leave the door open so I can hear Micha cry," Cyn called to Meg.

Slider, King, Rigid, Marco, and Remy were gathered around my couch, each of them eyeing it up.

"All in favor of the saw," Rigid called.

"Slider," I yelled as I walked down the stairs, flailing my arms.

"Fayth, what are you doing?" he asked.

I rolled my eyes. Like I could tell him what I was doing. I motioned to the couch and shook my head.

"Is this like charades?" Remy asked.

"Yeah, dude. She already said the only word she can. After that, it's either crazy hand gestures, or she has a pad of paper that she writes everything on," Marco explained. "If you really piss her off, she'll flip you off."

King, Rigid, and Slider busted out laughing while Cyn and Meg giggled behind me. I stomped my foot and pointed at Marco.

"So, what does it mean when she stomps and points?" Remy asked.

Marco stroked his chin and tilted his head. "I'm assuming it's the same as flipping me off, but she can't do that because I'm her kid."

King and Rigid laughed even harder, and Slider tried to smother his laugh with the back of his hand.

I moved towards Marco, and he took off running.

"Abort, abort," he shouted to Remy as they both ran out of the garage.

"Did anyone else feel like they were listening to commentary for a wildlife video?" King asked, still laughing.

Rigid bent over, bracing his arms on his knees, and wheezed uncontrollably. "Yes," he gasped.

I tossed my hands up in the air and stomped back into the house. There was no way I was going to get my point across to those buffoons right now. I grabbed my pad of paper off the kitchen island. *Cut it, and I cut you,* I scrawled.

I stomped back to the garage and tossed the pad of paper at Slider. Marco and Remy were standing to the side of the garage door and peeking in. I shook my fist at Marco, and they took off running again.

Slider picked up the pad of paper that had bounced off of his chest, read it, and then showed it to King and Rigid. "I'm going to have to veto the saw," Slider decided.

I crossed my arms over my chest and huffed. The threat of bloodshed seemed to be the only thing that got through to these guys.

"We'll figure out a way to get it in without cutting it, Fayth," King said reassuringly.

I nodded, satisfied with the fact I could trust King's word.

"Dinner in half an hour," Meg announced. "So, figure out how to get that couch in there so we have somewhere to sit beside monkey-piling into the recliner."

"Speaking of dinner," Cyn nodded over her shoulder, and we all glanced in the kitchen. Micha's little feet were kicking the blanket off of him, and I could hear him making little baby noises. "Little monster is going to be hungry in about five minutes."

I eagerly raised my hand to volunteer to feed Micha.

"Put your hand down, woman. You can only feed him if you have Cyn's boobs," Rigid called.

Cyn rolled her eyes. "Jesus, as nicely as Rigid put it, I'm breastfeeding. But as soon as the monster is done eating, he's all yours."

"I'll get dinner set out. You two go chat in the living room." Meg shooed us in the door.

"Put down the saw," Cyn called as Meg shut the door.

I worriedly looked over my shoulder, and Meg rolled her eyes. "I promise they won't cut up your couch. I'd like to think that Rigid was only joking, but you can never be too sure. King won't let anything happen to it."

I leaned against the island and watched Cyn grab little Micha out of his carrier. "Can you grab his diaper bag for me, Fayth? It's by the door."

I picked up the bag and followed Cyn into the living room. "Thanks," she said, smiling. She rummaged through it and pulled out a blanket. "It's so strange that you can't talk back to me," she mumbled.

I shrugged and couldn't help but agree. It was freaking weird, but there wasn't anything I could do about it.

"Don't get me wrong, I don't mean to be an ass. Hell, with Meg, half of the time I don't even say anything, and she does quite well holding up both sides of the conversation."

"I heard that," Meg called from the kitchen. "Just for that, you don't get your half of a chicken."

"Hey," Cyn called. "I'm nurturing your godson's life. I need to eat so he can eat."

"Then, maybe my godson's mother needs to learn when to keep her mouth shut."

Cyn rolled her eyes and positioned a blanket over her chest. "Your auntie is crazy," Cyn cooed to Micha.

"Again, I heard that," Meg yelled.

Cyn worked her shirt down, positioned Micha under the blanket, and reclined back in the chair.

I laid down on the floor and stared up at the ceiling.

"This still feels extremely weird to me. I think I'm going to be one of those mom's that stops breastfeeding early," Cyn confessed. "Rigid about hit the wall when I told him that."

"Hey," Meg hollered. "I never breastfed Remy, and he turned out pretty damn well. I even had that damn nurse at the hospital who told me I *needed* to breastfeed and then made me cry because my damn boobs didn't work, still didn't convince me to do what you are doing."

"I know, you've told me that story ten times already, Meg," Cyn laughed. "Did you breastfeed?" Cyn asked me.

I shook my head no. I had tried to also, but my milk never came in. I had been crushed when I had to feed Marco formula, but I had quickly gotten over it after I had visited one of my friends back then who was being run ragged by breastfeeding her son all of the time. I'm sure that wasn't the norm, but bottle-feeding is what worked best for Marco and me at the time.

"I'm telling ya, two more weeks and I'm done. Rigid is just going to have to deal with it. They're my boobs," she laughed.

The front door banged open, and I shot up to see what the hell was going on. Cyn stood, Micha pressed to her chest and the blanket fell down.

"Fayth, can you—" Slider's mouth dropped open, and he slapped his hand over his eyes. "Holy fuck!" He blindly tried to walk back out the door and slammed right into the door frame. "Help! Someone take my hand, get me the fuck out of here!" He blindly reached out his arm, and Rigid grabbed it and pulled him out the door.

Rigid peeked in and shook his head. "You saw my woman's tits, didn't you?" he yelled.

"I swear to Christ, I didn't!" Slider tried to walk back in the door but slammed into the door frame again because he still had his hand over his eyes. "All I saw was her shoulder and the back of the kid's head. I took Marco's advice and aborted before I saw any more."

"Cyn, put the blanket back over you and sit down," Rigid ordered.

Cyn rolled her eyes. "Another reason to give up on breastfeeding. You men are weirdos." She gently tossed the blanket back over Micha and sat back down.

I couldn't help but snicker as Slider blindly felt around, trying to walk.

"You can take your damn hand off of your eyes," Rigid laughed as Slider managed to make it in the door but turned left and slammed right into the hall closet.

"You couldn't have told me that ten seconds sooner?" Slider grumbled. He turned around, his hand still over his eye but peeked out between his fingers. "Are you sure I can look?"

I silently laughed and laid back down.

"Yes, asshole. You really think I would tell you to look if Cyn's tits were hanging out?" Rigid growled.

"Hey!" King called. "You think we could talk about Cyn's tits after we get the couch moved in? This thing isn't fucking light."

"How about we never talk about Cyn's tits again," Slider mumbled.

"That's the most intelligent thing you've said all day, Slider," Rigid replied and hit him upside the head. "And I never want any of you fuckers to say Cyn and the word 'tits' in the same sentence again," Rigid barked.

Rigid and Slider walked back out the door, and I turned over on my side to watch them maneuver the couch into the house. They had figured out how to get it in through the door, and in no time, the three-piece sectional was put together, and Marco and Remy were sprawled out on it.

"That fits perfectly in here," Meg called. "Definitely more room to sit down now."

"We still need to grab the kitchen table and chairs. Come on, guys." King knocked Remy's feet off of the couch. "You two can lay around after we get everything moved in."

"Yeah, yeah," Remy grumbled. He sat up and followed King out the door with Marco behind him.

I stood and moved over to the couch. I fluffed the cushions, straightening them and then sat down.

"Are they gone?" Cyn asked. She looked over at me, and I gave her a thumbs up. "Oh hell. I'm sorry. I'm an ass for assuming you can talk. I keep forgetting." Cyn stood, tucked her boob back in her shirt, and put Micha over her shoulder.

I shrugged. I couldn't be mad at her. Hell, half of the time I forgot that no words came out of my mouth. It wasn't a normal occurrence for someone who used to be able to talk to suddenly stop.

I held out my arms and wiggled my fingers, silently begging for Cyn to let me hold Micha.

"He's all yours," she laughed and laid him in my arms. "I'm gonna go grab a plate of food before the guys descend on it and devour it all. Do you want me to bring you a plate?" She walked over to the island where Meg was laying out all of the food.

I waited for her to look at me and nodded.

"I really need to remember you can't talk."

"It was nice to see you make an ass of yourself and not me for once," Meg said and pulled a couple of bowls out of the fridge.

"Hey, I was just feeding my kid. Slider was the one who made an ass of himself." Cyn grabbed two plates and piled them up with food. "Besides, you'll never live down the coffeepot with Marley."

"Pfft, please. I think you and I wrecking a bed is at the top for most embarrassing shit we've done," Meg replied and scoffed.

"True, true," Cyn agreed. "Although, that ended with you getting that huge-ass bed for cheap."

King walked in the front door with an end table "Cheap? That thing was far from cheap. Over a grand for a bed that I had to fucking fix is not cheap." King set the end table next to the recliner, and I knew as soon as everyone left, I was going to have to rearrange everything.

Meg rolled her eyes. "Please, you told me last night that bed was best money you've ever spent."

King looked over his shoulder and saw Marco and Remy walk in. "You know damn well why I said that last night. If you can't remember why, I'll remind you again tonight." King winked at Meg and headed back out the door.

"Jesus, I can't wait 'til I go to college and I don't have to go to bed with my headphones on," Remy mumbled to Marco.

I looked at Meg to see if she had heard Remy, but she was talking to Cyn about chicken. I silently laughed, and I couldn't help but think that Remy going to bed with headphones on was hilarious but also slightly embarrassing. I guess one of the good things about living with Leo was the house was so big that we never ran into those problems.

The guys came in with the rest of the furniture and quickly had it all set up.

"Here ya go," Cyn sang and sat down next to me.

Micha had fallen back asleep snuggled into my arms. I beamed at her, hoping she would figure out what I was trying to tell her. Her little guy was so adorable that I could hold him all day if she let me.

"You want me to take him so you can eat?" Rigid offered.

I shook my head no and held Micha closer to me. I wasn't going to give this baby up without a fight.

"Uh oh. I know that look. You're getting a fever, Fayth," Meg joked and sat down next to Cyn.

"Fever?" Slider asked, concerned.

"Yup, baby fever," Meg laughed.

"Don't worry, Meg had that too, but as soon as the little monster starts crying or needs his diaper changed, she's eager to give him back," Cyn laughed.

"Hey, that's because I'm the fun aunt. I'm here to do cool shit with, like go-carting and possibly playing mailbox baseball." Meg took a bite of chicken and pointed her chicken leg at King. "Speaking of that, we need to see where Remy's bat is."

"Meg," King said and shook his head. "No mailbox baseball. Can't you be the aunt to teach him how to bake, not destroy stuff?"

"Hell no. What fun is that?" Meg scoffed and rolled her eyes. "Amateurs. I've done this aunt gig three fucking times before with my sister. Trust me when I say I got this shit locked down."

"You do realize how many times you swore in that sentence, right? But you give the guys hell if they even say damn." King pointed his finger at Meg. "Get that shit locked down."

"Don't say shit," Meg scolded.

King tossed his hands up in the air. "I seriously don't know what to do with your mom," he said to Remy.

"Just agree with her. It's for the best." Remy patted King on the shoulder, grabbed his plate piled high with food, and followed Marco out to the garage. Apparently, hanging out with the adults wasn't cool.

"See, as much as you like to think that Remy is on your side, he's on mine. I gave that boy life," Meg laughed.

"I'm only on your side in hopes that you'll stop talking," Remy called before he shut the door to the garage.

"Hey!" Meg protested.

"Checkmate," Slider mumbled. "The kid has the last word."

"Hey, no one asked the peanut gallery," Meg said. She popped up from the couch and beelined it over to King.

"Oh hell, here we go. She's gonna give him hell," Cyn laughed.

Meg set her plate down, started talking with her hands, and went off on King.

Rigid stood in front of me with his arms held out. "I'll take the boy."

I held him close and shook my head.

"Give him up, woman."

Cyn elbowed me. "Just give him up. I'll come over this week without overprotective father here, and I'll let you hold him the whole time."

"I'm not overprotective," Rigid protested and grabbed Micha out of my arms. "I just missed my boy."

"Funny how you don't miss your boy in the middle of the night when he wakes up wet, or hungry."

"I don't have the right equipment to feed him," Rigid argued and winked at Cyn.

"Oh trust me, in two weeks, we'll both have the same equipment to feed him. A bottle."

Rigid rolled his eyes and gently rocked Micha in his arms. "We'll see about that."

"Oh, we certainly will." Cyn smirked.

I grabbed the plate Cyn had brought me and munched on the chicken and salads as I listened to everyone talk around me. I couldn't count how many times I wished I could join in the conversation, but nothing would come out. Slider's eyes stayed on me the whole time while he ate, and he barely spoke.

"That's it, we're going," Meg called from the kitchen.

I had just finished eating and stood from the couch, wondering why they were leaving already.

Rigid laid Micha in his carrier. "Us too. We need to get the little guy home for his bath."

Cyn sighed and stood next to me. "The man may drive me crazy with his overprotectiveness, but I can say with no doubt that he is one damn good dad."

I smiled at her and was glad she had someone like that. Raising a child with no father was a hard task I hoped Cyn never had to go through.

"I'll leave all of the leftovers," Meg called and started Saran-wrapping everything. "I'll put the extra food I bought in the fridge and pantry, Fayth, but I know you'll want to arrange things where you want them." Meg opened the fridge and put a few containers on the top shelf.

"How many chickens were left?" Cyn asked, grabbing the baby carrier.

"Only half. I swear Marco and Remy ate a chicken a piece." Meg shook her head and shut the fridge door. "The only good thing about him going to school in Chicago is my grocery bill will be cut in half."

"You say that now, until he calls you every week and gives you a sob story of how he doesn't have any food," King laughed.

Meg shrugged. "He's my baby."

"He is far from a baby, Meg." King put his arm over her shoulders and pulled her close.

"He'll always be my baby," she whispered. King pressed a kiss to the side of her head, and she burrowed into his side.

"All right, we're out. We'll get together this week, Fayth." Cyn waved and left out the front door with Rigid following behind her.

"Later," Rigid called.

"I'll grab Remy and meet you out by the truck." Meg pulled out of King's arm. "I'll come over with Cyn. We can catch up then." Meg squeezed my arm, waved to Slider, and headed out to the garage.

"That woman isn't going to know what to do with herself when Remy goes off to college," King sighed. "It's a miracle she's letting him go that far."

Slider began gathering dirty plates and dumped them into the sink. "He'll do good. He's got a good head on his shoulders."

"It's not him I'm worried about," King laughed. "I'll see you at the shop tomorrow." He grabbed a couple of chips and popped them into his mouth. "Things are picking up with the nice weather coming. Lots of bikes scheduled for this week."

Slider nodded. "I need to get mine up and running too."

"It's about damn time." King clapped him on the shoulder and nodded to me. "It was good seeing you again, Fayth," he muttered.

"I can get the dishes," Slider said as King walked out the door.

I shook my head and grabbed the dirty bowl out of his hands. He had moved in all of my furniture, there was no need for him to clean up from dinner too. I pointed at the TV and moved to the sink. I searched for my pad of paper but remembered I had thrown it at Slider in the garage.

"I'll go grab your paper," Slider said, reading my mind. He disappeared into the garage, and I turned on the water to fill the sink.

"Here, Firecracker." Slider slid the notebook across to the counter to me and turned to open the fridge.

I got the dishes. Go watch TV or whatever.

Slider grabbed a beer out of the fridge, popped the top, and I slid the notebook back down to him.

"What is considered as whatever?"

I shrugged. I had no idea what he did when he was at home, but I knew I didn't want to get in his way.

"I really ain't got much to do."

Well, he needed to find something else to do besides watch me do the dishes. *Go take Marco for a ride in your car.*

"If I take him for a ride, he's going to beg me to let him drive."

Then don't let him drive. You're the adult, Slider.

"Some days, it don't feel like it," he laughed and ran his fingers through his hair. He set his beer down and grabbed a set of keys off the top of the fridge. "I guess I'll finish my beer when we get back."

Slider opened up the door to the garage and hollered for Marco. "Start it, don't move it," he ordered and tossed the keys at him.

I heard Marco shout "hell yeah" before Slider shut the door. "You need anything while we are out?"

Ice cream? I was an absolute sucker for ice cream. Specifically, chocolate ice cream.

"Chocolate? Vanilla? Strawberry?" Slider asked.

I held up one finger.

"Chocolate?"

I nodded and gave him a thumbs up.

"Good, you can come with and pick out just the right one." Slider crossed his arms over his chest and leaned against the counter.

What? Why?

"I told you I'm not leaving your side, Fay. I meant it. If you want me to take Marco for a ride, you need to come with."

I motioned to the dishes. Who in the hell was going to do the dishes while we were off joyriding?

"They'll still be here when we come back, and Marco and I will help you with them."

Ha. That's funny. Marco would find every excuse possible not to do the dishes.

"Scout's honor." Slider help up his hand. "And I was a scout. I can show you my badges later," he said, winking at me. "One ride, we'll grab some ice cream, and then we'll be back in plenty of time to clean up."

I shook my head no and turned off the water. Slider was being a bit overprotective. Big A was in jail, and there wasn't any more danger. *I'll be fine for a half an hour by myself,* I wrote.

"I'm sure you will be, Firecracker, but I'm not willing to take the risk that you might not be. The sooner you get in the car, the sooner we'll be back."

"Are you ready?" Marco asked excitedly and bound into the kitchen. "You didn't say which car, so I tried both of them before I figured out it was the Corvette."

Slider grabbed a second set of keys off the fridge and tossed them to Marco. "Start the Camaro. Your mom is coming with us and there is no way you will be able to sit in the back."

"Oh, sweet." Marco returned to the garage, slamming the door behind him.

"The kid is excited, you can't let him down." Slider smirked.

He's excited about the car, not me.

Slider shrugged. "But the car doesn't leave unless you are in it with me. You stay, I stay. You leave, I leave."

Damn it. *Fine. Half an hour and you buy me the biggest chocolate sundae they have.*

Slider grabbed the paper and laughed while he read it. "Deal, Firecracker." He tossed the notepad on the counter and held his hand out for me to shake.

I reluctantly shook his hand and a smirk spread across his lips. Slider grabbed his sunglasses off of the counter and slid them over his eyes. He looked damn good with the glasses on, although he looked damn good no matter what he was wearing.

"Let's go for a ride."

****

Chapter 15

Slider

"Holy cow, I can't believe she ate all of that," Marco whispered.

Fayth licked the back of her spoon and laid her empty dish on the table at the end of the couch. After we had gotten back, Fayth made me move around the end tables and move the couch over a couple of feet before she let me touch my ice cream.

I had gotten a dish of the flavor of the day which was mint rocky road; Marco had decided on a twist cone, and Fayth had gotten a three-scoop chocolate sundae topped with hot fudge, and chopped up Kit Kats with whipped cream and a cherry on top. I was rather surprised she had finished it, also.

"I guess she likes chocolate ice cream," I whispered back.

Marco and I were sprawled out on the couch, and Fayth was laid back in the recliner while some shitty movie she had picked out played on the TV.

"I think that is an understatement at this point," Marco laughed. "I guess I know what I'm getting her for her birthday next month."

"Next month?" It was already the twenty-fourth of April.

"Yeah, I think it's the seventh." Fayth shook her head and glared at Marco. "Eighth?" She nodded and gave him the thumbs up.

"You should really know when your mom's birthday is," I chuckled.

"You're probably right."

He's a boy, Fayth wrote and held up the notepad to us.

"What does that have to do with anything?" Marco asked.

It means you're going to be a man, and men never remember birthdays. Fayth was getting damn good at writing fast.

"You have a point. I guess I'm in training to be a good man then, right, Slider?"

"Hey, speak for yourself. I happen to remember all important dates." I saw Fayth roll her eyes.

"What's your mom's birthday?" Marco quizzed.

"September fourteenth."

"What's your dad's birthday?"

"I didn't have one."

Fayth turned to look at me and tilted her head.

"He died before I was born, and from what I was told about him, I was better off that way." My mother said she never wanted to speak badly of the dead, but she made sure I became the exact opposite of the man he was. He had gotten my mother pregnant when she was only seventeen, run off with some blonde chick, and then died in a bar fight.

"Yeah, that's the same for my dad. He died when I was only three. I don't even remember him. Uncle Leo helped raise me."

That would explain the great bond between them and why Marco wanted to be like Leo. I had never known what happened to Marco's dad, because it wasn't any of my business.

Fayth held her hand over her head and tapped her wrist.

"Aww, come on mom. It's only ten. I'm sixteen years old," Marco protested.

She shook her head. *Bed. Now.* She held up the pad of paper and pointed to his room.

"This sucks. She hates when I talk about my dad. That's the only reason she's making me go to bed," Marco grumbled.

Fayth crossed her arms over her chest and gave Marco a look that only a mother could. I had seen that look many times from my own growing up.

"Head to bed, Marco. We've got a busy day tomorrow of unpacking all of your mom's stuff."

Marco nodded, kissed him mom on the cheek, and shuffled off to his room.

"He's really a good kid, Fayth." I used to think Marco was a spoiled brat when Fayth had first moved to Rockton. But my opinion of him had changed, mostly because the Marco I had just spent all day with was completely different from the sullen and moody teenager I first met.

She smiled and nodded.

"You don't like when he talks about his dad?"

She shook her head no. *He wasn't a good man,* she wrote.

"Did he hurt you?"

She shook her head no again and stood. *Tired,* she scrawled.

"I guess Marco was right when he said you didn't like talking about him."

It was a long time ago. Which bedroom is mine?

"Third door on the left."

She nodded, tossed the blanket she had been using over the back of the chair, and waved goodnight.

I knew that wouldn't be the last I saw her tonight.

She was about to find out the bed she would be sleeping in was also my bed.

"Slider!" she yelled.

I raised my arms over my head and clasped them behind my neck. The first step in my plan was set in motion. Now, it was time to see if it was going to work.

****

Chapter 16

Fayth

He had to be kidding. I looked down the hallway and counted the doors.

I was standing in the doorway of the third door on the left, and it sure looked like where Slider slept.

"Mom? Are you okay?" Marco asked after he opened his door and peeked his head out.

"Slider," I yelled. This had to be a joke. There was no way in hell I was going to sleep in the same bed as Slider with Marco just across the hall.

Slider appeared at the end of the hallway. "Yeah?"

I motioned to the room.

"What's wrong?"

Ah, the ass was going to play stupid. "Slider," I said disapprovingly.

"Firecracker, it's the only other bed I got, unless you want to sleep with Marco in his twin."

"Oh, hell no. I am not sleeping with you, Mom. As much as I love you and appreciate you bringing me into this world, this is my bed." Marco slammed the door, and I heard the lock flip into place.

Shit. What the hell was I going to do now?

****

Slider

My plan was lining up just how I had hoped it would. I was either going to piss Fayth off so much that she was going to speak, or I was going to end up in bed with her. I would be happy with either outcome.

She stomped her foot and shook her head.

"Is it really that bad to sleep in my bed?"

She shook her head again and pointed to Marco's room.

"He ain't gonna let you in there, Firecracker."

I heard her growl, and she marched towards me.

My theory was the only way Fayth was going to speak was if she were either pissed or terrified. I assumed when she had called my name the first time, she had been having a nightmare.

Now, I was going to get her so pissed that the words were just going to explode out of her mouth.

She slugged me in the arm, walked past me, and grabbed her notepad off of the recliner. *I CAN'T SLEEP WITH YOU!!!*

"All we'll be doing is sleeping."

She shook her fist at me, then angrily wrote. *MY SON IS IN THE NEXT ROOM. HAVE YOU LOST YOUR MIND?!? WHY DIDN'T THEY BRING MY BED WHEN THEY BROUGHT ALL OF THE OTHER FURNITURE?*

"There wasn't enough room. I told King to bring what could fit. Apparently, your bed didn't make the cut."

Go get it.

"Fayth, it's after ten. I'm not driving into town to your storage unit. Sleep in my bed."

She shook her head no and stomped her foot.

"You sure do stomp your foot a lot when you're pissed," I laughed.

She growled again, and I knew I was getting her worked up good.

I'm not sleeping with you tonight.

"What about tomorrow?"

She growled and shook her head. Growling was a new thing. Now, we were getting somewhere.

"Are you one of those girls who I need to take to dinner, spend a little money on, and then you'll sleep with me?"

Her face turned bright red, and I'm sure if she was able to, flames would have been shooting out of her ears.

No. I'm one of those girls who knows how to hide a body.

I threw my head back and laughed. I was going to have to be careful with her. She might have picked up a few tricks from Leo. I wasn't into sleeping with the fishes. "Now, now, Firecracker. No need to go threatening me."

I want my bed.

"Well, you can't have it. It's my bed or nothing."

I'm not sleeping with you. Her pen flew across the paper and she held it up to me.

"Is sleeping with me really that horrible. I mean, I've never been kicked out of bed before, Firecracker, and I have been in my fair share of beds."

Classy.

I shrugged. Sure not classy, but it was the truth. "Tell ya what, you sleep in my bed," she vehemently shook her head. I held up my hand and shushed her. She wasn't talking, but her head shake definitely spoke volumes. "And I'll sleep on the couch. At least until you let me sleep in my bed."

Fine. And that will be never.

"How about we just agree on tonight. I wouldn't want you to eat your words later on."

She growled again and tossed the pad of paper at me. She hissed, and I swear to Christ, it sounded like she had said "ass."

"Did you call me an ass?" I asked, shocked.

She reared her head back and her eyes got huge. She nodded.

"You," I pointed at her, "called me," I jammed my thumb into my chest, "an ass?"

She nodded and touched her lips.

"Well, I'll be damned. Now you can say Slider *and* ass. At this rate, you should be able to say a full sentence by your birthday."

She flipped me off and chucked her pen at my face.

I managed to swat it away before it hit me, and she flounced down the hallway to her room.

"Fayth," I called.

She turned around and glared at me.

"Sweet dreams, Firecracker," I growled and winked at her.

"Ass," she hissed and slammed the door behind her. I heard the lock fall into place, and I leaned against the wall.

Holy hell, it had actually worked.

Now, I needed to figure out how to get her so riled up that she was just start spewing words at me.

This was going to be more fun than I had bargained for. It would have been better if she had agreed to sleep with me, but there was always time for that later.

Beggars can't be choosers. I had Fayth in my house, and she was starting to talk.

I would have to say this had been a good day.

A damn good day.

****

Chapter 17

Fayth

"Say it."

I shook my head and grabbed the pan full of scrambled eggs off of the burner.

"Come on, Mom. Please, just say it once."

I scooped eggs onto three plates and set the pan back on the stove. Being able to only say two words, and one of those words being "ass," was not something I wanted to brag about.

Slider had gotten me so pissed off last night, the word "ass" had just ripped from my throat, and I was even more shocked by it than he was.

He had rolled off of the couch while I was making breakfast this morning, pressed a kiss to the side of my head, and told Marco I had said "ass" last night. Then, before I could find my paper fast enough to rip into him, he had disappeared into his bedroom, and I heard the water turn on in the bathroom. Now, I was dealing with Marco begging me to say "ass."

The toast popped up from the toaster, and I slathered them with butter.

"I don't know why you won't say it. You should be proud that you can say another word."

I rolled my eyes and pushed his plate towards him.

"What do you think your next word is going to be? I bet if I tell Gambler, they'll get a pool going on which word it'll be."

I bugged my eyes out and shook my head. There was no way in hell there was going to be a pool going on about me.

"I already told King," Slider announced and walked into the kitchen, pulling a t-shirt on over his head.

My gaze traveled over his toned and tanned chest before he tugged the shirt down, and I got an eye full of his nearly perfect body.

I turned back to the stove and braced my hands on the counter. What the hell was I doing eyeing up Slider? The man had made me so mad last night that I had felt like I was ready to explode.

"You think he'll tell Gambler? I'd totally get in on that bet. I'm guessing her next word will be douche," Marco said.

I spun around and pointed a finger at him. He knew not to talk like that, and I had a feeling he was taking advantage of the fact that I couldn't talk.

"Hey, let's lay off the bad words and leave those to your mom," Slider joked before winking at me.

"Ass," I whispered.

"Oh! She said it!" Marco yelled and jumped up.

I slapped my hand over my mouth, and Slider threw his head back and laughed.

"I think Slider is your good luck charm, Mom. First you say his name, and now he's the only one you'll talk to."

"Or I provoke her so much that she can't hold it in," Slider chuckled.

I pointed at Slider and then tapped my nose. He hit that one right on the head.

Slider grabbed a plate and sat down next to Marco at the island. "After breakfast, I need to run to the clubhouse for church. All of the girls will be there. You okay with hanging out with them during it?"

I nodded and grabbed the ketchup out of the fridge. I liked Meg and all of the girls. They were the closest thing to friends that I had.

"What the hell are you doing?" Slider asked, watching me squirt ketchup on my eggs.

"Dude, that's how she eats scrambled eggs."

"But I've seen her eat eggs before, and she's never put ketchup on them." Slider curled his lip as he watched me take a bite. "Well, that's different."

"She only does it on scrambled eggs. I gag every time she does it."

I rolled my eyes, grabbed my plate, and turned my back to Slider and Marco so I could eat my breakfast in peace without them talking about it.

"Are there any other weird food combinations your mom has?" Slider asked Marco.

"Hmm," Marco hummed. "Not really. She's normal for the most part, besides the ketchup on her eggs."

They could talk about me all they wanted. I was going to enjoy my eggs, and I didn't give a damn if they thought it was gross or not.

"Do I need to come with you?" Marco asked.

"Yeah. I know Remy is going to be there. I never realized how close you two were in age."

"Yeah, he's one year ahead of me. I saw him around school but never really talked to him before yesterday."

Shit! School. I had totally forgotten about that. I was going to have to call Marco's school back in Chicago to let them know he was transferring schools again. I wished I knew how long we were going to be in Rockton. I didn't want to get settled in here again and then have to go back to Chicago.

"Finish breakfast and then we'll head over there," Slider said. I heard his stool scrape backwards and then he walked in front of me to drop his dishes into the sink.

I looked down at my plate and then up at him. How in the hell had he eaten so fast? I barely had three bites.

"I'm a fast eater, Firecracker. You got coffee made?"

I nodded to the half-full coffee pot. I had already managed to have three cups of coffee while I was making breakfast.

Slider grabbed my cup and filled it. "No reason to dirty another dish," he muttered before he took a sip.

Slider drinking from my cup was more intimate than I would like to admit.

"I'm gonna change and then I'll meet you outside," Marco called.

Slider waved to him and leaned against the counter. He was wearing a tight black t-shirt and holey jeans, ripped at the knees. His standard black boots rounded out the outfit.

I glanced over my shoulder to make sure Marco wasn't there to witness the way my eyes ran over his body. I wasn't sure what I was thinking anymore. Slider always had a certain appeal to him, but I refused to acknowledge it. Now, it was like it was slapping me in the face, and I didn't want to ignore it. His right arm was covered in tattoos, while his left sported a half-sleeve. I had always wondered why he hadn't done a full sleeve, but never asked, because it really wasn't any of my business.

"You know what you're doing right now, Firecracker?" Slider asked, his voice low, and his eyes locked with mine.

I swallowed hard and shook my head no. I didn't have a clue what I was doing. All I knew was I was enjoying the sight of Slider's muscled arms.

"You're driving me crazy without even saying a word." He drained his cup in two swallows and set it in the sink. "Your eyes are taking off my clothes, and I can't help but like the fact that you're looking at me that way." He stepped forward and brushed my hair off of my shoulder. "Lord knows I've been looking at you like that for far too long. It's nice to know we're having the same thoughts."

I gulped and took a step back. I bumped into the counter, and Slider grabbed my plate out of my hand. "I can't wait for the day you start talking again, Firecracker. I'd love to know what's going through your mind right now. Your dark brown eyes tell me things have changed. I feel you watching me, but I'd like to feel more than your eyes on me."

"Slider," I whispered.

He leaned in and brushed his fingertips across my lips. "I pray for the day you say that while I'm balls deep, taking everything you have."

I gasped, and my jaw dropped. His finger slipped into my mouth, and I closed my lips around it.

"What are you doing to me?" he growled. I sucked on his finger, and he slowly pulled it out of my mouth. "Choose very carefully what you do next, Fayth," he whispered.

I licked my lips, and my eyes fell to his. I knew what my body wanted to do, but my mind was screaming no. Everything felt right when I was with Slider, even last night when he was being an ass to me. It always felt right, and I wondered if kissing him would feel right too.

"You have five seconds to tell me no before I kiss you."

I looked up, locked eyes with him, and saw need there. Slider wanted this as badly as I did, but I was too chicken to do anything about it.

"Three seconds," he warned.

I gulped and ran my hands up his arms. I didn't care what my mind wanted anymore. All I wanted to do was feel.

"Mom! Have you seen my black Nike hoodie?" Marco called from his room.

Slider jumped back, and my eyes darted to the floor. Whatever trance Slider and I were in was broken.

I grabbed my pad of paper. *It's in his bag.* I held it up to Slider but didn't look him in the eye. I was too embarrassed by what I had just done. Who the hell sucks someone's finger in the kitchen in the middle of the day?

"She said to check your bag," Slider hollered.

I picked up my plate, stepped around him, and dropped it into the sink. I didn't know what to do. It seemed like he wanted me, but was it for real? Was Slider really interested in someone like me? Hell, I couldn't even speak. I didn't really bring much to the table for a relationship.

"I'll get the truck started," Slider mumbled.

I nodded and heard him slip into the garage. I dropped my head, and my shoulders sagged. What in the hell was I doing?

The old Fayth never would have been so wanton with Slider. It was like I wasn't myself anymore. All I wanted to do was live in the moment, because I never knew when it was going to be my last.

"I'm gonna go out with Slider," Marco called as he ran across the kitchen. I nodded, but I doubted he had even seen me.

Marco was loving having Slider around, and even he could tell it was different from before. Slider used to stay outside most of the time, or hang out on the porch talking on his phone or just watching cars drive by.

I noticed him back then, but I knew we were different people who didn't want the same things. I longed for a quiet, simple life and a father for Marco who could teach him how to be a good man. Slider loved being in the club and having no one to answer to. If Slider were to be with me, it would be a complete one-eighty from the life he had been living.

I knew what I wanted now, but was I crazy for wanting it? Did Slider want the same thing, or was he just looking for right now, while I was looking for forever?

What the hell was I getting my heart into?

****

Chapter 18

Slider

"Get your ass in here."

I closed the door behind me and sat down next to Rigid. "You told me to get here when I could. What the hell crawled up your ass?" I asked King.

"Leo Banachi is what crawled up my ass," King growled.

Rigid snickered next to me, and I couldn't help but chuckle.

"Knock it off," Demon called. "You two are worse than a couple of rowdy teenagers."

King grabbed his gavel and slammed it down on the table. "If you two are done having a fucking laugh, you might want to listen up and hear what I have to say."

Well hell, King was not in a good mood at all. I sat back in my chair and kicked out my feet. Might as well be comfortable while he reamed my ass.

"Leo called me this morning. He's dealing with an issue that seems to be connected to Rockton," King explained.

"What the hell does Rockton have to do with anything in Chicago? We're small fish compared to Leo," Gambler commented, leaning his elbows on the table.

"We're not small fish. He's a fucking mob boss, we're an MC. Completely different," Hammer retorted.

"You're wrong, Ham. Leo is more like us than any of you realize. He's got men under him just like I have you all. He's runs his turf just like we run Rockton. Now, Leo takes it a step further by involving himself in things that we would rather have nothing to do with," King informed Hammer.

"So, tell us what the hell is headed to Rockton," Demon demanded.

"That's the thing, he has no idea who or what it is."

"How the fuck does that work?" Rigid asked.

"You remember the calls and messages we were getting before Fayth was shot?" We all nodded. "Well, it seems whoever was sending them has started again."

"But it was Big A who was sending them. The asshole is in jail now," I replied.

King nodded. "He is, but it seems he has someone on the outside who is trying to complete what he had set out to do before."

"But who? All of his men headed south when he lost it."

"That's what we need to figure out. Leo is indefinitely out of town, and he can't spare any men to come help."

"Well, we don't even know what the hell we need help with, so now what?" Rigid asked.

"Now, we start back at square one, and figure out who is connected to Big A that is still around Rockton." King steepled his hands in front of him and tapped his fingertips together. "I have a few leads, people that were around during the whole Cyn shit and have faded into the background."

"Who?" Demon asked.

"Cherry," King stated.

"I don't even know who the hell that is," I said.

"Fucking gash who used to hang around the club. She's Big A's cousin. Her brother was the one who beat Cyn," Rigid explained.

"You let her hang out in the club?" Why the hell would they let someone who was connected to Big A even step foot into the clubhouse, let alone be a hang-around.

"She was only around for a little bit before Meg and Cyn took care of her," King laughed.

"She knew she wasn't welcome around here after Rigid and Cyn hooked up."

"She works with Meg, Cyn, and Troy," King said.

"Yeah, from what I hear, the only reason she has a job is because she likes to spend time under the boss' desk," Rigid said, laughing.

"Sounds like a perfect girl for you, Turtle," Hammer joked, slugging Turtle in the arm.

"Man, fuck you. I ain't wanting a bitch like that. I'll take one like Gambler has though," Turtle said, flipping off Hammer.

"Are you looking at my woman?" Gambler growled.

Turtle held up his hands and shook his head. "Just observing."

"You're about to observe my foot kick your fucking ass." Gambler shoved his chair back, and it slammed against the wall.

Turtle moved behind Hammer. "Dude, it ain't like I'm touching her or anything."

"That's because she'd never let you touch her," Gambler boomed.

"All right, all right," King called. "Both of you sit the fuck down. Stop looking at his woman, Turtle, and chill the fuck out, Gambler."

Gambler pointed at Turtle. "I will destroy you if I ever see you looking at Gwen with anything more than a glance."

Turtle held up his hands and nodded.

"You think we can get back to figuring out who the hell is fucking with us?" I growled. Normally, I was up for a petty fight and egged them on, but this was different. Someone was out there fucking with us for Big A, and we had no idea who it was.

"There are a few of the guys who used to run with him that still hang around a bar outside of town. They don't try to hide the fact that they know Big A, so I doubt it is them, but I can run out there and see what I can find out," Hammer volunteered.

"Good. Take Turtle with, and let me know what you find out. We need to follow every lead that we have." King slammed his gavel on the table. "Everyone, keep your eyes open, and don't let your guard down. Something is going on, and we need to find out what it is."

"Gotta love it when our orders are to go to the bar," Hammer chuckled.

Hammer and Turtle walked past Gambler and me, and Gambler growled at Turtle.

"I swear to Christ, between the two of them, they *maybe* equal a whole brain," Demon said under his breath as Turtle and Hammer walked out.

"That's being generous," Rigid replied, laughing.

King kicked back in his chair. "Well, hopefully between the two of them, they can get a lead that we need. Right now, we're grasping at air."

"So, who's going to check on Cherry?" Gambler asked.

"Not fucking me. I'm sure Cyn would flip her shit if she knew that I was seeking out that gash," Rigid said, throwing his hands in the air. "Cyn is all hormonal after having Micha. I'm doing everything I can to stay on her good side."

"Meg would do the same. That's why I'm leaving Cherry to Slider and Demon." King smirked.

"What?" Demon shouted. "I'm the damn VP of this club. How the hell do I get the shit job? I've got an ol' lady too, who wouldn't appreciate me visiting Cherry. Have Slider and one of the other brothers go with him. Hell, tell Roam to get his ass back here from wherever the hell he is."

"Nope. It's you and Slider. Get it done, boys." King stood, nodded at us, and walked out of the room.

"This is bullshit. Paige is going to be pissed," Demon complained.

"Does she even know who Cherry is?" Rigid asked. "If you don't tell her who she is, she probably won't even care."

"I'm sure she doesn't know, but she's also friends with your baby mama and King's wife. It won't be long until she figures out just who she is." Demon ran his fingers through his hair and shook his head. "At least you don't have an ol' lady to worry about, Slider. How about I drive us, and you can do all of the talking."

I tapped my finger on my chin, and a grin spread across my lips. "I have an even better idea. You know how King said that Troy worked with Cherry too?"

Gambler, Rigid, and Demon all nodded.

"I think it's time to make Troy an honorary member of the Knights," I suggested.

"Is that even a thing?" Gambler asked.

"No," Demon growled, "but I think it's about to become something, at least for a day or two." Demon smiled at me and kicked back in his chair.

Rigid laughed and stood. "Better not let King know what you two are planning."

"He's not going to find out, although we're going to need your help. I can't leave Fayth alone. We're gonna have to figure out a way for you to watch her, but make sure we don't raise any eyebrows." I had no idea how the hell we were going to manage that.

"I think I have an idea," Rigid mumbled.

Demon elbowed him in the side. "Well, spill, fucker."

"Cyn and Meg have been talking about going to get tattoos. Maybe I'll try to talk Cyn into making it a girl thing or some shit like that."

"Fayth needs someone with her all of the time. She can't go out with just the girls," I reminded.

"Don't get your panties in a bunch. We ain't letting our girls go off on their own either. Gambler or I will be there."

"Hey," Gambler protested, "don't be signing me up for some tattoo field trip with a bunch of chicks."

"I'll go, but you'll have to stay home with Micha, then. He's a bit too young for his first trip to the tattoo parlor."

"I'll go to the tattoo parlor," Gambler agreed quickly. "I'm not ready to be alone with a baby."

"That's a good thing, because I really doubt Cyn would have left him alone with you, and even if she would have, you can bet your ass I would have vetoed that," Rigid drawled.

"I think I should be offended right now," Gambler said, feigning outrage.

"All right, that's settled. How about we plan on Friday? That should give you enough time to convince Cyn, right?" I asked Rigid.

"I'm sure it won't take much to convince her, it's just I have to do it in a way that she thinks that it's her own idea, and not mine."

"Well, it's only Saturday. That gives you all week." I stood and pulled my phone out of my pocket, checking to make sure Fayth hadn't messaged me. I knew she was only a couple of rooms away, but I had told her to if she needed me at all. "I'm gonna check on Fayth." There was nothing from her, so I shoved my phone in my pocket.

"She's with the girls. No need to check on her," Demon laughed. "They'll be cackling like a bunch of hens gathered around the bar while they all get drunk."

"And then we get to take them home and reap the benefit of drunk sex," Rigid said, wiggling his eyebrows up and down.

"Well, I know Fayth won't be out there talking, although she's probably gone through ten notebooks trying to keep up with your ol' ladies. The only words she can say are 'Slider' and 'ass.'"

"Ass?" Demon asked, laughing.

"Yeah, it's all part of my plan. Get her so pissed off, she has no choice but to talk."

Demon shook his head. "You might be playing with fire with that plan."

I shrugged. I had no idea what else to do. "What have I got to lose? She'll get pissed and not talk to me?" I asked, laughing.

Rigid and Gambler laughed. "Or, you'll lose her before you even have her," Demon warned.

I had to take what he said to heart. Demon knew too well what it was like to have someone and then blow it. He had been lucky to find Paige after fucking up royally.

"That won't happen," I vowed.

I wanted Fayth, and I was going to get her.

****

554

Chapter 19

Fayth

"Line 'em up," Meg called.

"How many is this?" Marley slurred next to me.

"Seven. Or was it three?" Cyn asked. She held up her hand and tried to count her fingers. "I think it was three," she said and held up five fingers. "Oh wait, I forgot to add my thumb," she mumbled.

I blinked slowly and tried to figure out what her thumb had to do with anything.

"Does your thumb count as ten?" Paige hiccuped.

"Who the hell cares," Meg insisted. "Just line up six more," she ordered Gwen.

Gwen set six shot glasses up and grabbed the almost-empty bottle of Rum Chata. "Gambler is going to be so pissed if I puke in his truck," she slurred and concentrated on the glasses in front of her.

"Give him a little something when you get home, and he won't even notice," Meg instructed.

"Make sure you brush your teeth, though," Cyn put in. "Thank God Ethel is watching Micha. I would be such a bad mom if Micha was here right now." Cyn rested her head on the bar, and I patted her on the back.

Meg waved her hand at Cyn and scoffed. "We're not that drunk. You could totally still take care of him." Meg slid halfway off her stool and grabbed onto the edge of the bar. "Or not," she mumbled and struggled to pull herself back up.

I had no idea how we had gotten here. Well, I actually did, but I couldn't believe it had happened so fast. One minute, we were all *oohing* and *ahhing* over pictures of Micha that Cyn had on her phone, and then the next thing I knew, the bottle of Rum Chata had been pulled out and it had been all downhill since then.

"All right, bottoms up, bitches," Gwen said, pushing a shot glass to each of us.

"What are we toasting this time?" Marley asked.

"Is there really anything left to toast?" Meg questioned. "How about tacos?"

"Tacos?" Cyn repeated and giggled.

"Hell yes, tacos. Why the hell not? They are the most important food group." Meg held up her shot glass.

"I didn't know tacos were part of that food octagon," Marley pondered.

"They're not," Troy called from the couch. He had driven Marley over after Meg had texted her to get her ass here. Since Troy wasn't part of the club, he was subjected to our downward spiral of Rum Chata.

"Then, what are they?" Meg called.

"Damn good eating," Troy yelled and held up his beer.

The girls all cheered and raised their glasses. "To damn good eating and tacos!" Cyn called. We all clumsily clanked glasses and tossed back our shots.

"Jesus Christ." King had come down the hallway and had his arms crossed over his chest. "We weren't even in church for half an hour." He smirked.

"We only had four," Meg called.

"I thought it was eight, or was it five." Cyn held up her hands again and tried counting her fingers.

"Don't count the thumb," Marley reminded her.

"Both of them?" Paige asked.

"I would count one," Troy suggested, as he laughed.

"Oh, good idea, babe," Marley called. "He's so smart," she said dreamily.

"How in the hell does this always happen?" King asked, shaking his head.

"It's the Meg effect," Troy called.

"Because Meg kicks ass! Woo!" Gwen yelled, raising the bottle in the air.

Another cheer went up, and we all ended up laughing, trying not to fall off of our stools.

Hammer and Turtle walked into the bar. "Damn, these chicks roll harder than we do."

"Yeah, and that's one party you two don't get to be a part of," King nodded at the door. "Go find out what I told you to."

Hammer and Turtle both grumbled under their breath but headed out the door.

"Where are Gambler, Demon, and those other two?" Paige hiccuped.

"I bet he yelled at them," Meg said, shaking her head.

"Why?" Cyn asked.

"Because he yelled at me before we came," Meg pouted.

Gwen leaned on the bar. "Oh, what for?"

"I didn't yell at you," King growled.

"Yes you did," Meg shouted, pointing her finger at King. "You told me to behave and not get everyone drunk."

King looked around and smirked. "I see you listened to me so well."

Meg stood up and shouted, "Hey! You're not drunk. So there. I did listen." Meg crossed her arms over her chest and leaned heavily against Cyn.

"I don't count."

"Well, then, Gambler and those three other guys aren't drunk," Meg smarted off.

"Oh, and neither were Hammer and Turtle," Marley chimed in.

"Booya!" Cyn shouted.

"Sweet Jesus." King shook his head. "It's a damn good thing I love you, woman."

Meg smiled. "And it's a damn good thing I let me love you."

King tilted his head. "I think I might need to cut you off, babe. I know you're done when I can't decipher what you're trying to say."

"You're too late, Lo." Meg shook her head and looked down. "I already cut myself off. Pukey Meg is going to make an appearance soon."

"Puke and rally!" Troy shouted.

Meg groaned and shook her head.

"Quiet from the peanut gallery. You're egging on my woman," King yelled at Troy.

"It's about damn time someone else eggs her on, normally it's the other way around," Troy replied.

Gambler walked to the end of the bar. "Grab me a beer, doll." Rigid, Demon, and Slider followed behind him and stood behind us.

Gwen waved her hand at Gambler and shook her head. "It's probably best for me not to walk right now."

Rigid approached Cyn and put his arm around her shoulders. "How drunk are you, beautiful?"

"On a scale of seventy to fifty-nine, I'm going to have to say twenty-nine," Cyn slurred.

"Huh?" Slider tilted his head to look at Cyn. "How in the hell does that make sense?"

"Thumbs!" Marley shouted. "She added too many thumbs," she mumbled while she stumbled over to Troy and fell on top of him.

"Looks like we missed the rager," Demon noted, walking behind the bar where he grabbed four beers out of the fridge.

"It really wasn't as exciting as you would think. All they did was talk, laugh like a pack of hyenas, and drink like camels." Troy grabbed Marley and situated her in his lap.

"I'm not a camel," she weakly protested.

"And, I haven't drank in nine months. I am a complete heavy weight," Cyn said while she reached up and patted Rigid's cheek.

"I think you mean lightweight, beautiful," Rigid corrected.

"Nope," Cyn said. "I'm too heavy to be a light weight. I have an ass and now a gut thanks to Micha. Although, he's too cute for me to be mad at him." Cyn batted her eyes at Rigid. "You still love me though, right?"

"You keep giving me babies like Micha, and there's no way in hell I'd stop loving you."

Cyn shook her head. "That's sweet, but I'm not giving you anymore babies. Micha is perfect. There is no way in hell we could do that again. We'd probably get Satan's baby or something."

"I'll convince you to give me at least two more." Rigid smirked.

"Then, you better get her liquored up *real good*," Paige said, laughing.

Slider scooted next to me and leaned down. "You doing okay, Firecracker, or am I going to have to carry you out to the truck?"

I nodded and plastered a goofy smile on my face intentionally.

"Learn any new words?" he asked.

I rolled my eyes and flipped him off.

"Still feisty," he whispered. "I just need to talk to Troy quick and then we'll head back to the house."

I nodded and grabbed a bottle of water Gambler had set in front of each of us.

Demon and Slider plopped down on the couch next to Troy.

"I wonder what they're talking about," Meg mumbled, watching Demon and Slider talk quietly to Troy.

I shrugged. I barely knew what was going on around here, let alone what Slider was talking to Troy about.

"You know how you were talking about getting those tattoos you've been wanting, beautiful?" Rigid asked Cyn.

"Yup. You told me they can be my push gift," she beamed.

"Don't you normally give like a necklace for that, not a tattoo?" Gwen questioned.

Cyn shook her head and laughed. "I thought you knew by now that we aren't normal."

"Bad ass bikers give their women tattoos when they squeeze a baby out, not jewelry," Meg snickered, her attention taken off of Troy.

"So, does that mean you aren't getting any new tattoos since you aren't pushing out any babies for me?" King asked Meg.

She flipped him off and shook her head. "You knew a long time ago that my baby making factory is closed. You want a baby, you're going to have to find a new wife, and I'll just buy my own tattoos," she smarted off.

"I think I'll stick with you, and Remy is good enough for me."

"Smart man," she mumbled.

"Next Friday, I'll stay with Micha, and you go out with the girls. Tattoo party," Rigid suggested.

"Really?" Cyn squealed. "Did you make us appointments?"

"No, but I figured you can go to Meg's chick. She can get you all in." Rigid nodded at Meg, and she gave him a thumbs up.

"Aye, aye, captain," she said with a salute.

"You say girls, who do you all mean?" Gwen asked.

"Every chick here, plus Ethel if she wants to go with you guys. King is going to have to go with you guys, though. Make sure you stay out of trouble," Rigid replied.

King sighed. "Meg is going, trouble will definitely be present."

"I promise to only give you what you can handle," she purred to King and blew him a kiss and winked.

"I'm gonna need another brother with," he chuckled.

"I'll go with you," Gambler offered.

King and Gambler bumped fists, and Gwen rolled her eyes.

"It's funny you two think you can handle us." Gwen smirked. "This is going to be fun."

"You in?" Cyn asked me.

I looked around and wondered when I became one of the girls. Never in my life had I been to a girls' night out.

"She's in," Slider called. "I need to get some shit done around the shop on Friday, and if King is going, I don't mind if she does."

I crossed my arms and glared at Slider. I was going to say yes, but Slider saying yes for me pissed me off. Since I was eighteen years old, I have been making my own decisions. Slider thinking he could decide for me was not going to go over well.

"Sweet." Cyn clapped her hands together. "Now I need to figure out which ones I wanted."

"I'll have to call Darby and see if we can book the whole night." Meg pulled her phone out of her pocket.

"Tell her she'll be tipped generously for dealing with you six." King popped the top to his beer. "I know Mom will want to go with y'all. She was telling me the other day that she missed hanging out."

"I just messaged her, but she texted back 'huh.'" Meg squinted at her phone and laughed. "Probably because I texted 'Friday tattoo girls night your ass.'"

Cyn spit out the water she had been drinking and laughed hysterically. "She probably thought you want to tattoo her ass."

"Use more words," Paige advised.

King grabbed Meg's phone out of her hand. "I'll take care of the texting and calling tonight. I'm surprised Gravel hasn't called me wondering what in the hell is going on."

Rigid pulled his phone out of his pocket and held it up to King. "That would be because he texted me and not you."

"Crazy," King said, shaking his head.

"We're gonna head home," Slider announced. "It's only one PM and you guys managed to get rip-roaring drunk. I think if we stay the rest of the day, it'll be all downhill from here."

Taking a nap was high on my list of things I wanted to do, so going home sounded like a solid plan.

"Oh, I'm taking your son," Meg said, pointing at me. "Remy asked if he could hang out with Marco tonight. I said yes as long as they stay at the clubhouse. My house is not big enough for four people, even if Remy and Marco stay in his room. I hope that's okay."

I shrugged. I wasn't about to say no. I knew Marco had the same problem I did. He never really had any friends who were truly his friends and not just nice to him because they knew who his uncle was.

Slider stood behind me and rubbed my back. "We'll pick him up in the morning."

King nodded. "Sounds like a plan."

"Oh, you just like it because that means you don't have to put your hand over my mouth when we have sex tonight," Meg said, rolling her eyes.

King nodded. "This is true."

"You wanna say bye to Marco?" Slider asked me.

I gave him a thumbs up and downed the rest of my water. Slider grabbed my hand and pulled me down the hallway and turned left. "They are in Roam's room. Remy stays in here when Roam is out of town."

I tilted my head and looked at Slider. Why would Roam be out of town all the time?

"Roam is a nomad. The guy can't seem to stay in one place for too long. He hasn't been around much lately, so I'm sure he'll be turning up soon." Slider stopped in front of third door on the left and raised his hand to knock.

"Come in," Remy called.

Slider pushed open the door and pulled me in behind him.

"Hey, Mom. Did Meg tell you she said it was okay for me to spend the night?"

I nodded and examined the room. The only items in the room were a queen size bed and a huge-ass TV on the wall. Remy was lying on the large throw rug on the floor on his stomach playing a video game, while Marco was sprawled out on the bed.

"Your mom and I are going to head back to the house. You want me to run back with some clothes for you?" Slider asked Marco.

"Nah, I'll be good. Remy said he had some clothes I can borrow."

"Slider," I said, looking up at him. Shit, I couldn't say what I wanted to. I had left my pad of paper on the bar, and now I was going to have to play charades. I pointed to the floor and shook my head.

Slider tilted his head at me, and I knew this was going to be more difficult than I thought. "Stay?"

I nodded and pointed at the door, then again shook my finger.

"Don't leave?"

Hell yes. This was easier than I thought it was going to be.

"Don't leave unless you have someone from the club with you," Slider told Marco. "Your mom and I will pick you up tomorrow."

"Sounds good," Marco mumbled.

I rolled my eyes and knew Marco was barely listening to Slider. I stomped my foot and pointed at Marco to get his attention. I pointed at my ear and then to Slider.

"Um, I think she wants you to listen to her," Remy laughed. He had paused his game so he could watch the show I was putting on.

"Yeah, I got that when she stomped her foot at me," Marco muttered.

"Look, just stay together, don't leave the clubhouse, and don't get in trouble. Shouldn't be hard at all," Slider replied.

Marco saluted him and Remy unpaused his game. They were both glued to the TV, and I knew they had listened as much as they were going to.

Slider grabbed my hand and pulled me out the door. "He'll be fine, Firecracker. Remy is a good kid."

We headed back down the hallway, skirted around the bar where everyone had paired up, and ducked out the front door.

Rain pelted us as we sprinted to the truck. Slider held the door open for me to leap in, then he rounded the truck and slipped in, drenched.

"Hell, I thought is wasn't supposed to rain until tonight," he muttered before he ran his hand through his hair and stuck the key in the ignition.

I hadn't known it was supposed to rain at all. I really was out of touch with everything going on. My wet hair was matted to my forehead and the grey long-sleeve shirt I had tossed on this morning was now molded to my body.

Slider cranked up the truck. "You okay?"

I nodded. We had left my pad of paper on the bar, so I was left with head nods and lame sign language.

We pulled out of the parking lot. "You need something to eat?"

We had been munching on chips and salsa while the guys had been in their meeting, but my stomach rumbled, letting me know chips wasn't a good enough lunch.

"Wanna hit the Kwik Trip on the way back? We can pick up a pizza to bake up at home," Slider suggested.

I shrugged. Gas station pizza wasn't really what I was hungry for. I waved my hand at him. He glanced over at me, and I pretended to act like I was writing.

He shook his head and pointed to the glove box. "There should be a napkin and a pen in there you can use. We're going to have to stock up on notepads and stash them everywhere," he said, laughing.

I popped open the glovebox and searched for the paper and pen.

"If you don't want pizza, what do you want?"

I finally found the pen and grabbed a blue, paper, heavy-duty towel. *Grocery store.* I held up the paper for him to read.

"Really? The store doesn't have easy food that we can just throw together."

I want good, not easy.

"All right, all right. The store it is. You got any plans on what you wanna make?"

We'll see. I'm just tired of eating out.

"No problem, Firecracker."

I wadded up the paper and tossed it on the floor. The sky was ominous, like it was going to rain all day, and I couldn't think of a better way to spend the time than cooking and just relaxing.

Now, hopefully Slider kept his distance, because I didn't think I would have much restraint if he didn't.

****

Chapter 20

Slider

"Holy hell." I took another bite and moaned. "This is insane," I mumbled.

Fayth smirked and took a sip of her wine.

"Why the hell didn't I know that you can cook like this?" I grabbed my beer and washed down the delicious taste of fried pork chop and mashed potatoes.

Fayth shrugged.

I couldn't tell you how many times I had groaned and wished I had a second stomach. "Firecracker, you sure are one big surprise."

She grabbed the pad of paper she had set next to her plate. *I like to cook.*

"Obviously, Fay. I think what you just did was way more than cooking."

She rolled her eyes. *Are you drunk?*

I laughed. "No, Firecracker. You got to be the drunk one today." After we had wandered around the store collecting all of the ingredients Fayth wanted, we had gone home where Fayth had helped unload everything then passed out for two hours.

After her cat-nap, she had woken bright-eyed and attacked all of the food we had bought. Two hours later, delicious smells were coming out of the oven, and my stomach was growling for whatever she had made.

It was all Meg's fault.

"It normally is, Firecracker. That woman is a loon and a half."

But I like her.

"We all do, Fay. It'd be pretty bad if we didn't like the prez's ol' lady." I finished the rest of my beer and set the empty bottle next to my plate. "So, what did you want to do tonight?"

Fayth shrugged and pushed her food around on her plate.

"Movie? Video games? Pool?"

She tilted her head and mouthed the word "pool."

"Yeah, down in the basement."

Her eyes bugged out. She grabbed her pad of paper and frantically wrote. *Like water?* She held the notepad up, and I busted out laughing.

I shook my head. "Firecracker, you really think there is a pool in my basement?"

She glared at me and tossed the notepad on the table.

"It's a pool table," I chuckled.

She crossed her arms over her chest and huffed a breath out.

"Come downstairs and I'll show you. I guess you really haven't had time to wander around and see everything." I grabbed my dirty dishes and stacked them in the sink. Fayth stayed at the table, glaring at me as I grabbed her dishes and set them in the sink. I walked back over to the table and held my hand out. "Come on, Firecracker. I promise not to beat you too bad," I said with a wink.

She growled low and batted my hand away. Pushing past me, she stomped over to the fridge, grabbed the second bottle of wine then looked around. She held up the bottle and acted like she was trying to open it.

I grabbed the corkscrew out of the drawer and two glasses out of the cabinet. Wine glasses were one of the many things I didn't have, so old fashioned glasses were going to have to do for tonight. "Come on, Firecracker. I promise not to laugh anymore."

She rolled her eyes.

"You know, if you keep rolling your eyes at me, I'm going to develop a complex." I moved toward the door that lead to the garage and looked over my shoulder. "Don't forget your paper, Firecracker," I called.

I heard her growl again, and I had to assume she was shooting daggers at me with her eyes as I turned left and opened the door that led to the basement. Her soft footsteps followed me down the stairs, and I flipped on the lights and waited at the bottom of the landing for her.

The basement was the one place in the house I had spent time making complete, but I still didn't spend a lot of time down here. There was a pool table at the far end of the room, a foosball table closest to us, a dart board on one wall, and a fifty-inch flat screen TV on the other wall. On one side of the pool table was a small bar I had stocked with various types of booze and there were eight barstools randomly placed around the perimeter of the room. It was a perfect man cave.

"Slider," she gasped and took it all in.

"I fucking love when you say that," I mumbled. I couldn't lie. My name being the first word Fayth spoke after the shooting made me want to puff my chest out and howl at the moon.

"Ass," she laughed.

"My second favorite word you say." I winked at her before I grabbed her hand and tugged her over to the bar where I took the wine from her. "Go rack 'em up, and I'll open the wine."

She wandered over to the rack where all the pool cues were and grabbed the triangle.

I popped open the cork, filled two glasses half full, and watched Fayth corral the balls into the triangle.

"You played before?" I asked, surprised she correctly placed each ball.

She shrugged and lifted the triangle off of the table. She hung it on the corner of the rack and looked over the pool cues.

"Here's your wine, Firecracker." She chose a cue and rubbed it between her hands. Something about the way she chose the correct pool cue, and the way she held it, made me think this was most definitely not the first time she had played. Part of me felt I was dealing with a pool shark in sheep's clothing.

She grabbed the glass out of my hand and paced back and forth, never taking her eyes from the table.

I grabbed my cue. "You wanna break?"

An innocent smile spread across her lips, and she slightly nodded. She lined up her shot, and I watch as all of the balls scattered, and she managed to sink a stripe and a solid.

"Impressive."

Fayth smirked and pointed to a solid.

"All right, Firecracker. You're solids, I'm stripes. Game on."

Fayth lined up her next shot and sunk another ball.

I grabbed my drink and watched her circle the table, looking for her next shot. I sat down on a stool next to the bar and waited.

I had a feeling it was going to be a bit before I had a chance to play, but I definitely had some good scenery until it was my turn.

Fayth bending over the table, presenting her ass to me, wiggling back and forth while she lined up her shot was a sight I gladly welcomed.

Pool was fastly becoming my favorite past time.

****

566

Chapter 21

Fayth

"Cheater."

I rolled my eyes and grabbed the triangle to rack the balls again.

"You didn't even give me a chance to go," Slider whined, leaning against his pool cue.

I hadn't, but that was because I kicked ass at pool. I had spent many nights in pool halls in Chicago during college, mainly because it drove Leo up the wall. He thought his innocent little sister shouldn't be spending her time with the dirty lowlifes of the city.

My nights at the pool hall were my chance to feel like a normal person and not like Leo Banachi's sister who no one wanted to talk to in fear they would piss him off.

"How in the hell did you learn to play pool like that?"

I finished racking the balls and grabbed the glass of wine Slider had poured me. It was actually my fourth glass of wine, and I was well on my way to being drunk for the second time today.

I grabbed my pen and tapped it against my chin. Should I tell him the truth, that I was a rebellious teenager who did anything to piss off my brother? *I like pool.* I couldn't help but smile as I held it up to him. Slider didn't need to know everything about me.

"There's more to that than what you're saying," he laughed. "I bet you did it to piss off your brother, and every time you went out, he sent his goons after you to bring you home."

Hmm. Now that was the truth. I could count on one hand how many times I had gone out without one of Leo's men lurking in the crowd, keeping an eye on me. I took another sip of my wine and decided he was just going to have to use his imagination.

"Hold up there, Firecracker," he called as I made my way over to the end of the pool table. "I know I should be a gentleman and let you go first, but I know if I do that, I'll never get a chance."

I motioned for him to go and leaned against my pool cue. I would get my turn, and then I would win, just like I had last time.

Slider broke, the balls scattering everywhere, and he managed to sink a solid. "Now, it's your turn to stand there and watch how it's done." He smirked. He lined up his next shot, and I couldn't help but notice how his black t-shirt stretched across his shoulders, and the sleeves of his shirt inched up, giving me a better view of his tattoos.

He managed to sink another solid, but the white ball followed behind, right into the pocket.

"Son of a bitch," he mumbled. He grabbed it and handed it to me. "Be gentle, Firecracker."

I rolled my eyes and set the white ball down. I had grown up with Leo Banachi, whose philosophy was take no prisoners. Slider was going down again.

I lined up my shots, making sure I was going to sink all of my balls, and managed to beat Slider again.

"Five. Five fucking shots was all it took to wipe the floor with me." He shook his head and looked at the table that only had solids on it.

"Darts? Foosball? Can I beat you at any of those, or are you ringer at those, too?" He filled his glass and drained the bottle of wine.

I shrugged. I sucked at both, but I wasn't going to tell him that.

"I think it's time for a bet." He hung up his cue. "If I win the next game, you need to say my name."

I rolled my eyes. Like that was a big loss. I pointed at myself.

"And if you win, I'll do whatever you want me to."

I tilted my head. Did he know what he was doing? My prize was way better than the one he would get if he won. I could say his name right now for him, and it wouldn't be a loss to me.

I nodded, agreeing with his terms and walked over to the foosball table. I figured foosball was the best chance I would have at winning. I sucked at darts and was barely able to hit the board most of the time.

"No, no. I get to pick the game. For all I know, you could be the world foosball champion."

I snorted and shook my head. That was far from the truth.

Slider opened the cabinet around the dartboard and turned it on. It was one of those fancy ones with all the lights and it kept score. He handed me three darts, and I couldn't miss the smirk on his lips. "You ready to know what it feels like to have your ass beat?"

I rolled my eyes and looked at the darts. I doubted any of three he had given me were going to make it to the board. I hoped he was okay with holes in his drywall, because that was where these were headed.

"You think you can beat me in this, too, Firecracker?"

No, I didn't. I was about to lose the bet, but did it really matter? I nodded at the stereo he had in the corner.

"You think putting on music is going to distract me?"

I shrugged. It couldn't hurt.

Slider walked over to the stereo, hit a couple buttons, and then we were surrounded with the thumping of AC/DC pouring out of the speakers.

I couldn't help but laugh at his choice of song. "Big Balls" was not exactly the song I thought he would choose.

"What's with the smile?" he asked. "You don't like my song of choice? AC/DC is classic."

He stood about ten feet away from the dartboard and motioned for me to stand next to him. "Now, are you going to act like you have no clue about darts, or are you going to just tell me you are going to kick my ass?"

I shook my head. There would be no ass-kicking from me this time.

"You go first, Firecracker." He motioned to the board.

Slider moved to the left, and I stood squarely in front of the board. I had played darts maybe a handful of times, and that was it. Flying projectiles just didn't appeal to me.

I held up the dart, squinted at the board, and mentally pictured the head sinking into the board. I exhaled, said a silent Hail Mary, and let the dart fly.

It didn't even make it all the way to the board before it nosedived and stuck into the carpet.

Slider busted out laughing, bent over with his hands on his knees, and wheezed. "Oh Christ, that was horrible."

I rolled my eyes and bumped him with my hip as I walked by him. He grabbed my hand before he tumbled over, and we both ended up on the floor, me on top of Slider.

"That wasn't very nice, Firecracker," he said softly. His brown eyes shone up at me, and his hand cupped my head. "Don't tell me you're a sore loser."

I shook my head. I wasn't, except when I got laughed at. "Slider," I said sternly.

"Ah, I didn't even have to win for you to say my name. Although, after that throw, it was inevitable that I was going to win." He ran his fingers though my hair and gently tugged my head down. "I'm gonna kiss you, Fay. Tell me to stop if you don't want me to."

I smiled. "Ass."

"And there is my other favorite word," he chuckled. "But I'm assuming I'm an ass because you can't tell me to stop, but I know you don't want me to."

I gently pulled back, and he instantly let go of the hold he had on me. I couldn't say stop, but I knew if I made any move that I didn't want this, he would let me go without hesitating.

Slider looked up with concern written all over his face. "Stop?"

I bit my lip and shook my head.

"Go?" he whispered, hopeful.

I leaned down, my body covering him and my lips hovered above his. "Yes," I barely whispered.

"Jesus Christ." He pushed up, his lips touching mine, and he delved his fingers into my hair.

His lips claimed mine, sucking and licking as I braced my arms on the plush carpet. One hand snaked around my waist and held me close. My lips moved against his, feeling and tasting what I had been craving since I had met Slider. The man had driven me crazy, but I couldn't fight the attraction I had to him.

"Slider," I moaned against his lips as his hand drifted over my ass and gently squeezed.

"Say yes again so I know I wasn't hearing things," he whispered.

I opened my eyes and looked down into his face. "Yes," I said clearly.

"Fucking perfect," he breathed out. He rolled us over, his body covering mine with one of his knees between my legs. "Tell me to stop," he growled. "If you don't, I'll take everything I want."

I slightly shook my head no. I didn't want him to stop. I wanted him to do everything but stop.

His lips devoured mine, and his hands roamed over my body. He pulled off my shirt, and his fingers lightly skated over my skin. His palm spanned my side, and he squeezed gently. "So fucking soft," he growled. His other hand cupped my breast through my bra, and I arched my back into him.

I needed him to touch me everywhere before my body combusted into flames. His touch was setting me on fire, and I never wanted it to end. I grabbed the hem of his t-shirt and pulled it up his back and over his head.

His hands left me for a second, and I missed his touch instantly. "Slider," I moaned when he tossed his shirt to the side.

"I'm right here, Fayth. I'm not going anywhere," he vowed. He grabbed my hand and pulled me up. He sat back on his ass and pulled me into his lap. "You were fucking made to be in my arms." He lifted me up, positioning me in his lap and held me close.

I ran my fingers through his hair, finally able to know what it felt like.

"I've had these dreams for a while. I would have this crazy, wild sex, but I never knew who I was fucking. Last night, I had the dream again, and it was you. I was fucking you until you screamed my name and begged me never to stop."

I gasped as Slider slammed his lips down on mine, his tongue invading my mouth. My hands roamed over his bare back, and his hands frantically worked the clasp of my bra free. His hands immediately cupped my breasts when my bra broke free.

He squeezed and twisted my nipples as his mouth assaulted me, teasing and tasting all at once. "What the fuck are you doing to me, Fay?" he growled against my lips. "I can't get enough of you."

I ground my hips into him, the feel of his rock hard dick bulging under his jeans driving me insane. That was for me. I was making Slider feel this way. No one else but me.

"Yes," I gasped when he leaned down and captured my nipple in between his teeth. The sharp bite of pain mixed with the pure ecstasy my body was feeling.

Slider's hand slid down my stomach, working on the button of my jeans when we heard a loud bang. His head whipped up.

"What the fuck was that?" he growled.

I had no idea what it was. I was in a pleasurable fog that I didn't want to come out of. Whatever it was could wait for later. I reached up, cupping Slider's head, and he looked down at me. "Stay here, don't move." He grabbed his shirt and quickly pulled it over his head.

His hands deftly grabbed my shirt, covering my breasts, and he stood, gently setting me on the ground. He walked over to the bar, reached under the shelf, and pulled out a handgun. "I want you on the other side of the pool table and stay down. Only come out if I tell you to, no one else."

I nodded dumbly, reaching behind me to fasten my bra.

"Do you know how to use a gun?" He reached under the bar again and pulled out a smaller gun.

I nodded and quickly stood. He pressed the gun into my hand and pressed a kiss to my lips. "Stay down, shoot if it's anyone but me," he instructed. He pushed me towards the pool table and headed to the stairs.

"Slider," I called, and he stepped on the first step.

His eyes hit me, and he nodded. I didn't want him to leave. We had no idea what was going on, and he was headed up there blindly. "I'll be back, Fayth. I promised to never let anything hurt you again, and I'll die keeping that promise."

He slowly made his way up the stairs, both hands on the gun.

I waited until I couldn't see him anymore, and I slowly sank down behind the table, the gun at my side.

I finally discovered what Slider's touch was like, and I might never get to feel it again.

I prayed to God that Slider was going to be okay, because I knew if he wasn't, I wasn't going to be okay either.

****

Chapter 22

Slider

I crept up the stairs and saw the door to the garage was wide open. A car door slammed, and I heard tires squeal down the driveway. I flattened myself against the wall by the garage door and glanced in the kitchen.

The table was tipped upside down and three of the chairs were knocked over. That would explain the loud bang Fayth and I had heard. Footsteps sounded in the garage, and I quickly whipped around, my arms extended and pointed my gun.

"It's about fucking time you got your head out of your ass."

"What the fuck are you doing here?" I asked as I kept my gun trained on Creed, one of Leo's men.

"Looks like I'm here to babysit you fuckers again." He walked toward me, stopping two feet away and crossing his arms over his chest. "You can put the fucking gun down," he growled.

"Leo said he couldn't spare any men." I lowered the gun to my side and clicked the safety into place.

"Yeah, and Leo also worries about his sister and nephew. He was able to spare me to come help, and it looks like it was in the nick of time." Creed pointed down the driveway. "Some fuck face was breaking into your house when I pulled up. He managed to get in through the front door. I tried to take him down in the kitchen, but the fucker managed to slip away."

"Who the hell was it?" I couldn't believe Fayth had been in the house, and we hadn't heard someone trying to break in.

"Not a fucking clue. I was hoping that you would have an idea. Leo said he talked to King about finding out who's still around that is connected to Big A."

"Yeah, he did, but that was just today. We haven't had a chance to find any leads yet."

Creed nodded. "That's what Leo told me, but I was hoping that you guys had managed to figure something out already."

"We have two leads that we're going to track down, and hopefully one of them pans out. You manage to get the plates on the car?" I stepped back and let Creed through the door.

"No, fucker had them blacked out. It was newer black Town Car. I'd never seen the car before."

"I don't know anyone who drives a car like that either."

"You got any ice? I managed to get a couple of punches in before the fucker took off." Creed held up his hand that was red and swollen.

"Looks like they were at least good punches. Ice is in the fridge," I said, pointing in the kitchen. "Grab what you need. I'll get Fayth."

"What, you hiding her in the basement?" Creed chuckled.

I shook my head and started down the stairs. "We were playing pool," I called up to him.

I walked down the stairs and picked up the darts we had dropped. "Fayth, it's me, Firecracker," I called as I set them back on the shelf.

I heard her click the safety into place, and she slowly rose from the side of the pool table. "Slider?" she asked meekly.

"I'm okay," I assured. "Someone was trying to break into the house, and thankfully Creed showed up in time to stop him."

Fayth's eyes bugged out, and she gasped.

I grabbed the gun out of her hand and laid it underneath the bar. "You okay?"

She nodded and looked down at the floor.

"Fayth." I hooked a finger under her chin and lifted her head to look at me. "What's wrong?"

She bit her lip and shook her head.

"Where's that fucking paper?" We weren't going upstairs until I figured out what had changed from when I went up the stairs to now. I handed her the pad of paper, and she walked over to the bar.

It took her a minute, but she finally started writing.

You kissed me.

I read while she wrote. "I did more than kiss you, Fay," I growled.

She shook her head. *Why?*

She didn't look up from the paper, just waited for my answer. "Because I've wanted to kiss you since the first day I saw you, but I knew if I did that, things would change."

So why now?

"Because if I wouldn't have kissed you then, it would have happened eventually, and it probably wouldn't have been in private. I've been a ticking time-bomb, waiting for the right time to explode, Fay. I couldn't resist you anymore."

She tapped her pen on the paper and looked up at me.

"Don't look at me like that, Firecracker. I could give two shits about Creed being upstairs. I'll take you right there on that pool table, and you won't see the sunlight until Tuesday."

It's Saturday!!

I smirked. "I know damn well what day it is."

We just almost had sex, and we didn't even hear a guy breaking into your house.

I ran my hand through my hair. Yeah, that was definitely running through my mind. Fayth was a distraction I didn't need, but I fucking wanted her. "You're too damn distracting, Firecracker."

"Ass," she hissed.

"I love when you talk dirty to me."

She rolled her eyes. *You're the dirty talker. Not me.*

I grabbed the empty bottle and glasses. "Yeah, but you damn sure like it, Fay. Don't tell me you didn't stop for a second and picture me pounding the hell out of you bent over that pool table."

Her mouth dropped out, and she smacked me with the notepad.

I leaned down, my lips hovering over hers. "Did you really say yes before, or did I imagine it?"

"Yes," she whispered.

"You do know this means I'm going to have to keep pushing you, because that's when you speak."

She rolled her eyes and moved to step away from me.

"Not so fast, Firecracker. Right now, I have to go upstairs and deal with some shit I'd really rather not, but you can bet that lush ass of yours that we will be continuing this later." She glared up at me, but I couldn't miss the spark of desire in her eyes. Fayth wanted this just as much as I did; we just had to find the right fucking time.

I wrapped my arm around her waist and pulled her close. "You can't get away from me that easily, Fay. I'll always be right here." I pressed my lips against hers, needing one more taste. She moaned slightly, her hand pushing against my chest, but her body melted into mine. "You're going to be mine, Fayth. Just you wait," I growled against her lips.

"Slider," she breathed out. He eyes were filled with desire, and I knew it wouldn't be long until I made her mine.

I was sick of waiting.

****

Fayth

"What the hell were you two doing down there?"

Slider had his arms braced on the counter, and he growled and glared at Creed. I smoothed down my shirt, making sure it wasn't pushed up and wrinkled.

"You wanna talk to Fayth with a different tone?" Slider snarled.

Creed moved the ice that was on his hand. "I wasn't talking to Fayth," he shot back.

They both stood there, staring at each other.

I cleared my throat and stood next to Slider and waved at Creed, hoping to break the tension between them.

"Fayth," he said, his eyes surveying me. Creed and I had dated after I had Marco, and he still acted like we were possibly going to be something. "You look different."

I smoothed down my shirt again and looked down at the counter.

"She looks the fucking same. You mind taking your eyes off of her now?" Slider stood straight and moved over to stand in front of me partially.

Creed looked between Slider and me. "Leo is going to shit himself when he hears this," he mumbled, shaking his head.

I slammed my hand down on the counter and pointed my finger at Creed.

Slider snickered next to me.

"Don't give me that look, Fayth."

I would give Creed any look I felt like.

"I'm here to look after you."

I pointed at Slider.

"He's here to look after you?" Creed chuckled. "I just found some guy breaking in while you two were downstairs doing God knows what."

577

I grabbed a pad of paper and a pen that I had stuck by the fridge. *No, you are here to report back to Leo.*

Creed shrugged. "I can't deny that."

You can go.

Creed threw his head back and laughed. "No can do. Leo told me to stay here until all this bullshit gets tied up."

No.

"See, now this is why we never would have worked. I tell you something, and you think you know better." Creed crossed his arms over his chest and glared at Slider. "He can have you."

"Oh, I can have her? You're giving me permission?" Slider barked.

Creed shrugged. "If that's what you want to call it."

I put my hand on his arm and shook my head.

This is Slider's house, I wrote and shoved it in Creed's face.

I knew that was going to shut up Creed. It was a big thing to all of Leo's men to respect where they were. Talking to Slider the way Creed was would not go over well with Leo.

Creed put up his hands. "My bad." He tossed the ice pack into the sink and grabbed his keys off of the counter. "I'm gonna grab my bag that I dropped in the bushes." Creed headed out the front door, and Slider turned to look at me.

"You dated that douchewad?"

I glanced to the right and nodded. It wasn't really my brightest moment. I had been trying to piss off Leo, and dating one of his men was an easy way to do it.

"He's not Marco's dad, is he?"

My jaw dropped, and I shook my head.

"I knew you had said that his dad had died, but I didn't know if you just didn't want to tell him that douche was his dad." Slider shrugged and leaned against the counter.

"Ass."

"I fucking love when you call me that." Slider grabbed me around the waist and pulled me into his arms. "Say it again before douchelord comes back," he growled against my lips.

"Ass," I whispered.

He slammed his lips down mine and gave me a quick, but thorough, kiss. "Don't forget what I said before. I'm not done with you."

Slider pulled out of my arms and grabbed his boots from near the back door. "I need to call King and let him know what happened. I'm going to be a bit."

I looked at the clock and saw it was already after nine. *I think I'm going to go to bed.* I held up the paper to Slider, and he nodded.

"Sounds good, Firecracker." Slider slipped out the back door, and I collapsed against the counter.

What a night. I was ready to go to bed and pass out.

Slider kissed me. Someone broke into the house. Slider kissed me again. Creed was here. Slider kissed me again.

I think I needed another drink after the day I just had.

Hopefully, tomorrow was going to be a better day, although I totally wouldn't mind if Slider kissed me again.

****

Chapter 23

Slider

"I was wondering if you were going to tear yourself away from Fayth."

I shoved my phone in my pocket and turned around to look at Creed who walked across the backyard. "You gonna talk shit the whole time you're here?"

Creed shrugged and crossed his arms over his chest. "I really don't think you know what the hell you're doing with her."

"I think you're fucking wrong, but I know that your damn opinion doesn't mean shit to Fayth and me."

"You may be right about that, but I can guarantee Leo's opinion matters to Fayth."

He was right, but I really didn't think Leo had a problem with me. Leo was the one who had called me and had told me to take Fayth back to Rockton. "I guess I'll have to have a chat with Leo. Make sure we're on the same page."

Creed looked at the house. "You call King? Let him know what the hell happened."

I nodded. "He's aware."

"You wanna tell me how the hell you didn't know someone was breaking into your house?"

"I fucked up."

"That seems to be a pattern with you, Slider. Your fuck up three months ago landed Fayth in the hospital."

I growled and flexed my hands at my sides. I didn't need my fuck-ups listed off to me. "You ever make a mistake in your life before, Creed?"

"Yeah, but not that anyone knows."

"Well, I made a mistake with Fayth before, and I've vowed to never let it happen again."

"You were damn close to it happening tonight."

I shook my head. "I'll die before anything happens to Fayth again. We don't even know what the guy was doing here. He could have just been trying to get my TV."

Creed shrugged. "That may be true, but you should have been there before he even had a chance to get in the house."

I ran my fingers through my hair. I was beating myself up enough over the fact I wasn't paying attention, I didn't need Creed to beat a dead horse. "I got it, Creed. There isn't anything else I can say."

"You're right. Now fucking do what you keep saying. You die before anything happens to Fayth. I'll make sure of it." Creed stalked to the front of the house and I looked up at the dark sky.

"Fuck," I mumbled.

I needed to prove I was going to keep Fayth safe.

It was time to stop fucking around and to keep my word.

No more distractions until everything was fucking tied up in a neat little bow.

Then, Fayth would be mine.

****

Chapter 24

Fayth

It was Friday afternoon, and I had never been more confused in my life.

I could count on one hand the amount of times Slider said more than one word to me. Something had changed the night of the break-in after I had went to bed, and I had no idea what it was.

"Remy's here, Mom," Marco called.

I peeked out of the bathroom and motioned for him to come to me.

"What?"

I grabbed my small pad of paper from my back pocket. *Be safe. Listen to whoever is at the clubhouse watching you guys.*

"I know, you've told me five times. You should have saved the paper the first time you wrote it." Marco shoved his hands in his pocket and leaned against the wall. "Can I come with you to get a tattoo? I'm sure they would let me if you were there with me."

I shook my head no. *Not happening, Marco. You can get a tattoo when you're thirty.*

"Thirty?" Marco scoffed. "I swear each time I asked you, you add two years."

Ask me again.

Marco rolled his eyes and gave me a quick hug. "I'll text you when we get back to clubhouse. Don't get the Mike Tyson special."

I heard Creed bust out laughing in the kitchen, and I sighed. *Be good, and call me if you need me.*

Marco nodded and headed to the front door.

"You about ready, woman?" Creed called.

I rolled my eyes and slammed the bathroom door. "Ass," I muttered as I looked in the mirror. Creed knew I only said a few words, but he didn't care.

Creed pounded on the door. "I'm gonna be in the car. Hurry your ass up."

I flipped off the bathroom door, wishing Creed could see it. The man had been driving me insane the past week. He was my shadow who wasn't very good at blending in.

Slider had suddenly become too busy and had decided that since Creed was in town, he could be my personal bodyguard. The only reason I had been okay with having someone with me at all times before was because it had been Slider. Now, all I wanted to do was knee Creed in the nuts and grab a bottle of wine.

I examined myself in the mirror and sighed. I looked good, but I sure didn't feel good. I missed Slider, and I had no idea how to tell him without sounding like some needy bitch. He was always on his phone, either texting or quietly talking, and I didn't want to bother him. Things were tense all over, and I knew what he was doing was important, but it still sucked he wasn't home much anymore.

I had thought he would have come to the tattoo parlor tonight, but he left over two hours ago, with just the explanation that he had other plans.

I fluffed up my hair, hoping to add more volume and grabbed my lip gloss. I tossed it into my small handbag and gave myself one last look. I had opted for tight dark blue jeans with the Harley Davidson shirt Slider had bought back in Chicago. Meg had sent over a pair of motorcycle boots that were on my feet, and I had a light jean jacket to throw on. In the mirror, I looked like someone I had never seen before, but I had never felt more comfortable.

I flipped off the bathroom lights and was surprised to see Slider walking in the front door as I pulled my jean jacket on. "Slider?"

Slider stopped in his tracks when he saw me, and his jaw dropped. "Fay?" His eyes traveled over my body, and I wished it was his hands instead. "Uh…"

A smile spread across my lips, and I grabbed my clutch off of the table. "Yes?"

"Is that what you are wearing tonight?" he asked and stepped closer.

I looked down, and nodded. "Yes."

"That's the shirt I bought, isn't it?"

I nodded. It sure as hell was, and I knew exactly what he was going to say next.

"You planning on keeping that coat on all night?"

I smirked and shrugged. I had planned on it, unless I got a tattoo, but he didn't need to know that.

"Keep your coat on," he said low.

I tossed my hair over my shoulder and just looked at him. If he wanted me to wear my coat all night, he needed to come along and keep an eye on me himself.

"Fayth," he growled.

"Slider," I whispered. I missed this damn man, and he was getting pissed at me over a damn shirt.

"That fucking shirt barely has a back."

I rolled my eyes. It had a back, it was just cut into strips. A lot of them.

"Turn around," he ordered.

I shook my head. He couldn't not talk to me all week and then just walk in here and expect me to do whatever he says. The man was insane.

I moved to step around him, but he grabbed my arm and spun me around. He pressed his front to my back, and he buried his nose in my hair. "I've missed you," he whispered.

My eyes closed, and I sighed.

"I'm sorry, Firecracker. Things are so fucked up right now, I can't see clear." He grabbed the front of my coat and pulled the sleeves off. "I've wondered what this shirt would look like on you. You looked like a biker's dream when I walked through the door."

The coat fell to my feet, and his hands traveled over my back. I sighed again and forgave him for the past few days he had ignored me. This man had quickly become my weakness, and I didn't even care. I needed him more than my next breath.

"I can't even remember what I walked in here for. You distract me just by being you."

I laughed and looked over my shoulder. "Slider," I whispered.

His eyes locked with mine, and I could feel the air charge with the attraction between us. "Fuck it," he growled. He delved his hands into my hair, and I spun around. My arms instinctively wrapped around his shoulders, and I held on as his lips assaulted my mouth. I gave him everything I had.

"I'll never get enough of you," he moaned against my lips.

I held him close, wishing I never had to let him go.

A horn blared from outside, and we jumped apart, both of us looking at each other like we had just gotten caught with our hand in the cookie jar.

"I need to go," he muttered as he wiped his hands on his jeans. "I just needed to grab something." I smirked and shook my head. "Well, grab something besides you," he laughed.

I nodded. He had important things to do, and I was in the way. I ducked my head and stepped around him towards the door.

He grabbed my arm again and turned me to face him. "I'm almost done, Fay. Just wait for me."

I leaned up on my tiptoes and pressed a kiss to his cheek. "Okay," I whispered.

Slider sputtered, amazed at the new word I could say. If he were around more, I would have shared with him a couple of other words that had decided to start falling out of my mouth.

"Fayth," he called as I sauntered over to the door.

I looked over my shoulder. "Yes?"

"You won't have to wait long."

I hoped not, because I couldn't be held responsible for what I would do if he did make me wait. I was not above crawling onto the couch where he slept and having my way with him.

I smiled and walked out the door.

Slider was going to have one hell of a surprise when he decided to spend more than five minutes with me.

God, please don't make that man wait much longer. My patience was gone, and I was ready for Slider to make me his.

****

Chapter 25

Slider

I watched Fayth climb into the car with Creed and waited 'til the taillights disappeared before I moved away from the window. My phone buzzed, and I pulled it out to see a text message from Troy.

I'm here. Where the fuck are you?

I should have been there too, but I realized I hadn't grabbed my gun and ran back to the house to grab it. *Be there in ten.*

I shoved my phone back in my pocket, stalked to the bedroom, and tossed open the closet door. After pushing the clothes to one side, I turned the combination on the wall safe. The lock clicked into place, and I swung the door open. I grabbed my .45 and an extra clip and slammed the safe shut.

The clothes swayed as I moved them back in front of the safe, and I slid the door back. The bed was a mess, and I knew if I got closer to it, I would be able to smell Fayth's sweet scent all over it. The past week had been torture not going to her room every night, but I knew I needed to stay focused, or one of us was going to end up hurt, or even worse, dead.

Hammer and Turtle had good luck when they had gone to the bar outside of town. They found out Big A was in contact with at least three of his old minions. Two of whom had been at the bar that night.

All they could tell Hammer and Turtle was Big A had asked them to keep an eye on the Knights and let him know if anyone started sniffing around. Of course, they didn't dispense this information until Hammer showed them the reason he had that nickname. The guy had a right hook that felt like you were being smashed in the face with a sledge hammer.

Apparently, the guy who had broken into my house was someone Big A had hired to toss it to scare Fayth back to Chicago. We weren't sure why he wanted her out of Rockton, yet.

They had also given us the name "Kramer," but we didn't know who that name belonged to, or how he came into play.

Tonight, Demon, Troy, and I were meeting at the clubhouse, and then were going to head over to the strip club. The fucking thing was finally about to open and word was Cherry was planning on applying for a job. We hoped we were going to find out more about what was going on with Big A, since she was related to him. We knew this might be a dead end, but we needed to check out every lead we had just to make sure we weren't missing anything.

I knew Fayth had been disappointed when she found out I wouldn't be going to the tattoo parlor with her, but King wouldn't let me get out of going to the strip club. He said he would help keep an eye on the girls, but I was still worried about Fayth.

This past week, I hadn't been with her as much as I should have been, and I felt guilty as hell. Creed had agreed to keep an eye on her for me since whenever I was around her, I was distracted as fuck.

My phone buzzed again, and I pulled it out to see Fayth had texted me.

I miss you, too.

Well, shit. I squeezed my phone in my hand and wished like hell I could be with her right now.

Soon enough, all of this shit would be over, and I would have Fayth in my arms.

Fucking soon.

****

Fayth

"You actually into that guy?"

I looked over at Creed and rolled my eyes.

We were on our way to the tattoo parlor where we were going to meet all of the girls. I grabbed my pen and wondered what I ever saw in Creed. *Not any of your business.*

"Come on, Fayth. You can tell me." He glanced over at me with a huge grin on his face.

I like him. That's all you get.

"I like ice cream, doesn't mean I'm going to have sex with it."

I rolled my eyes again. *Your weird sexual preferences don't matter to me.*

"At one point in time, they did, but I'm pretty sure they did only because you wanted to piss your brother off."

I shrugged and tossed the notepad on the dash. Using Creed the way I did wasn't really something I wanted to talk about.

"I get it, Fayth. I know I'm not the kind of man you want, but I find it hard to believe that Slider is going to be the guy who can handle you either."

I didn't want to be handled. I just wanted to be with someone who liked me for who I was, and not for who I was related to. Slider never cared that Leo was my brother and didn't give a shit about the things Leo could offer.

"Just make sure he treats you good. You know if he doesn't, Leo will make sure he does."

I rested my head against the window and sighed.

I knew what I wanted, and I knew Slider was the man who was going to give it to me.

I just wanted to be loved for me, and nothing else.

****

Chapter 26

Slider

"Are you fucking sure she's here?"

"Yeah, her name is at the bottom of the list."

Demon leaned back in his chair and stretched his arms over his head. "You think Hammer would have been smarter and put her name at the top of the fucking list."

"You do know you just said you assumed Hammer was smart, right?" I laughed and grabbed my beer. "It's a miracle he was able to read the sheet at all."

"I could be at home with Marley right now, but instead, I'm sitting here with you assholes watching some chicks shake their asses." Troy tossed his phone on the table and crossed his arms over his chest.

"Well, it's fucking official. We are all pussy-whipped if we'd rather be with our women than at a strip club." Demon laughed and pointed to the door. "Looks like our girl just walked in."

A dark-haired chick walked through the door, with tight black shorts barely covering her ass and a white t-shirt her tits were trying to bust out of. "Typical club girl," I mumbled as we watched her stroll over to the bar.

"That typical club girl is your type, brother," Demon replied.

I shook my head. "Used to be."

"Ah, you finally get your head out of your ass? I remember not too long ago you giving King and Rigid crap about giving up the club pussy." Demon nudged me with his shoulder.

"Things change," I muttered.

"Yeah, you found the one chick that does what none of these other chicks can do," Troy replied.

"Tell him what that one thing is, Troy," Demon said, smirking.

"She fucking loves you even when you're being a dick."

Demon busted out laughing. "That wasn't what I thought you were going to say, but that is definitely true."

Troy grabbed his beer, chugged the rest of it, and crushed the empty can. "Then, what the hell did you think I was going to say? I know Marley puts up with a lot of my shit, but she still manages to like me."

"About the same thing, just not in the same words. Our ol' ladies love us, these bitches love the idea of being an ol' lady and are always looking for the next best thing. Gwen could care less if I was part of the club."

"So, you need to find a chick who doesn't care?" I laughed.

Troy threw his crushed empty can at me. "You already found a chick."

"Don't tell me you haven't figured that shit out and locked her down yet?" Demon asked.

I shook my head and turned to watch Cherry. "We have an understanding."

"I hope that understanding ends with her in your bed at night."

"It does." I didn't need to tell them that she was in my bed, but I wasn't there with her.

"Let's get this fucking show on the road. If we're lucky, we can head over to the tattoo parlor after this and catch up with the girls." Demon motioned to the bartender, and we all sat back, ready to get this shit over with.

We were auditioning girls for the stage and for being waitresses. I firmly believed that if either Gwen or Marley knew Demon and Troy were here, they would have their balls cut off. And I'm pretty sure Fayth would feel the same way.

"Cherry Pie" poured out of the speakers and the first candidate wobbled her way onto the stage in way too high heels and her hair piled even higher on her head. Demon and Troy both looked bored watching her slink around on the stage.

We all couldn't help but laugh when her shoes proved to be more than she could handle, and she fell off the stage, landing on her ass.

Well, if anything, this was definitely going to be entertaining.

****

Chapter 27

Fayth

"How bad does it hurt?"

I held up two fingers and shrugged my shoulders. On a scale of one to ten, it didn't really hurt.

"Am I seriously the only one who doesn't have any tattoos?" Marley whined.

Cyn nodded. "Around here you are. Why don't you let Darby at that virgin skin of yours?" Cyn was sitting in the chair next to mine, her sleeve rolled up, waiting for her guy to start tattooing.

There were four artists working tonight, and Cyn, Meg, Gwen, and I were all getting inked at the same time. Paige was looking at all of the flash art, trying to find the perfect swallow she wanted on her wrist.

Marley had been going back and forth since we got here trying to decide if she was going to get a tattoo.

"Woman, get a tattoo if you want one. Don't get a tattoo if you don't want one. Just make up your mind," Meg called. She was lying on her stomach, her shirt pulled down, and a guy named Axel was working on the small crown she wanted on her shoulder.

"But, it's just so…permanent," Marley mumbled.

"Oh Lord, are you sure I can't drink while you're tattooing me?" Meg asked Axel as she looked over her shoulder at him.

"Yeah," he grunted.

"You're not a man of many words, are you, Axel?" Meg chirped.

Darby, who was doing my tattoo, giggled. "Axel is the silent giant." She picked up the tattoo gun and held it over my shoulder. "You should feel honored that he's talking to you, Meg. He doesn't even talk to Mabel."

"The chick up front?" Cyn asked. "How the hell does that work? I mean, Fayth doesn't talk, but that's because she can't."

"I talk," Axel growled.

Darby sat up, shocked. "So you do, Ax. You just never seem to talk to clients, or Mabel," she snickered.

"I'm always up for a good ribbing," Meg said, "but do you think you could continue this when Axel doesn't have a needle in my skin?"

"Ax slings ink like no one I've ever seen before, Meg. You've got nothing to worry about," Imogen, who was working on Gwen's tattoo on her forearm, said. "He did my back piece."

"Oh, I want to see," Meg called.

"Stay," Axel barked.

"Easy, Ax. I meant I want to see it after you're done with me," Meg replied. She reached behind her, flailing her arm.

"Stop," Axel grunted.

"I'm trying to pat you. You know, calm ya down."

Axel grabbed her arm and pressed it to her side. "I'm not a dog."

"Well, neither am I, but you told me to stay like I was one," Meg pouted.

"Why do I always get the talkers?" Axel complained.

Darby laughed and shook her head. "You have to realize that Mabel does that on purpose, right? I mean, she gave me the chick that doesn't talk, and you the one that talks a mile a minute."

"Hey, I think I should be offended by that," Meg whined. "Although, Lo says the same thing. Speaking of Lo, where did he go?" She looked around.

I pointed to the front door.

"Fayth and I saw him go out the front door with Creed a couple of minutes ago," Cyn told Meg.

"Hmm, I wonder what is going on. Lo has been acting weird the past week. Kind of like when he tried to hide the whole Big A threatening Gwen thing." Meg laid her head flat on the table. "I hoped with Big A being in jail that everything would be over. I was obviously wrong."

I had felt the same way as Meg all week. Except, I knew a bit more about what was going on. Not only were they still dealing with Big A, they were also dealing with whatever Leo sent me back to Rockton for.

"That's it, I'm doing it," Marley announced. "On my wrist." She thrust her wrist in my face. "A small cowboy hat."

I looked up at her and quirked my eyebrow. A cowboy hat was the last thing I expected her to say.

"For Troy, because Dad calls him cowboy all the time," Marley explained.

"I think that's perfect," Paige said as she stepped into the back of the shop.

"You do?" Marley spun around and thrust her wrist at Paige. "I've always thought about it, but I didn't know if that made me crazy, or if it would jinx Troy and me."

"Pshh, that's nonsense. Lo and I both have each other's names on us," Meg said, her face smushed into the table. "Yeah, it's in my birdcage."

"Maybe I'll get something else," Marley blurted out. "What did you guys all get again?"

Cyn rolled her eyes and pointed at me. "For the third time, Meg is getting a tiny crown, Gwen is getting a pair of scissors, comb, and blow dryer on her forearms, I'm getting the lotus I've been wanting, and Fayth is getting a pair of lips behind her ear."

"Lips?" Paige asked.

I nodded. I hadn't explained why yet, and I was hoping I wouldn't have to.

"I think you should get a tramp stamp, Marley. That way, Troy has something to look at when he's going at ya," Gwen laughed.

Marley tapped her chin. "You know…no, never mind. I'm not doing that. Troy would only want to do it doggie style then, and while I like that, I need variety."

"Oh Jesus," Axel rumbled under his breath.

"What are you getting?" Marley asked Paige.

"I'm going to get a swallow on my wrist."

"What does it mean?" Marley asked. Marley believed that every tattoo had to have some deep, hidden meaning.

"Uh, well. It means I think it's pretty, and I want it on my wrist," Paige laughed.

Marley sighed. "I still don't know."

"You sure I can't have that drink, Axel?" Meg asked.

Axel grunted and shook his head. "Thirty minutes, and then you can drink all you want."

Darby pulled back my hair, and I held it. "Deep breaths, tell me if I need to stop," she instructed me.

I closed my eyes and concentrated on breathing. The hum of the machine was next to my ear, and she smeared some goo on my neck.

"Here we go," she mumbled.

The needle pricked my skin and slowly moved over the stencil.

"Doing okay?" she asked.

I gave her a thumbs up, and she continued working on the outline.

"Scale of one to holy fuck balls, how bad does it hurt?" Marley asked me.

"I'd say from the grimace on her face, we're going to go with a six, possibly seven," Cyn said, trying to help me out.

"A six isn't too bad," Marley muttered. "Okay. I'm doing it. Totally going to do it," she said, psyching herself up. She rubbed her hands on her jeans and moved her head side to side.

"I'll get you in ten minutes," Darby said. "These lips won't take long." Darby stopped tattooing, giving me a few seconds of relief. I may have lied when I held up two fingers to Marley before. I felt like my brain was getting rattle around with each stroke of the needle.

"Ten minutes? That soon?" Marley gasped.

Darby shook her head and dipped her needle into the black ink. "I swear to you that you won't even notice me tattooing you. It'll just be like a mosquito bite."

Marley took a deep breath and nodded. "Okay, I'm totally doing this."

"Thank Christ," Meg said, laughing. "I was thinking we were going to have to strap you to the chair for a second there."

"Demon just texted me," Gwen said. "They were doing auditions at the club tonight, and he said they've already had two girls fall off the stage, and he thinks one of them broke their nose."

Cyn and Paige busted out laughing, while Meg snorted. "I think I would pay to see that."

"I think Troy is with them too," Paige giggled. "I asked him if he was going to be raring to go when he got home. He just rolled his eyes and took off in his truck. He didn't seem too enthused to be stuck with helping Demon and Slider."

"Slider?" I asked.

"Hey, I thought she couldn't talk," Axel said.

"She can only say her man's name and maybe like three other words," Meg told him.

It was more like shit-ton of words I could say now, but no one knew that. What I was more concerned about was the fact that Slider was at a strip club right now, and hoping that I didn't pass out from pain. I was starting to rethink ever getting a tattoo anywhere near my head.

"Yeah, he didn't tell you that King stuck them with interviewing the dancers and waitresses?" Cyn asked.

I waited 'til Darby stopped for a second and shook my head. He hadn't told me anything other than he had things he needed to take care of tonight.

"I wouldn't be too concerned, Fayth. Demon said Slider looked like he's about to fall asleep. Gambler just showed up, and they are placing bets on who is going to fall next." Gwen held up her phone to show me the text message.

I shrugged and tried to act like I didn't care. Obviously, Slider didn't want me to know what he was doing, but Demon and Troy were okay with telling Gwen and Marley.

"You okay with me going again?" Darby asked me.

I nodded and closed my eyes as the needle pierced my skin. I strained my ears to hear what the girls were saying and was able to pick up the majority of what they were talking about.

"Demon said they're going to stop by when they are done if we are still here." Gwen said.

"Who's stopping by?"

I opened my eyes and watched King walk over to Meg and look down at the tattoo she was getting. "You're crazy, you know that, right?" King mumbled under his breath.

"Axel doesn't like me," Meg pouted, completely ignoring King.

"Who the hell is Axel?" King demanded.

Meg pointed over her shoulder. "The guy doing my tattoo."

"You talking his ear off?" King asked.

Meg batted her eyes at King and shook her head. "No more than usual."

"You got a big tip coming your way, brother," King said, laughing. "You heard from Rigid?" he asked Cyn.

"Yeah, he's waiting for Micha to fall asleep. He sounded exhausted the last time I talked to him," Cyn snickered. "I think that man is finally realizing what I go through every day."

I tried to focus on the loud buzz of the tattoo gun in my ear, but all I could think about was Slider not telling me where he was going. I didn't ask him, so he didn't lie to me about it, but I still felt like he had lied to me.

"Switching to color," Darby muttered.

I thought about the tattoo I was getting and hoped I wouldn't regret it later on down the road.

My neck was the first place Slider had kissed me, and that was one kiss I never wanted to forget. Now, I would have a tattoo on my neck, reminding me of that day every single day.

Oh Lord, I hoped I hadn't just made a mistake.

It felt like Slider and I knew so much about each other, but there were still things he didn't know. I knew I would tell Slider any and everything about me, but I didn't know if that ran true for him.

Only time would tell.

****

Chapter 28

Slider

"We about done with this shit?"

"This is the last one before Cherry is up," Troy mumbled, tossing the notebook on the table. We had seen at least twenty girls audition to be a dancer, and maybe three of them were good enough to possibly go on stage. Demon figured three other ones were good enough to be waitresses, and the rest were shown the door.

The girl on the stage wobbled in the heels she was wearing, and Gambler sat up, ready to watch her fall, and take the money he had laid out on the bet that at least one more girl would take a digger.

"Timber," Demon whispered under his breath as the girl took one more step, stumbled, rolled her right ankle, and landed flat on her ass.

"Pay up, fuckers," Gambler gloated. "I told you she was going to fall. I saw her walk in, and she could barely make it across the room, there wasn't a chance in hell she was going to be able to dance on stage."

Gambler held out his hand, and Demon slapped a twenty in it. "You think we would have learned by now," he muttered.

"Next!" I called as the girl hobbled off.

Cherry was sitting at the bar and fluffed her hair while she stood. She tugged on her shorts and smoothed down her shirt before she sauntered up on stage. "Haven't seen you boys in a while," she purred.

I motioned to the bartender to clear out the room and all of the girls scattered out the door.

"Oh, I see how it is, you boys want me all to yourselves." Cherry made her way down the stage, and Demon put his hand up to stop her.

Troy curled his lip. "Is this chick for real?"

Cherry stopped and put her hands on her hips. "Oh, I see. You boys want a show first." Cherry fluffed her hair and bent over, her ass in the air and slowly stood, running her hands up her legs.

"For the love of God, make it stop," Troy shouted as he stood. His chair skidded backwards and slammed into the wall. Gambler had a hand over his eyes, and he was shaking his head.

I couldn't help but chuckle. We had become a sad bunch of men who didn't want to watch strippers. "You might want to keep your clothes on," I called to her. "I don't think Troy's eyes can take any more."

"We have a few questions to ask you, Cherry. Come have a seat," Demon said, motioning to the chair Troy had been sitting in.

Cherry stepped of the stage and strode over to the chair. "I figured you guys would want to see what I can do, not talk to me."

"We're more interested in what you know," Demon explained, resting his arms on the table.

Cherry's eyes darted between Demon and me. "I need a job, that's all I know."

"You know more than that, and you're going to tell us," I insisted. Cherry had nerve walking into a strip club owned by the Knights and thinking she could act like she owned the place.

"Well," she said, crossing her arms over her chest, "I guess you'll have to ask your questions, and I'll tell you if I know the answer."

"I can't decide if she's actually clueless, or if she has *cajones* the size of China," Gambler commented while he surveyed Cherry.

"I'm going to go with a little bit of both," Troy muttered.

"Is there actually a job here for me, or are you guys just being assholes like those bitches you guys date," she hissed.

Gambler made to stand up, but Demon grabbed his arm and held him back. "You might want to choose your words very carefully when you talk about the women in our lives," Demon sneered. "That also goes for the women in our brothers' lives too."

Cherry rolled her eyes and smacked her lips. "I'm suddenly forgetting everything I know. I think it's time for me to leave." Cherry stood, and Demon nodded at me.

I moved quickly, grabbing Cherry by the arm and twisting it behind her back. "You're hurting me," she shrieked.

I knew I wasn't hurting her. Hurting people was one of the things I knew how to do well, and the way I was holding her, anyone could break free from if they truly wanted to.

"We just have some questions for you, Cherry. You're the one who has the attitude," Demon replied. "Besides, I remember seeing you in this position before when you didn't heed King's warning the last time you were at the club."

Cherry growled and tried to jerk her arm out of my hold. "King should have been mine," she snarled.

"Obviously, King saw things differently," Troy said with a shrug.

"You're that bitch's best friend," Cherry spit out. "You're just as bad as she is."

"I'd like to take that as a compliment, and not an insult." Troy moved in close, inches away from Cherry's face. "You know why I'm taking that as a compliment?" Cherry shook her head. "Because if I took it as an insult, that would mean you were also insulting Meg, too, and Demon told you not to do that. I'd hate for you to find out the reason behind Slider's name."

The blood drained from Cherry's face, and she swallowed hard. I tighten the grip I had on her arm, and she arched her back. "I don't know anything," she gasped.

"I find that hard to believe. You have to know something, otherwise you wouldn't have strutted in here the way you did," Gambler said.

"I swear. I've only talked to Alfonso three times since he's been in jail."

"Alfonso?" Gambler scoffed. "I can see why he goes by Big A."

"It was my grandfather's name," Cherry bit out.

Gambler shrugged and laughed. "I feel bad for your grandfather now, too."

Cherry snarled, and I twisted her arm. This girl needed to learn how to not show what she was feeling. She was going to end up with a broken arm in no time.

"Tell me what your cousin has been telling you," Demon demanded.

"He told me you killed Nate," she spit out. "You killed my brother, and you're sitting here acting like you're better than me and my family."

"I know we're better than your family, because we don't beat women," Troy barked. "You ever wonder how Cyn got the shit beat out of her? YOUR MOTHER FUCKING BROTHER!"

Troy's words hit Cherry one by one, and the blood drained from her face. "He didn't," she whispered.

"He did. He fucking did, Cherry. You can believe that your brother was some great guy, but when it comes down to it, he was a cheater, a liar, and fucking coward who beat women." Troy slammed his fist down on the table.

"My brother wouldn't do that. He was an asshole, but he would never hit a woman."

Demon shook his head. "It's good for you that we're not asking about that, because you're not seeing that shit clearly. We need to know what your cousin has been telling you."

"There hasn't been anything except for just normal stuff," Cherry said, shaking her head.

"I want to hear it all, even if you think it has nothing to us," Demon demanded.

A lone tear streaked down her cheek. "I really don't know anything. I swear I haven't known anything this whole time. He just told my family a couple of months ago that Nate had gone back to Mexico, and he had died in a fight. I swear I had no idea he had tried to hurt Cyn."

"He hurt her, not fucking tried to," Troy growled.

Demon held up his hand, silencing Troy. We were all pissed off about the fact that Cyn had been hurt, but we had taken care of that problem by getting rid of Asshat, now we had to deal with Big A. "Just tell me every word he said to you, Cherry, and nothing will happen to you. We know that you have nothing to do with this, but if you don't tell us what you know, this might not end well for you."

Cherry looked around and nodded. "Fine, but I don't think me telling you about him finding a new doctor is really going to help with anything."

"How the hell does he have a new doctor if he's in jail?" Gambler asked.

"I don't know. The last two times I visited him, he told me I couldn't stay long because his doctor was also coming."

"Did you ever see this doctor?" I asked.

"No. I was always gone before he showed up," Cherry replied.

Demon nodded and leaned back in his chair. "What else did he tell you?"

"He always asked about my mom and me. We really didn't talk about much. My visits were only ten or fifteen minutes. The first visit he said he was sorry about my brother, and that he was going to make everything right. I didn't think much of what he said, because he's in jail. What the hell can he do while he's in there?"

"Apparently, enough," I mumbled.

"Look, I swear to you that I have no idea what Alfonso is planning. I wish none of this would have happened, and Nick was still here," she sobbed.

Troy rolled his eyes and crossed his arms over his chest. "I really doubt you've had a complete change of heart in the past ten minutes. You were mouthing off about Meg and Cyn not even five minutes ago."

"Honestly," she said, "I don't like them, but I don't want them dead. They both seem to get everything they want, while I'm sitting in a strip club begging for my life while wondering where my next meal is going to come from."

"So, that makes you a raging bitch?" Troy shook his head and sat down at the table next to us.

"Did he ever tell you what the doctor's name was?" Demon asked.

"No. All he said was he had an appointment with his doctor. I didn't ask any questions, because I've learned not to question Alfonso, even if it's an innocent question."

"You think we can figure out who this doctor is?" Gambler asked Demon.

Demon shrugged. "It's more than what we had before."

"Am I done?" Cherry asked.

"Is that all you know?" Demon asked her.

"That's all. I had no idea my brother was an ass, and that Alfonso was an even bigger ass."

Demon nodded at me, and I let go of Cherry's arm. "Better not be lying," I whispered.

She glared at me and rubbed her arm. "I don't have a reason to lie."

"You also really don't have a reason to be a bitch to the girls, but you still are," I replied.

Cherry rolled her eyes. "Can I go now? I have to find another job, and you guys just wasted my night."

Demon nodded at her, and she flounced over to the door.

"Come back next week, maybe we can find a waitressing job for you," Demon called.

"Really?" Cherry asked.

"If what you just told us pans out, and you don't go running back to your cousin, then we'll see what we can figure out, but just know, your attitude is going to have to do a one-eighty if you have any hopes of working here."

Cherry nodded and disappeared out the door.

"Fucking really?" Troy asked. "You do know that Meg and the girls are going to flip their shit when they find out you offered her a job, right?"

Demon shrugged. "It's not like the girls or any of us are going to be hanging out here. Besides, King has the final say." Demon picked up his beer. "That's not really the issue at hand right now. We need to figure out who this doctor is."

"I doubt he even is a doctor. It's gotta be code for something," Gambler said.

"He must still have some of his men working for him. Hammer and Turtle said that no one was with him anymore, but I find that hard to believe," I replied.

"Well, whatever, or whoever the doctor is, we need to figure it out." Demon glanced at the clock and shook his head. "King said we need to head over to the tattoo parlor when we were done. He said the girls were up to their normal antics."

"I bet ya it's Meg," Gambler mumbled.

"He didn't really say who, but it sure was fucking loud when he called earlier," Demon laughed.

"Gwen hasn't texted me in a while, so I can only imagine what's going on there." Gambler grabbed his phone off of the table and shoved it in his pocket. "I'm heading over there. The rest of you fuckers coming too?"

"Rolly, lock up for us, would ya?" Demon called to the bartender.

Rolly walked out from the back and nodded. "Will do. You want me to call back any of those girls you saw tonight?" Rolly was going to be the general manager of the club, and also a bartender when need be.

Demon pointed to the list on the table. "Circled ones are the ones you can call. There ain't many of them, though. We're going to have to run another ad in the newspaper."

Rolly nodded and chuckled. "I didn't figure you would have too many. Falling off the stage really isn't something we want."

"True that. Brother," Troy said, raising his fist in the air.

"What about the last one?" Rolly asked.

"We'll have to get back to you on that one. King is going to have to decide," Demon replied as he slid his leather jacket on.

"She had an attitude on her, but she had the look to her that would draw men into here," Rolly replied.

Rolly was right. Cherry wasn't bad to look at, it was just when she opened her mouth that she became ugly.

We all agreed but didn't like to.

"It sure feels good to be on the bike," Gambler said when we walked outside.

It was late April, and there was still a chill in the air, but we felt it was time to get back on our bikes. Winter was hell on a biker who couldn't ride.

"I was surprised that you actually got yours out, Slider. You were moping around so much the past months that I thought you were hanging it up." Demon swung his leg over his DynaGlide.

I shrugged. "Just didn't feel like riding before."

"But now you do?" Troy flipped his keys up in the air.

"Just finally felt like getting her ready," I replied as I straddled my bike.

"I think he means he finally got Fayth straightened, so now everything else can go back to normal," Gambler said, laughing.

I flipped him off and cranked up my bike. The motor roared beneath me, and it felt damn good. What would feel even better would be when I had Fayth on the back with me.

"Meet y'all at the tattoo place," Troy called, walking over to his truck.

Demon and Gambler both started up their bikes, and Demon circled his hand in the air and we took off towards town.

The tattoo parlor was only ten minutes away, but it felt like ten minutes too long. I missed Fayth, and I needed to see her again. I had told her she was going to have to wait until the Big A situation was under control, but I wasn't sure I could wait that long.

I needed to make her mine.

****

Chapter 29

Fayth

"Ow."

"Good lord, she hasn't even touched you yet."

"Ouch."

"Sweet Jesus. I need a drink, Axel," Meg called from the table she was sprawled out over.

All of us had our tattoos done, Paige included, and we were just waiting for Marley to be done. Well, it was more like we were waiting for Marley to even start.

Darby turned on the tattoo gun, and Marley about jumped out of her skin.

"Oh hell. I can't do this," she gasped.

I rolled my eyes and grabbed the half-empty bottle of wine off of the floor. This had been happening for the past hour, and we were all about to lose our minds.

Meg stood. "Good, we can go home."

"But I really want it," Marley whined.

"Oh, Mylanta. We're never going to get out of here," Cyn sighed.

"Look, either you're going to get it, or you're not. Decide, woman," Axel barked. The quiet man we had first met was gone and was replaced by an impatient giant who just wanted to go home. Marley had played musical tattoo artists for a bit, going from one to the other trying to decide who she wanted to tattoo her.

"I'm sticking with Darby. I know that," Marley said confidently.

Axel stood. "About fucking time. Good luck, Darby. Hopefully you aren't here when I come back in the morning." Axel headed out the backdoor with Imogen and Keegan following him.

"And then there was one," Gwen mumbled.

"Okay," Marley said before she took a deep breath. "Let's do this. No turning back. She closed her eyes and put her wrist on the table in front of Darby.

"Girl, grab that wrist and tattoo something on it before she changes her mind again," Paige said from the floor.

Cyn was sitting in the same chair she had started in, while I was sitting on the floor next to Paige, and Gwen and Meg were sprawled out on the tables. Three bottles of wine were being passed around, and the last of one was now firmly in my hand, and I didn't want to give it up.

"I'm going to have to run to the liquor store if we don't get this thing going soon." Gwen held up her empty bottle of wine.

"I have some up front," Darby replied, poising the tattoo gun over Marley's arm. "Last time, chick. You chicken out, you're going to have to come back, and I highly doubt you'll get anyone to tattoo you."

Marley shook her head. "I'm ready," she whispered.

We all held our breath, praying this would be the time Marley did it.

Darby gently pricked Marley's skin, and nobody moved.

Marley peeked open one eye and looked down at her wrist. "Is that it?" she asked Darby.

"For the most part, *chica*. Just about twenty more minutes of that, and you'll have your first tattoo." Darby dunked the needle back in the ink and looked up at Marley. "Ready for more?"

"Pfft, hell yes. You guys made it seem way worse than this." Marley smirked.

We all groaned, and I tossed back the last of the wine.

"How bad did the one on your neck hurt?" Cyn asked me.

I shrugged and held up my pinky and thumb a little apart. It had hurt, but not more than any other tattoo I had gotten. I had angel wings on my back for my mother who had passed away when I was sixteen, a firefly on my thigh, and Marco's initials on my ankle. I counted the angel wings as two because those suckers are huge.

"Can I see it again?" she asked.

I held back my hair, exposing the lips on my neck.

"Those are sexy as hell," she mumbled. "Why did you decided on those?"

I shrugged.

"It's about time the Cavalry got here," I heard King call from the front of the shop.

"Yeah, yeah, you know how shit goes," Gambler replied. "Where's the women?"

"In the back getting ready to kill Marley," King said, laughing.

"No shit, I would have figured it would have been Paige chickening out."

I looked over my shoulder and watched Gambler heading down the short hallway with Demon, King, Troy, and Slider following behind him.

"Hey, I'll have you know that I knew exactly what I wanted when I got here," Paige replied, pointing her finger at Gambler.

Troy stood next to Marley and looked down at her wrist. "How the hell were you causing trouble?"

"Well, you know. I wanted to make sure I got just the right tattoo, and in the right place," she said, beaming up at Troy.

"Your woman took almost two hours to get her ass in that chair with a needle in her skin," Meg called from the table. "I was ready to pour a bottle of wine down her throat and strap her to the chair."

"How'd you end up on the floor, Firecracker?"

I looked up, and Slider was standing over me, a smirk on his face.

"Slider," I said softly.

"You get a tattoo?"

I nodded and tilted my head to the right.

Slider kneeled next to me and brushed his fingertip across my neck. "Damn," he uttered.

"Sexy, right?" Cyn said.

"Sexy as hell," he whispered. He threaded his fingers through my hair and looked me in the eye. "You ready to go?" he asked quietly.

I nodded, and he grabbed my hand to hoist me off the floor.

He looked down at me. "You have fun?"

I nodded. I really did have a good time when I was with all of the girls. They were all funny and different in their own ways.

Creed walked through the back door. "You taking her home?"

"I planned on it," Slider growled.

"Good. I got some shit to take care of tonight, and I won't be around. You think you can keep an eye her while I'm gone?"

"Not an issue."

"Good. I'll see ya in the morning." Creed left without a glance at anyone.

"That man is an ass," Marley blurted out.

"Amen, sista," Gwen agreed. "A hot body, and an assy attitude."

"Hey," Gambler said, "you mind not looking at his hot body?"

Gwen grinned like the Cheshire cat. "So, you agree he has a hot body?"

"Burn," Paige said, laughing. She reached up, holding her hand out to me. I slapped her hand and she hooted, "Woo!"

"I don't think that was really a burn, baby," Demon said with a smirk.

Paige waved him off. "In my head it was, and Gwen is my sister."

"What the hell does that have to do with anything?" Demon asked.

"It's the ho code," Cyn piped up. "Just like the bro code, but you know, with ho's."

We all looked at each other and busted out laughing.

"The ho code sounds more like something you don't want to be a part of," King chuckled as he scooted Meg over and sat down on the edge of the table.

Meg elbowed him and rolled her eyes. "I'll be part of your ho code, Cyn."

Cyn turned and looked at Meg. "You didn't have a choice, you were in no matter what."

"What the hell are you getting a tattoo of?" Demon looked down at Marley's wrist. "Is that brown?"

"Yeah, it's a cowboy hat."

"Oh, yeah, I totally see it now if I turn my head to the side." Demon twisted his head to the right and squinted. "Yeah, totally a cowboy hat."

Darby stopped tattooing and glared at Demon. "You might want to sit down by your woman if you know what's best for you."

Demon raised his hands, moved over to Paige, and held his hand out to her. "Let's get out of here, the natives are getting restless," he said, motioning to Darby.

Paige shook her head and stood. "I think you need to keep your mouth shut around the native who had a tattoo gun in her hand," she giggled, and he grabbed her sweatshirt off the back of Cyn's chair.

"See, that's why I need you around." Demon wrapped his arms around Paige and pulled her into his side. "Lord knows what I'd get tattooed on me if you weren't here."

Darby grinned evilly at Demon and pointed the tattoo gun at him.

"Yup," Demon said, grabbing Paige and propelling her towards the door. "Definitely time to get the hell out of here."

"Bye!" Paige called over her shoulder as Demon pushed her out the door.

"You ready to get out of here too?" Gwen said and nudged Gambler's feet that were hanging off of the table.

"What?" Marley shrieked. "You guys can't all leave. What about the ho code?"

"Relax," Meg called. "Cyn and I will be here until the end of the world's longest tattoo. I just need to get up and get the booze up front." Meg moved her legs, and King slapped her on the ass.

"Sit, babe. I'll get it." He sauntered up front.

Cyn reclined back in her chair. "For the record, I'm only here because Meg is my ride."

Marley flipped off Cyn and stuck her tongue out.

Cyn blew her a kiss and whispered, "Ho code."

"Can we go back to the fact that you're getting a cowboy hat tattooed on your wrist?" Troy asked. His eyes had yet to leave Marley's arm, and it looked like he was thinking doubly hard.

"Serious?" Meg sat up and leaned her head on her hand. "You're getting good at the sarcastic ass, Troy. I can never tell if you're being serious or not anymore."

"It's a skill," Troy muttered. He looked at Marley. "What are you doing?"

Marley's eyes bugged out, and her mouth dropped. "I'm getting a cowboy hat tattoo."

"I see that, but why?"

"Uh, well, you see, I thought since my dad calls you cowboy, I would get a cowboy hat, you know because, I love you or something," Marley said, ducking her head.

"You know that's forever, right?" he asked her.

"Troy, kno—" Meg interrupted, but Troy held his hand up to silence her.

"This doesn't have anything to do with you, Meg," he barked.

Darby stopped tattooing and rolled away from Marley.

"Troy, I'm not stupid, I know a tattoo is forever," Marley said, her voice cracking.

I moved into Slider, and he put his arm around my waist. I had no idea what was going on with Troy and Marley, but it didn't seem good.

"That means something that represents me is on you forever. No going back," he remarked.

"I know," she said quietly.

Troy reached into his pocket and pulled out a ring box. Gwen and Meg gasped and put their hands over their mouths. "Holy fuck," Cyn, who had a front row seat, said.

Troy got down on one knee and opened up the ring box. "That tattoo is forever, and so is this ring."

Marley gasped and grabbed the ring out of his hand. "Holy buckets."

"Did she just say holy buckets?" Meg looked at King who was standing behind Slider and me.

"Yeah, babe. Shut the hell up," King ordered. Meg gasped and glared at King but stopped talking.

Troy took the ring back from Marley. "You don't get this until I get to say the spiel I've been practicing for a month, and you say yes."

"Yes," Marley shouted.

"Girl, you might want to hear that spiel before you say yes. He might ask you to iron his underwear every day and have fifteen kids," Gwen advised.

Gambler put his hand over her mouth. "Sorry man," he mumbled. "Apparently our women don't know how to act."

Gwen sputtered under Gambler's hand.

"I think you're good to keep going. Mine can't talk," Slider said, hitching his thumb at me.

Marley bust out laughing. "She could always object and say no."

I held up my hands and shook my head. I was all good with Troy proposing to Marley.

Troy cleared his throat and looked up into Marley's eyes. "I knew the second I laid eyes on you that you were unlike any woman I had ever met. We may have had a bumpy start, but I knew that you were going to be the one to bring me to my knees."

"Aww," Meg sighed.

Troy rolled his eyes and glared at her. "Two minutes, Meg. Just give me two minutes."

"This shit is hilarious." Gambler had pulled his phone out and was recording everything.

"Hell," Troy shook his head, "I fucking love you, Marley, and I want us to be together for as long as that tattoo is on your wrist. Marry me, and put me out of my misery." Troy took the ring out of the box and held it up. Marley reached out her hand and nodded.

"Yes. Yes times a million," she sobbed as he slipped the ring onto her finger.

Troy wrapped his arms around Marley's waist and lifted her up in the air.

"Careful of her wrist," Darby called.

Marley held her arm over her head and wrapped her other one around Troy's neck. "I love you," she shouted. "Now I have two things that will be with me forever. My tattoo and your ring."

"Um, how about three things," Gambler called. "Don't forget Troy."

Gwen elbowed Gambler in the side and rolled her eyes. "You might want to heed your own advice," she mumbled.

Gambler grabbed her around the waist and wrapped his arms around her. "You might want to watch what you say, or I might make you mine forever, too."

"Promises, promises," Gwen mumbled before she pressed a kiss to his cheek. "I don't think you could handle me forever."

"Hey, focus on me," Marley called, waving her hand in the air. "I'm getting married," she said with a huge smile on her face.

Cyn, Meg, Gwen, and I circled around her, and *oohed* and *aahed* over the gorgeous ring Troy had picked out.

"Holy hell, this thing is huge." Meg grabbed Marley's hand and held it up to her face. "You did well, homie." She smiled up at Troy. "And that also explains why you stopped volunteering to buy dinner for us at work. My dinner is on Marley's finger."

Troy shrugged. "Priorities," he mumbled.

"Well, fuck your priorities and go back to buying dinner every now and then," Meg said, moving over to Troy to give him a hug.

King, Gambler, and Slider all clapped Troy on the back and congratulated him after Meg finally released Troy.

"You ready to go?" Slider asked when Marley sat back down to finish her tattoo. I nodded and smothered a yawn with the back of my hand.

It was well after midnight, and the bottle of wine I had drank was starting to catch up with me.

Slider helped me put my coat on. "Did you check in on Marco?"

"Yes," I mumbled. It still felt weird to talk in front of everyone. I knew that eventually I would be babbling and going on like everyone else, but for now, I just liked to keep my words for Slider. I was still upset he hadn't talked to me all week and avoided me, but I couldn't fight the natural attraction I had when he was around.

"Good."

I hugged Meg, Cyn, and Gwen good-bye, and then Slider and I were out the front door. I looked up and down the street looking for Slider's truck but didn't see it anywhere.

"I got the bike, Fay," he drawled as he grabbed my hand and hauled me over to three bikes that were at the curb.

"Slider," I protested. I had never been on a bike before, and I didn't think my first time should be after I had downed a bottle of wine.

He grabbed a helmet out of a bag that was on the side of his bike and set it on my head. "You look the part of an ol' lady, now it's time to get you on the back of my bike." He strapped the helmet under my chin. "Trust me, Firecracker," he said against my lips. His arms wrapped around my waist, and he palmed my ass with his warm hands. "I'll never let anything happen to you." He kissed me quick and hard, leaving me breathless.

"Slow," I whispered.

Slider's eyes got huge. "Fay, you just said slow."

I nodded and checked to make sure the helmet was on tight. I trusted Slider, but I just needed to make sure my helmet wasn't going to go anywhere.

He cupped my cheek. "Something tells me you've got more to say than that."

I smirked and leaned in, my lips next to his ear. "Maybe," I whispered.

Slider wrapped his arms around me and swung me around. "Holy shit," he yelled. "You can fucking talk."

I buried my face in his neck and inhaled his scent. "Take me home," I whispered.

Slider pulled my head back and looked me in the eye. "Say it again."

"Take me home."

He set me on my feet and swung a leg over his bike. "Get on, Fay. You only needed to tell me twice, because I wanted to make sure I wasn't dreaming." He cranked the bike up and looked at me over his shoulder.

I did the only thing I could. I swung my leg over the bike and wrapped my body around him.

It may be my first time on a bike, but Slider was taking me home, and that was all that mattered.

******

Chapter 30

Slider

I pulled into the garage and killed the bike.

Fayth was wrapped around me, and I didn't want her to move.

I had taken the ride slow, making sure not scare her, but also because her warm body pressed against me was foreplay in itself. Every turn, her arms had tightened around me, and I wished I had an endless tank of gas so I could ride forever with Fayth behind me.

"Wow," she breathed out.

I looked over my shoulder, and she had a huge smile plastered on her face. "You're gonna blow my mind with every word you say. You know that, right?"

She laughed and reached up to unbuckle her helmet. "I hope so."

"Fuck me," I mumbled as I grabbed the helmet from her. She shimmied off of the bike and impatiently waited for me to do the same.

I hung the helmet on the handlebars, stood, and swung my leg over the bike. Fayth squealed when I grabbed her around the waist and lifted her up in my arms. "I need to hear every word you have to say." I had missed her voice fiercely, and I couldn't wait to hear her say my name while I sunk into her lush body.

"Hit the button," I mumbled, fumbling with my keys to open the door. She swatted at the garage door button and the door slowly sunk down. "How long have you been able to talk?" The lock flipped over, and I pushed open the door.

"You left me alone all week. I had time to practice," she said quietly.

Mind blown again. If I hadn't avoided her all week, I would have heard her voice sooner. She wrapped her legs around my waist, and I slammed the door shut behind us. I pressed her back against the wall and moved her hair off of her neck. "You ready to tell me what this tattoo is, because I have a pretty good idea what it means, but I want to hear those sweet words come out of your mouth." She tilted her head to the side, and I lightly traced a circle around the red lips on her neck.

"That was where you first kissed me," she whispered. She ran her fingers through my hair and squeezed her legs tight around me. "I never wanted to forget it."

"Does that mean every time I kiss you, you're going to get a tattoo to remember it? Because I plan on kissing every inch of your body tonight." I watched her eyes fill with desire.

She bit her lip and shook her head. "Just keep kissing me, and I'll never be able to forget."

I grabbed her head, pulling her face down to me and slammed her lips onto mine. I couldn't wait another second to taste her lips. She moaned low as my hands slid down her body and cupped her sweet ass. She arched her back, pressing her lush body against me and I knew I couldn't take much more torture. I needed to have her naked beneath me.

I walked us through the dark house, tossed my keys on the counter, and headed straight to the bedroom.

"Slider," she gasped when I tossed her onto the bed and flipped on the lights. "I need to see you. Naked," I growled, pulling off my cut and tossing it on the floor. "Undress, now," I demanded while I pulled my shirt over my head and sailed it across the room.

I toed my boots off and watched her scramble to get her coat and then her boots off.

She reached down and fumbled with the laces. "Damn laces," she mumbled.

I pulled my jeans down my legs, and she finally had the laces undone and tossed her boots on the floor. "You're behind, Firecracker."

She looked up at me, and she licked her lip, focusing on the bulge between my legs. "You could help me," she suggested quietly.

"Or I could watch you unwrap your body," I growled.

She grabbed the hem of her shirt and pulled it over her head. A bright pink bra encased her lush tits, and I couldn't help the growl that slipped from my lips while I watched her shimmy her jeans down her legs, her tits jiggling with each move. She was wearing matching panties that made me want to take them off with my teeth and devour her sweet pussy.

Fayth laid back on the bed, her bra and panties still on. "You're still wearing too many clothes," I insisted, and I walked over to the bed and stood over her.

"I think you need to help me with those," she purred. Her dark hair was fanned out around her, and she looked like heaven laying in my bed.

"I need to hear you, Fay. I know the second I touch you, I'm not going to be able to stop. Tell me you want me, and no one else," I demanded.

She ran her hands up her stomach and cupped her breasts. "I want you, Slider. You're all I can think about."

"Once I take you, I'll never be able to give you up," I warned. I had never wanted a woman like the way I wanted Fayth. She was something special, and I had no plans of letting her go.

"I don't want to be anywhere else." Something crossed her face, and a frown appeared on her lips. "But first, I need to know something," she whispered.

"What is it, Fay?" I reached down and brushed my hand against her arm.

"Where were you tonight?"

I swallowed hard. I hadn't told Fayth anything about where I had gone tonight, and at first, I had no plans on telling her, but I knew I couldn't lie to her. "I was with Demon, Troy, and Gambler out at the club."

"The clubhouse?"

I shook my head. "No. We were at the strip club the MC owns."

She leaned up on her elbows. "Why? You could have been with me."

"Trust me, Fay. I wanted to be with you more than anything. I had club business to take care of. We needed to ask a chick some questions, and the only way we could do that was at the club."

"Gwen said there were auditions," she mumbled.

I tilted my head and smirked. "You knew the whole night where I was, didn't you?" Fayth shrugged. "Drove yourself mad wondering what I was doing, didn't you?"

She grabbed the pillow that was under her head and tossed it at me. "Ass," she hissed.

"Ah, that's still going to be one of my favorite words you say." I tossed it on the floor.

"Auditions?"

I rolled my eyes and put one knee on the bed. "Yes, we watched girls audition, but I can tell you right now, none of those chicks had anything on you. It was more of a comedy show watching them wobbled around the stage trying to be sexy."

Now, it was her turn to roll her eyes. "A woman in her underwear is hardly a comedy show."

I stroked my chin. "You sure did learn a lot of words," I mumbled. "I think I might have liked it better when you couldn't throw sass at me." She reached for the other pillow next to her, but I lunged for it and grabbed her arms before she could get to it. "So feisty," I whispered, pinning her arms over her head. "I should start calling you wildcat instead of firecracker."

She growled low and struggled to get her arms out of my grip. "Slider, I'll show you wildcat." Her words surprised me, and she was able to wiggle out from my grip and wrap her arms around my neck. She twisted her body and rolled us over so she was laying on top of me.

I palmed her ass and pressed her against me. "I like the way you talk," I mumbled against her lips.

"I knew you were going to be my dirty talker, so I thought I'd try to keep up," she whispered.

"Jesus fucking Christ, you are like a damn dream come true." I was in awe, and she ground her pussy into my dick. "Just looking at you makes my dick fucking hard, Fay. Finally having you in my arms, I'm pretty sure I could fuck you into next week."

She moaned and pressed her lips to mine. I threaded my fingers through her hair, holding her in place, and took over the kiss. Her soft lips melted into mine, and my tongue slipped into her mouth. Her hands skated down my chest and gripped the waistband of my boxers.

I pushed my feet into the bed and rolled us back over, our lips and body remaining connected. I glided my hands down her sides, and my lips traveled down her neck. "Slider," she moaned. I gently nipped her earlobe, and she arched her back up. "Please," she pleaded on a whisper.

"Please what?" I whispered in her ear. "Let me hear you say what you want," I insisted.

She moaned, frustrated by my demand. "You. I want you."

"You want me doing what?" I asked. I ran my tongue across the line if her jaw, and my hands cupped her breasts.

"I just want you," she gasped. "Do whatever you want."

I sat back on knees and held my hand out to Fayth. "Then, we're going to need to get you completely naked."

She grabbed my hand and sat up, and my other hand instantly went to the clasp on her bra. As soon as the bra was free, she lifted her arm and covered her breasts. "Slider," she whispered.

"Trust me, Fay," I growled as I pulled the straps down her arms, and her arm moved away. I knew Fayth was going to be perfect when I finally got her naked, but finally seeing it, I was blown away. "Fuck me," I mumbled, and I circled her pert nipple with my thumb. "You're not allowed to wear clothes any more. I want you naked twenty-four-seven."

Fayth laughed and cupped her breasts, pushing them together. "I make the cut?"

I looked her in the eye and shook my head. "Firecracker, you blow everyone else away."

A sly smile spread across her lips. "Good to know," she whispered.

"Lay back down," I ordered.

She slowly laid back down and put her crossed arms above her head. "I think you still have too many clothes on."

I quickly pulled my boxers off and tossed them on the floor. "Better?" I stroked my cock.

She licked her lips and nodded.

"Except now, you have too many on." I nodded at her panties. "Take them off." I sat back on my knees and watched her hook her thumbs into the sides of her panties and slowly work them down her legs.

The lips of her pussy were wet with her desire, and all I wanted to do was bury my tongue in her sweet taste.

"Spread those lips, Fay. Let me see your clit," I ordered and cupped her pussy. "Show me what I'm doing to you."

"I just want you to touch me," she moaned and ran a finger up the slit of her pussy, spreading her slippery lips.

"Hold them open for me," I instructed, and I got down on my hands and knees and swiped my tongue over her clit. "You taste like heaven, Fay," I growled against her clit.

She gasped when I sucked on her clit and swirled my tongue around it. "Please," she pleaded. "Don't stop."

"I couldn't if I tried," I mumbled.

She dug her heels into the bed and spread her legs, and I fell in between them. My hands grabbed her ass, tilting her pussy up to me, and I devoured her. Her moans and cries surrounded me, and she held herself open to me, giving me the permission I had been craving from her. I needed to know that she wanted this as much as I did.

"Slider, please," she cried out.

My tongue slid over her clit, and my finger worked over her tight hole. "Say my name again," I growled. I rapidly pumped my finger in and out of her, bringing her closer to the edge.

"Slider, Slider," she repeated over and over.

"Enough," I boomed as I ripped my mouth away from her and climbed up her body. Her soft skin felt like velvet beneath my fingers, and I wanted to touch and memorize every inch of her. "I need you, Fayth. I need you more than my next breath."

She wrapped her arms around my shoulders and arched her body into me. "Take me, I'm here," she whispered into my ear.

"God dammit." My hands roamed over her body while my mouth devoured her in a kiss that neither of us were ever going to recover from. Fayth was giving me everything she had as her hands clawed at my back. I palmed her full tits, kneading and teasing her nipples.

"More," she gasped. My hand traveled down her stomach, feeling the way down her lush body, and committing every curve to memory.

I cupped her sweet pussy and a shiver ran through her body. "Only I can make you feel this way," I said against her lips. "Only me," I vowed.

She arched her body into me and moaned when my finger slipped into her wet pussy. "So fucking wet," I growled. I flicked her clit, and her eyes slammed shut.

"Please, God please," she pleaded.

"Tell me you need me. Tell me," I demanded.

"Slider, please. It's you, it's always been you."

"Son of a bitch," I moaned at her words.

"I need you so much," she whispered. "Please don't stop."

"Never," I vowed. I stroked my cock, feeling how rock hard I was, and knew Fayth was my meaning for everything now. I finally had her in my bed, and I wasn't going to let her go.

****

Chapter 31

Fayth

I was so close to falling over the edge, and Slider held all of the power in his hands. One touch from him made my body sing.

Slider leaned back on his knees and stroked his cock while he looked down at me. I missed the feel of his hands on me and knew that I would never feel anything like it again.

He grimaced, and his eyes were filled with desire. "You make me so fucking hard, Fay," he growled. A drop of precum seeped from the head of his dick, and I whimpered, wishing I could lick it off.

He parted the lips of my pussy with his other hand, and I moaned in anticipation. "Please," I gasped. I couldn't take much more.

"So fucking gorgeous and all fucking mine," he said quietly. He covered my body with his, and he slowly entered me. "So fucking tight," he groaned.

I rested my arms on his shoulders and wrapped my legs around his waist. I needed to feel Slider deep in me. "Shit," I gasped, and he hit rock bottom. I could feel his hard dick pulsing in me.

"I could cum right now, Fay," he gritted out.

I clenched the walls of my pussy, knowing that at any second, Slider was going to move. I needed him to move. I turned my head, and my lips were next to his ear. "Fuck me," I whispered. I was at my wits end, and I couldn't take it anymore.

Slider pulled out, then slammed back into me, both of us moaning in pleasure. "So fucking tight," he growled. His hands moved over my body, touching and teasing as he slammed into me over and over.

I dug my heels into the bed and spread my legs as far as I could. Slider grabbed my ass and tilted my hips up. "Yes, yes," I screamed. His lips devoured my mouth, his tongue thrusting in and out, keeping time with his hips.

"Fayth, son of…bitch," he called out. His eyes were closed while he frantically pounded into me, and I felt my release rising with each thrust.

"Slider," I moaned. He buried his face in my neck, and his hand snaked down my body. His finger flicked my clit, driving me insane with need. "Again," I pleaded, knowing I was seconds away from falling over the edge.

He continued to pound into me as I ran my hands over his back, feeling his muscles contract and bulge with each thrust. "Mine," he growled. "Fucking mine," he snarled. He flicked my clit, and my body exploded around him.

My pussy milked his cock, demanding every drop of cum he had to give me. "Fuck!" he shouted, thrusting into me one last time. "Holy fuck," he growled into my ear, and he collapsed on top of me.

I tiptoed my fingers up his back. "Can I say something?" I asked quietly.

"Firecracker, you can say anything you want after that."

"Was that amazing for you, or was it just me?"

Slider leaned back and looked down at me. "Amazing?"

I nodded, fearful Slider hadn't enjoyed that as much as I had.

"Fay, that was the most fucking amazing, out of this world sex I have ever had, and I plan on doing it again at least two more times before the sun comes up." He leaned down to brush a kiss against my lips. "But Firecracker, I need sustenance if I plan on staying up all night."

"I can make something," I replied.

"How about I cook for you? You're always cooking for Marco and me. I think it's about time the tables were turned, and you get waited on."

I smiled up at him. "I guess that sounds okay."

"Okay? I'm gonna show you better than okay." Slider rolled off of me and laid on his side with his arm propping up his head. "I'm gonna make you the Slider Special."

"Slider Special?" I giggled. "And what exactly is in that?"

"You're just going to have to haul your sexy ass out of bed and come find out."

"I thought you said I was going to get waited on? I figured that meant breakfast in bed." I glanced at the clock and saw it was way too early for breakfast. "Or snack in bed."

"See, normally I would say that you can stay here, but I just finally had you, and I don't want you that far away from me." Slider rolled off the bed and grabbed my robe that I had hanging on the back of the door. "Stand up, let me wrap you up, and then you can watch me make you something to eat."

I leaned up on my elbows. "What happens after we eat?" I asked coyly.

"Get your ass out of bed, and you'll find out." Slider grabbed my hand and pulled me up. He wrapped me in my robe and tied the sash tight around me.

"Wait," I called while he pulled me down the hall. "You're cooking naked?"

Slider stopped and looked down. "Shit. You head to the kitchen, and I'll meet you there once I figure out where I tossed my underwear," he mumbled and headed back into the bedroom.

I shuffled down the hallway, straight to the coffeemaker. By the time Slider made it to the kitchen, I had a pot of coffee going, and I was sitting on the counter waiting for him.

"Coffee?" he asked.

I shrugged. "I figure if you plan on keeping me up all night, I'm going to need a bit of caffeine."

Slider stood between my legs and pressed a kiss to my lips. "I guess I can't argue with that logic."

"You probably shouldn't argue with me at all," I said, smirking.

"There's that feistiness I love. I missed it when you weren't talking. Hell, I felt like I was missing a huge part of you when you couldn't talk."

"I felt the same way," I whispered.

"But now, you're back."

"Well, only you know I can talk."

He brushed my hair off of my shoulder. "You really saved it for me?"

"I had tried to tell you all week, but you kept running away from me whenever I tried. You were starting to give me a complex," I laughed.

He wound my hair around his hand and gently tugged on it. "I need you to be safe, Fay. You distract the hell out of me, and I was terrified that you were going to get hurt again because I couldn't keep it in my pants."

I put my arms on his shoulders and pulled him close. "Well, for the record, I'm glad you didn't keep it in your pants, and so far, there hasn't been some horrific accident."

"So far, no. But I'm not going to get too comfortable."

I looked up at him and shrugged. "When Big A shot me, it wasn't your fault."

"I never should have let you wander away from the cabin like you did. All I had to do was keep an eye on you and make sure nothing happened to you."

"Slider, I'm my own person, and I'll make my own decisions. I didn't think that I was in any harm. If I had known that Big A was going to go after me, I never would have walked into the woods like I had. Now we both know that we are all Big A's targets, nothing is going to happen."

"You don't know that, Fayth. Things are still going on, and we have no idea what they are."

"Is that why you were at the strip club tonight?"

"We were trying to find out what Big A has been up to."

"He's in prison. Can he really be up to much?" What the hell was the man capable of being in a maximum security prison?

"He was behind the guy who broke into the house, we think. He's got help on the outside that is doing all his bidding for him right now."

"So, did the girl you talked to tonight help at all?"

"Nah, not from what we can tell. There are a few leads that we are chasing down, but nothing has changed. The club is still on high alert."

I nodded. "So, that means your detective work at the strip club is over?"

Slider smirked and nodded. "For the time being."

"So, how many girls did you have to watch shake their asses before the chick you needed to talk to hit the stage?"

Slider laughed. "It wasn't exactly shaking their asses, it was more like wobbling around on stilts."

I rolled my eyes. "I'm sure it was so, so hard to watch half-naked women walk around."

"It sure as hell wasn't fun. Hell, Fayth, half of those women were two steps away from falling off the stage." Slider laughed and cupped my cheek. "Four of them did fall off stage, Fay. I can tell you right now, you were the only thing that was on my mind."

"You don't have to blow smoke up my ass, Slider." I knew what went on at a strip club. And although Slider said all of the women were horrible, I really doubted they were that bad to look out. I'm sure most of them had strapped on the tallest shoes they could find and teetered around the stage, but that didn't mean they weren't sexy.

"What's is going to take for you to believe me?" he asked, kissing my neck, right below my fresh tattoo.

"Hmm," I hummed. "Probably one of those Slider Specials."

"Is that all?"

"For now. I'm sure I'll think of more later."

"Oh, is that how it's going to go?" he chuckled. "I feel you're going to use this as a way to get anything you want." Slider kissed his way up my neck and nipped on my earlobe.

I shrugged. "I guess you're just going to have to wait and see."

Slider growled and stepped back. "I guess I'll just have to keep you occupied in bed so you don't think of other ways to blackmail me."

I busted out laughing. "I'm hardly blackmailing you. I'm just making sure you're not thinking of all of the girls you saw tonight."

Slider wrapped his arms around me and rested his forehead against mine. "It's you, Fayth. There isn't another chick on this Earth that I'm thinking of."

I smiled and pressed a kiss to his lips. "Let's hope it stays that way."

"You don't have a thing to worry about, Fay." Slider walked over to the fridge and surveyed everything inside. "Now," he said, looking over his shoulder at me, "are you ready for the Slider Special?"

I nodded and watched him pull out a jar of jelly and set it on the counter. "Jelly?"

"Oh yeah. You can't have a Slider Special without jelly."

My interest was piqued, and I had no idea what he was about to make.

"Now, all we need it bread, peanut butter, and milk."

"Wait, wait, wait. Are you telling me that a Slider Special is a peanut butter and jelly sandwich with milk?"

Slider shrugged. "If that's what you want to call it, but I prefer the Slider Special." Slider winked and headed to the pantry to grab the peanut butter and bread.

I hopped off of the counter and grabbed the milk from the fridge.

"Hey, get your ass back on that counter," Slider scolded. He set the bread and peanut butter on the counter. "I don't need an assistant."

"My bad," I laughed setting down the milk. "Can I at least get a cup of coffee?"

"Coffee, that's it," he said and pointed a finger at me. "I promised a Slider Special, and I aim to deliver."

I grabbed two coffee cups down from the cabinet and filled them while Slider constructed our sandwiches. I leaned against the counter, my coffee cup in hand, and sighed. The man who I had wanted the past few months was making me a peanut butter and jelly sandwich in his boxers, and I couldn't be happier.

There wasn't much more a girl could ask for.

****

Chapter 32

Slider

"We need to get up and go pick up Marco."

"I'm not the one who decided that we were going to stay up all night. I don't want to move from this bed, and it's all your fault." Fayth rolled over and buried her head in her pillow. "I'm too old for this," she muttered.

"You also need to get up and put some shit on your tattoo."

"Ugh, can you stop reminding me of all of the adulting I need to do?" she groaned.

I slapped her on the ass and hopped out of bed before she hit me with the arm she was flailing behind her back. "Rise and shine, Firecracker." I grabbed my boxers off the floor, slipped them on, and watched Fayth roll over and launch her pillow at me. "You go get Marco and leave me here to pass out."

I grabbed the pillow she had thrown and tossed it back on the bed. "No can do, Fay. Get your ass up, and I'll make breakfast."

"Oh Lord, please tell me it's not another Slider Special," she giggled.

"You're gonna have to get your ass out of bed and find out." I pulled my jeans on and headed down the hallway.

"Wait," Fayth called. "Is this going to be a shirtless breakfast?"

I shook my head. "For me it will be." The door to the garage opened, and Creed walked in. "I suggest you put some clothes on though, Fay. We've got company."

"What?" Fayth shrieked. "It's not Marco, is it?" she called.

"Just get some clothes on before you come out." I looked over my shoulder in time to see the bedroom door slam shut and heard Fayth muttering loudly about staying up all night and people not letting her sleep.

"You look fucking happy this afternoon," Creed said when I walked into the kitchen and flipped on the coffee pot.

"Afternoon?" I smirked. I knew exactly what time it was, and my happiness was thanks to the woman in my bedroom who was probably searching for her underwear that I had slipped into my pocket before I had left.

"You sure are a smug ass after you get laid," Creed mumbled, sitting down at the island. "Must be nice to take the whole day off and shack up with your woman."

"Coffee?" I grabbed three cups down from the cupboard. "And, it sure fucking is nice."

Creed nodded to coffee and pulled his phone out. "You Knights sure do have shit easy. Sleeping all day with your women, not going to fucking work," he mumbled while he typed on his phone.

"Or maybe, we just know how to work so that we have time for our women."

"Sure, keep telling yourself that. Meanwhile, we'll just pick up the slack," he laughed.

"Fuck you, fucker."

"Ah, it's good to see you boys are up to your usual banter," Fayth said, walking into the kitchen.

"Jesus, woman. Put some damn clothes on." Creed covered his eyes with his hand. "Wait," he said, shocked. "You're fucking talking." Creed turned to look at me. "Your dick is that magical that it made her talk?"

Fayth busted out laughing, and I couldn't help but think that it damn sure was. Creed didn't need to know Fayth was talking before last night, though.

"Looking to find out, Creed?" Fayth asked.

"What?" Creed held his hands up. "Look, I don't know what kind of kink you guys are into, but I don't want no part of it. You keep your magical dick over there, and I'll stay here," he said, pointing at me.

"And, what's wrong with my clothes? It's shorts and a t-shirt?" Fayth asked.

"What's wrong with it is I shouldn't be looking at another man's woman dressed like that," Creed said, averting his eyes and looking out the back door.

"Creed, I wore this same outfit last week, and you didn't have a problem with it," Fayth noted, putting her hands on her hips.

There wasn't anything wrong with what she was wearing. Maybe the shorts were a bit short, but I wasn't going to complain about it. It was just more of her I could see when we weren't in the bedroom.

"Last week you weren't knocking boots with that buffoon. Now, you're his, and I shouldn't be thinking of you, at all."

"Ya shouldn't have been thinking of her at all before," I growled.

Fayth leaned into me and laughed. "Easy killer," she whispered. She leaned up on her tiptoes and pressed a kiss to my cheek.

"All right, this shit is too weird for me right now. I'm gonna call Leo, let him know you had a miraculous recovery, leave out how it happened, and then I'm gonna go chop some wood or something," Creed opened the door and slipped out into the backyard.

"Chop some wood?" Fayth asked, laughing. "When did Creed become a comedian?"

I filled both of our cups and handed one to Fayth. "I think right around the time he realized you were mine, and he doesn't have a shot in hell with you anymore."

"Oh, I'm yours, am I?" Fayth smirked.

"I'm pretty sure that's what we established last night, and this morning, Fay." I set my cup down and wrapped my arms around her. "Do I need to fuck you right here to remind you?"

Fayth glanced out the back door. "You think that's possible?"

I pushed her up against the counter and whispered in her ear. "There's only one way to find out."

****

Fayth

Slider's hands slid down my back and cupped my ass. "Just say the word, Firecracker."

I glanced over my shoulder out the door where Creed had just gone and bit my lip. "He'll be on the phone for at least ten minutes," I muttered.

"Is that a yes?" Slider whispered.

"That's a you better fuck me hard and fast."

"How about good and fast?" His hands moved around to the waistband of my shorts, and he tugged them down my legs. "These are some damn short shorts," he muttered.

"I think that's why they call them shorts," I whispered.

"I'd love to have you spread out on this counter naked, but I think all I'm gonna be able to do is pull this tiny triangle you call underwear off and bend you over." He hooked his thumbs in the sides of my panties and looked me in the eye. "Last chance to back out."

I shook my head, and he pulled them down my legs. "No going back now," I whispered, stepping out of my shorts and panties. I cupped his dick through his jeans and whispered, "I'm ready for you."

Slider growled, spun me around, and pressed my back against his front. "I guess I didn't fuck you enough last night." His hand traveled up my stomach, pushing my shirt up, and he cupped my breast. "You're mine," he whispered in my ear.

A tremor rocked my body at his words, and his hand moved around to my back. "Slider," I moaned when he bent me over and ground his jean-clad dick into my bare ass.

"Shh," he whispered. "You don't want Creed to come in here and find you bent over with my dick buried in you, do you?"

"You'd stop if he came in," I whispered.

"Would I?" The sound of his zipper sliding down sent a thrill through me, and I realized Slider was going to fuck me with Creed not even twenty feet away. "Maybe if he saw me with my dick inside you, he'd realize that you really are mine."

"I am yours," I gasped as his hands grabbed my hips, and he pulled me against his bare dick.

Slider leaned down and whispered in my ear. "Spread your legs, grab your ankles, and hold the fuck on," he ordered.

I shuffled my feet apart and wrapped my fingers around my ankles. "Slider, I've never—"

"Shush," he insisted. "Just listen to me and do what I say." His hands parted the lips of my pussy, and he growled. "So fucking wet, just for me." He flicked my clit, and I gasped, certain I wouldn't be able to be quiet.

"Maybe we should go in the bedroom," I suggested.

Slider slapped my ass, the sound echoing around us. "Not happening. You want this, Fay. Don't fucking deny it." He slid his dick up and down the crack of my ass, and my body sang with anticipation.

He slowly pushed inside me, and I closed my eyes at the slight sting of pain when he slapped my ass again. The walls of my pussy spasmed around his dick, and I knew it wasn't going to take much for me to cum.

"How the fuck do you do this to me, Fay?"

"The feeling is mutual," I gasped when he was fully inside me.

Slider slowly pulled out, then slammed back in. "No one in my whole life has ever made me feel the way you do," he moaned, thrusting in and out. "No one," he insisted.

He slammed into me, his fingers digging into my hips to hold on. "Slider," I moaned.

He slapped my ass. "Quiet, unless you want an audience." I bit my lips and shook my head. "Good girl," he drawled.

I looked between my feet, saw Slider's jeans pooled around his feet and I pictured what we must look like. Slider powered into me, and I closed my eyes, feeling my release coming. "Please," I whispered over and over.

Slider's hand skated up my back and gathered my hair. He gently tugged my head back and the soft bite of pain was more than I could take. "Slider," I gasped while he rocked his hips into me hard and finally pushed me over the edge. My orgasm slammed into me, and I couldn't hold back the scream that ripped from my lips.

"Fuck, fuck," Slider chanted.

He let go of my hair, dug his fingers into my hips, and pounded into me. I held on, knowing if I let go of my ankles, we would end up a pile on the floor.

"Fayth," he growled low. He groaned, frantically thrusting into me, and I felt his dick spasming inside me. I clenched the walls of my pussy, milking his cock while he came inside me.

He thrust one last time, burying his cock deep inside me. "It's a damn good thing you're on the pill, because if you weren't, there sure would be a condom shortage. I plan on fucking you like that every morning now." He slapped my ass one last time and slowly pulled out.

I released my ankles and stood, blood rushing to my head. I held onto the counter and looked over my shoulder. "That definitely is one hell of a way to wake up," I purred.

Slider stood behind me, his chest heaving and sweat on his brow. "You're gonna be the death of me, woman."

"But what a way to go, huh?" I asked, laughing.

Slider shook his head and grabbed his pants from around his ankles. "Where did you find those panties?" he asked, nodding at the pale pink scrap of lace by the stove.

"Pulled them out of my bag. I couldn't find the ones I was wearing before."

Slider pulled my panties out of his pocket and held them up. "You mean these?"

I snatched them out of his hand and laughed. "Those would be the ones."

Slider pulled me to him and wrapped his arms around me. "You sure do make me damn happy, Fay."

"Stealing my underwear makes you happy?"

"Well, that, and you just being you."

I buried my face in his neck and sighed. I didn't know how I had gotten so lucky to have this man holding me, but I knew I was going to do everything I could to make sure he never stopped. "Do I get the breakfast Slider Special now?" I mumbled.

"I'm pretty sure you just had it," he chuckled.

I smacked his shoulder. "Ass."

"And we're back to me being an ass. Full circle, Firecracker."

I rested my head on his shoulder and smiled.

Full circle, and I was pretty damn happy with where we were.

****

Chapter 33

Slider

"You're an ass!"

I rolled my eyes and grabbed my jeans off of the floor. "No, I'm not."

"Then, why in the hell can't I come with you to the clubhouse?" Fayth asked, tugging the sheet up over her body.

I had just gotten done fucking her brains out, and her attitude was in full-force. "Because of what just happened here. I don't get shit done when you're around."

She sat up and clutched the sheet to her chest. "That's not true," she protested.

"Fay, I was changing the oil on my bike, and the next thing you know, we're in bed fucking like rabbits."

"You act like that's a bad thing," she pouted.

"It's not, but when I have things to do, you're a distraction that I can't pass up."

"So, you're just going to leave me at home when you have something to do? Why can't I come with you and hang out with the girls?"

"Because they aren't there. Meg and Cyn are going to be working, and I think the rest of them are at home or also working. King said just the guys were at the clubhouse."

"So, I have to stay here with Creed?"

I nodded. "Yes. I won't be gone long. Marco should be home from school soon. You won't be stuck with only Creed for long." I pulled my shirt on and grabbed a pair of socks out of my dresser.

"I guess I could start on dinner. You'll be home by then, right?"

I glanced at the clock on the dresser and nodded. "I'll be gone two hours." It was only two-thirty, and I didn't even think I would be gone that long.

Fayth bit her lip and nodded. "I guess I can find stuff to do while you're gone."

"You act like I'm leaving you for days, Firecracker," I said, pulling on my socks and then grabbing my boots from under the bed.

Fayth shrugged. "I guess I like having you around."

"And I like being around." It had been two weeks since Fayth and I fallen into bed together, and we had barely been out of it since. Whenever she was around, I couldn't keep my hands off of her. "But I need to get some shit done today, Fay. The less distractions, the better."

"Can I call Gwen and Paige and see if they want to come over?"

"Knock yourself out, Firecracker." I shoved my feet into my boots and quickly laced them up. I was already running behind. I had told King I would be there at two to work on a couple of cars he had lined up.

I leaned over Fayth and pressed a kiss to her lips. "Are you sure you have to leave?" she asked, tugging down the sheet.

My eyes fell on her lush, full breasts, and I shook my head. I stepped back and put my hand over my eyes. "No. Not happening. Your banging body with not distract me. King will kill me if I call in and tell him I'm not coming."

Fayth laughed. "Okay, you can look," she called.

I peeked between my fingers and saw she was adequately covered. "Get dressed, have the girls over, and try not to get too drunk."

"Yes, sir." She lifted her hand that was holding the sheet in place and saluted me. "Whoops," she whispered, grabbing the sheet. "I promise not to distract you until you get home."

"Promises, promises," I said. "Call me if you need me. I'll be back soon."

Fayth nodded, and I made my way down the hallway before she tried to persuade me to stay.

Creed was in the kitchen, headphones on his ears, and looking in the fridge. I clapped him in the back, and he jumped around.

"Jesus Christ, man," he cussed and tugged off the earphones.

"What's with those?" I asked.

"These? These are the only thing that is keeping me from hearing you bang my boss' sister." Creed tossed them on the counter and turned back to the fridge. "Bunch of fucking rabbits," he said under his breath.

I laughed and grabbed the keys to my bike off of the counter. "I gotta run to the garage for a bit. Keep an eye on Fayth for me? She was thinking of inviting some of the girls over."

Creed rolled his eyes and grabbed a container full of leftovers out of the fridge. "Great, me and a bunch of women."

"Don't act like you don't like it," I said, laughing.

"Yeah, yeah. I'll keep an eye on her. That's my job."

I glanced at the clock over the sink and knew I was going to have to book it to make it to the club before King reamed my ass out. "Later," I called as I stepped out the front door.

I swung my leg over my bike that I had pulled out of the garage earlier and cranked her up. The curtains in my bedroom moved to the side and Fayth stood there—naked from head to toe.

"Jesus Christ," I whispered. She blew me a kiss and cupped her tits in her hands.

I pulled my phone out of my pocket and dialed her number. She disappeared from the window and answered her phone. "Yes?" she said coyly.

"Giving me a little show?"

"Just reminding you of what you're missing."

"Behave," I muttered.

"Okay."

"Hey, Fay," I called before she hung up. "I'll never forget what I have, Firecracker." I shoved the phone in my pocket and slid my sunglasses over my eyes.

Fayth Banachi was the one woman I could never forget.

✳✳✳✳✳✳✳

Chapter 34

Fayth

"How does he not have margarita mix?" Gwen asked while she surveyed the small bar Slider had in the basement.

"Probably because he's a guy, and beer and whiskey are what he drinks," Paige said, twirling one of the handles on the foosball table.

"You know you're going to have to rectify this, right, Fayth?"

I laughed and grabbed a bottle of amaretto. "I promise the next time you come over that we will have a full bottle of margarita mix."

"Do you have sour?" she asked, eying the bottle in my hand.

"Of course. It's upstairs, though."

"Sweet. I brought some chips and salsa over. I figured we can snack while we watch you make dinner," Paige replied.

"Sounds like a plan to me," Gwen chimed in. "Lead the way, woman."

The door to the garage opened and closed, and I rolled my eyes. "Creed's declaration of staying in the garage the whole time lasted a whole five minutes," I laughed.

"Typical man, says one thing and does the other," Gwen agreed, shaking her head.

Gwen followed behind me, with Paige bringing up the rear.

"I see you lied about staying in the garage," I called to Creed when were halfway up the stairs. I heard his heavy footsteps in the laundry room, and I smiled over my shoulder at Gwen.

The smile on her lips fell and the color drained from her face.

"Hello, Fayth. It sure is nice to finally hear your voice."

I whipped my head around and saw Dr. Stevens standing on the landing. "Dr. Stevens?" What the hell was going on?

"Oh, and you have your friends with you. This will save me from paying them a visit later." He pulled a needle from behind his back and held it up. "Now, be a good girl, and let the doctor check you over."

Gwen grabbed my arm and yanked me down the stairs.

"Creed!" I called as I stumbled down the stairs.

Dr. Stevens shook his head. "Creed won't be bothering us anymore. He was always around—him and that biker you've been fucking aren't going to stop me this time."

****

Slider

King leaned against the fender and crossed his arms. "You gonna have this car done today?"

I was elbow-deep in an old Caddy, and only an hour into the job. "I'm hoping on it. Should only be another hour to get it all done."

"Good. This car has been sitting here for three days waiting for you."

"Sorry, brother."

King smirked and shook his head. "No need to apologize. I remember how it was the first time I got a taste of Meg, I couldn't get enough. Hell, I still can't get enough."

I wiped my hands on a towel and grabbed a wrench off of the cart next to me. "I definitely ain't complaining," I laughed. "She just distracts the hell out of me. Hell, when I was leaving today, she pulled back the curtains in our bedroom, naked as a jaybird, and blew me a kiss. The woman is going to be the death of me."

"Nice," King chuckled.

Yeah, it definitely had been nice. So nice that I hadn't been able to get the picture out of my head.

"Yo, your phone," King said, nodding at the workbench. "I gotta head up front. Holler when you're done with this."

King made his way across the shop, and I grabbed my phone and saw that it was Leo calling. "'Leo?"

"Slider? You with Fayth?"

"No, she's with Creed. I had some things to take care of. You need her?"

"No, I was just making sure that someone was with her."

"Why?" I tossed the dirty rag on the bench and leaned against it.

"Her doctor called me today. Asked if he could see her. Said he was interested in how she was doing."

"She's doing fine. She doesn't need to see the doctor."

"Well, he's on the way there. Hell, he's probably there already. He called me over two hours ago, but I didn't get the chance to call you right away."

"Wait, he called you?" I grabbed my keys off the bench. Why would he call Leo? What could he possibly need to see her for? Unless... fuck!

"Yeah, he said he needed to close out her case or some shit like that. He's her doctor," Leo reminded me.

"No, he's not, Leo. He's Big A's doctor."

All the pieces fell into place, and I sprinted across the shop and hollered for King.

"Son of a bitch," Leo barked. "Get to her now!"

King peeked his head out of his office. "What's up?"

"I know who the doctor is, and he's with Fayth right now."

****

Chapter 35

Fayth

"Wake her up!"

"I can't," Gwen said. "You knocked her out when you hit her over the head. What the hell did you expect to happen?"

Dr. Stevens growled and grabbed Gwen by her hair. "You might want to be careful of what you say to me. You don't want to end up like your sister."

Paige had tried to make a run for it when Dr. Stevens had skirted around the pool table to grab me, but she hadn't been quick enough. Now, she was laid out on the floor, with a huge gash on her forehead. Gwen growled back but didn't say anything.

His eyes fell on me and a sick, twisted smile spread across his lips. "I bet you never saw this coming, did you?" he sneered.

I shook my head and slightly moved backward. I was ten feet away from the bar, and I knew the only way we were going to make it out of here was if I was able to get the gun that Slider kept on the shelf.

"What are you doing?" he shouted at Gwen, his gaze shifting from me.

I slowly crab-walked backwards, careful not to draw attention to myself.

Gwen quickly looked at me, and I nodded at her.

"She needs help," Gwen shrieked, keeping Dr. Stevens' attention on her. "Why would you hit her like that?"

"Because I'm supposed to kill you bitches, so it doesn't really matter if I knock her out before I do." He snapped Gwen's neck back, and she yelped. "Although, I think I might want to have a little fun with you first. I like the ones that fight back." He licked his lips, and my skin crawled.

Gwen kicked him in the shin. "You're fucking disgusting," she spit out. "I'd rather be dead then have you touch me."

"All in due time, my dear." He pulled on her head, lifting her off the ground and onto her feet. "I could always fuck you when you're dead, too."

Jesus Christ, this guy was one sick fucker. I was almost to the bar when his eyes whipped over to me.

"What the hell do you think you are doing?" he shouted. "Get your ass over here," he demanded.

I needed to think fast. If he got me away from the bar, I knew he wouldn't let me over here again. I licked my lips shook my head. "I need a drink," I rasped out.

He didn't buy it, but it gave me time to figure out my next move. "Get the fuck over here, now!" he screamed.

I acted like his words had stunned me and shot up from the ground, and then stumbled over my feet. I fell backwards and landed behind the bar.

"Get the fuck up and get your clumsy ass over here."

The black 9mm was right where Slider had left it the last time we were down here, and I grabbed it as I hoisted myself. "No," I growled, lifting the gun and pointing it at his head. "Let her the fuck go."

****

Slider

I flew down the country roads, praying I wasn't too late.

King and half of the club were behind me, all of them hell-bent on getting to my house.

This was the time I cursed myself for buying a house outside of town. The ten minute drive felt like an hour, and each second that ticked by, I could feel Fayth slipping away from me.

I careened into the drive, and in one fluid movement, I knocked the kickstand down and shot off of my bike. The garage door was open, and Creed was lying in the middle of the floor, unconscious.

"Fucking wait," King called.

I pulled my gun out of the waistband of my jeans and shook my head. I couldn't fucking wait. That asshole had Fayth, and I had promised that nothing would happen to her. I was going to keep my promise this time.

"Call an ambulance," King barked. His footsteps sounded behind me, and I looked back to see he had his gun drawn.

"I got you," he said.

I nodded and slowly opened the door. I instantly heard Fayth yelling for the doctor to let someone go. I looked back at King and pointed down to the basement.

Somehow, Fayth had gotten trapped in the basement with the lunatic. That was probably the worst place to be. There was only one way out.

"You shoot me, I'll stick this needle in her!"

I stepped into the house, checked to make sure there wasn't anyone in the kitchen, and put one foot on the steps. King laid a hand on my shoulder and held me back. He pointed down at the ground and shook his head. "Lay down," he whispered.

Fayth was yelling at the doctor, and I prayed she could distract him long enough for me to get in a position. I laid down on my stomach, set the gun three steps lower, and slowly slid down the stairs.

Four steps down, I was able to see Fayth facing me, my 9mm in her hand, pointed at a guy who was holding Gwen by her neck.

"Get away from her," Fayth screeched again.

"You won't shoot me. I know what it takes to kill someone, and you don't have it in you."

Fayth shook her head and cocked the trigger. "Try me, fucker," she bellowed.

The doctor held something to Gwen's neck and laughed. "One stick of this needle, and she's dead," he threatened.

"One bullet between your eyes, and you're dead, asshole," Fayth spit out.

"You can't kill me!" he shouted. He lunged at Fayth, Gwen still under his arm.

I took my shot, knowing it wasn't a clear one, but I had to take it. Just as I pulled the trigger, Fayth moved the gun down and fired a bullet into his foot. He released Gwen just before my bullet ripped through his back and sent him careening onto the floor.

I flew down the stairs, King right behind me.

"Slider!" Fayth screamed and dropped the gun.

"Pick up the gun, Fayth!" King shouted.

The doctor was withering on the floor by her feet, and he reached for the gun. Gwen managed to land a kick in the doctor's side, and Fayth picked it up and pointed it down at him.

"You fucking bitch," he rasped from the floor. "You need to die."

King grabbed the gun out of Fayth's hand and gently shoved her over to me. "Go upstairs," I ordered as I put my arm around her.

"What about Paige?" she asked.

"There's an ambulance on the way," King said. "Go upstairs, now," he ordered.

Gwen grabbed Fayth's hand and tugged her up the stairs.

"You grab Paige, I've got him," I said.

"You sure about that?" King asked me.

The asshole had stopped moving, but his eyes were still open. "Yeah. He's mine."

King gathered Paige in his arms and made his way up the stairs.

I crouched next to the doctor. "What's your name?"

"Fuck...you," he wheezed.

I shook my head. "I don't really think you want those to be your last words, do you?"

"He's gonna kill you," he hissed.

"He can sure fucking try, but I'm pretty sure he's the one who isn't going to make it. He thinks he's the only one with connections?" I scoffed and tapped the barrel of the gun on his temple. "I know people on the inside who owe me favors." I glanced at the clock on the wall and laughed. "You know what's fucking ironic, you're both going to die at the same time."

"How?"

"Because at four o'clock this afternoon, Big A is going to take his last breath, and so will you." I stood and looked down at him. "Now, tell me your fucking name."

"What does it fucking matter to you?" he uttered.

"Because I like to know the names of every man I kill." He coughed and sputtered out blood. "The difference between you and me is that every man I've killed deserved to be dead. Now, tell me your fucking name."

"John," he gasped.

I cocked the trigger on my gun. "You told my woman she needed to die, right? Well you were fucking wrong." I put my finger on the trigger, the cold steel the only thing I felt as I aimed at his head. "You need to die."

****

639

Chapter 36

Fayth

"Here, lay her on the couch."

King laid Paige on the couch, and Gwen kneeled next to her. "Paige, Paige," she called, brushing hair from her face.

"What did he do to her?" King asked.

"Um, he hit her over the head. She tried to run up the stairs and he caught her," I mumbled.

King nodded. "She should be okay. The ambulance should be here any minute."

"What about Creed?" I asked.

"Not sure what was up with him. He was knocked out in the garage when we pulled up," King replied and grabbed his phone out of his pocket.

The garage door busted open, and Demon and Gambler ran in.

"What the fuck did he do to her?" Demon demanded while moving Gwen out of the way and gathering Paige in his arms.

"She's just knocked out," Gwen sobbed. Gambler wrapped his arms around her and buried his face in her neck.

Gwen sobbed uncontrollably, and she held onto Gambler.

"What happened to hi—" Demon asked, but was cut off by a gunshot.

Gwen and I both jumped and yelped.

"Slider took care of him," King said quietly.

Dr. Stevens was dead. Slider had killed him. I put my hand over my mouth to hide a sob and tears streaked down my cheeks.

Slider's heavy footsteps sounded up the stairs and the piercing whine of sirens moved closer. I looked towards the garage door and found Slider standing there.

"Slider," I whispered.

"I'm sorry, Fay," he said.

I shook my head and ran to him. "You saved me," I sobbed. "You saved me again." He wrapped his arms tightly around me, and I buried my face in his neck.

"It's okay, Fay. It's all over." He smoothed down my hair.

My sobs ripped through me, knowing that everything was over, and Slider was okay.

It was finally over.

****

Slider

"How did you know to come home early?" Fayth asked me.

We were lying in bed, her body covering mine, and her head was resting on my shoulder. "Your brother called and told me that your doctor was coming over."

"That still doesn't explain how you knew that I needed you."

"That chick we talked to at the strip club had told us that Big A was meeting with his doctor a lot lately. It didn't feel right when Leo told me your doctor had called asking about you."

Fayth sighed and ran her fingers over my chest. "I'm so sorry, Slider."

"It's not your fault, Fay. It's not anyone's fault. I'm just glad I was able to be there before something even worse happened to you. Although, you seemed to have a handle on things when I got there," I laughed.

Fayth looked up at me and smiled. "I have to say, your hiding spot for your gun is pretty amazing. If I hadn't known it was there, things might have ended completely different."

I pressed a kiss to the side of her head and rolled us over so I was on top of her. "But they didn't, Fay, and that's all that matters. This whole fucking thing is over."

"But what about Big A? Won't he just try to find someone else to hurt us?"

"We had him taken care of before today. I had a connection that was able to eliminate the problem completely."

"Do I want to know what happened?"

"I can tell you want to know, although it isn't pretty."

She shook her head. "As long as you say that he's never going to hurt us again, I don't need to know."

"I promise with everything I am, he will never hurt you, or anyone else we love."

She closed her eyes and sighed. "You're included in that, right?"

641

"Yeah, Fay. Of course."

"Good, because I love you, and if anything were to happen to you, I don't think I would make it."

"Fay, what…I…but…"

Fayth pressed a finger to my lips and shook her head. "I love you, Slider. You need to get used to it."

I kissed her finger and closed my eyes. "I'm not a good man, Fay."

"I'm not interested in a good man. I want a man who protects his brothers and family no matter what. I want you," she whispered.

"Keep saying that, Fay, and I'll never let you go."

"That's the plan, Slider. Although, even if you wanted to leave me, I'd have my brother find you and drag you back to me."

"Ah, that's right, my girl has mafia connections," I chuckled.

"That's right, and don't forget it. Now," she said, her hands skating up and down my back, "do you have something you need to tell me?"

I tapped my chin. "No, I think that's it."

"Slider," she scolded.

"All right, all right." I caged her in with my arms and pressed a kiss to her lips. "You're mine. You're everything I said I never wanted, and I love you Fayth Banachi. I'm never letting you go."

The End

Epilogue

Marley

"Put it down."

I looked over my shoulder at Troy and shook my head. "No."

"Sunshine, I'm telling you right now, put the spoon down, and stop fucking with the damn food. It. Will. Cook."

"But what if I don't want to put the spoon down?"

Troy slammed his hand down on the table and pointed his finger at me. "No more hanging out with Meg."

"What the hell does Meg have to do with it?"

"I have no idea, but I know she's behind this somehow."

I rolled my eyes and turned back to the pot of boiling potatoes. "I think they're done."

"They aren't, Marley. They have only been boiling for five minutes. There is no way in hell ten pounds of potatoes are done in five minutes."

I stomped my foot and turned around. "Dammit man, I told Meg that I would make the potato salad. Now, back the hell off and let me do what I need to do." I waved the spoon at him. "You said yourself that my cooking has been getting better."

"Well it damn well better be getting better. We've been together for five years, Sunshine."

"And I haven't killed you yet." I smirked.

Troy rubbed his stomach. "There was that one time with the shrimp and the rotten—"

I stomped my foot and pointed the spoon in his face. "We do not talk about the shrimp. Never," I ordered. I slapped the spoon into the palm of my hand. "It was one time, and Meg told me where to buy the shrimp."

"Marley, you had to have thought that buying shrimp from a gas station was not the best idea."

"Silence!" I shouted.

"I kill you," a tiny voice shouted from the highchair.

"Dammit, Troy. Have you been watching Comedy Central with Brock again?"

Troy shrugged. "What else am I supposed to do when he wakes up when I get home from work?"

"Put Paw Patrol on, or I don't know, put him back to bed!" I picked Brock up out of his chair. "You're the reason he sleeps all day."

"He's on a schedule," Troy insisted.

"A one-year-old should not be on the schedule of someone who works second shift."

"I kill you, I kill you," Brock chanted over and over and pointed at Troy.

"No more Comedy Central," I said, handing Brock off to him. "By the time he goes to school, he's going to be telling dirty jokes and telling everyone he's going to kill them."

"The kid's got a sense of humor. I'm just nurturing his need to hear jokes."

I rolled my eyes and took the pot of boiling potatoes off, then dumped them into the colander I had in the sink. "Your nurturing is a bit misguided."

Troy put his arm around me and spun me around. "Marley."

"Troy." This was his new thing. He thought just saying my name was going to calm me down, or defuse whatever situation we were in.

"Bok!" Brock shouted and threw his hands in the air. I couldn't help but laugh at the little boy who was a perfect mix of Troy and me.

"See, the kid has a knack of making people laugh," Troy pointed out.

"I pray our next one is more like me." I sighed, watching Brock try to give Troy a raspberry on his cheek.

"Maybe someday, right?" Troy said to Brock.

"How about a day about eight months from now?"

Troy's face turned white, and his eyes bugged out. Brock was drooling all over his cheek, still trying to give Troy a raspberry. "What did you just say?"

"Um, well. You remember that night about a month ago where I got rip-roaring drunk, and we had sex in the back of your truck?"

Troy nodded. "That's pretty hard to forget."

"Well, surprise. We made a baby that night."

Troy handed me Brock and shook his head. "That's it," he shouted. "There will absolutely be no more sex in my truck! We had Brock the same way."

"Da, Da, Da," Brock chanted, holding his arms out for Troy. Brock had become a Daddy's boy from their late night TV binging.

"Troy, that's ridiculous. You know that has nothing to do with it."

"I won't believe that until you prove it." Troy held up one finger. "Almost two years ago, we had had sex in the front seat of my truck. Bam! You're pregnant." He flipped up another finger. "One month ago, I let you take advantage of me in the bed of my truck. Bam! You're pregnant again," he proclaimed, pointing at my stomach. "No more truck sex. I'm putting my foot down."

"Bam, bam!" Brock repeated and held his arms over his head.

"Is that all you can think about right now? Where we had sex? I'm about to give you another baby and that's all you're worried about," I shouted, my voice cracking. I had been an emotional wreck all week, suspecting I was pregnant but wasn't for sure until I had been to the doctor's this afternoon.

"Well, you have to admit, it's more than a coincidence."

"Troy! I'm fucking pregnant!" I shouted.

Brock cried out, and his cute, little face scrunched up. I buried my face in his sweet scent and turned my back to Troy.

"Dammit, Marley, I'm sorry." He put his arms around me. "You know how I get. I can't see past my own nose sometimes."

Troy was right. I did know how he got, and that was one of the things I loved about him. He could see humor in anything. "You just need to reel it in sometimes," I whispered. Brock was playing with my hair, and Troy's hands rubbed my stomach.

"You're having my baby again, Marley." Troy stated.

"I sure am," I mumbled.

Troy sighed, and I turned around in his arms. "We're gonna have two kids under the age of two running around the house." I nodded. "Ol' Bandit isn't going to know what to think."

"He'll get used to it, just like he did with Brock."

Troy brushed my hair out of my face. "You're having my baby," he repeated.

I nodded and knew that it was finally sinking in.

Troy grabbed me around the waist and spun Brock and me around. Brock clapped his hands and laughed at his silly daddy.

Troy pressed a kiss to Brock's cheek and took him out of my arms. He set him in his highchair and dumped a pile of Cheerios in front of him.

"Troy, that's too many," I scolded.

Troy tossed the box of cereal on the counter and grabbed me around the waist. "Silence," he whispered.

"I kill you!" Brock shouted.

Troy pressed his forehead to mine, a goofy grin on his lips. "I promise not to let the new baby watch Comedy Central."

"Promises, promises," I whispered.

"I love you, Marley," he growled against my lips.

"I love you too, Troy."

****

Cyn

"Get in the car."

I grabbed my purse and hitched it over my shoulder.

"Get in the car now, Diamond," I heard Rigid say as I walked out the front door.

"You need to have a firm voice, Rigid." I walked up to the car and put my hands on my hips.

"I can't have more of a firm voice than I do, Cyn," he growled. "I wanted a big, burly Doberman, and you come home with a girl Doberman with a neon pink collar on, and you name her Diamond. How the hell can you be firm when saying Diamond?"

"Like this, Dad," Micha called from the open car door. "Come here, Diamond," he said, patting his knee. Diamond hopped into the car, and I slammed the door.

"You're losing your touch, Rigid. I'm going to have to start calling you Ashley. It seems to suit you better."

"You do that, and you're going to end up over my knee," he said menacingly.

"Promises, promises," I chided.

Rigid pushed me up against the car and caged me in with his arms. "You better be thankful we have somewhere to be, or I'd make good on my promise right now."

"Micha is staying the night at Gwen's tonight," I purred, running my hands up his arms.

"Are you just trying to get me riled up?" he asked.

"Maybe, but you'll never know for sure."

"Cynthia, you're trying my patience," he mumbled next to my ear.

I wrapped my arms around his waist and pulled him close. "Good," I whispered.

Rigid delved his hands into my hair and devoured my mouth.

"How the hell after five years, do you still drive me crazy?" he asked when we finally came up for air.

"Probably the same way you drive me crazy. Chemistry, big man," I said before pressing a kiss to his cheek.

"As soon as we get home, I'm going to show you chemistry," he mumbled.

I pressed a quick kiss to his lips and ran my fingers through my hair. "I can't wait."

****

Paige

"One more."

I shook my head and brushed on my lip gloss.

"Paige, come one. How can you not want one more?" Demon asked from where he sat on the edge of the tub, holding our three-month-old son, Braxton in his arms.

I heard running down the hallway and knew my two reasons for stopping at three were about to burst through the bathroom door.

"Ma, Mom, Mommy," Ryan and Riley yelled as they pounded on the bathroom door. I looked at Demon in the mirror and pointed at the door. "Our three-year-old twins are the reason I don't want any more. If I managed to make it through the terrible three's with those two, I think we'll be doing good."

"Come on, Paige, you know how boys are. Next time, we can have a girl," Demon pointed out.

I rolled my eyes and turned around. I leaned against the bathroom sink and crossed my arms over my chest. "You promised me with Braxton that he was going to be a girl. I'm pretty sure when he screamed bloody murder when he got circumcised says differently." I knew that Demon couldn't predict what we were going to have, but I still liked to point out that he was wrong about Braxton.

"That's because we had sex on a Tuesday with him. I figure we shoot for a Thursday, and bada bing bada boom, girl."

647

"Did you really just say bada bing bada boom?" The man was pulling every trick out of the bag to try to convince me to have another baby.

Demon shrugged and looked down at Braxton. "How can you not want to have another one of these?"

Ryan pounded on the door and demanded I open it to open his juice box. "Because that," I said, pointing at a sleeping Braxton, "turns into screaming banshees who need juice boxes opened at all hours of the night." I opened the door a crack and grabbed the juice box Ryan handed me. I poked the straw through the hole and handed it back to him. "You boys better not have gotten dirty," I called as they ran down the hallway to their room.

"One more, and then we're done," Demon promised.

"How about we just practice?" I suggested.

"Baby," Demon wiggled his eyebrows at me. "You know we don't need to practice. We've got this down pat now."

I shook my head and pushed off of the counter. "Enjoy the ones you've got, Demon, because they are all you're getting from this baby factory."

I patted him on the shoulder and opened the bathroom door.

"I love you, Paige," he called while I walked down the hallway. "Even if you won't give me any more babies."

"I love you, too, Demon."

"That's all you have to say?" he hollered.

"Do you need anything more?" I yelled back.

I heard him grumble and walk out of the bathroom. "No, but since you won't give me any more babies, you have to change Braxton. He just stunk me out of the bathroom." Demon handed Braxton off to me and shook his head. "I could feel him filling the diaper, baby," he grimaced.

"And you want another of these?" I laughed.

"Do you think we could get one that's potty trained?"

I shook my head. "I'm pretty sure that's not how it works."

Demon pressed a kiss to the side of my head. "Then, I think we're good with the three poop machines we have."

I busted out laughing. "Well, while I take care of this one, why don't you go make sure the other two are ready to go. We need to be to Meg's in half an hour and no matter what we do, we always seem to be an hour behind."

"I'm on it, baby." Demon headed down the hallway to the boy's room and yelled "what are you doing" when he jumped into their room. The boys busted out into giggles, and I smiled down at Braxton.

"I think we're pretty good at five, don't you bud?" Braxton smiled up at me, and I felt a rip roaring fart on my hand. "We're definitely good at five."

****

Gwen

"Oh God, help me out." I waved my hand at Gambler, who just stood by my door and watched me struggled to get up.

"Why the hell are you wearing heels?" he asked.

"Because I look hot in heels. Flats make me feel old."

Gambler grabbed my hand and hoisted me out of the car. Hoist was the most appropriate word for anything these days when it came to me getting up. My eighth month of pregnancy was not agreeing with me. "Yeah, well, flats keep you and my baby safe. Now, I'm going to have to follow you around all day making sure you don't fall over."

"You act like I'm a wobbling tower of Jenga pieces," I sneered, grabbing his shoulder to steady myself.

"I have never heard a more accurate description of you being eight months pregnant and teetering around in heels."

I slapped Gambler on the chest and looped my arm through his. "One more month," I mumbled.

Gambler helped me up the curb and looked down at me. "I love you, Gwen, and you do know we're at least doing this one more time, right?"

I nodded. "I love you, too, and I know. As soon as we're given the okay, we're onto baby two, but do you think we could just worry about this one right now? He's pretty feisty today," I said, rubbing my stomach where he had just kicked.

"He's ready to come out." He rubbed my stomach and the baby kicked again.

I shook my head. "Nope. He needs to stay in there and cook a little bit longer. We still have to finish unpacking all of the boxes, and then get the crib put together. Three weeks, at least."

"Let's hope he heard that," Gambler said and pulled me to Meg's house.

We had just moved into a three-bedroom ranch over by Slider's house, and we had both realized how stupid it was to move while pregnant. Gambler ended up doing ninety percent of the work while I either complained or slept. So, it actually wasn't that bad of a deal for me, it was Gambler who was getting the short end of the stick.

"I think we're the last ones here," I mumbled. Everyone was spread around Meg's backyard and deck.

"Yeah, it looks like we are, although I don't see Ethel or Gravel."

"You think they're okay?"

Gambler shrugged. "I sure fucking hope so."

****

Ethel

"What did he say?"

I looked over at Gravel and shook my head.

"Dammit, woman, tell me what the doctor said."

"Negative. It was negative," I sobbed.

Gravel slouched in his seat and sighed. "You about gave me a heart attack there. You know I'm old and my heart can't take that."

I set my phone on the dash and looked out the windshield. We were parked outside of Meg's house when the doctor called. I had been waiting all day yesterday for the phone call, and it never came. Gravel had insisted I contact the doctor myself, but I had fought him off. Thankfully, the doctor had finally called, or I knew Gravel would have barged into his office on Monday and demanded to know the results of a bump they had removed from my breast.

"So, it was nothing. No cancer?"

I nodded. "It was benign."

"Holy fuck, Ethel. I thought I was going to have to go through worrying about losing you all over again. Twice was enough."

I had to agree with him. Six years ago, I had been diagnosed the first time with breast cancer, then three years ago, I had relapsed and gone through chemo and treatment all over again. It was a hellacious few years, but I had made it through. "Negative," I said, laughing. "It was negative!" I shouted.

Gravel looked over at me like I had lost my marbles. "You okay over there, woman?"

"I'm great," I sobbed as the realization hit me. I had cheated death again. "I didn't know how much longer I had on this Earth, but I knew it wasn't going to be breast cancer that was going to take me out. "I love you, Gravel. I love you so much. You stood by me and helped me so much these past years. I never would have made it without you."

Gravel threaded his fingers through mine and pressed a kiss to the back of my hand. "You're a fighter, Ethel. I knew it the day I met you, and I know it now. Nothing is going to take you from your family. You won't let it."

I closed my eyes and nodded. "I love you, and I love that huge extended family we have waiting for us."

"Yeah, who would have known they would have thrown a shindig all because we tied the knot?" Gravel chuckled.

"It only took us forty years to get here," I laughed.

"Yeah, but we finally made it."

****

Fayth

"Eat it."

I shook my head and pushed my plate away. "No."

"I dare you," Slider coaxed and held the fork full of potato salad in front of my mouth. "You know you want to."

I leaned in and whispered softly. "I freakin' love Marley, Slider, but nothing on this Earth could make me put that in my mouth. I could tell the potatoes were raw the second I stuck my fork in it."

Slider shook his head and leaned back in his chair. "You're gonna hurt your friend's feelings if you don't at least try it."

"I don't have to try it to tell her that I tried it."

"That's lying, Mom," Marco said next to me. "You always told me that no matter what, always tell the truth. I think it's only fair that you tell Marley her food is crap."

"Hey, how come you didn't take any?" I asked him, looking at his plate that was full of food, but didn't have any raw potato salad on it.

"Because I asked Remy who made what when we were going through the line. He told me it was all good to eat besides the green bowl." Marco shoveled a fork full of beans into his mouth and sighed. "Way better than raw potatoes."

Slider laughed, and I glared at him. "And how the hell did you manage to not take any?"

"I saw Marley walk in with the bowl. You should really pick up on these things after five years, Fay." Slider winked and waved the fork in front of me again. "One bite won't kill you, Firecracker."

"Oh, you took some, too," Marley called as she walked over to our table with Troy trailing behind her. "How was it?"

Troy shook his head and waved his arms in the air. Slider smothered a laugh with the back of his hand and turned away from Marley. "Excuse him, he's got a horrible case of being an ass today," I explained to Marley while I kicked Slider under the table. "He was dropped on his head as a baby."

Marco choked on his food because he was laughing so hard, and I had to slap him on the back to get him breathing again.

Troy came up behind Marley and wrapped his arms around her. "Did you hear our news?" he asked, rubbing her belly.

Thank you, sweet baby Jesus, Troy was giving me an out so I didn't have to tell Marley how horrible her food was. "Oh my god," I gasped. "That's amazing!"

"Saved by the baby," Slider mumbled under his breath.

I managed to kick him under the table one last time before I stood and hugged Marley. "I'm so happy for you," I gushed, wrapping my arms around her.

"Yeah, we weren't going to tell anyone, but apparently Troy just can't keep it in."

Troy grimaced and shrugged. "You know me, I just can't keep a secret." He also couldn't stand to see his wife's feeling get hurt either.

Gwen and Paige came over, and Troy told them too.

Slider grabbed my arm and tugged me over to the side of the huge tent we were sitting under. "You know you're going to have to pay for those kicks, right?" he whispered in my ear and wrapped his arms around me.

"I don't know why you have to tease me so much."

"Because I like the way you blush when you try to lie," he said, brushing a finger down my cheek. "And, I wasn't going to make you eat that. I don't want you to choke on a raw potato."

"How chivalrous of you." I rolled my eyes.

"Is Marco heading back to Chicago with Remy tonight?" Slider glided his hands down my back and grabbed my ass.

"No, I think he's staying one more night, and then they are headed back."

"So, one more night and then I'm back to having you all to myself?"

"Yes, do you think you can control yourself for that long?" I chided.

"Probably, but that's only because I'm going to have you tonight."

"Slider," I scolded as I batted his hands away. "I can't take you anywhere without you trying to fuck me."

"That's because it's my favorite thing to do. Can you really blame me?" he whispered in my ear.

I couldn't blame him, but it would be nice for the man to have some self-control. "Five minutes, that's all you get. Everyone is going to wonder where we went if we're gone for longer than that."

Slider picked me up, and I couldn't help the yelp that escaped my lips. Everyone look over at us, and a guilty smile spread across my lips.

"We'll be right back, Ethel," Slider hollered over his shoulder and headed to the side of the house.

"Any kind of stealthiness we had going for us, you blew out of the water," I scolded.

"You really think I care?" Slider asked, pressing me against the side of Meg's house and running his hand up my thigh.

"No, but I would hope that you would care if I cared."

"That's a whole lot of caring that I just don't have time to care about, Fay."

I put my hands on Slider's shoulders and looked him in the eye. "Is it always going to be like this?"

"Like what?"

"Like we can't get enough of each other, and we have a huge group of friends that are like family?"

"It hasn't changed in the past five years, Fay. Why all of a sudden do you think it will?" Slider cupped my cheek and stroked his thumb along my jaw.

"Everything is perfect, Slider. I'm terrified it's all going to fall apart."

653

Slider shook his head. "And you know what you do when things are going good?" I shook my head no, because if I did, I wouldn't be terrified of change. "You hold on, and don't let go."

"But what happens if you crash?"

"You hold on even tighter and ride out the wave. As long as you have me and my brothers behind you, Fay, the good times will never stop."

I sighed and nodded. "You really do have it all figured out, don't you?"

Slider shrugged. "It's easy. As long as I have you loving me, nothing can break me."

"I love you so much, Slider," I whispered.

"I love you, too, Fay." Slider leaned close and brushed his lips against my ear. "But do you know what would make me love you more?"

"If I let you fuck me upside this house?" I giggled.

"Damn straight, Firecracker."

****

Meg

"I hope the cops don't drive by," I mumbled and sat down in Lo's lap.

"Why? What'd you do now, babe?"

"Ha, ha. You're so funny." I rolled my eyes and put my arm around his shoulders. "Slider is screwing Fayth against the side of the house."

"Again?" Lo asked. "They did that the last time we had a bonfire."

"Well, at least last time it was dark out. Now, it's the middle of the day, and any Tom, Dick, or Harry could drive by and see them going at it."

"You remember when we were like that?"

I scoffed and shook my head. "I'm pretty sure we never screwed in broad daylight."

"You don't remember one of those first nights we went out? You and Cyn sang horrible karaoke, and then I almost had you up against that brick wall?"

I pressed the back of my hand against Lo's forehead and checked for a fever. "I think you're getting Alzheimer's in your old age, or you're thinking of another girl. We never had sex against a brick wall. I may have let you feel me up, but there was no penetration."

He swatted my hand away. "Jesus, Meg. It damn well was you."

I shook my head. "You'll never hear me admit that out loud."

"Crazy," Lo muttered under his breath.

"But you love me." I laid my head on his shoulder and looked around at all of the people that had become family. "Did you talk to your mom?"

Lo nodded. "Negative," he mumbled.

"She beat it, Lo," I whispered.

Lo wrapped his arms around me and buried his face in my hair. Two weeks ago, Ethel had told us they had found another bump, and she was having it removed. Lo had lost it. I didn't know how he was going to make it through if he found out his mom had cancer for a third time.

"I fucking love you, Meg."

I relaxed in his arms and let him hold me. "I love you, too. I wouldn't have any of this if it weren't for meeting you."

"Well, thank God we met each other, because I know I wouldn't be here if it weren't for you either."

"Then, I guess we're good for each other, right?" I said smugly.

Lo pulled back my hair and kissed my neck. "I don't want anyone but you."

I looked around, taking in all of my friends eating and just hanging out. "Did you happen to try Marley's potato salad?"

Lo did a full body shiver and grimaced. "Hell yes. She managed to trap me over by the table, and I couldn't escape. Why the hell didn't Remy warn me that she brought the green bowl?"

"Did she force-feed you some?" I asked, laughing.

"Fed me like a damn baby," Lo growled.

I couldn't help but laugh at the idea of Lo—big, bad president of the Devil's Knights—being force-fed by sweet Marley. "Troy is going to have to break it to her sometime that she just should give up on cooking."

"And baking," Lo agreed. "She brought muffins to the shop last week, and I almost broke a tooth on the damn thing."

"But I bet you ate it though, right?"

"Yeah, because she stood there and waited for me to take a bite."

"You really are a good man," I said as I ran my fingers though his hair.

"Only for you, babe."

I sighed and watched Remy and Marco sitting at a table all by themselves. "When did my baby grow up?" I wondered out loud.

"He may be grown up, but you'll always be his mom, babe."

Remy had graduated high school five years ago, moved away to go to school in Chicago for two years, and now he was working on a pit crew for a nitro funny car. "I just wish he was home more."

"He's young, babe. This is the time he should be off, finding out who he is and sowing his oats."

"You mean having ten girlfriends at once and getting drunk every night?"

Lo shrugged. "I plead the fifth," Lo mumbled. I knew Remy told Lo more about his life than he did me, and it drove me crazy.

"Just as long as one of those wild oats he's sowing doesn't turn up pregnant."

"He's got a good head on his shoulders, babe. You did good by him." Lo gently patted my thigh. "Have a little faith in him, babe."

"Hmm," I hummed. "Here I thought once everything settled down, I could just relax and have no worries. Now, I have a whole new set of worries with Remy gone all of the time."

"Well, I guess I'm not doing my job well enough then. I'll have to try to distract you even more."

"And how exactly are you going to do that?" I asked as I turned in his arms.

"Well, there are at three other sides to the house that aren't being used." Lo wiggled his eyebrows.

I smacked his chest and waved my finger in his face. "Not happening, big man."

Lo shot up from the chair and tossed me over his shoulder. "Lo," I shrieked. "Put me down."

"Not happening, babe" He smacked my ass.

"Hey, you gotta copy Slider's move?" Gambler called when Lo ducked out of the tent.

"Nah, this shit has always been my move. You fuckers just copied them all," Lo hollered.

Everyone groaned and told Lo he was crazy.

Lo climbed the stairs to the deck. "I thought you were taking me to the side of the house?" I giggled.

He opened the screen door and ducked inside the house. "I was going to, but then I realized that really was a Slider move."

"So, you opted to go with a standard Lo move of sweeping me off my feet and taking me to bed?"

Lo made his way through the house and tossed me on the bed. "I figure why mess with something that ain't broken. I made you fall in love with me this way, so I'll just keep doing what works."

Lo covered my body with his and whispered, "I certainly did fall in love with you, Lo. You gave me one hell of a story to tell our grandkids one day."

"The one where you had your ass waving in the air, and you told me you don't eat?"

I giggled and nodded. "That would be the one. It's our story."

"It's always been our story, babe, because it's always been you."

"Always," I whispered.

Lo was mine, and I wouldn't have had it any other way. After all, our story had only just begun back then, and every day was an adventure I couldn't wait to live.

Life in the *Lo Daze* got better every day.

A word to my loyal readers:

Thank you so much for taking the ride with me with the Devil's Knights. I first published Loving Lo with the only thought of I needed to get this story out of my head. I was absolutely blown away by the response I received, and knew there was more to this series.
With each book I wrote, the more I found my voice and knew that writing was not only what I wanted to do, but it had become a need.
I have meet so many amazing (and some not so amazing LOL) people on this journey, and I honestly can't remember life before this amazing indie community. I've surrounded myself with those who only want the best for me, and can't wait to see what I pull out of my head next.
The Devil's Knights wouldn't be possible without each and every one of you buying my books, and following me as I navigate my way through this wonderful journey.

Did you really think this is the end of the Devil's Knights?
You can't silence Meg that easily…

Long live the #LoDaze.

Love, Winter

Grab Forever Lo.